Raves for
❀ *NOBODY'S BABY BUT MINE* ❀

"Four stars . . . True romance is back . . .
Nobody writes funnier romance than
Susan Elizabeth Phillips."
Detroit Free Press

"*Nobody's Baby* is a hoot, and Miss Phillips supplies
romance to go along with the chuckles. . . . Romance
fans (and I know you're out there) should check out
Susan Elizabeth Phillips's *Nobody's Baby But Mine.*"
Omaha World Herald

"Excellent . . . sexually charged and emotionally
wrenching . . . This is the most satisfying romance
I've read in quite a while."
Contra Costa Times

Kudos for
❀ *THIS HEART OF MINE* ❀

"Terrifically entertaining."
Milwaukee Journal-Sentinel

"Frothed with humor and passion . . . Phillips's
character development draws readers
into her Cinderella-type story."
Chicago Sun-Times

"Pure up-to-the-minute entertainment."
Publishers Weekly

Everyone adores *New York Times* bestselling author

SUSAN ELIZABETH PHILLIPS!

"[A] considerable talent."
Detroit Free Press

"One of the few writers whose books I buy
on the basis of name alone, knowing
I'll get my money's worth."
Milwaukee Journal-Sentinel

"Susan Elizabeth Phillips's bestselling novels have
helped to give romance fiction something it
long deserved—respectablity."
Chicago Sun-Times

"She writes a story that wraps around
your heart and doesn't let go."
Oakland Press

"Phillips is a master of her craft . . .
Funny, smart, satisfying."
Contra Costa Times

"She makes you laugh, makes you cry—
makes you feel good."
Jayne Ann Krentz

By Susan Elizabeth Phillips

Nobody's Baby But Mine

SUSAN ELIZABETH PHILLIPS

This Heart of Mine

AVON BOOKS
An Imprint of HarperCollinsPublishers

Nobody's Baby But Mine was originally published in mass market by Avon Books in 1997, and *This Heart of Mine* was originally published in hardcover by William Morrow in 2001 and in mass market by Avon Books in 2002.

HarperCollins books may be purchased for educational, business, or sales promotional use. For information please write: Special Markets Department, HarperCollins Publishers Inc., 10 East 53rd Street, New York, NY 10022.

FIRST EDITION

ISBN-13: 978-0-06-089470-2
ISBN-10: 0-06-089470-9

06 07 08 09 10 JTC/RRD 10 9 8 7 6 5 4 3 2 1

Nobody's Baby But Mine

To my mother

"Let me get this straight," Jodie Pulanski said. "You want to give Cal Bonner a *woman* for a birthday present."

The three offensive linemen, who were spending the November evening sitting in the back booth at Zebras, the DuPage County sports bar favored by the Chicago Stars football players, all nodded at once.

Junior Duncan gestured toward the waitress for another round. "He's going to be thirty-six, so we wanted to make this extra special."

"Bull," Jodie said. Everybody who knew anything about football knew that Cal Bonner, the Stars' brilliant quarterback, had been demanding, temperamental, and generally impossible to get along with ever since the season started. Bonner, popularly known as the "Bomber" because of his fondness for throwing explosive passes, was the top-ranked quarterback in the AFC and a legend.

Jodie crossed her arms over the form-fitting white tank top that was part of her hostess uniform. It didn't occur to either her or any of the three men at the table to consider the moral dimensions of their discussion, let alone notions of political correctness. This was, after all, the NFL. "You think if you get him a woman, he'll ease up on all of you," she said.

Willie Jarrell gazed down into his beer through a pair of thickly-lashed dark brown eyes. "Sonovabitch been kickin' so much ass lately, nobody can stand being around him."

Junior shook his head. "Yesterday, he called Germaine Clark a *debutante*. Germaine!"

Jodie lifted one eyebrow, which was penciled several shades darker than her brassy blond hair. Germaine Clark was All-Pro and one of the meanest defensive tackles in the NFL. "From what I've seen, the Bomber already has more women than he knows what to do with."

Junior nodded. "Yeah, but, the thing of it is, he doesn't seem to be sleepin' with any of them?"

"What?"

"It's true." Chris Plummer, the Stars' left guard spoke up. "We just found it out. His girlfriends have been talking to some of the wives, and it seems Cal's not using them for anything more than window dressing."

Willie Jarrell spoke up. "Maybe if he waited until they were out of diapers, he could get turned on."

Junior chose to take his remark seriously. "Don't say things like that, Willie. You know Cal won't date 'em till they're twenty."

Cal Bonner might be getting older, but the females in his life weren't. No one could remember him dating anyone over the age of twenty-two.

"Far as anybody knows," Willie said, "the Bomber hasn't slept with anybody since he broke up with Kelly, and that was last February. It's not natural."

Kelly Berkley had been Cal's beautiful twenty-one-year-old companion until she'd gotten tired of waiting for a wedding ring that wasn't ever going to come and run off with a twenty-three-year-old guitarist for a heavy metal band. Since then, Cal Bonner had been concentrating on winning football games, dating a new woman every week, and kicking his teammates' asses.

Jodie Pulanski was the Stars' favorite groupie, but although she hadn't yet turned twenty-three, none of the men suggested that she offer her own body as Cal Bonner's birthday present. It was a well-known fact he'd already rejected her at least a dozen times. That made the Bomber Public Enemy Number One on Jodie's personal hate list, even though she kept a collection of blue-and-gold Stars' jerseys in her bedroom closet, one jersey for every Stars player she'd slept with, and was always eager to add more.

"What we need is somebody who won't remind him of Kelly," Chris said.

"That means she needs to be real classy," Willie added. "And older. We think it would be good for the Bomber to try someone maybe twenty-five."

"Sort of dignified." Junior took a sip of beer. "One of those society types."

Jodie wasn't known for her brains, but even she could see the problem with that one. "I don't think too many society types are going to volunteer to be a man's birthday present. Not even Cal Bonner's."

"Yeah, that's what we was thinking, too, so we might have to use a hooker."

"But a real classy one," Willie said hastily, since everyone knew Cal didn't go for hookers.

Junior gazed glumly into his beer. "Problem is, we haven't been able to find one."

Jodie knew some hookers, but none of them were what she'd call classy. Neither were her friends. She ran with a group of hard-drinking, party-loving women, whose single goal in life was to sleep with as many professional athletes as they could. "What do you want from me?"

"We want you to use your connections and find somebody for him," Junior said. "His birthday's coming up in ten days, and we got to have a woman for him before then.''

"What's in it for me?''

Since all three of their jerseys already hung in her closet, they knew they'd have to go out on a limb. Chris spoke cautiously. ''You got a particular number you're interested in adding to your collection?''

"Other than number eighteen,'' Willie quickly interjected, eighteen being the Bomber's number.

Jodie thought about it. She'd rather screw over the Bomber than find him a woman. On the other hand, there was one particular number that she wanted real bad. ''As a matter of fact, I do. If I find your birthday present, number twelve's mine.''

The men groaned. ''Shit, Jodie, Kevin Tucker's got too many women as it is.''

"That's your problem.''

Tucker was the Stars' backup quarterback. Young, aggressive, and sublimely talented, he had been handpicked by the Stars to take over the starting position when age or injury prevented Cal from getting the job done. Although the two men were polite in public, both were fierce competitors, and they hated each other's guts, which made Kevin Tucker all the more desirable to Jodie.

The men grumbled, but eventually agreed that they'd make sure Tucker did his part if she found the right woman for Cal's birthday present.

Two new customers entered Zebras, and since Jodie was the bar's hostess, she got up to greet them. As she made her way to the door, she mentally sorted through her female acquaintances, trying to come up with one of them who would qualify, but she drew a blank. She had a lot of female friends, but not a single one of them was classy.

Two days later, Jodie was still mulling over the problem as she dragged her hangover into the kitchen of her parents' home in suburban Glen Ellyn, Illinois, where she was temporarily living until she got her Visa paid off. It was almost noon on Saturday, her parents were gone for the weekend, and she didn't have to be at work until five, which was a good thing because she needed time to recover from last night's partying.

She opened the cupboard door and saw nothing but a can of decaf. *Shit.* It was sleeting outside, and her head hurt too much to drive, but if she didn't have a quart of caffeine inside her by kickoff time, she wouldn't be able to enjoy the game.

Nothing was going right. The Stars were playing in Buffalo that afternoon, so she couldn't look forward to the players coming into Zebras after the game. And when she finally did see them, how was she going to break the news that she hadn't been able to find the birthday present? One of the reasons the Stars paid so much attention to her was because she could always get them women.

She gazed out the kitchen window and saw a light on at the geek's house next door. The geek was Jodie's private name for Dr. Jane Darlington, her parents' neighbor. She was a Ph.D. doctor, not a medical one, and Jodie's mom was always going on about what a wonderful person she was because she'd been helping the Pulanskis with mail and shit ever since they'd moved in a couple of years ago. Maybe she'd help Jodie out with some coffee.

She did a quick fix on her makeup and, without bothering to put on underwear, slipped into a pair of tight black jeans, Willie Jarrell's jersey, and her Frye boots. After grabbing one of her mother's Tupperware containers, she headed next door.

Despite the sleet, she hadn't bothered with a jacket, and by the time Dr. Jane got around to answering the bell, she was shivering. "Hi."

Dr. Jane stood on the other side of the storm door staring

at her through geeky, oversize glasses with tortoiseshell frames.

"I'm the Pulanskis' daughter Jodie. From next door."

Dr. Jane made no move to invite her inside.

"Listen, it's cold as hell out here. Can I come in?"

The geek finally pushed open the storm door and let her in. "I'm sorry. I didn't recognize you."

Jodie stepped inside, and it didn't take her more than two seconds to figure out why Dr. Jane hadn't been in any big hurry to admit her. The eyes behind the lenses were teary and her nose red. Unless Jodie was more hungover than she thought, Dr. Jane had been crying her nerdy little heart out.

The geek was tall, maybe five-eight, and Jodie had to look up as she extended the pink Tupperware container. "Can I bum a couple of scoops of coffee? There's nothing but decaf in the house, and I need something stronger."

Dr. Jane took the container, but she seemed to do it reluctantly. She didn't strike Jodie as the stingy type, so her reaction probably meant she wasn't in the mood for company. "Yes, I'll—uh—get you some." She turned away and headed for the kitchen, obviously expecting Jodie to wait where she was, but Jodie had a half hour to kill before the pregame show started, and she was curious enough to follow.

They passed through a living room that, at first glance, seemed pretty boring: off-white walls, comfortable furniture, boring-looking books everywhere. Jodie was getting ready to pass right through when the framed museum posters on the walls caught her attention. They all seemed to have been done by some lady named Georgia O'Keeffe, and Jodie knew she had a dirty mind, but she didn't think that explained why every one of the flowers looked like female sex organs.

She saw flowers with deep, dark hearts. Flowers with petals flopping over moist, secret centers. She saw—jeez.

It was a clamshell with this little wet pearl, and even some-body with the cleanest mind in the world would have to look twice at that one. She wondered if maybe the geek was a dike. Why else would she want to look at flower pussies every time she went into her living room?

Jodie wandered into the kitchen, which was pale lavender with pretty floral curtains hanging at the window, although these flowers were regular ones, not the X-rateds in the living-room paintings. Everything in the kitchen was cheery and cute except for the owner, who looked more dignified than God.

Dr. Jane was one of those neat, tweedy women. Her tai-lored slacks had small, tidy brown-and-black checks, and her soft, oatmeal-colored sweater looked like cashmere. De-spite her height, she was small-boned, with well-proportioned legs and a slender waist. Jodie might have felt envious of her figure except for the fact that she had no boobs, or at least none to speak of.

Her hair was jaw-length—pale blond with streaks of flax, platinum, and gold that couldn't have come from a bottle. It was arranged in one of those conservative hairstyles that Jodie wouldn't have been caught dead in—brushed loosely back from her face and held in place with a narrow brown velvet clip-on headband.

She turned slightly so that Jodie got a better look. Too bad about those big, geeky glasses. They hid a nice set of green eyes. She also had a good forehead and a decent nose, neither too big nor too small. Her mouth was sort of inter-esting, with a thin upper lip and a plump bottom one. And she had great skin. But she didn't seem to do much with herself. Jodie would have added a lot more makeup. All in all, the geek was a good-looking woman, but sort of intim-idating, even with those red-rimmed eyes.

She put the lid on the Tupperware and held it out toward Jodie, who was just about to take it when she spotted the

crumpled wrapping paper on the kitchen table and the small
pile of gifts lying next to it.

"What's the occasion?"

"Nothing, really. It's my birthday." Her voice had an
interesting huskiness to it, and for the first time Jodie noticed the tissues crumpled in her hand.

"Hey, no kidding. Happy birthday."

"Thank you."

Ignoring the Tupperware container in Dr. Jane's out-
stretched hand, Jodie walked over to the table and looked
down at the assortment of presents: a puny little box of
plain white stationary, an electric toothbrush, a pen, and a
gift certificate for Jiffy Lube. Pathetic. Not a pair of crotch-
less panties or a sexy nightie in sight.

"Bummer."

To her surprise, Dr. Jane gave a short laugh. "You're
right about that. My friend Caroline always comes through
with the perfect gift, but she's on a dig in Ethiopia." And
then, to Jodie's surprise, a tear skidded out from under her
glasses and slipped down her cheek.

Dr. Jane stiffened, as if it hadn't happened, but the presents really were pathetic, and Jodie couldn't help but feel
sorry for her. "Hey, it's not so bad. At least you don't have
to worry about the sizes being wrong."

"I'm sorry. I shouldn't . . ." She stiffened her bottom
lip, but another tear slid out from beneath her glasses.

"It's okay. Sit down, and I'll make us some coffee."
She pushed Dr. Jane down into one of the kitchen chairs,
then took the Tupperware container over to the counter
where the coffeemaker sat. She started to ask Dr. J. where
the filters were, but her forehead was all crumpled, and she
seemed to be taking deep breaths, so Jodie opened a couple
of cupboards until she found what she wanted and began
making a fresh pot.

"So what birthday is it?"

"Thirty-four."

Jodie was surprised. She wouldn't have taken Dr. J. for any more than her late twenties. "Double bummer."

"I'm sorry to be carrying on like this." She dabbed her nose with a tissue. "I'm not usually so emotional."

A couple of tears was hardly Jodie's idea of "carrying on," but for such an uptight chick, this was probably big-time hysterical. "I said it's okay. You got any doughnuts or anything?"

"There are some whole wheat bran muffins in the freezer."

Jodie made a face and headed back to the table. It was small and round with a glass top and metal chairs that looked like they belonged in a garden. She sat across from Dr. Jane.

"Who gave you the presents?"

She tried to manage one of those smiles that held people at a distance. "My colleagues."

"You mean the people you work with?"

"Yes. My associates at Newberry, and one of my friends at Preeze Laboratories."

Jodie didn't know about Preeze Laboratories, but Newberry was one of the most la-de-da colleges in the United States, and everybody was always bragging about the fact that it was located right here in DuPage County.

"That's right. Don't you teach science or something?"

"I'm a physicist. I teach graduate classes in relativistic quantum field theory. I also have special funding through Preeze Labs that lets me investigate top quarks with other physicists."

"No shit. You must have been a real brain in high school."

"I didn't spend much time in high school. I started college when I was fourteen." One more tear trickled down her cheeks, but, if anything, she sat even straighter.

"Fourteen? Get out of here."

"By the time I was twenty, I had my Ph.D." Something

inside her seemed to give way. She set her elbows on the table, balled her hands into fists, and propped her forehead on top of them. Her shoulders trembled, but she made no noise, and the sight of this dignified woman coming all unraveled was so pathetic that Jodie couldn't help feeling sorry for her. She was also curious.

"You got troubles with your boyfriend?"

She kept her head ducked and shook her head. "I don't have a boyfriend. I did. Dr. Craig Elkhart. We were together for six years."

So the geek wasn't a dike. "Long time."

She lifted her head, and although her cheeks were wet, her jaw had a stubborn set to it. "He just married a twenty-year-old data-entry clerk named Pamela. When he left me, he said, 'I'm sorry, Jane, but you don't excite me anymore.' "

Considering Dr. J's, basic uptight personality, Jodie couldn't exactly blame him, but it had still been a shitty thing to say. "Men are basically assholes."

"That's not the worst part." She clasped her hands together. "The worst part is that we were together for six years, and I don't miss him."

"Then what are you so broke up about?" The coffee was done, and she got up to fill their mugs.

"It's not Craig. I'm just . . . It's nothing, really. I shouldn't be going on like this. I don't know what's wrong with me."

"You're thirty-four years old and somebody gave you a Jiffy Lube gift certificate for your birthday. Anybody would be bummed."

She shuddered. "This is the same house I grew up in; did you know that? After Dad died, I was going to sell it, but I never got around to it." Her voice developed a faraway sound, as if she'd forgotten Jodie was there. "I was doing research on ultrarelativistic heavy-ion collisions, and I didn't want any distractions. Work has always been the center of my life. Until I was thirty, it was enough. But then one birthday followed another.''

''And you finally figured out all that physics stuff isn't giving you any thrills in bed at night, right?''

She started, almost as if she'd forgotten Jodie was there. Then she shrugged. ''It's not just that. Frankly, I believe sex is overrated.'' Uncomfortable, she looked down at her hands. ''It's more a sense of connection.''

''You don't get much more connected than when you're burning up the mattress.''

''Yes, well, that's assuming one burns it up. Personally . . .'' She sniffed and stood, slipping the tissues into the pocket of her trousers where they didn't presume to leave a bump. ''When I speak of connection, I'm thinking of something more lasting than sex.''

''Religious stuff?''

''Not exactly, although that's important to me. Family. Children. Things like that.'' Once again she drew her shoulders back and gave Jodie a brush-off smile. ''I've gone on long enough. I shouldn't be imposing on you like this. I'm afraid you caught me at a bad time.''

''I get it! You want a kid!''

Dr. J. delved into her pocket and yanked out the tissues. Her bottom lip trembled, and her entire face crumpled as she dropped back into the chair. ''Yesterday Craig told me that Pamela is pregnant. It's not . . . I'm not jealous. To be honest, I don't care enough about him anymore to be jealous. I didn't really want to marry him; I don't want to marry anybody. It's just that . . .'' Her voice faded. ''It's just . . .''

''It's just that you want a kid of your own.''

She gave a jerky nod and bit her lip. ''I've wanted a child for so long. And now I'm thirty-four, and my eggs are getting older by the minute, but it doesn't seem as if it's going to happen.''

Jodie glanced at the kitchen clock. She wanted to hear

the rest of this, but pregame was starting. "Do you mind if I turn on your TV while we finish this?"

Dr. J. looked confused, as if she weren't exactly sure what a TV was. "No, I suppose not."

"Cool." Jodie picked up her mug and headed for the living room. She sat down on the couch, put her mug on the coffee table, and fished the remote out from under some kind of brainy journal. A beer commercial was playing, so she hit the mute button.

"Are you serious about wanting a baby? Even though you're single."

Dr. Jane had her glasses on again. She sat in an over-stuffed chair with a ruffle around the bottom and the clam-shell painting hanging right behind her head, the one with that fat, wet pearl. She pressed her legs together, her feet side by side, anklebones touching. She had great ankles, Jodie noticed, slender and well shaped.

Once again that back stiffened, as if somebody had strapped a board to it. "I've been thinking about it for a long time. I don't ever plan to marry—my work is too important to me—but I want a child more than anything. And I think I'd be a good mother. I guess today I realized I have no way to make it happen, and that's hit me hard."

"I got a couple of friends who are single moms. It's not easy. Still, you've got a lot better paying job than they do, so it shouldn't be so tough for you."

"The economics aren't a problem. My problem is that I can't seem to come up with a way to go about it."

Jodie stared at her. For a smart woman, she sure was dumb. "Are you talking about the guy?"

She nodded stiffly.

"There've got to be a lot of them hanging around that college. It's no big deal. Invite one of them over, put on some music, give him a couple of beers, and nail him."

"Oh, it couldn't be anyone I know."

"So pick up somebody in a bar or something."

"I could never do that. I'd have to know his health history." Her voice dropped. "Besides, I wouldn't know how to pick someone up."

Jodie couldn't imagine anything easier, but she guessed she had a lot more going for her than Dr. J. "What about one of those, you know, sperm banks?"

"Absolutely not. Too many sperm donors are medical students."

"So?"

"I don't want anyone who's intelligent fathering my child."

Jodie was so surprised, she neglected to turn up the volume on the pregame show, even though the beer commercial had ended and they'd begun to interview the Stars' head coach, Chester "Duke" Raskin.

"You want somebody stupid to be the father of your kid?"

Dr. J. smiled. "I know that seems strange, but it's very difficult for a child to grow up being smarter than everyone else. It makes it impossible to fit in, which is why I could never have had a child with someone as brilliant as Craig or even chance a sperm bank. I have to take into account my own genetic makeup and find a man who'll compensate for it. But the men I meet are all brilliant."

Dr. J. was one weird chick, Jodie decided. "You think because you're so smart and everything that you've got to find somebody stupid?"

"I know I do. I can't bear the idea that my child would have to go through what I did when I was growing up. Even now . . . Well, that's neither here nor there. The point is, as much as I want a child, I can't just think about myself."

A new face on the screen caught Jodie's attention. "Oh, jeez, wait a minute; I got to hear this." She snatched the remote and hit the volume button.

Paul Fenneman, a network sportscaster, was doing a

taped interview with Cal Bonner. Jodie knew for a fact that the Bomber hated Fenneman's guts. The sportscaster had a reputation for asking stupid questions, and the Bomber didn't have any patience with fools.

The interview had been pretaped in the parking lot of the Stars Compound, which was located on the outskirts of Naperville, the largest town in DuPage County. Fenneman spoke into the camera, looking real serious, like he was getting ready to cover a major war or something. "I'm speaking with Cal Bonner, the Stars' All-Pro quarterback."

The camera focused on Cal, and Jodie's skin went clammy from a combination of lust and resentment. Damn, he was hot, even if he was getting old.

He stood in front of this big Harley hog wearing jeans and a tight black T-shirt that outlined one of the best sets of pecs on the team. Some of the guys were so pumped up they looked like they were getting ready to explode, but Cal was perfect. He had a great neck, too, muscular, but not one of those tree trunks like a lot of the players had. His brown hair had a little curl to it, and he wore it short so he didn't have to bother with it. The Bomber was like that. He didn't have any patience with stuff he thought was unimportant.

At a little over six feet, he was taller than some of the other quarterbacks. He was also quick, smart, and he had a telepathic ability to read defenses that only the finest players share. His legend had grown nearly as big as the great Joe Montana's, and the fact that it didn't look like Jodie would ever have number eighteen hanging in her closet was something she could never forgive.

"Cal, your team had four turnovers against the Patriots last week. What are you going to do against the Bills so that doesn't happen again?"

Even for Paul Fenneman, that was a stupid question, and Jodie waited to see how the Bomber would handle it.

He scratched the side of his head as if the question was

so complicated he had to think it over. The Bomber didn't have any patience with people he didn't respect, and he had a habit of emphasizing his hillbilly roots in situations like this.

He propped one boot up on the footpeg of the Harley and looked thoughtful. "Well, Paul, what we're gonna have to do is hang on to the ball. Now, not having played the game yourself, you might not know this, but every time we let the other team take the ball away from us, it means we don't have it ourselves. And that ain't no way to put points on the board."

Jodie chuckled. She had to hand it to the Bomber. He'd gotten old Paul right in the numbers with that one.

Paul didn't appreciate being made to look like a fool. "I hear Coach Raskin's been real happy with the way Kevin Tucker's been looking in practice. You're going to be thirty-six soon, which makes you an old man in a young man's game. Any worries Kevin'll be taking over as starter?"

For a fraction of a second, the Bomber's face stiffened up like a big old poker, then he shrugged. "Shoot, Paul, this ol' boy ain't ready for the grave yet."

"If only I could find somebody like him," Dr. Jane whispered. "He'd be perfect."

Jodie glanced over and saw her studying the television. "What are you talking about?"

Dr. J. gestured toward the screen. "That man. That football player. He's healthy, physically attractive, and not very bright. Exactly what I'm looking for."

"Are you talking about the *Bomber*?"

"Is that his name? I don't know anything about football."

"That's Cal Bonner. He's the starting quarterback for the Chicago Stars."

"That's right. I've seen his picture in the paper. Why

can't I meet a man like that? Someone who's a bit of a dim bulb.''

"Dim bulb?"

"Not very intelligent. Slow."

"Slow? The Bomber?" Jodie opened her mouth to tell Dr. Jane that the Bomber was the smartest, trickiest, most talented—not to mention meanest—sonovabitchen quarterback in the whole freakin' NFL when this big dizzy rush hit her smack in the middle of her head, an idea so wild she couldn't believe it had even come into her brain.

She sank back into the couch cushions. *Holy shit*. She fumbled for the remote and pushed the mute button. "Are you serious? You'd choose somebody like Cal Bonner to be the father of your baby?"

"Of course I would—assuming I could see his medical records. A simple man like that would be perfect: strength, endurance, and a low IQ. His good looks are an added bonus."

Jodie's mind ran in three different directions all at once. "What if . . ." She swallowed and tried not to get distracted by an image of Kevin Tucker standing naked right in front of her. "What if I could arrange it?"

"What are you talking about?"

"What if I could set it up so you could get Cal Bonner in bed?"

"Are you joking?"

Jodie swallowed again and shook her head.

"But I don't know him."

"You wouldn't have to."

"I'm afraid I don't understand."

Slowly, Jodie told her story, leaving out a part here and there—like what a badass the Bomber was—but pretty much being honest about the rest. She explained about the birthday present and the kind of woman the guys wanted. Then she said that with a little cosmetic enhancement, she thought Dr. J. herself could fit the bill.

Dr. J. got so pale she started looking like the little girl in that old Brad Pitt vampire flick. "Are you— Are you saying you think I should pretend to be a prostitute?"

"A real high-class one because the Bomber doesn't go for hookers."

She rose from her chair and began pacing around the room. Jodie could almost see her nerd brain working away like a calculator, adding up this and that, pushing plus buttons and minus buttons, getting a look of hope around her eyes and then sagging back against the fireplace mantel.

"The health records . . ." She gave a deep, unhappy sigh. "Just for a moment I thought it might actually be possible, but I'd have to know his health history. Football players use steroids, don't they? And what about STDs and AIDS?"

"The Bomber doesn't touch drugs, and he's never been too much for sleepin' around, which is why the guys are setting this up. He broke up with his old girlfriend last winter and doesn't seem to have been with anybody since."

"I'd still have to know his medical history."

Jodie figured between Junior and Willie, one of them could sweet-talk a secretary into giving her what she needed. "I'll have a copy of his medical records by Tuesday, Wednesday at the latest."

"I don't know what to say."

"His birthday is in ten days," Jodie pointed out. "I guess what it all comes down to is whether or not you've got the guts to go for it."

2

W_hat had she done?_ Jane Darlington's stomach took a turn for the worse as she made her way into the ladies' room at Zebras, where Jodie Pulanski had brought her to meet the football player who was driving her to Cal Bonner's condominium that very night. Ignoring the women chatting at the basins, she headed into the nearest stall, latched it, and leaned her cheek against the cold metal divider.

Was it only ten days since Jodie had shown up at her door and turned her life inside out? What insanity had possessed her to agree to this? After years of orderly thinking, what had convinced her to do something so reckless. Now that it was too late, she realized she'd made a high-school student's mistake and forgotten the second law of thermodynamics: order inevitably leads to disorder.

Maybe it was a regression. As a youngster, she was always getting herself into scrapes. Her mother had died several months after her birth, and she'd been raised by a cold, withdrawn father who only seemed to pay attention to her when she misbehaved. His attitude, combined with the fact that she was bored in school, had led to a series of pranks that had culminated in her elementary-school principal's house being painted a bright shade of pink by a local contractor.

The memory still gave her satisfaction. The man had been a sadistic child-hater, and he'd deserved it. Luckily, the incident had also forced the school authorities to see the light, and they began to accelerate her through the system so that she had no more time for mischief. She'd buried herself in her increasingly challenging studies while she shut herself off from a peer group that regarded her as a freak, and if she sometimes thought she liked the rebellious child she had been better than the intense, scholarly woman she had become, she'd simply regarded it as one more price she'd had to pay for the sin of being born different.

Now it seemed that rebellious child still lived. Or maybe it was simply fate. Although she had never placed any credence in mystical signs, discovering that Cal Bonner's birthday fell exactly at her most fertile time of the month had been too portentous for her to ignore. Before she'd lost her courage, she'd picked up the telephone and called Jodie Pulanski to tell her that she was going to go through with it.

By this time tomorrow, she might be pregnant. A distant possibility, it was true, but her menstrual cycle had always been as orderly as the rest of her life, and she wanted this so badly. Some people might think she was being selfish, but her longing for a baby didn't feel selfish. It felt right. People saw Jane as a person to be respected, to be held in awe. They wanted her intellect, but no one seemed to want the part of her that she most needed to share, her capacity to love. Her father hadn't wanted that, and neither had Craig.

Lately she had imagined herself sitting at the desk in her study lost in the data being displayed on the computer screen before her—the intricate calculations that might someday unlock the secrets of the universe. And then in her vision a noise would disturb her concentration, the sound of an imaginary child coming into her study.

She would lift her head. Cup her hand over a soft cheek.

"Mama, can we fly my kite today?"

In her vision she would laugh and turn from her computer, abandoning her search for the secrets of the universe to explore the heavens in a more important way.

The flush of the toilet in the next booth brought her out of her reverie. Before she could fly any kites, she had to get through tonight. That meant she had to seduce a stranger, a man who would know far more about seduction than someone who'd only had one lover.

In her mind she saw Craig's pale, thin body, naked except for the black socks he wore because he had poor circulation. Unless she had her period or he had one of his migraines, they'd made love nearly every Saturday night, but it was over quickly and not very exciting. Now she felt ashamed of having spent so long in such an unsatisfactory relationship, and she knew loneliness had driven her to it.

Male companionship had always been a problem for her. When she'd been in school, her classmates were too old for her, a problem that had persisted even after she had her degree. She wasn't an unattractive woman, and a number of her colleagues had asked her out, but they were twenty years her senior, and she'd been vaguely repulsed. The men who had attracted her, the ones her own age, were the graduate students taking her seminars, and dating them violated her sense of ethics. As a result, she'd earned the reputation of being aloof, and they'd stopped asking.

That had finally changed when she'd received the Preeze fellowship. She was investigating top quarks as part of the ultimate quest for every physicist, the search for the Grand Unification Theory, that simple equation, much like Einstein's $E=mc^2$, that would describe all the parts of the universe. One of the scientists she had met at a University of Chicago seminar had been Craig.

At first she'd thought she'd found the man of her dreams. But, although they could rethink Einstein's Gedanken experiment without ever growing bored, they never laughed, and they never exchanged the sort of confidences she'd always imagined lovers should share. Gradually, she accepted the fact that their physical relationship was little more than a convenience for both of them.

If only her relationship with Craig had better prepared her to seduce Mr. Bonner. She knew men didn't consider her sexy, and she could only hope he was one of those awful creatures who didn't care very much with whom he was sexually engaged as long as he was physically satisfied. She feared he would recognize her for the fraud she was, but at least she would have tried, at least she would have a chance. And she had no alternative. She'd never use a sperm bank and risk having a brilliant child who would grow up as she had, a lonely freak of nature who felt disconnected from those around her.

The sound of chatter faded as the women left the rest room. She knew she couldn't hide out forever, and she hated the image of herself cowering, so she finally opened the door. As she slipped out of the stall, she caught her reflection in the wall of mirrors and, for a fraction of a moment, thought it belonged to someone else.

Jodie had insisted she wear her hair down and had even brought over hot rollers to set it so that it now fell in a soft tousle around her face. Jane found the style a bit untidy, and she hoped Jodie was right when she insisted that a man would consider it sexy. She'd also permitted Jodie to do her makeup, which the young woman had applied with a heavy hand. Jane hadn't protested, however. Her ordinary application of antique rose lipstick and a dab of light brown mascara was hardly appropriate for a hooker, even a high-class one.

Her gaze finally dropped to the outfit she and Jodie had shopped for together. In the past ten days, Jane had grown to know Jodie Pulanski better than she wanted to. The younger woman was shallow and self-centered, interested only in clothes, going to bed with football players, and getting drunk. But she was also wily, and for reasons that Jane still didn't understand, she was determined to pull off this sordid encounter.

Jane had steered her away from black leather and studs toward a slimly cut ecru silk suit with a short skirt that molded to her body in a way that left few mysteries. The wrapped jacket was fastened at one side with a single snap, and the neckline dipped nearly to the waist, its soft draping camouflaging Jane's unimpressive bust line. A lacy white garter belt, pair of sheer stockings, and stiletto heels completed the outfit. When Jane had mentioned underpants, Jodie had scoffed.

"Hookers don't wear them. Besides, they'll only get in your way."

Jane's stomach pitched and the swell of panic she'd been suppressing all day rose up to suffocate her. What had she been thinking of? This whole idea was insane. She must have been deluded to believe she could go through with this bizarre plan. It had been one thing to map it out intellectually, but it was quite another to carry it through.

Jodie burst into the rest room. "What the hell's keeping you? Junior's here to pick you up."

Jane's stomach pitched. "I—I've changed my mind."

"Like hell. You're not going to chicken out on me now. Damn, I knew this would happen. Stay right here."

Jodie rushed out the door before Jane could protest. She felt flushed and cold at the same time. How had she gotten herself into this mess? She was a respectable professional woman, an authority in her field. This was madness.

She darted toward the door only to have it nearly hit her in the face as Jodie rushed back in carrying a bottle of beer. She opened her palm. "Swallow these."

"What are they?"

"What do you mean? They're pills. Can't you see that?"

"I told you I was farsighted. I can't see anything close without my glasses."

"Just swallow them. They'll relax you."

"I don't know . . ."

"Trust me. They'll take the edge off."

"I don't think it's a good idea to take strange medication."

"Yeah, yeah. Do you want a kid or not?"

Misery swelled inside her. "You know I do."

"Then swallow the fucking pills!"

Jane swallowed them, using the beer to wash them down, then shuddering because she hated beer. She protested again as Jodie dragged her out of the rest room and the cool fingers of air trickling under her skirt reminded her she wasn't wearing panties. "I can't do this."

"Look, it's no big deal. The guys are getting Cal drunk. They'll clear out as soon as you arrive, and all you have to do is keep your mouth shut and jump on him. It'll be over before you know it."

"It's not going to be quite that easy."

"Sure it is."

Jane noticed some of the men staring at her. For a moment she thought something was wrong—that she had a streamer of toilet paper dragging from her shoe or something—and then she realized they weren't looking at her critically, but sexually, and her panic mounted.

Jodie pulled her toward a dark-haired, no-neck monster standing at the bar wearing an olive green trench coat. He had heavy black eyebrows that had grown together until they looked like one giant caterpillar crawling over his brow.

"Here she is, Junior. Don't let anybody say Jodie Pulanski can't deliver."

The monster ran his eyes over Jane and grinned. "You

done all right, Jodie. She's real classy. Hey, what's your name, sweetheart?''

Jane was so rattled she couldn't think. Why hadn't she planned for this? Her eyes fell on one of the neon signs that she could read without her glasses. ''Bud.''

''Your name's Bud?''

''Yes.'' She coughed, stalling. Her adult life had been dedicated to the search for truth, and lying didn't come easily. ''Rose. Rose Bud.''

Jodie rolled her eyes.

''Sounds like a effin' stripper,'' Junior said.

Jane regarded him nervously. ''It's a family name. There were Buds who came over on the *Mayflower*.''

''Is that right.''

She began to elaborate in an attempt to be more convincing, but she was so anxious she could hardly think. ''Buds fought in all the major wars. They were at Lexington, Gettysburg, the Battle of the Bulge. One of my female Bud ancestors helped establish the Underground Railway.''

''No kidding. My uncle used to work for the Santa Fe.'' He tilted his head and regarded her suspiciously. ''How old are you, anyway?''

''Twenty-six,'' Jodie interjected.

Jane shot her a startled glance.

''She looks a little older than that,'' Junior said.

''She's not.''

''I got to hand it to you, Jodie. This one ain't nothin' like Kelly. Maybe she'll be just what the Bomber needs. I sure hope he doesn't get turned off by the fact that she's so old.''

Old! What kind of twisted value system did this man have that he regarded a woman in her late twenties as old? If he knew she was thirty-four, he'd dismiss her as ancient.

Junior cinched the belt on his trench coat. ''Come on, Rose; let's get you out of here. Follow me in your car.''

He started toward the door only to stop so suddenly she

nearly bumped into him. "Damn, I almost forgot. Willie said to put this on you."

He reached into his pocket. She stiffened as she saw what he withdrew. "Oh, no. I don't think—"

"Got to, babe. It's part of the job."

He encircled her neck with a fat pink bow. She lifted her hand to her throat, and her stomach pitched as she touched the loops of satin ribbon.

"I'd rather not wear this."

"Too bad." He finished tying it. "You're a gift, Rose Bud. A birthday present from the guys."

Melvin Thompson, Willie Jarrell, and Chris Plummer— three members of the Stars offensive line—watched Cal Bonner line up his last putt. They'd set a course across the carpet of the Bomber's spacious, but sparsely furnished, living room, where he and Willie were playing for a hundred bucks a hole. The Bomber was up four hundred.

"So who'd you rather bonk?" Willie asked Chris as Cal tapped his putt straight into the oversize Dunkin' Donuts commuter mug that marked the fifth hole. "Mrs. Brady or Mrs. Partridge?"

"That's easy." Chris was also a big fan of *Nick at Night*. "I'd do Mrs. Brady."

"Yeah, me, too. Man, was she hot."

It was Willie's turn to putt, and, as Cal moved out of the way, his right guard lined up for the same mug. "Somebody said her and Greg got it on in real life." Willie's putt rolled past on the right.

"No shit. Did you know that, Cal?"

Cal took a sip of scotch and watched Willie miss his second putt. "I don't even know what the hell you boys are talking about."

"Mrs. Brady on *The Brady Bunch*," Melvin explained, "and Mrs. Partridge on *The Partridge Family*. If you had the chance to fu—" He stopped himself just in time. "If you got to bonk one of them, which one would it be?''

The linemen had a side bet going on who could last the longest before uttering their favorite obscenity. Cal wasn't part of that bet because he'd refused to give up his freedom of expression, which was just fine with the rest of them since they knew he'd probably win. Although Cal could turn the field blue during a game, once he was out of uniform, he seemed to lose interest.

"I guess I'd have to give it some thought." Cal drained his glass and took the putter back after Willie finally tapped it in for a three. He eyed his next putt, a sharp dogleg left into a KFC bucket. He didn't play any game, not even a living-room putting contest, without the intention of winning. The urge to compete had taken him from Salvation, North Carolina, to the University of Michigan, where he'd led the Wolverines to two consecutive Big Ten Championships before he'd gone on to the National Football League and become one of its best quarterbacks.

Chris finished off his beer. "Here's one for you. Would you rather bonk that *Beauty and the Beast* chick or Pocahontas?''

"Pocahontas," Melvin replied.

"Yeah, Poc, for sure," Willie concurred.

"You know who I'd like to f—uh, bonk," Chris said. "Brenda Starr. Damn, she's hot."

Cal couldn't hold back a grin at that one. God, he loved these jerks. Week after week they put their asses on the line to protect him. He'd been riding them hard lately, and he knew they didn't like it, but the Stars had a chance of going all the way to the Super Bowl this year, and he wanted it bad.

It had been the worst year of his life. His brother Gabriel had lost his wife Cherry and only child Jamie, two people Cal had deeply loved, in a car accident. Since then, he couldn't muster the enthusiasm to do anything except play ball.

He banked his next putt off the TV cabinet, combining his touch on the golf greens with his skill at the pool table, and put the ball within inches of the KFC bucket.

"Hey, that's not fair," Willie protested. "You didn't say we could bank the shots."

"I didn't say we couldn't."

Melvin checked his watch and refilled Cal's glass from a bottle of very old, very expensive scotch. Unlike his teammates, Cal seldom got drunk, but this was his birthday, he had the blues, and he was trying to make an exception. Unfortunately, he had a cast-iron stomach, and it wasn't all that easy.

He smiled as he remembered his last birthday. Kelly, his former girlfriend, had planned a big surprise party for him, but she wasn't good with details, and he'd shown up before any of the guests. He thought maybe he should miss Kelly more, but what he mostly felt when he thought about her was embarrassment that she'd dumped him for a twenty-three-year-old guitarist who'd offered her a wedding ring. Still, he hoped she was happy. She'd been a sweet girl, even though she used to irritate the hell out of him.

He was a yeller, by nature. He'd didn't mean anything by it; it was just the way he communicated. But whenever he'd yelled at Kelly, she'd burst into tears instead of standing up to him. She made him feel like a bully, which meant he couldn't ever completely relax and just be himself around her.

It was a problem he'd always had with the girls he dated. He was naturally attracted to the nice ones, the ones who cared about other people and weren't just out for themselves. Unfortunately, girls like that tended to be wimps, and they'd let him run right over them.

A lot of the more aggressive women, the ones who might have been able to stand up to him, turned out to be money-grubbers. Not that he blamed a woman for looking out for herself, as long as she was up front about it.

Phoebe Calebow, the Stars' owner and his nominee for best woman in the world when she wasn't being a pain in the ass, said he wouldn't have so much trouble with females if he'd stop dating such young ones, but she didn't understand. Football was a young man's game. *He* was young, dammit! And since he could pick and choose when it came to women, why should he choose a desperate thirty-year-old who was starting to turn brown around the edges when he could have a beautiful young woman with some dew-sparkle still left on her? He refused to think of himself as anything but in his prime, especially now that he had Kevin Tucker breathing down his neck. Cal swore he'd burn in hell before he'd let that cocky sonovabitch take over his job.

He finished the last of his scotch and felt the beginnings of the faint buzz that told him he was finally getting to the place he wanted to be, the place where he'd forget about the deaths of two people he loved, where he'd forget about Kevin Tucker and getting older and the fact that it seemed like forever since he'd felt the inclination to take one of those eager little dew-sparklers he'd been dating to bed. At the same time he noticed Chris checking his watch for the third time in fifteen minutes. "Going somewhere, Chris?"

"What? Uh, no." He exchanged glances with Melvin. "Naw, I just wondered what time it was."

"Three minutes later than when you last looked." Cal picked up the putter and headed into the dining room, which had some kind of limestone floor and a pricey crystal chandelier, but no furniture. What was the point? He liked to keep things loose and easy, and he sure wasn't planning any fancy dinner parties. When he entertained his friends, he chartered a plane and flew everybody to Scottsdale.

Besides, he didn't believe in accumulating a lot of unnecessary possessions since living in the same place too long made him antsy, and the less he had, the easier it was to move. He was a great player because there was no clutter in his life. No permanent houses, no permanent women, nothing that could make him feel old and used up. Nothing that could cause him to lose his edge.

The doorbell rang, and Willie's head shot up. "That must be the pizzas I ordered."

All three of them charged toward the door.

Cal regarded them with amusement. All night, there had been something going on between them. Now it seemed he was about to find out what.

Jane stood in the spacious entry of Cal Bonner's luxury condominium. With the fat pink bow tied around her neck, she was gift-wrapped and special-delivered.

Her heart beat so rapidly she was surprised the men couldn't see the skin moving beneath the plunging neckline of her suit. She was also feeling a little muzzy, not at all like herself, and she suspected those pills Jodie had given her had kicked in.

Junior of the caterpillar eyebrow took her coat and whispered brief introductions to three men who could only be football players. The one named Chris was white with a prematurely receding hairline and the most massive neck she'd ever seen on a human being. Melvin was black, and his wire-rimmed glasses gave him a faintly scholarly look that was at odds with his enormous frame. Willie had warm coffee-colored skin that accented a pair of huge lady-killer eyes.

Junior finished his introductions and shoved his thumb in her direction. "Jodie done great, didn't she? I told you she'd come through."

The men assessed her, and Willie nodded. "Real classy. But how old is she?"

"Twenty-five," Junior replied, cutting another year off her mythical age.

"Nice legs," Chris said as he circled her. "Great ass,

too." He curved his hand over her right buttock and squeezed.

She whirled around and kicked him hard in the shin.

"Hey!"

Too late, she realized she'd made a big mistake. A woman who traded in lust would hardly react so violently to being fondled. She recovered quickly and regarded him with all the haughtiness of an upper-class call girl. "I don't give free samples. If you're interested in buying the merchandise, make an appointment."

Far from being offended, they started to laugh, and Willie nodded his approval. "You're just what the ol' Bomber needs."

"He's gonna be smilin' tomorrow," Melvin chuckled.

"Come on, boys. It's party time!"

Junior pushed her forward, and as she tottered across the limestone floor on her ridiculously high heels, they all started to sing. *Happy birthday to you, Happy birthday to you* . . .

Dry-mouthed and terrified, she reached the end of the foyer. On her next step, her heels sank into the white carpet. She turned, spotted Cal Bonner, and froze. Even through her narcotic-induced haze, one agonizing fact became completely clear. The television screen had lied.

He stood silhouetted against a wall of windows with nothing behind him but the cold November night. On television she'd seen a country hick with a good body and bad grammar, but the man staring at her from the other side of the room had nothing of the hick about him. She had chosen a warrior.

He cocked his head to the side and studied her. His gaze was cold and grim, and it sent frightening impressions running through her head.

Gray eyes so pale they were almost silver. Eyes that knew no mercy.

Crisp brown hair whose tendency to curl hadn't quite

been tamed by a no-nonsense cut. A man who made his own rules and answered to no one.

Hard muscle and sinewy strength. A physical animal.

Brutal cheekbones and a ruthless jaw. No softness there. Not even a speck of the gentler emotions. This man was a conqueror, designed by nature to make war.

A chill traveled along her spine. She knew without question that he would be ruthless with anyone he decided was his enemy. Except she wasn't his enemy, she reminded herself. He'd never know what she had planned for him. Besides, warriors didn't care about things like illegitimate offspring. Babies were a natural consequence of rape and pillage and not to be given a second thought.

Rough hands, accompanied by raucous male laughter, pushed her toward the man she had chosen to be the father of her child.

"Here's your birthday present, Cal."

"From us to you."

"Happy birthday, buddy. We cared enough to send the very best."

One final shove pitched her against him. She bumped into a muscular chest. A strong arm encircled her before she could fall, and she caught a faint whiff of scotch. She tried to pull away, but he hadn't yet made up his mind to release her, so that proved impossible.

Her sudden helplessness was frightening. He stood nearly a head taller than she, and there wasn't an ounce of fat on his lean, conditioned body. She had to force herself not to struggle to get free because she knew he would crush her if he sensed her weakness.

An image flashed through her mind, of her body naked beneath his, and she immediately pushed it away. If she thought about that part of it, she wouldn't have a prayer of pulling this off.

His cupped hand slid up her arm. "Well, now, I don't think I ever got a birthday present quite like this one. You

guys got more tricks up your sleeve than a deer's got
ticks.''

The sound of that deep, country drawl immediately
steadied her. He might have the body of a warrior, but he
was only a football player, and not a very intelligent one
at that. The knowledge of her own superior brainpower
gave her enough confidence to look up into those pale eyes
as he slowly released the grip that held her captive.

"Happy birthday, Mr. Bonner." She had intended her
voice to sound sultry, but instead it sounded professorial,
as if she were greeting a student who'd slipped into class
late.

"He's Cal," Junior said. "It's short for Calvin, but I'd
advise you not to call him that because it pisses him off
big time, and making the Bomber mad isn't something I'd
recommend. Cal, this is Rose. Rose Bud.''

He lifted one eyebrow. "You guys brought me a stripper?''

"That's exactly what I thought, but she's not. She's a
hooker.''

Distaste flickered across his expression, then disappeared. "Well, now, I thank y'all a whole lot for thinkin'
about me, but I'm gonna have to pass.''

"You can't do that, Cal," Junior protested. "We all
know how you feel about hookers, but Rose, here, ain't
your ordinary street corner whore. Hell, no. She's a real
classy whore. Her family came over on the *Mayflower* or
something. Tell him, Rose.''

She was so busy trying to absorb the fact that she—Dr.
Jane Darlington, a respected physicist with only one lover
in her past—was being called a whore that it took her a
moment to muster a haughty response. "A Bud served with
Miles Standish.''

Chris glanced toward Melvin. "I know him. Didn't he
play for the Bears back in the eighties?''

Melvin laughed. "Damn, Chris, did you spend any time

in the classroom while you were in college?''

"I was playing ball. I didn't have time for that shit. Besides, we're not talking about that now. We're talking about the fact that it's the Bomber's birthday, we got him the best freakin' present money could buy, and he wants to freakin' pass!''

"It's because she's too old," Willie exclaimed. "I told you we should have gone for somebody younger, but y'all kept sayin' how she wasn't supposed to remind him of Kelly. She's only twenty-four, Cal. Honest.''

Just like that, she'd lost another year.

"You can't pass." Chris stepped forward, a belligerent look in his eyes. "She's your birthday present. You got to fu—er—bonk her.''

Her skin grew hot, and since she couldn't be caught blushing, she turned away and pretended to study the living room. Its low-pile white carpet, gray sectional sofa, stereo equipment, and large-screen television were expensive but uninteresting. She noticed various containers tossed down on the carpet: a plastic cup, a KFC bucket, an empty cereal box. In addition to being a hayseed, Mr. Bonner was a slob, but since messiness wasn't genetic, it didn't concern her.

He flipped the golf putter he'd been holding from one hand to the other. "Tell you what, guys. People exchange presents all the time. How about I trade her in for a steak dinner?''

He couldn't do that! She would never find anyone more perfect to father her child.

"Shit, Bomber, she cost a hell of a lot more than a steak dinner!''

She wondered how much. Junior had handed her the money, which she'd tucked into her purse without looking, then slid under the front seat of her car. First thing tomorrow, she'd donate every dollar to the college scholarship fund.

He drained the liquor in his glass. "I appreciate the

thought, guys, but I guess I just don't feel like having a whore tonight.''

Anger hit her like a molecular collision. How dare he talk about her like that! Her emotions sometimes betrayed her, but her mind seldom did, and now it was shouting at her to do something. She couldn't give up this easily. He was ideal, and somehow she had to find a way to make him change his mind. Yes, he was physically terrifying. and she didn't believe he would be a gentle lover, but a few minutes rough handling wouldn't kill her, and hadn't she chosen him because he was her opposite in every way?

''Aw, come on, Bomber,'' Willie said. ''She's hot. I'm getting hard just looking at her.''

''Then take her.'' Bonner jerked his head toward the hallway. ''You know where the spare bedroom is.''

''*No!*''

They all turned to stare at her.

She thought of his cornpone accent and reminded herself that he wasn't anything more than a simpleminded football player. The pills gave her courage. All she had to do was outwit him. ''I'm not a piece of meat that gets passed around. I work under exclusive contract, and my contract calls for me to practice my craft only with Mr. Bonner.'' Avoiding his eyes, she looked toward the other men. ''Why don't you gentlemen leave now so he and I can discuss this privately?''

''Yeah, why don't we do that,'' Melvin said. ''Come on, guys.''

He didn't have to convince them. They rushed toward the foyer with a speed that was at odds with their size.

Melvin turned back to her at the last minute. ''We expect our money's worth, Rose. You give Bomber the works, you hear? Anything he wants.''

She gulped and nodded. A moment later, the front door slammed shut.

She and the man they called the Bomber were alone.

3

Jane watched the Stars' quarterback refill his glass from a bottle sitting on the coffee table. As he raised the tumbler to his lips, he studied her with pale piercing eyes that looked as if they could carry out a scorched-earth campaign all by themselves.

She had to come up with some way to seduce him before he threw her out, but what? She could simply strip off her clothes, but since her small-breasted body wasn't exactly pinup quality, that might be the quickest way to get thrown out. Besides, it was hard to get enthusiastic about undressing in front of a stranger who was standing in a fully lit room that had a wall of curtainless windows. When she'd envisioned the nudity part of this, she'd imagined someplace very dark.

"You might as well go on with 'em, Rosebud. I believe I told you I ain't much for hookers."

His atrocious grammar renewed her commitment. With every one of his linguistic mistakes, her unborn child's IQ dropped another few points.

She stalled for time. "I've always found it inadvisable to stereotype any group of people."

"You don't say."

"Condemning a person solely on the basis of ethnicity,

religion, or even that person's professional activities is il-
logical.''

"Is that so? What about murderers?''

"Murderers aren't, strictly speaking, a cohesive group,
so it's hardly the same thing.'' She knew that engaging him
in a debate probably wasn't the best method of turning him
on, but she was a much better debater than seducer, and
she couldn't resist driving her point home. "America was
founded on principles of ethnic diversity and religious freedom, yet blind prejudice has caused most of the evils in
our society. Don't you find that ironic?''

"Are you trying to tell me it's my patriotic duty as a
loyal son of Uncle Sam to show you the cracks in my
bedroom ceiling?''

She started to smile until she saw by his expression that
he was serious. In the face of such blessed brainlessness,
her unborn child's IQ took another welcome tumble down-
ward.

For a moment, she weighed the morality of deliberately
manipulating someone so dull-witted, not to mention defi-
cient in humor, but her need for the services of his warrior's
body won out over her principles. "Yes, I suppose in a
way it is.''

He upended his tumbler. "All right, Rosebud. I guess
I'm drunk enough to give you a chance before I throw you
out. G'wan and show me what you got.''

"I beg your pardon.''

"Let's see the goods.''

"The goods?''

"Your body. Your bag of tricks. How long you been a
hooker, anyway?''

"It's— Uh . . . Actually, you're my first client.''

"Your first client?''

"Please don't let that alarm you. I've been very well
trained.''

His face tightened and she remembered his distaste for

prostitutes, a fact that made this particular charade all the more difficult to carry off. When she'd pointed this out, Jodie had brushed it aside by saying that his teammates were going to get him drunk, and he wouldn't be as particular. But although Jane could see that he was imbibing, he didn't look very drunk.

Once again, she would have to lie. Maybe it was the pills, but she seemed to be getting a better grip on the whole process. It was simply a matter of inventing a new reality, embellishing it with a few pertinent details, and doing her best to retain eye contact throughout the process. "You're probably from the old school, Mr. Bonner, that still believes women in my profession can only get their training in one way, but that's not true any longer. I, for example, am not promiscuous."

His glass stalled in midair. "You're a hooker."

"True. But I think I mentioned that you're my first client. Up until now I've only been intimate with one man. My late husband. I happen to be a widow. A very *young* widow."

He didn't look as if he were buying any of this, so she began to embellish. "My husband's death left me in terrible debt, and I needed something that paid better than minimum wage. Unfortunately, with no marketable skills, I didn't have many choices. Then I remembered that my husband had always complimented me on the intimate aspects of our marriage. But please don't think that just because I've only had one partner, I'm not highly qualified."

"Maybe I'm missin' something, but I don't rightly see how somebody who claims to have had—What'd you say? One partner?—can be well trained."

He had a point. Her brain clicked away. "I was referring to the instructional videotapes my agency has all its new employees watch."

"They train you by watching videos?" His eyes narrowed, reminding her of a hunter looking down a gun sight. "Now, ain't that interesting."

She felt a little surge of pleasure as her child lost another few points on the Iowa Test of Basic Skills. Even a computer couldn't have picked a more perfect match.

"They're not ordinary videos. Nothing you'd want an impressionable child to see. But the old methods of on-the-job training aren't practical in our current era of safe sex, at least not for the more discriminating agencies."

"Agencies? Are you talking about whorehouses?"

Each time she heard that repellent word it stung a bit more. "The politically correct term is 'pleasure agency.' " She paused. Her head felt as if it were floating off her shoulders. "Just as prostitutes are better referred to as sexual pleasure providers or SPPs."

"SPPs? You sure are a reg'lar encyclopedia."

It was curious, but his accent seemed to be growing thicker by the minute. It must be the liquor. Thank goodness he was too dull-witted to realize how outlandish this conversation had become. "We have slide shows and guest lecturers who discuss their various specialties with us."

"Like what?"

Her mind raced. "Uh . . . Role playing, for example."

"What kind of role playing?"

What kind, indeed? Her mind shuffled through various scenarios, searching for one that didn't involve physical pain or degradation. "Well, we have something we call Prince Charming and Cinderella."

"What's that like?"

"It involves . . . roses. Making love on a bed of rose petals."

"Sounds a little too girly to appeal to me. You got anything spicier to offer?"

Why had she mentioned role playing? "Of course, but since you're my first customer, I think I can give you more value if we stick to the basics."

"Missionary stuff?"

She gulped. "My current specialty." He didn't look too excited by the prospect, although his face showed so little expression, it was hard to tell. "That, or—I think I might have a talent for being the—uh—the partner on top."

"Well, I guess you've just about overcome my prejudice against hookers."

"Sexual pleasure providers."

"Whatever. But the thing of it is, you're a little old for me."

Old! That *really* frosted her. He was thirty-six, but he had the nerve to regard a woman of twenty-four as old! Maybe it was her floating head, but the fact that she wasn't really twenty-four no longer made a difference. It was the principle that counted.

She mustered a look of sympathy. "I'm sorry, I must have misunderstood. I assumed you were able to handle a grown woman."

Whatever he was swallowing went down the wrong pipe and he choked.

Feeling decidedly malicious, she gestured toward his telephone. "Would you like me to call the office and have them send out Punkin'? If she has her homework done, she should be available."

He stopped coughing long enough to level her with a sonic blast from those eyes. "You're not twenty-four. Both of us know you're not a day under twenty-eight. Now go ahead and show me what you learned from those training films about warm-up activities. If you catch my interest, maybe I'll reconsider."

More than anything, she wanted to tell him to go to hell, but she wouldn't let her indignation, no matter how justified it might be, keep her from her goal. How could she entice him? She hadn't given any consideration to foreplay, assuming he would simply get on top of her, perform the deed, and roll off the way Craig had done it.

"What kind of warm-up activities have you preferred in the past?"

"Did you bring any Reddi Whip with you?"

She could feel herself blushing. "No, I didn't."

"How 'bout handcuffs?"

"*No!*"

"Dang. I guess it really don't matter then. I'm open-minded." He lowered himself into the room's largest arm-chair and waved a hand vaguely in her direction. "You go on there, Rosebud, and—whadyacall—improvise. I'll prob'ly like whatever you come up with."

Maybe she could do a seductive dance for him. She was a good dancer in private, but in public she tended to be awkward and self-conscious. Perhaps she could do a routine from one of her aerobics classes, although between her demanding work schedule and the fact that she preferred brisk walking as an exercise form, she usually dropped out before the session was over. "If you'd like to put on some of your favorite music . . ."

"Sure." He got up and walked over to the stereo cabinet. "I think I might have some highbrow stuff. I bet a SPS such as yourself loves longhair music."

"SPP."

"Isn't that what I said?" He slipped a compact disc into the machine, and as he resumed his seat, the living room was filled with the lively music of Rimsky-Korsakov's "Flight of the Bumblebee." A piece with such a frenzied tempo was hardly her idea of seductive music, but what did she know?

She performed a few shoulder rolls from the warm-up part of her aerobics class and tried to look sultry, but the quick pace of the music made it difficult. Still, the chemicals surging through her bloodstream spurred her on. She added some side stretches, ten on the right and then ten on the left so she wouldn't get lopsided.

Her hair brushed her cheeks as she moved in a manner

that she could only hope was alluring, but as he watched her with those scorched-earth eyes, she couldn't see any evidence that he was getting swept away with lust. She thought about touching her toes, but that didn't seem like a very graceful dance movement. Besides, she couldn't reach them without bending her knees. Inspiration struck.

One. Two. Three. Kick!

One. Two. Three. Kick!

He crossed his legs and yawned.

She experimented with a small hula routine.

He glanced at his watch.

It was hopeless. She stopped and let the bumblebee fly on without her.

"And here I was waitin' for you to get to the jumpin' jacks part."

"I don't dance well with people watching."

"Guess you should have spent a little more time with them training videos. Or a couple of old John Travolta movies." He got up and walked over to lower the volume on the music. "Can I be honest with you here, Rosebud?"

"Please."

"You're not turnin' me on." He reached into his back pocket and pulled out his wallet. "Let me give you a little extra for your time."

She could barely resist the urge to cry, despite the fact that she wasn't a crier by nature. He was going to kick her out, and she would have lost her best chance to have the child of her dreams. Desperation made her voice husky. "Please, Mr. Bonner. You can't dismiss me."

"I sure can."

"You'll . . . You'll get me fired. The Stars' account is a very important one to my agency."

"If it's so damned important, why did they send you? Anybody can see you don't know diddly about being a hooker."

"There's a—a convention in town. They were short-handed."

"So what you're sayin' is . . . I ended up with you by default."

She nodded. "And if they find out you weren't satisfied with my services, they'll fire me. Please, Mr. Bonner, I need this job. If they dismiss me, I'll lose my benefits."

"You get benefits?"

If prostitutes didn't get benefits, they certainly should. "They have an excellent dental plan, and I'm scheduled for a root canal. Couldn't we . . . Couldn't we just go into the bedroom?"

"I don't know, Rosebud . . ."

"Please!" With a sense of desperation, she snatched up his hands. Squeezing her eyes shut, she pulled them to her breasts and held them there, palms flat.

"Rosebud?"

"Yes?"

"What are you doing?"

"Letting you . . . feel my breasts."

"Uh-huh." His hands remained still. "Did any of those training videos suggest you take off your clothes first?"

"The jacket's very thin, so I'm sure it doesn't make any difference. As I'm certain you can tell, I don't have anything on under it."

The heat from his palms burned through the fragile silk into her skin. She didn't let herself imagine what those hands would feel like without the tissue-thin barrier. "You may move your hands on them if you like."

"I appreciate the offer, but— You plannin' on openin' your eyes anytime soon?"

She'd forgotten they were shut, and she quickly raised her lids.

It was a mistake. He was standing so near that she had to tilt her neck to gaze at him. From such close range, his features had blurred, but not quite enough to hide the fact that his mouth looked even harder than she'd first thought. She saw a small scar on the side of his chin, another near his hairline. He was all muscle and steel. There wasn't a playground bully on this planet who'd have the nerve to torment this man's child.

That's my swing, geek face! Get off it or I'll punch you.

Brainy Janie's got cooties . . . Brainy Janie's got cooties . . .

"Please. Couldn't we just go to your bedroom?"

She loosened her hands, and he slowly released her breasts. "You really want this bad, don't you, Rosebud?"

She nodded.

He gazed at her, and his warrior's eyes revealed none of his thoughts.

"I'm bought and paid for," she reminded him.

"That's right. You are." He seemed to be mulling it over. She waited patiently, giving his sluggish brain all the time it needed to work.

"Why don't you just go back to your employer and say we did the dirty."

"I have a very transparent face. It would immediately be apparent that I was lying."

"There doesn't seem to be any other way out of this, then, does there?"

Her hopes began to soar. "I'm afraid not."

"All right, Rosebud; you win. I guess we'd better head on upstairs." He slipped his index finger under the pink ribbon. "You sure you didn't bring any handcuffs with you?"

She felt her throat move against his finger as she swallowed. "I'm sure."

"Let's get it over with, then."

He tugged on the ribbon as if it were a dog collar. Her heart thudded as he led her out into the foyer and up the carpeted steps without releasing her. The side of her body brushed against his. She tried to move away, but he held her captive.

As they climbed the stairs, she regarded him through the corners of her eyes with apprehension. She knew it was only her imagination, but he seemed to have grown taller and bigger. Her gaze swept from his chest to his hips, and her eyes widened. Unless she was mistaken, he wasn't quite as detached as he seemed. Beneath those jeans he seemed to be fully aroused.

"In here, Rosebud."

She stumbled as he drew her through the doorway into the master bedroom, still trying to figure out how someone as inept as she had managed to excite him. She reminded herself that she was female, and he had a caveman mentality. In his drunken state, he must have decided that any woman would do. She should be grateful he was dragging her into his cave by the ribbon instead of her hair.

He flipped a switch. Recessed lighting illuminated a king-size bed made up with blankets, but no comforter. It sat opposite a wall that held a row of windows covered with plantation shutters. There was a chest of drawers, a comfortable chair, a set of bedside tables, but very little clutter.

He released her ribbon and turned away to shut the door. She gulped as he twisted the lock. "What are you doing?"

"Some of my buddies have the key to this place. I'm guessin' you'd just as soon we didn't have any company. 'Course if I'm wrong . . ."

"No, no. You're not wrong."

"You sure? Some PSSs specialize in groups."

"SPPs. And those are level threes. I'm only a level one. Could we turn out the lights, please?"

"How am I going to see you if we do that?"

"There's quite a bit of moonlight coming in through those shutters. I'm certain you'll be able to see just fine. And it'll be more mysterious that way."

Without waiting for permission, she made a dash for the light switch and flicked it off. The room was immediately bathed in the wide bars of moonlight slipping through the shutters.

He walked over to the bed and turned his back to her. She watched him draw his knit polo shirt over his head. The muscles of his shoulders rippled as he tossed it aside. "You can put your clothes on that chair there."

Her knees trembled as she walked toward the chair he had indicated. Now that the moment of reckoning had come, she was nearly paralyzed with a fear that even narcotics couldn't quite overcome. It had been one thing to plan this encounter in the abstract, but it was quite another to face the reality of having sex with a stranger. "Maybe you'd like to talk a bit first. Get to know each other a little better."

"I lost interest in talking when we walked through that bedroom door."

"I see."

His shoes hit the floor. "Rosebud?"

"Yes?"

"Leave the bow on."

She clutched the back of the chair for support.

He turned to her and, with a flick of his fingers, opened the button on his jeans. Bars of moonlight fell across his naked chest and down over his hips. His arousal was so pronounced she couldn't tear her eyes away from it. Had she done that?

He spoiled her view by sitting on the edge of the bed to pull off his socks. His bare feet were straight and narrow, much longer than Craig's had been. So far everything about him was larger than Craig. She took a long, steadying breath and slipped out of her heels.

Wearing only his unbuttoned jeans, he lay down on the bed and leaned against the pillows. She reached for the snap at the side of her jacket. He crossed his arms behind his head and watched.

As her fingers touched the snap, ripples of panic turned her skin to gooseflesh, and she fought to reassure herself. What difference did it make if he saw her naked? It wasn't as if she had anything unusual beneath her clothes, and she needed him so desperately. Now that she had seen him, she couldn't imagine anyone else siring her child.

But her hand felt as if it were paralyzed. She noticed that his zipper had crept down, revealing a narrow blade of hair bisecting a flat abdomen.

Do it! her brain screamed. *Let him see you!* But her fingers wouldn't move.

He watched her, saying nothing. There was no kindness in that hard-eyed gaze. No gentleness. Nothing to reassure her.

As she tried to shake off her paralysis, she remembered that Craig hadn't liked sexual foreplay. He'd told her that with men, the end result was all that mattered. Cal would probably appreciate it if she simply let him get to it. She began walking toward the bed.

"I got some rubbers in the top drawer in the bathroom, Rosebud. Go get 'em."

Even though his request made everything more complicated, she was pleased with this evidence of his survival skills. He might not be book smart, but he had street smarts, a valuable asset to pass on to a child.

"No need," she said softly. "I came prepared."

She extended her leg slightly, then tugged on her skirt with her left hand. The white silk crept up to her thigh. She reached underneath, and as she withdrew the condom she had tucked in the top of her stocking, she was hit full force by the moral implications of what she was doing. She had deliberately sabotaged the condom, and this was thievery.

Studying particle physics either distanced people from God or brought them closer. For her, the latter had happened, and she was defying everything she believed in. At the same time, she began to rationalize. He had no use for what she wanted, and she wasn't harming him in any way by taking it. He was merely a device. This would have absolutely no negative effect on him.

Setting aside her qualms, she peeled apart the package and handed the condom to him. Even in the dim light, she wasn't taking any chances that he would notice the package had been tampered with.

"Well, now, aren't you an efficient little thing."

"Very efficient." Drawing a steadying breath, she tugged her skirt just high enough so that she could kneel on the edge of the mattress. Then she straddled his thighs, determined to get this over with as quickly as she could.

He gazed up at her, his arms crossed behind his head, the condom between his fingers. Staying on her knees, she garnered her courage and reached for the open waistband of his jeans. Her fingertips brushed the taut skin of his abdomen, and the next thing she knew, she was flat on her back.

With a hiss of alarm, she gazed up at him. His weight pressed her into the mattress, and the heels of his hands pinioned her shoulders so she couldn't move. "Wh-what are you doing?"

His mouth tightened into a hard, thin line. "The game's over, lady. Who the hell are you?"

She gasped for breath. She didn't know whether it was his weight or her own fear, but her lungs felt as if they'd collapsed. "I—I don't know what you mean."

"I want the truth, and I want it now. Who are you?"

She'd underestimated his street smarts, and she knew she couldn't afford another convoluted explanation. Her only chance to salvage this situation lay in simplicity. She thought of Jodie Pulanski and forced herself to look directly into his eyes.

"I'm a big fan."

He regarded her with disgust. "That's what I figured. A bored society bimbo with a hankerin' for football jerseys."

Bimbo! He thought she was a *bimbo!* The novelty of it distracted her, and it took a moment to recover. "Not all jerseys," she said hastily. "Just yours."

She hoped he wouldn't ask her the number because she had no idea. The personal research she'd done had centered on his medical records: low cholesterol, twenty-twenty vision, no family history of chronic disease, only a variety of orthopedic injuries that were of no concern to her.

"I should kick your ass out of here."

Despite his words, he didn't move, and as she felt him pressed hard against her thigh, she knew why. "But you won't."

For a long moment, he said nothing. Then he reared back, releasing her shoulders. "You're right. I guess I'm drunk enough to forget that I gave up groupies years ago."

He moved to the side of the bed and shucked his jeans. With the bars of moonlight falling across his body, there was something primitive about him and elementally male. She looked away as he tugged on the sabotaged condom. This was it, then.

Her mouth went dry as he turned back and reached for the snap that held her jacket together. She flinched and made an instinctive grab for his hand.

He clenched his teeth in something that resembled a snarl. "Make up your mind, Rosebud, and do it fast."

"I want to . . . I want to keep my clothes on." Before he could respond, she gripped his wrist and shoved his hand under her skirt. Once she'd done that, she released him, because if he couldn't take it from there by himself, she was doomed.

She needn't have worried.

"You sure are full of surprises, Rosebud." He stroked up the length of her stocking, then moved higher, tracing the path of the garter to the point where it met the lacy belt. Now he knew exactly how little she had on beneath her skirt.

"You don't believe in wasting any time, do you?"

She could barely force the words through the constriction in her throat. "I want you. Now."

She willed herself to open her legs, but the muscles in her thighs were so rigid, she could barely force them apart. He stroked them, soothing her as if she were a cat with an arched back.

"Relax, Rosebud. For somebody who wants it so bad, you sure are tense."

"An—anticipation." *Please give me my baby. Just give me my baby and let me out of here.*

His fingers brushed the soft hair at the juncture of her thighs, and she wanted to die from the embarrassment of it. She winced as his touch grew more intimate, then tried to turn the sound into a moan of passion. She had to relax. How could she possibly conceive when she was so tense?

"Am I hurting you?"

"No. Of course not. I've never been more aroused."

He gave a snort of disbelief and began to push her skirt to her waist, only to have her grab it at the top of her thighs. "Please don't do that."

"I'm startin' to feel like a sixteen-year-old again, makin' out in the alley behind Delafield's Drugstore." His voice had a husky sound to it she hadn't heard before, giving her the impression that he didn't find that particular fantasy entirely unpleasant.

What would it have been like, she wondered, to be the teenage girl making out with the town football hero in the alley behind the drugstore? When she had been sixteen, she was in college. At best, her male classmates had treated her as a kid sister; at worst, they had made snide remarks about "the little bitch who broke the grade curve."

He trailed his mouth over the bodice of her jacket. She felt the moist heat of his breath on her breast, and she nearly leaped off the bed as his lips found the bump of her nipple.

A hot rush of desire, as unexpected as it was overwhelming, rushed through her. He closed his mouth over her nipple and teased it through the silk with the tip of his tongue. Sensation flooded through her body, waves of it, crashing in on her.

She fought against what was happening. If she permitted herself to derive even a moment's pleasure from his caress, she would be no better than the prostitute she was impersonating. This had to be a sacrifice, or she could never live with herself.

But Craig had always ignored her breasts, and the sensations were so sweet.

"Oh, please . . . Please don't do that." Desperately, she reached out for him and tried to draw him on top of her.

"You're mighty hard to please, Rosebud."

"Just do it. Do it, will you!"

She heard something that sounded like anger in his voice. "Whatever the lady wants."

His fingers opened her. And then she felt an awful pressure as he pushed himself inside. She turned her cheek into the pillow and tried not to cry.

He cursed and began to pull away.

"No!" She clutched at his hips and dug her fingernails into those hard buttocks. "No, please don't!"

He went still. "Then wrap your legs around me."

She did as he said.

"Tighter, dammit!"

She tightened her grip, then squeezed her eyes shut as he began to move slowly inside her.

The stretch hurt, but she had expected his brutal warrior's strength to inflict pain. What she hadn't expected was how quickly the pain changed to warmth. His movements were unhurried—deep, slow thrusts of silk and steel that unfurled ribbons of pleasure inside her.

Sweat from his body dampened the fragile barrier of her clothing. He reached under her and caught her hips in his hands. He tilted them up, angling his own body in such a way that hot spasms licked at her. Her excitement grew even as she fought to suppress it. Why couldn't Craig have loved her like this just once?

The fact that she was finding pleasure in having sex with a stranger shamed her, and as the sensations intensified, she tried to concentrate on her research by conjuring up thoughts of the top quark that obsessed her. But her mind refused to focus on subatomic particles, and she knew she had to act or he would push her to orgasm, something that would be unforgivable. She steeled herself, even as her brain warned her of the danger of inciting a warrior.

"Are you . . . going to take all day?"

He went absolutely still. "What did you say?"

She gulped, and her voice held a soft croak. "You heard me. I thought you were supposed to be a great lover? Why is it taking you so long?"

"So long?" He drew back far enough to glare down at her. "You know something, lady? You're crazy!" And then he lunged.

She bit her lip to keep from crying out as he drove deep. Again and again.

She clung to him with her thighs and her arms, meeting his fierce thrusts with a grim determination. She would stay with him, and she would feel nothing.

But her body rebelled. Those intolerable pleasure waves grew strong. She gasped. Climbed.

And then his muscles stiffened. Every part of him went rigid, and she felt the moment when he spilled himself inside her.

She clutched her hands into fists, her own pleasure forgotten. *Swim! Swim, all you warrior babymakers! Swim, all you sweet little brainless babymakers!* With a rush of tenderness for the gift he was giving her, she turned her lips to his damp shoulder and gave him a soft kiss of gratitude.

He slumped forward, his weight heavy on her.

She kept her thighs clutched around his hips, not letting him go even as she felt him begin to withdraw. Just a little longer. Not yet.

The power of her will was no match for his strength. He pulled away and sat up on the edge of the bed. Bracing his elbows on his knees, he stayed there, staring into space and breathing deeply. The bow that had been fastened around her neck had come untied, and, as she moved, it slipped onto the pillow.

Bars of moonlight slashed across his back, and she thought she had never seen anyone who looked so lonely. She wanted to reach out and touch him, but she couldn't intrude on his privacy. The wrongness of what she had done struck her like a blow. She was a liar and a thief.

He rose and headed for the bathroom. "I want you gone when I come out."

4

As Cal stood under the locker-room shower, he found himself thinking about Rosebud instead of the grueling practice he had just completed or the fact that his shoulder ached, his ankle throbbed, and nothing on him seemed to be recovering as quickly as it used to. It wasn't the first time he'd thought about Rosebud since his birthday night two weeks ago, but he couldn't explain why she kept popping into his mind or why he'd been so immediately attracted to her. He only knew that the instant she had walked into his living room with that fat pink bow around her neck, he'd wanted her.

Her appeal confounded him because she wasn't his type. Although she was attractive with her blond hair and those light green eyes, she wasn't in the same league with the beautiful girls he'd been dating. Her skin was outstanding, he'd give her that, sort of like French vanilla ice cream, but she was too tall, too flat-chested, and too damned old.

He ducked his head and let the shower water splash over him. Maybe he'd been drawn in by all her contradictions: the intelligence in those green eyes that fought the cocka-mamie story she'd told him, a funny aloofness in her manner that kept running headlong into her clumsy attempts to seduce him.

He'd quickly figured out that she was an upper-crust groupie looking for a cheap thrill by pretending to be a hooker, and he hadn't liked the idea that he was attracted to a woman like that, so he'd told her to leave. But he hadn't put any real energy behind it. Instead of being irritated by her lies, he'd mainly been amused by her desperate earnestness as she'd spun out one story after another.

But it was what had happened in his bedroom that he couldn't forget. Something had been very wrong. Why had she refused to take off her clothes? Even when they were going at it, she wouldn't let him undress her. It had been strange, and so damned erotic he couldn't quit thinking about it.

He frowned, remembering that she hadn't let him make her come. That bothered him. He could read people pretty well, and although he'd known she was a liar, he'd figured she was essentially harmless. Now he wasn't so sure. It was almost as if she had some hidden agenda, but he couldn't imagine what it was beyond putting a check mark in front of his name before she moved on to her next celebrity jock.

Just as Cal was rinsing the shampoo out of his hair, Junior yelled into the shower room. "Hey, Bomber, Bobby Tom's on the phone. He wants to talk to you."

Cal slapped a towel around his hips and hurried to the telephone. If it had been anybody else in the football world from the NFL commissioner to John Madden, he'd have told Junior he'd call back. But not Bobby Tom Denton. They hadn't played together until the last few years of B.T.'s career, but that made no difference. If B.T. wanted his right arm, Cal figured he'd probably give it to him. That's how much respect he had for the former Stars' player who, in his opinion, had been the best wide receiver in NFL history.

Cal smiled as that familiar Texas drawl came over the phone lines. "Hey, Cal, you comin' down to Telarosa for my charity golf tournament in May? Consider this your personal engraved invitation. Got a big barbeque in the works and more beautiful women than even you're gonna know what to do with. 'Course, with Gracie lookin' on, I'll have to leave it up to you to entertain them. That wife of mine keeps me on a real tight leash.''

Since injuries had prevented Cal from playing in B.T.'s last few tournaments, he hadn't met Gracie Denton, but he knew Bobby Tom well enough to realize there was no woman in the world who could keep him on a leash.

"I promise to do my part, B.T.''

"That'll make Gracie real happy. Did you know she got herself elected mayor of Telarosa right before Wendy was born?''

"I'd heard.''

Bobby Tom went on to talk about his wife and new baby girl. Cal wasn't too interested in either, but he pretended to be because he knew it was important to B.T. to act as if his family was the center of his life now that he was retired, and that he didn't miss football at all. Bobby Tom never complained about being forced from the game by blowing out his knee, but Cal knew it still had to be ripping his guts apart. Football had been B.T.'s life, just like it was Cal's, and without those games to look forward to, Cal knew his former teammate's existence was as empty as a Tuesday night stadium.

Poor B.T. Cal gave the former wide-out high marks for not whining about the injustice of being forced out of the game, even as he promised himself he wouldn't let anything in the world push him into retirement until he was ready. Football was his life, and nothing would ever change that. Not age. Not injuries. Nothing.

He finished his conversation, then went to his locker to dress. As he pulled on his clothes, his thoughts drifted away from Bobby Tom Denton and back to his birthday night. Who was she, damn it? And why couldn't he get her off his mind?

*   *   *

"You made me come all the way over here today just so you could ask me about my transportation expenses to the Denver conference?" Jane never lost control in professional situations, but as she looked at the man who governed her day-to-day activities at Preeze Laboratories, she wanted to scream.

Dr. Jerry Miles lifted his head from the papers he'd been studying on his desk. "You may regard these kinds of details as minor annoyances, Jane, but as the director of Preeze Laboratories, I assure you they're not minor to me."

He thrust his hand back through his limp, too-long graying hair as if she'd frustrated him beyond bearing. The gesture seemed as studied as his appearance. Today Jerry's uniform consisted of a snagged, yellow polyester turtleneck sweater, threadbare navy jacket with a dandruff-flecked collar, and rusty corduroy slacks now mercifully concealed by the desk.

It wasn't Jane's habit to judge people by their clothing—most of the time she was too preoccupied even to notice—but she suspected Jerry's unkempt appearance was deliberately cultivated to conform to the image of the eccentric physicist, a stereotype that had died out a good decade earlier, but which Jerry must believe would camouflage the fact that he could no longer keep up with the exploding body of knowledge that made up modern physics.

String theories mystified him, supersymmetry left him baffled, and, unlike Jane, he couldn't handle the complex new mathematics that scientists such as she were practically inventing on a daily basis. But despite his shortcomings, Jerry had been appointed director of Preeze two years ago, a maneuver engineered by the older and more conservative members of the scientific establishment, who wanted one of their own to head such a prestigious institution. Jane's association with Preeze had been a hellish snarl of bureaucracy ever since. By contrast, her position on the Newberry College faculty seemed remarkably uncomplicated.

"In the future," Jerry said, "we're going to need more documentation from you to justify this sort of expense. Your cab fare from the airport, for example. Outrageous."

She found it mind-boggling that a man in his position could find nothing better to do than harrass her about something so inconsequential. "The Denver airport is quite far from the city."

"In that case, you should have used the hotel shuttle."

She could barely swallow her frustration. Not only was Jerry scientifically incompetent, but he was a sexist, since her male colleagues didn't have to undergo this kind of scrutiny. Of course, they hadn't made Jerry look like a fool either.

When Jane had been in her early twenties and still operating in a fog of idealistic zeal, she had written a paper that had patently disproved one of Jerry's pet theories, which had been a slapdash piece of work that had nonetheless garnered him accolades. His stock within the scientific community had never been the same, and he'd neither forgotten nor forgiven her.

Now, his brow furrowed, and he launched into an assault on her work, not a simple thing since he comprehended so little of it. As he pontificated, the depression that had dogged her ever since her failed attempt to get pregnant two months earlier, settled in deeper. If only she were carrying a child now, everything might not seem so bleak.

As a fierce seeker of the truth, she knew what she had done that night was morally wrong, but she was confused by the fact that something about it had seemed so right, maybe the fact that she could not have chosen a better candidate to be her baby's father. Cal Bonner was warrior, a man of aggression and brute strength, all qualities she lacked. But there was something more, something she couldn't entirely explain, that spoke of his absolute suitability. An internal female voice, ancient and wise, told her what logic couldn't explain. It would be Cal Bonner or no one.

Unfortunately that internal voice didn't tell her how she was to find the courage to approach him again. Christmas had come and gone, but as desperately as she wanted a baby, she couldn't imagine arranging another sexual coupling.

The sight of Jerry Miles's lips thinning into a cat-that-ate-the-canary smile yanked her back to the present. "... tried to avoid this, Jane, but in view of the difficulties we've been having over the past few years, I don't seem to have a choice. As of now, I'm requiring that you submit a report to me by the last day of each and every month detailing your activities and bringing me up to date on your work."

"A report? I don't understand."

As he began to elaborate on what he wanted from her, she couldn't hide her shock. No one else was required to do anything like this. It was bureaucratic busywork, and the very idea went against the essense of everything Preeze stood for.

"I won't do it. This is blatantly unfair."

He regarded her with a faintly pitying look. "I'm sure the Board will be unhappy to hear that, especially since your fellowship is up for review this year."

She was so outraged, she could barely speak. "I've been doing excellent work, Jerry."

"Then you shouldn't mind preparing these reports for me each month so I can share your enthusiasm."

"No one else has to do this."

"You're quite young, Jane, and not as well established as the others."

She was also a woman, and he was a sexist jerk. Years of self-discipline prevented her from saying any of this out loud, especially since she would end up hurting herself more than him. Instead, she rose to her feet, and, without a word, marched from his office.

She fumed as she rode down to the main floor in the elevator and stalked across the lobby. How much longer was she going to have to put up with this? Once again, she regretted the fact that her friend Caroline was out of the country. She very much needed a sympathetic ear.

The gray January afternoon held that ugly hint of permanence that always seemed to hang over northern Illinois at this time of year. She shivered as she climbed into her Saturn and sped toward the elementary school in Aurora where she was scheduled to do a science program for the third graders.

Some of her colleagues teased her about her volunteer work there. They said that having a world-renowned theoretical physicist teaching elementary-school children, especially disadvantaged ones, was like having Itzhak Perlman teaching beginning violin. But the state of science education in the elementary schools disturbed her, and she was doing her small part to change it.

As she hurried into the assembly room where the third graders were waiting and set down the supplies she'd brought with her for the experiments, she forced herself to put aside thoughts of Jerry's newest act of bureacratic sadism.

"Dr. Darling! Dr. Darling!"

She smiled at the way the third graders had corrupted her last name. It had happened during her first visit two years ago, and since she hadn't bothered to set them straight, the appellation had stuck. As she returned their greetings and gazed into their eager, mischievous faces, her heart twisted. How she wanted a child of her own.

She felt an unexpected rush of disgust directed entirely at herself. Was she going to spend the rest of her life filled with self-pity because she didn't have a child, but not doing anything to correct the situation? It was no wonder she hadn't been able to conceive a warrior's baby. She didn't have a backbone!

As she began her first experiment, using a candle and an empty oatmeal box, she made up her mind. From the beginning she'd known her chances of conceiving after only one attempt were slight, and now it was time to try again—this weekend, when her fertility was at its peak.

She knew from her dedicated perusal of the newspaper's sports' section that the Stars would be in Indianapolis for the AFC Championship quarterfinals this weekend. According to Jodie, Cal was going to his family home in North Carolina shortly after the season was over, so if she put this off any longer, he might be gone.

Her conscience chose that moment to remind her that what she was doing was immoral, but she firmly silenced that nagging voice. On Saturday, she would put her misgivings behind her and head for Indianapolis. Maybe this time the legendary quarterback could score a touchdown just for her.

It had rained all day in Indianapolis, delaying the Stars' Saturday morning flight out of Chicago and backing up the schedule. By the time Cal left the hotel bar on Saturday night and headed for the elevator, it was nearly midnight, an hour past the team's normal game-night curfew. He passed Kevin Tucker, but neither man spoke. They'd already said everything they had to at a press conference a few hours earlier. They both hated the public ass-kissing they were forced to do, but it was part of the job.

At every one of these conferences, Cal was forced to look the reporters straight in the eye and go on and on about Kevin's talent and how much he appreciated his support and how both of them only wanted what was best for the team. Then Kevin would start in about all the respect he had for Cal and how privileged he was just to be part of the Stars. It was all bull. The reporters knew it. The fans knew it. Cal and Kevin sure knew it, but, still, they had to go through the motions.

When Cal got to his room, he loaded a videocassette of the Colts' last game into the VCR that the hotel had provided and kicked off his shoes. As he lay back on the bed to watch, he pushed thoughts of Kevin Tucker aside to concentrate on the Colts' defensive line. He fast-forwarded to the second quarter and pushed the play button, then watched until he found what he wanted. He hit the rewind button and watched again.

With his gaze firmly fixed on the screen, he unwrapped his pillow mint and ate it. Unless his eyes were playing tricks, their safety had a bad habit of signaling a blitz by looking twice toward the sideline. Cal smiled and tucked the information away.

Jane stood in front of Cal Bonner's hotel-room door dressed in the ecru silk suit and taking deep breaths. If tonight didn't work, she would have to learn to live with self-pity because she couldn't go through this again.

She realized she'd forgotten to take off her glasses, and she quickly stuck them into her purse, then hitched the gold-chain strap higher on her shoulder. If only she had some of Jodie's little relaxation pills, this might be easier, but tonight she was on her own. Summoning all her willpower, she raised her hand and knocked.

The door swung open. She saw a bare chest. Blond chest hair. A pair of green eyes.

"I—I'm sorry. I seem to have the wrong room."

"I guess that depends on who you're looking for, buttercup."

He was young, perhaps twenty-four or twenty-five, and arrogant. "I was looking for Mr. Bonner."

"Aren't you lucky, then, because you found something better. I'm Kevin Tucker."

She finally recognized him from the televised games

she'd been watching, although he looked younger without his helmet. "I was told Mr. Bonner was in 542." Why had she trusted Jodie to get the correct information?

"You were told wrong." His mouth grew faintly sullen, and she gathered that she'd insulted him by not recognizing him.

"Do you happen to know where he might be?"

"Oh, I know, all right. What kind of business do you have with the old man?"

What kind of business, indeed? "It's private."

"I'll just bet it is."

His leer annoyed her. This young man definitely needed to be put in his place. "I happen to be his spiritual advisor."

Tucker threw back his head and laughed. "Is that what they call it? Well, I sure hope you can help him deal with all his problems about getting old."

"I keep the conversations I have with my clients confidential. Could you please tell me his room number?"

"I'll do you one better. I'll take you there."

She saw wily intelligence in his eyes and knew that even with his good looks and glow of health, he was far too bright ever to be a candidate to father her child. "You don't have to do that."

"Oh, I wouldn't miss it for the world. Just let me get my key."

He got his key, but he didn't bother with either a shirt or shoes, and he padded barefoot down the hallway. They rounded a corner and went down another corridor before they stopped in front of 501.

It was difficult enough facing Cal without having an onlooker, so she quickly extended her hand and shook his. "Thank you very much, Mr. Tucker. I appreciate your help."

"No problem." He withdrew his hand and banged his knuckles twice against the door.

"I believe I can take it from here. Thank you again."

"You're welcome." He made no move to leave.

The door swung open, and Jane caught her breath as she once again found herself face-to-face with Cal Bonner. Next to the youthful glory of Kevin Tucker, he looked more battleworn than she remembered, and, if anything, more formidable: a case-hardened King Arthur to Tucker's callow Lancelot. She hadn't remembered quite how powerful his presence was, and she fought an instinctive urge to step back.

Tucker's drawl seemed deliberately insolent. "Look what I found wandering around, Calvin. Your personal spiritual advisor."

"My what?"

"I was given Mr. Tucker's room number by mistake," she said hastily. "He graciously offered to escort me here."

Tucker smiled at her. "Did anybody ever tell you that you talk funny? Like you should be narrating wildlife films on public television."

"Or be somebody's damn butler," Cal muttered. His pale eyes raked her. "What are you doing here?"

Tucker crossed his arms and leaned back against the doorjamb to watch. Jane had no idea what had transpired between these two men, but she knew they weren't friends.

"She came here to give you spiritual advice on dealing with the problems of old age, Calvin."

A small muscle twitched at the corner of Cal's jaw. "Don't you have some training films to watch, Tucker?"

"Nope. I already know everything God does about the Colts' defense."

"Is that so?" He regarded him with those seasoned campaigner's eyes. "Did you happen to notice their safety signals whenever they're about to blitz?"

Tucker stiffened.

"I didn't think so. Go do your homework, kid. That

golden arm of yours ain't worth a damn 'til you learn how to read a defense.''

Jane wasn't entirely certain what they were talking about, but she understood that Cal had somehow put Kevin in his place.

Tucker pulled away from the doorjamb and winked at Jane. "You'd better not stay too long. Old guys like Calvin need their beauty sleep. Now you feel free to stop by my room when you're done. I'm sure he won't have worn you out."

Although the young man's gall was amusing, he still needed to be put in his place. "Do you require spiritual advice, Mr. Tucker?''

"More than you can imagine."

"Then I'll pray for you."

He laughed and took off down the hall, all youthful strut and blatant disrespect. She smiled in spite of herself.

"Why don't you go right along with him, Rosebud, since you think he's so damn funny?"

She turned her attention back to Cal. "Were you that cocky when you were young?''

"I wish everybody'd quit talkin' about me like I've got one foot in the damn grave!"

Two women rounded the corner and came to a stop as they caught sight of him. He grabbed her arm and pulled her inside. "Get in here."

As he shut the door behind her, she glanced around the room. The pillows were bunched up against the headboard of the king-size bed, and the spread was rumpled. Static flickered on the silent screen of the television.

"What are you doin' in Indianapolis?"

She swallowed. "I think you know the answer to that." With a boldness she couldn't believe she possessed, she slid the palm of her hand down over the light switch by the door.

The room plunged into a darkness that was relieved only

by the flickering silver light from the television screen.

"You don't believe in messin' around, do you, Rose-bud?"

Her courage was rapidly flagging. This second time was going to be even more difficult than the first. She dropped her purse to the floor. "What's the point? We both know where this is headed."

With a thudding heart, she looped her fingers over the waistband of his slacks and pulled him toward her. As his hips pressed against hers, she felt him grow hard, and it was as if every cell in her body came alive.

For someone who had always been timid with the opposite sex, playing the femme fatale was a powerful experience. She sank her fingers into his buttocks and pressed her breasts to his chest. Running her hands up along his sides, she curled her body against him, moving seductively.

But her sense of power was short-lived. He pinioned her to the wall and caught her chin in a rough grasp. "Is there a Mr. Rosebud?"

"No."

His grip tightened. "Don't mess with me, lady. I want the truth."

She met his eyes without flinching. In this, at least, she didn't have to lie. "I'm not married. I swear."

He must have believed her because he released her chin. Before he could question her further, she pushed her hands between them and released the snap on his slacks.

As she struggled with the zipper, she felt his hands on the bodice of her jacket. She opened her mouth to protest just as he pulled it apart.

"No!" She snatched at the gaping silk, ripping a seam in the process as she covered herself.

He immediately stepped away from her. "Get out of here."

She clutched the jacket together. He looked furious, and she knew she'd made a mistake, but the only way she could keep this from becoming unbearably sordid was to preserve her modesty.

She forced herself to smile. "It's more exciting this way. Please don't spoil it."

"You're making me feel like a rapist, and I don't like it. You're the one who's after me, lady."

"It's my fantasy. I came all the way to Indianapolis so I could feel ravaged. With my clothes on."

"Ravaged, huh."

She clutched the jacket tighter over her bare breasts. "With my clothes on."

He thought for a moment. If only she could read his mind.

"You ever done it against a wall?" he asked.

The prospect excited her, and that was the last thing she wanted. This was about procreation, not lust. Besides, it might be harder to get pregnant that way. "I prefer the bed."

"I guess the person doing the ravaging gets to decide that, doesn't he?"

The next thing she knew, he had shoved her against the wall and pushed her skirt up far enough to catch the back of her thighs. He splayed them, lifted her off the floor, and stepped into the nakedness between.

The hard strength of his body should have frightened her, but it didn't. Instead, she looped her arms around his shoulders and held on.

"Put your legs around me." His voice was a low, husky command, and she instinctively obeyed.

She felt him free himself, and she expected him to enter her roughly, but he didn't. Instead, he touched her with one gentle fingertip.

She buried her face in the side of his neck and sank her teeth into her bottom lip to keep from crying out. She concentrated on the intrusion instead of the pleasure, on the embarrassment of opening herself like this to a stranger's touch. She had made herself his whore. That was all she meant to him, a slut to be used for a few moments of sexual pleasure and then discarded. She nurtured her humiliation so she wouldn't experience desire.

His finger traced the entry to her body. She shuddered and focused on the strain in her splayed thighs, the uncomfortable pull of her muscles, anything except that silken stroking. But it was impossible. The sensations were too sweet, so she dug her fingernails into his back and bucked against him.

"Ravage me, damn it!"

He cursed, and the sound was so savage, she flinched. "What the hell's wrong with you?"

"Just do it! Now!"

With a low growl, he caught her hips. "Damn you!"

She bit her lip as he thrust inside her, then gripped his shoulders tighter so she wouldn't lose him. All she had to do was hang on.

The heat from his body burned through his shirt into her breasts. The wall bruised her spine, and he had spread her legs so far apart the muscles ached. She no longer had to worry about suppressing her pleasure. She wanted only for him to finish.

He thrust so deeply inside her that she winced. He would have made love to her if she had given him any sign at all, but she hadn't wanted that. She had been determined to take no pleasure, and he'd granted her wish.

His shirt grew damp beneath her palms, and he used her so that he made her feel as if he were punishing them both. She barely held on to him through his orgasm. When it happened, she tried to will her body to absorb the essence of his, but her badly bruised soul wanted only to escape.

Seconds ticked by before he finally withdrew. He slowly stepped away from her and lowered her to the floor.

Her legs were so rubbery, she could barely stand. She

refused to look at him. She couldn't bear this thing she had done, not once, but twice.

"Rosebud . . ."

"I'm sorry." She bent down to snatch up her purse and grabbed the doorknob. With her jacket clutched together in one hand and her thighs wet, she ran out into the hallway.

He called her name. That silly name she had taken from a beer sign. She couldn't tolerate his coming after her and watching her fall apart, so she lifted her hand and waved without looking back. It was a jaunty wave, one that said, *So long, sucker. Don't call me. I'll call you.*

The door slammed behind her.

He'd gotten the message.

5

The following evening Cal sat in his accustomed place toward the back of the chartered plane that was returning the Stars to Chicago from Indianapolis. The lights were out in the cabin, and most of the players either slept or listened to music through headsets. Cal brooded.

His ankle ached from an injury he'd received in the fourth quarter. Afterward, Kevin had gone in to replace him, been sacked three times, fumbled twice, and still thrown the ball fifty-three yards for the winning touchdown.

His injuries were coming faster now: a shoulder separation at training camp, a deep thigh bruise last month, and now this. The team physician had diagnosed a high ankle sprain, which meant Cal wouldn't be able to practice this week. He was thirty-six years old, and he tried not to remember that even Montana had retired at thirty-eight. He also wasn't dwelling on the fact that he didn't recover as quickly as he used to. In addition to his ankle injury, his knees throbbed, a couple of his ribs hurt, and his hip felt as if it had a hot poker shoved right through it. He knew he'd spend a good part of the night in his whirlpool.

Between the ankle injury and the disastrous incident with Rosebud, he was more than glad to have this weekend behind him. He still couldn't believe that he hadn't used a

69

rubber. Even when he was a teenager, he'd never been that careless. What really galled him was the fact that he hadn't even thought about it until after she'd left. It was as if the minute he'd set eyes on her, his brain had gone into hibernation, and lust had taken over.

Maybe he'd taken one too many blows to the head because he sure as hell felt like he was losing his mind. If it had been any groupie other than Rosebud, he would never have let her into his room. The first time he'd had an excuse since he'd been half-drunk, but this time there weren't any excuses. He'd wanted her, and he'd taken her; it had been as simple as that.

He couldn't even figure out what her appeal was. One of the perks of being an athlete was picking and choosing, and he'd always chosen the youngest and the most beautiful women. Despite what she'd said, she was at least twenty-eight, and he had no interest in women that old. He liked them fresh and dewy, with high, full breasts, pouty mouths, and the smell of newness about them.

Rosebud smelled like old-fashioned vanilla. Then there were those green eyes of hers. Even when she was lying, she'd looked at him dead on. He wasn't used to that. He liked flirty, fluttery eyes on women, but Rosebud had no-nonsense eyes, which was ironic considering the fact that nothing about her was honest.

He brooded all the way back to Chicago and kept at it right on into the next week. The fact that he was held out from practice made him even more bad-tempered than usual, and it wasn't until Friday that his rigid self-discipline finally kicked in, and he blocked out everything except the Denver Broncos.

The Stars were playing in the semifinals for the AFC Championship, and despite his sore shoulder, he managed to perform. Injuries, however, hampered their defense, and they weren't able to stop the Broncos' passing attack. Denver won, twenty-two to eighteen.

Cal Bonner's fifteenth season in the NFL came to an end.

* * *

Marie, the secretary Jane shared with two other members of Newberry's Physics Department, held out several pink message slips as Jane walked into the office. "Dr. Ngyuen at Fermi called; he needs to speak with you before four o'clock, and Dr. Davenport has scheduled a departmental meeting for Wednesday."

"Thanks, Marie."

Despite the secretary's sour face, Jane could barely resist giving her a hug. She wanted to dance, sing, jitterbug on the ceiling, then race through the corridors of Stramingler Hall and tell all her colleagues that she was pregnant.

"I need your DOE reports by five."

"You'll have them," Jane replied. The temptation to share the news was nearly irresistible, but she was only a month along, Marie was a judgmental sourpuss, and it was too early to tell anyone.

One person knew, however, and as Jane collected her mail and walked into her office, a nagging worry burrowed through her happiness. Two nights ago Jodie had dropped by the house and spotted the books on pregnancy that Jane had unthinkingly left stacked on the coffee table. Jane could hardly hide her condition from Jodie forever, and she didn't try to deny it, but she was uneasy about trusting someone so self-centered to keep quiet regarding the circumstances surrounding her child's conception.

Although Jodie had promised that she'd carry Jane's secret to the grave, Jane didn't have quite that much faith in her integrity. Still, she had seemed genuinely happy and sincere in her desire to keep the secret, so, as Jane closed herself in her office and flipped on her computer, she decided not to waste any more energy worrying about it.

She logged on to the electronic preprint library at Los Alamos to see what new papers on string theory and duality had been posted since yesterday. It was an automatic act, the same one performed daily by every top-level physicist in the world. The general public opened a newspaper first thing in the morning. Physicists connected with the library at Los Alamos.

But this morning, instead of concentrating on the list of new papers, she found herself thinking about Cal Bonner. According to Jodie, he was spending most of February traveling around the country fulfilling his commercial endorsement obligations before he left for North Carolina in early March. At least she wouldn't have to worry about bumping into him at the corner grocery store.

The knowledge should have been comforting, but she couldn't quite shake off her uneasiness. She determinedly turned her attention back to her computer screen, but the words wouldn't come into focus. Instead, she found herself envisioning the nursery she wanted to decorate.

She'd already decided it would be yellow, and she would paint a rainbow running up the walls and across the ceiling. Her mouth curved in a dreamy smile. This precious child of hers was going to grow up surrounded by everything beautiful.

Jodie was pissed. The guys had promised her a night with Kevin Tucker if she came up with the Bomber's birthday present, but it was the end of February, more than three months later, and they still hadn't delivered. Watching Kevin flirt with one of her girlfriends didn't sweeten her mood.

Melvin Thompson had rented Zebras for a party, and all the players who were still in town were there. Although Jodie was officially working, she'd been sipping from everybody's drinks all night so she was finally ready to confront Junior Duncan when she found him in the back room shooting pool with Germaine Clark shortly after midnight.

"I need to talk to you, Junior."

"Later, Jodie. Can't you see me and Germaine have a game going?"

She wanted to pull the cue right out of his hands and bash him over the head with it, but she wasn't quite that drunk. "You guys made me a promise, but I still don't have number twelve hanging anywhere near my closet. You might have forgot about Kevin, but I sure haven't."

"I told you we're working on it." He aimed for the center pocket and missed. "Shit."

"That's what you've been saying for three months, and I'm not buying it anymore. Every time I try to talk to him, he looks at me like I'm invisible."

Junior stepped aside so Germaine could take his turn, and she was happy to see that he looked a little uncomfortable. "The thing of it is, Jodie, Kevin's been givin' us a few problems."

"Are you sayin' he doesn't want to sleep with me?"

"It's not that. It's just that he's been seeing a couple other women, and it's gotten sort of complicated. Tell you what? How 'bout I fix you up with Roy Rawlins and Matt Truate?"

"Get real. If I'd wanted those two benchwarmers, I could have screwed them months ago." She crossed her arms. "We had a deal. If I found you a hooker for the Bomber's birthday present, I got a night with Kevin. I lived up to my part of the bargain."

"Not exactly."

The sound of that Carolina drawl coming from directly behind her sent a shiver down her spine, just like somebody'd stomped right over her grave. She turned and looked into the Bomber's pale gray eyes.

Where had he come from? The last time she'd seen him, a couple of blondes had been trying to make time with him at the bar. What was he doing back here?

"You didn't come up with a *hooker*, did you, Jodie?"

She licked her lips. "I don't know what you're talking about."

"I think you do." She jumped as he curled his long fingers around her arm. "Excuse us, guys. Jodie and me are going to step outside and have ourselves a little chat."

"You're crazy! It's freezing out there."

"We won't stay long." Without giving her a chance to argue, he pulled her away from the pool table and toward the back door.

All day the radio had been warning that temperatures would be dipping into the single digits that night, and as they hit the alley, their breath made vapor clouds in the air. Jodie shivered, and Cal regarded her with grim satisfaction. He was finally going to have his questions answered.

Mysteries had always made him edgy, both on the football field and in real life. In his experience a mystery generally meant somebody was getting ready to run a play that wasn't in the book, and he didn't like those kinds of surprises.

He knew he could have pressed the guys for some answers, but he didn't want them to suspect how much time he'd spent thinking about Rosebud. Until he'd overheard Jodie's conversation with Junior, it hadn't occurred to him to talk to her.

No matter how hard he tried, he couldn't seem to put the matter of Rosebud to rest. He found himself worrying about her at the strangest times. Who could predict how many hotel rooms she'd stumbled into recently, with her story about SPPs and spiritual advisors? For all he knew, she'd moved on to the Bears by now, and he couldn't help wondering which one of them she wasn't undressing for.

"Who is she, Jodie?"

She wore only her hostess uniform, a clingy scooped-neck top with a zebra-striped short skirt, and her teeth were already chattering. "A hooker I found out about."

Part of his brain whispered a warning that maybe he

should let it go at that. How did he know he wasn't poking into things he was better off not knowing? But one of the factors that made him a great quarterback was his ability to sense danger, and for some reason he didn't understand, the hairs on the back of his neck had begun standing up.

"You're bullshitting me, Jodie, and I don't like it when people do that." He let go of her arm, but, at the same time, he moved a few inches closer, trapping her between himself and the brick wall.

Her eyes darted to the side. "She's somebody I met, okay?"

"I want a name."

"I can't— Look, I can't do that. I promised."

"You shouldn't have."

She started rubbing her arms, and her teeth began to chatter. "Jesus, Cal, it's colder than hell out here."

"I don't even feel it."

"She's . . . Her name is Jane. That's all I know."

"I don't believe you."

"This is bullshit!" She jerked to the side, trying to push past him, but he shifted his weight, blocking her way. He knew he was scaring her, and that was just fine with him. He wanted to get this over with as quickly as possible.

"Jane what?"

"I forget." She clutched her arms tighter and hunched her shoulders.

Her defiance annoyed him. "Hanging around the guys means a lot to you, doesn't it?"

She regarded him warily. "It's okay."

"I think it's a lot more than okay. I think it's the most important thing in your sad little life. And I know you'd be real upset if none of the players came in to Zebras anymore. If none of them wanted to hang out with you, not even the backups."

He knew he had her, but she made one last stab at defying him. "She's a nice lady having a hard time, and I'm not going to hurt her."

"Name!"

She hesitated, then gave in. "Jane Darlington."

"Keep talking."

"That's all I know," she said sullenly.

He lowered his voice until it was barely more than a whisper. "This is your last warning. Tell me what I want to know, or I'll make you off-limits to every player on the team."

"You're a real shit."

He didn't say a thing. He just stood there and waited.

She rubbed her arms for warmth and regarded him with belligerence. "She's a physics professor at Newberry."

Of all the things he had expected to hear, that one wasn't even on the list. "A *professor?*"

"Yeah. And she works at one of those labs, too. I don't know which one. She's a geek—real smart—but she doesn't have a lot of guys, and . . . She didn't mean any harm."

The more answers he got, the more the skin on the back of his neck tightened. "Why me? And don't try to tell me she's a Stars' groupie because I know that's not true."

She was shaking with the cold. "I promised her, okay. This is like her whole life and everything."

"I've just run out of patience."

He could see her trying to figure out whether she was going to protect her own hide or rat on her friend. He knew the answer even before she spoke.

"She wanted to have a kid, all right! And she doesn't want you to know about it."

A chill shot through him that had nothing to do with the temperature.

She regarded him uneasily. "It's not like she's going to show up when the kid's born and ask for money. She's got a good job, and she's smart, so why don't you just forget about the whole thing.''

He was having a hard time dragging enough air into his lungs. ''Are you telling me she's pregnant? That she used me to get herself pregnant?''

''Yeah, but it's not like it's really your kid. It's like you're just a sperm donor. That's the way she thinks about it.''

''A sperm donor?'' He felt as if he were going to explode—as if the top of his head was about to blow right off. He hated any kind of permanence—he wouldn't even live in the same place for very long—yet now he'd fathered a child. He had to fight to stay in control. ''Why me? Tell me why she choose me?''

A thread of fear reappeared beneath her hostility. ''You're not going to like this part.''

''I'll just bet you're right.''

''She's this genius. And being so much smarter than everybody else made her feel like a freak when she was growing up. Naturally she didn't want that for her kid, so it was important for her to find somebody who wasn't like her to be the sperm donor.''

''Wasn't like her? What do you mean?''

''Somebody who . . . Well, who wasn't exactly a genius.''

He wanted to shake her until every one of her chattering teeth hit the ground. ''What the hell are you trying to say? Why did she choose me?''

Jodie eyed him warily. ''Because she thinks you're stupid.''

''The isotope's three protons and seven neutrons are unbound.'' Turning her back on the eight students in her graduate seminar, six males and two females, Jane continued sketching on the board. ''Take one neutron away from Li-11, and a second one will also leave. Li-9 stays behind, binding it and the two remaining neutrons as a three-body system.''

She was so intent on explaining the complexity of neutron halos in isotopes of lithium that she paid no attention to the slight disturbance that was arising behind her.

"Li-11 is called a Borromean nucleus along with . . ." A chair squeaked. She heard whispers. "Along with . . ." Papers rustled. More whispers. Puzzled, she turned to investigate the source of the disturbance.

And saw Cal Bonner leaning against the sidewall, his arms crossed, fingers tucked under his armpits.

All the blood rushed from her head, and for the first time in her life, she thought she was going to faint. How had he found her? What was he doing here? For a moment she let herself pretend that he wouldn't recognize her in her professional attire. She wore a conservative double-breasted woolen dress, and her hair was pulled into the French twist that kept it out of her way when she worked. She had her glasses on—he'd never seen her with glasses. But he wasn't fooled for a moment.

A thick silence fell over the room. Everyone in her class seemed to recognize him, but he paid no attention to their reactions. He only looked at her.

She had never been the target of such undisguised hatred. His eyes were narrowed and deadly, hard lines bracketed his mouth, and, as she watched him, she felt as unbound as the nucleus of the isotope she had just been describing.

With so many curious eyes looking on, she had to pull herself together. There were ten minutes left in the class. She needed to get him out of here so she could finish. "Would you wait for me in my office until I'm done here, Mr. Bonner? It's just down the hall."

"I'm not going anywhere." For the first time he turned to stare at her eight graduate students. "Class is over. Get out."

The students scrambled to their feet, closing their notebooks and grabbing their coats. Since she couldn't engage in a public battle with him, she addressed them as calmly as possible. "I was nearly done anyway. We'll pick up here on Wednesday."

They filed out of the room within seconds, darting curious glances at the two of them as they left. Cal uncoiled from the wall, shut the door, and punched the lock.

"Open the door," she said immediately, filled with alarm at being confined with him in this small windowless classroom. "We can talk in my office."

He resumed his earlier position. Leaning against the doorjamb, he crossed his arms and tucked the fingers in his armpits. His forearms were tan and muscular. A strong blue vein throbbed there.

"I'd like to take you apart."

She sucked in air as panic raced through her. His posture suddenly seemed full of significance, the sign of a man forcibly restraining himself.

"Nothing to say? What's the matter, Dr. Darlington? You sure were full of words when we met before."

She fought to calm herself, hoping against hope that he had simply discovered she wasn't who she'd said she was and had come here to redeem his warrior's pride. *Please don't let it be anything else,* she prayed.

He walked slowly toward her, and she took an involuntary step backward.

"How are you living with yourself?" he sneered. "Or is that genius brain of yours so big it's taken over the place where your heart should be? Did you think I wouldn't care, or were you just counting on me never finding out?"

"Finding out?" Her voice was barely a whisper. She bumped into the chalkboard as dread slithered down her spine.

"I care, Professor. I care a lot."

Her skin felt hot and clammy at the same time. "I don't know what you're talking about."

"Bull. You're a liar."

He purposefully advanced on her, and she felt as if she were trying to swallow great lumps of cotton. "I want you to leave."

"I'll just bet you do." He drew so close his arm brushed her own. She caught the scent of soap, wool, and fury. "I'm talking about the baby, Professor. The fact that you set out to get yourself pregnant with my kid. And I hear you hit the jackpot."

All the strength left her body. She sagged against the chalk tray. *Not this. Please, God, not this.* Her body felt as if it were closing down, and she wanted to curl in on herself.

He didn't say anything; he simply waited.

She drew a deep, shuddering breath. She knew it was useless to deny the truth, but she could barely form her words. "It doesn't have anything to do with you now. Please. Just forget about it."

He was on her in a second. She gave a guttural scream as he gripped her by the shoulders and jerked her away from the board. His lips were pale with suppressed rage, and a vein pulsed at his temple. "Forget about it? You want me to forget?"

"I didn't think you'd care! I didn't think it would matter to you!"

His lips barely moved. "It matters."

"Please . . . I wanted a baby so badly." She winced as his fingers dug into her arms. "I didn't mean to involve you. You weren't ever supposed to know. I've never—I've never done anything like this before. It was an . . . an ache inside me, and I couldn't come up with another way."

"You had no right."

"I knew—I knew what I was doing was wrong. But it didn't seem wrong. All I could think about was having a baby."

He slowly released her, and she sensed he was barely

holding onto his self-control. "There were other ways. Ways that didn't involve me."

"Sperm banks weren't a viable option for me."

His eyes raked her with contempt, and the menace in his soft Carolina drawl made her want to cringe. "Viable? I don't like it when you use big words. See, I ain't a hotshot scientist like you. I'm just a dumb jock, so you'd better keep everything real simple."

"It wasn't *practical* for me to use a sperm bank."

"Now why's that?"

"My IQ is over 180."

"Congratulations."

"I didn't have anything to do with it, so it's not something I'm proud of. I was born that way, but it can be more of a curse than a blessing, and I wanted a normal child. That's why I had to be very careful in my selection." She twisted her hands in front of her, trying to think how she could say this without angering him even more. "I needed a male with—uh—average intelligence. Sperm bank donors tend to be medical students, men like that."

"Not Carolina hillbillies who make their living throwing a football."

"I know I've wronged you," she said quietly, her fingers twisting one of the brass buttons on the front of her dress, "but there's nothing I can do at this point except apologize."

"You could have an abortion."

"No! I love this baby with all my heart, and I would never do that!"

She waited for him to argue with her, but he said nothing. She spun away, hugging herself with her arms and moving to the side of the classroom so she could put as much distance between them as possible, protecting herself, protecting her baby.

She heard him coming toward her, and she felt as if she were being regarded through the crosshairs of a high-powered rifle. His voice was whispery and strangely disembodied. "This is the way it's going to be, Professor. In a few days, the two of us are taking a trip across the state line into Wisconsin, where the press won't be likely to sniff us out. And once we're there, we're getting married."

She caught her breath at the venom in his expression.

"Don't plan any rose-covered cottage because this is going to be a marriage made in hell. As soon as the ceremony's over, we're each going our own way until after the baby's born. Then we'll get a divorce."

"What are you talking about? I'm not marrying you. You don't understand. I'm not after your money. I don't want anything from you."

"I don't much care what you want."

"But why? Why are you doing this?"

"Because I don't believe in stray kids."

"This child won't be a stray. It's not—"

"Shut up! I've got a whole ton of rights, and I'm going to make sure every one of them is spelled out, all the way down to a joint custody agreement if I decide that's what I want."

She felt as if all the air had been sucked from her lungs. "Joint custody? You can't have it. This baby is mine!"

"I wouldn't bet on that."

"I won't let you do this!"

"You lost any say in the matter when you came up with your nasty little scheme."

"I won't marry you."

"Yeah, you will. And you know why? Because I'll destroy you before I let a kid of mine be raised as a bastard."

"It's not like that anymore. There are millions of single mothers. People don't think anything of it."

"I think something of it. Listen to me. You put up a fight, and I'll demand *full* custody of that baby. I can keep you in court until I bankrupt you."

"Please don't do this. This is my baby! Nobody's baby but mine!"

"Tell it to the judge."

She couldn't say anything. She had moved into a bitter, pain-filled place where speech was impossible.

"I'm used to rolling around in the mud, Professor, and to tell you the truth, it doesn't bother me all that much. I even kind of like it. So we can either do this in private and keep it clean, or we can go public and make it nasty, not to mention real expensive. One way or another, I'm calling the shots."

She tried to absorb what he was saying. "This isn't right. You don't want a child."

"A kid is the last thing I want, and I'll curse you to hell until the day I die. But it's not his fault that his mother is a lying bitch. It's like I said; I don't believe in strays."

"I can't do this. It's not what I want."

"Tough. My lawyer'll get in touch with you tomorrow, and he'll have a big fat prenuptial for you to sign. The way it's written, both of us will come out of the marriage with exactly what we took in. I can't touch your assets, and you sure as hell can't touch mine. My financial responsibility is to the kid."

"I don't want your money! Why won't you listen? I happen to be able to take care of this child all by myself. I don't want anything from you."

He ignored her. "I have to be back in North Carolina soon, so we're getting this over with right away. By this time next week, the two of us are going to be married, and after that, we'll use my lawyer to communicate about the kid and set up transfers back and forth."

He was destroying all her wondrous plans. What a mess she'd made of everything. How could she hand her child over to this barbarian, even for short visits?

She was going to fight him. He had no right to stake a claim to her baby! She didn't care how many millions of dollars he had or how expensive a court fight would be—this child was hers. She wouldn't let him barge in and take over. He had no right—

Her indignation slammed headlong into her conscience. He did have a right. He had every right. Thanks to her deviousness, he was the child's father, and whether she liked it or not, that gave him a say about the future.

She made herself face the truth. Even if she could afford a lengthy court battle with him, she wouldn't do it. She had gotten into this situation by turning her back on her principles, convincing herself that the end justified the means, and look where that had led her. She couldn't do it any longer. From this point on, she must base every decision on only one criterion: what was best for this child?

She grabbed her notes from the lectern and made her way to the door. ''I'll think about it.''

''You do that. You've got until four o'clock Friday afternoon.''

''Dr. Darlington barely made the deadline.'' Brian Delgado, Cal's lawyer, tapped the prenuptial agreement that lay in the center of his desk. ''She didn't get here until nearly four, and she was very upset.''

''Good.'' Even after a week, Cal couldn't contain his rage over what she'd done to him. He could still see her standing in the classroom wearing that dark orange dress with a double row of gold buttons fastening her up tight. For a moment he hadn't recognized her. Her hair had been swept back into one of those efficient hairdos, and big glasses covered up her green eyes. She'd looked more like the CEO of a company than any woman he'd ever had in his life.

He stalked over to the windows, where he stared blindly down at the parking lot. In two more days he'd be a married man. *Son of a bitch.* Everything inside him rebelled, everything except the moral code he'd been raised with that told him a man didn't abandon his kid, even a kid he didn't want.

The idea of this kind of permanence made him feel as if he were strangling. Permanence was for after his career, for the time when was too damned old to throw a ball, not for now, while he was still in his prime. He'd do his duty by this kid, but Dr. Jane Darlington was going to pay the price for manipulating his life. He didn't let anybody push him around. Never had and never would.

He ground out the words. "I want her punished for this, Brian. Find out everything you can about her."

"What exactly are you looking for?"

"I want to know where she's vulnerable."

Delgado was still young, but he had the eyes of a shark, and Cal knew he was the right man for the job. Delgado had been representing Cal for the past five years. He was smart, aggressive, and no leaks had ever come out of his office. Sometimes Delgado could be overeager in his desire to please his most valuable client—a few times he'd gone off half-cocked—but Cal figured there were worse faults. So far he'd handled this mess with speed and efficiency, and Cal didn't doubt that he'd handle the rest of it equally well.

"She's not going to get away with this, Brian. I'm marrying her because I have to, but that's not the end of it. She's going to discover she picked the wrong man to push around."

Delgado looked thoughtful as he tapped the prenup with the top of his pen. "She seems to lead a quiet life. I don't imagine I'll find too many skeletons."

"Then find out what's important to her and bring her down that way. Put your best people on it. Investigate her work life and her professional life. Find out what matters most to her. Once we know that, we'll know exactly what we're going to take away."

Cal could almost see the wheels turning in Delgado's

mind as he sifted through the challenges of the job he'd been given. Another less aggressive attorney might have balked at an assignment like this, but not Brian. He was the sort who enjoyed feasting on a kill.

As Cal left the office, he made up his mind to protect the people he most cared about from what Jane Darlington had done. His family still mourned the deaths of Cherry and Jamie, and he wouldn't add to their wounds. As for the baby . . . People'd been calling him a tough son of a bitch for as long as he could remember, but he was also fair, and he wouldn't let the kid be punished for its mother's sins.

He shied away from thinking any more about the baby. He'd deal with those responsibilities later. For now, all he cared about was revenge. It might take a while, but he was going to hurt her, and he'd do it in a way she'd never forget.

The night before the wedding, Jane was so full of dread she couldn't eat or sleep, but, as it turned out, the actual ceremony proved to be anticlimactic. It took place at the office of a Wisconsin judge and lasted less than ten minutes. There were no flowers, no friends, and no kiss.

At the end of the ceremony, Brian Delgado, Cal's attorney, told her that Cal would be returning to North Carolina in another week and that Delgado would handle any necessary communications. Other than his brusquely delivered wedding vows, Cal didn't speak to her at all.

They left the ceremony in separate cars just as they had arrived, and by the time she got home, Jane was lightheaded with relief. It was over. She wouldn't have to face him again for months.

Unfortunately, she hadn't counted on the *Chicago Tribune*. Two days after the ceremony, a *Tribune* sports writer, acting on a tip he received from an anonymous Wisconsin county clerk, broke the story of the secret marriage of the city's most famous quarterback to Dr. Jane Darlington, a distinguished professor of physics at Newberry College.

The media circus began.

6

"I'll never forgive you for this," Jane hissed as she snatched up the two halves of her seat belt and shoved them together.

"Just remember who showed up with a bow around her neck." Cal jabbed the stubs from their boarding passes into the pocket of his sport coat and settled into the seat beside her. He bristled with hostility, and she couldn't remember ever being in the presence of such naked hatred.

It was Monday, only five days since their makeshift wedding ceremony, but everything had changed. The flight attendant serving the first-class passengers stopped beside their seats, calling a temporary halt to the bitter verbal battle that had been going on between them in one form or another since the *Trib* story had been published three days earlier. She held out a tray with two glasses of champagne.

"Congratulations! The crew's so excited about having both of you on board today. We're all big Stars' fans, and we're thrilled about your marriage."

Jane forced a smile as she took the champagne. "Thank you."

Cal said nothing.

The flight attendant's gaze slipped over Jane, assessing the woman who had managed to snag the city's most prom-

inent bachelor. Jane was beginning to grow accustomed to
the flicker of surprise on people's faces when they saw her
for the first time. They undoubtedly expected Cal Bonner's
wife to look and dress like a Victoria's Secret model, but
Jane's well-cut tweed jacket, camel trousers, and bronze
silk shell fell short of the mark. All of her clothes were of
good quality, but conservative. The classic styles suited her,
and she had no desire to make herself over into a fashion
butterfly.

She'd arranged her hair in a loose French twist, a style
she had always liked because it was neat and timeless. Her
friend Caroline said it was too stuffy, but she'd also admitted it did a good job of setting off Jane's rather delicate
bone structure. Her jewelry was minimal, small gold knots
in her ears and the plain gold wedding band Cal's attorney
had purchased for the ceremony. It looked strange on her
finger, and she pretended it wasn't there.

As she resettled her glasses, she considered Cal's well-
known partiality for very young women. He would undoubtedly have been much happier if she'd shown up in a
miniskirt and rhinestone bra. She wondered what would
happen when he discovered how old she really was.

Just looking at the belligerent thrust of that hard, square
jaw unnerved her. If the man had ever held an elevated
thought in his head, he concealed it. Sitting next to him,
she felt like a detonated smart bomb.

"Drink this." She passed her champagne glass over to
him as the flight attendant moved away.

"Why should I?"

"Because I'm pregnant, and I can't. Or do you want
everybody to know about that, too?"

He glared at her, downed the contents, and thrust the
empty glass back at her. "Next thing, you'll turn me into
a damned alcoholic."

"Since you've had a drink in your hand most of the
times I've been with you, I doubt you have far to go."

"You don't know crap."

"Charming vocabulary. Pungent."

"At least I don't sound like I swallowed a dictionary. How much longer do you figure it'll take you to finish burpin' up all them big words?"

"I'm not certain. But if I do it slowly enough, maybe you'll be able to understand a few of them."

She knew that sparring with him like this was infantile, but it was better than the hostile silences that left her nerves ragged and her eyes searching for the nearest exit. Instead of reassuring her, the fact that he had been making an obvious effort to avoid the slightest physical contact between them left her feeling as if he didn't trust himself to hold back if he ever got his hands on her. She didn't like being frightened, especially when she knew she was so very much in the wrong, and she'd made up her mind to meet his belligerence aggressively. No matter what, she wouldn't let him suspect she was afraid.

Her emotional upheaval was only one of the changes that the catastrophic events of the past few days had produced. She'd arrived at Newberry on Friday morning, two days after their wedding, to find an army of reporters shouting questions at her and shoving microphones in her face. She'd pushed through the crowd and made a mad dash for her office, where Marie had met her with an awestruck look and an enormous stack of phone messages, including one from Cal.

She'd reached him at his home, but he cut off her questions with a snarl, then read her the press release his attorney had written. It stated that the two of them had been introduced by mutual friends several months ago, and that their decision to marry had been sudden. It listed her academic credentials and described his pride in her professional accomplishments, a sentiment he'd accompanied with a derisive snort. Then it announced that the couple would be spending the next few months honeymooning in

Cal's hometown of Salvation, North Carolina.

Jane had erupted. "That's impossible! I have classes to teach, and I'm not going anywhere."

His sneer carried over the phone line. "As of five o'clock today, you're taking one of them—what do you call 'em?—a temporary leave of absence."

"I certainly will not be."

"Your college says different."

"What are you talking about?"

"Ask your boss." He slammed the phone down.

She'd immediately marched into the office of Dr. William Davenport, head of Newberry's Physics Department, where she discovered Cal was giving the college a major endowment as a token of his appreciation for their flexibility regarding her work schedule in the upcoming months. She'd felt impotent and humiliated. With nothing more than the stroke of a pen over his checkbook, he'd taken control of her life.

The flight attendant stopped to pick up their glasses. As soon as the woman disappeared, she vented her smoldering resentment on Cal. "You had no right to interfere in my career."

"Get off it, Professor. I bought you a few extra months vacation. You should be thanking me. If it wasn't for me, you wouldn't have all this free time to do research for that lab you work for."

He knew far too much about her, and she didn't like it. It was true that being temporarily relieved of her teaching schedule would benefit her research for Preeze, although she wasn't going to admit that to him. Her computer equipment was already en route to North Carolina, and with the aid of a modem, the change in location wouldn't affect her work. Under other circumstances, she would have been delighted with three months free time, but not when she hadn't arranged for it herself, and not when she had to spend any part of it with Calvin Bonner.

"I could do my research a lot better in my office at home."

"Not with a whole army of reporters camped out on your doorstep asking why the city's most famous newlyweds are livin' in two different states." His eyes flicked over her as if she were debris. "I go to Salvation this time every year and stay until training camp starts in July. Maybe that giant brain of yours can come up with a convincing excuse for not bringing my brand-new bride along, but I can't seem to think of anything."

"I don't understand how you can perpetrate a fraud like this on your family. Why don't you just tell them the truth?"

"Because, unlike you, nobody in my family's a good liar. It'd be all over town before long, and then the whole world would have the details. Do you really want the kid to grow up knowing how we met?"

She sighed. "No. And stop calling her 'the kid.' " Once again she wondered if the baby would be a boy or a girl. She hadn't made up her mind whether she'd let them tell her after she'd had her ultrasound.

"Besides, my family's been through enough in the past year, and I'm not puttin' them through any more."

She remembered Jodie mentioning the death of Cal's sister-in-law and nephew. "I'm truly sorry about that. But whenever they see us together, they'll know something's wrong."

"That's not going to be a problem because you won't be spending a lot of time with them. They'll meet you, they'll know who you are, but don't plan on getting chummy. And one more thing. If anybody asks how old you are, don't tell 'em you're twenty-eight. If you get pressed, admit to twenty-five, but no older."

What was going to happen when he found out she was thirty-four, not twenty-eight? "I'm not going to lie about my age."

"I don't see why not. You lied about everything else."

She fought back another wave of guilt. "Nobody's going to believe I'm twenty-five. I won't do it."

"Professor, I'd seriously advise you not to piss me off any more than you already have. And don't you have contact lenses or something so you don't have to wear those damned egghead glasses all the time?"

"They're actually bifocals." She took a certain pleasure in pointing that out.

"Bifocals!"

"The kind with an invisible line. There's no correction at the top, but magnification at the bottom. A lot of *middle-aged* people wear them."

Whatever unpleasant response Cal was about to make was cut off as a burly passenger struggling toward the coach section with two large carry-on bags banged one of them into his arm. She stared at the man in fascination. It was fifteen degrees outside, but he was wearing a nylon tank top, presumably so he could show off his muscles.

Cal noticed her interest in the man's attire and gave her a calculated look. "Where I come from, we call those muscle tops wife-beater shirts."

He'd obviously forgotten he wasn't messing with one of his little love bunnies. She smiled sweetly. "And here I thought hillbillies never hit their sisters."

His eyebrows slammed together. "You don't have any idea what hillbillies do, Professor, but I suspect you'll be finding out soon."

"Hey, sorry to interrupt, Cal, but I was wondering if you'd autograph this for my kid." A middle-aged businessman thrust a pen at Cal, along with a memo pad that bore the name of a pharmaceutical company. Cal complied, and before long another man appeared. The requests continued until the flight attendants ordered everyone to their seats. Cal was polite to the fans and surprisingly patient.

She took advantage of the interruption to begin reading

a journal article written by one of her former colleagues on the decay products of the six-quark H particle, but it was difficult to focus on nonlinear physics with her own world so far out of kilter. She could have refused to go with him to Salvation, but the press would have hounded her and cast a shadow over her child's future. She simply couldn't risk it.

No matter what, she had to keep their tawdry story from becoming public knowledge. The humiliation she'd face, as gruesome as that would be, wasn't nearly as bad as what that information would do to her child growing up. She had promised herself she would base all her decisions on what was best for this baby, and that was why she had finally agreed to go with him.

She pushed her glasses more firmly on her nose and once again began to read. Out of the corner of her eye, she saw Cal glaring at her, and she decided it was a good thing she didn't have psychic ability because the last thing she wanted to do was read his mind.

Bifocals! Cal thought. God, how he hated those glasses. He mentally cataloged all that he disliked about the woman sitting next to him and concluded that, even if he set aside the issue of her character, there was a lot to choose from.

Everything about her was too serious. She even had serious hair. Why didn't she loosen it up from that damned thingamabob? It was a great color, he'd give her that. He'd had a couple of girlfriends with hair that color, but theirs had come out of a bottle, and Jane Darlington's could only have come from God.

With the exception of that small lock of hair that had escaped its confines to make a silky S behind her ear, this was one serious woman. Serious hair and serious clothes. Pretty skin, though. But he sure as hell didn't like those big nerdy *bifocals*. They made her look every one of her twenty-eight years.

He still couldn't believe he'd married her. But what else

could he have done and still been able to live with himself? Let his kid grow up without a father? With the way he'd been raised, that wasn't even a possibility.

He tried to feel good about the fact that he'd done the right thing, but all he felt was rage. He didn't want to be married, damn it! Not to anybody. But especially not to this uptight prig with her liar's heart.

For days he'd been telling himself she was no more permanent than a temporary live-in girlfriend, but every time he spotted that wedding band on her finger, he felt a sickening premonition. It was as if he were watching the scoreboard clock tick off the final days of his career.

"I can't imagine buying a car without seeing it first." Jane gazed around at the interior of the new hunter green Jeep Grand Cherokee that had been waiting for them in the parking lot at the Asheville airport with the key hidden in a magnetic case under the front bumper.

"I hire people to do this kind of thing for me."

His nonchalance about his wealth made her waspish. "How pretentious."

"Watch your language, Professor."

"It means wise," she lied. "You might try working it into a sentence sometime with a person you really admire. Tell them you think they're pretentious, and they'll feel warm and fuzzy all day."

"Thanks for the suggestions. Maybe I'll use it next time I'm on TV."

She regarded him suspiciously, but couldn't see even a trace of mistrust in his expression. It occurred to her that these last few days were turning her into a bitch.

She stared glumly out the window. Despite the gloom of the chilly, overcast March day, she had to admit the country was beautiful. The mountainous contours of western North Carolina formed a stark contrast to the flat Illinois landscape where she'd grown up.

They crossed the French Broad River, a name that would have made her smile under other circumstances, and headed west on Interstate 40 toward Salvation. Ever since she'd first heard the name of Cal's hometown, something about it had struck a chord in the back of her mind, but she couldn't remember what.

"Is there some reason I should recognize the name Salvation."

"It was in the news a while back, but most of the locals don't like to talk about it."

She waited for more information and wasn't too surprised when none was forthcoming. Next to the Bomber, she was a magpie. "Do you think you could let me in on the secret?"

He took so long responding that she thought he was ignoring her, but he finally spoke. "Salvation was where G. Dwayne Snopes settled. The televangelist."

"Wasn't he killed in some kind of small plane crash a few years ago?"

"Yeah. While he was on his way out of the country with a few million dollars that didn't belong to him. Even at the height of his career, the town's leaders never thought much of him, and they don't like having Salvation's name associated with him now that he's dead."

"Did you know him?"

"We met."

"What sort of man was he?"

"He was a crook! Any fool could figure that out."

The nuances of polite conversation were obviously beyond his mental capabilities. She turned away and tried to enjoy the scenery, but being plunged into a new life with a dangerous stranger who hated everything about her made it tough.

They eventually left the highway for a winding two-lane road. The gears of the Jeep ground as they headed up one side of a mountain and then curved down the other. Rusty double-wide mobile homes sitting in weedy lots at the side of the road provided a sharp contrast to the gated entrances of posh residential developments built for retirees around lush golf courses. Her stomach was beginning to get queasy from the switchbacks when Cal turned off the highway onto a gravel road that seemed to go straight up.

"This is Heartache Mountain. I need to stop and see my grandmother before we get settled. The rest of my family's out of town now, but she'll kick up a fuss if I don't bring you to see her right away. And don't go out of your way to be nice. Remember that you won't be around for long."

"You want me to be rude?"

"Let's just say I don't want you winning any popularity contests with my family. And keep the fact that you're pregnant to yourself."

"I wasn't planning on announcing it."

He swung into a deeply rutted lane that led to a tin-roofed house badly in need of paint. One of the shutters hung crookedly, and the front step that led up to the porch sagged. In view of his wealth, she was shocked by its condition. If he cared about his grandmother, he could surely have spared a little money to fix up this place.

He turned off the engine, climbed out of the car, and came around the front to open her door. The courtesy surprised her. She remembered that he'd done the same when she'd gotten into the car at the airport.

"Her name's Annie Glide," he said as she got out, "and she'll be eighty next birthday. She's got a bad heart and emphysema, but she's not ready to give up yet. Watch that step. Damn. This place is going to fall down right around her ears."

"Surely you can afford to move her out of here."

He looked at her as if she'd lost her mind, then walked to the door and slammed his fist against it. "Open up, you old bat, and tell me why this step isn't fixed!"

Jane gaped at him. This was the way he treated his dear old granny?

The door squeaked open, and Jane found herself staring at a stoop-shouldered woman with bleached blond hair sticking out in tufts all over her head, bright red lipstick, and a cigarette hanging out of the corner of her mouth. "You watch the way you talk to me, Calvin James Bonner. I can still whup you, and don't you forget it."

"Have to catch me first." He plucked the cigarette out of her mouth, ground it beneath the toe of his shoe, and folded her in his arms.

She gave a wheezy cackle and patted his back. "Wild as the devil and twice as bad." She peered around his back to scowl at Jane, who was standing at the top of the steps. "Who's that?"

"Annie, this is Jane." His voice developed a steely note. "My wife. Remember I called to tell you about her. We got married last Wednesday."

"Looks like a city gal. You ever skinned a squirrel, city gal?"

"I—uh—can't say as I have."

She gave a dismissive snort and turned back to Cal. "What done took you so long to come see your granny?"

"I was afraid you'd bite me, and I had to get my rabies shots up to date."

This sent her into a gale of witchy laughter, culminating in a coughing spasm. Cal looped his arm around her and steered her into the house, cussing her out for her smoking the entire time.

Jane pushed her hands into the pockets of her jacket and thought about how there weren't going to be any easy successes for her the next few months. Now she'd failed the squirrel-skinning test.

She wasn't anxious to go inside, so she walked across the porch to the place where a brightly colored wind sock whipped from the corner of the roof. The cabin was tucked into the side of the mountain and surrounded by woods, with the exception of a clearing to the side and back for a garden. The way the mist clung to the distant mountain peaks made her understand why this part of the Appalachian chain was called the Smokies.

It was so quiet she could hear a single squirrel rustling through the bare branches of an oak tree. Until that moment, she hadn't realized how noisy a town, even a peaceful suburban one, could be. She heard the crack of a twig, the caw of a crow, and breathed in the damp, chill scent of March woodlands not yet ready to leave winter behind. With a sigh, she crossed the porch to the door. She already knew enough about Annie Glide to realize the old woman would take any retreat as a sign of weakness.

She stepped directly into a small, cluttered living room that was a curious amalgam of the old and gaudy with the new and tasteful. A rich, thick-piled smoky blue carpet held an assortment of worn furniture upholstered in everything from faded brocade to threadbare velvet. The gilded coffee table had a broken leg crudely repaired with silver duct tape, and faded red tassels held fragile lace curtains back from the windows.

There was an obviously expensive stereo cabinet complete with a compact disc player sitting on a wall perpendicular to an old stone fireplace. The rough-hewn mantel held an assortment of clutter including a guitar-shaped ceramic vase filled with peacock feathers, a football, a stuffed pheasant, and a framed photograph of a man who looked familiar, although Jane couldn't quite place him.

Through a small archway off to the left she could see part of a kitchen with a peeling linoleum floor and a state-of-the-art cooking range. Another doorway presumably led to bedrooms in the back.

Annie Glide lowered herself with a great deal of effort into an upholstered rocker while Cal paced in front of her, glowering. ''. . . then Roy said you pulled your shotgun on him, and now he tells me he won't come out here again without a five-hundred-dollar deposit. Nonrefundable!''

"Roy Potts don't know the difference between a hammer and his colon."

"Roy is the best damn handyman in these parts."

"Did you bring me my new Harry Connick, Jr. CD? Now that's what I really want, not some fool handyman nibbin' into my business."

He sighed. "Yeah, I brought it. It's out in the car."

"Well, go on and get it for me." She waved him toward the door. "And move that speaker when you get back. It's too close to my TV."

As soon as he disappeared, she speared Jane with her blue eyes. Jane felt a curious desire to throw herself on her knees and confess her sins, but she suspected the cantankerous woman would simply smack her in the head.

"How old are you, gal?"

"I'm thirty-four."

She thought that one over. "How old does he think you are?"

"Twenty-eight. But I didn't tell him that."

"You never told him different, either, did you?"

"No." Although she hadn't been invited to sit, she found a place at the end of an old velvet couch. "He wants me to tell everyone I'm twenty-five."

Annie rocked for a while. "You gonna do it?"

Jane shook her head.

"Cal told me you're a college professor. That must mean you're a real smart lady."

"Smart about some things. Dumb about others, I guess."

She nodded. "Calvin, he don't put up with much foolishness."

"I know."

"He needs a little foolishness in his life."

"I'm afraid I'm not too good at that sort of thing. I used to be when I was a child, but not much anymore."

Annie looked up at Cal as he came in the door. "When I heard how fast you two got married, I thought she might have done you bad like your mama done your daddy."

"The situations aren't the same at all," he said tonelessly.

Annie tilted her head toward Jane. "My daughter Amber wasn't nothin' more than a little white-trash gal spendin' all her time runnin' after boys. Laid her a trap for the richest one in town." Annie cackled. "She caught him, too. Cal here was the bait."

Jane felt sick. So Cal was the second generation of Bonner male trapped into marriage by a pregnant female.

"My Amber Lynn likes to forget she growed up dirt-poor. Isn't that so, Calvin?"

"I don't know why you're always giving her such a hard time." He walked over to the CD player, and a few moments later, the sounds of Harry Connick, Jr. singing "Stardust" filled the cabin.

Jane realized Connick was the man in the photograph on the mantel. What a strange old woman.

Annie leaned back in the chair. "That Connick boy has got him one beautiful voice. I always wished you could sing, Calvin, but you never could manage it."

"No, ma'am. Can't do much but throw a football." He sat down on the couch next to Jane but not touching her.

Annie closed her eyes, and the three of them sat quietly listening to the honey-sweet voice. Maybe it was the gray day, the deep quiet of the woods, but Jane felt herself begin to relax. Time ticked away, and a curious alertness came over her. Here in this ramshackle house lying in the shadows of the Great Smoky Mountains, she began to feel as if she were on the verge of finding some missing part of herself. Right here in this room that smelled of pine and must and chimney smoke.

"Janie Bonner, I want you to promise me something."

The feeling faded as she heard herself being addressed

for the first time by her married name, but she didn't get a chance to tell Annie she'd be using her maiden name.

"Janie Bonner, I want you to promise me right now that you'll look out for Calvin like a wife should, and that you'll think about his welfare before you think about your own."

She didn't want to do any such thing, and she struggled to hide her dismay. "Life's complicated. That's a hard thing to promise."

" 'Course it's hard," she snapped. "You didn't think bein' married to this man was gonna be easy, did you?"

"No, but . . ."

"Do what I say. You promise me right now, gal."

Under the force of those sharp blue eyes, Jane's own will dissolved, and she found she couldn't deny this old woman. "I promise that I'll do my best."

"That's good enough." Once again, her lids closed. The creak of her rocker and her wheezy breathing underscored the smooth molasses voice coming from the speakers. "Calvin, promise me you're gonna look after Janie Bonner like a husband should and that you'll think about her welfare before you think about your own."

"Aw, Annie, after all these years of waitin' for the right girl to come along, you think I wouldn't take care of her once I found her?"

Annie opened her eyes and nodded, having failed to notice either the malevolent gaze Cal shot at Jane or the fact that he hadn't promised a single thing.

"If I'd of made your mama and daddy do this, Calvin, maybe things would of been easier for them, but I wasn't smart enough, then."

"It didn't have anything to do with being smart, you old hypocrite. You were so happy to see your daughter catch a Bonner that you didn't care about anything else."

Her mouth pursed and Jane saw where her crimson lipstick had bled into the age lines around her lips. "Bonners always thought they was too good for Glides, but I guess we showed them. Glide blood runnin' true and strong in all three of my grandsons. At least it is in you and Gabriel. Ethan's always been a sissy boy, more Bonner than Glide.''

"Just because Ethan's a preacher doesn't make him a sissy.'' He rose from the couch. ''We have to go now, but don't you think I've forgotten about that front step. Now where are you hiding those damn cigarettes?''

"Somewhere you won't find them.''

"That's what you think.'' He headed for an old bureau next to the kitchen door where he dug into the bottom drawer and pulled out a carton of Camels. ''I'll be taking these with me.''

"You just want to smoke 'em yourself.'' She rose from the rocker with great difficulty. ''When Calvin comes back, you come with him, Janie Bonner. You got a lot to learn 'bout bein' married to a country boy.''

"She's working on a real important research project,'' Cal said, ''so she's not going to have much time for visiting.''

"Is that true?'' Jane thought she saw a flash of hurt in the old woman's eyes.

"I'll come visit whenever you like.''

"Good.''

Cal's jaw clenched, and she realized she'd displeased him.

"Now go away.'' Annie shooed them toward the door. ''I want to listen to my Harry without all this talk.''

Cal opened the door for Jane to slip through. They had just reached the car when Annie's voice stopped them.

"Janie Bonner!''

She turned to see the old woman regarding them through the screen door.

"Don't you wear nothin' to bed, not even in the winter, you hear me, gal? You go to your husband the way your Maker made you. Stark naked. Keeps a man from strayin'.''

Jane couldn't summon an appropriate response, so she waved and got in the car.

"That'll be the day," Cal muttered as they drove away from the house. "I'll bet you wear clothes in the shower."

"It really galls you, doesn't it, that I didn't strip for you?"

"The list of what you've done that galls me, Professor, is so long I don't know where to start. And why did you tell her you'd come back whenever she likes? I brought you here because I had to, but that's it. You're not spending any more time with her."

"I already told her I'd come back. How do you suggest I get out of it?"

"You're the genius. I'm sure you can figure something out."

7

As they drove down off the mountain, Jane saw an old drive-in movie theater on the right. The screen still stood, although it was damaged, and a deeply rutted gravel lane led to a ticket booth that had once been painted yellow, but had faded to a dirty mustard. The overgrown entrance was marked with an enormous starburst-shaped sign outlined in broken bulbs with the words, *Pride of Carolina*, written inside in flaking purple-and-yellow script.

Jane couldn't tolerate the thick silence that had fallen between them any longer. "I haven't seen a drive-in in years. Did you used to come here?"

Somewhat to her surprise, he answered her. "This is where all the high-school kids got together in the summer. We'd park in the back row, drink beer, and make out."

"I'll bet it was fun."

Jane didn't realize how wistful she'd sounded until he shot her a curious glance. "You never did anything like that?"

"I was in college when I was sixteen. I spent my Saturday nights in the science library."

"No boyfriends."

"Who was going to ask me out? I was too young for

105

my classmates, and the few boys I knew who were my own age thought I was a freak.''

She realized too late that she'd just given him a golden opportunity to take another verbal swipe at her, but he didn't do it. Instead he turned his attention back to the road as if he regretted having even such a short conversation with her. She noticed that the hard edges of his profile made him seem very much a part of these mountains.

They'd approached the outskirts of Salvation before he spoke again. "I've always stayed at my parents when I visit, but since I couldn't do that this year, I bought a house.''

"Oh?'' She waited for him to offer a few details, but he said nothing more.

The town of Salvation was small and compact, nestled in a narrow valley. The quaint downtown section held an assortment of stores, including a charmingly rustic restaurant, a shop that featured twig furniture, and the pink-and-blue caboose-shaped Petticoat Junction Cafe. They passed an Ingles grocery store, then crossed a bridge. Cal turned onto another winding, climbing road, then pulled into a lane paved with fresh gravel and came to a stop.

Jane stared at the two wrought-iron gates directly in front of them. Each held a pair of gold praying hands at its center. She swallowed, barely repressing a moan. "Please tell me this isn't yours.''

"Home sweet home.'' He got out of the car, pulled a key from his pocket, and fiddled with a control box on a stone pillar to the left. Within seconds, the gates with their praying hands swung open.

He climbed back in the car, put it into gear, and drove forward. "The gate operates electronically. The realtor left the controls inside.''

"What is this place?'' she said weakly.

"My new house. It's also the only piece of real estate in

Salvation that'll give us enough privacy to hide our nasty little secret from the world.''

He rounded a small curve, and Jane caught her first glimpse of the house. "It looks like Tara on steroids.''

The gravel drive ended in a motor court that formed a crescent in front of a white, colonial plantation house. Six massive columns stretched across the front, along with a balcony of elaborate gold grillwork. A fanlight of jewel-toned colored glass topped the double-wide front door, while three marble steps led to the veranda.

"G. Dwayne liked to do things in a big way," Cal said.

"This was his house?" Of course it was. She'd known it the moment she'd seen the praying hands on the gates. "I can't believe you bought the house of a crooked tele-vangelist.''

"He's dead, and I need privacy." He stopped the Jeep in front, then craned his neck to look up at the ornate fa-cade. "The realtor guaranteed I'd like it.''

"Are you saying this is the first time you've seen it?''

"G. Dwayne and I weren't close, so he never put me on his guest list.''

"You bought a house without looking at it?" She thought about the car she was riding in and didn't know why she was even surprised.

He climbed out without replying and began to unload. She got out, too, and stooped down to pick up one of her suitcases, only to have him brush her aside. "You're in my way. Get inside. It's unlocked.''

With that gracious invitation, she mounted the marble stairs and opened the front door. As she stepped inside and caught her first glimpse of the interior, she saw that it was even worse than the outside. The open foyer had at its cen-ter an overly grandiose fountain with a marble sculpture of a Grecian maiden pouring water from an urn balanced on her shoulder. The fountain was running, thanks, no doubt, to the realtor who had unloaded this monstrosity on Cal, and the multicolored lights hidden beneath the water gave the whole thing a certain Las Vegas look. Hanging above the foyer like an inverted wedding cake was an enormous crystal chandelier made up of hundreds of prisms and tear-drops held together with gold swags and filigree.

Turning to the right, she entered a sunken living room that was furnished with fake French rococo furniture, elaborately fringed draperies, and an Italian marble fireplace complete with cavorting cupids. Perhaps the room's most vulgar piece was the coffee table. Its round glass top was supported by a center column shaped like a kneeling blackamoor, naked except for a crimson-and-gold loincloth.

She moved on to the dining room where a pair of crystal chandeliers topped a table that could easily seat twenty. But the most oppressive of the downstairs rooms was the study, which was outfitted with Gothic arches, thick, olive green velvet drapes, and dark, heavy furniture including a massive desk and a chair that looked as if it could have belonged to Henry VIII.

She reentered the foyer just as Cal was bringing in his golf clubs. As he leaned them against the side of the fountain, she looked up toward the second floor, which was surrounded by a balcony of grillwork that was even more ornate than the balcony outside. "I'm afraid to see the upstairs."

He straightened and regarded her with cold eyes. "You don't like it? I'm hurt. Hillbillies like me spend our whole lives dreaming of owning a beautiful place like this."

She barely repressed a shudder as she turned away and headed upstairs, where she wasn't surprised to find more swags, fringe, velvet, and gilt. She opened a door at one end and stepped into the master bedroom, which was a nightmare of red, black, and gold. It held still another chandelier along with a king-size bed resting on a platform. A red-brocade canopy decorated with heavy gold-and-black tassels topped the bed. Something caught her eye, and as she walked closer, she saw that the underside of the canopy held an enormous mirror. She quickly backed away, only to realize that Cal had entered the room behind her.

He went over to the bed and looked under the canopy to see what had caught her attention. "Well, what do you know? I always wanted me one of these. This house is even better than I thought it'd be."

"It's awful. Nothing more than a monument to greed."

"Doesn't bother me none. I wasn't the one who cheated the God-fearing."

His narrow-mindedness maddened her. "Think of all those people sending Snopes money they squeezed out of their food budget and social security checks. I wonder how many malnourished children went into that ceiling mirror?"

"A couple dozen for sure."

She shot him a quick look to see if he was joking, but he had wandered over to explore an elaborate ebony cabinet that held electronic equipment.

"I can't believe how callous you're being about this." She didn't even know why she was trying to make someone so self-involved and intellectually impaired see beyond his limits.

"You'd better not say that in front of G. Dwayne's creditors. More than a few of them are finally getting paid because I bought this place." He slid out a deep drawer in the cabinet. "He sure did have a taste for porn. There must be a couple dozen X-rated videos in here."

"Perfect."

"You ever see *Slumber Party Panty Pranks*?"

"That does it!" She stomped over to the cabinet, dug into the drawer, and filled her arms with the cassettes. The pile was so large, she had to brace it under her chin as she headed out the door to find a garbage can. "Starting now, this house is G-rated."

"That's right," he called after her. "The only use you've got for sex is to get yourself knocked up."

She felt as if she'd been kicked in the stomach. She stopped at the top of the stairs and turned to face him.

He glared at her with those damn-the-torpedo eyes, his hands splayed on his hips, chin jutted forward, and she wouldn't have been surprised if he'd told her to meet him outside so they could settle this with their fists. Once again, she realized how woefully ill equipped she was to handle this man. Surely there had to be a better way than sniping.

"Is this how we want to live for the next three months?" she asked quietly. "With the two of us attacking each other?"

"Works for me."

"But we'll both be miserable. Please. Let's call a truce."

"You want a truce?"

"Yes. Let's stop all these personal attacks and try to get along."

"No dice, Professor." He stared at her for a long moment, then walked forward, his steps unhurried, but still threatening. "You're the one who started this dirty little war, and now you're going to live with the consequences." He brushed past her and headed down the stairs.

She stood there with her heart pounding as he disappeared out the front door. Moments later, she heard the sound of the Jeep driving away. Deeply depressed, she dragged herself to the kitchen, where she deposited the videotapes in the trash.

The requisite Snopes's family crystal chandelier hung over an island workspace topped with black granite that made it look like a crypt, an effect that was enhanced by the shiny black marble floor. The connecting breakfast nook had a charming bay window and a beautiful view. Unfortunately, the view had to fight a built-in banquette upholstered in blood red velvet and wallpaper printed with metallic red roses so full-blown they seemed on the verge of decay. The entire area looked as if it had been decorated by Dracula, but at least the view was pleasant, so she decided to settle in there until she felt more able to cope.

For the next few hours, she alternated between putting away the groceries that had been delivered, making phone calls to tie up loose ends in Chicago, writing a quick note to Caroline, and brooding. As evening approached, the quiet in the house grew thick and oppressive. She realized her last meal had been a very early breakfast, and though she had little appetite, she began putting together a small meal from the badly stocked pantry.

The groceries that had been delivered included multiple boxes of Lucky Charms, cream-filled chocolate cupcakes, white bread, and bologna. It was either hillbilly gourmet or the dream diet of a nine-year-old boy—either way, it didn't appeal to her. She preferred her food fresh and as close to its natural state as possible. Deciding on a grilled cheese sandwich made from Styrofoam white bread and rubbery slices of artificial cheese, she settled on the red velvet banquette to eat.

By the time she'd finished, the events of the day had caught up with her, and she wanted nothing more than to stumble into bed and sleep, but her suitcases weren't in the foyer. She realized Cal must have put them away while she'd been exploring the house. For a moment, she remembered that awful master bedroom and wondered if he thought she was going to share it with him. She immediately dismissed the idea. He'd been avoiding even the slightest physical contact with her; she certainly didn't have to worry about him being sexually aggressive.

The knowledge should have comforted her, but it didn't. There was something so overwhelmingly male about him that she couldn't help feeling threatened. She simply hoped her superior intelligence would win over his physical strength.

The colored lights of the fountain in the foyer below threw grotesque fun-house shadows on the walls as she made her way upstairs to find a bedroom for herself. With a shudder, she headed toward the door at the end of the hallway, choosing it only because it was farthest from the master bedroom.

The charming little nursery she found surprised her. Simply decorated with blue-and-white-striped wallpaper, it held a comfortable rocker, white enameled bureau, and matching crib. Above it hung a needlework prayer mounted in a simple frame, and she realized this was the only religious object she'd seen inside the house. Someone had designed this little boy's nursery with love, and she didn't believe it had been G. Dwayne Snopes.

She sank down in the wooden rocker that sat by a window with tieback curtains and thought about her own child. How could it ever grow strong and happy with two parents constantly at war? She remembered the promise she'd made Annie Glide to put Cal's welfare before her own and wondered how she had let the old lady trap her into agreeing to something so impossible. It seemed even more ironic in view of the fact that he had promised nothing in return.

Why hadn't she been wilier and ducked the old lady's prodding as he'd done? Still, in light of the wedding vows she'd spoken, what difference did one more broken promise make?

As she rested her head against the back of the rocker she searched for a way to make peace with him. Somehow she had to accomplish it, not because of what she'd said to Annie, but because it was best for the baby.

A little after midnight, Cal sealed himself in the study to call Brian Delgado at home. While he waited for his attorney to answer the phone, he viewed the room's Gothic furnishings with distaste, including the trophy heads mounted on the walls. He liked his blood sport to involve able-bodied men, not animals, and he made up his mind to get rid of them as soon as possible.

When Brian answered, Cal was in no mood to chitchat, so he got right to the point. "What have you found out?"

"Nothing yet. Dr. Darlington doesn't seem to have any skeletons in her closet—you were right about that—maybe because her personal life has been almost nonexistent."

"What does she do with her spare time?"

"She works. That seems to be her life."

"Any blots on her professional record?"

"Problems with her boss at Preeze Labs, but that looks more like professional jealousy on his part. High-level particle physics still seems to be pretty much a boys' club, especially with the older scientists."

Cal frowned. "I hoped you'd have more by now."

"Cal, I know you want this handled yesterday, but it's going to take a while unless you want to attract all kinds of attention."

He shoved his hand through his hair. "You're right. Take the time you need, but handle it. I'm giving you complete authority to act. I don't want this pushed aside."

"Understood."

They talked for a few minutes about the terms Cal was being offered to renew his contract with a fast-food chain, and then they discussed a proposed endorsement for an athletic clothing manufacturer. Cal was just ready to hang up when a thought occurred to him.

"Send one of your people out tomorrow to buy up a batch of comic books. Soldier of fortune stuff, action heroes—have them throw in a couple of Bugs Bunny. I'll need four or five dozen."

"Comic books?"

"Yeah."

Brian asked no more questions, even though Cal knew he wanted to. Their conversation ended, and he headed upstairs in search of the woman who had so deviously altered his life.

He didn't feel even a pang of guilt for wanting revenge. The gridiron had taught him a lot of survival lessons, and one of them was fundamental. If somebody laid a dirty hit on you, you had to strike back twice as hard or pay for it in the future, and that was something he wouldn't risk. He had no intention of living the rest of his life looking over his shoulder trying to figure out what she might be up to next. She needed to understand exactly who she'd tangled with and exactly what the consequences would be if she ever tried to deceive him again.

He found her in the nursery curled up in a rocker with her glasses resting in her lap. In her sleep she appeared vulnerable, but he knew what a lie that was. From the beginning, she'd been cold-blooded and calculating as she'd gone about getting what she wanted, and in the process she'd altered the course of his life in a way he'd never forgive. And not only his life, he reminded himself, but the life of an innocent child.

He'd always liked kids. For over ten years he'd spent a lot of his time working with underprivileged ones, although he'd done his best to keep that information from the press because he didn't want anybody trying to make him over into Saint Cal. When he finally got around to getting married, he'd always figured he'd stay that way. He'd grown up in a stable family, and it bothered him to watch his buddies and their ex-wives shuffle their kids back and forth. He'd sworn he'd never do that to a child, but Dr. Jane Darlington had taken the choice away from him.

He walked farther into the room and watched the blade of moonlight caught in her hair turn it into silver. One stray lock curled softly over her cheek. She'd taken off her jacket, and her silk top clung to her breasts so that he could watch their gentle rise and fall.

Asleep, she looked younger than the formidable physics professor who'd instructed her class on Borromean nuclei. That day there had been something parched about her, as if she'd been closed up inside so long that all her juices had dried up, but asleep and bathed in moonlight she was different—dewy, renewed, plumped up—and he felt the stirrings of desire.

His physical reaction bothered him. The first two times he'd been with her he hadn't known what she was like. Now he knew, but his body didn't seem to have gotten the message.

He decided it was time for the next scene in their unpleasant melodrama, and he pressed the toe of his shoe down on the front of the rocker. The chair tilted, and she startled awake.

"Bedtime, Rosebud."

Her green eyes flew open and immediately darkened with wariness. "I—I must have fallen asleep."

"Big day."

"I was looking for a bedroom." She slipped on her glasses, then pushed her hands through her hair, where it had fallen forward over her face. He watched silvery blond drizzles trickle through her fingers.

"You can take the Widow Snopes's room. Come on."

He could see that she didn't want to follow him, but she wanted another argument even less. It was a mistake for her to telegraph her emotions the way she did. It made the game too easy.

He led her down the hallway, and as they came closer to the master bedroom, her nervousness grew. He felt a grim satisfaction watching it happen. What would she do if he touched her? So far, he'd avoided any physical contact, not quite trusting himself to stay in control. He'd never hit a woman—could never even have imagined doing such a thing—but the urge to damage her was primal. As he observed her nervousness, he knew he had to test her.

They reached the door just before his own. He extended his hand toward the knob and deliberately brushed her arm.

Jane jumped as she felt his touch and spun to face him. His eyes were full of mockery, and she realized he knew exactly how nervous he was making her. There was something dangerous about him tonight. She had no idea what he was thinking; she only knew that they were alone in this big, ugly house, and she felt defenseless.

He pushed open the door. "We've got connecting bedrooms, just like those old-time houses used to have. I guess G. Dwayne and his wife didn't get along real well."

"I don't want a connecting bedroom. I'll sleep in one of the rooms at the other end of the hall."

"You'll sleep wherever I tell you."

Prickles of alarm skidded up her spine, but she lifted her head and met his gaze. "Stop bullying me."

"This isn't bullying. Bullies can't back up their threats. I can."

His lazy drawl held an edge of menace, and her stomach twisted. "Exactly what are you threatening?"

His gaze slid over her, lingering at the hollow of her neck, her breasts, passing down to her hips, then returning to her eyes. "You cost me my peace of mind, not to mention a wad of cash. To my way of thinking, that means you've got some big debts to pay off. Maybe I just want you close by while I decide when I'm going to start collecting."

The sexual threat was unmistakable, and she should have been enraged—certainly frightened—but instead, a curious jolt passed through her, as if her nerve endings had received an electrical shock. She found her reaction deeply disturbing, and she tried to move away from him, only to back into the doorjamb.

He lifted his arm and splayed one hand on the edge of the frame, just next to her head. His leg brushed the side of hers, and all of her senses grew alert. She saw the hollows beneath his cheekbones, the rim of black that surrounded the irises of his pale gray eyes. She caught the faint scent of laundry detergent on his knit shirt and something else, something that shouldn't have a smell, but did. The scent of danger.

His voice was a husky whisper. "The first time I strip you naked, Rosebud, it's going to be in broad daylight because I don't want to miss a thing."

Her palms grew damp, and an awful wildness rose inside her. She felt a suicidal desire to peel her silk shell over her head, unfasten her slacks, to strip herself naked for him right here in the hallway of this sinner's house. She wanted to answer his warrior's challenge with one of her own, a challenge as ancient and powerful as the first woman's.

He moved. It was almost nothing. A slight shift of his weight, but it brought the chaos of her thoughts back in order. She was a middle-aged physics professor whose only lover wore socks to bed. What kind of opponent was she for this seasoned sexual warrior who seemed to have chosen sex as a weapon to subjugate her?

She was deeply shaken and just as determined not to let him use her weakness to his advantage. She lifted her gaze to his. "You do what you have to, Cal. I'll do the same."

Did she imagine a flicker of surprise on his face? She couldn't be certain as she turned into the room and shut the door.

The sun streaming through the windows awakened her the next morning. She propped herself up on the pillows and admired the Widow Snopes's bedroom, which was painted a pale blue with chalk white trim and soft iris accents. Its simple cherry furniture and braided rugs gave the room the same homey feel as the nursery.

Jane glanced uneasily toward the door that led to a master bath linking her bedroom with Cal's. She vaguely remembered hearing a shower running earlier, and she could only hope he'd already left the house. Last night she had placed her own toiletries in a smaller bathroom down the hall.

The Jeep was gone by the time she had finished dressing, gotten unpacked, and made her way to the kitchen. She found a note from Cal on the counter with the number of a grocery store that delivered and instructions to order whatever she wanted. She ate a piece of toast, then phoned in a list of items more suitable to her taste buds than foam-filled chocolate cupcakes.

Not long after the groceries arrived, another deliveryman showed up with her computer equipment. She had him carry it to her bedroom, where she spent the next few hours setting up a workspace for herself on a table she moved in front of the window, so she could gaze at the mountains whenever she remembered to look up from her computer screen. For the rest of the day, she worked, stopping only long enough to take a walk outside.

The grounds around the house nearly made up for the interior. Shadowed by the surrounding mountains, they were a bit overgrown, and it was too early for anything to be in bloom, but she loved their feeling of isolation and slightly abandoned look. She saw a rough path leading up the side of the nearest mountain and began to follow it, but after less than ten minutes, she found herself gasping for breath from the effects of the altitude. As she turned back, she decided she'd make herself go a bit farther each day until she reached the notch at the top.

By the time she went to bed that night, she still hadn't seen Cal, and he was gone when she awakened the next morning. Late that afternoon, however, he walked into the foyer as she came downstairs.

He gave her that familiar contemptuous look, as if she'd crawled out from under a rock. "The realtor hired a couple of women to keep the house clean while it was on the market. She said they did a good job, so I told them to stay on. They'll be coming a couple times a week starting tomorrow."

"All right."

"They don't speak much English, but they seemed to know what they're doing. Stay out of their way."

She nodded and thought about asking him where he had been until two o'clock in the morning, the time she'd heard the toilet flush in the adjoining bathroom, but he had already turned to leave. As the door shut, she wondered if he was going off to be with another woman.

The thought depressed her. Even though their marriage was a sham, and he didn't owe her fidelity, she wished he'd give it to her, just for the next three months. A premonition of disaster settled over her, a sense of impending doom that made her so uncomfortable, she hurried back to her computer and buried herself in work.

Her days settled into a routine, but the uneasiness never quite went away. To keep it at bay, she worked most of the time, although she managed a walk each day. She barely saw Cal, something that should have eased her mind, but didn't, since she realized he had virtually imprisoned her. She had no car, he didn't offer to lend her his, and the only people she saw were deliverymen and the two Korean cleaning women. Like a feudal lord with a moated castle, he had deliberately cut her off from the town and its people. She wondered what he planned to do when his family returned.

Unlike a medieval noblewoman, she could have put an end to her imprisonment anytime she wanted. A phone call to a taxi company would have done the job, but she didn't have any real desire to go out. With the exception of the prickly Annie Glide, she knew no one here, and although she would have enjoyed seeing something of the area, she couldn't resist the luxury of uninterrupted time.

Never in her life had she been able to devote herself so completely to pure science. There were no classes to teach, no faculty meetings to attend, no errands to run, nothing to distract her from her research. With her computer, modem, and telephone, she was linked to everything she needed, from the Los Alamos electronic library to the data coming in from crucial experiments being conducted in the world's billion-dollar supercolliders. And work kept her uneasy thoughts at bay.

She began to lose track of time as she absorbed herself in the mathematics of duality, applying theoretical physics to unravel mathematical puzzles. Using a free-flowing mathematics of intuition, she pondered convoluted curves and mirror symmetry. She applied quantum field theory to count holes in four-dimensional space, and wherever she went, she left scribbled notes to herself—ideas scratched on the backs of pizza coupons that came in the mail, formulas written with a stubby golf pencil over the margins of the morning newspaper. One afternoon she walked into her bathroom only to see that she'd unthinkingly used her antique rose lipstick to draw a doughnut shape that was remodeling into a sphere on the bathroom mirror. With that, she knew she had to get out.

She grabbed her white Windbreaker, emptied the notes she'd stuffed into the pockets on previous walks, and left through the French doors at the rear of the house. As she made her way across the yard toward the path up the side of the mountain that she'd been climbing a little higher each day, her thoughts returned to the problems of convoluted curves. Would it be possible . . .

The shrill call of a bird blasted through her conjecture and made her aware of her surroundings. What was she doing pondering quantum geometry in the middle of all this beauty? If she weren't careful, she'd become so strange that no child would want her as a mother.

As she climbed higher, she forced herself to observe the world around her. She drew in the rich scents of pine and leaf mold and felt the sun shining with new warmth. The trees had a fragile green lacework on them. Spring was arriving, and before long these mountain slopes would be alive with blooms.

But instead of being buoyed by the beauty, her spirits drooped, and the premonition of disaster that had been nagging at the edges of her consciousness for days grew stronger. By immersing herself so completely in her work, she had kept herself from thinking, but with the quiet of the damp woods around her, that was no longer possible.

As her breathing grew labored, she made her way to a rocky area off to the side of the path where she could rest. She was so tired of living with guilt. Cal would never forgive her for what she had done, and she could only pray that he wouldn't take his hostility out on their child.

She remembered his veiled sexual threat the night they had arrived and realized she had no idea if he'd really try to force himself on her. She shivered and looked down on the valley, where she saw the house with its dark-shingled roof and crescent-shaped motor court. She watched a car turn into the gated lane. Cal's Jeep. Had he come back to grab a fresh comic book from his collection?

They were scattered all over the house: *X-Men, The Avengers, The Vault of Horror*, even *Bugs Bunny*. Every time she saw a new comic book, she sent up a silent prayer of thanksgiving that at least this one thing had gone right. Intelligence tended toward the norm. Surely his mental slowness would balance her own genius and keep her child from being a freak. She silently expressed her gratitude by making certain his comics were never disturbed, not even by the cleaning women.

But that gratitude didn't extend to her imprisonment. As much as the isolation helped her work, she realized she was giving him too much power by tolerating it. What would he do, she wondered, if she didn't return? He knew she went for walks, but how would he react if she didn't come back? What if she made her way beyond the gates, found a telephone, and took a taxi to the airport?

The idea of upsetting him elevated her spirits a few small notches. Leaning back on her elbows, she tilted her face and enjoyed the sunshine until she felt the chill of the rocky ledge through her wool slacks. Then she rose and gazed back down into the valley.

The house and its owner lay beneath her; the mountains rose above. She began to climb.

8

Cal stalked into the family room with Jane's purse clutched in his hand and strode over to the French doors that led to the deck, but he still couldn't see any sign of her. That meant only one thing. She'd taken off up the mountain.

He knew she walked most days, but when he'd asked her about it, she'd told him she never went far. Well, she'd obviously gone far today, so far she'd gotten lost! For someone with an IQ of 180, she was the stupidest woman he'd ever met.

"Damn!" He flung the purse down on the couch. The latch flew open and the contents spilled.

"Something wrong, C-Man?"

"What? Uh, no." Cal had forgotten about his youngest brother Ethan. When Ethan had shown up at the gate twenty minutes earlier, Cal had made up an excuse about having to return a phone call and stuck him in here while he'd tried to find a clue to his missing wife's whereabouts.

Buying himself a few days' extra time before he introduced Jane to his family was proving to be even tougher than he'd thought. Ethan had been back from his ski trip for three days, his parents from their vacation for two, and all of them had been hounding him.

"I was looking for my wallet," he lied. "I thought Jane might have put it in her purse."

Ethan rose from an easy chair near the fireplace, which was large enough to roast a Honda, and walked over to peer out the patio doors. Cal's anger softened a bit as he gazed at his brother. While he and Gabe had shone on the playing fields, Ethan had made his mark in school theatrical productions. Although he was a decent athlete, organized sports held no appeal for him simply because he'd never been able to grasp the importance of winning.

Blond, more slightly built than either Cal or Gabe, and heartbreakingly handsome, he was the only one of the three Bonner brothers who took after their mother, and his male-model good looks had caused him to endure an endless amount of ribbing from Cal and Gabe. He had thickly lashed light brown eyes and a nose that had never been broken. His dark blond hair was conservatively cut and always combed. Normally he favored oxford shirts, neatly pressed Dockers, and penny loafers, but today he wore an ancient Grateful Dead T-shirt and jeans. On Ethan, the outfit looked like Brooks Brothers.

Cal frowned at him. "Did you iron that T-shirt?"

"Just a little touch-up."

"Jesus, Eth, you've got to stop doin' crap like that."

Ethan smiled his Christ smile solely because he knew how much it irritated his big brother. "Some of us take pride in our appearance." He regarded Cal's muddy boots with distaste. "Others of us don't care how we look."

"Can it, asshole." Cal's language always deteriorated when he was around Ethan. There was just something about the kid's unflappability that made him want to cuss. Not that it bothered Ethan one bit. As the youngest of three boys, his brothers had toughened him up at an early age. Even as children, Cal and Gabe had sensed that Ethan was more vulnerable than they were, so they'd made sure he could take care of himself. Although no one in the Bonner family ever admitted it, all of them secretly loved Ethan best.

Cal also respected him. Ethan had gone through a wild period, during college and into his early twenties, where he'd drunk too much and slept with too many women, but when he'd received the call, he'd made up his mind to live as he preached.

"Visiting the sick's part of my job," Ethan said. "Why don't I just look in on your new wife?"

"She wouldn't like it. You know how women are. She wants to be all fixed up before she meets the family, so she can make a good first impression."

"When do you think that's going to be? Now that Mom and Dad are back in town, they're champing at the bit to meet her. And Annie's really rubbing it in because she's seen her and we haven't."

"It's not my fault all of you chose now to go gallivanting around the country."

"I've been back from my ski trip for three days."

"Yeah, well, it's like I told everybody when I came over for dinner last night, Jane got sick right before you got back. Damned flu. She should be feeling better in a few days—next week at the latest—and then I'll bring her over to the house. But don't expect to see much of her. Her work's real important to her, and she can't spend too much time away from her computer right now."

Ethan was only thirty, but he regarded him through old, wise eyes. "If you need to talk, C-Man, I'm willing to listen."

"There's nothing for me to talk about except the way everybody in this family wants to stick their noses in my business."

"Not Gabe."

"No, not Gabe." Cal jammed his hands into the back pockets of his jeans. "I wish he would."

They each fell silent, preoccupied with thoughts of their

wounded middle brother. He was down in Mexico, on the run from himself.

"I wish he'd come home," Ethan said.

"He left Salvation years ago. It's not home to him anymore."

"I guess no place is home without Cherry and Jamie."

Ethan's voice tightened, and Cal looked away. Anxious to break the mood, he began picking up the contents of Jane's purse. Where was she? These past two weeks he'd forced himself to stay away and let his temper cool.

He also wanted her to feel her isolation and understand that he was the one holding the key to her prison. Unfortunately she didn't seem affected.

Ethan came over to help. "If Jane's flu is this bad, maybe she should be in the hospital."

"No." Cal reached for a small calculator and pen so he didn't have to look at his brother. "She's been pushing herself pretty hard, but she'll feel better as soon as she gets some rest."

"She sure doesn't look like one of your bimbos."

"How do you know what she looks—?" He lifted his head and saw Ethan studying her photo on the driver's license that had fallen out of her wallet. "None of the women I dated were bimbos."

"They weren't exactly rocket scientists." He laughed. "This one practically is. I still can't believe you married a physicist. The way I remember it, the only thing that got you through high-school physics was the fact that Coach Gill taught the class."

"You're a damned liar. I got an A in that class."

"Deserved a C."

"B minus."

Ethan grinned and waved the driver's license. "I can't wait to tell Dad I won my bet."

"What bet?"

"The age of the woman you married. He said we'd have

to schedule the wedding ceremony around her Girl Scout meetings, but I said you'd come to your senses. I believed in you, bro, and looks like I was right."

Cal was irritated. He hadn't wanted everybody to know that Jane was twenty-eight, but with Ethan staring at the date of birth on her driver's license, he couldn't deny it. "She doesn't look a day over twenty-five."

"I don't know why you're so sensitive. There's nothing wrong with marrying someone your own age."

"She's not exactly my age."

"Two years younger. That's not a big difference."

"Two years? What the hell you talkin' about?" He snatched the license away. "She's not two years younger than me! She's—"

"Uh-oh." Ethan backed away. "I think I'd better go."

Cal was too stunned by what he saw on the license to hear the amusement in his brother's voice, nor did he notice the sound of the front door closing a few moments later. He couldn't take in anything except the date on the driver's license he held in his hand.

He scrubbed the laminate with his thumb. Maybe it was just a smear on the plastic that made the year of her birth look like that. Or maybe it was a misprint. Damned DMV couldn't get anything right.

But he knew it wasn't a misprint. There was no mistaking those grim, condemning numbers. His wife was thirty-four years old, and he'd just taken the sack of a lifetime.

"Calvin, he'll be comin' to fetch you before long," Annie Glide said.

Jane set down the tea she'd been sipping from an ancient white ceramic mug that bore the remains of an American flag decal and gazed at Annie across the cluttered living room. Despite its unorthodox decor, this house felt like a home, a place where a person could belong. "Oh, I don't think so. He doesn't know where I am."

"He'll figure it out soon enough. Boy's been roamin' these mountains ever since he was in diapers."

She couldn't imagine Cal ever wearing diapers. Surely he'd been born with a belligerent attitude and a full set of chest hair. "I can't believe how close your house is to his. The day I met you it seemed as if we drove several miles before we got to those awful gates."

"You did. Road winds all the way 'round Heartache Mountain goin' through town. This morning, you just took the shortcut."

Jane had been surprised when she'd reached the notch in the mountain and looked down the other side to see the tin roof of Annie Glide's cabin. At first she hadn't recognized it, but then she'd spotted the colorful wind sock flying at the corner of the porch. Even though it had been nearly two weeks since they'd met, Annie had greeted her as if she'd been expected.

"You know how to make corn bread, Janie Bonner?"

"I've made it a few times."

"It's no good lest you fold in a little buttermilk."

"I'll remember that."

"Before I took so sick, I used to make my own apple butter. Nothin' as good as cold apple butter on warm corn bread. You got to find you real soft apples when you make it, and watch yourself peelin' 'em 'cause ain't nobody on earth likes to bite into a big tough ol' piece of peel when they're expectin' good smooth apple butter."

"If I ever make any, I'll be careful."

Annie had been doing this ever since Jane had arrived, tossing out recipes and bits of folk wisdom: ginger tea for colds, nine sips of water for hiccups, beets to be planted on the twenty-sixth, twenty-seventh, or twenty-eighth of March, but no later or they'd be puny.

Despite the improbability of her ever using any of this information, she'd found herself taking it all in. Annie's advice represented the continuity between one generation and the next. Roots went deep in these mountains, and as someone who had always felt so very rootless, each tidbit seemed like a solid link with a family that had a history and traditions, everything she craved.

"... and if you're gonna make you some dumplin's, put a egg in that dough and a pinch of sage." She started to cough, and Jane regarded her with concern. When she recovered, she waved her hand displaying fingernails painted a bright cherry red. "Listen to me goin' on. It's a wonder you haven't just said, 'Annie, shut your yap; you done wore out my ears.' "

"I love listening to you."

"You're a good girl, Janie Bonner. I'm surprised Calvin married you."

Jane laughed. Annie Glide was the most unexpected person. The only one of her grandparents Jane had ever known had been her father's self-centered and narrow-minded mother.

"I miss my garden. Had that worthless Joey Neeson plow for me a couple weeks ago, even though it goes against my grain to have strangers 'round here. Calvin, he's always sending strangers up here to fix things, but I won't have it. Don't even like family nibbin' in my business, let alone strangers." She shook her head. "I was hopin' I'd be strong enough to get my garden put in this spring, but I was foolin' myself. Ethan said he'd come by to help me, but that poor boy has so much work with his church, I didn't have the heart to do nothin' but tell him weren't no sissy boy plantin' my garden." She gave Jane a sideways glance from her crafty blue eyes. "Sure am gonna miss my garden, but I won't have strangers plantin' for me."

Jane saw right through the old woman's wiles, but it didn't occur to her to be annoyed. Instead, she felt curiously flattered. "I'll be happy to help you if you show me what to do."

Annie pressed her hand to her chest. "You'd do that for me?"

Jane laughed at her feigned amazement. "I'll enjoy it. I've never had a garden."

"Well, now, that's just fine. You make Calvin bring you over here first thing tomorrow, and we'll get those 'taters in right away. It's real late—I like to do it at the end of February, during the dark of the moon—but they still might turn out if we get 'em in right away. Then we plant onions, and after that some beets."

"It sounds great." She suspected the old woman wasn't eating as well as she should, and she stood. "Why don't I fix us a little lunch? I'm getting hungry."

"Now that's a real good idea. Amber Lynn's back from her trip, and she done brung over some of her bean soup yesterday. You can heat that up. 'Course she don't make it like I taught her, but, then, that's Amber Lynn for you."

So Cal's parents had returned. As she headed to the kitchen, she wondered how he was explaining not bringing her to meet them.

Jane served their soup in one china bowl and one plastic. She accompanied it with squares of corn bread from a pan on the counter. As they ate at the kitchen table, she couldn't remember enjoying a meal more. After two weeks of isolation, it was wonderful just being around another person, especially one who did more than bark out orders and glare at her.

She cleaned up the dishes and was bringing a mug of tea to Annie in the living room when she noticed three diplomas among the clutter of paintings, ceramic ballerinas, and wall clocks hanging next to the doorway.

"Those belong to my grandsons," Annie said, "but they give 'em to me. They knowed it always bothered me the fact I had to quit school after sixth grade, so each of 'em give me their college diplomas the same day they graduated. That there's Calvin's hangin' at the top."

Jane fetched her glasses from the kitchen table and gazed at the top diploma. It was from the University of Michigan, and it stated that Calvin E. Bonner had received a Bachelor of Science degree . . . with highest distinction.

Summa Cum Laude.

Jane's hand flew to her throat. She whirled around. "Cal graduated *summa cum laude*?"

"That's what they call it when a body's real smart. I thought you, bein' a professor, would of knowed that. My Calvin, he was always smart as a whip."

"He—" She swallowed and fought to go on as a roaring sounded in her ears. "What did he get his degree in?"

"Now didn't he tell you that? Lot of athletes, they take real easy classes, but my Calvin, he wasn't like that. He got hisself a degree in biology. Always liked roamin' in the woods, pickin' up this 'n' that."

"Biology?" Jane felt as if she'd just taken a punch in the stomach.

Annie narrowed her eyes. "Strikes me strange you don't know any of this, Janie Bonner."

"I guess the subject never came up." The room began to sway, and she felt as if she were going to faint. She turned awkwardly, sloshing hot tea over her hand, and stumbled back into the kitchen.

"Janie? Somethin' wrong?"

She couldn't speak. The handle broke off the mug as she dropped it into the sink. She pressed her fingers to her mouth and fought a rising tide of horror. How could she have been so stupid? Despite all her conniving, she'd brought about the very disaster she'd tried so hard to avoid, and now her child wasn't going to be ordinary at all.

She clutched the edge of the sink as hard reality overcame her rosy daydreams. She'd known Cal had attended the University of Michigan, but she hadn't believed he'd been serious about it. Didn't athletes take the minimum number of courses to get by and then leave before they graduated? The fact that he'd majored in biology and graduated with honors from one of the most prestigious universities in the country had such brutal ramifications she could barely take them in.

Intelligence tended toward the mean. That fact screamed at her. The one quality she prized in him—his stupidity— was nothing more than an illusion, an illusion he had deliberately perpetuated. By not seeing through it, she'd condemned her child to the same life of isolation and loneliness she'd lived herself.

Panic clawed at her. Her precious child was going to be a freak, just like her.

She couldn't let that happen. She'd die before she'd permit her child to suffer as she'd suffered. She'd move away! She'd take the baby to Africa, some remote and primitive part of the continent. She'd educate the child herself so that her precious little one would never know the cruelty of other children.

Her eyes stung with tears. What had she done? How could God have let something so cruel happen?

Annie's voice penetrated her misery. "That'll be Calvin now. I told you he'd come after you."

She heard the slam of a car door, the pounding of footsteps on the front porch.

"*Jane!* Where is she, dammit?"

Jane charged into the living room. "You *bastard!*"

He stalked forward, his face twisted. "Lady, you've got some *explaining* to do!"

"God, I *hate* you!"

"Not any more than what I think of *you!*" Cal's eyes blazed with anger and something else that was now so clear Jane couldn't believe she hadn't seen it all along—a keen, biting intelligence.

She wanted to throw herself at him and scratch that intelligence from his eyes, chop open his cranium and pluck it from his brain. He was supposed to be stupid! He read comic books! How could he betray her like this?

The last of her self-control shredded, and she knew she had to get away before she fell apart. With an exclamation of fury, she whirled around and dashed back into the kitchen, where she flew out the rickety back door.

As she began to run, she heard a roar of rage coming from behind her. "You get back here! Don't make me run after you, or you'll be sorry!"

She wanted to hit something. She wanted to throw herself in a deep hole and let the earth close in on top of her, anything to stop the awful pain raging inside her body. This baby that she already loved more than she'd ever loved anything was going to be a freak.

She didn't hear him come up behind her, and she gasped when he spun her around. "I told you to *stop*!" he shouted.

"You've ruined *everything*!" she screamed back.

"Me?" His face was pale with rage. "You damned *liar*! You're an old lady! A goddamn old lady!"

"I'll *never* forgive you for this!" She balled her hand into a fist and hit him in the chest so hard the pain shot into her arm.

He was spitting fury. He began to grab her by both arms, but she had been transported into a place of vengeance and she wouldn't be restrained. This man had harmed her unborn child, and she, who had never hit another person, wanted his blood.

She went wild. Her glasses flew off, but she didn't care. She kicked and clawed and tried to damage him in any way she could.

"You stop this right now! *Stop it*!" His bellow shook the very treetops. Once again he tried to restrain her, but she sank her teeth into his upper arm.

"Ouch!" His eyes widened with outrage. "That hurt, dammit!"

The violence felt good. She lifted her knee to slam it into his groin and found her feet swept out from under her.

"Oh, no, you don't . . ."

He went down with her, breaking her fall with his own body, then twisting to pinion her against the ground.

The fight had taken everything out of her, but he was a man who took hits for a living, and he wasn't even winded. He was, however, enraged, and he let her have it.

"You settle down right now, you hear me? You're acting like a crazy woman! You *are* crazy! You lied to me, cheated me, and now you're trying to *kill* me, not to mention the fact that you can't be doing that baby any good with your carryin' on. I swear to God I'm going to have you locked up in a mental ward and shot full of Thorazine."

Her eyes stung with tears that she didn't want him to see, but couldn't hold back. "You've ruined everything."

"Me?" He bristled with outrage. "I'm not the one who's acting like a lunatic. And I'm not the one who told everybody I was twenty-eight fucking years old!"

"I never told you that, and don't you curse at me!"

"You're thirty-four! *Thirty-four!* Were you ever planning on mentioning that to me?"

"When was I supposed to mention it? Should I have told you when you were stalking me in my classroom, or when you were screaming at me over the telephone? How about when you pushed me on the airplane? Or maybe I should have let you know after you locked me up in your house? Is that when I should have told you?"

"Don't try to weasel out of it. You knew it was important to me, and you deliberately misled me."

"Deliberately? Now there's a big word for a dumb jock. Do you think it's cute putting on that asinine hillbilly act and making everyone think you're a moron? Is that your idea of a good time?"

"What are you talking about?"

She spit the words at him. "University of Michigan. *Summa cum laude.*"

"Oh, that." Some of the tension left his body, and his weight eased on her.

"God, I hate you," she whispered. "I would have had a better chance at a sperm bank."

"Exactly where you should have gone in the first place."

Despite his words, he no longer sounded quite so angry, but acid churned in her stomach. She knew she had to ask him, even though she dreaded hearing the answer, and she forced out the words. "What's your IQ?"

"I have no idea. Unlike you, I don't keep it tattooed on my forehead." He rolled to the side, which allowed her to struggle to her feet.

"Then your SATs. What were they?"

"I don't remember."

She regarded him bitterly. "You're a liar. Everybody remembers their SATs."

He swiped at some wet leaves on his jeans as he rose.

"Tell me, dammit!"

"I don't have to tell you anything." He sounded annoyed, but not particularly dangerous.

That didn't calm her. Instead, she once again felt a swell of hysteria. "You tell me right now, or, I swear to God, I'll find some way to murder you! I'll put ground glass in your food! I'll stab you with a butcher knife while you're sleeping! I'll wait until you're in the shower and throw in an electrical appliance! I'll—I'll club you in the head with a baseball bat some night when you walk in the door!"

He stopped brushing his jeans and gazed at her with what looked more like curiosity than apprehension. The fact that she knew she was only making herself appear more irrational further inflamed her. "Tell me!"

"You are some bloodthirsty woman." Looking faintly bemused, he shook his head. "That electrical appliance thing . . . You'd need an extension cord or something to reach all the way into the shower. Or maybe you weren't planning to plug it in."

She gritted her teeth, feeling prodigiously foolish. "If it wasn't plugged in, it wouldn't electrocute you, now would it?"

"Good point."

She took a deep breath and tried to regain her sanity. "Tell me your SATs. You owe me that much."

He shrugged and bent over to pick up her glasses. "Maybe fourteen hundred, or somethin' like that. Mighta been a little lower."

"*Fourteen hundred*!" She punched him as hard as she could, then stomped away from him into the woods. He was a hypocrite and a fraud, and she felt sick down to the very depth of her soul. Even Craig wasn't as smart as this man.

"That's dumb compared to you," he called after her.

"Don't ever speak to me again."

He came up next to her, but didn't touch her. "Come on, Rosebud, you've got to settle down enough so I can take you apart for what you've done to me, which is a whole lot worse than my damned SATs."

She whirled on him. "You didn't do anything to *me*! You've done it to my child, don't you see that? Because of you, an innocent child is going to grow up to be a freak."

"I never told you I was stupid. You just assumed."

"You said *ain't*! That first night we were together, you said *ain't* twice!"

A muscle twitched at the corner of his mouth. "A little local color. I'm not apologizin'."

"There are comic books all over the house!"

"I was just livin' up to your expectations."

She collapsed then. She turned her back to him, crossed her arms against the nearest tree trunk, and rested her forehead against her wrist. All the humiliations of her childhood returned to her: the taunts and cruelties, the awful isolation. She had never fit in, and now, neither would her child.

"I'm going to take the baby to Africa," she whispered. "Away from civilization. I'll teach her myself, so she doesn't have to grow up with other children taunting her."

A surprisingly gentle hand settled over the small of her back and began to rub. "I'm not going to let you do that to him, Rosebud."

"You will once you see what a freak she is."

"He's not going to be a freak. Is that how your father felt about you?"

Everything within her went still. She pulled away from him and fumbled in the pocket of her Windbreaker for a tissue. She took her time blowing her nose, wiping her eyes, regaining her self-control. How could she have let herself fall apart like this? It was no wonder he thought she was crazy.

She gave her nose a final blow. He held out her glasses, and she put them on, ignoring the strands of moss caught in one hinge. "I'm sorry for causing such a dreadful scene. I don't know what came over me. I've never hit anyone in my life."

"Feels good, doesn't it?" He grinned, and to her amazement, a dimple popped into the hard plane of his cheek. Stunned, she gazed at it for several long moments before she was able to pick up her train of thought.

"Violence doesn't solve anything, and I could have hurt you quite badly."

"I'm not trying to get you cranked up again, Rosebud, but you don't have a whole lot going for you when it comes to packin' a punch." He took her arm and began steering her back toward the house.

"This is my fault. Everything's been my fault from the beginning. If I hadn't let myself buy into every conceivable stereotype about athletes and Southerners, I would have been a more astute judge of your mental abilities."

"Uh-huh. Tell me about your father."

She nearly stumbled, but his hand on her elbow steadied

her. "There's nothing to tell. He was an accountant for a company that manufactured paper punches."

"Smart man?"

"An intelligent man. Not brilliant."

"I think I'm getting the picture here."

"I don't have any idea what you're talking about."

"He didn't have a clue what to do with you, did he?"

She picked up her pace. "He did his best. I really don't want to discuss it."

"Did it occur to you that your problems as a kid might have had more to do with your old man's attitude than with the size of your brain?"

"You don't know anything."

"That's not what my diploma says."

She couldn't respond because they had reached the back of the house, and Annie waited for them at the screen door. She glared at her grandson. "What's wrong with you? You get a pregnant woman upset like that, it'll put a mark on the baby, for sure."

"What do you mean?" He bristled with belligerence. "Who told you she's pregnant?"

"You wouldn't have married her otherwise. You don't have that much sense."

Jane was touched. "Thank you, Annie."

"And you!" Annie turned on her. "What was in your head carryin' on like that? If you go berserk every time Calvin upsets you, that baby's gonna strangle on the cord long before it has a chance to catch its first breath."

Jane thought about addressing the physiological improbability of that happening, but decided to save her breath. "I'll be more careful."

"Next time he makes you mad, just take a shotgun to him."

"Mind your own business, you old bat," Cal growled. "She's got enough ideas of her own for doin' me in."

Annie tilted her head toward Jane, and a sadness seemed

to come over her. "You listen to me, Janie Bonner. I don't know what happened between you and Calvin so he ended up marryin' you, but from what I saw a few minutes ago, the two of you don't have no love match goin'. He's married you, and I'm glad about that, but I'm tellin' you right now that if you did anything havey cavey to bring him around, you'd better make sure Amber Lynn and Jim Bonner never find out about it. They're not as broad-minded as me, and if they even suspect you've hurt their boy, they'll cut you off at the knees, you understand what I'm sayin'?"

Jane swallowed hard and nodded.

"Good." She turned to Cal. The sadness faded, and her old eyes grew sly. "I'm surprised somebody with such a bad case of the flu as Janie here had enough strength to walk over the mountain."

Cal cursed softly under his breath. Jane stared at Annie. "What do you mean? I don't have the flu?"

Cal grabbed her arm and began to pull her away. "Come on, Jane, you're going home."

"Wait a minute! I want to know what she meant by that."

Cal drew her round the side of the house, but not before she heard Annie's cackle. "You remember what I told you about that cord gettin' twisted, Janie Bonner, 'cause I think Calvin's about to upset you again."

9

"**Y**ou told everybody in your family I had the flu?" Jane said as they drove down off the mountain. It was easier talking about this small deception than the larger one.

"You got a problem with that?"

"I expected to meet your parents. I thought that's why you brought me here."

"You'll meet 'em. When I decide to introduce you."

His arrogance was like setting a spark to tinder. This was the result of letting him spend the last few weeks calling all the shots, and it was time she put a stop to it. "You'd better decide soon because I'm not going to let you keep me cooped up any longer."

"What are you talkin' about, cooped up? Here I've gone out of my way to make sure you can work without a lot of people bothering you, and you're complaining."

"Don't you dare act like you're doing me a favor!"

"I don't know what else you'd call it."

"How about *imprisonment? Incarceration? Solitary confinement?* And just so you don't accuse me of going behind your back, I'm breaking out of the joint tomorrow to help Annie plant her garden."

"You're *what?*"

Think about Annie and her garden, she told herself, instead of the fact that her child would be another misfit. She snatched off her glasses and began cleaning the dirt from them with a tissue, concentrating on the job as if it were a complicated equation. "Annie wants to get her garden in. If the potatoes aren't planted in the next few days, they'll be puny. We're also planting onions and beets."

"You are *not* putting in a garden for her. If she wants a garden, I'll hire Joey Neeson to help her."

"He's worthless."

"You don't even *know* Joey."

"I'm just repeating what I heard. The reason nothing's getting done is because she doesn't want strangers around her place."

"Well, that's just too bad because you're not doing it for her."

She opened her mouth to launch another attack, but before she could get the first word out, he cupped her head and pushed her down on the seat so that her cheek squashed against his thigh.

"What are you doing?" She tried to sit up, but he held her down.

"My mom. She's coming out of the shoestore."

"I'm not the only one who's gone crazy! You have completely lost your mind!"

"You're not meeting my family until I decide you're meeting them!" While he held her fast, he steered with his opposite knee and waved. Damn! Why couldn't his parents have stayed away longer, like another two months or so? He knew he had to let them meet the Professor, but he'd hoped to postpone it as long as he could. Now his elderly wife had ruined everything with her morning's trek over the mountain.

He glanced down. Her cheek lay mashed against his thigh, and her hair felt soft under his fingers. She was always so tidy, but now her French braid had pretty much given up the ghost. Silky blond tendrils tumbled over his hand and across the faded denim of his jeans. She sure did have pretty hair, even decorated with twigs and bits of dried leaves. The elastic band holding the braid together was barely hanging on, and he had to resist the urge to pull it off and loosen the rest with his fingers.

He knew he had to let her up soon, since she was madder than a wet hen and starting to sputter, but he kind of liked the idea of her head in his lap, even if she was spitting nails. He noticed that she didn't have more than a speck of makeup left on her face. Still, without those glasses, she looked kind of cute. Sort of like seventeen going on twenty-five. Maybe he could still pass her off as—

As if she'd let him. Damn, but she was one hardheaded woman. He remembered how many times he'd wished Kelly hadn't been quite so sweet. Kelly was a beautiful girl, but he'd never been able to have a decent fight with her, which meant he couldn't ever entirely relax. One thing he had to say about the Professor—she sure knew how to have a good fight.

He frowned. Were his feelings toward her softening? *Hell, no.* He had a long memory, and he wouldn't ever forget how she'd tricked him. It was just that he seemed to have lost the white-hot rage that had carried him through the first couple of weeks. Maybe it had finally burned itself out when she'd leaned her head against that tree trunk and told him she was taking the baby to Africa.

Except for what she'd done to him, he was beginning to realize that she was probably a decent person. Too damn serious and uptight as hell. Still, she worked hard—he'd seen lots of evidence of that from those equations she left like mouse droppings all over the house—and she'd made her way in a man's world. The fact that she wanted to help Annie spoke well of her, even though it made things twice as tough for him. Maybe his feelings *had* softened a little. She'd been so upset today when she found out he wasn't the dummy she'd counted on that he'd actually felt guilty. Her old man sure had done a number on her.

Once again he looked down at her and saw that a blond lock had escaped from her French braid and now curled in a figure eight over his zipper. He nearly groaned aloud. He'd been hard ever since he pushed her into his lap. Even earlier, if he counted that skirmish they'd had when they were lying on the ground at Annie's. But instead of easing up, it was getting worse, and if she turned her head even a little bit, she'd see that his zipper wasn't close to lying flat. No question about it. Fighting with the Professor had turned him on, and he was beginning to think it was time he did something about it. So far he'd had nothing but inconvenience from this marriage; it was about time he took advantage of its one convenience.

"Ouch! Damn it!" He snatched his hand away from her head and rubbed his thigh. "That's twice now you bit me! Don't you know that human saliva is a hundred times more dangerous than an animal's?"

"I supposed you learned that while you were getting your *summa cum laude* degree in biology!" She struggled to sit back up and shoved her glasses on. "I hope you get gangrene and they do the amputation without anesthetic. And they use a chain saw!"

"I'm going to see if my house has an attic where I can lock you up, just like men used to do in the old days when they found out they were stuck with a crazy wife."

"I'll bet if I were eighteen instead of thirty-four, you wouldn't be thinking about locking me up. You'd be stuffing me full of bubble gum and showing me off all over town! Now that I know you're an intelligent man, your attraction to infants seems even more peculiar."

"I am *not* attracted to infants!" He turned into the lane that led to the house.

"You certainly don't seem very confident of your ability to handle a grown woman."

"I swear, Jane— Damn!" He slammed on the brakes and reached over to push her back down on the seat, but he was too late. His father had already spotted her.

He cursed and reluctantly lowered the window. As he stopped his car well behind the muddy red Blazer, he called out, "What's up, Dad?"

"What do you think is up? Open this damn gate and let me in!"

Great, he thought with disgust. This was just great, a perfect addition to a miserable day. He punched the button that controlled the gate, nodded at his father, and hit the accelerator, shooting past the Blazer too quickly for the old man to get a good look at Jane.

Those softer feelings he'd been experiencing toward her only moments earlier vanished. He didn't want her meeting his parents. Period. He hoped it wouldn't occur to his father to mention any of the activities that had been taking up so much of his time. The less Jane knew about his private life, the better he liked it.

"You follow my lead," he said. "And whatever you do, don't let him know you're pregnant."

"He'll find out eventually."

"We're going to make it later. A lot later. And take off those damned *bifocals*!" They reached the house, and Cal hustled her inside before he went back out to greet his father.

Jane heard the door slam and knew he was upset. Good! Mr. Summa cum laude deserved to be upset. Biting her lip, she made her way to the kitchen. When she got there, she pressed her hand over her waist. *I'm sorry, little one. I didn't know. I'm so sorry.*

She plucked a few shreds of dried leaves out of her messy hair. She should try to straighten herself up before Cal's father came in, but she couldn't summon the energy to do more than push her glasses up on her nose while she tried to figure out how she was going to raise a genius.

She heard Cal's voice. "... and since Jane was feeling a lot better today, we went over to see Annie."

"Seems if she was feelin' better, you might have driven her into town to meet your parents."

She dropped her Windbreaker on one of the counter stools and turned to face the men coming into the kitchen.

"Dad, I went over this with you and Mom last night at dinner. I explained..."

"Never mind." Cal's father stopped as he caught sight of her.

Her mental image of him as a jolly old man with a round belly and fringe of white hair had dissolved the instant she'd caught sight of him at the gate. Now she felt as if she were staring at an older version of Cal.

He was equally imposing—big, handsome, rugged—and he looked exactly right in his red flannel shirt, rumpled slacks, and scuffed leather boots. His thick dark hair, worn longer and shaggier than his son's, had a few strands of silver, but he appeared to be no older than his early to mid-fifties, much too young and too good-looking to have a thirty-six-year-old son.

He took his time assessing her, and she didn't have any difficulty recognizing that straight-on, no-holds-barred gaze as a mirror of his son's. As she returned his scrutiny, she knew she would have to prove herself worthy. Still, he gave her a warm smile and extended his hand.

"I'm Jim Bonner. Glad we're finally getting to meet."

"Jane Darlington."

His smile disappeared as his eyebrows slammed together. He released her hand. "Most women around here take their husband's name when they get married."

"I'm not from around here, and the name is Darlington. I'm also thirty-four years old."

Behind her back, she heard a choking sound. Jim Bonner laughed. "You don't say."

"I certainly do. Thirty-four and getting older by the second."

"That's enough, Jane." The warning note in Cal's voice advised her not to reveal any more secrets, but he might not have spoken.

"You don't look sick."

"I'm not." She felt something brush her back and realized she'd lost the elastic holding her French braid.

"She started feeling better a couple of hours ago," Cal interjected. "Must not have been the flu after all."

Jane turned far enough to give him a faintly pitying look—she wasn't going to support him in his lies—but he pretended not to see.

Jim picked up an X-Man comic from the counter and regarded it quizzically. "Book-Of-The-Month-Club?"

"Jane reads them for relaxation. You want a beer, Dad?"

"No. I'm on my way to the hospital."

Concern drove away the caustic remark Jane had been about to make regarding the comic. "Is something wrong?"

"How about a sandwich?" Cal said too quickly. "Jane, make Dad and me a couple of sandwiches."

"I'll be happy to make your father a sandwich. You can fix your own."

Jim raised one eyebrow at his son in an expression Jane suspected meant something like, *After all these years, is this the best you could do for a wife?*

She refused to be cowed. "Are you having some tests done? I hope you're not ill."

Cal shot forward. "You've got some dirt on your face, sweetheart, from that walk you took at Annie's. Maybe you'd better go upstairs and get cleaned up."

"There's no big mystery about it," Jim said. "I'm a doctor, and I have patients to visit."

For a moment she couldn't move as the magnitude of the mistake she'd made once again drove its way home.

She whirled on Cal. "Your father's a *doctor*? How many more family skeletons do you have locked up?"

Her own heart might be breaking, but he seemed amused. "I know you were hopin' for a moonshiner, sweetheart, but I guess this just isn't your lucky day. Although, come to think of it—Dad, didn't you tell me your great-grampa had a still someplace up in the mountains?"

"That's what my father told me." Jim studied Jane. "Why do you care?"

Cal didn't let her reply, which was a good thing, because the lump in her throat had grown too large to permit speech. "Jane's sort of a hillbilly groupie. She's a city girl herself, but she likes all that backwoods stuff, and she's been real disappointed to find out we wear shoes."

Jim smiled. "I guess I could take mine off."

A woman's voice, soft and Southern, sounded from the foyer. "Cal, where are you?"

He sighed. "In the kitchen, Mom."

"I was passing by, and I saw the gate open." Like Cal's father, the woman who appeared in the doorway looked too young to have a thirty-six-year-old son, and she also seemed much too sophisticated to be the daughter of Annie Glide. Pretty, trim, and stylish, she wore her light brown hair in a short, trendy cut that curved behind her ears and emphasized a pair of clear blue eyes. Discreet frosting camouflaged whatever strands of gray had emerged. Her tall figure set off slim black trousers topped by a loosely cut fleece jacket in grape-colored wool with an abstract silver pin on the lapel. In comparison, Jane felt like a street urchin with her dirty face and leaf-flecked hair falling willy-nilly.

"You must be Jane." She walked forward, one hand extended in welcome. "I'm Lynn Bonner." Her greeting was warm, but as Jane took her hand, she received the impression of a deep reserve. "I hope you're feeling better. Cal said you were under the weather."

"I'm fine, thank you."

"She's thirty-four," Jim announced from his spot next to the counter.

Lynn looked startled, and then she smiled. "I'm delighted."

Jane found herself warming to Lynn Bonner. Jim sat down on one of the counter stools and stretched out his legs. "Cal said she's a hillbilly groupie. She sure is gonna love you, Amber."

Jane saw Cal shoot his father a puzzled look. She noted a faint trace of insolence in Jim Bonner's tone that hadn't been there before, but his wife showed no reaction. "I'm sure Cal told you we just got back from a combined vacation and medical conference. I was so sorry you weren't feeling well enough to join us for dinner last night. We'll make it up on Saturday. Jim, if it doesn't rain, you can grill."

Jim crossed his ankles. "Shoot, Amber, since Jane here likes hillbilly ways so much, why don't you forget grilling and make her some of those Glide family specials. We could have beans and fatback, or how 'bout some of that souse like your mama used to fix. You ever eat souse, Jane?"

"No, I don't believe I have."

"I can't imagine Jane wanting that," Lynn said coolly. "Nobody eats souse anymore."

"Maybe you could bring it back in fashion, Amber. You could tell all your ritzy friends about it next time you go to one of those big charity affairs in Asheville."

Cal had been staring at his parents as if he'd never seen them before. "When did you start calling Mom Amber?"

"It's her name," Jim replied.

"Annie uses it, but I've never heard you do it."

"Who says people have to keep doing things the same way?"

Cal glanced toward his mother, but she made no comment. Clearly uncomfortable, he turned away and once again opened the refrigerator door. "Are you sure nobody wants a sandwich? How about you, Mom?"

"No, thanks."

"Souse is part of the Glide family heritage," Jim said, unwilling to give up that particular avenue of conversation. "You haven't forgotten about that, have you, Amber?" He stabbed his wife with eyes so remote that Jane experienced a surge of sympathy for Cal's mother. She knew exactly how it felt to be on the receiving end of a gaze like that. Without waiting for an answer, he turned to Jane. "Souse is like sausage, Jane, but it's made from a hog's head, minus the eyeballs."

Lynn smiled a bit stiffly. "It's disgusting. I don't know why my mother ever made it. I just talked to her on the cell phone; that's how I knew you were feeling better. She seems to have taken to you, Jane."

"I like her." Jane was as anxious to change the subject as her new mother-in-law. Not only were the undercurrents of tension between Cal's parents disconcerting, but her stomach hadn't been entirely predictable lately, and she didn't want to take any chances with a discussion of eyeballs and a hog's head.

"Cal told us you're a physicist," Lynn said. "I'm so impressed."

Jim rose from the stool. "My wife didn't graduate from high school, so she sometimes gets intimidated when she meets people with advanced degrees."

Lynn didn't seem at all intimidated, and Jane found herself beginning to dislike Jim Bonner for his not-so-subtle put-downs. His wife might be willing to ignore his behavior, but she wasn't. "There certainly isn't any reason to be intimidated," she said evenly. "Some of the most foolish people I know have advanced degrees. But why am I telling you this, Dr. Bonner? I'm sure you've observed the same thing firsthand."

To her surprise, he smiled. Then he slipped his hand

inside the back of his wife's coat collar and rubbed her neck with the familiarity of someone who'd been doing exactly that for nearly four decades. The intimacy of the gesture made Jane realize she'd stepped into water far too deep for her, and she wished she'd kept her mouth shut. Whatever marital disharmony was going on between them had undoubtedly been going on for years, and it was none of her business. She had enough of her own marital disharmony to worry about.

Jim stepped away from his wife. "I've got to get going, or I'll be late for my rounds." He turned to Jane and gave her arm a friendly squeeze, then smiled at his son. "It was nice meeting you, Jane. See you tomorrow, Cal." His affection for Cal was obvious, but as Jim left the kitchen, she noticed that he didn't so much as glance at his wife.

Cal set a package of sandwich meat and cheese on the counter. As they heard the sound of the front door closing, he gazed at his mother.

She regarded him with perfect equanimity, and Jane noticed the invisible "No Trespassing" sign she had been wearing disappeared now that her husband had gone.

He looked troubled. "Why's Dad calling you Amber? I don't like it."

"Then you'll have to speak with him about it, won't you?" She smiled at Jane. "Knowing Cal, he won't think to take you any place but the Mountaineer. If you'd like to see some of the local shops, I'd be happy to show you around. We could have lunch afterward."

"Oh, I'd love that."

Cal stepped forward. "Now, Jane, you don't have to be polite. Mom's understanding." He slipped his arm around his mother's shoulders. "Jane can't spare any time from her research right now, but she doesn't want to hurt your feelings. She's saying yes when she really wants to say no."

"I understand completely." Lynn's expression said she

didn't understand at all. "Of course, your work is more important than socializing. Forget I said anything."

Jane was appalled. "No, really—"

"Please. You don't need to say another word." Turning her back on Jane, she hugged Cal. "I have to get to a meeting at church. Being the minister's mother is becoming a full-time job; I wish Ethan would get married." She glanced over at Jane, her eyes cool. "I hope you can spare some time for us on Saturday night."

Jane felt the rebuke. "I wouldn't miss it."

Cal escorted his mother to the door, where they spoke for a few moments. Afterward, he returned to the kitchen.

"How could you do that?" she said. "You made me seem like a snob to your mother?"

"What difference does it make?" He straightened his leg to pull his car keys from the right pocket of his jeans.

"Difference? It was a direct insult to her."

"So?"

"I can't believe you're being so obtuse."

"Now I get it." He set his keys on the counter. "You want to be the dearly beloved daughter-in-law. That's it, isn't it?"

"I simply want to be courteous."

"Why? So they can start to like you, and then have their guts ripped out when they find out we're getting a divorce?"

Uneasiness settled in the pit of her stomach. "Exactly what are you saying?"

"They've already mourned one daughter-in-law," he replied quietly. "I'm not going to have them mourn another. When they find out about our divorce, I want them cracking a bottle of champagne and celebrating their oldest son's narrow escape from a bad marriage."

"I don't understand." Even though she did.

"Then let me spell it out. I'd appreciate it very much if

you made sure that my parents can't stand the sight of you."

Her hands began to tremble, and she clasped them together in front of her. Until that moment, she hadn't realized that she'd been entertaining a subtle, but nonetheless powerful, fantasy of being made to feel part of Cal's family. For someone who had always wanted to belong, this was the final irony. "I'm the designated bad guy."

"Don't look at me like that. You came into my life uninvited and turned everything upside down. I don't want to be a father right now; I sure as hell don't want to be a husband. But you took away my choice, and now you have to make some of that up to me. If you've got an ounce of compassion in that heart of yours, you won't hurt my parents."

She turned away and blinked her eyes. He couldn't have asked anything that would disturb her more. Once again she would be the outsider, and she wondered if this was always to be her role in life? Would she always stand on the fringes gazing in at other people's families, at the bonds that seemed to come so easily to everyone else? But this time, if Cal had his way, she would be more than an oddity. This time she was to be loathed.

"A big chunk of my life is here in Salvation," he said. "My friends. My family. You'll just be around for a couple of months and then disappear."

"Leaving behind nothing but bad memories."

"You owe me," he said softly.

There was a sense of justice in what he was asking that was almost eerie in its perfection. What she had done to Cal was immoral, which was why she'd been dogged by guilt for months, and now she had a chance to serve penance. He was right. She hadn't done anything to deserve a place in his family. And she owed him.

He fiddled with his keys on the counter, and she realized he was uncomfortable. It was rare to see him looking anything but self-confident, and it took her a moment to understand. He was afraid she wouldn't go along with his wishes, and he wanted a way to convince her.

"You might have noticed my parents are a little tense with each other right now. That weren't like this before Cherry and Jamie died."

"I know they married when they were teenagers, but they're even younger than I expected."

"I was my dad's high school graduation present. Mom was fifteen when she got pregnant, sixteen when I was born."

"Oh."

"They kicked her out of school, but Annie told us that mom stood under the stadium during his graduation ceremony, wearing her best dress even though nobody could see her, just so she could hear him give the valedictory address."

Jane considered the thirty-year-old injustice. Amber Lynn Glide, the poor mountain girl, had been kicked out of school for being pregnant while the rich boy who'd gotten her that way stood at the podium and received the community's accolades.

"I know what you're thinking," Cal said, "but he didn't get off scot-free. He had it plenty rough. Nobody expected him to marry her, but he did, and he had to support a family while he went through college and med school."

"With help from his parents, I'll bet."

"Not at first. They hated my mom, and they told him if he married her, they wouldn't give him a penny. They kept their word for the first year or so, but then Gabe came along, and they finally kicked in for tuition."

"Your parents seem very troubled."

He immediately grew defensive. She realized it was one thing for him to comment on the problem, but quite another for her to. "They're just upset, that's all. They've never been very demonstrative, but there's nothing wrong with their marriage, if that's what you're getting at.''

"I'm not getting at anything.''

He snatched up his keys from the counter and made his way toward the door that led to the garage. She stopped him before he got there.

"Cal, I'll do what you want with your parents—I'll be as obnoxious to them as I can—but not with Annie. She's halfway to the truth, anyway.'' Jane felt a kinship with the old woman, and she had to have at least one friend or she'd go crazy.

He turned to look at her.

She squared her shoulders and lifted her head. "That's the deal. Take it or leave it.''

He slowly nodded. "All right. I'll take it.''

10

Jane groaned as she rose to turn off her computer, then slipped out of her clothes to prepare for bed. For the past three days, she'd spent her mornings helping Annie plant her garden, and every muscle ached.

She smiled as she folded her jeans and put them away in the closet, then pulled out her nightshirt. Usually she bristled around dictatorial people, but she loved having Annie boss her around.

Annie had bossed Cal, too. On Wednesday morning he'd insisted on driving Jane to Heartache Mountain. When they'd gotten there, Jane had pointed out the front step and suggested he stop hiring other people to do what he should do himself. He'd set to work with a great deal of grumbling, but it wasn't long before she'd heard him whistling. He'd done a good job on the step and then made some other needed repairs. Today he'd bought several gallons of paint at the hardware store and begun scraping the exterior of the house.

She slipped into a short-sleeved gray nightshirt with an appliqué of Goofy on the pocket. Tomorrow night she would be dining with Cal's parents. He hadn't mentioned her promise to distance them, but she knew he hadn't forgotten.

Although she was tired, it was barely eleven o'clock, and she felt too restless to go to bed. She began to tidy her work area and found herself once again wondering where Cal went at night. She suspected he was seeing other women, and she remembered the reference Lynn had made to the Mountaineer. She'd asked Annie about it today and learned that it was a private club of some sort. Was that where he met his women?

Even though this wasn't a real marriage, the idea hurt. She didn't want him sleeping with anyone else. She wanted him sleeping with her!

Her hands stilled on the stack of printouts she'd been straightening. What was she thinking of? Sex would only make an already complex situation impossible. But even as she told herself that, she remembered the way Cal had looked today with his shirt off while he'd stood on the ladder and scraped the side of Annie's house. Watching those muscles bunch and flex every time he moved had made her so crazy she'd finally grabbed his shirt, thrown it at him, and delivered a stern lecture on the depletion of the ozone layer and skin cancer.

Lust. That's what she was dealing with. Pure, unadulterated lust. And she wasn't going to give in to it.

She needed something to do that would distract her, so she carried her overflowing trash can downstairs and emptied it in the garage. Afterward, she gazed out the kitchen bay window at the moon and found herself contemplating the ancient scientists—Ptolemy, Copernicus, Galileo—who'd tried to unravel the mysteries of the universe with only the most primitive of instruments. Even Newton couldn't have envisioned the tools she used, from the powerful computer on her desk to the world's giant particle accelerators.

She jumped as the door behind her opened, and Cal walked in from the garage. As he moved across the kitchen, it occurred to her that she had never seen a man so at home

in his body. Along with his jeans, he wore a wine red hen-
ley, the kind made out of waffle-knit underwear fabric, and
a black nylon parka. Tiny needle-points of sensation prickled at her skin.

"I thought you'd be in bed," he said, and she wondered
if she imagined the slight huskiness she heard in his voice.

"Just thinking."

"Dreaming about all those potatoes you planted?"

She smiled. "As a matter of fact, I was thinking about
Newton. Isaac," she added.

"I've heard the name," he said dryly. The hem of his
parka flopped over his wrists as he pushed his hands into
his jeans pockets. "I thought you modern-day physicists
had forgotten all about old Isaac in your passion for the
Big Guy."

Hearing Einstein referred to in that way amused her.
"Believe me, the Big Guy had a lot of respect for his pred-
ecessor. He just didn't let Newton's laws limit his thinking."

"I still think that's disrespectful. Isaac did all that work,
then old Albert had to come along and upset it."

She smiled again. "The best scientists have always been
rebels. Thank God they still don't execute us for our theories."

He tossed his parka over one of the counter stools.
"How's the search for the top quark coming?"

"We found it in 1995. And how do you know what kind
of work I'm doing?"

He shrugged. "I make it my business to know things."

"I'm investigating the *characteristics* of the top quark,
not looking for it."

"So how many top quarks fit on the head of a pin?"

"More than you can imagine." She was still surprised
that he knew anything about her research.

"I'm asking you about your work, Professor. I promise

you that I can at least grasp the concept, if not the particulars.''

Once again she'd let herself forget how bright he was. Easy to do with that muscular jock's body standing in front of her. She pulled her thoughts up short before they could move any farther in *that* direction. ''What do you know about quarks?''

''Not much. They're a basic subatomic particle, and all matter is made up of them. There are—what?—six kinds of quarks?''

It was more than most people knew, and she nodded. ''Top and bottom quarks, up and down, strange and charm. They got their names from a song that's in James Joyce's *Finnegans Wake*.''

''See, that's part of the problem with you scientific types. If you'd take your names from Tom Clancy books—things people actually read—then the general public would understand what you do better.''

She laughed. ''I promise if I discover something important, I'll name it Red October.''

''You do that.'' He looped his leg over a stool, then regarded her expectantly. She realized he was waiting for her to tell him more about her work.

She walked to the corner of the counter and rested one hand on the granite top. ''What we know about the top quark is quite surprising. For example, it's forty times heavier than the bottom quark, but we don't know why. The more we understand about the top quark's characteristics, the closer we come to exposing the cracks in the standard model of particle physics. Ultimately, of course, we're looking for the final theory that will lead us to a new physics.''

''The Theory of Everything?''

''The name is facetious. It's more accurately called the Grand Unification Theory, but, yes, the Theory of Everything. Some of us think the top quark will unlock a small part of it.''

"And you want to be the Einstein of this new physics.''

She busied herself wiping a speck from the granite with the tip of her finger. ''There are brilliant physicists all over the world doing the same work.''

"And you're not intimidated by any one of them, are you?''

She grinned. "Not a bit.''

He laughed. "Good luck, Professor. I wish you well.''

"Thank you.'' She waited for him to change the subject—most people's eyes began to glaze over when she talked about her work—but instead, he got up, grabbed a bag of taco chips from the pantry, and slouched down into the red velvet banquette in the alcove, where he began questioning her about the way the supercolliders worked.

Before long, she found herself sitting across from him munching on taco chips as she described the Tevatron collider at Fermilab as well as the new collider being built by CERN in Geneva, Switzerland. Her explanations merely induced more of his questions.

At first she answered eagerly, thrilled to find a layman who was genuinely interested in particle physics. It was cozy sitting in this warm kitchen late at night, munching on junk food and discussing her work. It almost felt as if they had a real relationship. But the fantasy evaporated when she realized she was explaining the components of the lepton family to him, and, much worse, that he was taking it in.

Her stomach twisted as she absorbed how easily he grasped these difficult concepts. What if her baby turned out to be even more brilliant than she feared? The idea made her dizzy, so she jumped into a complicated explanation of the Higgs boson that soon left him behind.

"Afraid you lost me, Professor.''

If only she could scream at him that she'd lost him because he was too dumb to understand, but all she could say was, "It gets pretty hairy." She rose from the table. "I'm tired. I think I'll turn in for the night."

"All right."

She decided this would be as good a time as any to put an end to her imprisonment. He was in a fairly good mood, so maybe he'd handle the news better. "By the way, Cal, I need to do something about getting a car. Nothing fancy, just basic transportation. Who should I see?"

"No one. If you have to go some place, I'll take you."

As quickly at that, his affability vanished. He rose from the table and walked out of the kitchen, putting an end to the discussion.

But she wasn't nearly done, and she followed him across the cavernous family room toward the study. "I'm used to my independence. I need my own car." And then, waspishly, "I promise I won't wave at your friends when I drive through town."

"No car, Professor. That's the way it's going to be." Once again, he walked away from her, this time disappearing into the study. She compressed her lips and marched forward. This was ridiculous. Cal seemed to have forgotten they lived in the twentieth century. And that she had her own money.

She stopped in the doorway. "Unlike your girlfriends, I'm old enough to have my driver's license."

"The joke's wearing thin."

"Except it's not exactly a joke, is it?" She regarded him thoughtfully. "Are you sure all this has to do with protecting your parents? Are you sure it isn't more about keeping me locked up so my advanced age and general lack of bimbo qualities don't embarrass you in front of your friends?"

"You have no idea what you're talking about." He sprawled down behind the massive wooden desk.

She regarded him dispassionately. "I'm not even close

to being the kind of woman all your buddies expected you to marry, am I? I'm not pretty enough to be your wife, my breasts aren't big enough, and I'm too old. Big time embarrassment for the Bomber.''

He crossed his ankles and propped his boots on the desk. "If you say so."

"I don't need your permission to buy a car, Cal. I intend to do it whether you like it or not."

He hit her dead on with those scorched-earth eyes. "Like hell."

Completely exasperated and in no mood to enter into a full-fledged battle, she turned toward the door. Tomorrow she'd do as she liked, and he could just live with it. "I've had all of you I can take for right now. Good night."

"Don't you walk away from me!" He moved so quickly that she didn't see him coming, and before she could get through the doorway, he'd blocked it. "Did you hear me?"

She splayed her hands on her hips and glared up at him. "Back off, buster!"

Seconds ticked away, each one crackling with tension. His forehead wrinkled and his lips tightened, but at the same time, she detected something that seemed almost like anticipation in his eyes, as if he wanted to fight with her. It was the most astonishing thing. She was used to people who avoided conflict, but Cal seemed to enjoy it, and, to her surprise, she was more than willing to join in.

Before she got a chance, however, he dropped his gaze and the corner of his mouth curled. "Goofy."

She'd been called many things, but never that, and her temper flared. "*What* did you say?"

"Your nightshirt." He reached down and, with the tip of his finger, traced the cartoon appliqué that lay on the upper slope of her breast. "Goofy."

"Oh." Her anger deflated.

He smiled and began using his fingernail, running it back and forth over the outline of the figure. The skin of her breast tightened, and her nipple hardened in response. She hated reacting to something that was obviously a calculated move on his part. No wonder he had a big ego; he could probably turn women on in his sleep.

"I hope you're arousing yourself because you're not doing a thing to me."

"Is that so?" He glanced down at the front of her nightshirt where the evidence clearly pointed to the contrary.

He was so arrogant; so sure of himself. She needed some small measure of revenge, so she shook her head and regarded him sadly. "You haven't figured it out yet, have you, Cal?"

"Figured what out?"

"Never mind." She sighed. "I guess you're probably a fairly nice guy underneath all that bluster, and I don't want to hurt your feelings."

An edge of belligerence crept into his voice. "Don't you worry about my feelings. What haven't I figured out yet?"

She made a helpless, fluttery gesture that was surprisingly effective considering the fact that she'd never done anything like that before. "This is silly. I really don't want to talk about it."

"Talk!"

"All right, then. To be blunt, the thing you don't seem to be able to grasp is the fact that you're not my type. You just don't turn me on." *Liar, Liar, pants on fire.*

He dropped his hand. "I don't turn you on?"

"Now I've made you angry, haven't I?"

"Angry? Why the hell should I be angry?"

"You look angry."

"Well, that just goes to show that you're not as perceptive as you think."

"Good. Besides, I'm sure my lack of response to you is simply a problem with my perception. It probably doesn't have anything to do with you."

"Damn right."

A little shrug. "I've just always preferred a different type of man."

"What type is that?"

"Oh, men who aren't quite as large. Not quite as loud. Gentle men. Scholarly men."

"Like Dr. Craig Elkhart?" He spit out the name.

"What do you know about Craig?"

"I know he dumped you for a twenty-year-old secretary."

"She wasn't a secretary. She was a data-entry clerk. And he didn't dump me."

"That's not the way I heard it. The guy dumped you like a load of wet cement."

"He most certainly did not. We parted by mutual agreement."

"Mutual, my ass."

"You're just throwing up a smoke screen because I wounded your pride when I said I wasn't attracted to you."

"I've met a lot of women who were liars, but you take the cake. Admit it, Professor. I turn you on so much you can hardly stand it. If I put my mind to it, I could have you naked and begging in thirty seconds flat."

"There's nothing more pathetic than an aging man boasting of his flagging sexual prowess."

"Flagging!"

She watched a slow flush spread across his cheekbones and knew she'd really done it. She'd pushed him past his limit, and now she absolutely had to shut up. "Don't worry, Cal. Somewhere there's a woman who'll care enough to take her time with you."

The flush spread to his ears.

She patted his chest. "And if that doesn't work, I've heard they're doing wonders with implants."

Those pale eyes widened, almost as if he couldn't believe what he was hearing.

"I think there are also some nonsurgical devices based

on air pressure and vacuum. I could probably even design something for you, if it came to that."

"That's it!" The flush receded, and before she knew what was happening, he'd dropped his shoulder, pushed it not ungently against her stomach, and upended her.

"Upsey-daisy, sweetheart."

She found herself staring at the seat of his jeans. Faded denim stretched tight over slim, hard-muscled hips. She began to feel dizzy and wasn't certain she could entirely blame it on the blood rushing to her head. "Cal?"

"Uh-huh?"

"Please put me down."

"In a minute." He headed out into the foyer, moving carefully in deference to her pregnancy. He'd hooked one of his arms behind her knees to hold her in place, and he patted the back of one bare thigh as he mounted the stairs. "Just stay real still, now, and everything'll be fine."

"Where are we going?"

"We're paying the Evil Queen a visit."

"Evil queen? What are you talking about? Put me down!"

They reached the top of the stairs. "Quiet, now. I have to concentrate real hard so I don't turn too fast and slam that head of yours right into the wall, givin' you a nasty concussion that would lower your IQ to somewhere in the vicinity of human and make you behave like a reasonable human being."

"My bedroom's over there."

"The Evil Queen's this way." He marched toward his own bedroom.

"*What* evil queen? What are you talking about? And put me down right this minute or I'll scream bloody murder, then do the job for real!"

"I already hid all the electrical appliances, and I'm not taking a shower without locking you in the closet first." He dropped his shoulder, and she found herself being low-

ered onto something soft. She looked up into her own reflection.

Her hair was tousled, her nightshirt twisted around her
thighs, and her skin rosy. Cal stood next to the bed. He
leaned forward and gazed up at the mirror mounted above
the bed.

"Mirror, mirror, on the wall, who's gonna be the most
naked lady of all?"

The Evil Queen! She snatched a pillow and threw it at
him. "Oh, no, you don't." She vaulted toward the other
side of the bed, only to have him grab her nightshirt and
pull her back down.

"Time for good ol' Goofy to make himself scarce so the
grown-ups can play."

"I don't want to play with you, and don't you dare try
to pull off my nightshirt, you arrogant ass!"

The mattress sagged as he straddled her thighs. "And
you've got a very nice one yourself, I couldn't help but
notice. What say we take a closer look?" He reached for
the hem of the nightshirt.

"Don't, Cal." She slapped her hands down, but even as
she pressed the garment to her thighs, she knew she wanted
to let him take it off her. Why couldn't she? They were
married, weren't they?

Still straddling her, he leaned back on his right calf.
"You don't seriously think we're going to live here for
three months without getting intimate."

Her heart pounded, her body pulsed with need, and her
brain cried out the truth. He didn't have the slightest bit of
affection for her. She was nothing more than a sexual convenience. She gritted her teeth. "Have you forgotten that
you don't like me?"

"True, but one thing doesn't necessarily have anything
to do with the other. You don't like me, either."

"That's not exactly so."

"You do like me?"

"I don't *dislike* you. You're probably a decent person. In your own twisted way, I know you think you're doing the right thing about all this, but I just wish you were different."

"Dumber."

"That. And not so big. Everything about you is too big for me—not just your body, but your personality, your bank account, your temper, and, definitely, your ego."

"Don't you talk to me about temper! I'm not the one going around trying to electrocute people. And if we're throwing out things that are too big, what about that gargantuan brain of yours?" He drew his leg over her and resettled himself at the end of the bed, where he leaned against the bedpost.

She knew she'd done the right thing, but it was still painful. She pointed out the obvious. "To you, I'm just an available body."

"You're my wife."

"A technicality." She sat up so she was leaning against the headboard. "You want me to be unpleasant to your parents and stay away from your friends but, at the same time, you expect me to make love with you. Can't you understand how I might find that a little demeaning?"

"No." He gazed at her, and his flared nostrils and tight lips dared her to argue with him. He was going to take his stand, even though he knew it was indefensible.

"I guess I shouldn't be surprised you feel like that since it's typical of the way celebrity athletes traditionally treat their groupies. Women are good enough for a quick romp in bed, but not good enough to be part of a big shot's life."

"Are you saying you want to be part of my life? That's pretty hard to believe, Professor, considering the fact that you don't seem to like anything about me."

"You're deliberately misinterpreting. I'm merely saying that I refuse to sleep with you at night knowing you don't like me, especially when you want to keep me locked up during the day. Don't deny that you'd behave differently if one of your bimbos had done what I did.''

"None of my bimbos is smart enough to plan what you did! And I don't have any bimbos!''

She lifted one eyebrow. ''A man like you wants his wife to be a reflection of himself. You want youth and beauty standing next to you because that's how you want everyone to see you, as young and healthy, a perfect physical specimen who doesn't have a worry about anything, certainly not about Kevin Tucker taking away your job.''

He threw his leg over the side of the bed and stood. ''This is the most boring conversation I ever had.''

"Just another sign of how incompatible we are because I think the conversation's pretty fascinating. What are you going to do when your playing days are over, Cal?''

"I don't have to worry about that for a long time.''

"I've seen you limp when you get out of the car after you've been sitting for a long time, and I have a feeling those thirty-minute showers I hear you take in the morning aren't about personal cleanliness. Your body has taken a beating, and it's not going to do it much longer.''

"Now you're an expert on orthopedics.''

"I know what I see.''

"I'm not buying you a car.'' He headed for the door.

"I didn't ask you to,'' she called after him. ''I intend to buy my own.''

"No, you're not.'' He poked his head back in the door. ''And I *am* taking you to bed.''

She untangled herself from the covers and pushed her nightshirt down as she stood up. ''I'm not going to bed with a man who dislikes me.''

"We'll work on that part of it.''

"We've never had a date.''

"We've already *done it* twice!''

"That was nothing more than a medical procedure.''

His eyes narrowed.

"We've never even kissed," she went on, driving her point home.

"Now that's something we can fix real easy." He advanced on her, a sense of purpose glittering in his eyes.

"Cal, I didn't mean . . ." She couldn't go on. She wanted to kiss him.

He encircled her wrists with his hands. The bedpost bumped against her spine. "Consider this a scientific experiment, Professor."

He leaned forward, drawing her hands behind her back and around the bedpost at the same time. She felt as if she'd been tied to a stake, except his gentle fingers were the only bonds holding her in place.

As he gazed down, her heart gave a nervous kick against her ribs. "Let's see how you taste."

His head dipped and his lips brushed hers. They were soft and warm, slightly parted, barely touching. Her eyes drifted shut. She felt as if she were being grazed by a feather and wondered how someone so strong could have such a tender touch.

He continued to tease her with his mouth. The barest brush, the slightest touch. Her senses swirled. She wanted more and she went up on tiptoe, slanting her mouth across his and deepening the kiss.

He drew back. Another graze. A glance.

She leaned into him again, and he nipped her bottom lip. Was that a warning that only the quarterback called the play? Her body throbbed with frustration.

He rewarded her obedience by closing his lips over hers and lightly tracing the bow with the tip of his tongue. She moaned. If he gave this much attention to a simple kiss, what would he do if she let him get to the rest of her?

She couldn't stand it any longer, and once again she reared up on her tiptoes. This time he didn't object. The gentle tantalizer disappeared, and he took full possession of what she offered. With his hands occupied shackling hers behind the bedpost, he could only use his mouth on her, and he used it well, filling her with his tongue and leaning into her so she could feel his passion.

She pressed her own body against his and lost herself in a new way of kissing, a mating that was more erotic than any sex act she'd ever experienced. She could be male and female, the possessor and the possessed. She moved her body against him, using it as if she were a snake, rubbing breasts and belly, thighs and hips. Her body burned with the thrill of everything that had been missing for her, and in her passion, she had a brief glimpse of how it might be if they were more to each other than bodies.

She heard a moan, but this time it didn't come from her. It was hoarse, muffled, urgent. Her hands were suddenly free, while his were on her thighs, sliding beneath her nightshirt.

Oh, yes. She wanted him there. *Hurry. Touch my softest place. My sweetest place.* Her body urged him to boldness while her mind and heart cried out not to give herself so cheaply. She wanted to be courted, to be wooed and won, even if only for her body. Just once in her life, she wanted to feel what other women felt when men pursued them.

His fingers touched the soft curls. "Stop!" Her exclamation sounded as if it were part command, part howl.

"No."

"I mean it, Cal." She gasped for breath, struggled for control. "Get your hands out from under my nightshirt."

"You want me here. You know you do."

He was still pressed hard against her, and she wished she'd touched him there first, before she'd told him to stop. Just one quick touch so she could see how he felt against her hand. "I want you to stop."

He jerked away from her. "This is stupid! This is so damn stupid I can't believe it! The two of us are trapped together in this stinking marriage. We can't stand each other, and the only consolation we're going to find is in bed, but you're too damn stubborn to cooperate!''

He'd proven her point in spades, and she swallowed her hurt so she could let him know it. ''I *knew* you didn't like me.''

''What are you talking about?''

''You just said it. You just said that *we* can't stand each other, even though I already said *I* didn't dislike you. So that leaves you. You just admitted how you felt about me.''

''I did *not* say that.''

''You most assuredly did.''

''Well, I didn't mean it.''

''Ha!''

''Rosebud . . .''

''Don't you call me that, you jerk! Sex is just another form of sport to you, isn't it? Something to do when you're not on the football field or drinking beer with your buddies. Well, I don't feel that way about it. You want to have sex with me, fine! You can have sex with me! But on my terms.''

''And exactly what terms are those?''

''You're going to have to *like* me first! A lot!''

''I already like you a lot!'' he roared.

''You are pathetic!'' With an exclamation made up of equal parts fury and frustration, she snatched a pillow from the bed, threw it at his head, and flounced back to her bedroom.

Moments later, she heard a loud thud, as if somebody's fist might very well have connected with a wall.

11

Cal's parents lived on a hilly residential street shaded by mature trees and lined with older homes. Vines that would soon bloom with clematis and morning glory clung to the mailboxes, and empty white latticework planters waiting to be filled with colorful blooms perched on front porches.

The Bonner house sat at the top of a steep slope carpeted with ivy and rhododendron. It was a graceful two-story cream stucco topped by a roof of curving pale green Spanish tiles, with the shutters and trim painted the same light green. Cal pulled the Jeep under the porte cochere off to the side, then came around the front to open the door for her.

For a moment his eyes lingered on her legs. He hadn't commented on her soft, taffy-colored skirt and sweater ensemble, even though she'd rolled the skirt twice at the waistband so that a good three inches of thigh showed through her pale hose. She thought he hadn't noticed and figured her thirty-four-year-old thighs weren't any match for all those long-stemmed aerobicized legs he was used to, but now the flicker of admiration in his eyes made her wonder if she'd misjudged.

She couldn't remember ever being so confused. Last

night she'd felt as if she'd run through an entire gamut of emotions with him. When they'd talked in the kitchen, there had been a sense of companionship she'd never expected. There had also been laughter, anger, and lust. Right now, the lust disturbed her most.

"I like your hair," he said.

She'd left it down, along with abandoning her glasses and taking twice her normal time to apply her makeup. The way his gaze slid over her made her think it was more than just her hair he liked. Then he frowned.

"No funny business tonight, you hear me?"

"Loud and clear." She deliberately stuck a burr under his saddle so she'd stop thinking about last night. "Don't you want to throw your coat over my head to make sure none of the neighbors get a good look at me? Now what am I saying? If any of them spot me, you can just tell them I'm the mother of one of your girlfriends."

He grabbed her arm and steered her toward the front door. "One of these days I'm going to slap a piece of duct tape right over that smart mouth of yours."

"Impossible. You'll already be dead. I spotted an electric hedge trimmer in the garage."

"Then I'm going to tie you up, toss you in a closet, throw in a dozen rats crazed from hunger, and lock the door."

She lifted her eyebrow. "Very good."

He grunted and opened the front door.

"We're in here," Lynn called out.

Cal led her into a beautifully decorated living room done almost entirely in white, with accent pieces in peach and soft mint green. Jane barely had a chance to take it in before her attention was caught by one of the most beautiful men she had ever seen.

"Jane, this is my brother Ethan."

He walked forward, took her hand, and looked down at

her through kind blue eyes. "Hello, Jane. We finally meet."

She could feel herself melting, and she was so surprised by her reaction to him that she barely managed to acknowledge his greeting. Could this blond-haired, finely chiseled, soft-spoken man really be Cal's brother? Gazing into his eyes, she felt the same swell of emotion she sometimes experienced when she saw a newborn baby or a photograph of Mother Teresa. She found herself sneaking a glance at Cal, just to see if she'd missed something.

He shrugged. "Don't look at me. None of us can figure it out."

"We think he might be a changeling." Lynn rose from the couch. "He's the family embarrassment. Goodness knows, the rest of us have a list of sins a mile long, but he makes us look even worse in comparison."

"For very good reason." Ethan regarded Jane with absolute sincerity. "They're all the spawn of Satan."

By now Jane had more than a passing acquaintance with the Bonner sense of humor. "And you probably mug old ladies in your spare time."

Ethan laughed and turned to his brother. "You finally caught yourself a live one."

Cal muttered something inaudible, then glared at her with a silent reminder that she was supposed to be alienating everybody, not buddying up. She hadn't forgotten, but neither had she let herself think too much about that part of it.

"Your father had a delivery," Lynn said, "but he should be back any minute now. Betsy Woods's third. You remember; she was your first prom date. I think your father has delivered the babies of every old girlfriend any of you boys ever had."

"Dad took over the practice from his own father," Ethan explained. "For a long time Dad was the only doctor around here. He's got help now, but he still works too hard."

The discussion reminded her that she needed to find a doctor soon. And it wouldn't be Jim Bonner.

As if she'd conjured him, he appeared in the archway. He looked rumpled and tired, and Jane saw an expression of concern flicker across Lynn's features.

As Jim came into the room, his big voice boomed. "How come nobody has a drink?"

"I have a pitcher of margaritas waiting in the kitchen." Lynn's forehead smoothed, and she moved toward the door.

"We'll come with you," Jim said. "I can't stand this room, not since you and that fancy decorator ruined it. All this white makes me feel as if I can't sit down."

Jane thought the room was lovely and found Jim's remark uncalled-for. The four of them followed Lynn into the kitchen, whose warm pine and tasteful accessories gave it a cozy country charm. Jane wondered how Cal could stand their own garish house after being raised in such a comfortable place.

Jim shoved a beer at his son, then turned to Jane. "Would you like a margarita?"

"I'd rather have a soft drink."

"Baptist?"

"Pardon?"

"Are you a teetotaler?"

"No."

"We have some nice white wine in the house. Amber's made herself over into something of a wine expert, haven't you, honey?" His words sounded like those of a proud husband, but their bite told a different story.

"That's enough, Dad." Cal's voice held a touch of steel. "I don't know what's going on here, but I want it to stop."

His father straightened, and their eyes clashed. Although Cal's posture remained relaxed, the hard glint in his eyes warned his father that he'd stepped over the line.

Jim obviously wasn't used to having anyone challenge his authority, but Cal didn't show the slightest inclination to back down. She remembered that only yesterday he'd denied that anything was wrong with his parents' marriage.

Ethan broke in with a request for a beer and a casual remark about a town council meeting. He must be the family peacemaker. Tensions eased, and Lynn asked Jane about her morning with Annie. Jane heard the coolness in her voice and knew she must be wondering why her new daughter-in-law had so much time to spend helping her mother put in a garden but refused to spare a few hours for sightseeing with her.

Jane glanced at Cal. She saw an expression of resignation in his face. He didn't expect her to keep her word.

She felt a moment of sadness, but it did no good wishing for the impossible when she knew she owed him this. "It's been a bother, but don't tell her that. She simply doesn't understand that every hour she pulls me away from my research is an hour I can never regain."

There was a moment of strained silence. Jane refused to look at Cal. She didn't want to see his relief as she embarrassed herself in front of his family. With a sense of dread, she turned the screw. "I know her garden is important to her, but, really, it hardly compares with the work I'm doing. I tried to explain that to her, but she's so . . . I don't mean to imply she's ignorant, but, let's be frank, her understanding of complex issues is limited."

"Why the hell does she even want you there?" Jim barked.

Jane pretended not to pick up on his belligerence, which was so like his son's. "Who can account for the whims of an old lady?"

Cal broke in. "I'll tell you what I think? Jane's got a cantankerous nature, just like Annie's, and I think that's why Annie loves having her around. The two of them have a lot in common."

"Lucky us," Ethan muttered.

Her cheeks burned, and Cal must have sensed that she'd

gone as far as she could because he turned the conversation to a discussion of Ethan's skiing trip. Before long they were all seated at the dinner table.

Jane did her best to look bored while she drank in every detail. She observed the easy affection between the two brothers and the unconditional love Jim and Lynn had for their sons. Despite the problems between her in-laws, she would have given anything to belong to this family instead of the distant father she'd grown up with.

Several times during the meal the conversation turned toward Jim's work: an interesting case he had, a new medical procedure. Jane found his descriptions too gory for the dinner table, but it didn't seem to bother anyone else, and she concluded they were all accustomed to it. Cal, in particular, kept pressing his father for details.

But Jane was most fascinated by Lynn. As the meal progressed, she spoke of art and music, as well as a reading group discussion she was leading on a new novel. She was also an excellent cook, and Jane found herself feeling increasingly intimidated. Was there anything this former mountain girl didn't do well?

Ethan nodded toward the table's centerpiece, a crystal vase holding an arrangement of lilies and dendrobium orchids. "Where'd you get the flowers, Mom? Since Joyce Belik closed her shop after Christmas, I haven't seen anything like that around here."

"I picked the arrangement up when I was in Asheville on Thursday. The lilies are getting a little limp, but I'm still enjoying them."

For the first time since they'd begun to eat, Jim addressed his wife directly. "Do you remember the way you used to decorate the table right after we got married?"

She was still for a moment. "It was so long ago I've forgotten."

"Well, I haven't." He turned toward his sons. "Your mother'd pick dandelions out of somebody's backyard, stick 'em in an old pickle jar, and show 'em off to me when I came in from class like they were some exotic flower I'd never seen before. She'd get as excited about a jar full of dandelions as other women get about roses.''

Jane wondered if Jim had intended to embarrass his wife with this reminder of her humble roots, but if so, his strategy backfired. Lynn didn't seem at all embarrassed, but his own voice had deepened with an emotion that surprised her. Maybe Jim Bonner wasn't as contemptuous of his wife's humble roots as he pretended to be.

"You used to get so annoyed with me," she said, "and I can't blame you. Imagine. Dandelions on the dinner table.''

"It wasn't just flowers she used for centerpieces. I remember one time she scrubbed up a bunch of rocks she thought were pretty and set them in a bird's nest she found.''

"You very rightly pointed out that a bird's nest on the kitchen table was disgusting and refused to eat until I threw it out.''

"Yeah, I did, didn't I?'' He rubbed his fingers on the stem of his wineglass and frowned. "It might have been unsanitary, but it sure was pretty.''

"Really, Jim, it was no such thing.'' She smiled, cool, serene, unaffected by the currents of old emotions that seemed to have claimed her husband.

For the first time since they'd sat down, he met Lynn's eyes straight on. "You always liked pretty things.''

"I still do.''

"But now they have to have labels on them.''

"And you enjoy those labels much more than you ever enjoyed dandelions or birds' nests.''

Despite her promise to distance herself from the family, Jane couldn't bear the idea of witnessing any more unpleasantness.

"How did you manage in those first years after you were married? Cal said you had no money."

Cal and Ethan exchanged a glance that made Jane wonder if she'd stumbled on a forbidden topic. She realized her question was overly personal, but since she was supposed to be obnoxious, what difference did it make?

"Yeah, Dad, exactly how did you manage?" Ethan said.

Lynn dabbed at the corners of her lips with her napkin. "It's too depressing. Your father hated every minute of it, and I don't want his dinner spoiled."

"I didn't hate every minute of it." Jim seemed pensive as he leaned back in his chair. "We lived in this ugly two-room apartment in Chapel Hill that looked out over an alley where people'd throw rusted bedsprings and old couches. The place was hopeless, but your mother loved it. She tore pictures out of *National Geographics* and hung them on the walls. We didn't have any curtains, just two window shades that had turned yellow, and she made tissue-paper flowers out of pink Kleenex to pin across the bottoms. Things like that. We were poor as church mice. I stocked grocery shelves when I wasn't in class or studying, but she had the worst of it. Right up until the day Cal was born, she got up at four in the morning to work all day in a bakery. But no matter how tired she was, she'd still find time to pick those dandelions on her way home."

Lynn shrugged. "Believe me, working in that bakery wasn't nearly as difficult as the farm chores I'd been doing on Heartache Mountain."

"But you were pregnant," Jane pointed out, trying to imagine it.

"I was young and strong. In love." For the first time, Lynn looked slightly ruffled. "After Cal was born, we had medical bills on top of everything else, and since I couldn't work in the bakery and still take care of him, I began experimenting with cookie recipes."

"She'd start baking as soon as she'd given him his two

o'clock feeding, work until four, then go back to sleep for an hour or so until he woke again. After she'd fed him, she'd wake me up for class. Then she'd wrap everything up, load Cal into an old buggy she'd found in a junk shop, pack the cookies around him, and walk to campus where she'd sell them to the students, two cookies for twenty-five cents. She didn't have a license, so whenever the campus cops came around, she'd cover up everything but Cal's head with this big blanket."

She smiled at Cal. "Poor thing. I knew nothing about babies, and I nearly suffocated you in the summer."

Cal regarded her fondly. "I still don't like a lot of covers on me."

"The cops never caught on," Jim said. "All they saw was a sixteen-year-old mountain girl in a pair of worn-out jeans pushing a dilapidated buggy with a baby everybody figured was her little brother."

Ethan's expression grew thoughtful. "We always knew you had it tough, but you'd never tell us any of the details. How come?"

And why now? Jane wondered.

Lynn rose. "It's an old and boring story. Poverty's only charming in retrospect. Help me clear the table for dessert, will you, Ethan?"

To Jane's disappointment, the conversation shifted to the much less interesting topic of football, and if Jim Bonner's troubled gaze kept straying back to his wife, no one else seemed to notice.

As boorish as his behavior had been that afternoon, Jane was no longer quite so eager to pass judgment. There was something sad lurking in the depths of his eyes that touched her. When it came to Cal's parents, she had the feeling that nothing was quite what it seemed.

For her, the most interesting moment came when Ethan asked Cal how his meetings were going, and she learned what her husband was doing with his time. Cal had been enlisted by the local high-school principal, an old classmate of his, to visit county businessmen and persuade them to get involved with a new vocational program for high-risk students. He also seemed to be giving Ethan a considerable amount of money to expand a drug program for county teens, but when she pressed for more details, he changed the subject.

The evening dragged on. When Jim asked her a question about her work, she patronized him with her explanation. Lynn issued an invitation to join her book group, but Jane said she had no time for ladies' social gatherings. When Ethan said he hoped he'd see her at Sunday services, she told him she wasn't a believer.

I'm sorry, God, but I'm doing the best I can here. These are nice people, and they don't need any more heartache.

It was finally time to go. Everyone was rigidly courteous, but she didn't miss Jim's frown as he said good-bye or the deep concern in Lynn's eyes as she hugged her son.

Cal waited until he'd pulled out of the driveway before he looked over at her. "Thanks, Jane."

She stared straight ahead. "I can't go through that again. Keep them away from me."

"I will."

"I mean it."

"I know that wasn't easy for you," he said softly.

"They're wonderful people. It was horrible."

He didn't speak again until they reached the edge of town. "I've been thinking. What say the two of us go out on a date sometime soon?"

Was this to be her reward for humiliating herself tonight? The fact that he'd chosen this particular time to extend his invitation made her waspish. "Do I have to wear a paper bag over my head in case somebody might see me?"

"Now why d'you have to go and get all sarcastic on me? I asked you out, and all you have to say is yes or no."

"When?"

"I don't know. How about next Wednesday night?"

"Where are we going?"

"Don't you worry about that. Just wear the tightest pair of jeans you've got and maybe one of those slinky halter tops."

"I can barely button my tight jeans, and I don't have a slinky halter top. Even if I did, it's too cold."

"I imagine I can keep you pretty warm, and don't worry about buttons." The deep timbre of sexual promise she heard in his voice made her shiver. He glanced over, and she felt as if he were stroking her with his eyes. He couldn't have made his intentions any clearer. He wanted her, and he intended to have her.

But the question remained, was she ready for him? Life had always been serious business for her, and nothing could ever make her a casual sort of person. Could she deal with the pain that would await her in the future if she let down her guard with him?

Her head had begun to ache, and she turned to look out the window without answering him. She tried to distract herself from the sizzling undercurrents that vibrated between them by turning her thoughts to his parents, and as the Jeep passed through the silent streets of Salvation, she began sorting through what she'd learned about them.

Lynn hadn't always been the reserved, sophisticated woman who had entertained so graciously tonight. But what about Jim? Jane wanted to dislike him, but all evening she'd caught glimpses of yearning in his eyes when he'd looked at his wife, and she couldn't seem to work up a good solid dislike for a man who had feelings like that.

What had happened to the two high school kids who had once been in love? she wondered.

Jim wandered into the kitchen and poured himself the last cup of decaf. Lynn stood at the sink with her back to him. She always had her back to him, he thought, although it didn't make much difference because, even when she faced him, she never let him see anything more than the polite mask she wore for everyone except their sons.

It was during her pregnancy with Gabe that Lynn had begun transforming herself into the perfect doctor's wife. He remembered how he'd welcomed her increasing reserve and the fact that she no longer publicly embarrassed him with bad grammar and overexuberance. As the years passed, he'd grown to believe that Lynn's transformation had prevented their marriage from turning into the disaster everyone had predicted. He'd even thought he was happy.

Then he'd lost his only grandson and a daughter-in-law he'd adored. Afterward, as he'd witnessed his middle son's bottomless grief and been helpless to cure it, something inside him seemed to have snapped. When Cal had phoned him with the news that he'd married, he'd finally begun to feel hopeful again. But then he'd met his new daughter-in-law. How could Cal have married that cold, supercilious bitch? Didn't he realize she was going to make him miserable?

He cradled the coffee mug in his hands and looked over at his wife's slim, straight back. Lynn was shaken to the core by Cal's marriage, and both of them were trying to come up with a reason why he'd chosen so badly. The physicist had a subtle sex appeal that he'd seen right away, even if Lynn hadn't, but that didn't explain why Cal had married her. For years they'd both despaired over his preference for women who were too young and intellectually limited for him, but at least all of them had been sweet-natured.

He felt helpless to deal with Cal's problems, especially when he couldn't even deal with his own. The conversation at the dinner table had brought it all back to him, and now he felt the passage of time ticking away so loudly he wanted to shove his hands over his ears because he couldn't go back to fix all the places where he'd made the wrong choices.

"Why haven't you ever said anything about that day I bought the cookies from you? All this time, and you've never said a word."

Her head came up at his question, and he waited for her to pretend she didn't know what he was talking about, but he should have realized that wouldn't be her way. "Goodness, Jim, that was thirty-six years ago."

"I remember it like it was yesterday."

It had been a beautiful April day during his freshman year at UNC, five months after Cal was born, and he'd been coming out of a chem lab with some of his new friends, all of them upperclassmen. Now he didn't remember their names, but at the time he'd craved their acceptance, and when one of them had called out, "Hey, it's the cookie girl," he'd felt everything inside him turn cold.

Why did she have to be here now, where his new friends could see her? Anger and resentment turned to acid inside him. She was so damned hopeless. How could she embarrass him like this?

As she'd brought the buggy with the wobbly wheels to a stop, she'd looked thin and ragged, barely more than a child, a raw mountain girl. He forgot everything he loved about her: her laughter, the way she'd come so eagerly into his arms, the little spit hearts she'd draw on his belly before she'd settled beneath him so sweet and giving he couldn't think of anything but burying himself inside her.

Now as he watched her come closer, every poisonous word his parents had said shrieked in his ears. She was no good. A Glide. She'd trapped him and ruined his life. If he ever expected to see a penny of their money, he had to divorce her. He deserved something better than a roach-infested apartment and a too-young mountain girl, even one so tender and joyous she made him weep with love for her.

Panic welled inside him as his new friends called out to

her. "Hey, Cookie Girl, you got any peanut butter?"

"How much for two packs of chocolate chip?"

He wanted to run, but it was too late. His new friends were already examining the cookies she'd baked that morning while he slept. One of them leaned forward and tickled his son's belly. Another turned back to him.

"Hey, Jimbo, come on over here. You haven't tasted anything until you've tried this little girl's cookies."

Amber had looked up at him, laughter dancing in eyes as blue as a mountain sky. He could see her waiting for the moment he would tell them she was his wife, and he knew she was savoring the humor of the situation as she savored everything about their life together.

"Yeah, uh . . . okay."

Her smile remained bright as he walked toward her. He remembered that her light brown hair had been pulled into a ponytail with a blue rubber band, and that she'd had a wet spot on the shoulder of his old plaid shirt where Cal must have drooled.

"I'll take the chocolate chip."

Her head tilted quizzically to the side—*You goof, when are you gonna tell 'em?*—but she continued to smile, continued to enjoy the joke.

"Chocolate chip," he repeated.

Her faith in his honor was infinite. She waited patiently. Smiled. He slipped his hand in his pocket and drew out a quarter.

Only then, when he held out the money, did she understand. He wasn't going to acknowledge her. It was as if someone had turned out a light inside her, extinguishing her laughter and joy, her faith in him. Hurt and bewilderment clouded her features. For a moment she only stared at him, but, finally, she reached into the buggy for the cookies and held them out with a trembling hand.

He tossed her the quarter, one of four she'd given him that morning before he'd left for class. He tossed her the quarter as if she were nothing more than a street corner beggar, then he laughed at something one of the other guys said and turned away. He didn't look at her, just walked away while the cookies burned in his hand like pieces of silver.

It had happened more than three decades ago, but now his eyes were stinging. He set the coffee on the counter. "What I did was wrong. I've never forgotten it, never forgiven myself, and I'm sorry."

"Apology accepted." She flicked on the faucet, putting a deliberate end to the subject. When she turned off the water, she said, "Why did Cal have to marry her? Why couldn't they just have lived together long enough for him to see what kind of woman she is?"

But he didn't want to talk about Cal and his cold wife. "You should have spit in my face."

"I just wish we'd met Jane ahead of time."

He hated her easy dismissal of his wrong, especially when he suspected she hadn't dismissed it at all. "I want you back, Lynn."

"Maybe we could have changed his mind."

"Stop it! I don't want to talk about them! I want to talk about us, and I want you back."

She finally turned, and she gazed at him out of blue, mountain sky eyes that revealed nothing. "I never left."

"The way you were. That's what I want."

"You *are* in a mood tonight."

To his dismay, he could feel his throat closing up, but even so, he couldn't be silent. "I want it the way it was at the beginning. I want you silly and funny, imitating the landlady and teasing me for being too serious. I want dandelions back on the dinner table, and fatback and beans. I want you to start giggling so hard you wet your pants, and when I walk in the door, I want you to throw yourself at me like you used to."

Her forehead crinkled with concern. She walked over to

him and rested her hand on his arm in the same comfort-place she'd been touching for nearly four decades. "I can't make you young again, Jim. And I can't give you back Jamie and Cherry and everything the way it used to be."

"I know that, dammit!" He shook her off, rejecting her pity and her suffocating, never-ending kindness. "This isn't about them. What happened has made me realize I don't like the way things are. I don't like the way you've changed."

"You've had a hard day. I'll give you a back rub."

As always, her sweetness made him feel guilty, unwor-thy, and mean. It was the meanness that had been driving him lately and telling him to push her so far, to hurt her so badly, that he'd destroy the icy reserve and find the girl he'd thrown away.

Maybe if he gave her some evidence that he wasn't as bad as he knew himself to be, she'd soften. "I've never screwed around on you."

"I'm glad to know that."

He couldn't let it go at that, giving her only the part of the truth he wanted her to see. "I had chances, but I never went all the way. Once I got myself right to the motel door—"

"I don't want to hear this."

"But I backed off. God, I felt good about that for at least a week. Smug and self-righteous."

"Whatever you're doing to yourself, I want you to stop it right now."

"I want to start over. I thought maybe on our vacation . . . but we hardly talked to each other. Why can't we start over?"

"Because you'd hate it now just as much as you hated it then."

She was as unreachable as a distant star, but he still needed to touch her. "I loved you so much, you know that, don't you? Even when I let my parents talk me into agreeing to a divorce, I still loved you.''

"It doesn't matter now, Jim. Gabe came along, and then Ethan, and there wasn't any divorce. It was all so long ago. There's no sense in stirring up the past. We have three wonderful sons and a comfortable life.''

"I don't want to be comfortable!" Fury exploded inside him, fueled by frustration. "Goddammit! Don't you understand anything? Jesus, I hate you!" In all their time together, he had never once touched her in violence, but now he grabbed her arms and shook her. "I can't stand this any longer! Change back!''

"Stop it!" Her fingers dug into his upper arms. "Stop it! What's wrong with you?''

He saw the fear on her face, and he jerked away, appalled by what he'd done.

Her icy reserve had finally melted, leaving rage behind, an emotion he'd never until that moment seen on her face.

"You've been torturing me for months!" she cried. "You belittle me in front of my own sons. You poke at me and jab me and draw blood in a thousand ways every day! I've given you everything, but it's still not enough. Well, I won't put up with it anymore! I'm leaving you! I'm finished!" She raced from the kitchen.

Panic welled inside him. He started to run after her, but then stopped just as he reached the door. What would he do when he caught her? Shake her again? Christ. What if he'd finally pushed her too far?

He drew a deep breath and told himself she was still his own Amber Lynn, sweet and gentle as a mountain afternoon. She wouldn't leave him no matter what she said. She just needed time to calm down, that was all.

As he heard her car peel out of the driveway, he kept repeating the same thing to himself.

She wouldn't leave him. She couldn't.

*   *   *

Lynn's chest was so tight that she had to gasp for breath as she raced along the narrow, winding road. It was a treacherous piece of highway, but she'd been driving it for years, and not even her tears made her slow down. She knew what he wanted from her. He wanted her to open her veins again and bleed with love for him the way she once had. Bleed with love that would never be returned.

She struggled for breath and remembered that she'd learned her lesson years ago when she'd been little more than a baby, naive and ignorant at sixteen, utterly convinced that love could conquer the enormous gap between them. But that naïveté hadn't lasted. Two weeks after she'd told him she was pregnant with Gabe—Cal had only been eleven months old—her innocence was shattered forever.

She should have seen it coming, but of course she hadn't. When she'd told him she was pregnant, she'd bubbled over with happiness even though Cal wasn't yet a year old, and they were barely managing as it was. He had sat frozen as she'd babbled on.

"Just think, Jim! Another sweet baby! Maybe it'll be a girl this time, and we can name her Rose of Sharon. Oh, I'd love to have me a girl! But a boy'd might be better so Cal'd have somebody to roughhouse with."

When his expression didn't change, she'd started to get scared. "I know it'll be a mite hard for a while, but my baking business is goin' real good, and just think how much we love Cal. And we'll be real careful from now on to make sure there ain't no more. Tell me you're happy about the baby, Jim. Tell me."

But he hadn't said anything; he'd just walked out the door of their little apartment, leaving her alone and frightened. She'd sat for hours in the dark until he'd returned. He hadn't said a word. Instead, he'd pulled her into bed and made love to her with a ferocity that had driven away her fear.

Two weeks later, while Jim was in class, her mother-in-

law had come to see her. Mildred Bonner had told her that
Jim didn't love her and wanted a divorce. She'd said he'd
planned to break the news to her the same night Lynn had
announced that she was pregnant again, but now he felt
honor-bound to stick by her. If Lynn truly loved him, Mildred said, she would let him go.

Lynn hadn't believed her. Jim would never ask for a
divorce. He loved her. Didn't she see the evidence every
night in their bed?

When he came home from studying at the library, she
told him about his mother's visit, expecting him to laugh
it off. Only he didn't. "What's the use of talking about it
now?" he said. "You got pregnant again, so I can't go
anywhere."

The rose-colored world she'd built shattered at her feet.
Everything had been an illusion. Just because he loved to
have sex with her didn't mean he loved her. How could
she ever have been so foolish? He was a Bonner and she
was a Glide.

Two days later his mother came to the apartment again,
a fire-breathing dragon demanding that Lynn set her son
free. Lynn was ignorant, uneducated, a disgrace to him! She
could only hold him back.

Everything Mildred said was true, but as much as Lynn
loved Jim, she knew she wasn't going to let him go. On
her own, she could have managed, but her children needed
a father.

She found some hidden reservoir of strength that gave
her the courage to defy his mother. "If I ain't good enough
for him, then you'd better fix me up so's I am, because me
and my babies ain't goin' nowhere."

It hadn't happened easily, but gradually the women had
formed a fragile alliance. She'd accepted Mildred Bonner's
guidance in everything: how to talk, how to walk, what
food to fix. Mildred insisted that Amber sounded like a
white trash name, and she must call herself Lynn.

While Cal played at her feet, she devoured the books on Jim's English reading lists and exchanged baby-sitting with another woman so she could sneak into some of the larger lecture halls and lose herself in history, literature, and art, subjects that fed her poet's soul.

Gabe was born, and his family loosened the purse strings enough to take over Jim's school expenses and her medical bills. Money was still tight, but they were no longer desperate. Mildred insisted they move into a better apartment, one she furnished with Bonner family pieces.

Lynn's transformation was so gradual that she was never certain when Jim grew aware of it. He continued to make love to her nearly every night, and if she no longer laughed and teased and whispered naughty words in his ear, he didn't seem to notice. She grew more restrained out of the bedroom as well, and his occasional approving glances rewarded her for her self-control. Gradually, she learned to keep her love for her husband locked away where it would embarrass no one.

He finished his undergraduate work and entered the grueling years of medical school, while her world was defined by the needs of her young sons and her continuous efforts at self-improvement. When he finished his residency, they returned to Salvation so he could join his father's practice.

The years passed, and she found contentment with her sons, her work in the community, and her passion for the arts. She and Jim had their separate lives, but he was unfailingly considerate of her, and they shared passion, if not intimacy, in the bedroom. Gradually the boys left home, and she found a new serenity. She loved her husband with all her heart and didn't blame him too much for not loving her back.

Then Jamie and Cherry had died, and Jim Bonner had fallen apart.

In the months that followed the deaths, he'd begun

wounding her in so many countless ways she sometimes felt as if she were slowly bleeding to death. The unfairness left her reeling. She'd become everything he'd wanted, only now he didn't want that. Instead, he seemed to want something that she no longer had within herself to give.

12

Annie called Jane shortly before eight o'clock on Monday morning and announced she wasn't up to doing any gardening for a few days, and she didn't want either of them bothering her until she asked. As far as she was concerned, she said, a pair of newlyweds should have something better to do anyway than pester an old lady to death.

Jane smiled as she hung up the phone and returned to the oatmeal she was cooking. When she was an old lady, she hoped she had the guts to be as good at it as Annie.

"Who was that?"

She jumped and dropped her spoon as Cal, all bedroom-rumpled and gorgeous, wandered into the kitchen. He wore jeans and an unbuttoned flannel shirt. His hair was tousled, and he was barefoot.

"Don't sneak up on me like that!" She told herself the unwelcome thudding in her heart was caused by fright and not the sight of him so disheveled and outrageously handsome.

"I wasn't sneaking. I'm just a quiet walker."

"Well, stop it."

"You are one grouchy fud."

"Fud?"

"P.H.D. Us dumb jocks call you guys fuds."

She snatched up a clean spoon and jabbed it back into the oatmeal. "Us fuds call you guys dumb jocks, which just goes to show how smart some of us fuds really are."

He chuckled. What was he doing here? He was usually gone by the time she came downstairs for breakfast. Even on the mornings last week when he'd stayed around to drive her to Annie's, they hadn't eaten together. He'd been in his study.

"Who was on the phone?" he repeated.

"Annie. She doesn't want us bothering her today."

"Good."

He walked over to the pantry and came out with one of the half dozen boxes of Lucky Charms he kept there, along with potato chips, cookies, and candy bars. She watched from the stove as he poured a mountain of the multicolored cereal into a serving bowl, then walked over to the refrigerator, where he got the milk.

"For a doctor's son, you have an abysmal diet."

"When I'm on vacation, I get to eat what I like." He grabbed a spoon, slung one leg over the counter stool, and sat with his knees splayed, bare heels hooked over the rungs.

She tore her eyes away from those long, narrow feet only to shudder at the sight of him digging in. "I'm making plenty of oatmeal. Why don't you eat some of it instead of that stuff?"

"For your information, this isn't stuff. It happens to be the culmination of years of scientific research."

"There's a *leprechaun* on the box."

"Cute little guy." He gestured toward her with his milky spoon. "You know what the best part is? The marshmallows."

"The marshmallows?"

"Whoever thought of adding all those little marshmallows was one smart guy. I've got it written in my contract that the Stars have to keep the training table stocked with Lucky Charms just for me."

"This is fascinating. I'm talking with a man who graduated *summa cum laude*, and yet I could swear I'm in the presence of an idiot."

"The thing I wonder about is this . . . As good as Lucky Charms are, maybe there's another cereal just waiting to be invented that's even better." He took another bite. "That's what I'd do with myself if I had a brain as big as yours, Professor. Instead of messing around with that top quark, I'd come up with the best breakfast cereal in the world. Now, I know that'd be hard. They've already added chocolate and sprinkles and peanut butter, not to mention all these different-colored marshmallows, but answer me this— Has anybody thought about M&Ms? No, ma'am, they haven't. Nobody's been smart enough to figure out there's a big market for M&Ms in breakfast cereal."

She absorbed this as she watched him eat. He sat there at the counter—bare feet, naked chest showing through his unbuttoned shirt, muscles rippling like liquid steel every time he moved. A gorgeous picture of dumbness. Except this gorgeous dummy was smart as a fox.

She filled her bowl and carried it over to the counter along with a spoon. "Peanut or plain?"

He thought it over. "It prob'ly wouldn't pay to get too fancy right off. I'd go with plain."

"Wise decision." She added her own milk and sat down next to him.

He glanced over at her. "You're really going to eat that?"

"Of course I am. This is cereal as God intended."

He reached over without an invitation and scooped up a heaping spoonful that included all the brown sugar melting at the center.

"Not bad."

"You took my brown sugar!"

"But you know what'd really be good on it?"

"Now let me think . . . M&Ms?"

"You are one smart lady." He picked up the Lucky Charms box and shook a few on top of her oatmeal. "This'll give you the crunch that's missing."

"Gee, thanks."

"I do like those marshmallows."

"So you've said." She pushed the Lucky Charms to the side, and took another bite. "You know, don't you, cereal like that is made for children?"

"Then I guess I'm a kid at heart."

The only thing about him that reminded her of a kid was his immature attitude toward women. Was that what had kept him out until three in the morning? Picking up younger women?

She saw no need to keep herself in suspense any longer. "Where were you last night?"

"Checking up on me?"

"No. I wasn't sleeping very well, and I heard you come in late, that's all."

"Where I was doesn't have anything to do with you."

"It does if you were with another woman."

"Is that what you think?" He let his gaze ramble down over her body in what she could only interpret as a gesture of psychological warfare. She was wearing a red T-shirt with Maxwell's Equations printed on it, although the final equation disappeared into the waistband of her slacks where she'd tucked it in. His eyes lingered on her hips, which certainly weren't as slim as the hips he was accustomed to seeing on his women. Still, she took heart from the fact that he didn't look all that critical.

"It's crossed my mind." She pushed away her oatmeal and studied him. "I just want to know what the rules are. We haven't talked about this, and I think we should. Are we free to sleep with other people while we're married or not?"

His eyebrows shot up. "*We?* What's this *we?*"

She kept her expression carefully blank. "I beg your pardon? I'm not following you."

He shoved his hand through his hair. It had grown a bit longer in the last few weeks, and a spike stuck up on one side. "We're married," he said gruffly. "That's it."

"That's what?"

"It!"

"Uhmm."

"You're a married woman, and a pregnant one, to boot, in case you forgot."

"And you're a married man." She paused. "In case you forgot."

"Exactly."

"So does that mean we're going to mess around with other people while we're married or we're not?"

"It means *we're* not!"

She concealed her relief as she rose from the stool. "Okay. No messing around, but we can carouse until all hours of the night with no explanation and no apologies, right?"

She watched him mull that one over and wondered how he'd work around it. She wasn't entirely surprised when he didn't try. "I get to carouse. You don't."

"I see." She picked up her oatmeal bowl and carried it to the sink. She could feel him waiting for her to rip into him, and she knew him well enough to suspect he was relishing the challenge of defending a position he knew very well was indefensible. "Well, I suppose from your point of view that's only logical."

"It is?"

"Of course." She gave him a silky smile. "How else can you possibly convince the world you're still twenty-one?"

*   *   *

On Wednesday night she took her time dressing for the mysterious date she'd finally agreed to go on, despite her misgivings. She showered, powdered, and perfumed. Then she was ashamed of herself for placing so much importance on the occasion. But she'd had such a good day, it was hard to be annoyed with herself for long. Her work had gone well, and she was enjoying the fact that Cal seemed to be hanging around the house a lot more this week. Today he'd even made an excuse to accompany her on her walk, saying he was afraid she'd get so preoccupied solving some damn formula that she'd get lost.

She didn't like admitting how much she enjoyed being around him. She'd never met anyone who made her laugh as he did, while his razor-sharp mind kept her on her toes. It was ironic that the intelligence that made him so attractive to her was also the source of her greatest concern.

She pushed the unhappy reminder of her baby's future aside and thought about the battered red Ford Escort that had been delivered a few hours ago and hidden away behind an old shed in the far corner of the estate. Buying a used car by telephone might defy conventional wisdom, but she was satisfied with her purchase. True, the car wasn't anything to look at with its dented door, broken front grillwork, and bad touch-up job, but it had fit comfortably into her budget, and all she needed was basic transportation to get her through the next few months until she returned to Chicago and the perfectly good Saturn waiting in her garage.

She also didn't intend to keep the car hidden, but she knew Cal was going to be furious, and she wanted to enjoy her evening before she broke the news to him that her imprisonment was at an end.

She smiled as she finished dressing. She'd followed his instructions about wearing jeans, but instead of the halter top, she'd chosen a mulberry silk blouse and a pair of semitrashy gold hoop earrings that were more appropriate for one of Cal's baby dolls than a theoretical physicist. She couldn't figure out why she liked them so much.

She unbuttoned the top button of her silk blouse and watched it fall open to show the lacy top of her black bra. She studied herself, sighed, and rebuttoned the blouse. For now, trashy earrings were as far as she was prepared to go.

Cal came out into the foyer as she descended the stairs. He wore an old Stars' T-shirt that outlined all of those beautifully developed chest muscles and was tucked into a pair of jeans so tight, faded, and threadbare he might as well have been naked.

His gaze traveled over her like a lazy stream on a hot summer day. She flushed, then stumbled on the step and had to grab for the rail.

"Something wrong?" he inquired innocently.

Jerk. He knew very well what was wrong. He was a walking, talking sexual fantasy. "Sorry. I was contemplating Seiberg-Witten theory. Quite tricky."

"I'll bet." His eyes swept over her in a way that made her feel her primping time hadn't been wasted. "Couldn't find a halter top, huh?"

"They were all in the wash."

He smiled, and as she watched that unexpected dimple pop into the hard plane beneath his cheekbone, she wondered what she was doing with a man like this? He was so far out of her league, he might have come from another solar system.

She realized she'd forgotten her jacket and turned on the stairs to go back and fetch it.

"Runnin' scared already?"

"I need a jacket."

"Wear this." He went to the closet and pulled out his gray zippered sweatshirt. She came down to meet him, and as he set it around her shoulders, his hands lingered there for a moment. She caught the heady scent of pine, soap, and something that was unmistakably Cal Bonner, an intoxicating hint of danger.

The soft folds of the shirt settled over her hips. She glanced down at it and wished she were one of those women who looked cute in men's clothes, but she suspected she merely looked pudgy. He didn't appear to find anything wrong with her, however, so she took heart.

He'd left the Jeep in the motor-court, and, as always, he opened the door for her. As he started the car and headed down the drive toward the highway, she realized she was nervous, and she wished he'd say something to break the tension, but he seemed content to drive.

They passed through town, where the stores were closed for the night, along with the Petticoat Junction Cafe. Down one of the side streets, she saw a lighted building with a number of cars parked around it. She deduced that was the Mountaineer.

They reached the edge of town and drove around Heartache Mountain. Just as she'd decided he was taking her to Annie's, he slowed the Jeep and turned into a badly rutted gravel lane. The headlights picked out a ramshackle structure no bigger than a tollbooth sitting just beyond the heavy chain that stretched across the road.

"Where are we?"

"See for yourself." He stopped the car and pulled a flashlight from under the seat. After he'd lowered the window, he shone the beam outside.

She ducked her head and saw a starburst-shaped sign made up of broken lightbulbs, peeling purple paint, and the words, *Pride of Carolina*. "*This* is where you're taking me for our date?"

"You said you'd never gone on a drive-in date when you were a teenager. I'm making it up to you."

He grinned at her dumbfounded expression, flicked off the flashlight, and got out of the car to unfasten the chain that barred the road. When he returned, he drove forward, jarring her as the car hit the ruts.

"My first date with a multimillionaire," she grumbled, "and this is what I get."

"Don't hurt my feelings and tell me you've already seen the movie."

She smiled and grabbed the door handle to keep from banging against it. Despite her grumbling, she wasn't exactly displeased with the idea of being alone with him at this abandoned drive-in. It would benefit their baby, she told herself, if she and Cal got to know each other a little better.

The Jeep's headlights swept the deserted lot, which looked like an eerie science-fiction landscape with its concentric mounds of earth and row upon row of metal speaker poles. The car lurched as he headed toward the rear of the drive-in, and she grabbed the dashboard with one hand while she instinctively covered her abdomen with the other.

He glanced over. "Waking the little guy up?"

It was the first time he'd acknowledged her pregnancy with anything other than hostility. She felt as if a blossom had slowly unfurled inside her, and she smiled.

He turned into the back row. "He can go back to sleep in a minute. That is, if he's not too busy solving equations."

"You won't think it's so funny when she starts grouping her Cheerios in multiples of ten while the other kids are gumming away at them."

"I swear, you're the most worryin' woman I've ever met. You act like having a brain is the worst tragedy on earth. The boy'll be fine. Just look at me. Having a brain didn't bother me any."

"That's because you keep yours under lock and key."

"Well, lock yours up for a while so we can enjoy the damn movie."

There was nothing much she could say to that, so she didn't try.

He moved to the center of the last row, just in front of a sagging chain-link fence, and pulled into one of the spaces so that the front wheels were elevated by the dirt mound. He picked up the speaker, brought it into the car, hung it on top of the steering wheel, then closed the window to shut out the chilly night air. She refrained from mentioning that the speaker had no cord.

He turned off the headlights and the engine, plunging them into darkness relieved only by a sliver of quarter moon. She shifted her attention to the distant screen, which was bisected by a silvery shaft of moonlight. "We should have gotten here earlier so we could get better seats."

"The back row's the best."

"Why is that?"

"No little kids lookin' through the windows. I like my privacy when I'm makin' out."

She swallowed hard. "Did you bring me here to make out?"

"Pretty much."

"Oh."

"You got a problem with that?" The moon slipped beneath a bank of clouds, leaving them in darkness. He flicked on the overhead light, and she saw the corner of his mouth kick up, making him the very picture of a self-satisfied man. He twisted toward the backseat, reached down, and came up with a large bag of grocery-store popcorn.

Her brain was flashing out warning signals at the exact speed of light, but she was in no mood to listen. She'd wanted to be courted, and he was doing that, even if he'd chosen a peculiar way to go about it. And no matter what he said, she didn't think he still hated her because he smiled too much when they were together.

He was also wily as a fox, she reminded herself, and

he'd made no secret of the fact that he desired her. Since his moral code seemed to dictate fidelity, at least for the next few months, he either had to seduce her or go without. She wanted to believe he would be pursuing her even if they weren't caught in this impossible situation, but she couldn't quite make that leap of faith. Maybe she could strike a compromise.

"I don't have a problem with it as long as you understand that I won't go all the way on a first date."

He opened the bag and took out a handful of popcorn. "I respect you for that. 'Course, maybe we should discuss exactly how you're calculating when we had our first date. I seem to remember a surprise birthday—"

"Cal . . ."

He tossed the popcorn into his mouth. "There's some beer and juice in a cooler in the backseat. See if you can reach over there and get it."

She turned around and saw a small Styrofoam cooler resting on the seat. She knelt and reached back for it, only to find herself being gently, but forcibly, upended. As she awkwardly scrambled to balance herself on the rear seat, she heard a chuckle that had a faintly diabolical sound to it.

"Good idea, sweetheart. I'll just come right back there with you."

Before she could react, he had let himself out the driver's door, opened the back, and settled down next to her.

"Jeez . . ." She straightened her blouse. "Fathers must have locked up their daughters when they saw you coming."

"I didn't develop my best moves 'til I was in college."

"Why don't you just be quiet and watch the movie."

"Hand me one of those beers first."

She did as he asked, taking a can of apple juice for herself and refusing the popcorn. He sipped his beer; she sipped her juice. They both leaned their heads back against the seat in companionable silence, with the dome light glowing above them.

He stretched his arm across the seat behind her. "This movie's making me horny."

Her heart gave a queer thump in her chest. "Which part? Where Maria sings about the hills being alive with the sound of music? Or is it that *do re mi* thing the kids are doing?"

A grin flicked across that hard mouth. "It's Maria, all right. You've just got to wonder what's underneath that apron she's wearing."

The discussion was definitely getting dangerous. She couldn't remember feeling more at sea and less in touch with herself. She decided to buy a little time with a change of subject. "What have you been doing with your time when you're not meeting with the local business leaders?"

At first she didn't think he'd answer, but he shrugged. "I work out at the Y, visit friends, take care of some business. Today I spent a couple of hours at Dad's office. He likes it when I hang around." He frowned.

"Something wrong?"

"Not really. I don't know. I guess the problems he and Mom are having are more serious than I thought." The crease in his forehead deepened. "He said she's gone to stay with Annie for a while. I thought he meant overnight, but it seems she's been there since the weekend, and today he told me she doesn't have any plans to come back."

"Oh, dear."

"I can't understand her doing something like this. It really has him upset." He drained his beer and glared at her. "I don't want to talk about it anymore, so would you mind keeping your questions to yourself."

He was the one who'd volunteered the information, but she didn't call him on it.

He jabbed his empty can toward the distant screen. "With all your chattering, I can't keep my mind on the movie, and Maria's singing one of my favorite songs. Damn, but that woman looks good naked.''

"Maria does not sing naked in *The Sound of Music*!''

''I've got perfect eyesight, and that woman is naked as the day she was born. You can even see her—''

"You're mistaken. The person who's naked is Baron von Trapp. And he is certainly one impressive figure of a man.''

"You call *that* impressive? That puny—''

''I do.''

"Man-oh-man, if you think that's impressive, I could sure make you one happy woman.''

"Braggart.'' Had she gone completely crazy? She was deliberately baiting him.

"You, on the other hand, might have warts on your belly for all I know.''

''I do not have warts on my belly.''

"Says you.'' He took her apple juice from her hand, and tossed it, along with his beer can, into the cooler, which he picked up and put in the front seat. "Okay, you can show me now.''

"Show you what?''

''I'm being serious here. If you've got warts, my boy's gonna end up with them, and if that's true, I need time to prepare myself.''

"You are a certifiable lunatic.''

"Just unzip your jeans a little bit there. Enough for me to get a peek.''

"No!''

"Okay, then. I'll have to go by feel.''

She slapped his hands away as he reached for the snap. "I told you I'd make out with you! I didn't say I'd let you give me a medical exam.''

By the time she realized what she'd said, he was grinning as if he'd just won the lottery. "That's right, you did say you'd make out. Well, come on now, honey. Show me your stuff.''

"I will not."

"Coward."

"I won't be baited."

"You're scared to make out with me." In one motion, he pulled off her bulky sweatshirt and tossed it on top of the discarded cooler. "Scared you won't be able to handle me. You are one big scaredy-cat."

"I am not."

"Scared to show me what you've got. Scared you won't measure up to all those thousands of women in my past."

"There aren't *thousands* of women in your past."

His grin looked so much like a fox's that she could almost see the chicken feathers stuck to his mouth.

Her heart thudded against her ribs. She was frightened, aroused, and amused all at the same time, which made it difficult to frown and sound grouchy. "Oh, all right. I guess I'll make out with you. But keep your hands to yourself."

"That's not fair since I'm gonna let you put yours wherever you want."

A dozen locations sprang to mind. "I'm sure I won't want to."

"I seriously hope that's not true." He switched off the dome light and plunged them into darkness so thick she felt as if the stars had been turned off.

Her eyes gradually adjusted enough to make out his shape, if not his features. He cupped her shoulder, and she felt him come close. "Maybe you just need me to remind you where some of the best places are." His lips brushed past her trashy hoop earring and settled on the tender spot beneath. "This one, for example, is a nice warm-up spot."

She caught her breath and wondered how he knew she was sensitive there. "If you're going to talk through this, could you at least manage to say *ain't* a few times so I can fantasize?"

His lips tugged on her earlobe, right next to the gold

wire, and his elbow bumped against the door. "Who could you fantasize about that's better than me?"

"Well . . ." She struggled to speak as her skin turned to goose flesh. "There's this studmuffin physicist who used to be a top-quark hunter at Fermilabs . . ."

"I doubt he says *ain't.*" He played at the corner of her mouth. "You're supposed to be showing me what you're made of. So far I'm doing all the work here."

She lost what remained of her restraint and tilted her head just far enough for her lips to meet his. The contact jolted her so that she forgot all about playing games, and as their kiss deepened, she abandoned herself to the pleasure of the erotic. She tasted beer and popcorn, along with a hint of toothpaste and something dangerous that reminded her of thunder.

"You are the damnedest woman," he whispered.

She kissed him again. He pulled her shirttail free, and his big hands, strong and possessive, settled on the skin beneath. His thumbs trailed up the small ridges of her spine 'til they came to her bra, then he whispered against her open mouth. "We have to get rid of this, Rosebud."

She didn't even consider arguing. As she enjoyed the sweet invasion of his tongue, he made short work of the buttons on her blouse, despite the fact that the darkness kept him from seeing exactly what he was doing, then he released the front hook on her bra. His movements were accompanied by bumps and thuds as he banged against one part of the car or another.

He bent to take her in his mouth. Her nipples were tender from her pregnancy, and when he began to suckle her, she bucked and dug her fingers into his hair. The exquisite pain of the gentle suction left her wanting both to cry out for him to stop and beg him not to.

She knew she had to touch him as he was touching her, and she dragged at his T-shirt. The interior of the car had grown hot and steamy, and the soft cotton felt damp beneath her hands. Her shoulder bumped against the window, and she felt the moisture that had congealed on it seep through her blouse.

He helped her free his T-shirt, then turned his attention to her jeans. He pitched her shoes into the front seat, then tugged at the denim while she explored the contours of his bare chest.

She gave an oof of surprise when he whipped off her jeans and her naked bottom came in contact with the cold upholstery. The shock jolted her and suddenly everything seemed to be happening too fast. She needed to think this over, weigh the facts, consider her options. "I didn't . . . I don't . . ."

"Hush." His husky whisper filled the steamy interior as he cupped her thigh and pushed it away from its mate. She heard a soft curse.

"It's too dark," he muttered. "I still can't see you."

She stroked the contours of his pectorals and trailed her thumb over the hard point of his nipple. "Go by feel," she whispered.

He did better than that. He went by taste, and she thought she would die from this pleasure she had dreamed of but never experienced.

"You don't—" She gasped. "You don't have to do that."

His chuckle wasn't altogether steady, and she moaned when his hot whispery breath fell on her. "Mind your own business."

Once again he dropped his head, and she felt as if all the parts of her were unraveling. She banged her elbow against the steamy window when she gripped his bare, damp shoulders. He swore and bumped against the seat as he shifted his weight, but none of it mattered.

It was too exquisite, too miraculous. She climbed and spiraled, but just as she felt herself beginning to slip over the edge, he drew back. "Oh, no, you don't. Not without me."

She lay open and vulnerable before him. His breathing came fast and heavy. "God, this was a stupid idea. We should be doing this in the bedroom where we can see each other, but I can't wait that long. I need you now."

She reached for the snap on his jeans and felt the hard, thick shape of him. His breath caught on a hiss as she took her time unzipping, exploring until his restraint broke with a hoarse exclamation. "No more, Rosebud. I can't take anymore."

"Wimp." She dropped her mouth to his chest and licked a special trail all her own.

He gave a sound that was part chuckle and part moan. At the same time, he leaned back and lifted her so she straddled him. She had lost all of her clothing except the blouse that hung open from her shoulders. He had only lost his T-shirt. Although she had freed him from his jeans, the space was too confined for her to remove them completely. His chest was bare, however, as bare as her bottom, and she nipped him with her teeth.

He uttered a strangled exclamation, but she loved her position of supremacy, and she had no pity. Even though her feet were wedged awkwardly against the back of the front seat, she didn't let that prevent her from kissing him how and where she would.

While darkness deprived her of sight, her other senses grew more acute, and she suspected from his touches, tastes, and deep, intimate caresses that it was the same for him.

The faintest thread of moonlight caught a glimmering rivulet rolling down the steamy windows, and the sweat from their bodies was slick on her palms. He cupped her bare bottom in his big hands and lifted her. "Now, sweetheart. Now."

She moaned as he guided her down upon him, but her

body accepted him without question. She gave a sob and pressed her breast to his mouth. He caressed her with lips, teeth, and tongue until she had to draw back and move on him before she went crazy.

Even as he grasped her hips, he didn't try to force her into his rhythm but let her find her own. She raised and lowered herself upon him, rubbing the tips of her breasts against the soft hair of his chest and returning his deep, devouring kisses. She felt strong and sure as she met his passion. Sensation built upon sensation until reality slipped away and she felt as if she were being hurled through a supercollider, flying past the speed of light through a narrow underground passage toward the place where everything came apart.

And then she cried out as all the molecules that made up who she was fragmented: atoms dissociated, nuclei detached, everything broke open, shattered, and, at the end, left her more complete than she had ever been.

He went rigid with her cry. His teeth sank into the side of her neck, not hurting her, but holding her as he spilled himself within her depths. For a fraction of time she felt his utter defenselessness, and she sagged forward, protecting him as he found his ease.

Their hearts thundered together, one pressed against the other. She turned her lips to his hair.

Finally he stirred beneath her, a shift of his hand, a movement in his leg. Only gradually did she grow aware of the strain in her splayed thighs and the cramp in her calf. The air inside the car was so thick with heat it was hard to draw breath, but she didn't want to move. This intimacy was too precious to her.

"What am I going to do with you?" he muttered against her breast.

You could try loving me.

The unspoken thought jarred her, then filled her with dismay. Was this the destructive path her subconscious was taking? She wanted him to fall in love with her? When had she lost touch with reality? What made her entertain, even in her fantasies, the notion that this man who wanted no attachments could love her, especially when no one else had ever been able to?

"You're going to take me home," she said briskly. "That was quite pleasant, but I have a great deal of work to do tomorrow, and I need my rest."

"Quite *pleasant*?"

It had been earth-shattering, but she could no more confess that to him than she could explain how their coming together had given her an entirely new understanding of high-speed subatomic particle collisions.

God. Why was she thinking of that now? Everything people believed about her was true! She was a complete geek.

She reached for her clothes. Her panties were lost somewhere in the dark, so she drew her jeans on without them, pulling them up over her wetness.

He threw open the door, and as the dome light flashed on, she drew her blouse across her breasts. He glanced down at her as he zipped his jeans. "You're not bad, Professor, for someone who isn't a big-time player."

His casual dismissal of what had been so important to her made her want to weep. Fool! But what did she expect? Did she think he was going to declare his undying love for her simply because she'd finally given him what he must have known he'd get all along?

They rode home in silence. He went into the house with her, and she felt his gaze as she climbed the stairs to her room.

She hesitated, then looked down at him watching her from the foyer below. "Thank you for a lovely evening."

She'd meant to sound brisk, but her words had a wistful quality. She didn't want the evening to end this way. What if she held out her hand and invited him into her bed? The idea chilled her. Was that the only way she could keep him at her side?

He slouched against the front door and looked bored. "Yeah, it was great."

He couldn't have found a clearer way to tell her he was finished with her. With a man like Cal Bonner, she realized, the game was everything, and once it was over, he lost interest. Heartsick and angry, she turned and headed for her room.

Moments later, she heard him drive away.

13

Pleasant! She'd said it was *pleasant!* Cal sat at his favorite table in the corner of the Mountaineer and brooded. Usually there weren't any empty seats around him, but tonight everybody'd seemed to realize he had a giant mean-on, and they'd given him wide berth.

No matter how easily she'd dismissed what had happened between them, he knew Professor Rosebud had never had a better lover than she'd had tonight. There'd been none of that nonsense they'd gone through before, with her pushing his hands away. No, sir. He'd had his hands all over her, and she hadn't uttered a single protest.

But what stuck in his craw—what really stuck like a big old chunk of hard-boiled egg—was the fact that he'd just had some of the best sex of his life, and he'd never felt more unsatisfied.

Maybe it was his fault for getting cute. Why hadn't he just grabbed her right there in the house, carried her upstairs, and romanced her in his bed with all the lights on and that big mirror overhead? He could have done his best work there, not that he hadn't been pretty damn good tonight, but if they'd been in his bed, he would have seen everything he wanted to see. In duplicate.

He reminded himself this was the third time the two of

them had gone at it, but he wasn't any closer to seeing her naked now than he'd been that first night. It was getting to be an obsession. If only he hadn't turned off the dome light, he could have looked his fill, but despite that sassy mouth of hers, he'd known she was skittish, and he'd wanted her so much he hadn't been thinking straight. Now he had to face the consequences.

He understood his nature well enough to know that the only reason he found himself thinking about her a few thousand times a day was because he still didn't feel as if he'd really made love to her. How could he when he didn't know what she looked like? Once he found out, it'd be over. Instead of growing stronger every day, this attraction he felt toward her would disappear, and he'd be his old self again, ready to roam the fertile fields of dewy young females with flawless faces and sweet temperaments, although he was giving serious consideration to raising his minimum age requirement to twenty-four, since he was getting tired of everybody baiting him.

His thoughts strayed back to the Professor. Damn, but she was one funny lady. Sharp as a tack, too. Over the years, he'd developed a certain smugness about the fact that he was smarter than most everybody else, but that razor-sharp brain of hers made it hard to sneak much past her. Instead, she marched right alongside him, her brain cells clicking away, matching him step for step and move for move. He could almost feel her peering into every dusty corner of his mind and making a generally accurate assessment of whatever it was she found there.

"Reliving those three interceptions you threw against the Chiefs last year?"

His head shot up, and he found himself looking into the face of his nightmares. *Son of a bitch.*

Kevin Tucker's lips curled in a cocky grin that reminded Cal the kid didn't have to spend thirty minutes standing under a hot shower every morning just to work the kinks out.

"What the hell are you doing here?"

"Heard this is a beautiful part of the country, and I decided to take a look. I rented one of those vacation villas north of town. Nice place."

"You just happened to choose Salvation?"

"Strangest thing. I'd already crossed the city limits before it even occurred to me that this was where you lived. Can't imagine how I forgot that."

"Yeah, I can't imagine."

"Maybe you could show me some of the local sights." Kevin turned toward the bartender. "Sam Adams for me. Get the Bomber here another of whatever he's having."

Cal was drinking club soda, but he hoped Shelby kept her mouth shut about that.

Kevin sat down without an invitation and leaned back in the chair. "I didn't get a chance to congratulate you on your marriage. It sure surprised everybody. You and your new wife must have had a good laugh over the way I took her for a groupie that night she came to your hotel room."

"Oh, yeah, we laughed real hard about that."

"A physicist. I can't get over it. She didn't exactly look like your standard groupie that night, but she sure as hell didn't look like a scientist, either."

"Just goes to show."

Shelby brought the drinks over herself and gave Kevin the eye. "I saw you play fourth quarter against the 49ers last year, Mr. Tucker. You looked real good."

"I'm Kevin to you, dollface. And thanks. The old man here taught me everything I know."

Cal bristled, but he could hardly punch Kevin out with Shelby watching. It took her forever to finish flirting with Pretty Boy, but she finally left them alone.

"How 'bout cutting the bullshit, Tucker, and tell me why you're really here."

"I already told you. Just a little vacation. Nothing more."

Cal swallowed his fury, knowing the more he pressed, the more satisfaction Tucker'd get out of it. Besides, he had a pretty good idea why Kevin had shown up in Salvation, and he didn't like it one bit. The kid was playing a psych-out game. *You can't get away from me, Bonner. Not even during the off-season. I'm here, I'm young, and I'm in your face.*

Cal made his way to the kitchen at eight the next morning. He was in no mood for the nine o'clock meeting Ethan had scheduled with their local state representative so the three of them could discuss the teen drug program, and he wasn't looking forward to the lunch he'd set up with his mother to try and talk some sense into her, but neither could be postponed. Maybe if he'd had more sleep he wouldn't be so out of sorts.

But he knew he couldn't blame his foul mood on either lack of sleep or the stiffness in his joints. It was that sex viper he'd married who was responsible. If she didn't have this compulsion for keeping her clothes on, he'd have slept like a baby last night.

As he walked into the kitchen, he saw Jane sitting at the counter munching some kind of nutritious-looking bagel with honey squeezed on top. For a moment the homeyness of the scene made it hard for him to breathe. This wasn't what he wanted! He didn't want a house and a wife and a kid on the way, especially not with Kevin Tucker holed up five miles away. He wasn't ready for this.

He noticed that the Professor looked as neat as always. Her gold turtleneck was tucked into a pair of khaki slacks that were neither too tight nor too loose, and she'd pulled her hair back with a narrow, tortoise-colored clip-on headband. As usual, she hadn't bothered with much more makeup than a swipe of lipstick. There wasn't one thing sexy about her appearance, so why did she look so delectable to him?

He grabbed a fresh box of Lucky Charms from the pantry, then collected a bowl and spoon. He slapped the milk carton down on the counter with more force than necessary and waited for her to rip into him about the way he'd run off last night. He knew it hadn't exactly been gentlemanly, but she'd hurt his pride. Now he was going to have to pay the price, and the last thing he wanted to hear at eight in the morning was a screaming banshee.

She raised both of her eyebrows over the tops of her glasses. "Are you still drinking 2 percent milk?"

"Something wrong with that?" He ripped open the cereal box.

"Two percent isn't low-fat milk despite what millions of Americans think. For the sake of your arteries, you should really switch to skimmed, or at least 1 percent."

"And you should really mind your own damned business." The Lucky Charms clattered into his bowl. "When I want your—" He broke off in mid-sentence, unable to believe what he was seeing.

"What's wrong?"

"Will you look at this?"

"My goodness."

He stared incredulously into a mound of dry cereal. All the marshmallows were missing! He saw lots of beige-colored frosted oat cereal, but not a single marshmallow. No multicolored rainbows or green shamrocks, no blue moons or purple horseshoes, not a single yellow whatchamacallit. Not one solitary marshmallow.

"Maybe someone tampered with the box," she offered in that cool scientist's voice.

"Nobody could have tampered with it! It was sealed up tighter than a drum when I opened it. Something must have gone wrong at the factory."

He sprang up from his stool and headed back into the

pantry for another box. This was all he needed to make a lousy morning worse. He emptied his old cereal in the trash, ripped open the new box, and poured it in the bowl, but all he saw was frosted oat cereal. No marshmallows.

"I don't believe this! I'm going to write the president of General Mills! Don't they have any quality control?"

"I'm sure it's just a fluke."

"Doesn't make any difference whether it's a fluke or not. It shouldn't have happened. When a person buys a box of Lucky Charms, he's got expectations."

"Would you like me to fix you a nice wheat bran bagel with a little honey on it? And maybe a glass of skimmed milk to go along."

"I don't want a bagel, and I sure as hell don't want skimmed milk. I want my Lucky Charms!" He stalked into the pantry and pulled out the remaining three boxes. "I'll guaran-damn-tee you one of these is going to have marshmallows in it."

But none of them did. He opened all three boxes, and there wasn't a single marshmallow in any of them.

By now the Professor had finished her bagel, and her green eyes were as cool as the missing marshmallow shamrocks. "Perhaps I could make you some oatmeal. Or Wheatena. I believe I have Wheatena."

He was furious. Wasn't there anything in life he could count on these days? The Professor had him spinning mental cartwheels; Kevin Tucker had materialized out of nowhere; his mom had moved out on his dad; and now the marshmallows were missing from five boxes of his favorite breakfast cereal. "I don't want anything!"

She took a sip of milk and regarded him with perfect serenity. "It really isn't healthy to start the day without a good breakfast."

"I'll risk it."

He wanted to whip her up off that stool, toss her over his shoulder, and carry her up to his bedroom so he could finish what he'd started last night. Instead, he yanked his keys from his pocket and stalked out to the garage.

He wouldn't just write the president of General Mills, he decided. He was going to sue the whole damned company! Everybody from the board of directors right down to the shipping clerks. By damn, he'd teach General Mills not to ship out inferior cereal. He jerked open the door of his Jeep, and that was when he saw them.

Marshmallows. Hundreds of tiny marshmallows covering the seats. Red balloons, pink hearts, blue moons. They were scattered everywhere. Across the dashboard, on the front seat, and all over the backseat.

A red veil descended over his eyes. He slammed the door shut and charged into the kitchen. He was going to kill her!

She sat at the counter sipping a cup of tea. "Forget something?"

"Yeah, I forgot something all right. I forgot to smack you silly!"

She didn't look the slightest bit intimidated. Damn it! No matter what he threatened, no matter how loud he yelled, she didn't even cringe, probably because she knew he wouldn't touch her. Now he had to satisfy himself by pumping up the volume. "*You* are going to pay for this!"

He grabbed one of the Lucky Charm boxes and turned it over, spilling the cereal everywhere. He yanked open the sealed flap on the bottom, and sure enough, a neat slit in the inner bag had been carefully resealed with Scotch tape.

He gritted his teeth. "Don't you think this was just a little childish?"

"It certainly was. And immensely satisfying." She took a sip of tea.

"If you were pissed off about the way I took off last night, why didn't you just say so?"

"I prefer docudrama."

"I can't believe anybody could be so damned immature!"

"I could have been a lot more immature—emptying the marshmallows in your underwear drawer, for example—but I believe revenge should be subtle."

"Subtle! You ruined five perfectly good boxes of Lucky Charms and spoiled my whole day in the process."

"What a pity."

"I ought to . . . I swear I'm . . ." Damned if he wasn't carrying her upstairs right now and making love to her until she begged his forgiveness.

"Don't mess with me, Calvin. You'll only get hurt."

Seriously. He was seriously going to kill her. He regarded her through narrowed eyes. "Maybe you'd better explain why you got upset enough to do this. It's not like anything really important happened last night, is it? You yourself said it was—How did you put it? Oh, yeah. You said it was *quite pleasant.* Now to my way of thinking, *pleasant* doesn't add up to *important.*" He regarded her closely. "But maybe it was more than pleasant for you. Maybe it was more important than you want to let on."

Was it his imagination or did something flicker in the depths of those melted shamrock eyes. "Don't be ridiculous. It's your lack of courtesy I found offensive. It would merely have been good manners on your part to have stayed around instead of running off like a teenager hurrying to tell his buddies he'd scored."

"Manners? Is that what five boxes of mutilated Lucky Charms is all about?"

"Yes."

Just one good shot. He was already late for his meeting, but he couldn't leave until he got off one good shot. "You're about the lowest breed of human being there is."

"What?"

"Right up there with the Boston Strangler and the Son of Sam."

"Don't you think that's a little extreme?"

"Not hardly." He shook his head and regarded her with disgust. "I married a damned cereal killer."

14

Jane smiled as she headed toward Heartache Mountain in her battered Escort late that afternoon. She'd spent nearly four hours last night sorting through all that cereal, but it had been worth it to see the expression on Cal's face. One day soon he'd figure out that he couldn't walk all over her. She hoped the marshmallow exercise would point him in the right direction.

Why did he have to be so thoroughly intriguing? Of all the pitfalls she had imagined in this marriage, growing to care so much about him had not been one of them. As much as he irritated her, she loved the fact that her intelligence didn't intimidate him, as it did so many others. She felt alive when she was with him: her blood pumping, her brain at full alert, all senses engaged. Until now, she'd only felt that way when she was engrossed in her work.

Everything would have been so much easier if she could dismiss him as an egotistical, self-centered jock, but he was far more complex than that. Beneath that belligerent good ol' boy exterior lay, not only a keen mind, but a highly developed sense of humor. In light of the marshmallow incident and the fact that he would soon find out about her car, she rather hoped it kicked in soon.

She pulled up in front of Annie's house and turned off

the ignition. The Escort shuddered for several seconds before it finally shut down. As she'd hoped, Lynn's car was nowhere in sight, so she was still at lunch with Cal, which gave Jane a chance to check on Annie.

She climbed the front steps and let herself in without knocking, just as Annie had ordered her to do the last time she'd been here. *You're family now, missy, in case you forgot.*

"Annie?" She walked farther into the empty living room.

To her dismay, Lynn Bonner poked her head through the kitchen door, then came slowly forward as she saw her daughter-in-law.

Jane noted the pallor of Lynn's complexion beneath her makeup and the dark smudges under her eyes. Plainly dressed in jeans and an old pink pocket T-shirt, she bore little resemblance to the well-groomed, stylish hostess who had presided so graciously at the dinner table five days earlier. She wanted to express her concern, but realized even that small gesture would do more harm than good. She wasn't going to add to Lynn's troubles, and that meant playing the bitch. "I didn't know you were here. I thought you were having lunch with Cal."

"His morning meeting ran long, and he had to cancel." Lynn set the dish towel she'd been holding over the back of the wing chair. "Did you stop by for any particular reason?"

"I came to see Annie."

"She's napping."

"Tell her I was here, then."

"What did you want to see her about?"

Jane began to say she'd been concerned about Annie, but stopped herself just in time. "Cal told me I had to drive up today to check on her." Did lies count with God when they were uttered with good intentions?

"I see." Lynn's blue eyes grew frosty. "Well, I'm glad

duty forced you to stop by because I want to talk to you. Would you like a cup of coffee or tea?"

The last thing she needed was a private chat with Cal's mother. "I really can't stay."

"This won't take long. Have a seat."

"Maybe another time. I have a dozen really important things to do."

"Sit!"

If Jane hadn't been so anxious to get away, she would have been amused. Apparently Cal hadn't received all his leadership abilities from his father, but then, she supposed any woman who had raised three strong-willed sons knew something about exercising her authority. "All right, but just for a few moments." She took a place at the end of the couch.

Lynn sat in Annie's upholstered rocker. "I want to talk with you about Cal."

"I'm not comfortable talking about him behind his back."

"I'm his mother, and you're his wife. If that doesn't give us a right to talk about him, I don't know what does. After all, we both care about him?"

Jane heard the faint question mark at the end of that statement and understood that Lynn wanted her to confirm her feelings for Cal. Instead, she kept her face carefully expressionless. Cal was right. Lynn and Jim had endured enough grief without having to mourn the failure of his marriage. Let them celebrate, instead, the end of a disastrous alliance. Maybe it would give them something to share.

Lynn's posture grew more rigid, and Jane's heart went out to her. She regretted the pain she was causing her now, but knew that, in the end, it was kinder this way. Her in-laws seemed destined for heartbreak, but at least she could make it as short-lived as possible.

"In some ways Cal is like his father," Lynn said. "They

both have a lot of bluster, but they're more easily hurt than people imagine." A shadow crossed Lynn's face.

Maybe a simple concession on her part would somehow ease her mother-in-law's mind enough to end this conversation. "Cal is a special person. I knew that the moment I met him."

She immediately realized her mistake because a spark of maternal hope ignited in her mother-in-law's eyes, and she could see Lynn nurturing the possibility that the frosty, snobbish bride her eldest son had brought home wasn't as bad as she appeared to be.

Jane's hands tightened in her lap. She hated causing this woman pain. There was something frail about Lynn, a sadness that lay just beneath that sophisticated veneer. No matter how bad Jane made herself look, she couldn't hold out false hopes. In the end that would be more cruel than anything else.

She forced her stiff lips into a thin smile. "If anyone ever doubts that he's special, all they have to do is ask him. He does have an ego."

Lynn's chin shot up at the same time her fingers gripped the arm of the chair. "You don't seem to like him very much."

"Of course I do, but no one's perfect." Jane felt as if she were suffocating. She had never been deliberately cruel in her life, and even though she knew she had to do this, it made her ill.

"I can't understand why you married him."

Jane had to get out of here before she fell apart, and she lurched to her feet. "He's rich, intelligent, and he doesn't interfere with my work. Is there anything else you want to know?"

"Yes." She released her hold on the arm of the chair and stood. "Why in the hell did *he* marry *you*?"

Jane knew she had to drive the final nail into the coffin of Lynn's hopes. "That's easy. I'm smart, I don't interfere

with his work, and I'm good in bed. Look, Lynn, don't get
yourself in a tangle over this. Neither Cal nor I have a big
emotional investment in this marriage. We hope it works
out, but if it doesn't, we'll both survive. Now if you'll
excuse me, I need to get back to my computer. Tell Annie
if she wants anything to call Cal.''

"I want him to finish paintin' my house.''

Jane's head snapped around, and she was dismayed to
see Annie standing in the doorway that led to the back
bedroom. How long had she been there, and how much had
she overheard? Annie was unpredictable. She obviously
hadn't informed Lynn that Jane was pregnant, but what had
she said? Beneath the wrinkles and blue eye makeup, the
old woman regarded her with what could only be compassion.

"I'll tell him," Jane said.

"You do that." Annie gave a short nod and walked into
the kitchen.

Jane hurried to her car, tears stinging her eyes. Damn
Cal for making her come to Salvation! Damn him for forcing her into this marriage and believing it would be so easy
to distance his parents!

But as she jabbed the key into the ignition, she knew the
fault didn't lie with Cal. It was hers alone. She was to
blame for everything, and the wrong she'd done had spread
until it touched more people than she could ever have imagined.

She swiped at her eyes with the back of her hand and
drove blindly down the lane, thoughts of the butterfly effect
swirling through her mind. It was a concept that scientists
who studied chaos theory talked about, the notion that
something as simple as a butterfly's wings stirring the air
in Singapore could cause a ripple effect that would eventually affect weather systems in Denver. The butterfly effect
could also be a mini morality lesson, and she remembered
talking to her third graders about it, telling them that any

good deed, no matter how small, could keep multiplying until it had changed the whole world forever for the better.

Her deed had done the same thing, but in reverse. Her selfish act was causing pain to an increasing number of innocent people. And there was no end in sight. The harm kept spreading, the butterfly effect multiplying. She had hurt Cal, she was hurting his parents, and, worst of all, her bad judgment was going to hurt their baby.

She was too upset to work, so she drove into town and went to the drugstore. As she came out, she heard a familiar voice.

"Hey, beautiful. Did you pray for me?"

She whirled around and found herself looking into a pair of cocky green eyes. For absolutely no reason that she could think of, her flagging spirits lifted a few notches. "Hello, Mr. Tucker. I didn't expect to see you here."

"Why don't you call me Kevin? Even better, how about calling me *honey* and really pissing off the old man."

She smiled. He reminded her of a young golden retriever: attractive, overly eager, full of restless energy and unlimited self-confidence. "Now let me guess. You've shown up in Salvation to cause Cal as much trouble as possible."

"Me? Now why would I do something like that? I love the old guy."

"If someone doesn't put you in your place soon, there's no justice in the world."

"My place is sitting on the bench, and I don't like it one bit."

"I'm sure you don't."

"Let me buy you some lunch, Jane—I can call you Jane, can't I? Why are you driving that old heap around? I didn't know they still allowed cars like that on the road. Whose is it?"

She opened the door of the Escort and set her packages inside. "It's mine, and don't talk about it like that, or you'll hurt its feelings."

"That car's not yours. The Bomber'd never let you drive a junker like that in a million years. Come on, let's go have some lunch at the Mountaineer. It's the best meal in town."

He grabbed her arm, and she found herself being swept around the corner toward a small, tidy-looking wooden house with a roughly carved sign on the porch indicating this was the bar she'd been hearing about. The entire time they walked, he talked.

"Did you know this is a dry county? There are no bars. The Mountaineer is what they call a bottle club. I even had to buy a membership card to get in. Don't you think that's bogus? You can still drink in this county, but you have to have a membership card to do it."

He led her up the stairs, across a wooden porch, and into a small entryway where a young woman in jeans stood next to an old classroom lectern that held a reservation book. "Hi there, sweetheart. We need a table for two. Someplace cozy." He flashed his membership card.

The hostess smiled at Kevin and directed them through a small, spartan dining room that looked as if it had originally served as the living room of the house, but was now furnished with half a dozen square wooden tables, all of which were empty. Two steps led down into an open area with a brick floor, mahogany bar, and large stone fireplace whose hearth held a rush basket full of old magazines. Country music played in the background, but the noise wasn't deafening, and an assortment of local people sat at the round tables and barstools enjoying their lunches. The hostess led them to a small table tucked near the fireplace.

Jane had never been a fan of bars, but she had to admit this one was cozy. The walls were hung with nostalgic advertising signs, yellowed newspaper stories, and football memorabilia including a blue-and-gold Stars' jersey emblazoned with the number eighteen. Next to the jersey hung an assortment of framed magazine covers, all of them picturing her husband.

Kevin glanced over at them as he held out a cane-backed chair for her. "As good as the food is, the view sure could spoil your appetite."

"If you didn't want that kind of view, you shouldn't have come to Salvation."

He snorted as he took his seat. "The whole town's brainwashed."

"Grow up, Kevin."

"I should have known you'd be on his side."

She laughed at the injured expression on his face. "I'm his wife! What did you expect?"

"So? You're supposed to be this genius or something, aren't you? Can't you be fair-minded?"

She was saved from replying by the arrival of the waitress, who regarded Kevin with rapacious eyes, but he was absorbed in the menu and didn't seem to notice. "We'll have a couple of burgers, fries, and beer. Make it Red Dog."

"Will do."

"And two side orders of coleslaw."

Jane could barely resist rolling her eyes at his highhandedness. "Make that a cobb salad for me, no bacon, light with the cheese, dressing on the side, and a glass of skimmed milk."

Kevin grimaced. "You serious?"

"Brain food."

"Whatever."

The waitress left. While they waited for their orders to arrive, Jane listened to a monologue whose central subject seemed to be Kevin Tucker. She bided her time until their food arrived, then she got down to business. "Exactly what are you up to?"

"What do you mean?"

"Why did you come to Salvation?"

"It's a nice place."

"There are a lot of nice places." She drilled him with

her schoolmarm eyes. "Kevin, put down those fries and tell me exactly what you're doing here." She realized she felt protective of Cal. How strange, especially considering how upset she was with him.

"Nothing." He shrugged and returned a handful of fries to their blue plastic basket. "Just having a little fun, that's all."

"What do you want from him, other than his job?"

"Why would I want anything from him?"

"You wouldn't be here otherwise." She rubbed her thumb along her milk glass. "Sooner or later he'll have to retire, and then the job'll be yours. Why can't you just wait?"

"Because I should have it now!"

"Apparently the coaches don't agree."

"They're fools!"

"You seem to go out of your way to give him a hard time. Why is that? Just because you're rivals doesn't mean you have to be enemies."

His expression grew sullen, making him look younger than his years. "Because I hate his guts."

"If I hated someone as much as you seem to hate Cal, I'd do my best to stay away from him."

"You don't understand."

"Explain it."

"I— He's a real prick, that's all."

"And?"

"He's— I don't know." He looked down. Nudged the edge of his plate. "He's a fairly decent coach."

"Ahh."

"What's that mean?"

"Nothing. Just *ahh*."

"You said it like it was supposed to mean something."

"Does it?"

"Do you seriously think I'd want him coaching me, having him on my ass all the time yelling at me that my arm's worthless because I don't have a football brain to go with it? Believe me, that's the last thing I need. I'm a damned good quarterback without his help."

But an even better one with Cal's help, Jane imagined. So that's why Kevin was here. It wasn't just Cal's job he coveted; he also wanted Cal to coach him. But unless she missed her guess, he didn't have a clue how to ask him and still hold on to his pride. She tucked the information away.

For his part, Kevin was transparently anxious to change the subject. "I'm sorry about that night at the hotel. I thought you were another groupie; I didn't know the two of you were an item."

"That's all right."

"You sure kept your relationship a secret."

Not for the first time, she wondered about Junior and the other players who had arranged her birthday night visit. What had they made of all this? And more important, had they kept their mouths shut?

She decided to probe a bit. "A few people knew we were seeing each other."

"Guys on the team?"

"A few."

"They never told me."

So Cal's friends hadn't talked.

"You sure don't seem like his type."

"Maybe you don't know Cal as well as you think."

"Maybe I don't want to." He sank his teeth into his burger, taking a bite too large to pass muster with any authority on etiquette. Still, his enthusiasm was contagious, and she realized she was hungry.

As she ate, he entertained her with funny stories, most of which were risqué. The fact that he was the central subject of each one should have put her off, but it didn't. She had the feeling that his self-centeredness resulted from a lack of confidence he was determined to conceal from the world. Although there were a lot of reasons why she shouldn't, she couldn't help liking Kevin Tucker.

He finished his beer and grinned at her. "Are you interested in cheating on the Bomber? Because if you are, I think you and me could have a good thing going."

"You're impossible."

He smiled, but his eyes were sober. "I know on the surface, we don't have too much in common, and you're a couple of years older than me, but I like being with you. You understand things. And you're a good listener."

"Thank you." She couldn't help smiling back. "I like being with you, too."

"But you probably wouldn't be interested in an affair, would you? I mean, you only got married a couple of weeks ago."

"There *is* that." She knew she shouldn't be enjoying this, but her confidence had been badly shattered last night, and Kevin Tucker was adorable. Still, she had enough sins on her conscience without pumping up her ego at the expense of his. "How old are you?"

"Twenty-five."

"I'm thirty-four. Nine years older than you."

"I don't believe it. You're nearly as old as the Bomber."

" 'Fraid so."

"I don't care." His lips tightened into a stubborn line. "The Bomber might care about all that age stuff, but it doesn't mean anything to me. The only thing is . . ." He looked vaguely chagrined. "As much as I hate the Bomber's guts, I've sort of made it a policy not to screw around with married women."

"Good for you."

"You like that?"

"It speaks well of you."

"Yeah, I guess it does." He looked pleased and reached across the table and took her hand. "Promise me something, Jane. If you and the Bomber split, promise that you'll give me a call."

"Oh, Kevin, I really don't think—''

"Well, now, isn't this cozy.''

A deep, belligerent voice cut her off, and her head snapped up in time to watch Calvin James Bonner charging toward them looking like a blast furnace about to erupt. She half expected to see ribbons of smoke sliding from his nostrils, and she tried to pull her hand away from Kevin's grasp, but, naturally, he held her fast. She should have known he wouldn't miss such a golden opportunity to aggravate her husband.

"Hey, there, old man. Me and the missus was just havin' ourselves a little chat. Pull up a chair and join us.''

Cal ignored him and gave Jane a visual blast with enough power to explode a mushroom cloud over the western half of North Carolina. "Let's go.''

"I'm not quite finished with my lunch.'' She gestured toward her half-eaten salad.

"Oh, you're finished, all right.'' He snatched the salad out from under her and dumped what was left of it on Kevin's plate.

Her eyes widened. Was she wrong, or could she possibly be witnessing a major jealousy tantrum? Her spirits rose several more notches even as she tried to figure out how she wanted to handle this. Should she make a scene in public or in private?

Kevin took the decision out of her control by springing to his feet. "You son of a bitch!''

A fist flew, and the next thing she knew, Kevin was lying on the floor. With a hiss of alarm, she jumped up and rushed to him. "Kevin, are you all right?'' She glared up at her husband. "You cretin!''

"He's a pansy. I barely touched him.''

Kevin spouted a mouth-soaper of an obscenity, and as he scrambled to his feet, she reminded herself that she was dealing with two overgrown male children, both of whom were hot-tempered and intensely physical. "Stop it right now!'' she exclaimed as she rose. "This isn't going any farther.''

"You want to settle it outside?'' Cal sneered at Kevin.

"No! I'm gonna kick your ass right here.''

Kevin shoved Cal in the chest. Cal stumbled backward, but didn't fall.

Jane's hands flew to her cheeks. They were starting a barroom brawl, and unless she was mistaken, one of the things they were fighting over was her! She pushed the enticing thought away by reminding herself that she abhorred violence, and she had to put a stop to it.

"There will be *no* ass kicking!'' She used her sternest voice, the one that she occasionally employed with rowdy third-grade boys. But *these* boys paid no attention. Instead, Cal threw Kevin into a barstool, then Kevin dragged Cal against the wall. A framed *Sports Illustrated* cover showing her husband taking off his helmet came crashing down.

Jane knew she couldn't overpower them physically, so she tried another tactic. Reaching behind the bar, she snatched up one of the dispenser hoses, aimed it at the two brawlers, and pushed the trigger. It was either water or club soda, she couldn't tell which, but it lost too much of its power by the time it reached them to have any effect.

She spun toward the onlookers, who'd gotten up from their chairs to watch, and implored several of the men. "Do something, will you? Stop them!''

They ignored her.

For a moment she considered letting them beat each other's brains out, but they were too strong, and she didn't have the stomach for it. She swept up a full beer pitcher from the top of the bar, rushed over, and flung it at them.

They gasped, sputtered, and went right back to pulverizing each other as if nothing had happened. It was an unpleasant reminder of exactly how tough they were.

Kevin slammed his fist into Cal's stomach, then Cal delivered a solid punch to Kevin's chest. None of the busi-

nessmen or retirees watching showed any inclination to
help, so she knew she was on her own, but the only other
action she could think of went against her grain. Still, she
couldn't come up with a better idea so she sat down on a
barstool, dragged in a huge gulp of air, and began to scream
at the top of her lungs.

The sound was annoying, even to her, but she kept at it.
The onlookers immediately shifted their attention from the
fight to the crazed blonde sitting on a barstool wailing like
a banshee. Cal got so distracted that he allowed Kevin to
catch him in the side of his head. Then Kevin lost his focus
and ended up on the floor.

She sucked in more air and kept screaming.

"Will you stop it!" Cal bellowed, staggering away from
the wall.

She was starting to get dizzy, but she forced herself to
let loose a fresh stream of shrieks.

Kevin scrambled up from the floor, his chest heaving.
"What's wrong with her?"

"She's hysterical." Cal wiped the beer from his eyes
with the back of his hand, dragged in some air, and lurched
toward her with a purposeful gleam in his eye. "I'm going
to have to slap her."

"Don't you dare!" she yelped.

"Got to." The gleam in his eye now had a faintly diabolical cast to it.

"Touch me and I'll scream!"

"*Don't touch her!*" three people in the crowd called out
at once.

She crossed her arms over her chest and glared at the
onlookers. "You could have helped, you know, and then
this wouldn't have been necessary."

"It's only a bar fight," Kevin grumbled. "No reason to
make such a big deal out of it."

Cal took her arm and pulled her down off the barstool.
"She's a little high-strung."

"I'll say." Kevin pulled up his shirttail to wipe the beer from his face. A cut on his cheekbone was bleeding, and one eye had puffed up.

A middle-aged man wearing a starched white shirt and black bow tie regarded her curiously. "Who is she, anyway?"

Cal pretended not to hear.

"Darlington," she said, holding out her hand to shake. "Jane Darlington."

"She's my wife," Cal muttered.

"Your wife?" The man looked faintly bewildered as he took her hand.

"The same," she replied.

"This is Harley Crisp. He runs the local hardware store." Jane had never heard a more begrudging introduction.

Harley dropped Jane's hand and turned to Cal. "How come when she finally showed up here, she was with Tucker and not you?"

Cal clenched his jaw. "They're old friends."

Jane realized everyone in the bar was now assessing her, and none of them looked particularly friendly.

"Nice you could finally spare the time to come meet the people who live here, Miz Bonner," Harley said.

She heard several other hostile murmurs, including one from the attractive bartender, and knew that the story of Cal's chilly scientist wife who thought she was more important than everyone else had spread.

Cal diverted the crowd's attention by directing the bartender to put the damages on Kevin's lunch tab. Kevin looked sulky, like a kid who'd been sent to his room. "You threw the first punch."

Cal ignored him. Instead, he grabbed Jane with a hand still damp from beer and headed toward the front door.

"Nice to have met you all," she tossed back over her

shoulder at the hostile crowd. "Although I would have appreciated a little more help."

"Will you shut up?" he growled.

He drew her across the porch and down the steps. She saw the Jeep parked at the curb, and it reminded her she had one more battle to fight. Being married to Cal Bonner was becoming an increasingly complicated business.

"I have my own car."

"Hell you do." His lip was bleeding and beginning to swell on one side.

"I do."

"You don't."

"It's parked in front of the drugstore even as we speak." She reached into her purse, withdrew a tissue, and held it out to him.

He paid no attention. "You bought a car?"

"I told you I was going to."

He braked to a stop. She dabbed the tissue gently against his lip, only to have him jerk away. "And I told you you weren't."

"Yes, well, I'm a bit too old and a lot too independent to pay attention to you."

"Show me." He spit out the words like bullets.

She remembered Kevin's unkind comments about her Escort and felt a moment of trepidation. "Why don't I just meet you at the house?"

"Show me!"

Resigned, she walked down the block to the town center, then turned toward the drugstore. He stalked silently at her side and his heels seemed to strike white-hot sparks as they hit the pavement.

Unfortunately, the Escort's appearance hadn't improved. As she came to a stop next to it, he looked stunned. "Tell me this isn't it."

"All I needed was basic transportation. I have a perfectly good Saturn waiting for me at home."

He sounded as if he were strangling on a bone. "Has anybody seen you drive this?"

"Hardly anybody."

"Who?"

"Only Kevin."

"Shit!"

"Really, Cal, you need to watch your language, not to mention your blood pressure. A man of your age—" She saw her mistake and quickly changed direction. "It's perfectly fine for what I need."

"Give me those keys."

"I will not!"

"You win, Professor. I'll buy you a car. Now give me the damn keys."

"I have a car."

"A real car. A Mercedes, a BMW, whatever you want."

"I don't want a Mercedes or a BMW."

"That's what you think."

"Stop bullying me."

"I haven't even started."

They were beginning to attract a crowd, which wasn't surprising. How often had the people of Salvation, North Carolina, seen their local hero standing in the middle of town dripping beer and blood?

"Give me those keys," he hissed.

"In your dreams."

Luckily for her, the crowd made it impossible for him to snatch them away as he wanted. She took advantage of that to shove past him, open the door, and jump into the car.

He looked like a pressure cooker about to explode. "I'm warning you, Professor. This is the last drive you're taking in that junker, so enjoy every minute of it."

This time his high-handedness didn't amuse her. Obviously the marshmallows hadn't done the trick, and it was time to take stronger measures. Mr. Calvin Bonner needed to figure out for once and for all that he couldn't run a marriage like he ran a football play.

She gritted her teeth. "You know what you can do with your warnings, buster. You can take them and—"

"We'll talk about this when we get home." He hit her dead on with those nuclear winter eyes. "Now drive!"

Seething, she peeled out of the parking place. The car blessed her by backfiring. She set her jaw and headed for home.

She'd had it.

15

Jane used the small screwdriver she always carried in her purse to disable the automatic gates. Now they would remain shut and it had taken her less than two minutes. When she reached the house, she parked the Escort in the driveway, stomped inside, and fetched some twine that she secured in a tight figure eight around the twin knobs set side by side in the double front door. She fashioned a wedge from several cooking utensils and used it to secure the back door.

She was checking the bolts in the French doors that opened off the family room when the intercom began to buzz. She ignored it and headed for the garage, where she used the small ladder that was stored there to unplug the automatic door opener from its ceiling outlet.

The angry buzzing of the intercom assaulted her ears as she stalked back into the kitchen. She yanked all the first-floor draperies closed and pulled the phone off the hook. When that was done, she grabbed her screwdriver, made her way to the intercom, and punched the button.

"Cal?"

"Yeah, listen Jane, there's something wrong with the gate."

"There's something wrong, all right, buster, but it

238

doesn't have anything to do with the gate!'' With a twist of her wrist, she loosened the connection, and the buzzer fell silent. Afterward, she stalked upstairs, booted up her computer, and set to work.

It wasn't long before she heard the rattling of doors accompanied by a determined pounding. When it grew so loud it disturbed her concentration, she tore a tissue in two and wadded the pieces in her ears.

Blessed quiet.

An *Escort!* Cal hauled himself up onto the lower section of roof that jutted out over the first-floor study. First she'd sabotaged his Lucky Charms, and now she'd embarrassed him in front of the entire town by driving a ten-year-old Escort! He couldn't explain why both offenses seemed a lot worse than the fact that she'd managed to lock him out of his own house. Maybe because he was enjoying the challenge of getting back in, not to mention the anticipation of the fight they were going to have after he'd managed it.

He walked as lightly as he could across the roof because he didn't want the damn thing to spring a leak the next time it rained. As he glanced up at the dark clouds skidding across the darkening sky, he figured that rain might not be too far off.

He reached the end of the roof, where it met up with the corner of the balcony that extended across the front of the house, and experienced a moment of disappointment because there wasn't a bigger gap to make this more of a contest. Still, the grillwork railing was too shaky to hold his weight, so that made it a little more interesting.

Using the bottom edge of the balcony as a handhold, he lowered himself over the side and, legs dangling, worked his way along the balcony's edge until he came to the corner column. A clap of thunder reverberated, and rain began to pelt him, plastering his shirt to his back. He wrapped his legs around the column for support, then, bracing one hand on the wobbly grillwork, shinnied up the slippery surface and lowered himself over the railing.

The lock in the French doors that led into his bedroom was flimsy, and it annoyed him that Miss Big Brain hadn't done anything to secure it. She probably thought he was too *old* to make it this far! The fact that his lip hurt, his ribs ached, and his bad shoulder throbbed like a sonovabitch fueled his irritation, and as he jimmied the doors open, his temper flared up again. She should at least have had enough respect for him to shove a chair in front of the knob!

He walked across his dark bedroom into the hallway and moved toward the light that spilled out from her room. She sat with her back to the door and all her formidable concentration focused on the columns of incomprehensible data scrolling past on her computer screen. Puffs of blue tissue stuck out of both ears, making her look like a cartoon rabbit. He thought about marching up behind her and giving her the fright of her life by pulling the tissues out. It was exactly what she deserved, but since she was pregnant, he modified his plan. Not that he believed Annie's dire warnings about marked babies and twisted cords, but still, he wasn't taking any chances.

The smell of beer clung to him like barroom smoke as he made his way downstairs. He was wet, sore, completely pissed off, and every bit of it was her fault! His blood pounded in anticipation as he reached the foyer. Throwing back his head, he bellowed out her name.

"*Jane Darlington Bonner!* You get down here right this minute!"

Jane's head shot up. His roar penetrated her homemade ear plugs. So, he'd managed to find a way inside. As she pulled out the wads of tissue and tossed them in the basket, she wondered how he'd done it. Some amazing feat of bravado, no doubt, since the great quarterback wouldn't dream of demeaning himself by anything as obvious as breaking a window. Despite her pique, she felt a certain amount of pride.

As she rose from her desk and discarded her glasses, she tried to figure out why she had no desire to lock herself in her room. She'd never liked conflict and never been all that good at it—witness her dismal skirmishes with Jerry Miles. Maybe she wasn't anxious to avoid this battle because it would be with Cal. All her life she'd been so polite, so dignified, so careful not to offend. But Cal was impatient with politeness, unimpressed by dignity, and impervious to offense. She didn't have to watch what she said or mind her manners. She could simply be herself. As she crossed the room, her pulses hummed, and her brain cells went on full alert. She felt completely and wondrously alive.

From the foyer below, Cal watched her approach the top of the stairs. Her trim little butt swayed from side to side inside her slacks, and her green knit top emphasized a pair of breasts so unimpressive in their size he couldn't figure out why he was so anxious to set eyes on them. Her hair, pulled away from her face with barrettes like an upper-crust schoolgirl's, swung back and forth, as saucy as her mouth.

She looked down at him, but instead of being scared as she should have been, he could swear he saw a spark of mischief in her eyes. "Somebody looks mad," she drawled, all spunk and sass.

"You—" He slammed his hands on his hips. "—are going to pay for this."

"What are you gonna do, big guy? Spank me?"

Just like that, he got hard. Damn it! How did she keep doing this to him? And what kind of kinky talk was that for a respectable college professor?

An unwilling vision of that sweet little butt curving beneath his palm shot through him. He clenched his jaw, narrowed his eyes, and gave her a look so mean-assed he was ashamed of himself for using it on a poor, defenseless, pregnant female. "Maybe a bare-butt spanking is exactly what you need."

"Really?" Instead of fainting from fear the way any sensible woman would have done, she got this calculating look on her face. "Might be fun. I'll think about it."

Just like that she turned on her heel and swept back to her room, leaving him standing at the bottom of the stairs in her dust. He was stunned. How did she manage to keep turning the tables on him like that? And what did she mean, she'd think about it?

He remembered that mangled Escort sitting in the drive right where his kickass Jeep should have been and charged up the stairs after her. He wasn't half done with this fight!

Jane heard him coming and was ashamed of the thrill of anticipation the sound of those pounding feet gave her. Until these past few weeks, she hadn't realized how heavily the mantle of maintaining her dignity had weighed on her shoulders. But Cal had no more use for dignity than a dog for panty hose.

He flew through her bedroom door and jabbed his finger in the general direction of her forehead. "Starting right now, the two of us are going to get a few things straight. I'm the head of this household, and I expect respect! I don't want to hear another piece of sass out of you. Do you understand what I'm saying?"

His confrontation techniques undoubtedly worked very well with men, but she felt a flash of sympathy for those poor young girls he'd chosen as his past companions. He must have devastated those curvaceous little infants.

But for some reason the picture of him yelling at a defenseless twenty-year-old beauty queen wouldn't take shape in her mind, and it didn't take her long to understand why. He would never do it. Cal was incapable of unleashing the full force of his anger on someone he regarded as weaker than himself. The knowledge gave her a deep sense of pride.

"Your lip is bleeding again," she said. "Go in the bathroom, and I'll fix it."

"I'm not going anywhere until we settle this."

"Pretty please. I've always fantasized about tending a wounded warrior."

That gave him pause. He got this dangerous, squinty-eyed look that made her knees a little wobbly. He was 190 pounds of dynamite getting ready to detonate, so why wasn't she afraid?

He stuck a thumb in the pocket of his jeans. "I'll let you patch me up under one condition."

"What's that?"

"After you're done, you sit quietly—and I mean with your mouth shut—while I take you apart."

"Okay."

"Okay?" His roar nearly blew out her eardrums. "Is that it? Lady, you must not understand what I've got in mind because if you did, you wouldn't be standing there telling me 'okay'!"

She smiled just because she knew it would further irritate him. "I believe that open communication is important to a marriage."

"We're not talking about open communication. We're talking about me taking you apart limb by limb." He paused and thrust out his jaw. "Hand to bare butt."

"Whatever." She waved breezily as she set off toward the bathroom.

She almost felt sorry for him. He was an intensely physical man cursed with a strong moral conscience, which made it extremely difficult for him to have a truly satisfactory fight with a female. She finally understood why he loved football with its hard hits and thick rule book so much. To Cal, the combination of rough body contact and swift justice would be the best of all worlds.

This presented a definite problem in his relationships with women.

She crossed the cryptlike bathroom to the medicine cabinet and began a search of its contents. "I hope there's something in here that really stings."

When he made no comment, she turned, then gulped as she saw him pulling his shirt over his head. As he stretched, his scraped rib cage grew more prominent, and his navel formed a narrow oval. She saw the tufts of silky hair under his arms, the scar on his shoulder. "What are you doing?"

He tossed the shirt aside and popped the button on his jeans. "What do you think I'm doing? I'm taking a shower, or don't you remember you poured a pitcher of beer over my head, then locked me out of my own house in the middle of a savage thunderstorm? And that front gate you sabotaged had better be back in service first thing tomorrow morning or there's gonna be some big-time hell to pay." He pulled down his zipper.

She turned away, making the movement as casual as possible. Luckily the bathroom contained enough mirrors that by tilting her head she had a full view. Unfortunately, it was only of his back. Still that was pretty magnificent. Broad shoulders tapered to narrow hips and tight, flat buttocks. There was a red mark on one side of his spinal column from his fight with Kevin. She frowned at the collection of old scars and new scars and thought of all his aging warrior's body had endured.

He swung open the door of the cylindrical shower stall, which looked as if it belonged on the starship *Enterprise*, and stepped in. Unfortunately, the frosting on the bottom half of the glass kept her from seeing more.

"You're exaggerating about the savage thunderstorm," she called out above the sound of the water. "It just started raining."

"*Before* I made it over the top of the balcony."

"Is that how you got in?" Impressed, she turned toward the shower.

"Only because *you* didn't have enough confidence in me to secure those top doors."

She smiled to herself at the injured note in his voice. "I'm sorry. I wasn't thinking."

"Obviously not." He ducked his head under the spray. "Do you want to join me?"

She yearned to say yes, but his voice held a silky seductive note that reminded her of a snake slithering up the Tree of Knowledge, so she pretended not to hear. While he showered, she searched through the drawers of the vanity trying to locate some antibiotic ointment.

She found a tube of Crest Tartar Control squeezed up from the bottom and a column of neatly capped deodorant. His black comb was spanking clean and still had all its teeth. The drawer also held dental floss, a pair of shiny silver nail clippers, shaving cream and several razors, along with Extra Strength Tylenol, and a large tube of Ben Gay. And condoms. A whole box of them. The fact that he would be using these condoms with someone other than herself gave her a pang so sharp she ached.

Pushing the image aside, she knelt to look under the sink and found more Ben Gay, three cartons of Epsom salts, and a tube of antibiotic ointment. The water shut off and, moments later, the shower door clicked.

"Tucker's using you," he said. "You know that, don't you?"

"That's not true." She turned in time to watch him wrap a thick black towel around his waist. His chest was still wet, the dark hair matted.

"Sure it is. He's using you to get back at me."

The fact that he didn't believe Kevin could find her attractive stung enough that it forced her to retaliate. "That may be true, but there's also a subtle sexual chemistry between Kevin and me."

He'd been in the process of pulling a hand towel from the rack to dry his hair, but his arm stalled in mid-reach.

"What are you talking about? What sexual chemistry?"

"Sit down so I can fix your lip. It's bleeding again."

Droplets from his wet hair flew as he took an abrupt step forward. "I won't sit down! I want to know what you mean."

"An older woman, a *very* attractive younger man. It's been happening since the beginning of time. But don't worry. He won't mess around with married women."

His eyes had narrowed into mean-street slits at her description of Kevin. "Is that supposed to be comforting?"

"Only if the idea of Kevin and me together is discomfiting."

He snatched the towel and vigorously rubbed his hair. "You know he's only interested in you because you're wearing my ring. If it weren't for that, he wouldn't pay any attention to you."

He'd found her most vulnerable spot, and, just like that, the fun went out of the game. His meaningless threats of violence hadn't bothered her, but the fact that he believed she was too geeky for another man to find attractive stung to the quick. "No, I don't know that." She headed toward her bedroom.

"Where are you going?" he called after her. "I thought you were going to patch me up?"

"The antibiotic is on the vanity. Do it yourself."

He followed her into her bedroom, coming to a stop just inside the door. "Does Kevin— Does he mean something to you?" He flung down the hand towel. "How the hell could he mean anything to you? You don't even know him!"

"Our discussion is over."

"I thought you believed in open communication?"

She said nothing, but gazed out the window, wishing he'd go away.

He came up behind her, and she heard a curious gruffness in his voice. "I hurt your feelings, didn't I?"

She slowly nodded.

"I didn't mean to. I just— I don't want you to get hurt, that's all. You don't have a lot of experience with jocks. They can be—I don't know—hard on women, I guess."

"I know." She turned back to him in time to watch a crooked rivulet of water slide toward a flat brown nipple. "I think I've had enough high drama for today. You'd better go."

He came closer instead, and when he spoke, his voice held a surprising note of tenderness. "We didn't even get to the bare-butt spanking."

"Maybe some other time."

"How 'bout we just do the bare-butt part?"

"I don't think it's a good idea for us to bare anything to each other for a while."

"Now why do you say that?"

"Because it makes everything too complicated."

"Last night wasn't complicated. At least not 'til you got all snooty."

"Me!" Her head shot up. "I've never been snooty in my life!"

"Oh, yeah?" Her renewed feistiness must have been what he was waiting for because the glimmer of battle once again flared in his eyes. "Well, I happen to have been at that drive-in with you, and, believe me, you were snooty."

"When?"

"You know very well."

"I don't."

"That *quite pleasant* crap."

"I don't know what— Oh, that." She regarded him more closely. "Did what I said bother you?"

"Hell, no, it didn't bother me. You think I don't know how good I am? And if you don't realize it, well, I guess that's your problem and not mine."

He looked sulky, and she realized she had hurt his feelings last night. The knowledge touched her. Despite his seemingly boundless self-confidence, he had insecurities like everyone else. "It was more than pleasant," she admitted.

"Damn right."

"I'd say it was— It was—" She regarded him out of the corner of her eye. "What word am I looking for?"

"Why don't you start out with pretty damn terrific?"

Her spirits made a quantum leap upward. "Terrific? Yes, that's a good start. It was definitely terrific. It was also . . ." She waited.

"Exciting, and sexy as hell."

"That, too, but . . ."

"Frustrating."

"Frustrating?"

"Yeah." A combative thrust to that square jaw. "I want to see you naked."

"You do? Why?"

"Because I do."

"Is this a guy thing?"

His truculence faded, and one corner of his mouth—the uninjured corner—curled. "You could say that."

"Believe me when I tell you that you're not missing much."

"I'm probably a better judge of that than you are."

"Oh, I'm sure that's not true. You know those endlessly long legs you see on models? Those legs that go all the way up to their armpits?"

"Uh-huh."

"I don't have them."

"Is that a fact."

"My legs aren't short, but they're not exceptionally long, either. Just average. And as for breasts— Do you consider yourself a breast man?"

"They've been known to catch my attention."

"Mine won't. Now my hips are a different matter. They're huge."

"Your hips are not huge."

"I look like a pear."

"You do not look like a pear."

"Thank you for the vote of confidence, but since you haven't seen me naked, you're not exactly a competent judge."

"We can take care of that right now."

He was at his most enticing: gray eyes glinting, that unexpected dimple on display just beneath his cheekbone, funny, warm, sexy. And she was at her most vulnerable. In a flash of insight that nearly knocked her from her feet, she realized that she was in love with him. Deeply and forever in love. She loved his masculinity, his intelligence, his complexity. She loved his sense of humor and his loyalty to his family, as well as that old-fashioned moral code that dictated he watch out for a child. Even one he didn't want.

There was no time to think about it, no place to run so she could ponder the enormity of what had happened. She watched him lift his arm and trace the curve of her jaw with his thumb. "I like you, Rosebud. I like you a lot."

"You do?"

He nodded.

She noted that he'd said he liked her, not loved her, and swallowed the lump in her throat. "You're just saying that to get me naked."

The creases of amusement deepened at the corners of his eyes. "It's tempting, but this is too important to lie about."

"I thought you hated me."

"I did. But it's hard to hold on to a good—and entirely *justifiable*—hatred with you."

Hope sprang inside her. "You forgive me?"

He hesitated. "Not exactly. It's a pretty big thing to forgive."

Once again, she felt a great wave of guilt sweeping through her. "You know I'm sorry, don't you?"

"Are you?"

"I—I can't be sorry about the baby, but I am sorry about the way I used you. I didn't think of you as a real person, just a dehumanized object that could give me what I wanted. If anyone treated me that way, I'd never forgive them, and if it's any consolation, you should know that I'll never forgive myself."

"Maybe you could do what I've been doing and work on separating the sin from the sinner."

She gazed into his eyes, trying to see through them to his heart. "Do you really not hate me anymore?"

"I already told you that I like you."

"I don't see how you could."

"I guess it just happened."

"When?"

"When did I decide I liked you? That day at Annie's when you found out I was smart."

"And you found out I was old."

"Don't remind me. I still haven't recovered from that. Maybe we could say the DMV made a mistake on your license."

She ignored the hopeful glimmer in his eyes. "How could you have decided you liked me that day? We had a terrible fight."

"Beats me. It just happened."

She considered what he was revealing. Nothing could be farther from a declaration of love, but his words did show a certain warmth of feeling. "I'll need to think about it."

"About what?"

"Whether or not I'm going to get naked."

"All right."

That was another thing she liked about him. For all his bullying and bluster, he knew how to distinguish what was important from the trivial, and he seemed to understand he couldn't hurry her on this.

"There's one more thing we have to settle."

She regarded him warily, then sighed. "I like my car. It has personality."

"So do a lot of psychopaths, but that doesn't mean you want one in your house. Now here's the way it's going to be—"

"Cal, please don't waste your breath giving me one of your high-handed lectures because I'll only end up locking you out of the house again. I asked you to help me find a car, you refused, so I did it myself. The car stays. And it won't even hurt your reputation. Think about it. When people see me driving around in it, they'll take it as one more sign of how unworthy I am to be your wife."

"You've got a point there. Everybody who knows me knows I wouldn't be keeping any woman around for very long who drove a heap like that."

"I won't even comment on what that says about your sense of values." He had a wonderful sense of values. It was his taste in women that needed an overhaul.

He grinned, but she refused to let it effect her. She wouldn't be so easily won over. "I want your word of honor that you won't touch my car. No driving it away or sending a tow truck when I'm not looking. The car is mine, and it stays. And just so we understand each other, I'm telling you right now that if you lay a finger on my Escort, you'll never enjoy another box of Lucky Charms in this house."

"More marshmallow sabotage?"

"I never repeat myself. Think rat poison."

"You are the most bloodthirsty woman I've ever met."

"It's a slow and painful death. I don't recommend it."

He laughed and headed back into the bathroom, where he shut the door only to pop his head back out. "All this arguing has stirred up my appetite. How 'bout we scrounge up something to eat as soon as I get dressed?"

"All right."

As the rain continued to fall outside, they dined on soup, salad, and sandwiches, with a side order of taco chips.

While they ate, she managed to wheedle a few more details out of him about his work with teenagers and discovered he'd been devoting his time to disadvantaged kids for years. He'd help fund rec centers, made speeches to recruit volunteers for after-school tutoring programs, set up intramural leagues, and lobbied the Illinois state legislature to improve their drug- and sex-education programs.

He shrugged off her comment that not all celebrities would be willing to give up so much time with no obvious reward to themselves. It was just something to do, he growled.

The hallway clock struck midnight and, gradually, their conversation dwindled. An awkwardness settled between them that hadn't been there before. She toyed with an uneaten bread crust. He shifted his weight in the kitchen chair. She'd been so comfortable all evening, but now she felt awkward and self-conscious.

"It's late," she finally said. "I think I'll head up to bed." She picked up her plate as she stood.

He rose, too, and removed it from her hand. "You cooked. I'll clean up."

But he didn't head toward the sink. Instead, he stayed where he was and gazed at her with hungry eyes. She could hear his unspoken question. *Tonight, Rosebud? Are you ready to cut through all this pretense and do what we both want?*

If he had reached out for her, she would have been lost, but he didn't do that, and she understood that this time she would have to make the first move. His eyebrows rose in a silent dare.

Wings of a panic beat at her breastbone. The new knowledge that she had fallen in love with him made all the difference. She wanted sex between them to matter.

The powerful brain that had guided her throughout her life refused to function, and confusion gripped her. She felt paralyzed, and the most she could manage was a polite, social smile. "I've enjoyed tonight, Cal. I'll fix the gate first thing tomorrow."

He said nothing; he merely watched her.

She tried to think of some casual comment to defuse the tension, but nothing came to mind. He stood there watching her. She knew he was aware of her uneasiness, but he didn't seem to share it. Why should he when he didn't share her feelings? Unlike her, he hadn't fallen in love.

She turned away, enveloped by a sense of loss. As she left the kitchen, her brain told her she was doing the right thing, but her heart told her she was a coward.

Cal watched her disappear through the doorway, and disappointment filled him. She was running away, and he wasn't sure why. He hadn't pushed her tonight. He'd given her space, made certain the conversation stayed on safe topics. As a matter of fact, he'd been enjoying himself so much he'd nearly forgotten about sex. Nearly, but never entirely. He wanted her too much to put it out of his mind. She'd enjoyed their lovemaking last night—he knew she had—so why was she denying both of them one of life's most basic pleasures?

He carried the dishes from their dinner to the sink and rinsed them off. His disappointment turned into irritation. Why did he let her bother him so much?

Disgusted with himself, he stalked upstairs, but entering his bordello bedroom only made his mood grow bleaker. A crack of thunder rattled the windows, and he realized the storm had intensified. Good. It matched his mood. He sat down on the side of the bed and yanked off one shoe.

"Cal?"

He looked up to see the bathroom door swing open, but just then a blinding flash of lightning shook the walls, and the house was plunged into darkness.

Several seconds ticked by, and then he heard a soft giggle.

He flung down his other shoe. "We just lost our electricity. You want to tell me what's so funny about that?"

"It's not exactly funny. It's more of a good news/bad news situation."

"In that case, hit me with the good news first."

"They're both sort of rolled up into one."

"Stop stalling."

"All right. Now don't get mad, but . . ." Smothered laughter drifted toward him. "Cal . . . I'm naked."

16

One month later

Cal poked his head into her bedroom through the connecting bathroom door. A glint shone in his eyes. "I'm taking a shower. You want to get in with me?"

She slid her gaze over his deliciously naked body, so beautifully delineated in the morning light, and had to resist the urge to lick her lips. "Maybe another time."

"You don't know what you're missing."

"I think I do."

The inadvertently wistful note in her voice seemed to amuse him. "Poor little Rosebud. You've really boxed yourself into a corner, haven't you?" With a cocky smile, he disappeared into the bathroom.

She stuck out her tongue at the empty doorway, propped her cheek on her bent elbow, and thought about that April night one month ago when she'd made her impulsive decision to take off her clothes and go to him. The unexpected electrical failure just as she'd walked into his bedroom had marked the beginning of a night of pleasure and passion that she would never forget. She smiled to herself. In the month that had passed since then, Cal had gotten very good at making love by touch.

She'd gotten rather good at it herself, she thought with

255

a certain amount of pride. Maybe his lusty nature and lack of inhibition had freed her from her own inhibitions. She would do anything . . . everything . . . except let him see her naked.

It had become a game. She would only make love with him at night with the lights out, and she always awakened sometime before dawn so she could return to her own room or slip into his if they'd fallen asleep in her bed. He could have changed the rules. He could have overpowered her, or left her so breathless at high noon with his kisses that she relented, but he never did. He was a competitor, and he didn't want to win by guile, only by her total surrender.

Her insistence on making love in the dark had begun as a gentle form of sexual teasing, but as one week faded into another and she realized how deeply she had fallen in love with him, something changed. She began to worry about how he would react when he finally saw her. She was now four months pregnant, and although she bloomed with health, her waist had thickened to the point where she couldn't come close to fastening her slacks and her days wearing tucked-in blouses were a thing of the past. With her expanding belly and unimpressive breasts, she could never compete with all those beauties in his past.

But it was more than the shortcomings of her body that made her hesitant. What if mystery was the lure that drew him to her bed each night? Mystery and the enticement of the unknown? Once his curiosity was satisfied, would he lose interest?

She wanted to believe it wouldn't matter, but she knew how much Cal loved a challenge. Would he enjoy her company as much if she bent to his will? She seemed to be the only woman in his life, with the exception of his mother and grandmother, who stood up to him.

He was an intelligent, decent man with a generous heart. But he was also domineering and competitive. Was it only the novelty of her rebellion that made him seek her company, both in and out of bed?

She faced the fact that her time for playing games had run out. She needed to stop being a coward, take off her clothes so he could see her, and face the truth. If he didn't want her for who she was, but only for the challenge of conquering her, then what they had together was worthless. She had to do it soon, she decided. It was crazy to keep this going on any longer.

She got out of bed and made her way to her bathroom. After she'd taken her morning vitamins and brushed her teeth, she returned to her room, and, with one hand on her growing belly, wandered over to the window so she could gaze out at the May morning. The mountainside was alive with blooms: dogwood, rhododendron, flame azaleas, along with budding mountain laurel. Her first Appalachian spring was more beautiful than she could ever have imagined. Violets, trillium, and lady slippers had unfolded in the woods where she walked, and wisteria bloomed at the side of the house along with a white shower of blackberry blossoms. She had never experienced such a breathtaking, joyous May.

But, then, she'd never been in love, either.

She understood how vulnerable she'd made herself, but as the guarded look Cal had carried in his eyes for so long was replaced by laughter and tenderness, she began to believe that he might be falling in love with her. Two months ago the idea would have been absurd, but now it didn't seem so impossible.

For people who should have nothing in common, they never ran out of subjects to talk about or things to do. While she spent her mornings at the computer, Cal worked out and took care of his local commitments, but they spent most afternoons and many evenings together.

Cal had finished painting Annie's house while she'd put in the garden. They'd visited Asheville several times together, where they'd dined at some of the city's best restaurants and walked the grounds of the Biltmore Estate with busloads of tourists. They'd hiked some of the easier trails in the Great Smoky Mountain National Park, and he'd taken her to see Connemara, Carl Sandberg's home, where she'd been enchanted by the beautiful setting and he'd taken pictures of her playing with the goats that were kept there.

By unspoken agreement, they didn't go into Salvation together. When Jane had shopping to do, she went alone. Sometimes she ran into Kevin, and the two of them lunched together at the Petticoat Junction Cafe, where she ignored the hostile stares of the locals. Luckily, she could still conceal her pregnancy with loose-fitting dresses.

She and Cal continued to fight when he got high-handed, but it was generally a good kind of fighting, and he never displayed any of the cold hatred that had been so much a part of him in those early weeks. Instead, he roared away to his heart's content, and she refused to ruin his pleasure by not fighting back. The truth was, she enjoyed their battles as much as he.

She heard the shower cut off. Since there was no sense exposing herself to additional temptation, she gave him a few minutes to dry off and wrap a towel around himself before she rapped softly on the partially open bathroom door, then let herself in.

He stood at the sink with the black bath towel looped so low on his hips she was surprised it didn't drop off. As he spread shaving cream across his jaw, he took in her cherry red Snoopy nightshirt.

"When are you gonna show a little mercy, Professor, and stop encitin' me with those sexy negligees?"

"Tomorrow night I'm wearing Winnie-the-Pooh."

"Be still my heart."

She smiled, lowered the lid on the toilet, and took a seat. For a while she contented herself with watching him shave, but then she returned to the subject of yesterday's argument.

"Cal, explain to me once more why you won't spend a little time with Kevin?"

"Are we back to this again?"

"I still don't understand why you won't coach him. He really respects you."

"He hates my guts."

"That's only because he wants to move up in the world. He's young and talented, and you're standing in his way."

His muscles tensed. He didn't like the fact that she spent time with Kevin, but since she'd made it clear that she regarded him as a friend, and since Cal had apparently told Kevin he'd break both his arms if he so much as touched her, they'd settled into an uneasy truce.

He tilted his head and shaved under his chin. "He's not as talented as he thinks. He's got a great arm—no doubt about that. He's quick and aggressive, but he has a lot to learn about reading defenses."

"Why don't you teach him?"

"It's like I said, I don't see the logic in training my competition, and I also happen to be the last person in the world he'd take advice from."

"That's not true. Why do you think he's still hanging around Salvation?"

"Because he's sleeping with Sally Terryman."

Jane had seen the curvaceous Sally in town several times, and she decided Cal had a point, but since it wasn't the one she wanted to make, she ignored it. "He'd be a lot better player if you worked with him, and you'd be leaving something important behind when you retire."

"Which won't be for a long time." He ducked his head and rinsed off the shaving cream.

She knew she was treading on dangerous ground and stepped carefully. "You're thirty-six, Cal. It can't be much longer."

"Which just goes to show what you know." He grabbed a hand towel and dried his face. "I'm at the top of my game. There's no reason for me to retire."

"Maybe not right away, but certainly in the foreseeable future."

"I've got a lot of good years left."

She thought of the shoulder he rubbed when he thought no one was looking, the whirlpool he'd had installed in the bathroom, and knew he was fooling himself.

"What are you going to do when you retire? Do you have some business ventures lined up? Are you going into coaching?"

His back muscles tensed ever so slightly. "Why don't you just stick to those top quarks, Professor, and leave my future to me?" He headed into his bedroom, whipping off his towel as he walked over to his bureau and pulled out a pair of briefs. "You remember, don't you, that I'm taking off for Texas later this afternoon."

He'd changed the subject. "Some kind of golf tournament, I think you said."

"The Bobby Tom Denton Invitational."

"He's a friend of yours?" She got up from the toilet and leaned against the doorframe that led into his bedroom.

"Honey, don't tell me you've never heard of Bobby Tom Denton. He's only the most famous wide-out to ever play football."

"Wide-out?"

"Wide receiver. They're the ones quarterbacks throw to. I want to tell you, the day he blew out his knee and had to retire was one of the worst days in the history of pro ball."

"What's he doing now?"

He yanked on a pair of khakis. "Mostly putting up a good front. He lives in Telarosa, Texas, with his wife Gracie and their new baby. He acts like his family and the charity foundation he runs are all he needs in life."

"Maybe they are."

"You don't know Bobby Tom. From the time he was a little kid, he lived to play ball."

"It sounds as if he's doing some important work."

"The Denton Foundation?" He pulled a dark brown polo shirt over his head. "It does a lot of good, don't get me wrong. This golf tournament alone brings in a couple hundred thousand for a whole bunch of good causes, but I guess the way I look at it, there are lots of people in this country who could run something like that, but there's only one guy in the world who can catch a football like B.T."

In Jane's opinion, running a charitable foundation seemed a lot more important than catching a football, but she knew when to hold her tongue. "Retirement could be exciting. Think about yourself, for example. You'll have the chance to start a whole new life while you're still young."

"I like the life I have."

Before she could say anything else, he closed the distance between them and pulled her into his arms, where he proceeded to kiss her until she was breathless. She felt him harden through his slacks, but it was daytime, and he drew back with obvious reluctance to gaze down at her through heated eyes. "You ready to cry 'uncle' yet?"

Her eyes drifted to his mouth, and she sighed. "Just about."

"You know, don't you, that I won't make it easy on you. I'm not going to be satisfied with anything less than stripping you naked in broad daylight."

"I know."

"I might even make you walk around outside."

She regarded him glumly. "I wouldn't be surprised."

" 'Course I wouldn't make you do something like that stark naked."

"You're all heart."

"I'd prob'ly let you wear one of those nice pairs of high heels you've got."

"A man in a million."

He started to kiss her again. Then he was cupping her breasts, and they were both breathing so hard she didn't ever want to stop. Just that morning she'd told herself she was going to stop playing games with him, and now was the time. With one hand she reached for the hem of her nightshirt.

The telephone rang. She inched her nightshirt higher and continued kissing Cal, but the phone's persistence ruined the mood.

He groaned. "Why isn't the answering machine picking up?"

She let go of the nightshirt. "The cleaning women were here yesterday afternoon. They must have turned it off by mistake."

"I'll bet it's Dad. He was going to call me this morning." He relinquished her with reluctance, rested his forehead against hers for a few moments, then kissed the tip of her nose.

She couldn't believe it. She'd finally worked up the nerve to let him see her pudgy body, and the stupid phone had to ring! Giving him his privacy, she headed for her bathroom, where she showered, then dressed. Afterward, she made her way to the kitchen.

Cal was slipping his wallet into the pocket of his khakis. "That was Dad on the phone. He and Mom are meeting for lunch in Asheville today. I hope he can convince her to put an end to this craziness and move back home. I can't believe she's being so stubborn."

"There are two people involved in that marriage."

"And one of them is bullheaded."

She'd given up arguing with him about this. He was convinced that his mother was at fault in his parents' separation because she was the one who'd moved out, and nothing Jane said could persuade him that there might be another side to the story.

"Do you know what Mom told Ethan when he offered her some pastoral counseling? She told him to mind his own business."

She lifted an eyebrow at him. "Ethan might not be the best person to offer counsel."

"He's her pastor!"

She barely resisted rolling her eyes. Instead, she patiently pointed out the obvious. "You and Ethan are both too involved personally to be counseling either one of them."

"Yeah, I guess." As he picked up his car keys from the counter, he frowned. "I just don't understand how something like this could happen."

She gazed at Cal's troubled face and found herself wishing Lynn and Jim could settle their differences, not only for themselves but for their sons. Cal and Ethan loved their parents, and this estrangement was painful for them.

Once again she wondered what had happened to Lynn and Jim Bonner. For years they seemed to have managed to live together very well. Why had they separated now?

Jim Bonner strode into the Blue Ridge dining room at the Grove Park Inn, Asheville's most famous hotel and resort. It had always been one of Lynn's favorite places, and he'd asked her to meet him here for lunch. Perhaps its pleasant associations would soften his stubborn wife's heart.

The Grove Park Inn had been constructed at the turn of the century to serve as a luxurious refuge from the summer heat for the nation's wealthy. Built into the side of Sunset Mountain from rough-hewn granite, the massive structure was either ugly or splendid, depending on your viewpoint.

The Blue Ridge dining room, like the rest of the hotel, was furnished in the rustic charm of the Arts and Crafts movement. He walked down several steps that led to a lower dining area and spotted Lynn sitting at a small table positioned by the tall windows that overlooked the mountains. He drank in the sight of her.

Since he refused to visit her on Heartache Mountain, he either had to telephone or watch for her when he knew she'd be coming to town. He made excuses to drop by church on Wednesday evenings when she met with the worship committee and kept his eyes peeled for her car in the Ingles grocery store lot.

For her part, she seemed to do her best to avoid him. She always chose times when she knew she wouldn't run into him to stop at the house, either when he had office hours or was making his hospital rounds. He'd been relieved when she'd agreed to meet him today.

His pleasure at the sight of her faded into irritation. This past month didn't seem to have changed her, while he felt bruised and old. She wore a loosely woven lavender-and-cream jacket that he'd always liked, along with silver earrings and a silky top and skirt. As he pulled out the heavy wooden chair across from her, he tried to convince himself those were marks of sleeplessness he saw under her eyes, but they were probably only shadows cast by the light coming in through the windows.

She gave him the same cordial nod she used to greet strangers. What had happened to the enchanting young mountain girl who'd giggled uncontrollably and decorated his dinner table with dandelions?

The waiter approached, and Jim ordered two glasses of their favorite wine, only to have Lynn request a Diet Pepsi instead. After the waiter left, he regarded her inquisitively.

"I've gained five pounds," she explained.

"You're on hormone replacement therapy. You have to expect some weight gain."

"It's not the pills that are doing it to me; it's Annie's cooking. If something doesn't have a stick of butter in it, she doesn't think it's edible."

"Sounds to me as if the best way to get those five pounds off would be to come home."

She paused for a moment before she spoke. "Heartache Mountain has always been my home."

He felt as if a cold draft had blown across the back of his neck. "I'm talking about your real home. Our home."

Instead of responding, she picked up the menu and began to study it. The waiter delivered their drinks and took their order. While they waited for their food, Lynn spoke of the weather and a concert she had attended the week before. She reminded him to have the air conditioner checked and talked about some new road construction. It made him ache inside. This beautiful woman who used to speak only from her heart now never did.

She seemed determined to avoid anything personal, but he knew she wouldn't be able to avoid talking about their sons. "Gabe called from Mexico last night. Apparently neither of his brothers has seen fit to tell him you've moved out."

Concern furrowed her brow. "You didn't say anything, did you? He's got enough to deal with as it is. I don't want him worrying."

"No, I didn't say anything."

Her relief was visible. "I'm so worried about him. I wish he'd come home."

"Maybe someday."

"I'm worried about Cal, too. Have you noticed?"

"He looks fine to me."

"Better than fine. I saw him in town yesterday, and I've never seen him look happier. I don't understand it, Jim. He's always been a good judge of character, and that woman's going to break his heart. Why can't he see her for what she is?"

Jim grew grim at the thought of his new daughter-in-law. He'd seen her on the street a few days earlier, and she'd walked right past him, just as if he didn't exist. She'd refused to show up at church, declined social invitations from some of the nicest women in town, and even failed to attend a testimonial dinner for Cal the Jaycees had given. The only person she'd give the time of day to seemed to be Kevin Tucker. None of it boded well for his son.

"I don't understand it," Lynn went on. "How can he be so happy when he's married to such a . . . a . . ."

"Cold-hearted bitch."

"I hate her. I can't help it. She's going to hurt him badly, and he doesn't deserve it." Her brow furrowed, and her voice developed a huskiness that indicated the depth of her upset. "All these years we've waited for him to settle down and marry someone nice, someone who loved him, but look who he's picked—a woman who doesn't care about anyone but herself." She regarded him with troubled eyes. "I wish there was something we could do."

"We can't even straighten out our own troubles, Lynn. How could we expect to solve Cal's?"

"It's not the same thing. He's— He's vulnerable."

"And we're not?"

For the first time, she sounded vaguely defensive. "I didn't say that."

Bitterness tightened his chest and rose like bile in his throat. "I've just about had it with this cat and mouse game you're playing. I'm warning you, Lynn; I'm not going to put up with it much longer."

He realized right away that he'd made a mistake. Lynn didn't like being backed into a corner, and she always met aggression with her own brand of quiet stubbornness. Now she regarded him levelly. "Annie told me to tell you she doesn't want you calling the house."

"Well, that's just too bad."

"She's really angry with you."

"Annie's been angry with me since I was eight years old."

"That's not true. Her health is making her cranky."

"If she'd stop putting a stick of butter in everything, she might start feeling better." He leaned back in the chair. "You know why she doesn't want us talking. It's because she's got a good thing going having you on Heartache Mountain full-time to take care of her. She won't give that up easily."

"Is that what you think?"

"You bet it is."

"You're wrong. She's trying to protect me."

"From me? Yeah, right." His voice softened. "Damn it, Lynn, I've been a good husband to you. I don't deserve to be treated like this."

She looked down at her plate, and then up at him, her eyes full of pain. "It's always about you, isn't it, Jim? From the very beginning everything has revolved around you. What you deserve. How you felt. What kind of mood you were in. I've built my life around trying to please you, and it hasn't worked."

"That's ridiculous. You're blowing this whole thing out of proportion. Look, forget everything I said that night. I didn't mean any of it. I was just—I don't know—having some kind of mid-life crisis or something. I like you the way you are. You've been the best wife a man could ever have. Let's just forget all of this happened and go back to the way things were."

"I can't do that because *you* can't do it."

"You don't know what you're talking about."

"Someplace inside you there's this knot of resentment that formed the day we got married and has never gone away. If you want me back, it's only out of habit. I don't think you like me very much, Jim. Maybe you never have."

"That's absurd. You're overdramatizing this whole thing. Just tell me what you want, and I'll give it to you."

"Right now I want to please myself."

"Fine! Please yourself. I'm not standing in your way, and you don't have to run away to do it."

"Yes, I do."

"You're going to blame me for everything, aren't you? Go ahead! You explain to your sons what a bad guy I am, then. And while you explain it, remind them that *you're* the one who's walking out on a thirty-seven-year marriage, not me."

She regarded him levelly. "You know what I think? I think you walked out on our marriage the day we said our vows."

"I knew you'd start throwing up the past at me. Now you're going to blame me for the sins of an eighteen-year-old boy."

"That's not what I'm doing. I'm just tired of living with the part of you that's still eighteen, the part of you that still hasn't dealt with the fact that you knocked up Amber Lynn Glide and had to take the consequences. The boy who thinks he deserves something better has never gone away." Her voice grew soft and weary. "I'm tired of living with the guilt, Jim. I'm tired of always feeling as if I have to prove myself."

"Then stop doing it! I haven't made you live that way. You've done it to yourself."

"And now I have to figure out how to undo it."

"I can't believe how selfish you're being. Do you want a divorce, Lynn? Is that what all this is leading up to? Because if you want a divorce, you just tell me now. I'm not living in this limbo forever. Just tell me right now."

He waited to see her shock. What he had suggested was unthinkable. But there was no shock, and he began to panic. Why didn't she tell him to stop talking so crazy, that their situation wasn't nearly bad enough to even think about divorce? But once again, he'd miscalculated.

"Maybe that would be for the best."

He went numb.

She got a faraway look on her face, almost dreamy. "You know what I wish? I wish we could start all over. I wish we could meet each other again with no past history, just two strangers getting acquainted. Then, if we didn't like what we found, we could walk away. And if we did like what we found . . ." Her voice grew thick with emotion. "The playing field would be level. There'd be a—a balance of power."

"Power?" Fear churned inside him. "I don't know what you're talking about."

She regarded him with a look of pity that cut right through him. "You really don't, do you? For thirty-seven years you've had all the power in our relationship, and I've had none. For thirty-seven years I've had to live with the fact that I was a second-class citizen in our marriage. But I can't live that way anymore."

She spoke so patiently, like an adult explaining something to a child, and it enraged him.

"Fine!" He lost his ability to think clearly and acted on raw emotion. "You can have your divorce. And I hope you choke on it."

He threw down a wad of bills he didn't bother to count, shot up from his chair, and stalked from the dining room without a backward look. As he hit the hallway, he realized he was sweating. She'd turned his life upside down from the day he'd met her.

She wanted to talk about *power*! From the time she was fifteen years old, she'd had the power to twist his life out of shape. If he hadn't met her, everything might have been different. He wouldn't have come back to Salvation and been a family doctor, that's for sure. He'd have gone into research, or maybe he'd have hooked up with one of the big international outfits and traveled around the world to do the work on infectious diseases he'd always dreamed about. A million possibilities would have been open to him if he hadn't been forced to marry her, but because of her, he hadn't explored any of them. He'd had a wife and children to support, so he'd gone back to his hometown with his tail between his legs and taken over his father's practice.

Resentment seethed inside him. He'd had the course of his life irrevocably changed when he was still too young to understand what was happening. She'd done that to him, the same woman who'd sat in that dining room and told him she had no power. She'd fucked up his life forever, and now she blamed him.

He stopped in his track as all the blood rushed from his head. Jesus. She was right.

He sagged down on one of the couches that sat along the wall and dropped his head into his hands. Seconds lapsed, turning into minutes as all the mental barriers he'd erected against the truth grew transparent.

She'd been right when she'd said he'd always resented her, but his bitterness had become such an old, familiar companion he hadn't recognized it for what it was. She was right. After all this time, he still blamed her.

The many ways he'd punished her over the years came flying back in his face: the fault-finding and subtle put-downs, his blind stubbornness and refusal to acknowledge her needs. All those little punishments he'd inflicted against this woman who was the closest thing he had to a soul.

He pushed his fingertips into his eye sockets and shook his head. She was right about everything.

17

Jane's hands trembled as she stroked almond-scented lotion over every inch of her thirty-four-year-old body, including her rounding belly. Sunlight streamed through her bedroom window, and in the next room Cal's suitcase lay open on his bed, ready for his late afternoon flight to Austin. She'd made up her mind this morning, and now she wanted to do it before she lost her nerve.

She brushed her hair until it shone, then stared at her naked body in the mirrored wall behind the whirlpool. She tried to imagine how it would look to Cal, but all she could think about was how it wouldn't look. It wouldn't look like it belonged to a twenty-year-old centerfold.

With an exclamation of disgust, she stalked back into her bedroom, snatched up her prettiest robe, an apricot silk with a border of deep green laurel leaves at the hem and sleeves, and jabbed her arms into it. She was a physicist, for goodness sakes! A successful professional woman! Since when did she decide to measure her self-worth in terms of her hip size?

And since when could she respect a man who viewed her as only a body? If her measurements didn't meet Cal's standards, then it was long past time she found that out. They couldn't have a lasting relationship if the only thing that kept him interested in her was the mystery of what she looked like naked.

She wanted a real relationship more than she'd ever wanted anything. It hurt too much to be afraid all the caring was one-sided. She needed to stop procrastinating and find out if anything lasting existed between them, or if she were merely another touchdown for Cal Bonner to score.

She heard the faint whir of the garage door sliding open, and her heart jumped into her throat. He was home. Misgivings shot through her. She should have picked a more convenient time, a day when he wasn't getting ready to fly halfway across the country to a golf tournament. She should have waited until she was calmer, more sure of herself. She should have—

Her cowardice disgusted her and she resisted a nearly irresistible urge to grab every article of clothing in her closet and stuff herself into all of them until she was the size of a polar bear. Today she would begin the process of discovering whether she'd given her heart away in vain.

Taking a deep breath, she secured the robe's sash in a bow and padded barefoot into the hallway.

"Jane?"

"I'm up here." As she stopped at the top of the stairs, the thudding of her heart made her feel light-headed.

He appeared in the foyer below. "Guess who I—" He broke off as he looked up and saw her standing above him at one o'clock in the afternoon wearing nothing but a slinky silk robe.

He smiled and tucked the fingers of one hand in the pocket of his jeans. "You sure do know how to welcome a guy home."

She couldn't have spoken if she wanted to. Heart pounding, she lifted her hands to the robe's sash while her heart whispered a silent prayer. *Please let him want me for myself and not just because I'm a challenge. Please let him love me just a little bit.* Her clumsy fingers tugged on the robe's sash, and her gaze locked with his as the frail garment parted. With a shrug of her shoulders, she let it slide down her body and fall in a puddle at her feet.

Warm sunlight washed her body, revealing everything: her small breasts and rounding belly, her *huge* hips and very ordinary legs.

Cal looked dazed. She rested one hand lightly on the banister and moved slowly down the steps, wearing nothing but a fragile veil of almond-scented lotion.

Cal's lips parted. His eyes glazed.

Her foot touched the bottom step, and she smiled.

He licked his lips as if they had gone very dry and spoke in a voice that held a slight croak. "Turn around, Eth."

"Not on your life."

Jane's head shot up. With a gasp of dismay, she saw the Reverend Ethan Bonner standing in the archway just behind Cal.

He studied her with undisguised interest. "I hope I didn't show up at a bad time."

With a strangled moan, she spun around and dashed back up the stairs, all too aware of the view she presented them from behind. She scrambled for her robe and, crumpling it in front of herself, fled to her bedroom, where she slammed the door and sagged against it, more mortified than she had ever been in her life.

It seemed as if only a few seconds passed before she heard a soft rapping. "Honey?" Cal's voice held the tentative note of a man who knew he only had a few minutes to disarm a ticking bomb.

"I'm not here. Go away." To her dismay, tears stung her eyes. She had thought about this for so long, placed so much importance on it, and now it had ended in disaster.

The door bumped against her. "Step back now, sweetheart, and let me in."

She moved away, too dispirited to argue. With the silk

robe still crumpled in front of her, she pressed her bare back to the adjacent wall.

He entered gingerly, like a soldier expecting land mines. "You all right, sweetheart?"

"Stop calling me that! I've never been so embarrassed."

"Don't be, honey. You made poor Eth's day. Hell, you probably made his whole year, not to mention mine."

"Your brother saw me *naked*! I stood there on the stairs, naked as the day I was born, making a complete fool of myself."

"Now that's where you're wrong. There was nothing foolish about the sight of you naked. Why don't you let me hang that robe up for you before it gets ruined."

She clutched it more tightly to her midriff. "He was *looking* at me the whole time, and you didn't say a word. Why didn't you warn me we weren't alone?"

"You sort of took me by surprise, sweetheart. I wasn't thinking straight. And Eth couldn't help looking. It's been years since he's seen a beautiful naked woman in the flesh. I'd be worried about him if he hadn't looked."

"He's a minister!"

"It was a blessed event. You sure you don't want me to hang that robe up?"

"You're making a joke out of this."

"Absolutely not. Only an insensitive jerk would think something this traumatic was funny. Tell you what. I'll go downstairs right this minute and kill him before he gets away."

She refused to smile. Instead, she decided to pout. It was something she'd always wanted to do, but until that moment, she'd never quite been able to figure out how to. Now it seemed to come naturally. "I've just received the shock of my life, and you're treating it as a big joke."

"I'm a pig." He drew her a few inches away from the wall and rubbed his hands along her bare spine. "If I were you, I'd tell me to get lost because I don't even deserve to breathe the same air as you."

"That's so true."

"Honey, I'm really getting worried about that pretty robe. Squashed up between us, it's getting ruined. Don't you think you should let me have it?"

She pressed her cheek to his chest, enjoying the warm stroking of his hands along her back, but still not quite done with her pout. "I won't ever be able to look him in the eye again. He already thinks I'm a heathen. This will prove it."

"True, but Ethan's had a lifelong attraction to women with sin in their blood. It's sort of his tragic flaw."

"He can't have missed the fact that I'm pregnant."

"He'll keep his mouth shut if I ask him to."

She sighed, giving up her pout. "I'm going to have to go through with this, aren't I?"

He cupped her cheek and gently stroked his thumb along her jaw. "I'm pretty sure you passed the point of no return when you hit that top step."

"I suppose."

"But if you don't mind, since you've waited this long, hold out for just a few seconds more so I can open those curtains the rest of the way and get more light in here."

She sighed as he made his way to the window. "You're not going to make this easy, are you?"

"Nope." He tugged on the cord, letting the bright early-afternoon sunlight flood into the room.

"What about Ethan?"

"My brother's no fool. He's long gone by now."

"You take off your clothes first."

"No way. You've seen me naked dozens of times. It's my turn."

"If you think I'm going to be undressed while you lie there fully clothed . . ."

"That's exactly what I think." He walked over to her bed and stacked the pillows against the headboard. Then he kicked off his shoes and stretched out, crossing his arms behind his head like someone about to enjoy a good movie.

She was torn between amusement and irritation. "What if I've changed my mind?"

"We both know you've got too much pride to back off now. Tell me if you want me to close my eyes."

"As if you would." Why had she made such a big deal out of this? For a brilliant woman, she was a complete idiot. Damn him anyway. Why hadn't he just pulled that robe out of her hands and put an end to all this? But, no. That was too easy. Instead, he lay there with the glint of challenge in those gray eyes, and she knew he was testing her mettle. Her irritation grew. This was *his* test, not hers. He was the one who had something to prove, and it was time to give him his chance.

She shut her eyes and dropped the robe.

Dead silence.

A dozen thoughts ran through her mind, all of them horrible: he hated her body, he'd fainted from the sight of her hips, her pregnant belly repulsed him.

The last thought lit the fuse to her temper. He was a *worm*! Lower than a worm! What kind of man was repulsed by the body of the woman carrying his child? He was the lowest form of life on earth.

Her eyes flew open. "I knew it! I knew you'd hate my body!" She slammed her hands on her hips, marched over to the bed, and glared down at him. "Well, for your information, mister, all those cute little sex kittens in your past might have had perfect bodies, but they don't know a lepton from a proton, and if you think that I'm going to stand here and let you judge me by the size of my hips and because my belly's not flat, then you're in for a rude awakening." She jabbed her finger at him. "This is the way a grown woman looks, buster! This body was designed by God to be functional, not to be stared at by some hormonally im-

balanced jock who can only get aroused by women who
still own Barbie dolls!''

"Damn. Now I've got to gag you.'' With one swift motion, he pulled her down on the bed, rolled on top of her,
and covered her lips with his own.

His kiss was deep and fierce. It started at her mouth, then
traveled on to her breasts, her belly, the backs of her knees,
with several thrilling stops in between. Her irritation faded
as need took its place.

She wasn't certain when he got rid of his own clothes
because she quickly lost herself in the pleasures of feeling
that strong, solid body beneath her hands and lips. For a
man of action, he'd always been a leisurely lover, and today
was no exception. As the bright sunlight pooled over their
bodies, he satisfied his curiosity by exploring every inch of
her, turning her this way and that, across the light, toward
the light until she begged him.

"Please . . . I can't take any more.''

He nuzzled her breast with his lips and his husky breath
fell hot over her damp skin. "You're going to have to take
a lot more before we're through.''

She punished him for his teasing with a torment of her
own, using her mouth on him in the way she knew he
loved, but the deep, moist taking also served to inflame her
own need, so that when he finally reached his limit, she
had also reached hers. He covered her with his body and
entered her. She immediately climaxed.

"Now see what you've done,'' she complained when she
came back to earth.

His eyes were the deep gray of a spring thunderstorm,
his voice smoky with the most delicious sort of menace as
he pushed himself deep inside her. "Poor honey. I guess
I'll have to start all over again with you.''

"I'm not interested anymore,'' she lied.

"Then close your eyes and think about something else
'til I'm done.''

She laughed and he kissed her, and in no time at all they were lost in each other. She had never felt so free. In shedding her clothes, she had also shed the last of her defenses.

"I love you," she whispered, as he entered her. "I love you so much."

He kissed her lips as if he were sipping her words. "Sweet . . . My sweet. So beautiful . . ."

Their bodies found a rhythm as ancient as time, and they climbed together through every barrier that separated them. As he loved her with his body, she knew with a fierce certainty that he also loved her with his heart. It could be no other way, and the knowledge catapulted her over the top. Together, they touched creation.

They spent the next few hours in various states of undress. He allowed her to wear a pair of powder blue sandals, but nothing else. She allowed him to wear his black bath towel, but insisted he keep it draped around his neck.

They ate a late lunch in bed, where they played sexual games with the juicy slices of an orange. Afterward, as they showered together, she knelt before him with the water pouring over them and loved him until they both lost control.

They were insatiable. She felt as if she'd been created only to please this man and, in turn, take pleasure only from him. She had never been so well loved, so certain of her powers as a woman. She felt brilliant and strong, soft and giving, utterly fulfilled, and although he hadn't spoken the words, she knew in the very center of her being that he loved her. Such intensity of emotion couldn't be coming only from her.

He postponed leaving until he had barely enough time to get to the airport. As the Jeep flew down the driveway, she smiled and hugged herself.

Everything was going to be all right.

*   *   *

The best country western band in Telarosa, Texas, played a lively two-step, but Cal turned down invitations to dance from a Dallas Cowboy cheerleader and a knockout Austin socialite. He was a pretty good dancer, but tonight he wasn't in the mood, and not just because he'd played a semilousy round of golf in the tournament that day. Depression had settled on him as thick and dark as mountain midnight.

Part of the reason for his depression sidled up next to him, looking a lot more cheerful than a man who'd given up football should ever look. A blond-haired baby girl, who showed every sign of being a future mankiller, snuggled in the crook of his arm, occupying the same space all those game balls used to take up. As far as Cal could tell, the only times Wendy Susan Denton hadn't been glued in her daddy's arm were when Bobby Tom had been swinging a golf club or letting her mother nurse her.

"Did Gracie show you the new addition we put on the house?" Bobby Tom Denton said. "With the baby and everything, we decided we wanted more room. Plus, ever since Gracie was elected mayor of Telarosa, she's needed a home office."

"Gracie showed me, B.T." Cal glanced around him, looking for an escape route, but he couldn't find one. It occurred to him that having spent a few minutes alone with B.T.'s wife, Gracie Snow Denton, had been one of the few pleasures of this weekend. At the time, Bobby Tom had been charming sports' reporters and carrying Wendy around, so Cal hadn't been forced to look at that delicate wiggling bundle and see his own future.

To his surprise, Cal liked Wendy's mom a lot, even though Mayor Gracie wasn't the type of woman anybody ever figured a legend like Bobby Tom would marry. He'd always hung around with gorgeous bombshells, while Gracie was pretty much a cute BB. She sure was nice, though. Straightforward and genuinely caring about people. Sort of like the Professor, although she didn't have the Professor's habit of fading out in the middle of a conversation to ponder some theory only she and a dozen other people on the planet could possibly understand.

"Gracie and I sure had ourselves some fun designing the new addition on the house." Bobby Tom grinned and pushed his Stetson back on his head. Cal decided Bobby Tom could give Ethan a few lessons when it came to being movie-star handsome, although B.T. had more character lines in his face than the reverend. Still, he was a good-looking son of a gun.

"And did she tell you about the brick street I bought from that town in West Texas? Gracie found out they were tearing it up to put in asphalt, so I went over there and made a deal with them for it. Nothin' like used brick for beauty. Be sure you take a look at the back of the house and see what we did with it."

Bobby Tom went on about antique brick and wide-plank flooring as if they were the most important things in the world, while the baby nestled blissfully in the crook of his arm sucking her fists and making goo-goo eyes at her adoring papa. Cal felt as if he were suffocating to death.

Just two hours earlier, Cal had overheard a conversation the great wide receiver was having with Phoebe Calebow, the Stars' owner, about *breast-feeding*! It seemed B.T. wasn't sure Gracie was *doing it* right. He didn't think she was taking it *seriously* enough. Bobby Tom, who'd never taken anything but football seriously, had acted as if breast-feeding a baby was the most important topic in the world!

Even now, the memory made Cal start to sweat. All this time Cal had figured Bobby Tom was just putting on a front, pretending everything was wonderful in his life, but now he knew Bobby Tom *believed* it. He didn't seem to realize anything was wrong. The fact that the greatest wide-out in the history of pro ball had turned into a man who was centering his life around a wife and a baby and wide-plank flooring was horrifying! Never in a million years would Cal have thought that the legendary Bobby Tom Denton could have forgotten who he was, but that's exactly what had happened.

To his relief, Gracie came up and drew Bobby Tom away. Just before they walked off, Cal saw the look of utter contentment on his face as he gazed down at his wife, and it felt like a kick delivered to his very own stomach.

He finished off his beer and tried to tell himself he'd never once looked at the Professor like that, but the thing was, he couldn't be sure. The Professor'd been turning him inside out lately, and who knew what kind of goofy expression he had on his face when he was near her.

If only she hadn't told him she loved him, he might not feel so panicky. Why did she have to say those words? At first when she'd said them, he'd felt kind of good about it. There was something satisfying about winning the approval of a woman as smart and funny and sweet as the Professor. But that insanity had vanished when he'd hit Telarosa and run head-on into Bobby Tom Denton's life after football.

Bobby Tom might be happy with all this permanency crap, but Cal knew he couldn't ever be. There was nothing waiting for him on the other side of playing ball, no charity foundation to run, no honest work he could care about, nothing that would let him hold up his head like a man should. And that, he admitted to himself, was the crux of it.

How could a man be a man without honest work? Bobby Tom had the Denton Foundation, but Cal didn't have B.T.'s talent for making money multiply. Instead, he pretty much let it sit around in a few accounts here and there and pick up interest. Cal didn't have any worthy life waiting for him on the other side of the goal line. All the other side of the goal line held for him was exactly nothing.

It also held Jane, and yesterday afternoon when he'd said good-bye to her, he'd known she was no longer thinking about the short term like he was. She was thinking about wide-plank flooring and monogrammed bath towels and where they should settle down when they were old. But he wasn't even close to being ready for that, and he didn't want her telling him she loved him! Next thing, she'd be asking him to look at paint chips and pick out wall-to-wall carpeting. Now that she'd said the words, she was going to expect him to do something about it, and he wasn't ready for that. Not yet. Not when the only worthy work he knew how to do was throw a football. Not now when he was facing the toughest season of his life.

While Cal was playing golf in Texas, Jane took long walks up the mountain and daydreamed about the future. She considered places they might live and ways she could rearrange her schedule so she could occasionally go on road trips with him. On Sunday afternoon she pulled the ugly rose metallic wallpaper from the walls of the breakfast nook and made a pot of homemade chicken noodle soup.

When she awakened on Monday morning to the sound of the shower, she realized Cal had returned some time after she'd fallen asleep last night and was disappointed that he hadn't slipped into bed with her. In the past few weeks she'd gotten into the habit of keeping him company while he shaved, but the bathroom door remained firmly shut, and it wasn't until she made her way to the kitchen for breakfast that she finally met up with him.

"Welcome home." She spoke softly and waited for that moment he would take her in his arms. Instead, he muttered something unintelligible.

"How was your golf game?" she asked.

"Crap."

That explained his bad mood.

He carried his cereal bowl over to the sink and splashed it full of water. As he turned, he stabbed one finger toward the bare walls of the breakfast nook where she'd stripped off the wallpaper. "I don't like coming home and finding my house torn apart."

"You can't have liked those awful roses."

"It doesn't matter whether I liked them or not. You should have talked to me before you took it on yourself to start redecorating my house."

The tender lover she'd spent the weekend daydreaming about had disappeared, and uneasiness crept through her. She'd begun to think of this awful place as her house, too, but obviously he didn't regard it the same way. She drew a deep breath and repressed her hurt as she struggled to speak reasonably. "I didn't think you'd mind."

"Well, I do."

"All right. We can pick out some new paper. I'll be happy to put it up for you."

A look of abject horror crossed his face. "I don't pick out wallpaper, Professor! Not ever! And neither do you, so just leave it alone." He snatched up his car keys from the counter.

"You want to leave the wall like that?"

"You bet I do."

She debated whether she was going to tell him to go to hell or cut him some slack. Despite her hurt, she decided on the later. She could always tell him to go to hell later. "I made some homemade chicken noodle soup. Will you be back in time for dinner?"

"I don't know. You'll see me when you see me. Don't try to tie me down, Professor. I won't have it." With that, he disappeared into the garage.

She sat down on one of the kitchen chairs and told herself not to overdramatize what had just happened. He was jet-lagged, upset about performing badly in the golf tournament in front of his friends, and that had made him surly. There was no reason to believe his withdrawal had anything to do with what had happened between them the day he'd left. Despite this morning's churlish display, Cal was a decent man. He wasn't going to turn against her just because she'd taken off her clothes in broad daylight and told him she loved him.

She made herself eat half a piece of toast while memories of all the reasons she'd been reluctant to let him see her naked came back to her. What if her fears had proved correct? What if she'd stopped being a challenge to him, and he was no longer interested in having her in his life? Two days ago, she'd been so certain he loved her, but now she wasn't sure. About anything.

She realized she was brooding and got up, but instead of going to work, she found herself wandering through the house. The telephone rang, two quick tones that indicated a call was coming in on Cal's business line, which she never answered.

As she passed the door of his study, the machine clicked on, and she heard a voice she remembered all too well. "Cal, it's Brian. Look, I have to talk to you right away. While I was on vacation, I figured out how we can do this. Nothing like a white sand beach to unlock the brain cells; I'm just sorry it took so long. Anyway, I met with someone over the weekend to make sure it was possible, and it looks like we have a winner. But if we're going to act on it, we should do it now." He paused and his voice dropped. "I didn't want to use your fax for obvious reasons, so I sent a report to you express mail on Saturday that explains everything. You should get it this morning. Call me as soon as you read it." He chuckled. "Happy anniversary."

She remembered Cal's attorney, Brian Delgado, all too well: greedy eyes, arrogant carriage, disdainful manner. Something about the call disturbed her, probably that gloating note she'd heard in his voice. What an unpleasant man.

She glanced at her watch and saw that it was nine o'clock. She'd already wasted too much time this morning brooding, and she wasn't going to add Brian Delgado's call to her worry list. Returning to the kitchen, she poured herself a mug of coffee and carried it to her room, where she turned on her computer and logged in.

The date flashed, and the hair on the back of her neck prickled. For a moment she didn't understand why, but then she finally took in what she was seeing, and it came to her. *May 5.* She and Cal had been married two months ago today. *Happy anniversary.*

She pressed her fingertips to her lips. Was it a coincidence? She remembered Delgado's gloating. *I didn't want to use your fax for obvious reasons* ... What obvious reason? The fact that she might read this mysterious report before Cal saw it? She jumped up from her chair and went down to the study, where she sat behind the desk replaying the message and thinking.

Shortly before ten, the FedEx carrier arrived. She signed for the package, then carried it into Cal's study. Without a moment's hesitation, she ripped it open.

The report was several pages long and contained numerous typos, indicating that Delgado had probably prepared it himself. No wonder. Heartsick, she read every damning detail of Delgado's proposal and tried to absorb the fact that all the time Cal had been making love to her, he'd also been plotting revenge.

Over an hour passed before she could bring herself to go upstairs and pack. She called Kevin and asked him to come over. When he saw her packed suitcases, he immediately began to protest, but she refused to listen. Only after she threatened to carry the computer downstairs herself did he finally do as she wanted and load it into her car. Afterward, she made him leave, then she settled down to wait for Cal to come home. The old Jane would have slipped away, but the new one needed to face him down for the last time.

18

Jane hadn't left!

Cal spotted her through the sliding doors in the family room as she stood in the backyard looking up at Heartache Mountain. Muscles he hadn't even realized were tense began to ease. She was still here.

He'd been working out at the Y when Kevin had burst into the weight room with the news that his wife had packed up her computer and was getting ready to head back to Chicago. It had taken Kevin a couple of hours to track him down, and as Cal had sped home, still dressed in his sweat-soaked T-shirt and gray athletic shorts, he'd been terrified she might already have gone.

He still didn't understand why she wanted to do something so drastic. Granted, he'd been surly and rude this morning. He'd regretted it ever since, and he'd already made up his mind to get back in plenty of time to eat her homemade chicken noodle soup. But Jane wasn't one to run from a fight. He could easily imagine her taking a cast-iron skillet to his head, but he couldn't imagine her just packing up and leaving.

Now she stood below him, all buttoned up and battened down, and it occurred to him that the only person he knew whose clothes were as neat as hers were his younger brother's. She'd chosen one of those high-waisted cotton dresses to travel in, a creamy buttery color, with big tan buttons going all the way up the front. It fit her so loosely no one could tell she was pregnant, but she somehow still managed to look tidy and trim. The dress's full skirt covered most of her legs, but not those slender little ankles or the narrow feet tucked in a pair of simple leather sandals.

A tortoiseshell headband held her hair neatly back from her face. He watched the sunlight play in the golden strands and thought how pretty she looked. She was a classic, his wife, and as he watched her, he felt a jumble of emotions: tenderness and lust, confusion and resentment, anger and longing. Why did she have to go and get all temperamental on him now? One bad disposition was more than enough for any family, and that bad disposition belonged to him.

But his disposition wasn't the real problem. A couple of hours in the bedroom, and he could make her forget all about what a prick he'd been this morning, let alone any asinine ideas she had about going back to Chicago. No, the real problem lay deeper. Why did she have to tell him she loved him? Didn't she understand that once those three words were spoken, nothing could ever be the same?

If only she'd come into his life ten years earlier, before he'd had to deal with getting older and the fact that he couldn't see anything but a blank space waiting for him after he stopped playing ball. It was easy for the Professor to think about settling down. She had worthwhile work to do that would keep her busy for the rest of her life. He didn't, and now he couldn't get past the feeling that his life was careening in a direction he wasn't ready for it to take, a direction that might suit Bobby Tom Denton, but sure as hell wasn't right for him.

As he reached for the handle on the sliding glass door, he felt certain of only one thing. Jane had worked herself into a serious snit, and the best place to coax her out of it was under the sheets. But before he could get her there, he had some serious making up to do.

"Hey, Professor."

Jane turned toward Cal's voice and shaded her eyes with her hand. He was rumpled, sweat-stained, and gorgeous as he walked out on the deck. Something caught in her throat, something large and painful that made her feel as if she were choking.

He leaned on the rail and gave her a wolfish grin. "I've been working out, and I haven't had time to shower, so unless you're in the mood for some really raunchy sex, you'd better run upstairs right now and turn that water on for me."

She pushed her hands in the pockets of her dress and slowly mounted the wooden stairs. How could he behave like this when he had done something so unforgivable?

"Brian Delgado called this morning." She stepped onto the deck.

"Uh-huh. What say you get right in the shower with me so you can scrub my back?"

"Delgado sent you a report. I read it."

That finally got his attention, although he didn't look particularly alarmed. "Since when did you get interested in reading about my contracts?"

"The report's about me."

His grin vanished. "Where is it?"

"On your desk." She looked him square in the eye and tried to swallow the bubble of pain that choked her voice. "You need to make a decision about me right away because you only have two days before the Preeze board of directors meets. Luckily, your attorney's already done the initial work. He's met with Jerry Miles, and the two of them have most of the sordid details sketched out. All you need to do is sign a check with lots of zeros."

"I don't know what you're talking about."

"Don't you dare lie to me!" She balled her hands into fists. "You told Delgado to ruin me!"

"I'm going to call him right now and straighten this out. It's a misunderstanding." He turned toward the sliding doors, but she moved forward before he could open them.

"A misunderstanding?" She couldn't hide her bitterness. "You give your attorney orders to destroy my career, and you call that a misunderstanding?"

"I never told him that. Just give me an hour, and then I'll explain everything."

"Explain it now."

He seemed to realize she deserved something more, and he moved away from the door toward the deck railing. "Tell me what was in that report."

"Delgado set it up with Jerry Miles, the director of Preeze, that you'll give the labs a grant on the condition that they get rid of me." She took a deep, unsteady breath. "Jerry's waiting to hear from you before he fires me, then he's planning to announce your generosity to the board of directors when they meet on Wednesday."

Cal cursed softly under his breath. "Wait till I get hold of that son of a bitch. This isn't the first time Delgado's gone off half-cocked."

"You're saying this whole thing is his idea?"

"Damn right it is."

Emotion stuck in her throat. "Don't do this, Cal. Don't play games with me."

Outrage flashed in his eyes. "You know I wouldn't do something like this!"

"Then you didn't have him investigate me? You didn't tell him to find out where I was most vulnerable and use it against me?"

He rubbed his chin with the back of his knuckles, looking more ill at ease than she'd ever seen him. "That was a long time ago. It's complicated."

"I'm very bright. Explain it."

He wandered back toward the sliding doors, and her heart sank as she noticed he couldn't meet her eyes. "You have to remember how things were between us when all this started. I've never been a man to let anyone get the best of me, and I wanted you punished." He tucked one thumb in the waistband of his shorts, then pulled it back out again. "I did tell Brian I intended to get even, and I ordered him to have you investigated so I could strike back at you."

"And what did your investigation turn up?"

"That you don't have any dark secrets." He finally looked at her. "That you're brilliant and dedicated. And that your work means everything to you."

"You hardly needed a team of detectives to figure that out."

"I didn't know that at the time."

"So you decided to take my work away from me," she said quietly.

No!" He gripped the door handle. "After the first few weeks, I cooled off and dropped the whole thing. I let it go!"

"I don't believe you. No lawyer would put something like this into motion without authorization."

"He had my authorization. Not for this, but ..." He pushed the door open and moved into the house. "I just never got around to telling him to back off, that's all!"

"Why is that?" she asked as she followed him.

"We just didn't talk about it." He stopped next to the fireplace. "There were a bunch of other things going on. One of my endorsements got screwed up. The whole thing was a mess, and it took a while to get straightened out. Then he went on vacation, and I ducked a couple of his calls."

"Why?"

"I wasn't in the mood to deal with contracts."

"I wasn't a contract."

"No. But I just didn't think what was happening between us was any of his damned business!" He looked frustrated. "It never occurred to me that he'd try to take action against you without my go-ahead."

"But it sounds as if you'd already given him that."

"Yes, but—" He opened his hand in a gesture that was oddly vulnerable. "Jane, I'm sorry. I didn't think for a minute he'd do anything without talking to me."

She should have felt better. After all, he hadn't been actively plotting against her this past month, but she still felt awful. "This wouldn't have happened if you'd picked up the phone and told him to call off his dogs. Why didn't you do it, Cal? Were you afraid you were going to lose your macho by backing off?"

"It just wasn't important, that's all. Things had settled down between us, and revenge was the last thing on my mind."

"Too bad you didn't let your bloodsucker know that."

He plowed his hand through his already rumpled hair. "Look, no harm's been done. I have no intention of giving Preeze a penny, and if anybody there tries to get rid of you, I'll slap them with a discrimination lawsuit so fast they won't know what hit them."

"It's my business, Cal, not yours."

"Just give me a couple of hours. I'll straighten it all out, I promise."

"And then what?" she asked quietly.

"Then you won't have to worry about anything like this again."

"That's not what I mean. After you straighten it out, what happens between us?"

"Nothing happens. Everything will be the way it was." He moved toward his study. "I'm going to make my phone calls, then I'll unload your car and we can go out to eat. I can't believe you even considered running away."

She followed him to his study, then stopped in the doorway. She rubbed her arms, but the chill she felt came from inside instead of outside. "I don't think we're going to be able to go back to the way things were."

"Sure we can." He moved toward his desk. "I swear to God, I'm going to fire Delgado."

"Don't blame him for what you started," she said softly.

He spun back toward her, his body rigid. "Don't you dare say that! *You're* the one who started this, and don't you forget it!"

"How can I when you throw it in my face every chance you get?"

He glared at her, and she glared back at him. Then she looked away. This game of assigning blame accomplished nothing.

She pushed her hands into the pockets of her dress and reminded herself that her worst fear had been groundless. He hadn't been plotting against her at the same time they were making love. But the awful knot in her stomach wouldn't go away. What had happened was merely a symbol of all the problems that lurked between them, problems she'd ignored or glossed over as if they didn't exist.

She remembered how hopeful she'd been only a few days earlier that he loved her. She remembered all the dream castles she'd built in her head. It was ironic that a person who'd been trained in the scientific method could be so swift to abandon logic for wishful thinking.

She withdrew her hands from her pockets and clasped them in front of her. "I need to know where we're headed, Cal, and what your feelings are toward me."

"What do you mean?"

The discomfort in his voice indicated that he knew exactly what she meant. "How do you feel about me?"

"You know how I feel."

"Actually, I don't."

"Then, you must not have been paying attention."

He was going to make this even more difficult than it

already was, but she wouldn't back away. The time for daydreaming had passed. She needed to know exactly where she stood. "The only direct remark I can ever remember you making is that you like me."

"Of course, I like you. You know that."

She met his eyes squarely and forced herself to speak the words that wanted to remain stuck in the back of her throat. "I told you I loved you."

His gaze dropped, and she realized he couldn't look her in the eye. "I'm— I guess I'm flattered."

She dug her fingernails into her palms. "I don't think so. I think my honesty has scared you to death. And I also think you don't love me back."

"What the hell does something like that mean anyway?" He stalked to his desk. "We've gotten along together better than either of us ever could have imagined, and we're going to have a baby. Why do we have to stick a label on it? I care about you, and in my mind that counts for a lot." He dropped down into his chair as if the discussion had come to an end.

She wouldn't leave it there. Perhaps she'd gained a bit of wisdom in the last few months, or maybe it was simply stubbornness, but it was time he added something more to this relationship than sex and a few laughs. "I'm afraid caring isn't enough for me when I think about our future."

He gestured toward her with an impatient hand. "The future will take care of itself. Neither of us wants to be boxed in right now."

"The last time we talked about it, the idea was that we'd get a divorce as soon as the baby is born. Do you still want that?"

"It's way ahead. How do I know what's going to happen?"

"But that's still your plan?"

"That was the original plan."

"And now?"

"I don't know. How can either of us know? One day at a time."

"I don't want to measure time in days any longer."

"Well, that's the way it has to be for now."

He wouldn't commit, and she could no longer accept anything less. Tears pushed at her eyes, but she refused to let them fall. She had to bail out now, while she still retained her dignity, and she intended to do it honestly.

"I'm afraid I can't handle this anymore, Cal. I didn't mean to fall in love with you—I know you didn't ask me to—but that's what happened. I seemed destined to screw up where you're concerned." She licked her dry lips. "I'm going back to Chicago."

He shot up from the desk. "Like hell you are!"

"I'll contact you after the baby's born, but until then, I'd appreciate it if you'd communicate with me through my lawyer. I promise I won't make things tough for you when it comes to visitation."

"You're running away." He glared down at her, clearly on the attack. "You don't have the guts to stay and work this out, so you want to run away."

She struggled to speak calmly. "What is there to work out? You're still going to want a divorce."

"I'm not in any hurry."

"But you're still planning on it."

"So what? We're friends, and there's no reason for it to turn nasty."

Pain swelled in her chest as he confirmed what she already knew. He didn't view their marriage as permanent. He was merely marking time. She turned away from him and walked out into the foyer.

He was beside her in an instant. A vein throbbed at his temple, and his expression was stark. She wasn't surprised. A man like Cal didn't take well to ultimatums.

"If you think I'm going to come running after you, you're wrong! Once you go out that door, our marriage is

over for sure. You're out of my life, do you hear me?''
She nodded stiffly and blinked away the tears.
"I mean it, Jane!"
Without a word, she turned and walked from his house.

Cal didn't stand around to watch her drive away. Instead,
he kicked the door shut and stalked into the kitchen, where
he grabbed a bottle of scotch from the pantry. For a moment he couldn't make up his mind whether to drink it or
smash it against the wall. He'd be damned before he let her
push him into something he wasn't ready for.

He wrenched off the cap and tilted the bottle to his lips.
The scotch burned all the way down. If this was the way
she wanted things, then fine. He dashed the back of his
hand across his lips. It was about time his life got back to
normal.

But instead of feeling better, he wanted to throw back
his head and howl. He took another swallow and nursed
his grievances against her.

He'd offered her more than he'd ever offered any
woman—he'd offered her his damned friendship!—and
what did she do? She threw it right back in his face just
because he didn't feel like getting down on one knee and
volunteering for a life sentence picking out fucking *wallpaper*!

His hand clenched around the bottle. He wouldn't give
in. There were lots of women out there who were younger
and prettier, women who didn't see the need to pick fights
with him over every little thing, who'd do what he said and
then leave him alone. That's what he wanted. Someone
young and beautiful who'd leave him alone.

He took another swig then went into his study where he
set about the business of getting seriously drunk.

Jane knew she couldn't leave until she'd said good-bye
to Annie. Neither could she give in to her grief right now,

so she blinked her eyes and took big, shuddering gulps of air as she drove to the top of Heartache Mountain. Lynn's car wasn't in sight, and she was grateful she could say good-bye to Annie without a hostile witness.

The house looked so different from when she'd first seen it. Cal had painted it white. He'd fixed the crooked shutters and the broken step. As she entered and called out Annie's name, she pushed away the memory of the laughter they'd shared while they'd worked.

When she reached the kitchen, she saw Annie through the screen door. She was sitting outside in the sun snapping green beans from a pottery bowl on her lap. As Jane watched the rhythmic motion of Annie's gnarled fingers, she wanted to take the bowl from her and snap the beans herself. Bean snapping was one task that hadn't been influenced by technology. It was performed exactly the same way now that it had been hundreds of years ago. It suddenly seemed to her that snapping those beans would bring something solid into her life, a link with all the women who had come before her, all the women throughout history who'd snapped beans and survived the heartache of men who didn't love them back.

She bit her lip, then stepped outside. Annie turned her head. " 'Bout time you decided to stop by."

She sat down in the tubular lawn chair next to Annie and regarded the bowl that rested in her lap on top of a piece of newspaper to collect scraps. At that moment, its contents seemed precious and utterly necessary to her well-being. "Can I do those?"

"I don't like waste."

"All right." Her hands trembled as she took the bowl. With utmost concentration, she bent her head, pulled out a bean, and carefully snapped off the ends. Apparently she didn't take off too much because Annie didn't criticize. She let the ends drop into her lap and focused on breaking the beans into bite-sized lengths.

"Those is store-bought beans. The ones from my garden'll be a lot better."

"I wish I were going to be here long enough to see them
come in." Her voice sounded almost normal. A little tone-
less, maybe. A shade tight. But almost normal.

"They'll be ready long before Cal has to leave for
trainin' camp and the two of you head back to Chicago."

Jane didn't say anything. Instead, she picked up another
bean, pushed her thumbnail into the end, and tore it off.

For the next few minutes she applied herself only to the
beans, while Annie watched a bluebird hop from one
branch to another in her magnolia tree. But instead of bringing her peace, Annie's quiet and the warmth of the sun on
her skin, along with the peaceful repetition of this woman's
task, made her defenses too complicated to keep in place,
and they slowly crumbled.

A tear slipped over her bottom lid, trailed down her
cheek, and splashed onto the bodice of her cotton dress.
Another fell and then another. A shuddering little hiccup
slipped out. She continued to break the beans and stopped
fighting her grief.

Annie watched the bluebird fly away and then followed
the path of a squirrel in the same tree. One of Jane's tears
dripped into the beans.

Annie began to hum softly under her breath. Jane finished the last bean, then searched frantically through the
bowl for one she might have overlooked.

Annie reached into the pocket of her old apron, drew out
a pink tissue, and handed it over. Jane blew her nose and
began to speak. "I—I'm going to miss you s-so much,
Annie, but I can't stand it anymore. I have to go away.
H-he doesn't love me."

Annie pursed her lips with disapproval. "Calvin, he
don't know what he feels."

"He's old enough to have figured it out by now." She
gave her nose an angry blow.

"Never knew a man who hated getting older so much. Usually, it's women who'll fight the years."

"I couldn't leave without saying good-bye." She had to get away, and she nearly dropped the beans as she stood.

"Set those right down before you spill 'em all over the ground."

Jane did as she said. Annie struggled out of her chair. "You're a good girl, Janie Bonner. He'll come to his senses soon."

"I don't think so."

"Sometimes a wife needs a little patience."

"I'm afraid I'm fresh out." More tears rolled down her cheeks. "Besides, I'm not a real wife."

"Now that's plain nonsense."

She didn't have any words left to argue, so she wrapped the small, frail-boned woman in her arms. "Thanks for everything, Annie, but I've got to go." After a gentle hug, she pulled away and turned toward the house.

That was when she saw Lynn Bonner standing on the back step.

19

"**Y**ou're leaving my son?''

Lynn looked angry and confused as she stared at Jane. She moved down into the yard, and Jane's heart sank. Why had she stayed so long? Why hadn't she simply said her good-byes to Annie and left? She quickly turned away and dashed her hand across her damp cheek.

Annie stepped into the breach. "I got snap beans for dinner, Amber Lynn, and I'm makin' 'em with fatback whether you like it or not.''

Lynn ignored her and walked toward Jane. "Tell me why you're leaving Cal.''

As Jane turned to face her, she tried to slip back into the cool persona Lynn expected. "Be grateful,'' she managed. "I've been a terrible wife.''

But those dishonest words threatened to unleash a fresh flood of tears. She'd been the best wife he'd ever have, damn it! The best wife she'd known how to be! She turned away.

"Have you?'' Lynn sounded deeply troubled.

Jane had to get out of here before she completely shattered. "I have a plane to catch. It would be best if you'd talk to Cal. He can explain better.''

She began moving toward the side of the house, but

she'd barely taken two steps before Lynn's astonished exclamation brought her to a halt.

"My God, you're pregnant!"

She whipped around and saw Lynn staring at her midsection. Automatically, her gaze dropped, and only then did she notice the protective hand she'd unconsciously placed there. The gesture had pressed her dress against her body and outlined her gently rounded abdomen. She snatched it away, but she was too late.

Lynn looked bewildered. "Is it Cal's?"

"Amber Lynn Glide!" Annie snapped. "Where are your manners?"

Lynn seemed more shaken than accusatory. "But how am I supposed to know if it's his or not when I don't understand anything about this marriage? I don't know what they see in each other or how they got together. I don't even know why she was crying." Her voice caught. "Something's very wrong here."

The final threads of Jane's badly frayed emotions unraveled, and as she saw the lines of suffering etched into Lynn's face, she knew she had to tell her the truth. Cal's desire to protect his parents had been well-meaning, but now it had grown destructive. If she'd learned anything in these past four months, she'd learned that deception only led to hurt.

"It's Cal's baby," she said quietly. "I'm sorry you had to find out like this."

Lynn's hurt was obvious. "But, he never— He didn't say anything. Why didn't he tell me?"

"Because he was trying to protect me."

"From what?"

"From you and Dr. Bonner. Cal didn't want either of you to find out what I'd done to him."

"Tell me!" Her expression grew as fierce as a mother lion whose cub had been threatened, never mind that her cub was now king of the jungle. "Tell me everything!"

Annie picked up the pottery bowl. "I'm goin' inside and fix my beans the way I like. Janie Bonner, you stay right here till you get this settled with Amber Lynn, you hear me?" She shuffled toward the back porch.

Jane's legs wouldn't hold her any longer, and she sank down into the lawn chair. Lynn took the other chair and sat facing Jane. Her jaw was set, her manner confrontational. Jane found herself remembering the scrappy young girl who'd baked cookies at two in the morning so she could support her husband and her baby. The expensive yellow linen dress and chunky amber jewelry didn't hide the fact that this woman knew how to fight for her own.

Jane clasped her hands in her lap. "Cal wanted to spare you and his father pain. You've been through so much this past year. He thought—" She dropped her gaze. "The bald truth is that I desperately wanted a child, and I tricked him into getting me pregnant."

"You did what?"

Jane forced her head back up. "It was wrong. Unconscionable. I didn't intend for him ever to find out."

"But he did."

She nodded.

Lynn's lips had grown thin and taut. "Whose decision was it to get married?"

"His. He threatened to take me to court and sue for custody if I didn't do what he wanted. Now that I know him better, I doubt that he'd have carried out his threat, but I believed him at the time."

Taking a deep breath, she described the morning she'd opened the door to Jodie Pulanski, then told Lynn about the men's plan for his birthday. She explained her own yearning for a child as well as her concern about finding someone to father it. She spoke without embellishment, refusing to justify her behavior in any way.

When she described her reaction to seeing Cal on television and her subsequent decision to use him, Lynn pressed her fingers to her lips, and a gasp of horror mingled with a strangled laugh that held an edge of hysteria. "Are you saying you chose Cal because you thought he was *stupid*?"

She thought about trying to explain to Lynn how he'd used *ain't* and looked so dumb and gorgeous but gave it up. There were some things a doting mother would never understand. "Obviously I misjudged him, although I didn't figure that out until several weeks after we were married."

"Everybody knows Cal is smart as a whip. How could you have believed anything else?"

"I guess some of us aren't as smart as we think we are." She continued with her story, ending with the exposure of their marriage in the media and her decision to come with him to Salvation.

Lynn's face showed a flash of anger, but to Jane's surprise, it wasn't directed at her. "Cal should have told me the truth from the beginning."

"He didn't want anyone in the family to know. He said none of you were good liars, and the story would come out if he told you."

"He didn't even take Ethan into his confidence?"

Jane shook her head. "Last Friday Ethan saw me . . . Well, he figured out that I was pregnant, but Cal swore him to secrecy until he could tell you himself."

Lynn's eyes narrowed. "There's more. This doesn't explain your hostility to us."

Jane's clasped hands cramped in her lap, and once again she had to force herself to meet Lynn's gaze. "I told you that I'd already agreed to a divorce as soon as the baby was born. You'd recently lost one daughter-in-law you cared about, and it seemed cruel to let you get attached to another. Not that you necessarily would have," she said hastily. "I know I'm not what you had in mind for Cal. But, still, it wouldn't have been right for me to barge into your family when I wasn't planning on staying."

"So you decided to behave as badly as possible."

"It—it seemed like the kindest thing to do."

"I see." Her expression gave away little, and Jane realized she was once again confronting the self-possessed woman she'd first met. She regarded Jane through steady blue eyes. "What were your feelings toward Cal?"

Jane hesitated, then skittered around the truth. "Guilt. I've done him a terrible wrong."

"People said I tricked Jim into getting me pregnant, but it wasn't true."

"You were fifteen, Lynn. I'm thirty-four. I knew exactly what I was doing."

"And now you're compounding that wrong by running out on him."

After everything she'd revealed, she would have expected her mother-in-law to be glad to be rid of her. "He's not . . . He's not ready for a permanent marriage, so it doesn't make much difference when I leave. Something came up, and I have to get back to my job. It's better this way."

"If it's better, why were you crying your eyes out?"

She felt her nostrils quiver and knew she was once again on the verge of losing control. "Don't push this, Lynn. Please."

"You've fallen in love with him, haven't you?"

She lurched to her feet. "I have to go. I promise you can have as much contact with this child as you want. I'd never try to keep your grandchild away from you."

"Do you mean that?"

"Of course."

"You won't try to keep the baby from us?"

"No."

"All right, I'm going to hold you to it." She stood. "Starting now."

"I don't understand."

"I'd like my contact with my grandchild to start now."

Her softly pitched voice belied the stubborn set of her mouth. "I don't want you to leave Salvation."

"I have to."

"So you're already breaking your word?"

Her agitation grew. "The baby's not born yet? What do you want from me?"

"I want to know who you are. Since the day we met, you've thrown up so many smoke screens I have no idea."

"You already know I tricked your son in the most underhanded, dishonest way possible. Isn't that enough?"

"It should be, but somehow it's not. I have no idea what Cal's feelings are toward you except that he's been happier than I can remember in a long time. And I also have to ask myself why Annie's so taken with you. My mother's difficult, but she's no fool. So what has she seen that I haven't?"

Jane rubbed her arms. "What you want is impossible. I won't go back to Cal."

"Then you can stay here with Annie and me."

"Here?"

"Isn't this house good enough for you?"

"It's not that." She started to say something about her job, but she couldn't muster the energy. There had been too much drama that day, and she was exhausted. The thought of driving to Asheville and getting on a plane was overwhelming.

Another bluebird lighted on the magnolia tree, and she realized that what she really wanted was to stay on Heartache Mountain. Just for a little while. Lynn was going to be her baby's grandmother, and she already knew the truth. Would it be so terrible to stay here just long enough to show her that she wasn't a bad person, simply a weak one?

Her legs felt shaky. She yearned for a cup of tea and a cookie. She wanted to watch the bluebirds in the magnolia tree and let Annie boss her around. She needed to sit in the sun and snap beans.

Lynn's eyes held both dignity and silent supplication, and Jane found herself responding to it. "All right, I'll stay. But only for a few days, and you have to promise me you won't let Cal come up here. I don't want to see him again. I can't."

"Fair enough."

"Promise me, Lynn."

"I promise."

Lynn helped her unload her suitcase and showed her into the small spare room at the back of the house that held a narrow iron bed and an old black Singer sewing machine. The walls were covered in faded yellow paper printed with blue cornflowers. Lynn left her alone to unpack, but Jane was so tired that she fell asleep, fully dressed, and didn't awaken until Lynn called her for dinner.

The meal proved to be surprisingly peaceful, despite Annie's complaints that Lynn hadn't mixed any butter in the mashed potatoes. Just as they finishing cleaning up, the telephone on the kitchen wall jangled. Lynn answered, and it didn't take Jane long to figure out who was calling.

"How was your golf trip?" Lynn twisted the phone cord around her finger. "That's too bad." She glanced at Jane and her forehead puckered. "Yes, you heard right. She's here. Yes . . . Talk to her?"

Jane shook her head and regarded her pleadingly. Annie stood up from the table where she'd been supervising the cleanup and, with a grunt of disapproval, made her way into the living room.

"I don't think Jane wants to talk right now . . . No, I can't make her come to the phone . . . I'm sorry, Cal, but I really don't know what her plans are, except that she doesn't want to see you." She scowled. "You watch your tone of voice with me, young man, and you can just pass on your own messages!"

There was a long pause, but whatever Cal said didn't seem to satisfy her because her expression grew more fierce. "That's all well and good, but you and I have a lot to talk about, including the fact that you have a wife who's four months pregnant, and you neglected to mention it!"

Time ticked by. Lynn's frown gradually eased and puzzlement took its place. "I see . . . Is that so?"

Jane was beginning to feel like an eavesdropper, so she joined Annie in the family room, where the old woman dozed on the couch while one of the evening news magazines played on television. She had just taken a seat in the rocker when Lynn came in from the kitchen.

She stopped just inside the doorway and crossed her arms over her chest. "Cal told me a different story from the one you told, Jane."

"Oh?"

"He didn't mention anything about you tricking him."

"What did he say?"

"That the two of you had a brief affair, and you got pregnant."

Jane smiled, feeling a little better for the first time all day. "That was nice of him." She looked over at Lynn. "You do know he's lying, don't you?"

Lynn gave a noncommittal shrug. "I guess for right now I'm reserving judgment about everything."

Annie's head popped up from the couch, and she scowled. "Unless either one of you's got somethin' to say that's more important than Mr. Stone Phillips, I suggest you both hush up."

They hushed up.

Later that evening after Jane had fallen asleep, Lynn sat on the couch trying to sort out her thoughts while her mother watched VH-1 with the volume muted, undoubtedly hoping one of Harry Connick, Jr.'s videos would come on. She missed Jim so much: the noises he made as he banged through the house, the soothing murmur of his voice in the middle of the night as he calmed a frantic parent on the telephone.

She missed the solid feel of that big warm body curled around her at night, even the way he always left the newspaper folded wrong side out. She missed living in her own house and being the boss of her own kitchen, but she also felt a strange kind of peace she hadn't experienced in years.

Jim was right. He'd lost the girl he'd married long ago, but she was wiser than to think he wanted that girl back. It was himself he wanted back, the way he'd been in high school, when all of life's possibilities still lay ahead of him.

As for herself, she knew there had been too many changes for her ever to be that happy, free-spirited person again. But neither was she the cool and controlled Mrs. Doctor Bonner, who had been well trained by her mother-in-law to repress all vulgar excesses of emotion.

So who was she? A woman who loved her family, that was certain. She took joy in the arts and needed these mountains around her as surely as she needed air to breathe. She was also a woman who could no longer accept second best from the man she'd loved since she was fifteen.

But Jim was proud and stubborn. By not capitulating when he'd mentioned divorce, she'd waved a red flag in his face. He never made idle threats, and if she didn't move back into the house and resume their marriage, he would get his divorce. That's the way he was, stubborn to a fault, just like his son. Both of them would break before they'd bend.

Her problems with Jim went back more than three decades, but what about Cal? She could read between the lines of what Jane had told her well enough to understand that Jane wanted a lifelong commitment, but Cal wouldn't give it to her.

What was it about her son that made him fight marriage and commitment so ferociously? He'd been raised in a loving family. Why was he so resistant to having one of his own?

Even as a very young child, competition had been everything to him. She remembered teaching him hopscotch when he was so small he'd barely been able to walk, let alone hop on one leg. She'd been little more than a child herself, and he'd been her play companion as well as her son. She'd drawn a chalk outline on the old sidewalk outside the apartment where they'd been living, and she'd never forget the sight of that bottom lip caught between his teeth, all his toddler's concentration focused on beating her. Now she suspected that the permanent ties of a wife and family had become one more symbol of the fact that the most important part of his life was coming to an end, and he had nothing to take its place.

Cal would undoubtedly have called his father right after he'd talked with her and told him about the baby. She'd been married to Jim long enough to know he'd be overjoyed at the idea of having new life in their family, and like her, he'd be concerned about Cal's happiness. Unlike her, however, he wouldn't be at all concerned about the feelings of the young woman sleeping in the spare room.

Lynn gazed over at her mother. "Cal must care about Jane, or he wouldn't have lied to me the way he did."

"Calvin loves her. He just don't know it yet."

"Neither do you. Not for a fact." Even though she'd asked for it, her mother's know-it-all attitude irritated her. Or maybe she wasn't yet ready to let go of her hurt that Annie knew Jane better than she did.

"You can believe what you want." Annie sniffed. "I know some things."

"Like what?"

"She don't put up with any of his nonsense for one. He likes that about her. She's a fighter, too, and she ain't afraid to go after him. Janie Bonner's as good as they come."

"If she's such a fighter, why is she leaving him?"

"I guess her feelin's got too much for her. She has a powerful love for that son of yours. You should see the way the two of 'em look at each other when they don't think nobody's watchin'. 'Bout set your eyeballs on fire.''

She remembered Cal's recent happiness, along with the tears in her daughter-in-law's eyes, and thought there was a good chance her mother was right.

Annie regarded her with shrewd eyes. "That baby of theirs is gonna be a smart little cuss.''

"It seems inevitable.''

"You ask me, it ain't good for a special child like that to grow up all by itself. Look how bein' an only child traum'tized Janie Bonner into gettin' in this predicament in the first place.''

"You have a point.''

"She told me she felt like a freak growin' up.''

"I can see how she would.''

"A child like that needs brothers and sisters.''

"But the parents would have to be living under the same roof for that to happen.''

"You're sure 'nough right about that.'' Annie leaned back in her rocker and sighed. "Seems me and you don't have much choice, Amber Lynn. Looks like we're gonna have to catch ourselves another Bonner.''

Lynn smiled to herself as she walked out on the porch after her mother had gone to bed. Annie enjoyed believing the two of them had single-mindedly laid a trap for Jim. It wasn't so, but Lynn had given up trying to tell her mother that. Annie believed what she wanted to believe.

It was nearly midnight and chilly enough that she zipped the front of an ancient Wolverine sweatshirt from Cal's college playing days. She stared up at the stars and thought how much better she could see them from the top of Heartache Mountain than from their house in town.

The sound of an approaching car broke her concentration. All the men in her family were night owls, so it could only be Cal or Ethan. She hoped it was her oldest son come to claim his wife. Then she remembered her promise to

Jane that she would keep him away and frowned.

As it turned out, the car that appeared at the top of the lane didn't belong to either Cal or Ethan, but to her husband. She couldn't believe it. Not once since the night she'd left had Jim driven up here to see her.

She remembered the bitterness of their parting on Friday and wondered if he'd come to dangle the business card of his divorce lawyer in front of her. She had no idea how anybody got a divorce, beyond making an appointment with a lawyer. Was that how it happened? A person made an appointment with a lawyer, and, before they knew it, their marriage was over?

Jim got out of the car and moved toward her with that long graceful stride that had set her heart to beating for as long as she could remember. She should have expected him. Cal would have talked to him by now, and the prospect of a new grandchild would give him another excuse to browbeat her. She braced herself against one of the freshly painted posts that held up the tin roof of the porch and wished he hadn't found her so unworthy.

He came to a stop below the bottom step and gazed up at her. For a long time he said nothing—he merely studied her—but when he finally spoke, there was an odd formality in his voice. "I hope I didn't scare you showing up here so late."

"It's all right. As you can see, I'm still awake."

He dropped his gaze and for a moment she had the curious feeling he wanted to bolt, but that couldn't be so. Jim never ran from anything.

He looked up at her, and his eyes held that stubborn glint she knew so well. "I'm Jim Bonner."

She stared at him.

"I'm a doctor in town."

Had he lost his mind? "Jim, what's wrong?"

He shifted his weight as if he were nervous, but the only

time she had ever seen his confidence shaken was when
Jamie and Cherry had died.

He clasped his hands together and then immediately
dropped them to his sides. "Well, to be honest, I've got a
thirty-seven-year marriage that's on the rocks. I've been
pretty depressed about it, and instead of taking to the bottle,
I thought it might help me if I found a little female companionship." He drew a deep breath. "I heard in town there
was a nice lady living up here with her old battle-ax of a
mother, and I thought maybe I'd stop by and see if that
lady'd like to go out to dinner with me some time. Or
maybe catch a movie." A flicker of amusement caught at
the corner of his mouth. "That is if you don't have any
qualms about dating a married man."

"You're asking me out on a date?"

"Yes, ma'am. I'm kind of rusty at this sort of thing, so
I hope I'm going about it right."

She pressed her fingers to her lips, and her heart swelled.
During lunch on Friday she'd told him she wished they
could meet as strangers so they could start all over to see
if they liked each other, but he'd been so angry at the time,
she hadn't thought he'd even heard her. After all these
years, she had never imagined he could surprise her, but he
just had.

She resisted the urge to throw herself in his arms and tell
him all was forgiven. She didn't hold herself so cheaply
that this small bit of effort on his part, as much as she
appreciated it, could erase decades of not being good
enough. She wondered how far he was willing to take this.

"We may not be compatible," she replied, testing the
waters.

"Maybe not. I guess we won't be able to decide unless
we give it a try."

"I don't know. My mother might not like it."

"Now you leave your mother to me. I'm real good with
old ladies, even mean and crazy ones."

She nearly laughed. Imagine stubborn, hardheaded Jim Bonner doing something this romantic. She was charmed and touched, but not completely. Something saddened her, and it took a moment to figure out what. She'd spent most of her life feeling like a beggar for Jim's affection—always agreeable, always the one to make concessions and appease. He'd never had to put himself out for her because she'd never made any demands. She had never put a single road-block in his way, and now she was getting ready to run back to him just because he'd made one small effort to please her.

She could still remember the feel of his randy teenager's hands on her. Those first few times they'd had sex, she hadn't liked it very much, but it had never occurred to her to say no, even though she would rather have been sitting in the back booth at the drugstore sharing a Coke and gossiping about their classmates. Suddenly that made her angry. He'd hurt her when he'd taken her virginity. Not deliberately, but it had hurt nonetheless.

"I'll think about it," she said quietly. Then she gathered the sweatshirt tighter around her and went back inside.

A moment later, a spray of gravel hit the house as he peeled away, driving for all the world like an angry eighteen-year-old.

20

For two weeks, Cal stayed away from Heartache Mountain. During the first week, he got drunk three
times and took a swing at Kevin, who'd refused his demand
to get the hell out of Dodge. During the second week, he
started to go after her half a dozen times, but his pride
wouldn't let him. He wasn't the one who'd run away! He
wasn't the one who'd screwed everything up with unreasonable demands.

He also had to face the fact that he wasn't absolutely
sure any of those stubborn women would let him in the
house. Apparently the only men welcome there were Ethan,
who didn't count because he was Ethan, and Kevin Tucker,
who sure as hell *did* count. Cal seethed as he thought of
Tucker driving up to Heartache Mountain whenever he
pleased, getting fed and fussed over, of Tucker, who somehow or another seemed to have moved into Cal's own
house!

The first night Cal had gotten drunk at the Mountaineer,
Tucker had swiped his keys, as if Cal weren't smart enough
to have already figured out he wasn't in any condition to
drive. It was the same night Cal had swung at him, but his
heart hadn't been in it, and he'd missed. Next thing he
knew, he was slumped in the passenger seat of Tucker's

seventy-thousand-dollar Mitsubishi Spyder while Kevin drove him home, and he hadn't been able to get rid of the kid since.

He was pretty sure he hadn't told Kevin he could stay. As a matter of fact, he distinctly remembered ordering him out of his house. But Kevin had stuck around like a damned watchdog, even though he had a perfectly good rental house, not to mention Sally Terryman. The next thing Cal knew, the two of them were watching game films and he was showing Kevin how he always went to his first option instead of being patient, reading the defense, and finding the open man.

At least watching films with Kevin kept his mind off the fact that he missed the Professor so bad his teeth ached, which didn't mean he was any closer to figuring out what to do about it. He wasn't ready to be married forever and ever, not when he needed all his energy focused on playing ball, and not when he had no other life's work waiting for him. But he also wasn't nearly ready to lose Jane. Why couldn't she have left things as they were instead of making demands?

Crawling on his hands and knees up Heartache Mountain so he could beg her to come back was unthinkable. He didn't crawl for anybody. What he needed was a reason to go up there, but he couldn't think of a single one he wanted to admit out loud.

He still didn't understand why she'd stayed around instead of flying back to Chicago, but he was glad it had happened, since it was giving her time to come to her senses. She'd said she loved him, and she wouldn't have said those words if she didn't mean them. Maybe today was the day she'd be woman enough to admit her mistake and come back to him.

The door chimes sounded, but he wasn't in the mood for company, and he ignored them. He hadn't been sleeping too well or eating much more than an occasional bologna sandwich. Even Lucky Charms had lost their appeal—they held too many painful memories—so he'd been substituting coffee for breakfast. He rubbed a hand over his stubbly jaw and tried to remember how long it had been since he'd shaved; but he didn't feel like shaving. He didn't feel like doing anything except watching game films and yelling at Kevin.

The door chimes rang again, and he frowned. It couldn't be Tucker because somehow the sonovabitch had gotten a house key of his own. Maybe it was—

His heart made a queer jolt in his chest, and he banged his elbow on the doorframe as he made a dash for the foyer. But when he yanked the door open, he saw his father standing on the other side instead of the Professor.

Jim stormed in waving a supermarket tabloid folded open to an article. "Have you seen this? Maggie Lowell shoved it at me, right after I gave her a Pap. By God, if I were you, I'd sue that wife of yours for every penny she has, and if you don't do it, I will! I don't care what you say about her. I had that woman's number from the beginning, and you're too blind to see the truth." His tirade abruptly ended as he took in Cal's appearance. "What the hell have you done with yourself? You look terrible."

Cal snatched the tabloid out of his father's hand. The first thing he saw was a photograph of himself and the Professor that had been snapped at O'Hare the morning they'd left for North Carolina. He looked grim; she, dazed. But it wasn't the photograph that made his stomach drop to the bottom of his feet. It was the headline below it.

I Trapped the NFL's Best (And Dumbest) Quarterback into Marriage by Dr. Jane Darlington Bonner.

"Shit."

"You'll have a lot more to say than that when you read this piece of crap!" Jim exclaimed. "I don't care if she's pregnant or not—the woman's a compulsive liar! She says in here that she posed as a hooker and pretended to be your *birthday present* so she could get herself pregnant. How did you ever get tangled up with her?''

"It's like I told you, Dad. We had a fling, and she got pregnant. It was just one of those things.''

"Well, apparently the truth wasn't exciting enough, so she had to go and invent this outlandish story. And you know what? The people who read this rag are going to believe it's the truth. They're actually going to believe that's the way it happened.''

Cal crumpled the tabloid in his fist. He'd wanted a good excuse to go see his wife, and now he had it.

It was blissful, this life without men, or so they told themselves. Jane and Lynn lazed like cats in the sun and didn't comb their hair until noon. In the evening, they fed Annie her meat and potatoes, then smeared cottage cheese on ripe pears for themselves and called it supper. They stopped answering the phone, stopped wearing bras, and Lynn tacked a poster of a muscular young man in a Speedo to the kitchen wall. When Rod Stewart came on the radio, they danced with each other. Jane forgot her inhibitions, and her feet flew like dove's wings over the carpet.

To Jane, the rickety old house was everything a home should be. She snapped beans and filled the rooms with wildflowers. She put them in carnival glass tumblers, china bud vases, and a Bagels 2 Go commuter mug Lynn found on the top shelf. She didn't know exactly how she and Lynn had developed such an attachment to each other; maybe it was because their husbands were so much alike, and they didn't need any words of explanation to understand the other's pain.

They allowed Kevin into their women's house because he entertained them. He made them laugh and feel desirable even with pear juice trickling down their chins and seed-pods caught in their hair. They let Ethan in, too, because they didn't have the heart to turn him away; but they were glad when he left since he couldn't hide his worry.

Lynn gave up her women's club meetings and coordinated outfits. She forgot to color her hair or do her nails, which grew ragged at the cuticle. Jane's computer stayed in the trunk of her Escort. Instead of trying to unlock the Theory of Everything, she spent most of her hours lying on an old wicker chaise that sat in the corner of the front porch, where she did nothing but let her baby grow.

They were blissfully happy. They told each other so every day. But then the sun would set and their conversation would begin to lag. One of them would sigh while the other stared out at the gathering dusk.

Along with the night, loneliness settled over the rickety old house on Heartache Mountain. They found themselves yearning for a heavier tread, a deeper voice. During the day, they remembered that they had been betrayed by the men they'd loved too well, but at night their house of women no longer seemed quite so blissful. They got into the habit of going to bed early to make the nights shorter and then rising at dawn.

Their days developed a pattern, and there was nothing to separate that particular morning two weeks after Jane had come to stay on Heartache Mountain from any of the others. She fed Annie her breakfast, did some chores, and took a walk. Just after she got back, a particularly bouncy tune from Mariah Carey came on VH-1, and she made Lynn stop ironing the curtains she'd washed so they could dance. Then she relaxed on the porch. By the time the lunch dishes were put away, she was ready to work in the garden.

The muscles in her arms ached as she tilled the soil between the garden rows, using a hoe to uproot the weeds that threatened her precious bean plants. The day was warm, and it would have been smarter to do this in the morning, but schedules had lost their allure for her. In the morning she had been too busy lying on the chaise growing her baby.

She straightened to rest her back and propped her palm on the handle of the hoe. The breeze caught the skirt of the old-fashioned calico print housedress she wore and whipped it against her knees. It was soft and threadbare from many washings. Annie said it had once been her favorite.

Maybe she'd get Ethan or Kevin to unload her computer if either came to visit today. Or maybe she wouldn't. What if she started to work and Rod Stewart came on the radio? She might miss a chance to dance. Or what if, while she lost herself in equations, a new crop of weeds grew up near her bean plants and threatened them with suffocation?

No. Work was not a good idea, even though Jerry Miles was almost certainly plotting behind the scenes to finish off her career. Work was definitely not a good idea when she had beans to weed, a baby to grow. Although the Theory of Everything beckoned her, she'd lost the stomach for bureaucracy. Instead, she gazed at the mountain sky and pretended it marked the boundary of her life.

That was how Cal found her. In the garden, with her palm curled over the handle of a hoe and her face lifted to the sky.

His breath caught in his throat at the sight of her standing against the sun in a faded calico housedress. Her French braid was coming undone so that blond wisps formed a corona about her head. She looked as if she were part of the sky and the earth, a joining of the elements.

Sweat and the breeze had molded the dress to her body, displaying, as clearly as if she were naked, the shape of her breasts and the hard round belly where his baby grew. She'd unfastened two of the buttons at the top of the dress's scoopy neck, and the sides fell apart in a V over a damp, dusty chest.

She was brown as a berry: her arms and legs, her dirt-smudged face, that moist V of skin that pointed to her breasts. She looked like a mountain woman, one of those strong, stoic creatures who had eked a living out of this unforgiving soil during the depression.

With her face still lifted to the sky, she wiped the back of her arm across her forehead, leaving a dirty streak in its place. His mouth went dry as the fabric stretched tight over those small high breasts and caught just beneath her rounding belly. She had never been so beautiful to him as she was at that moment, standing without any cosmetics in his grandmother's garden and looking every one of her thirty-four years.

The tabloid newspaper rustled against his thigh, and Annie's voice rang out from behind him. "You get off my land, Calvin. Nobody invited you here!"

Jane's eyes flew open, and she dropped the hoe.

He turned in time to see his father charging around the side of the house. "Put that shotgun down, you crazy old coot!"

His mother appeared on the back porch and stopped behind Annie. "Well, now, aren't we just a picture of *Psychology Today*'s Family of the Year."

His mother. Although he'd spoken to her over the phone, she'd ducked his dinner invitations, and he hadn't seen her in weeks. What had happened to her? She never used sarcasm, but her voice fairly dripped with it. Shocked, he took in the other changes.

Instead of one of her expensive casual outfits, she wore a pair of black jeans unevenly cut off at mid-thigh, along with a green knit top that he seemed to remember having last seen on his wife, although there hadn't been a dirt smudge on it at the time. Like Jane, she wore no makeup. Her hair was longer than he'd ever seen it, and untidy, with threads of gray showing up that he hadn't known were there.

He felt a flash of panic. She looked like an earth mother, not like *his* mother.

Jane, in the meantime, had dropped the hoe and marched

across the yard toward the steps. Her bare feet were tucked into dirty white Keds with slits in the sides and no shoe-laces. As he watched, she silently took her place on the porch with the other women.

Annie remained in the middle with the shotgun still aimed at his gut, his mother stood on one side of her, Jane on the other. Despite the fact that none of them were ex-ceptionally large, he felt as if he were staring at a trio of Amazons.

Annie had drawn her eyebrows on crooked that morning, giving her a decidedly malevolent look. "You want this girl back, Calvin, you're gonna have to set yourself to a serious courtship."

"He doesn't want her back," Jim snapped. "Look what she's done." He snatched the newspaper from Cal's hand and shoved it toward the women.

Jane moved down onto the top step, took it from him, and bent her head to study the page.

Cal had never heard his father sound so bitter. "I hope you're proud of yourself," he snarled at Jane. "You set out to ruin his life, and you've done a damn good job of it."

Jane had taken in the gist of the article, and her gaze flew up to meet Cal's. He felt the impact in his chest and had to tear his eyes away. "Jane didn't have anything to do with that newspaper story, Dad."

"Her name's on the damn by-line! When are you going to stop protecting her?"

"Jane's capable of a lot of things, including being stub-born and unreasonable"—he shot her a hard-eyed look—"but she wouldn't do that."

He saw that she wasn't surprised by the way he'd come to her defense, and that pleased him. At least she trusted him a little. He watched her clutch the tabloid to her chest as if she could hide its words from the world, and he made up his mind Jodie Pulanski would pay for the pain she was causing her.

His father continued to look thunderous, and he realized he was going to have to give him at least part of the truth. He'd never tell him what Jane had done—that was nobody's business but his—but he could at least explain her behavior toward his family.

He took a protective step forward as his father closed in on her. "Are you getting regular prenatal care, or have you been too busy with your damn career to see a doctor?"

She met the old man square in the eye. "I've been seeing a doctor named Vogler."

His father gave a begrudging nod. "She's good. You just make sure you do what she tells you."

Annie's arm was starting to shake, and Cal could see the shotgun was getting too heavy for her. He caught his mother's eye. She reached out and took it away. "If anybody's going to shoot either one of them, Annie, I'll do it."

Great! His mother had turned crazy, too.

"If you don't mind," he said tightly, "I'd like to speak with my wife alone."

"That's up to her." His mother looked at Jane, who shook her head. That really pissed him off.

"Anybody home?"

The female triumvirate turned in one body, and all of them began to smile like sunbeams as his backup quarterback came strolling around the corner of the house like he owned the place.

Just when he'd thought things couldn't get worse . . .

Kevin took in the women on the porch, the two Bonner men standing below, and the shotgun. He arched his eyebrow at Cal, nodded at Jim, then moved up on the porch to join the women.

"You beautiful ladies told me I could stop by for some of that fried chicken, so I took you at your word." He leaned against the post Cal had painted only a month earlier. "How's the little guy doing today?" With a familiarity that indicated he'd done it before, he reached out and patted Jane's belly.

Cal had him off the porch and flat on the ground within seconds.

The shotgun blast nearly knocked out his eardrums. Bits of dirt flew into his face and stung his bare arms. Between the noise and the fact that the dirt had temporarily blinded him, he didn't have time to land his punch, and Kevin managed to roll out from beneath him.

"Damn, Bomber, you've done more damage to me this spring than happened all last season."

Cal swabbed the dirt from his eyes and lurched to his feet. "Keep your hands off her."

Kevin looked peeved and turned to Jane. "If he acted this way to you, it's no wonder you left him."

Cal gritted his teeth. "Jane, I'd like to talk to you. Now!"

His mother—his sweet, reasonable mother—stepped in front of her as if Jane were her kid instead of him! And his old man wasn't helping any. He just stood there looking at his mom as if he didn't understand anything.

"What are your intentions toward Jane, Cal?"

"That's between the two of us."

"Not exactly. Jane has family now to look after her."

"You're damn right she does! I'm her family."

"You didn't want her, so right now Annie and I are her family. That means we're the ones looking out for her best interests."

He saw that Jane's eyes were glued to his mother's face, and he took in her stunned, happy expression. He remembered the cold sonovabitch who'd raised her, and in spite of everything—the shotgun, his mother's desertion, even Kevin Tucker—he couldn't help but feel glad that she'd finally found herself a decent parent. If only she hadn't found *his* decent parent.

But his warmth cooled as his mother gave him the same I-mean-business look that, twenty years earlier, had meant turning over his car keys.

"Are you going to honor those wedding vows you made to Jane, or are you still planning to get rid of her after the baby's born?"

"Stop making it sound like I've got a contract out on her!" He jabbed his thumb at Tucker. "And could we discuss this in private, without Bozo here listening in?"

"He stays," Annie interjected. "I like him. And he cares about you, Calvin. Don't you, Kevin?"

"I sure do, Mrs. Glide. I care a lot." Tucker shot him a Jack Nicholson smirk, then turned to Lynn. "Besides, if he doesn't want Jane, I do."

Jane had the gall to smile.

But his mother had always been single-minded when she needed to be. "You can't have it both ways, Cal. Either Jane's your wife, or she's not. What's it going to be?"

He'd reached the end of his rope, and his temper snapped. "All right! No divorce. We'll stay goddamned married!" He glared at the three women. "There! Are you finally satisfied? Now I want to talk to my wife!"

His mother flinched. Annie shook her head and clucked her tongue. Jane gave him a look of utter contempt and swept into the house, taking the tabloid newspaper with her.

The screen door slammed, and Kevin let out a low whistle. "Damn, Bomber, maybe instead of watching all those game films, you should have been reading a few books on female psychology."

He knew he'd blown it, but he also knew he'd been pushed past the point of reason. They'd publicly humiliated him, making him look like a clown in front of his wife. With a furious glare at all of them, he spun on his heel and stalked away.

Lynn wanted to cry as she watched him disappear. Her heart went out to him, this stubborn oldest son who'd also been her play companion. He was furious with her, and she could only hope she was doing the right thing and that someday he would understand.

She expected Jim to rush after Cal. Instead, he walked the rest of the way to the porch, but he turned to Annie instead of her. Knowing his feelings about her mother, she waited for his customary display of belligerence, only to be surprised.

"Mrs. Glide, I'd like permission to take your daughter for a walk."

She caught her breath. This was the first time Jim had come to the house since that night two weeks ago when she'd turned him down. In the days that followed, she'd known she'd done the right thing, but at night when her defenses were down, she'd wished it could have been different. Never had she expected him to swallow his pride enough to repeat his performance as the polite suitor.

Annie, however, didn't seem to find anything odd about it. "You stay in sight of the house," she warned him.

A muscle ticked in his jaw, but he gave her a stiff nod.

"All right, then." Her mother's bony knuckles dug into the small of her back. "You go on now, Amber Lynn; Jim asked you nice and proper. And you be polite, not snippy like you've been with me lately."

"Yes, ma'am." Lynn moved down off the step, wanting to laugh even as she felt her eyes tear.

Jim's hand curled around her own. He gazed down at her, and the warm golden flecks in his hazel eyes suddenly reminded her how tender he'd been through her three pregnancies. When she was at her fattest, he'd kissed her belly and told her she was the most beautiful woman in the world. As her hand nestled like a small bird in his larger one, she thought how quick she was to forget the good and remember the bad.

He led her toward the path that curved into the woods.

Despite her mother's words, they were soon out of sight of the house.

"Pretty day," he said. "A little warm for May."

"Yes."

"It's quiet up here."

It astonished her that he was still willing to address her as if they'd just met. She rushed to join him in this new place where neither had ever hurt the other. "It's quiet, but I love it."

"You ever get lonely?"

"There's a lot to do."

"What?"

He turned to gaze at her, and she was struck by the intensity in his expression. He wanted to know how she spent her day! He wanted to listen to her! With a sense of delight, she told him.

"All of us get up early. I like to walk in the woods as soon as the sun's up, and when I get back, my daughter-in-law—" She faltered, then glanced at him from the corner of her eye. "Her name is Jane."

He frowned, but said nothing. They moved deeper into the woods where rhododendron and mountain laurel stretched on each side of the path, along with clusters of violets, trillium, and a burgundy carpet of galax. A pair of dogwood celebrated with a splash of white blossoms their escape from the fungus that had destroyed so many of the species in the Carolina mountains. Lynn inhaled the rich, moist scent of earth that smelled new.

"Jane has breakfast ready when I'm done walking," she went on. "My mother wants bacon and eggs, but Jane fixes whole grain pancakes or oatmeal with a little fresh fruit, so Annie is generally trying to pick a fight with her as I'm coming into the kitchen. Jane's wily, though, and she does a better job of getting her way with Annie than anyone else in my family. When breakfast is over, I listen to music and clean up the kitchen."

"What kind of music?"

He knew exactly what kind. Over the years he'd switched their various car radios from her classical stations to his country and western hundreds of times. "I love Mozart and Vivaldi, Chopin, Rachmaninoff. My daughter-in-law likes classic rock. Sometimes we dance."

"You and . . . Jane?"

"She's developed a passion for Rod Stewart." Lynn laughed. "If he comes on the radio, she makes me stop whatever I'm doing and dance with her. She's like that with some of the newer groups, too—ones you've never even heard of. Sometimes she has to dance. I don't think she did much of it when she was growing up."

"But she— I heard she's a scientist," he said cautiously.

"She is. But mostly now she says she just wants to grow her baby."

Time ticked by as he took that in. "She sounds like an unusual person."

"She's wonderful." And then, impulsively, "Would you like to come back for supper tonight so you can get to know her better?"

"Are you inviting me?" His face registered both surprise and pleasure.

"Yes. Yes, I think I am."

"All right, then. I'd like that."

They walked for a while without speaking. The path narrowed, and she moved off it, leading him toward the creek. They'd come here dozens of times when they were kids and sat side by side on an old log that had long since rotted away. Sometimes they'd simply watched the water rush over the mossy rocks, but most of the time, they'd made out. Cal had been conceived not far from here.

He cleared his throat and lowered himself onto the trunk of a yellow buckeye that had fallen along the edge of the creek bed in some forgotten storm. "You were pretty tough on my son back there."

"I know." She sat next to him, but not quite touching. "I have a grandchild to protect."

"I see."

But she could tell he didn't see at all. Just weeks ago, his uncertainty might have made him snap at her, but now he seemed more contemplative than irritated. Was he beginning to trust her?

"Do you remember that I told you my marriage was breaking up?"

She felt herself tensing. "I remember."

"It's my fault. I just want you to know that if you're thinking about . . . seeing me."

"All your fault?"

"Ninety-nine percent. I blamed her for my own shortcomings and didn't even realize it." He braced his forearms on his knees and gazed at the rushing water. "For years I let myself believe I'd have become a world-famous epidemiologist if I hadn't been forced to marry so young, but it wasn't until after she left me that I figured out I was kidding myself." He clasped his hands together, those strong, healing hands that had served as the gateway for both birth and death in this county. "I would never have been happy away from these mountains. I like being a country doctor."

She was touched by the depth of emotion she heard in his voice and thought he might finally have rediscovered a part of himself that he'd lost. "What about her one percent?"

"What?" He turned his head.

"You said you were 99 percent to blame. What about her one percent?"

"Even that wasn't really her fault." She didn't know if it were a trick of the light or a reflection from the water, but his eyes seemed full of compassion. "She didn't have many advantages when she was growing up, and she never had much formal education. She says I always looked down on her because of it, and she's probably right—she is about most things—but I think now she might have made it easy for me to look down on her because, even though she's accomplished more than most people could in two lifetimes, she's never thought much of herself.''

Her mouth snapped open, but then she shut it. How could she refute what was so patently true?

For a moment she let herself contemplate how far she had come in her life. She saw all the hard work and self-discipline that had been necessary for her to become the woman she'd wanted to be. As if from a distance, she viewed who she was and found she liked what she saw. Why had it taken her so long to accept herself? Jim was right. How could she have expected him to respect her when she didn't? In her mind that accounted for more than one percent of the blame, and she told Jim so.

He shrugged. "I guess I don't much care what the number is." He picked up her hand, which rested on her thigh, and ran his thumb along the ragged edge of one of her fingernails, then up over the ridge of her wedding band. He didn't look at her, and his voice held a soft, gravelly note that was filled with emotion. "My wife is so much a part of me, she's like the breath coming into my body. I love her very much."

His simple, emotion-filled statement shook her, and her words snagged in her throat. "She's very lucky."

He lifted his head and gazed at her. She recognized the moisture gathering in the corners of his eyes as tears. In thirty-seven years, she had never once seen her husband cry, not even the day they'd buried Cherry and Jamie.

"Jim . . ." She slipped into his arms and found that old familiar place that God had created just for her out of Jim's bone and muscle and flesh. Feelings she couldn't express choked her, making her brain fuzzy, so that the next words she spoke weren't what she'd intended at all. "You should know I don't sleep with men on the first date."

"Is that so?" His voice was husky.

"It's because I started having sex when I was too young." She drew away from him, looked down into her lap. "I didn't want to, but I loved him so much that I didn't know how to say no."

She glanced up to see how he'd taken her statement. She didn't want to throw more guilt in his face; she merely needed him to understand how it had been.

His smile held a hint of sadness, and he brushed the corner of her mouth with his thumb. "Did it turn you against sex for life?"

"Oh, no. I was blessed with a wonderful lover. Maybe a little clumsy when he got started, but it didn't take him long to get it right." She smiled.

"I'm glad to hear that." His thumb trailed over her bottom lip. "You should know right now that I don't have a lot of sexual experience. I've only been with one woman."

"That's nice."

He pushed her hair back from her face on one side with his fingers. "Did anybody ever tell you you're beautiful? A lot messier than my wife but still a traffic-stopper."

She laughed. "I couldn't stop traffic if I had a red light in the middle of my forehead."

"That just goes to show what you know." He took her hand and drew her to her feet. As his head dipped, she realized he was going to kiss her.

The brush of his lips was gentle and familiar. He kept his body away from hers so only their mouths touched, along with their hands, which were linked at their sides. Their kiss quickly lost its gentleness and grew urgent with passion. It had been so long for them, and there was so much they needed to express that lay beyond words. But she loved his courtship and wanted more time.

He drew back as if he understood and regarded her with glazed eyes. "I—I have to get back to my office. I'm already going to be late for my afternoon appointments. And when we make love, I don't want to be rushed.''

She felt heavy-limbed and wobbly with anticipation. She tucked her hand in his as they moved back to the path.

"When you come over for dinner, maybe we'll have some time to talk, and you can tell me about your work."

A smile of pure pleasure lit his face. "I'd like that."

She realized that she couldn't remember the last time she'd asked him anything beyond a cursory, "How was your day?" This business of listening to each other was going to have to go both ways.

His smile faded, and his forehead creased. "I don't suppose I could bring my son along when I come to dinner?"

She hesitated for only a moment before she shook her head. "I'm sorry. My mother wouldn't allow it."

"Aren't you a little old to be taking orders from your mother?"

"Sometimes she has a feeling about how things should go. Right now, she has feelings about who should come to the house and who shouldn't."

"And my son isn't welcome?"

She regarded him unhappily. "I'm afraid not. I hope . . . soon. It's really in his hands, not Annie's."

His jaw set in its familiar stubborn line. "It's hard to believe you're letting an old woman who's half-crazy make decisions about something so important."

She drew him to a stop and pressed a kiss to the corner of that stubborn jaw. "Maybe she's not as crazy as you think. After all, she was the one who told me I had to take this walk with you."

"You wouldn't have done it otherwise?"

"I don't know. I have a lot at stake in my life right now, and I don't want to make a mistake. Sometimes mothers know what's best for their daughters." She regarded him levelly. "And their sons."

He shook his head, and his shoulders slumped in resignation. "All right. I guess I know when I'm in over my head."

She smiled and had to restrain herself from kissing him again. "We eat early. Six o'clock."

"I'll be there."

21

Lynn showed Jane off to Jim that night as if she were a beloved child brought before a stranger to display her tricks. She sang Jane's praises until he began to look dazed, then shooed the two of them into the living room so they could patch up whatever differences remained between them.

As Jane took a seat in Annie's chair, the resemblance between father and son made her ache, and she wanted to move next to him on the couch and fold herself into those sturdy Cal-like arms. Instead, she drew a deep breath and told him how she had met Cal and what she had done.

"I didn't write the tabloid article," she said, when she reached the end of her story, "but nearly every word of it was true."

She expected his censure.

"I guess Ethan would have a few things to say here about divine providence being responsible for getting you and Cal together," he said.

He surprised her. "I don't know about that."

"You love Cal, don't you?"

"With all my heart." She dropped her gaze. "But that doesn't mean I'm going to be an afterthought in his life."

"I'm sorry he's giving you such a hard time. I don't

think he can help it. The men in our family are pretty hard-headed.'' He looked uncomfortable. ''I guess I have a confession of my own.''

''Oh?''

''I called Sherry Vogler this afternoon.''

''You called my doctor?''

''I couldn't relax about your pregnancy until I made sure everything was all right. She gave you a clean bill of health, but I couldn't bully her into telling me whether I have a grandson or a granddaughter on the way. She said you'd decided to wait, and I had to wait, too.'' He looked sheepish. ''I know I was out of line talking to her behind your back, but I don't want anything to happen to you. Are you angry?''

She thought of Cherry and Jamie and then of her own father, who'd never seemed to care at all. The next thing she knew, she was smiling. ''I'm not angry. Thanks.''

He shook his head and grinned. ''You're a nice lady, Janie Bonner. The old bat was right about you, after all.''

''I heard that!'' the old bat called from the next room.

Later that night as Jane lay sleepless in her narrow iron bed, she smiled at the memory of Annie's indignation. But her smile faded as she thought of all she would be losing when she left here: Jim and Lynn and Annie, these mountains that seemed to be more a part of her every day, and Cal. Except how could she lose something she'd never had?

She wanted to close her eyes and cry her heart out, but she punched the pillow instead and pretended it was Cal. Her anger faded, and she lay back to stare at the ceiling. What was she doing here? Was she subconsciously waiting for him to change his mind and realize he loved her? Today had shown her that wasn't going to happen.

She remembered the humiliating moment this afternoon when he'd shouted out that he would stay married. His offer had cut her to the quick. The words she'd longed to hear had been uttered on the cusp of his anger, and there hadn't been an ounce of true meaning behind them.

She made herself face the truth. He might very well come around, but it would be out of duty instead of love because he didn't feel the same way about her that she felt about him. She had to accept that and start living her life again. It was time for her to leave Heartache Mountain.

The wind had whipped up outside, and the room had grown chilly. Although it was warm under the covers, the cold seemed to have settled into her bones. She curled deeper into the bedclothes and accepted the fact that she had to leave. She'd always be thankful that she'd taken these two weeks for herself, but now she had to stop hiding and resume her life.

Miserable, she finally fell asleep, only to be jolted awake by a crash of thunder and a cold, wet hand settling over her mouth. She sucked in her breath to scream, but the hand clamped down tighter, and a deep, familiar voice whispered in her ear. "Shhh . . . It's me."

Her eyes shot open. A dark shape loomed over her. Wind and rain blew in through the window next to her bed and whipped the curtains against the wall. He eased his hand from her mouth and reached out to close the window just as a boom of thunder shook the house.

Rubber-limbed from the fright he'd given her, she struggled to sit up. "Get out!"

"Lower your voice before Medea shows up with her handmaiden."

"Don't you dare say anything bad about either one of them."

"They'd eat their own children for dinner."

This was too cruel. Why couldn't he just leave her alone? "What are you doing here?"

He planted his hands on his hips and scowled down at her. "I came to kidnap you, but it's wet and cold out there, so I'll have to do it some other time."

He lowered himself onto the straight chair that sat at the

sewing machine next to her bed. Beads of water glistened in his hair and on his nylon parka. As another flash of lightning lit the room, she saw that he was still just as unshaven and haggard-looking as he'd been this afternoon.

"You planned to kidnap me?"

"You don't seriously think I'm going to let you stay here much longer with these crazy women, do you?"

"It's none of your business what I do."

He ignored that. "I had to talk to you without those vampires listening in. For one thing, you need to stay away from town for the next few days. A couple of reporters have shown up anxious to check out that tabloid article."

So that was why he'd shown up tonight. Not to bring her a declaration of undying love, but a warning about the press. She struggled to swallow her disappointment.

"They're a bunch of bloodsuckers," he growled.

She sat higher in the pillows and met his gaze straight on. "Don't do anything to Jodie."

"Fat chance."

"I mean it."

He glared at her, and a flash of lightning picked out the hard glitter of her eyes. "You know damn well she's the one who sold that story to the tabloid."

"The damage is done, and there's nothing more she can do, so what's the point?" She pulled the quilt to her chin. "It'd be like squashing an ant. She's pitiful, and I want you to leave her alone."

"It's not in my nature to let somebody hit me without hitting them back."

She stiffened. "I know."

"All right." He sighed. "I'll leave her alone. I guess we don't have to worry too much about it anyway. Kevin held a press conference this evening, and he says he's holding another one tomorrow for the next batch of reporters who show up. Believe it or not, he's pretty much defused the whole thing."

"Kevin?"

"Your knight in shining armor." She didn't miss the bite of sarcasm in his tone. "I walked into the Mountaineer to get a beer and found him holding court with a bunch of reporters. He told them that the story was true."

"What?"

"But only up to a point. He said the two of us had been dating for months before that fateful night. According to him, the birthday thing was a surprise you'd arranged. Middle-age kinkiness, I believe he called it. I've got to say, the kid was pretty convincing. By the time he was done, even I believed that's the way it happened."

"I told you he was a sweetie."

"Oh, yeah? Well, your sweetie also made it clear that the only reason you and I started to date was because *he'd* just dumped you, and you were so upset about it he passed you on to me as a consolation prize."

"That jerk."

"My sentiments exactly."

Despite his words, he didn't sound all that upset with Kevin. He rose and pushed the chair aside. She stiffened as he sat on the edge of the bed.

"Come on home, sweetheart. You know I'm sorry about what happened before, don't you?" He closed his hand over her arm, where it lay beneath the covers. "I should have called Brian as soon as my feelings toward you changed, but I guess I wasn't ready to face what was happening. We can work it out. We just need to be alone for a while to do it."

He was breaking her heart. "There's nothing to work out."

"There's the fact that we're married, and we have a baby coming. Be reasonable, Jane. We just need a little time."

She hardened herself against the frailty inside her that made her want to agree. She refused to be another weak-willed woman victimized by her emotions. "My home is in Chicago."

"Don't say that." Once again, the edge of anger was back in his voice. "You've got a perfectly good home on the other side of this mountain."

"That place is yours, not mine."

"That's not so."

A rap sounded on the door, startling them both. Cal shot up from the edge of the bed.

"Jane?" Lynn called out. "Jane, I heard something. Are you all right?"

"I'm fine."

"I heard voices. Do you have a man in there?"

"Yes."

"Why'd you have to go and tell her that?" Cal hissed.

"Do you want him there?" Lynn asked.

Jane fought the tide of misery rising in her chest. "No."

There was a long pause. "All right, then. Come in my room. You can sleep with me."

Jane pushed back the covers.

Cal caught her arm. "Don't do this, Jane. We need to talk."

"The time's past for talking. I'm going back to Chicago tomorrow."

"You can't do that! I've been doing a lot of thinking, and I have things to tell you."

"Go tell them to somebody who cares." She jerked free and rushed from the room.

Jane was going to bolt, and Cal couldn't let it happen. Not in a million years. He loved her!

He'd learned from his father that the women got up early, so he arrived at Heartache Mountain right at dawn. He hadn't slept at all since he'd climbed back out into the rain from Jane's bedroom window last night. Now that it was too late, he saw the mistake in his strategy.

He should have told her he loved her the minute he came into her room, while he still had his hand over her mouth. Instead, he'd gone on about kidnaping and reporters, jabbering away instead of getting to the heart of the matter, the only part of what he had to say that meant anything. Maybe he'd been ashamed that it had taken him so long to figure out what should have been obvious to him for a long time.

The reality of his feelings had hit him like a lightning bolt. Yesterday afternoon he'd been struck by the truth as he'd driven hell-for-leather off the mountain right after he'd made a fool of himself by yelling out that he'd stay married. The expression on her face—the look of absolute contempt—had devastated him. Her good opinion meant more to him than any sportswriter's. She was everything to him.

Now he understood that loving her wasn't a new feeling, only his acceptance was new. Looking back, he figured he'd probably fallen in love with her when he'd tackled her in Annie's backyard that day he'd found out how old she was.

More than anything in his life, he knew he couldn't let this marriage break up. As much as the idea of ending his career scared him, it didn't scare him half as much as losing her. That meant he had to get her to listen to him, but first, he had to make certain she stayed put.

The front door of Annie's house was locked with the new dead bolt he'd installed not two weeks earlier. He figured there wasn't a chance in hell they'd open it for him, so he kicked it in and made his way to the kitchen.

Jane stood at the sink in her Goofy nightshirt with her hair all rumpled and her mouth open in an oval of surprise. As she took in his appearance, her eyes widened with alarm.

He'd caught a glimpse of himself in the mirror as he'd come through the living room, and he wasn't surprised by her reaction. With his outlaw's stubble, red eyes, and trigger-happy temper, he looked like the meanest hombre this side of the Pecos. Which was just fine with him. Let all of them know right from the beginning that he meant business.

Annie sat at the table with an old flannel shirt pulled on over pink satin pj's. She hadn't put on her makeup yet, and she looked every one of her eighty years. As he stalked across her kitchen floor, she started to sputter and struggle to her feet. He walked right past her and snatched the shotgun from its resting place in the corner.

"Consider yourselves disarmed, ladies. And nobody leaves here without my permission."

Taking the shotgun with him, he stalked back out through the front of the house to the porch, where he leaned the antique weapon against the house and slouched down into the old wooden rocker that sat near the front door. He propped his heels on the red-and-white Igloo cooler he'd brought with him. It held a six-pack of beer, a package of bologna, some frozen Milky Ways, and a loaf of Wonder bread, so they could just forget about starving him out. Then he leaned back and closed his eyes. Nobody threatened his family. Not even his own family.

Ethan showed up around eleven o'clock. Cal hadn't heard much noise from inside: some muted conversation, water running, Annie coughing. At least she wasn't smoking these days. No way would his mother and Jane let her get away with that.

Ethan stopped on the bottom step. Cal noted with disgust that he'd ironed his T-shirt again.

"What's going on here, Cal? And why's your Jeep blocking the road?" He walked up onto the porch. "I thought they wouldn't let you in the house."

"They won't. Hand over your car keys if you plan to go inside."

"My car keys?" He eyed the shotgun propped against the house.

"Jane thinks she's leaving today, but since she can't get

that rattletrap she drives out of here with my car in the way, she'll try to convince you to drive her. I'm just making sure you don't get tempted.''

"I wouldn't do that to you. I hope you know that you look like a Wanted poster.''

"You might not mean to give her your keys, but the Professor's nearly as smart as God. She'll figure out something.''

"Don't you think you're getting just a little paranoid?''

"I know her. You don't. Hand 'em over.''

With a great deal of reluctance, Ethan withdrew his car keys and passed them to Cal. "Have you thought about just sending her a couple dozen roses? It works for most men.''

Cal gave a snort of disgust, got up from the rocker, and walked over to open the broken door. He stuck his head inside just long enough to call out, "Hey, Professor. The Reverend's come to visit. The same one who saw you naked as a jaybird.''

Pulling back, he held the door open for Ethan to enter, then resumed his seat in the rocker. As he extracted a frozen Milky Way from the cooler, he decided his lack of principles were a match for her brains any day.

Kevin showed up an hour later. Cal knew he should thank him for the press conferences, but old habits died hard. He scowled at him instead.

"What the hell's going on, Bomber? Why are there two cars blocking the road?''

He was getting more than a little tired of explaining himself. "You don't go inside unless you hand over your keys.''

Unlike Ethan, the kid didn't give him any argument. He shrugged, pitched them over, and stuck his head in the front door. "Don't shoot, ladies. It's the good guy.''

With a snort, Cal crossed his arms over his chest, tucked his chin, and shut his eyes. Sooner or later she was going to have to come out and talk to him. All he had to do was wait.

At one o'clock, the old man arrived. Damn people kept coming, but nobody was leaving.

Jim jerked his head toward the road. "It looks like a parking lot."

Cal held out his hand. "Give me your keys if you want to go inside."

"Cal, this has to stop."

"I'm doing my best."

"Can't you just tell her you love her?"

"She won't give me a chance."

"I hope you know what you're doing." Jim tossed over his keys and went inside.

Cal hoped so, too, and he wasn't going to admit he had doubts. Especially not to his old man.

Cal's feelings for Jane were so clear to him now, he couldn't believe he'd ever been confused. The thought of living his life without her left him with an emptiness nothing would ever fill, not even football. If only he could forget the way he'd thrown her love back at her that day she'd left him. It was the most precious gift he'd ever received, and he'd tossed it away like week-old garbage. Now she was doing the same to him.

Despite her brief flirtation with the dark side to get herself pregnant, she had more integrity than anybody he knew, and he had to put his trust in the belief that, once she loved somebody, it would last forever. Still, when he looked the truth straight on, he knew he deserved what was happening to him because he hadn't possessed the good sense to value what God had given him. He also knew he'd sit out here for the rest of his life if that's what it took to get her back.

The afternoon dragged on. The blare of rock music coming from the backyard signaled that an impromptu party had broken out, but still Jane didn't appear to talk to him.

He smelled charcoal and heard Ethan calling out, "Gin!" At one point Kevin ran around the side of the house to catch a Frisbee somebody had thrown. Everybody seemed to be having a great time except him. He was a stranger in his own family, and they were dancing on his grave.

He straightened as he saw two figures moving through the woods on the east side of the house. For a moment he thought Jane had convinced someone to help her sneak away on foot, but just as he got ready to bolt out of the chair, he recognized his father and mother.

They stopped near an old white ash he'd climbed when he was a kid. His father pressed his mother against the trunk. She wrapped her arms around his neck, and the next thing he knew, they were going at it like a couple of teenagers.

His parents' estrangement was finally over, and he smiled for the first time in days. But his smile faded as he saw the direction his father's hands were taking and realized he was getting ready to feel up his mother!

With a shudder, he turned the rocker around. There were some things he didn't want to witness, and that was right at the top of his list.

For the next couple of hours he dozed on and off between brief visits from Kevin and Ethan, neither of whom seemed to have any idea what to talk about. Ethan settled on politics, while Kevin rather predictably picked football. His father was noticeably missing, but he didn't let himself dwell on what the old man and his mother might be doing. He heard nothing from Jane.

It was close to dusk when his mother appeared. She was badly mussed, and the redness on her neck looked suspiciously like beard burn. A bit of dried leaf clung to her hair, just behind her ear, giving further evidence that she and the old man had been doing something more than collecting wildflowers out in those woods.

She gazed down at him, and her forehead creased with

worry. "Are you hungry? Would you like me to bring you a plate of food?"

"Don't do me any favors." He knew he sounded surly, but he felt as if she had betrayed him.

"I'd invite you inside, but Annie won't allow it."

"You mean Jane won't allow it."

"You've hurt her, Cal. What do you expect her to do?"

"I expect her to come out here so we can talk."

"So you can yell at her, you mean?"

Yelling was the last thing on his mind, and he started to tell her that only to find himself once again alone on the front porch. For someone who'd set out to protect his parents from his personal life, he'd made an unholy mess of it.

Night settled over the mountain, and failure twisted at his belly. He leaned forward and dropped his head into his hands. She wasn't going to come out. How had he screwed things up so badly?

The screen door creaked on its hinges, and he looked up to see her. His boots dropped to the floor, and he straightened in the chair.

She had on the same thing she'd worn the day she'd left him: that buttery cotton dress with the big tan buttons down the front. This evening there was no headband in her hair. It fell helter-skelter around her beautiful face and looked just as it did when they'd finished making love.

She slipped her hands into the pockets. "Why are you doing this?"

He wanted to sweep her right off the porch and into the woods where he'd love her until she was the one with beard burn and dry leaves in her hair. "You're not leaving, Jane. Not without giving us a chance to work this out."

"We've had lots of chances, and we've blown every one."

"You mean *I* have. I promise you I won't blow the next one."

He rose from the rocker and moved toward her. She took an instinctive step back against the railing. He forced himself not to go any closer. He wasn't the only one who didn't like being backed into a corner.

"I love you, Jane."

If he'd expected his announcement to sweep her off her feet, he'd badly miscalculated. Instead of showing pleasure, her big, sad eyes seemed to swallow her face.

"You don't love me, Cal. Don't you see? This has turned into another game for you. Last night you finally realized that you were going to lose, but you're a champion, and losing isn't acceptable. Champions do whatever it takes to win, even saying things they don't really mean."

He stared at her, flabbergasted. She didn't believe him! How could she think this was just about winning? "You're wrong. That's not it at all. I mean what I said."

"Maybe right this second you do, but remember what happened after you saw me naked. The game was over, Cal, and you lost interest. This is the same way. If I agreed to take you back, you'd lose interest."

"I didn't lose interest after I saw you naked! Where did you get that crazy idea?" He realized he was yelling, and frustration made him want to yell even louder. Why was it so impossible for him to communicate like a normal person?

He swallowed hard and ignored the film of sweat that was breaking out on his forehead. "I love you, Jane, and once I make up my mind about something, it's made up for good. We're alike that way. Call off your watchdogs."

"They're not my watchdogs, they're yours!" Agitation showed in her expression. "I've tried to get them to leave, but they won't do it. They've got this idea that you need them. *You!* Ethan's told me all the sentimental stories from your childhood, and Kevin has described every touchdown you've ever made or even thought about making. As if I care! Your father's narrowed in on your academic accomplishments, which is the last thing I want to hear about!''

"I'll bet my mother hasn't been singing my praises."

"For a while she concentrated on the good causes you support. Then she began to explain how she used to play hopscotch with you, but she started to cry and had to walk away, so I'm not sure what she was trying to tell me."

"And Annie? What did she say?"

"That you're a spawn of Satan, and I'm better off without you."

"She did not."

"Close enough."

"Jane, I love you. I don't want you to go."

Her face twisted with pain. "Right now you love the challenge of me, but that's not enough to build a life on." She hugged herself and rubbed her arms. "These past few weeks have finally cleared the cobwebs from my brain. I don't know what I was thinking of to believe we could have a lasting relationship. It can't always be raging fights and knockdown arguments. You feed on that, but I need someone who's going to be there for me after the challenge is gone."

"For all your brains, you don't understand anything!" God, he was yelling again. He took a deep breath and lowered his voice. "Can't you just take a chance that I mean exactly what I say?"

"It's too important to take chances."

"Listen to me, Jane. This isn't about fights and challenges. I love you, and I want to stay married for the rest of our lives."

She shook her head.

Pain cut through him. He was spilling his guts, but she wasn't buying any of it. He couldn't think of a single thing that would convince her.

She spoke softly. "I'm leaving tomorrow, even if I have to use the police to get me out. Good-bye, Cal." She turned away and walked inside.

He squeezed his eyes shut as despair washed through him. He was weak-kneed and aching, just as if he'd taken a career-ending hit. Except he wasn't going to give up. Not ever.

As much as the idea of public declarations upset his sense of privacy, he couldn't think of anything else to do but take his case to the people. Clenching his jaw, he followed her inside.

22

Annie had her eyes glued to VH-1, where a Whitney Houston video mutely flickered. His parents sat on the couch holding hands and gazing at each other as if they were posing for a DeBeers anniversary ad. Ethan and Kevin had pulled kitchen chairs up to the gateleg table in the corner and were playing cards. All of them looked up at Cal as he walked in. Jane had already disappeared.

He felt foolish, but he knew that reaction came from pride, an emotion he couldn't afford right now when he needed the entire team behind him. He struggled to compose himself. "Jane doesn't think I'm serious about loving her."

Ethan and Kevin regarded him over the top of their cards. His mother's forehead creased. "Do you know that she likes to dance? Not those country and western line dances, but rock and roll."

He didn't exactly see how that was going to help him right now, but he filed it away.

"I'm sick of all this commotion!" Annie slapped the remote on the arm of her chair. "Jim Bonner, you go get Janie right this minute and make her come out. It's time things got settled around here, so I can have some peace and quiet."

"Yes, ma'am." With a flicker of a smile at his wife, Jim rose from the couch and headed toward the spare bedroom.

Jane looked up from the suitcase she'd been packing and saw Jim standing in the doorway. "What's wrong?"

"You have to come out in the living room now and face Cal."

"I already faced him, and I don't want to do it again."

"You have to. Annie says."

"No."

One eyebrow shot up. "What did you say?"

"I said no?" Unfortunately, it came out as a question instead of a statement, but there was definitely something intimidating about this man and his raised eyebrow.

"Right now I'm the closest thing you've got to a father, and I'm telling you to get yourself out there!"

Bemused, she watched as he jabbed his hand in the general direction of the living room. She couldn't help comparing the authoritarian look in his eyes with the way her own father had always regarded her, as if he were vaguely repulsed.

"No arguments. March!"

She thought about asking him if he intended to ground her if she disobeyed, but decided that wasn't a good idea. "Jim, this isn't going to work."

He walked over and pulled her into his arms for a reassuring squeeze. "He needs to have his say. He deserves that."

She rested her cheek against his shirt front. "He already had his say on the front porch a few minutes ago."

"Apparently he didn't finish." He gently pushed her away and gave her a nudge toward the door. "Go on now. I'm right behind you."

Cal looked even more dangerous in the living room than he'd looked on the porch, where the light had been dimmer. She noted his narrowed gunslinger's eyes and cattle rustler's expression. She wanted to believe that the three other men present would come to her rescue if he proved to be completely unreasonable, but she suspected that they were on his side.

Cal ignored her as she made her way to stand near the television, the farthest point in the room from the place he occupied near the kitchen door. As if she were invisible, he addressed the room's other occupants.

"Here are the facts . . . I love Jane, and she loves me. I want to stay married, and she wants to stay married. All of you are standing in the way." He fell silent.

Seconds ticked by. One after the other.

"That's it?" Ethan finally asked.

Cal nodded.

Kevin tilted his head toward her. "Hey, Jane, he says we're in the way. If we weren't here, would you go off with him?"

"No."

"Sorry, Bomber. You'll have to think of something else."

Cal glared at Kevin. "Will you get the hell out of here? This doesn't have anything to do with you. I mean it, Tucker. I want you out of here. Now!"

Jane saw that Kevin was only prepared to defy Cal so far, and he'd reached his limit. But as he began to rise, Annie's words forced him back in his seat. "He's part of this, and he stays!"

Cal turned on her. "He's not family!"

"He's the future, Calvin, the same future that you don't want to look at."

Her words seemed to infuriate him. He reached into his pocket, drew out a set of keys, and fired them at Kevin, who came slowly to his feet as he caught them.

"Sorry, Mrs. Glide, but I just remembered a previous engagement."

Jane rushed toward him, finally seeing a way out of this mess. "I'll go with you."

Everyone in the room seemed to stiffen.

"That," Kevin said, ". . . is a really bad idea."

"Sit down, Jane." Jim spoke in his firm paternal voice. "It's too late for you to get a plane out tonight, anyway, so you might as well hear Cal out. Kevin, thanks for your concern."

Kevin nodded, shot Jane a sympathetic smile, gave Cal a worried look, and left.

She sank down into a chair near Annie's. Cal stuck his hands in his pockets and cleared his throat, still addressing his family instead of her. "She thinks I only want her because she's playing hard to get, and that once the challenge is gone, I won't be interested. I told her that's not true, but she doesn't believe it."

"You do like a challenge," Lynn pointed out.

"Trust me . . . living with somebody who's trying to discover the Theory of Everything is more than enough challenge. Do you have any idea what it's like to see mathematical formulas scrawled on the front page of your newspaper first thing in the morning, or on the bottom of a grocery list when all you want to do is remember to buy beer? Or how about all over the lid of your cereal box before you even have your eyes open?"

"I never wrote on your cereal box!" Jane bolted out of the chair.

"You sure as heck did! Right across the lid of my Lucky Charms."

"You're making this up. He's making it up! I admit I sometimes doodle a bit, but—" She broke off as she remembered a morning several weeks ago when a cereal box had been the only thing available. Resuming her seat, she spoke stiffly. "That sort of thing constitutes an irritation, not a challenge."

"For your information, Professor, sometimes I can be talking right to you, and without any warning, you're gone." He splayed his hands on his hips and stalked toward her. "Physically you're standing right there in front of me, but your brain has taken off into hyperspace."

She shot up her chin. "An irritation, not a challenge."

"I'm going to kill her." Gritting his teeth, he slumped down onto the couch next to his parents and glanced over at his brother. "You see what I'm up against?"

"On the other hand," Ethan said, "she looks real good naked."

"Ethan!" Mortified, Jane turned to Lynn. "It's not the way it sounds. It was an accident."

Lynn's eyes widened. "A strange accident."

"You're getting off the subject," Annie said. "Personally, I believe Calvin. If he says he loves you, Janie Bonner, he means it."

"I believe him, too," Lynn said.

"Me, too," Jim offered.

Ethan remained silent.

Jane looked toward him as if he were her lifeline.

He regarded her with a hint of apology. "I'm sorry, Jane, but there isn't even any question about this."

She had let herself entertain the fantasy that they were her family, looking out for her best interests, but now that the chips were down, blood called out only to blood. They weren't the ones who'd wake up every morning wondering if this would be the day her husband was going to lose interest in her.

"You're all wasting your breath." Cal leaned forward, resting his lower arms on his knees and speaking in a hard flat voice. "Bottom line is, she's a scientist, and scientists require proof. That's what you want, isn't it, Jane? You want me to prove my feelings to you, just like you prove those equations you scribble all over the house."

"Love doesn't work that way," Lynn pointed out.

"She won't accept that, Mom. Jane needs something tangible to stick in her equations. And you know why that is?

Because nobody's ever really loved her before, and she doesn't believe it can happen now.''

She drew back in the chair as if he'd struck her. There was a ringing in her ears, a searing sensation inside her head.

Cal shot to his feet. "You want proof of the way I feel? Okay, I'm going to give it to you." In three quick steps he was looming over her. Without warning, he swept her into his arms and carried her toward the door.

"Stop it, Cal! Put me down."

Lynn jumped to her feet. "Cal, this isn't a good idea."

"I've done it your way," he shot back. "Now I'm doing it mine." He kicked the front door open and carried her outside.

"You can't settle this with sex," Jane hissed. She gathered her anger around her as a shield to protect her broken heart. Why didn't he understand he couldn't use strong-arm tactics to solve something this complex? He was ripping her apart, and he didn't even seem to be aware of it.

"Who said anything about sex? Or is that wishful thinking?"

She sputtered with outrage as he bore her off the front porch and began walking toward the road. Although she wasn't close to being petite, he acted as if she weighed hardly anything. His breathing remained normal, his arms steady, even as he carried her down the road toward three cars that blocked the way.

He lowered her to the ground in front of his Jeep, pulled a batch of keys from his pocket, and threw several sets on the hood. Then he steered her toward his father's Blazer, which blocked the other two cars. "Get in."

"Cal, this is just postponing the inevitable."

He pushed her inside and shut the door.

She turned her head to the window. If she wasn't careful, he would wear her down, and she would agree to stay with him. That would be disastrous. Better to endure the pain now than have to go through it again when he realized he'd made a mistake.

The Professor needs something tangible to stick in her equations. And you know why that is? Because nobody's ever really loved her before, and she doesn't believe it can happen now.

She rejected Cal's words. This was his problem, not hers. She wasn't so lacking in self-esteem that she would throw away love that was honestly offered. Maybe it was true that no one had ever really loved her, but that didn't mean she wasn't ready to grab it when the real thing came along.

Did it?

Cal turned out onto the highway, interrupting the painful path of her thoughts. "I appreciate the fact that you didn't air all our dirty linen in front of my family."

"I can't imagine there's even a piece of underwear elastic they haven't seen."

"It's okay, Jane. I won't snap your head off if you bring up the subject. I know I've done that before, but it won't happen again. It doesn't take a lot of insight to know that you see me as pretty aimless right now, and I appreciate the fact that you didn't hit me with that in front of my family."

"Aimless?"

"Just because I don't know what I'm going to do when I stop playing ball doesn't mean I'm not worthy of you. I know you might think that, but everything will change as soon as I get things figured out. I just need a little more time to sort through my options, that's all."

She stared at him, flabbergasted. This was the first time he'd acknowledged that he wouldn't be playing football forever. But what did that have to do with her feelings toward him? Not for a moment had she regarded his lack of plans for the future as a roadblock.

"I've never said I don't believe you're worthy."

"You don't have to say it. I know what you're thinking. Worthy people work."

"You work."

It was as if she hadn't spoken. "You're a physicist. That's worthy work. My father's a doctor; Ethan's a minister. The guys down at the Mountaineer are teachers, plumbers, backhoe operators. They tend bar or build houses. They work. But what am I?"

"You're a football player."

"And then what?"

She caught her breath, still unable to believe he was willing to admit his professional career was coming to an end. "Only you know the answer to that."

"But, you see, I don't know the answer. I don't have any idea what I'm going to do with the rest of my life. God knows, I've got enough money tucked away for three lifetimes, but I've never seen money as the mark of anybody's worth."

She finally understood. All along, Cal's refusal to acknowledge either his age or the fact that he'd soon be forced to retire hadn't been rooted in pigheadedness, but despair over finding work that would satisfy him.

She didn't know why she was so surprised. This was the same man who'd insisted on marrying a woman he hated just so his child would be legitimate. Beneath all that macho strut, Cal had a strong set of old-fashioned values. Those values dictated that a man without worthy work didn't deserve respect.

"Cal, there are so many things you could do. You could coach, for example."

"I'd be a terrible coach. You might not have noticed, but I don't have a lot of patience with stupidity. If I told somebody something once and he didn't get it, I wouldn't have the patience to tell him a second time. That's not the way to build a successful football team."

"What about Kevin? He says he's learned more about football from you than anyone."

"That's because he catches on the first time."

"You're very good on television. Why don't you think about broadcasting?"

"I can't work up any enthusiasm for it. Once in a while it's okay, but not for a life's work. Not for me."

"You have a degree in biology. You could use that."

"My degree is fifteen years old. I don't remember a darned thing. I only got it because I like science and the outdoors."

"You have a lot of experience in business. Maybe you could start a company."

"Business bores me. Always has. Always will." He glanced over at her, but didn't quite meet her eyes. "I've been thinking that maybe I could work on my golf game. In a couple of years, I might be able to qualify for the pro tour."

"I thought you were a mediocre golfer."

"Not exactly mediocre," he said defensively. "A little better than that." He sighed. "Never mind. Stupid idea."

"You'll think of something."

"Darn right I will, so if that's what's holding you back, put it right out of your mind. I've got no intention of spending the rest of my life lazing around and living off my money. I couldn't dishonor you like that."

He meant that he couldn't dishonor himself. She wondered how long this had been twisting away inside him? "Your future job prospects aren't what's between us, Cal. You still don't understand. I can't stand having my love tossed back in my face again. It's too painful."

He flinched. "You'll never know how sorry I am about that. I had a panic reaction. Some people take a lot longer to grow up than others, and I guess I'm one of them." He reached over and covered her hand with his. "You're the most important thing in the world to me. I know you don't believe it, but I'm going to prove it to you."

Releasing her, he swung the Blazer into a parking place in front of the hardware store, then cursed softly under his breath. "It's closed for the night. I didn't even think about that."

"You're bringing me to the hardware store to prove you love me?"

"I promise I'll take you dancing soon. Rock and roll, not country and western." He got out of the car, came around to open the door for her, and drew her out to stand next to him. "Come on."

Completely mystified, she let him lead her into the narrow alley that ran between the pharmacy and hardware store. When they reached the back door, he tested the knob, but the door was locked. The next thing she knew, he'd kicked it in.

A security alarm shrieked.

"Cal! Have you gone crazy?"

"Pretty much." Grabbing her arm, he pulled her inside. What was he doing?

He manacled her wrist with his fingers and drew her past lawn chairs and lighting fixtures to the paint section. The alarm continued its disconcerting wail. "The police are going to come!" she exclaimed.

"Don't you worry about the police; Odell Hatcher and I have been friends for years. You just worry about whether or not we can find the right wallpaper for that kitchen of ours."

"*Wallpaper?* You brought me here to pick out *wallpaper?*"

He looked at her as if she were dull-witted. "How else am I supposed to prove my feelings for you?"

"But . . ."

"Here we are." He settled her, not ungently, onto one of the stools that lined the counter in the wallpaper department, then turned to regard the shelves, which were stocked with dozens of wallpaper books. "Damn, I didn't know it was going to be this complicated." He began reading off the shelf labels. "*Bathrooms. Dining rooms. Vinyls. Flocks.* What the hell is a flock? Don't they have something with— I don't know—horses or something? Do you see a horse category?"

"Horses?"

For the first time, a shadow of a smile tugged at the corner of his mouth, as if he were beginning to realize just how ridiculous this was. "You could help out a little bit here instead of just saying things back to me."

The wail of a police siren joined the security alarm, and tires screeched in front of the store. "Stay right here," he ordered. "I'll take care of this. On second thought, maybe you'd better crouch down behind the counter just in case Odell has his gun out."

"Gun! I swear, Calvin Bonner . . . when this is over, I'm going to—"

Her threat died on her lips as he pulled her from the stool and pushed her to her knees on the carpet behind the counter.

"Odell, it's me!" he called out. "Cal Bonner."

"Get out of the way, Cal!" a rough voice replied. "We got a robbery goin' on here. Don't tell me they took you hostage!"

"There's no robbery. I kicked in the door because I have to pick out some wallpaper. My wife's here, too, so if you've got any ideas about firing that gun you've got in your hand, forget it. Tell Harley I'll settle up with him tomorrow. And help me turn off this damned alarm."

It took Cal a good fifteen minutes, along with the appearance of Harley Crisp, the hardware store owner, before the alarm was turned off and things set straight.

While Cal was talking his way out of a breaking and entering charge, Jane got up from behind the counter and sat on the stool so she could ponder how, in Cal's mind, picking out wallpaper constituted proof of his love. She couldn't see even the smallest link. He'd been angry with her for stripping off the wallpaper, but what did replacing it have to do with love? There was certainly a link in his mind, however, and if she forced him to explain his logic, he'd give her that incredulous look that called into question the results of all the IQ tests she'd ever taken.

As confusing as this was, she did understand one thing. To Cal's way of thinking, this late-night shopping expedition proved his love, and that was that. A traitorous warmth began to sneak through her.

Harley Crisp finally closed the door behind him, taking along a sizable chunk of Cal's cash. They were left alone in the store.

Cal looked down at her with an expression that was suddenly uncertain. "You don't think all this is stupid, do you? You do understand about the wallpaper?"

She didn't have a clue, but nothing would make her admit it, not while he was gazing at her with his heart in his eyes and a forever kind of love softening his voice.

"What I really wanted to do for you, sweetheart, was win a football game," he said huskily. "Dan Calebow did that for Phoebe once, and I wanted to do it for you, except the season hasn't started yet, and winning a game wouldn't count with you. Besides, compared to this, that'd be so easy it wouldn't prove anything. I wanted to do something hard. Really hard." He waited, an expectant look on his face.

"Pick out wallpaper?" she offered tentatively.

His eyes came alive, as if she'd just given him the keys to the universe. "You do understand." With a groan, he pulled her off the stool and into his arms. "I was scared to death you wouldn't. I promise I'll figure out the work thing just as soon as I can."

"Oh, Cal . . ." Her words caught on a happy sob. She didn't have the faintest idea how he'd sorted all this out in his mind. She didn't understand about breaking into the hardware store or picking out wallpaper, but she knew this was real. Cal's feelings for her weren't about the challenge she presented to him. He was giving her his warrior's heart, and she wouldn't let those old wounds from her childhood keep her from taking it.

They gazed deeply into each other's eyes and saw a pathway into their own souls.

"It's a real marriage now, sweetheart," he whispered. "Forever and ever."

And then, right there in the hardware store, he pulled her down onto the carpet behind the counter and began making love to her. Naturally, he didn't want her wearing even a single stitch of clothes, and she felt the same about him.

When they were naked, he surprised her by reaching for his jeans. She propped herself up on one elbow and watched him withdraw a bedraggled pink bow from the pocket, its pom pom loops flattened almost, but not quite, beyond recognition.

"You kept it," she said.

He leaned forward to nuzzle her breast. "At first I had the idea of making you eat it, then I was going to tie you up with it while I let those rats nibble on you."

"Uhmm." She lay back and did some nibbling of her own. "What are you going to do with it now?"

He muttered something that sounded like, "You'll think it's stupid."

"I will not."

He drew back and gazed at her. "Promise you won't laugh."

She nodded solemnly.

"You were the best birthday present I ever got."

"Thank you."

"I wanted to give you something back, but I've got to

warn you that it's not half as good as my present. Even so, you have to keep it."

"All right."

He draped the pink bow around his neck and grinned. "Happy birthday, Rosebud."

23

"I swear, Jane, this is the craziest thing I ever let you talk me into. I don't know why I listened."

Cal had listened because he'd been jumping through hoops this past month trying to please her as she grew bigger than a house and grouchier than a bear. Even now, she wanted to bash him over the head, just on general principles. But she loved him too much. So she settled for snuggling into his big arms instead.

They sat in the back of a black stretch limousine heading for Heartache Mountain. The trees that lined the road were splashed with October's colors: yellows, oranges, and reds. This would be her first mountain autumn, and she'd been aching to see it, as well as get reacquainted with the friends she'd made before they'd had to leave Salvation. Cal and his family had dragged her to every important function, and it hadn't been long before the townspeople's resentment toward her had disappeared.

As the limo neared Salvation her anticipation grew. Cal had ordered the car because the hamstring injury that had him sidelined for the next few weeks also kept him from driving, and he wouldn't let her behind the wheel until after the baby was born. It was probably just as well. Her back was killing her from those awful airline seats, and she felt too crummy to concentrate on the mountain roads. She'd been having Braxton-Hicks contractions for several weeks, those practice contractions that lead up to the real thing, but they'd been worse than normal this afternoon.

He kissed the top of her head. She sighed and snuggled closer. If she'd needed anything more to convince her of Cal's love, these past few weeks had done it. As her pregnancy had advanced to its final week, she'd become demanding, moody, and generally bitchy. In response, he'd been unendingly affectionate and obnoxiously good-humored. Several times she'd tried to prick his temper just for the challenge of it, but instead of rising to the bait, he'd laughed at her.

Easy for him to be so happy, she thought sourly. He wasn't the one carrying around a thousand pounds of future Olympic athlete and Nobel laureate. He wasn't stuck in this oversize tent of a dress with a stupid Peter Pan collar; an aching back; nagging, unproductive contractions; and a pair of feet she hadn't seen in weeks! On the other hand, he was sidelined for the next few games, so he wasn't exactly on top of the world. Still, his injury was the reason they were able to fly home to Salvation in the middle of the season.

She reached down to rub his thigh. It wasn't his hamstring, but it was the closest thing she could comfort. Her eyes filled with ever-ready tears as she thought of the pain he'd been in on Sunday when that ignorant cretin who played for the Bears had sacked him on fourth and two. Cal had been playing a glorious game up until then, and if Jane could have gotten her hands on that Neanderthal after the game, she would have taken him apart.

Kevin had pretended to be sympathetic when Cal had been helped off the field, but Jane wasn't fooled. Kevin reveled in every moment of playing time he could get, and she knew he would make the most of the next two weeks while Cal was out. If she weren't so annoyed with him, she'd be proud of his progress this season. Even Cal was proud of him, although he'd never admit it.

Sometimes she thought Kevin spent more time at their house than he spent at his own. They had sold her home in Glen Ellyn and settled in Cal's condo until they decided where they were going to live permanently. For some reason, Cal had insisted on participating in every decision about paint color and furniture purchases, right down to throw pillows. He and Kevin had assembled the baby's crib together, and put up bright yellow shutters in the sunny second-story bedroom that was to be the nursery.

Even Kevin didn't know that Cal was going to announce his retirement at the end of the season. Cal wasn't entirely happy about it, since he still didn't know what he would do with himself, but he was tired of fighting his injuries. He also said he'd learned there were more important things in life than playing football.

"Women are not supposed to fly when they're nine months pregnant," he growled. "It's a wonder they didn't arrest me for bringing you on that plane."

"They wouldn't have dared. You celebrities can get away with anything." She gave him the pouty lip that made her feel so deliciously like a bimbo. "Yesterday I realized I couldn't stand the idea of having our baby in Chicago. I want to be near family."

He was a sucker for the pouty lip, and he nipped it between his own before he went on with his complaint. "You could have decided that a month ago, and I'd have sent you out here while it was still safe to travel."

"Then we'd have been split up, and neither of us could have stood that."

It was true. They needed each other in more ways than they could ever have imagined. Not only had they found passion together, but they'd found contentment, as well as an energy that had spilled over into their jobs. Cal was well on his way to breaking his all-time passing record, and her work had never gone better.

Just after they'd returned to Chicago, she'd been awarded the Coates' Prize in Physics for a paper she'd done on duality. Unbeknownst to her, the rumors about the prize had been circulating for weeks, making Jerry Miles's vendetta against her look foolish. In August, he'd been dismissed and replaced with one of the most respected physicists in the country, a man who had convinced Jane to take a permanent position at Preeze. He'd even gone so far as to bribe her with several eager young physicists to serve as her staff.

At that moment, however, Cal didn't have his wife's blossoming professional career on his mind, but her physical well-being, and she tried to ease his worries. "Be logical, Cal. I talked to Dr. Vogler this morning. She knows my medical history, and she's perfectly capable of delivering this baby."

"I still say you could have made up your mind about this a long time ago."

Her desire to have their baby here had grown stronger as her pregnancy advanced, but she wouldn't even consider leaving Cal behind in Chicago. His injury over the weekend had given her the chance she needed.

The baby twisted, and her spine felt as if it were being clamped by a giant fist. He'd go ballistic if he realized she was in this much pain, and she barely bit back a gasp.

It was gradually occurring to her that Cal was right, and getting on that plane had been a stupid thing to do. Still, first-time labor took forever, and Jim and Lynn would be waiting for her. Her father-in-law would tell her if he thought she should call Vogler.

Luckily, Cal was distracted and didn't notice anything wrong. "What's that on the inside of your wrist?" He picked up her hand.

She could barely catch her breath. "Uh . . . It's nothing."

She tried to snatch it away, but he held fast. "It's just a little pen mark. I must have marked myself accidentally."

"Now that's real strange. This looks a lot more like an equation than an accidental squiggle."

"We were coming in for landing," she sniffed, "and I couldn't get to my notebook." She caught her breath as the baby scored a 9.7 with a triple axel double toe loop. This time her back pain hit along with a fierce contraction that seemed to last forever, but might still only be a Braxton-Hicks. She swallowed a groan, which would really upset him, and distracted herself from the pain by trying to start a quarrel.

"You don't fight with me anymore."

"That's not true, sweetheart. We've been fighting ever since you told me we had to go on this trip."

"We've been arguing, not fighting. You haven't yelled once. You never yell anymore."

"I'm sorry, but I just can't seem to work up a good mad at you."

"Why not? Even *I* can't stand myself!"

"Crazy, isn't it. I can't explain."

She glared at him. "You're doing it again."

"What?"

"That thing that irritates me."

"Smiling?"

"Yes. That."

"Sorry." His hand settled over her drum-tight abdomen. "I'm so happy, I can't seem to stop."

"Try harder!"

She suppressed her own smile. Who would ever have thought a warrior like Cal Bonner would put up with this much nonsense? But he didn't seem to mind. Maybe he understood how wonderful it felt to be completely unreasonable and still see all that unqualified love shining back. How could she ever have doubted his feelings for her?

When Cal Bonner made up his mind he was in love, he stuck to it.

Cal had talked her out of her fear of having a brilliant child by making her understand that most of the misery in her childhood came, not from her intelligence, but from being raised by a distant, unfeeling parent. That was something their child would never have to worry about.

He leaned forward and peered out the window. "Damn!"

"What's wrong?"

"Can't you see? It's starting to rain!" His voice grew agitated. "What if we're up on that mountain and you decide to go into labor, but the road gets washed out so we can't get back down? What are we going to do then?"

"That only happens in books."

"I was crazy to let you talk me into this."

"We had to come. I told you. I want to have the baby here. And I dreamed Annie was on her deathbed."

"You called her as soon as you woke up this morning. You know she's all right."

"She sounded tired."

"She probably stayed up all night planning a new hate crime against our father."

She smiled. He always did that now. He referred to his mother and father as if they belonged to her as well. Not only had he given her his love, he'd given her his parents, too.

Emotions she couldn't control bubbled up inside her. Her smiled faded, and she started to cry. "You're the most wonderful husband in the world, and I don't deserve you."

She thought she heard a long-suffering sigh, but it could have been the hiss of tires on wet pavement.

"Would it make you feel better if I told you that I'm writing down every unreasonable thing you've done this past month, and I promise to take it out of your hide as soon as you're back to normal?"

She nodded.

He laughed and kissed her again as the limousine began to climb Heartache Mountain. "I love you, Janie Bonner. I really do. The night you barged into my house with that pink bow tied around your neck was the luckiest night of my life."

"Mine, too," she sniffed.

All the lights were on at Annie's, and Jim's red Blazer was parked in front. She'd seen her in-laws two weeks earlier when they'd flown to Chicago to watch Cal play and behaved like newlyweds the whole time. That night, Cal had thrown a pillow over his head and announced that they were buying a new guest room bed. One that didn't squeak!

She was anxious to see Jim and Lynn, and she didn't wait for the driver to open the door for her.

"Hold on, Jane! It's raining, and—"

She was already waddling toward the porch. Even though Cal was limping on his bandaged leg, he caught her elbow before she reached the steps and steadied her. The door burst open, and Lynn flew out.

"Cal, what were you thinking of? How could you have let her do this?"

Jane burst into tears. "I want to have my baby here!"

Lynn exchanged a look with Cal over the top of her head.

"The smarter they are," he murmured, "the harder those hormones hit 'em."

Jim appeared behind Lynn and hugged Jane as he drew her inside. Another spasm hit her. She groaned and sagged against him.

He caught her shoulders and pushed back far enough so he could look down at her. "Are you having contractions?"

"Some back pain, that's all. A few Braxton-Hicks."

Annie cackled from her rocker by the TV. Jane lumbered over, intending to give her a hug, but found she couldn't lean down that far. Annie squeezed her hand instead. "'Bout time you come back to see me."

"How often are you having these back pains?" Jim asked from behind her.

"Every couple of minutes, I guess." She gasped and pressed her hand to her back. *"Bugger!"*

Cal limped across the carpet. "Are you trying to tell me she's in labor now?"

"I wouldn't be surprised." Jim steered her away from Annie and sat her on the couch, where he put his hand on her abdomen and glanced at his watch.

Cal looked wild-eyed. "The county hospital's a good ten miles from here! Ten miles on these roads'll take us at least twenty minutes! Why didn't you say something, honey? Why didn't you tell me you were having contractions?"

"Because you'd rush me off to the hospital, and they'd send me home. Most of this back pain is from that airline seat, anyway. *Owww!"*

Jim checked his watch. Cal's expression was frantic. "Dad, we've got to get her off the mountain before the road washes out in the rain!"

"It's barely sprinkling, Cal," his mother pointed out, "and that road hasn't washed out in ten years. Besides, first babies take their time."

He paid no attention, darting to the door instead. "The limo's already left! We'll put her in the Blazer. You drive, Dad. I'll get in the backseat with her."

"No! I want to have our baby *here!"* Jane wailed.

Cal shot her a horrified glance. "Here!"

She sniffed and nodded.

"Wait just a minute." His voice grew dangerously low, giving her a small thrill of pleasure that penetrated her misery. "When you kept saying you wanted to have our baby *here*, I thought you meant this area in general and, more specifically, the county hospital!"

"No! I meant *here*! Annie's house." She hadn't meant any such thing until just this moment, but now she knew she couldn't find a more perfect birthing nest.

Cal's eyes reflected a weird combination of frenzy and fear as he twisted toward his father. "My God! She's on her way to becoming the most famous physicist in the country, and she's *dumb as a post*! You are *not* having your baby in this house! You're having it at the county hospital!"

"Okay." She smiled at him through her tears. "You're yelling at me."

He groaned.

Jim patted her hand. "Just to be safe, why don't you let me check you first, honey? Is that all right? Do you mind going into the bedroom so I can see how far along you are?"

"Can Cal come, too?"

"Of course."

"And Lynn? I want Lynn there."

"Lynn, too."

"And Annie."

Jim sighed. "Let's go, everybody."

Cal put his arm around her and led her toward Lynn's old room. Just as they passed through the door, a spasm hit her that was so strong she gasped and grabbed the doorframe. This one lasted forever, and only after it was over did she notice what else had happened.

"Cal?"

"What, sweetheart?"

"Look down. Are my feet wet?"

"Your feet? Are your—" He made a queer, strangled sound. "Your water broke. *Dad! Jane's water broke!*"

Jim had gone into the bathroom to wash, but Cal had yelled so loudly he had no difficulty hearing him. "All right, Cal. I'll be there in a minute. I'm sure there'll be plenty of time to get her to the hospital."

"If you're so damn sure, why do you have to check her first?"

"Just to be safe. The contractions are fairly close."

Cal's muscles went rigid. He steered her toward the double bed, while Lynn fetched a stack of towels, and Annie pulled back the wedding ring quilt. Jane refused to sit until Lynn had the bed protected, so Cal reached under her dress and pulled down the sodden brown maternity tights he'd helped her into that morning. By the time he had them off, along with her shoes and panties, Lynn had spread a piece of plastic sheeting and some towels over the bed. Cal eased her down on it.

Annie chose a whitewashed wooden chair at the side of the room and settled in to watch the proceedings. As Jim came back into the room, Jane finally absorbed the fact that he intended to give her a pelvic and began to feel embarrassed. He might be a doctor, but he was also her father-in-law.

Before she could think too much, another contraction hit, this one with double the intensity of the last. A scream slipped past her lips, and through the wrenching pain, it occurred to her that something didn't seem right. It wasn't supposed to happen this way.

Jim delivered a few softly uttered instructions to his son. Cal held her knees open during the examination. Lynn clasped her hand and hummed "Maggie May."

"Damn, I've got a foot," Jim said. "It's a breech."

She gave a hiss of alarm, and then another pain hit.

"Cal, get under her," Jim ordered. "Hold her in your lap and keep her legs open; you're going to get wet. Jane, don't push! Lynn, run out to the car and get my bag."

Pain and fear encompassed her. She didn't understand. What did Jim mean, he had a foot? What did her foot have to do with it? She gazed frantically at Jim as Cal leaped into the bed. "What's happening? I can't be having the baby now. It's too fast. Something's wrong, isn't it?"

"The baby's breech," he replied.

She uttered a deep groan, then cried out in pain. Breech births were high-risk, and the babies were delivered by C-section in well-equipped operating rooms, not in mountain cabins. Why hadn't she insisted they drive right to the hospital. She had endangered their precious baby by coming here first.

"The head was down when she went to the doctor on Wednesday," Cal said. Ignoring his injured leg, he slid behind her.

"Sometimes they turn," Jim answered. "It's rare, but it happens."

Cal lifted her onto his lap. With her back pressed to his chest, and his legs straddling her, he clasped her knees to keep them separated.

Her baby was in trouble, and all thoughts of modesty fled. Sitting in his lap with his powerful warrior's body encircling her, she knew he would fight the world to keep their baby safe.

Jim gave Jane's knee a gentle squeeze. "This is going to go very fast, honey. Not anything like you expected. Right now I'm going to get the other foot down, and you can't push. Cal, we have to be careful of the cord in this position. Keep her from pushing."

"Breathe, sweetheart. Breathe! That's it. Just like we practiced. You're doing great."

Pain consumed her. She felt as if she were being devoured by an animal, but Cal made her breathe with him, all the time murmuring words of love and encouragement. Funny words. Tender words.

The urge to push grew stronger, impossible to resist, and horrible sounds came from her throat. She had to push!

But Cal, the leader of men, refused to let her give in. He threatened and cajoled, and she did as he said because he gave her no other choice. She panted as he ordered, then blew out great puffs of air that ended in a scream as she fought the natural instincts of her body.

"That's it!" Jim exclaimed. "That's it, honey! You're doing great."

She could no longer distinguish one pain from another. It wasn't at all like the childbirth films they'd seen, where the couple played cards and walked in the hallways, and where there was resting time between contractions.

Minutes ticked by and her world was reduced to a thick fog of pain and Cal's voice. She followed him blindly.

"Breathe! That's it! That's it, sweetheart! You're doing great." It was as if she could feel his strength passing into her body, and she drew on it.

His voice grew hoarse. "Keep breathing, honey. And open your eyes so you can see what's happening."

She looked down and saw Jim guiding the baby feetfirst from the birth canal. She and Cal cried out together as the head appeared. Ecstasy flooded through her, a sense of absolute bliss, at the sight of their child in his grandfather's strong, capable hands. Jim quickly suctioned the mouth and nose with an ear syringe Lynn handed him, then gently laid the infant on Jane's belly.

"A girl!"

The baby made a mewing sound. They reached down to touch the wet, squirming, bloody infant. Jim cut the cord.

"Cal!"

"She's ours, sweetheart."

"Oh, Cal . . ."

"God . . . She's beautiful. You're beautiful. I love you."

"I love you! Oh, I love you!"

They murmured nonsense, kissed each other, and cried. Tears streamed down Lynn's face, too, as she picked up the baby and wrapped her in a towel. Jane was so intent on the baby and her husband that she barely noticed either the fact that Jim had delivered the placenta or the broad grin on his face.

Lynn laughed and murmured nonsense of her own as she used a soft, damp washcloth to do a quick cleanup where Annie could see.

Annie Glide regarded her great-granddaughter with satisfaction. "This one's going to be a crackerjack. A real crackerjack. Just you wait and see. Glide blood runs true."

Lynn gave a watery laugh, then brought the baby back to Jane, but Cal's capable, quarterback's hands scooped her up first. "Come here, sweetheart. Let's get a good look at you."

He held the baby in front of Jane so they could drink in the sight of her tiny, wizened face together, then he dropped his lips to the miniature forehead. "Welcome to the world, sweetheart. We're so glad you're here."

Bemused and utterly at peace, Jane watched father and daughter get acquainted. She found herself remembering that moment so long ago when she'd cried out to Cal, *This is my baby! Nobody's baby but mine!* As she gazed around the room at two grandparents who looked as if they'd been handed the stars, a cantankerous great-grandmother, and a father who was falling head over heels in love even as Jane watched, she realized how wrong she had been.

Right then, she knew she'd found it. The ultimate Theory of Everything.

Cal's head shot up. "I just figured it out!" His hoot of laughter startled his newborn daughter's eyes open, but she didn't cry because she already had his number. Big, loud, softhearted. A pushover.

"Jane! Mom! Dad! I know what I'm going to do with my life!"

Jane stared at him. "What? Tell me?"

"I can't believe it!" he exclaimed. "After all this worry, it's been staring me in the face the whole time."

"Why didn't you tell me you was worried, Calvin?" a querulous voice piped up from the corner. "I could of told you what you needed to know years ago."

They turned to stare at her.

She scowled at them. "Anybody with half a brain could have figured out Calvin was destined to be a mountain doctor, just like his daddy and granddaddy afore him. Bonner blood runs true.''

"A doctor?'' Jane twisted her head and gazed at him in astonishment. "Is she right? You're going to be a doctor?''

Cal glared at his grandmother. "Don't you think you could have said something a long time ago?!''

She sniffed. "Nobody asked me.''

Jane laughed. "You're going to be a doctor? That's perfect!''

"By the time I'm done, I'm going to be an *old* doctor. You think you can handle having your husband go back to school?''

"I can't think of anything I'd enjoy more.''

At that moment Rosie Darlington Bonner decided she'd been ignored long enough. This was her big moment, darn it, and she wanted some attention! After all, she had lots to do. There were pesky little brothers to welcome into the world, friends to make, trees to climb, parents to appease, and, most of all, great novels to write.

There were also *lots* of math tests to flunk along the way, not to mention an unfortunate experience in chem lab with a cretin of a science teacher who didn't appreciate good literature. But maybe it was better the two people looking down at her with those goofy expressions on their faces didn't know about the chem lab yet . . .

Rosie Darlington Bonner opened her mouth and howled. *Here I am, world! Ready or not!*

Author's Note

It's said we're attracted to what we fear the most, and I'm beginning to believe that's true, since this is my second book that involves science and technology, an area in which I am—let's be honest—a complete doofus.

A number of books were extremely helpful in my research, even though I only understood a fraction of them, and I'd like to acknowledge the following: Paul Davies, *God and the New Physics*; James Gleick, *Chaos: Making a New Science*; Leon Lederman (with Dick Teresi), *The God Particle*. Also Mudhusree Mukerjee's article, "Explaining Everything," in *Scientific American*, January 1996, proved to be extremely useful.

Thanks to my husband, Bill, for being my viewing companion as I watched superstar Professor Richard Wolfson's sixteen-part videotaped lecture series on "Einstein's Relativity and the Quantum Revolution," produced by The Teaching Company. Professor Wolfson and Bill—God bless them both!—had a wonderful time.

A big thank you to everyone at Avon Books for their support, especially my editor, Carrie Feron, and her wonderfully competent assistant, Ann McKay Thoroman. Continued appreciation to my agent, Steven Axelrod.

A number of people were especially helpful in the preparation of this book. I'd like to acknowledge Dr. Robert Miller, Pat Hagan, Lisa Libman, my buddy Diane, and all the Phillips family cereal eaters. Speaking of cereal... Thanks Bryan, Jason, and Ty, even though you should have been studying instead. Go Boilers!

And to my readers—You'll never know how much your letters mean. Thank you.

Susan Elizabeth Phillips

Susan Elizabeth Phillips
www.susanephillips.com

This Heart of Mine

To Jill Barnett

for her talents as a matchmaker

Acknowledgments

Thank you to everyone who has rallied around me with handy facts and personal expertise, especially Steve Axelrod, Jill Barnett, Christine Foutris, Ann Maxwell, Bill Phillips, John Roscich, Betty Schulte, the Windy City RWA moms, and Chris Zars. Also the incomparable Creative Fest team of Jennifer Crusie, Jennifer Greene, Cathie Linz, Lindsay Longford, and Suzette Vann. Barbara Jepson has simplified my life immeasurably. Carrie Feron continues to earn my undying gratitude with wisdom, friendship, and editorial guidance. I am hugely indebted to all the people at Morrow/Avon who do so much for me. Thanks, Ty, for lending Molly your condo, and Zach, for writing Kevin and Molly such pretty love songs. Most of all, thanks to my readers for insisting that Kevin have his own story. In order to tell it, I've taken a few liberties with time passage and the ages of characters associated with the Chicago Stars football team. I hope those of you who care about this sort of thing will forgive me.

Susan Elizabeth Phillips
www.susanelizabethphillips.com

Chapter 1

Daphne the Bunny was admiring her sparkly violet nail polish when Benny the Badger zoomed past on his red mountain bike and knocked her off her paws.

"Oh, you pesky badger!" she exclaimed. "Somebody needs to squeeze the air out of your tires."

Daphne Takes a Tumble

THE DAY KEVIN TUCKER NEARLY KILLED HER, MOLLY SOMERVILLE swore off unrequited love forever.

She was dodging the icy places in the Chicago Stars headquarters parking lot when Kevin came roaring out of nowhere in his brand-new $140,000 fire-engine-red Ferrari 355 Spider. With tires shrieking and engine snarling, the low-slung car sprang around the corner, spewing slush. As the rear end flew toward her, she flung herself backward, hit the bumper of her brother-in-law's Lexus, lost her footing, and fell in a cloud of angry exhaust.

Kevin Tucker didn't even slow.

Molly gazed at the fading taillights, gritted her teeth, and picked herself up. Dirty snow and muck clung to one leg of her excruciatingly expensive Comme des Garçons pants, her Prada tote was a mess, and her Italian boots had a scratch. "Oh, you pesky quarterback," she muttered under her breath. "Somebody needs to castrate you."

He hadn't even *seen* her, let alone noticed that he'd nearly killed her! Of course, that was nothing new. Kevin Tucker had spent his entire career with the Chicago Stars football team not noticing her.

> Daphne dusted off her fluffy white cottontail, rubbed the dirt from her shimmery blue pumps, and decided to buy herself the fastest pair of Rollerblades in the whole world. So fast she could catch up with Benny and his mountain bike . . .

Molly spent a few moments contemplating chasing Kevin in the chartreuse Volkswagen Beetle she'd bought used after she'd sold her Mercedes, but even her fertile imagination couldn't conjure up a satisfactory conclusion to that scene. As she headed toward the front entrance of Stars headquarters, she shook her head in self-disgust. The man was reckless and shallow, and he only cared about football. Enough was enough. She was finished with unrequited love.

Not that it was really love. Instead, she had a pathetic crush on the jerk, which might be excusable if she were sixteen, but was ludicrous for a twenty-seven-year-old woman with a near-genius IQ.

Some genius.

A blast of warm air hit her as she entered the lobby through a set of glass doors emblazoned with the team logo, consisting of three interlocking gold stars in a sky blue oval. She no longer spent much time at the Chicago Stars headquarters as she'd done when she was still in high school. Even then she'd felt like a stranger. As a dyed-in-the-wool romantic, she preferred reading a really good novel or losing herself in a museum to watching contact sports. Of course she was a dedicated Stars fan, but her loyalty was more a product of family background than natural inclination. Sweat, blood, and the violent clashing of shoulder pads were as foreign to her nature as . . . well . . . Kevin Tucker.

"Aunt Molly!"

"We've been waiting for you!"

"You'll never ever guess what happened!"

She smiled as her beautiful eleven-year-old nieces came flying into the lobby, blond hair streaming behind them.

Tess and Julie looked like miniature versions of their mother, Molly's older sister, Phoebe. The girls were identical twins, but Tess was enveloped in jeans and a baggy Stars sweatshirt, while Julie wore black capris and a pink sweater. Both were athletic but Julie loved ballet, and Tess triumphed at team sports. Their sunny, optimistic natures made the Calebow twins popular with their classmates but a trial to their parents, since it never occurred to either girl to turn down a challenge.

The twins screeched to a stop. Whatever they'd been about to tell Molly vanished as they stared at her hair.

"Omigod, it's red!"

"Really red!"

"That's so cool! Why didn't you tell us?"

"It was sort of an impulse," Molly replied.

"I'm gonna dye my hair just like it!" Julie announced.

"Not your best idea," Molly said quickly. "Now, what were you going to tell me?"

"Dad is like so mad," Tess declared, eyes wide.

Julie's eyes grew even larger. "Him and Uncle Ron have been fighting with Kevin again."

Molly's ears perked up, even though she'd turned her back forever on unrequited love. "What did he do? Other than nearly run me over."

"He did?"

"Never mind. Tell me."

Julie took a gulp of air. "He went skydiving in Denver the day before the Broncos game."

"Oh, boy . . . " Molly's heart sank.

"Dad just found out about it, and he fined him ten thousand dollars!"

"Wow." As far as Molly knew, this was the first time Kevin had ever been fined.

The quarterback's uncharacteristic recklessness had started just before training camp in July, when an amateur motorcycle dirt track racing event had left him with a sprained wrist. It was unlike him to do anything that could jeopardize his performance on the field, so everyone had been sympathetic, especially Dan, who considered Kevin the consummate professional.

Dan's attitude had begun to shift, however, after word reached him that during the regular season Kevin had gone paragliding in Monument Valley. Not long after, the quarterback bought the high-performance Ferrari Spider that had knocked Molly over in the parking lot. Then last month the *Sun-Times* reported that Kevin had left Chicago after the Monday postgame meetings to fly out to Idaho for a day of heli-skiing in a secluded back bowl at Sun Valley. Since Kevin hadn't been injured, Dan had only given him a warning. But the recent skydiving incident had obviously pushed her brother-in-law over the edge.

"Dad yells all the time, but I never heard him yell at Kevin until today," Tess reported. "And Kevin yelled back. He said he knew what he was doing and he wasn't hurt and Dad should stay out of his private business."

Molly winced. "I'll bet your dad didn't like that."

"He really yelled then," Julie said. "Uncle Ron tried to calm them down, but Coach came in, and then he started yelling, too."

Molly knew that her sister Phoebe had an aversion to yelling. "What did your mom do?"

"She went to her office and turned up Alanis Morissette."

Probably a good thing.

They were interrupted by the pounding of sneakers as her five-year-old nephew, Andrew, came flying around the corner, much like Kevin's Ferrari. "Aunt Molly! Guess what?" He hurled himself against her knees. "Everybody yelled, and my ears hurt."

Since Andrew was blessed with not only his father's good looks but also Dan Calebow's booming voice, Molly sincerely doubted that. Still, she stroked his head. "I'm sorry."

He looked up at her with stricken eyes. "And Kevin was soooo mad at Daddy and Uncle Ron and Coach that he said the F word."

"He shouldn't have done that."

"Twice!"

"Oh, dear." Molly resisted a smile. Spending so much time inside the headquarters of a National Football League team office made it inevitable that the Calebow children heard more than their share of obscenities, but the family rules were clear. Inappropriate language in the Calebow household meant heavy fines, although not as heavy as Kevin's ten thousand dollars.

She couldn't understand it. One of the things she most hated about her crush—her *ex*-crush—on Kevin was the fact that her crush was on *Kevin,* the shallowest man on earth. Football was all that mattered to him. Football and an endless parade of blank-faced international models. Where did he find them? NoPersonality.com?

"Hi, Aunt Molly."

Unlike her siblings, eight-year-old Hannah walked toward Molly instead of running. Although Molly loved all four children equally, her heart held a special place for this vulnerable middle child who didn't share either her siblings' athletic prowess or their bottomless self-confidence. Instead, she was a dreamy romantic, a too-sensitive, overly imaginative bookworm with a talent for drawing, just like her aunt.

"I like your hair."

"Thank you."

Her perceptive gray eyes spotted what her sisters had missed, the grime on Molly's pants.

"What happened?"

"I slipped in the parking lot. Nothing serious."

Hannah took a nibble from her bottom lip. "Did they tell you about the fight Kevin and Dad had?"

She looked upset, and Molly had a pretty good idea why. Kevin showed up at the Calebow house from time to time, and like her foolish aunt, the eight-year-old had a crush on him. But unlike Molly, Hannah's love was pure.

Since Andrew was still wrapped around her knees, Molly held her arm out toward Hannah, who cuddled against her. "People have to take the consequences of their actions, sweetheart, and that includes Kevin."

"What do you think he'll do?" Hannah whispered.

Molly was fairly certain he'd console himself with another model who had a minimal mastery of the English language but maximum mastery of the erotic arts. "I'm sure he'll be fine once he gets over being angry."

"I'm afraid he'll do something foolish."

Molly brushed back a lock of Hannah's light brown hair. "Like skydiving the day before the Broncos game?"

"He prob'ly wasn't thinking."

She doubted that Kevin's small brain had the capacity to think about anything except football, but she didn't share that observation with Hannah. "I need to talk to your mom for a few minutes, and then you and I can leave."

"It's my turn after Hannah," Andrew reminded her as he finally released her legs.

"I haven't forgotten." The children took turns having overnights at her tiny North Shore condo. Usually they stayed with her on weekends instead of a Tuesday night, but the teachers had an in-service education day tomorrow, and Molly thought Hannah needed a little extra attention.

"Get your backpack. I won't be long."

She left them behind and headed down a corridor lined with photographs that marked the history of the Chicago

Stars. Her father's portrait came first, and she saw that her sister had freshened up the black horns she'd long ago painted on his head. Bert Somerville, the founder of the Chicago Stars, had been dead for years, but his cruelties lived on in both his daughters' memories.

A formal portrait of Phoebe Somerville Calebow, the Stars' current owner, followed, and then a photograph of her husband, Dan Calebow, from the days when he'd been the Stars' head coach instead of the team's president. Molly regarded her temperamental brother-in-law with a fond smile. Dan and Phoebe had raised her from the time she was fifteen, and both of them had been better parents on their worst day than Bert Somerville on his best.

There was also a photo of Ron McDermitt, the Stars' longtime general manager and Uncle Ron to the kids. Phoebe, Dan, and Ron had worked hard to balance the all-consuming job of running an NFL team with family life. Over the years it had involved several reorganizations, one of which had brought Dan back to the Stars after being away for a while.

Molly made a quick detour into the restroom. As she draped her coat over the sink, she gazed critically at her hair. Although the jagged little cut complimented her eyes, she hadn't left well enough alone. Instead, she'd dyed her dark brown hair a particularly bright shade of red. She looked like a cardinal.

At least the hair color added some flash to her rather ordinary features. Not that she was complaining about her looks. She had an all-right nose and an all-right mouth. They went along with an all-right body, which was neither too thin nor too heavy, but healthy and functional, for which she was grateful. A glance at her bustline confirmed what she'd accepted long ago—as the daughter of a showgirl, she'd been shortchanged.

Her eyes were nice, though, and she liked to believe their

slight tilt gave her a mysterious look. As a child she used to wear a half-slip over the bottom half of her face as a veil and pretend she was a beautiful Arabian spy.

With a sigh she swiped at the muck on her ancient Comme des Garçons pants, then wiped off her beloved but battered Prada tote. When she'd done her best, she picked up the quilted brown coat she'd bought on sale at Target and headed for her sister's office.

It was the first week of December, and some of the staff had begun to put up a few Christmas decorations. Phoebe's office door displayed a cartoon Molly had drawn of Santa dressed in a Stars uniform. She poked her head inside. "Aunt Molly's here."

Gold bangles clinked as her blond bombshell of an older sister threw down her pen. "Thank God. A voice of sanity is just what I— Oh, my God! What did you do to your hair?"

With her own cloud of pale blond hair, amber eyes, and drop-dead figure, Phoebe looked rather like Marilyn Monroe might have looked if she'd made it into her forties, although Molly couldn't imagine Marilyn with a smear of grape jelly on the front of her silk blouse. No matter what Molly did to herself, she'd never be as beautiful as her sister, but she didn't mind. Few people knew the misery Phoebe's lush body and vamp's beauty had once caused her.

"Oh, Molly . . . not again." The consternation in her sister's eyes made Molly wish she'd worn a hat.

"Relax, will you? Nothing's going to happen."

"How can I relax? Every time you do something drastic to your hair, we have another *incident*."

"I outgrew *incidents* a long time ago." Molly sniffed. "This was purely cosmetic."

"I don't believe you. You're getting ready to do something crazy again, aren't you?"

"I am not!" If she said it frequently enough, maybe she'd convince herself.

"Only ten years old," Phoebe muttered to herself. "The brightest and best-behaved student at the boarding school. Then, out of nowhere, you hack off your bangs and plant a stink bomb in the dining hall."

"Nothing more than a gifted child's chemistry experiment."

"Thirteen years old. Quiet. Studious. Not a single misstep since the stink-bomb incident. Until you started combing grape Jell-O powder through your hair. Then presto change-o! You pack up Bert's college trophies, call a garbage company, and have them hauled away."

"You liked that one when I told you about it. Admit it."

But Phoebe was on a roll, and she wasn't admitting anything. "Four years go by. Four years of model behavior and high scholastic achievement. Dan and I have taken you into our home, into our *hearts*. You're a senior, on your way to being valedictorian. You have a stable home, people who love you . . . You're vice-president of the Student Council, so why should I worry when you put blue and orange stripes in your hair?"

"They were the school colors," Molly said weakly.

"I get the call from the police telling me that my sister— my studious, brainy, Citizen of the Month sister!—deliberately set off a fire alarm during fifth-period lunch! No more *little* mischief for our Molly! Oh, no . . . She's gone straight to a class-two *felony*!"

It had been the most miserable thing Molly had ever done. She'd betrayed the people who loved her, and even after a year of court supervision and many hours of community service, she hadn't been able to explain why. That understanding had come later, during her sophomore year at Northwestern.

It had been in the spring, right before finals. Molly had found herself restless and unable to concentrate. Instead of studying, she read stacks of romance novels, drew, or stared at her hair in the mirror and yearned for something pre-Raphaelite. Even using up her allowance on hair extensions hadn't made the restlessness go away. Then one day she'd walked out of the college bookstore and discovered a calculator that she hadn't paid for tucked in her purse.

Wiser than she'd been in high school, she'd rushed back inside to return it and headed for Northwestern's counseling office.

Phoebe interrupted Molly's thoughts by jumping to her feet. "And the last time . . . "

Molly winced, even though she'd known this was where Phoebe would end up.

" . . . the *last* time you did something this drastic to your hair—that awful crew cut two years ago . . . "

"It was trendy, not awful."

Phoebe set her teeth. "The last time you did something this drastic, you gave away *fifteen million dollars!*"

"Yes, well . . . Getting the crew cut was purely coincidental."

"*Ha!*"

For the fifteen millionth time, Molly explained why she'd done it. "Bert's money was strangling me. I needed to make a final break from the past so I could be my own person."

"A poor person!"

Molly smiled. Although Phoebe would never admit it, she understood exactly why Molly had given up her inheritance. "Look on the bright side. Hardly anybody knows I gave away my money. They just think that I'm eccentric for driving a used Beetle and living in a place the size of a closet."

"You adore that place."

Molly didn't even try to deny it. Her loft was her most precious possession, and she loved knowing she earned the money that paid her mortgage each month. Only someone who'd grown up without a home that was truly her own could understand what it meant to her.

She decided to change the subject before Phoebe could

start in on her again. "The munchkins told me Dan hit Mr. Shallow with a ten-thousand-dollar fine."

"I wish you wouldn't call him that. Kevin's not shallow, he's just—"

"Interest-impaired?"

"Honestly, Molly, I don't know why you dislike him so much. The two of you couldn't have exchanged even a dozen words over the years."

"By design. I avoid people who speak only Gridiron."

"If you knew him better, you'd adore him as much as I do."

"Isn't it fascinating that he mainly dates women with limited English? But I guess it prevents a silly thing like conversation from interfering with sex."

Phoebe laughed in spite of herself.

Although Molly shared almost everything with her sister, she hadn't shared her own infatuation with the Stars' quarterback. Not only would it be humiliating, but Phoebe would confide in Dan, who'd go ballistic. Her brother-in-law was more than a little protective where Molly was concerned, and unless an athlete was happily married or gay, he didn't want Molly anywhere near him.

At that moment the subject of her thoughts burst into the room. Dan Calebow was big, blond, and handsome. Age had treated him kindly, and in the twelve years since Molly had known him, the added lines in that virile face had only given him character. His was the kind of presence that filled a room by reflecting the perfect self-confidence of someone who knew what he stood for.

Dan had been head coach when Phoebe had inherited the Stars. Unfortunately, she hadn't known anything about football, and he'd immediately declared war. Their early battles had been so fierce that Ron McDermitt had once suspended Dan for insulting her, but it wasn't long before their anger turned into something else entirely.

Molly considered Phoebe and Dan's love story the stuff of

legend, and she'd long ago decided that if she couldn't have what her sister and brother-in-law had together, she didn't want anything. Only a Great Love Story would satisfy Molly, and that was as likely as Dan rescinding Kevin's fine.

Her brother-in-law automatically wrapped an arm around Molly's shoulders. When Dan was with his family, he always had an arm around someone. A pang shot through her heart. Over the years she'd dated a lot of decent guys and even tried to convince herself she was in love with one or two of them, but she'd fallen out of love the moment she realized they couldn't come close to filling the giant shadow cast by her brother-in-law. She was beginning to suspect no one ever would.

"Phoebe, I know you like Kevin, but this time he's gone too far." His Alabama drawl always grew broader when he was upset, and now he was dripping molasses.

"That's what you said last time," Phoebe replied. "And you like him, too."

"I don't understand it! Playing for the Stars is the most important thing in his life. Why is he working so hard to screw that up?"

Phoebe smiled sweetly. "You could probably answer that better than either one of us, since you were a pretty big screwup until I came along."

"You must have me confused with someone else."

Phoebe laughed, and Dan's glower gave way to the intimate smile Molly had witnessed a thousand times and envied just as many. Then his smile faded. "If I didn't know him better, I'd think the devil was chasing him."

"Devils," Molly interjected. "All with foreign accents and big breasts."

"It goes along with being a football player, which is something I don't ever want you to forget."

She didn't want to hear any more about Kevin, so she gave Dan a quick peck on the cheek. "Hannah's waiting. I'll have her back late tomorrow afternoon."

"Don't let her see the morning papers."

"I won't." Hannah brooded when the newspapers weren't kind to the Stars, and Kevin's fine was sure to be controversial.

Molly waved her good-byes, collected Hannah, kissed the sibs, and set off for home. The East-West Tollway was already backing up with rush-hour traffic, and Molly knew it would be well over an hour before she got to Evanston, the old North Shore town that was both the location of her alma mater and her current home.

"Slytherin!" she called out to the jerk who cut her off.

"Dirty, rotten Slytherin!" Hannah echoed.

Molly smiled to herself. The Slytherins were the bad kids in the Harry Potter books, and Molly had turned the word into a useful G-rated curse. She'd been amused when Phoebe, then Dan, had started to use it. As Hannah began to chatter about her day, Molly found herself thinking back to her conversation with Phoebe and those years right after she'd finally come into her inheritance.

Bert's will had left Phoebe the Chicago Stars. What remained of his estate after a series of bad investments had gone to Molly. Since Molly was a minor, Phoebe had tended the money until it had grown into fifteen million dollars. Finally, with the emancipation of being twenty-one, along with her brand-new degree in journalism, Molly had taken control of her inheritance and started living the high life in a luxury apartment on Chicago's Gold Coast.

The place was sterile and her neighbors much older, but she was slow to realize she'd made a mistake. Instead, she'd indulged herself in the designer clothes she adored and bought presents for her friends as well as an expensive car for herself. But after a year she'd finally admitted that the life of the idle rich wasn't for her. She was used to working hard, whether in school or at the summer jobs Dan had insisted she take, so she'd accepted a position at a newspaper.

The work kept her busy, but it wasn't creative enough to be fulfilling, and she began to feel as if she were playing at life instead of living it. Finally she decided to quit so she could work on the epic romantic saga she'd always fantasized about writing. Instead, she found herself tinkering with the stories she made up for the Calebow children, tales of a spunky little bunny who wore the latest fashions, lived in a cottage at the edge of Nightingale Woods, and couldn't stay out of trouble.

She'd begun putting the stories on paper, then illustrating them with the funny drawings she'd done all her life but never taken seriously. Using pen and ink, then filling in the sketches with bright acrylic colors, she watched Daphne and her friends come alive.

She'd been elated when Birdcage Press, a small Chicago publisher, bought her first book, *Daphne Says Hello,* even though the advance money barely covered her postage. Still, she'd finally found her niche. But her vast wealth made her work seem more like a hobby than a vocation, and she continued feeling dissatisfied. Her restlessness grew. She hated her apartment, her wardrobe, her hair . . . A jazzy little crew cut didn't help.

She needed to pull a fire alarm.

Since those days were behind her, she'd found herself seated in her attorney's office telling him she wanted all of her money put into a foundation that would help disadvantaged children. He'd been flabbergasted, but she'd felt completely satisfied for the first time since she'd turned twenty-one. Phoebe had been given the opportunity to prove herself when she'd inherited the Stars, but Molly had never had that chance. Now she would. When she signed the papers, she felt feather-light and free.

"I love it here." Hannah sighed as Molly unlocked the door of her tiny second-floor loft a few minutes' walk from downtown Evanston. Molly gave her own sigh of pleasure. Even though she hadn't been gone long, she always loved the moment when she walked inside her own home.

All the Calebow children regarded Aunt Molly's loft as the coolest place on earth. The building had been constructed in 1910 for a Studebaker dealer, then used as an office building and eventually a warehouse before being renovated a few years ago. Her condo had floor-to-ceiling industrial windows, exposed ductwork, and old brick walls that held some of her drawings and paintings. Her unit was both the smallest in the building and the cheapest, but the fourteen-foot ceilings gave it a spacious feeling. Every month when she made her mortgage payment, she kissed the envelope before she slipped it into the mailbox. A silly ritual, but she did it just the same.

Most people assumed that Molly still had a stake in the Stars, and only a few of her very closest friends knew she was no longer a wealthy heiress. She supplemented her small income from the Daphne books by writing articles freelance for a teen magazine called *Chik*. There wasn't much left at the end of the month for her favorite luxuries—great clothes and hardback books, but she didn't mind. She bargain-shopped and used the library.

Life was good. She might never have a Great Love Story like Phoebe's, but at least she was blessed with a wonderful imagination and an active fantasy life. She had no complaints and certainly no reason to be afraid that her old restlessness might be rearing its unpredictable head. Her new hairstyle was nothing more than a fashion statement.

Hannah threw off her coat and crouched down to greet Roo, Molly's small gray poodle, who'd scampered to the door to greet them. Both Roo and the Calebows' poodle, Kanga, were the offspring of Phoebe's beloved Pooh.

"Hey, stinker, did you miss me?" Molly tossed down her mail to plant a kiss on Roo's soft gray topknot. Roo reciprocated by swiping Molly's chin with his tongue, then crouching down to produce his very best growl.

"Yeah, yeah, we're impressed, aren't we, Hannah?"

Hannah giggled and looked up at Molly. "He still likes to pretend he's a police dog, doesn't he?"

"The baddest dog on the force. Let's not damage his self-esteem by telling him he's a poodle."

Hannah gave Roo an extra squeeze, then abandoned him to head for Molly's workspace, which took up one end of the open living area. "Have you written any more articles? I loved 'Prom-Night Passion.'"

Molly smiled. "Soon."

In keeping with the demands of the marketplace, the articles she freelanced to *Chik* were almost always published with suggestive titles, although their content was tame. "Prom-Night Passion" stressed the consequences of backseat sex. "From Virgin to Vixen" had been an article on cosmetics, and "Nice Girls Go Wild" followed three fourteen-year-olds on a camping trip.

"Can I see your new drawings?"

Molly hung up their coats. "I don't have any. I'm just getting started with a new idea." Sometimes her books began with idle sketches, other times with text. Today it had been real-life inspiration.

"Tell me! Please!"

They always shared cups of Constant Comment tea before they did anything else, and Molly walked into the tiny kitchen that sat opposite her work area to put water on to boil. Her minuscule sleeping loft was located just above, where it looked out over the living space below. Metal shelves on the downstairs walls overflowed with the books she adored: her beloved set of Jane Austen's novels, tattered copies of the works of Daphne Du Maurier and Anya Seton, all of Mary Stewart's early books, along with Victoria Holt, Phyllis Whitney, and Danielle Steel.

Narrower shelves held double-deep rows of paperbacks—historical sagas, romance, mysteries, travel guides, and reference books. Her favorite literary writers were also well represented, along with biographies of famous women and some of Oprah's less depressing book club selections, most of which Molly had discovered before Oprah shared them with the world.

She kept the children's books she loved on shelves in the sleeping loft. Her collection included all the Eloise stories and Harry Potter books, *The Witch of Blackbird Pond*, some Judy Blume, Gertrude Chandler Warner's *The Boxcar Children*, *Anne of Green Gables*, a little Sweet Valley High for fun, and the tattered Barbara Cartland books she'd discovered when she was ten. It was the collection of a dedicated bookworm, and all the Calebow children loved curling up on her bed with a whole stack piled around them while they tried to decide which one to read next.

Molly pulled out a pair of china teacups with delicate gold rims and a scatter of purple pansies. "I decided today that I'm calling my new book *Daphne Takes a Tumble*."

"Tell me!"

"Well . . . Daphne is walking through Nightingale Woods minding her own business when, out of nowhere, Benny comes racing past on his mountain bike and knocks her off her feet."

Hannah shook her head disapprovingly. "That pesky badger."

"Exactly."

Hannah regarded her cagily. "I think somebody should steal Benny's mountain bike. Then he'd stay out of trouble."

Molly smiled. "Stealing doesn't exist in Nightingale Woods. Didn't we talk about that when you wanted somebody to steal Benny's jet ski?"

"I guess." Her mouth set in the mulish line she'd inherited from her father. "But if there can be mountain bikes and jet skis in Nightingale Woods, I don't see why there can't be stealing, too. And Benny doesn't mean to do bad things. He's just mischievous."

Molly thought of Kevin. "There's a thin line between mischief and stupidity."

"Benny's not stupid!"

Hannah looked stricken, and Molly wished she'd kept her mouth shut. "Of course he's not. He's the smartest badger in Nightingale Woods." She ruffled her niece's hair. "Let's have our tea, and then we'll take Roo for a walk by the lake."

Molly didn't get a chance to look at her mail until later that night, after Hannah had fallen asleep with a tattered copy of *The Jennifer Wish*. She put her phone bill in a clip, then absentmindedly opened a business-size envelope. She wished she hadn't bothered as she took in the letterhead.

Straight Kids for a Straight America

The radical homosexual agenda has targeted your children! Our most innocent citizens are being lured toward the evils of perversion by obscene books and irresponsible television shows that glorify this deviant and morally repugnant behavior . . .

Straight Kids for a Straight America, SKIFSA, was a Chicago-based organization whose wild-eyed members had been appearing on all the local talk shows to spew their personal paranoia. If only they'd turn their energies to something constructive, like keeping guns away from kids, and she tossed the letter in the trash.

Late the next afternoon Molly lowered one hand from the steering wheel and ran her fingers through Roo's topknot. Earlier she'd returned Hannah to her parents, and now she was on her way to the Calebows' Door County, Wisconsin, vacation home. It would be late when she got there, but the roads were clear and she didn't mind driving at night.

She'd made the decision to travel north impulsively. Her conversation with Phoebe yesterday had exposed something she'd been doing her best to deny. Her sister was right. Having her hair dyed red was a symptom of a bigger problem. Her old restlessness was back.

True, she wasn't experiencing any compulsion to pull a fire alarm, and giving away her money was no longer an option. But that didn't mean that her subconscious couldn't find some new way to commit mayhem. She had the uneasy sensation she was being drawn back to a place she thought she'd left behind.

She remembered what the counselor had told her all those years ago at Northwestern.

"As a child, you believed you could make your father love you if you did everything you were supposed to. If you got the best grades, minded your manners, followed all the rules, then he'd give you the approval every child needs. But your father was incapable of that kind of love. Eventually something inside you snapped, and you did the worst thing you could think of. Your rebellion was actually healthy. It kept you functioning."

"That doesn't explain what I did in high school," she'd told him. "Bert was dead by then, and I was living with Phoebe and Dan. They both love me. And what about the shoplifting incident?"

"Maybe you needed to test Phoebe and Dan's love."

Something odd had fluttered inside her. "What do you mean?"

"The only way you can make certain their love is unconditional is to do something terrible and then see if they're still around for you."

And they had been.

So why was her old problem coming back to haunt her?

She didn't want mayhem in her life anymore. She wanted to write her books, enjoy her friends, walk her dog, and play with her nieces and nephew. But she'd been feeling restless for weeks, and one look at her red hair, which really was awful, told her she might be on the verge of going off the deep end again.

Until that urge faded, she'd do the sensible thing and hide away in Door County for a week or so. After all, what possible trouble could she get into there?

Kevin Tucker had been dreaming about Red Jack Express, a quarterback delayed sneak, when something woke him up. He rolled over, groaned, and tried to figure out where he was, but the bottle of scotch he'd befriended before he'd fallen asleep made that tough. Normally adrenaline was his drug of choice, but tonight alcohol had seemed like a good alternative.

He heard the sound again, a scratching at the door, and it all came back to him. He was in Door County, Wisconsin, the Stars weren't playing this week, and Dan had slapped him with a ten-thousand-dollar fine. After he'd done that, the son of a bitch had ordered him to go up to their vacation house and stay there till he got his head together.

There wasn't a damn thing wrong with his head, but there was definitely a problem with the Calebows' high-tech security system—because somebody was trying to break in.

Chapter 2

So what if he is the hottest guy at your school? It's
the way he treats you that counts.

"Is He Too Hot to Handle?"
Molly Somerville for Chik

KEVIN SUDDENLY REMEMBERED THAT HE'D BEEN TOO PREOCCUPIED
with his scotch to set the house's security system. A lucky
break. Now he had a shot at a little entertainment.

The house was cold and dark as sin. He threw his bare feet
over the edge of the couch and bumped into the coffee table.
Cursing, he rubbed his shin, then hopped toward the door.
What did it say about his life that tangling with a burglar
would be this week's bright spot? He just hoped the son of a
bitch was armed.

He dodged a chunky shape that he thought might be an
armchair and stepped on something small and sharp, probably one of the Legos he'd seen scattered around. The house
was big and luxurious, set deep into the Wisconsin woods,
with trees on three sides and the icy waters of Lake Michigan
at the rear.

Damn, it was dark. He headed toward the scratching
sound, and just as he reached it, heard the click of the latch.
The door began to open.

He felt that adrenaline rush he loved, and in one smooth

motion he shoved the door against the wall and grabbed the person on the other side.

The guy was a lightweight, and he came flying.

He was a pansy, too, from the sound of that scream as he hit the floor.

Unfortunately, he had a dog. A big dog.

The hair stood on the back of Kevin's neck as he heard the low, bloodcurdling growl of an attack dog. He had no time to brace himself before the animal clamped down on his ankle.

With the reflexes that were making him a legend, he lunged toward the switch, at the same time steeling himself for the crunch of his anklebones. Light flooded the foyer, and he realized two things.

He wasn't being attacked by a rottweiler. And those panicked sounds weren't coming from a guy.

"Aw, shit . . . "

Lying on the slate floor at his feet was a small, screaming woman with hair the color of a 49ers jersey. And clamped to his ankle, ripping holes in his favorite jeans, was a small, gray . . .

His brain skidded away from the word.

The stuff she'd been carrying when he'd grabbed her lay strewn all around. As he tried to shake off the dog, he spotted lots of books, drawing supplies, two boxes of Nutter Butter cookies, and bedroom slippers with big pink rabbits' heads on the toes.

He finally shook off the snarling dog. The woman scrambled to her feet and assumed some kind of martial arts pose. He opened his mouth to explain, only to have her foot come up and catch him behind the knee. The next thing he knew, he'd been sacked.

"Damn . . . It took the Giants a good three quarters to do that."

She'd been wearing a coat when she hit the floor, but the only thing between him and the slate was a layer of denim. He winced and rolled to his back. The animal pounced on his chest, barking dog breath into his face and slapping him in the nose with the tails of the blue bandanna fastened around his neck.

"You tried to kill me!" she screamed, the fiery little wisps of 49er hair flashing around her face.

"Not on purpose." He knew he'd met her before, but he couldn't for the life of him remember who she was. "Could you call off your pit bull?"

Her panicked look was giving way to fury, and she bared her teeth just like the dog. "Come here, Roo."

The animal snarled and crawled off Kevin's chest. It finally hit him. *Oh, shit . . .* "You're, uh, Phoebe's sister. Are you okay"—he searched for a name—"Miss Somerville?" Since he was the one lying on the slate floor with a bruised hip and puncture wounds in his ankle, he considered the question something of a courtesy.

"This is the second time in two days!" she exclaimed.

"I don't remember—"

"The *second* time! Are you demented, you stupid badger? Is that your problem? Or are you just an *idiot!*"

"As to that, I— Did you just call me a badger?"

She blinked. "A bastard. I called you a bastard."

"That's all right then." Unfortunately, his lame attempt at humor didn't make her smile.

The pit bull retreated to his mistress's side. Kevin pushed himself up off the slate and rubbed his ankle, trying to recall what he knew about his employer's sister, but he remembered only that she was an egghead. He'd seen her a few times at Stars headquarters with her head buried in a book, but her hair sure hadn't been this color.

It was hard to believe that she and Phoebe were related, because she wasn't even close to being a fox. Not that she was a dog either. She was just sort of ordinary—flat where Phoebe was curvy, small where Phoebe was large. Unlike her sister's, this one's mouth didn't look as if it had been designed to whisper dirty words under the sheets. Instead, Little Sis's mouth looked as if it spent its days shushing people in the library.

He didn't need the evidence of all those scattered books to tell him she was the kind of woman he least liked—brainy and way too serious. She was probably going to be a talker, too, an even bigger strike against her. In the spirit of fairness, though, he had to give Little Sis high marks for eye power. They were an unusual color, somewhere between blue and gray, and they had a sexy slant to them, just like her eyebrows, which he realized were almost meeting in the middle as she scowled at him. Damn it. Phoebe's sister! And he'd thought this week couldn't get any worse.

"Are you all right?" he asked.

Those blue-gray irises turned the exact color of an Illinois summer afternoon right before the tornado siren went off. He'd now managed to piss off every member of the Stars' ruling family, except maybe the kids. It was a gift.

He'd better mend his fences, and since charm was his long suit, he flashed a smile. "I didn't mean to scare you. I thought you were a burglar."

"What are you doing here?"

Even before her screech, he could see that the charm thing wasn't working.

He kept an eye on that kung fu leg of hers. "Dan suggested I come up here for a few days, to think things over . . . " He paused. "Which I didn't need to do."

She slapped the switch, and two sets of rustic iron wall sconces came on, filling the far corners with light.

The house was built of logs, but with six bedrooms and ceilings that soared up two stories to the exposed roof beams, the place didn't bear any resemblance to a frontier log cabin. Big windows made the woods seem part of the interior, and the huge stone fireplace that dominated one end of the room could have roasted a buffalo. All the furniture was big, overstuffed, and comfortable, designed to take the abuse of a large family. Off to the side a wide staircase led to a second floor complete with a small loft at one end.

Kevin bent over to pick up her things. He examined the rabbit slippers. "Don't you get nervous wearing these during hunting season?"

She snatched them from his hand. "Give them to me."

"I wasn't planning on wearing them. It'd be a little hard to keep the guys' respect."

She didn't smile as he handed them over. "There's a lodge not too far from here," she said. "I'm sure you can find a room for the night."

"It's too late to throw me out. Besides, I was invited."

"It's my house. You're uninvited." She tossed her coat on one of the couches and headed for the kitchen. The pit bull curled his lip, then stuck his pompon straight up, just as if he were giving Kevin the finger. Only when the dog was certain his message had been delivered did he trot after her.

Kevin followed them. The kitchen was roomy and comfortable, with Craftsman cabinets and a daylight view of Lake Michigan through every window. She dropped her packages on a pentagon-shaped center island surrounded by six stools.

She had an eye for fashion, he'd give her that. She wore close-fitting charcoal pants and a funky, oversize metallic-gray sweater that put him in mind of a suit of armor. With that short flaming hair, she could be Joan of Arc right after the match had been struck. Her clothes looked expensive but not new, which was odd, since he remembered hearing that she'd inherited Bert Somerville's fortune. Even though Kevin was wealthy himself, he'd come into his money long after his character had been formed. In his experience, people who'd grown up wealthy didn't understand hard work, and he hadn't met many of them he liked. This snobby rich girl was no exception.

"Uh, Miss Somerville? Before you kick me out . . . I'll bet

you didn't let the Calebows know you were coming up here, or they'd have told you the place was already occupied."

"I have dibs. It's understood." She threw the cookies in a drawer and slammed it shut. Then she studied him, all uptight and mad as hell. "You don't remember my name, do you?"

"Sure I know your name." He searched his mind and couldn't come up with a thing.

"We've been introduced at least three times."

"Which was totally unnecessary, since I've got a great memory for names."

"Not mine. You've forgotten."

"Of course I haven't."

She stared at him for a long moment, but he was used to operating under pressure, and he didn't have any trouble waiting her out.

"It's Daphne," she said.

"Why are you telling me something I already know? Are you this paranoid with everyone, Daphne?"

She pursed her lips and muttered something under her breath. He could swear he heard the word "badger" again.

Kevin Tucker didn't even know her name! *Let this be a lesson,* Molly thought as she gazed at all that dangerous gorgeousness.

Right then she knew she had to find a way to protect herself from him. Okay, so he was drop-dead good-looking. So were a lot of men. Granted, not many of them had that particular combination of dark blond hair and brilliant green eyes. And not many had a body like his, which was trim and sculpted rather than bulky. Still, she wasn't stupid enough to be taken in by a man who was nothing more than a great body, a pretty face, and an on/off charm switch.

Well, she *was* stupid enough—witness her late, unlamented crush on him—but at least she'd known she was being stupid.

One thing she wouldn't do was come across as a fawning groupie. He was going to see her at her absolute snottiest! She conjured up Goldie Hawn in *Overboard* for inspiration. "You're going to have to leave, Ken. Oh, excuse me, I mean *Kevin*. It is Kevin, right?"

She must have gone too far because the corner of his mouth kicked up. "We've been introduced at least three times. I'd think you'd remember."

"There are just so many football players, and you all look alike."

One of his eyebrows arched.

She'd made her point, and it was late, so she could afford to be generous, but only in the most condescending way. "You can stay tonight, but I came here to work, so you'll have to vacate tomorrow morning." A glance out the back windows showed his Ferrari parked by the garage, which was why she hadn't seen it when she'd pulled up in front.

He deliberately settled on a stool, as if to show her he wasn't going anywhere. "What kind of work do you do?" He sounded patronizing, which told her he didn't believe it was anything too arduous.

"*Je suis auteur.*"

"An author?"

"*Soy autora,*" she added in Spanish.

"Any reason you've given up English?"

"I thought you might be more comfortable with a foreign language." A vague wave of her hand. "Something I read . . . "

Kevin might be shallow, but he wasn't stupid, and she wondered if she'd crossed the line. Unfortunately, she was on a roll. "I'm almost certain Roo has recovered from his little problem with rabies, but you might want to get some shots, just to be on the safe side."

"You're still mad about the burglar thing, aren't you?"

"I'm sorry, I can't hear you. Probably a concussion from the fall."

"I said I was sorry."

"So you did." She moved aside a pile of crayons the kids had left on the counter.

"I think I'll head upstairs to bed." He rose and started toward the door, then paused for another look at her awful hair. "Tell me the truth. Was it some kind of football bet?"

"Good night, Kirk."

As Molly entered her bedroom, she realized she was breathing hard. Only a thin wall separated her from the guest room where Kevin would be sleeping. Her skin tingled, and she felt an almost uncontrollable urge to take the scissors to her hair, even though there wasn't much left to cut. Maybe she should dye it back to its natural color tomorrow, except she couldn't give him the satisfaction.

She'd come here to hide out, not sleep next to the lion's den, and she grabbed her things. With Roo following, she hurried down the hall to the big, dormitory-style corner room the three girls shared and locked the door.

She sagged against the jamb and tried to settle down by taking in the room's sloping ceiling and the cozy dormers designed for daydreaming. Two of the walls displayed a Nightingale Woods mural that she'd painted while everyone in the family got in her way. She'd be all right, and in the morning he'd be gone.

Sleep, however, was impossible. Why hadn't she let Phoebe know she was driving up here, as she usually did? Because she hadn't wanted more lectures about her hair or warnings about "incidents."

She tossed and turned, watched the clock, and finally flicked on the light to sketch some ideas for her new book. Nothing worked. Usually the sound of the winter wind battering the solid log house soothed her, but tonight that wind urged her to throw off her clothes and dance, to leave the studious, good girl behind and cross over to the wild side.

She tossed back the covers and jumped out of bed. The room was chilly, but she felt flushed and feverish. She wished she were home. Roo lifted one sleepy eyelid, then closed it again as she made her way to the padded bench in the nearest dormer.

Frost feathers decorated the windowpanes, and snow swirled in thin, dancing ribbons through the trees. She tried to concentrate on the night beauty, but she kept seeing Kevin Tucker. Her skin prickled, and her breasts tingled. It was so demeaning! She was a bright woman—brilliant, even—but, despite her denial, she was as obsessed as a sex-starved groupie.

Maybe this was a perverse form of personal growth. At least she was obsessing over sex instead of the Great Love Story she wouldn't ever have.

She decided it was safer to obsess over the Great Love Story. Dan had saved Phoebe's life! It was the most romantic thing Molly could imagine, but she supposed it had also given her unrealistic expectations.

She gave up on the Great Love Story and went back to obsessing over sex. Did Kevin speak English while he was doing it or had he memorized a few handy foreign phrases? With a groan, she buried her face in the pillow.

After only a few hours' sleep she awakened to a cold, gray dawn. When she looked out, she saw that Kevin's Ferrari was gone. *Good!* She took Roo outside, then showered. While she dried off, she forced herself to hum a little ditty about Winnie the Pooh, but as she pulled on a well-worn pair of gray pants and the Dolce & Gabbana sweater she'd bought before she gave away her money, the pretense of pretending she was happy faded.

What was wrong with her? She had a wonderful life. She was healthy. She had good friends, a terrific family, and an entertaining dog. Although she was nearly always broke, she didn't mind because her loft was worth every penny it cost her. She loved her work. Her life was perfect. More than perfect, now that Kevin Tucker was gone.

Disgusted with her moodiness, she shoved her feet into the pink slippers the twins had given her for her birthday and padded down to the kitchen, the bunny heads on the toes waggling. A quick breakfast, then she'd get to work.

She'd arrived too late last night to pick up groceries, so she pulled a box of Dan's Pop-Tarts from the cupboard. Just as she was slipping one into the toaster, Roo began to bark. The back door opened, and Kevin came in, his arms loaded with plastic grocery bags. Her idiotic heart skipped a beat.

Roo snarled. Kevin ignored him. "Morning, Daphne."

Her instinctive burst of pleasure gave way to annoyance. *Slytherin!*

He dumped the bags on the center island. "Supplies were running low."

"What difference does it make? You're leaving, remember? *Vous partez. Salga.*" She enunciated the foreign words and was gratified to see that she'd annoyed him.

"Leaving isn't a good idea." He gave a hard twist to the cap on the milk. "I'm not making any more waves with Dan right now, so you'll need to go instead."

Exactly what she should do, but she didn't like his attitude, so she let her inner bitch take over. "That's not going to happen. As an athlete, you won't understand this, but I need peace and quiet because *I* actually have to *think* when I work."

He definitely caught the insult but chose to ignore it. "I'm staying here."

"So am I," she replied, just as stubbornly.

She could see that he wanted to toss her out but couldn't do it because she was his boss's sister. He took his time filling his glass, then settled his hips against the counter. "It's a big house. We'll share."

She started to tell him to forget it, that she'd leave after all, when something stopped her. Maybe sharing wasn't as crazy as it sounded. The quickest way to get over her fixation would be to see the Slythcrin beneath the real man. It had never been Kevin as a human being who attracted her because she had no idea who he really was. Instead, it was the illusion of Kevin—gorgeous body, sexy eyes, valiant leader of men.

She watched him drain the glass of milk. One belch. That's all it would take. Nothing disgusted her more than a man who belched . . . or scratched his crotch . . . or had gross table manners. Or what about the losers who tried to impress women by pulling out a fat roll of bills held together with one of those garish money clips?

Maybe he wore a gold chain. Molly shuddered. That would do it for sure. Or was a gun nut. Or said, *"You duh man."* Or in any of a hundred ways couldn't measure up to the standard set by Dan Calebow.

Yes, indeed, there were a million pitfalls awaiting Mr. Kevin I'm-too-sexy-for-my-Astroturf-green-eyes Tucker. One belch . . . one crotch scratch . . . even the slightest glimmer of gold around that gorgeous neck . . .

She realized she was smiling. "All right. You can stay."

"Thanks, Daphne." He drained the glass but didn't burp.

She narrowed her eyes and told herself that as long as he kept calling her Daphne, she was halfway home.

She found her laptop computer and carried it up to the loft, where she set it on the desk, along with her sketch pad. She could work on either *Daphne Takes a Tumble* or the article "Making Out—How Far to Go?"

Very far.

It was definitely the wrong time to work on an article about any kind of sex, even the teenage variety.

She heard the sound of game film being played below and realized Kevin had brought video with him so he could do his homework. She wondered if he ever cracked a book or went to an art film or did anything that wasn't connected with football.

Time to get her mind back on her work. She propped one foot on Roo and gazed out the window at the angry white-caps rolling over the gray, forbidding waters of Lake Michigan. Maybe Daphne should return to her cottage late at night only to find everything dark. And when she walked inside, Benny could jump out and—

She had to stop making her stories so autobiographical.

Okay . . . She flipped open her sketch pad. Daphne could decide to put on a Halloween mask and scare— No, she'd already done that in *Daphne Plants a Pumpkin Patch*.

Definitely time to phone a friend. Molly picked up the phone next to her and dialed Janine Stevens, one of her best writing pals. Although Janine wrote for the young adult market, they shared the same philosophy about books and frequently brainstormed together.

"Thank God you called!" Janine cried. "I've been trying to reach you all morning."

"What's wrong?"

"Everything! Some big-haired woman from SKIFSA was on the local news this morning ranting and raving about children's books being a recruiting tool for the homosexual lifestyle."

"Why don't they get a life?"

"Molly, she held up a copy of *I Miss You So* and said it was an example of the kind of filth that lures children into perversion!"

"Oh, Janine . . . that's awful!" *I Miss You So* was the story of a thirteen-year-old girl trying to come to terms with the persecution of an artistic older brother who'd been branded as gay by the other kids. It was beautifully written, sensitive, and heartfelt.

Janine blew her nose. "My editor called this morning. She said they've decided to wait until the heat dies down, and they're going to postpone my next book for a *year*!"

"You finished it almost a year ago!"

"They don't care. I can't believe it. My sales were finally starting to take off. Now I'm going to lose all my momentum."

Molly consoled her friend as best she could. By the time she hung up, she'd decided that SKIFSA was a bigger menace to society than any book could ever be.

She heard footsteps below and realized that the game film was no longer running. The only good thing about her conversation with Janine was that it had distracted her from thinking about Kevin.

A deep male voice called up to her. "Hey, Daphne! Do you know if they've got an airfield around here?"

"An airfield? Yes. There's one in Sturgeon Bay. It's—" Her head shot up. *"Airfield!"*

She vaulted out of her chair and made a rush for the railing. "You're going skydiving again!"

He tilted his head to gaze up at her. Even with his hands in his pockets, he looked as tall and dazzling as a sun god.

Will you please burp!

"Why would I go skydiving?" he said mildly. "Dan's asked me not to."

"Like that's going to stop you."

Benny pumped the pedals of his mountain bike faster and faster. He didn't notice the rain falling on the road that led through Nightingale Woods or the big puddle just ahead.

She raced down the stairs, even though she knew she should stay as far away from him as possible. "Don't do it. There were flurries all night. It's too windy."

"Now you're tantalizing me."

"I'm trying to explain that it's dangerous!"

"Isn't that what makes anything worth doing?"

"No plane's going to take you up on a day like today." Except that celebrities like Kevin could get people to do just about anything.

"I don't think I'd have too much trouble finding a pilot. If I did plan to go skydiving."

"I'll call Dan," she threatened. "I'm sure he'll be interested to hear just how lightly you've taken your suspension."

"Now you're scaring me," he drawled. "I'll bet you were one of those bratty little girls who tattled to the teacher when the boys misbehaved."

"I didn't go to school with boys until I was fifteen, so I missed the opportunity."

"That's right. You're a rich kid, aren't you?"

"Rich and pampered," she lied. "What about you?" Maybe if she distracted him with conversation, he'd forget about skydiving.

"Middle class and definitely not pampered."

He still looked restless, and she was trying to think of something to talk about when she spotted two books on the coffee table that hadn't been there earlier. She looked more closely and saw that one was the new Scott Turow, the other a rather scholarly volume on the cosmos that she'd tried to get into but set aside for something lighter. "You *read*?"

His mouth twitched as he slouched into the sectional sofa. "Only if I can't get anybody to do it for me."

"Very funny." She settled at the opposite end of the couch, unhappy with the revelation that he enjoyed books. Roo moved closer, ready to guard her in case Kevin took it into his mind to tackle her again.

You wish.

"Okay, I'll concede that you're not quite as . . . intellectually impaired as you appear to be."

"Let me put that in my press kit."

She'd set her trap quite nicely. "That being the case, why do you keep doing such stupid things?"

"Like what?"

"Like skydiving. Skiing from a helicopter. Then there's that dirt-track racing you did right after training camp."

"You seem to know a lot about me."

"Only because you're part of the family business, so don't take it personally. Besides, everybody in Chicago knows what you've been up to."

"The media make a big deal out of nothing."

"It's not exactly nothing." She kicked off her rabbit's-head slippers and tucked her feet under her. "I don't get it. You've always been the poster boy for pro athletes. You don't drive drunk or beat up women. You show up early for practice and stay late. No gambling scandals, no grandstanding, not even much trash talk. Then all of a sudden you freak out."

"I haven't freaked out."

"What else can you call it?"

He cocked his head. "They sent you up here to spy on me, didn't they?"

She laughed, even though it compromised her role as a rich bitch. "I'm the last person any of them would trust with team business. I'm sort of a geek." She made an X over her heart. "Come on, Kevin. Cross my heart, I won't say a thing. Tell me what's going on."

"I enjoy a little excitement, and I'm not apologizing for it."

She wanted more, so she continued her exploring mission. "Don't your lady friends worry about you?"

"If you want to know about my love life, just ask. That way I can have the pleasure of telling you to mind your own business."

"Why would I want to know about your love life?"

"You tell me."

She regarded him demurely. "I was just wondering if you find your women in international catalogs? Or maybe on the Web? I know there are groups that specialize in helping lonely American men find foreign women because I've seen the pictures. 'Twenty-one-year-old Russian beauty. Plays classical piano in the nude, writes erotic novels in her spare time, wants to share her dandy with a Yankee doodle.' "

Unfortunately, he laughed instead of being offended. "I date American women, too."

"Not many, I'll bet."

"Did anybody ever mention that you're nosy?"

"I'm a writer. It goes with the profession." Maybe it was her imagination, but he didn't look as restless as when he'd sat down, so she decided to keep poking. "Tell me about your family."

"Not much to tell. I'm a PK."

Prize kisser? "Pathetic klutz?"

He grinned and crossed his ankles on the edge of the coffee table. "Preacher's kid. Fourth generation, depending on how you count."

"Oh, yes. I remember reading that. Fourth generation, huh?"

"My father was a Methodist minister, son of a Methodist minister, who was the grandson of one of the old Methodist circuit riders who carried the gospel into the wilderness."

"That must be where your daredevil blood comes from. The circuit rider."

"It sure didn't come from my father. A great guy, but not exactly what you'd call a risk taker. Pretty much an egghead." He smiled. "Like you. Except more polite."

She ignored that. "He's no longer alive?"

"He died about six years ago. He was fifty-one when I was born."

"What about your mother?"

"I lost her eighteen months ago. She was older, too. A big reader, the head of the historical society, into genealogy. Summers were the highlight of my parents' lives."

"Skinny-dipping in the Bahamas?"

He laughed. "Not quite. We all went to a Methodist church campground in northern Michigan. It's been in my family for generations."

"Your family owned a campground?"

"Complete with cabins and a big old wooden Tabernacle for church services. I had to go with them every summer until I was fifteen, and then I rebelled."

"They must have wondered how they hatched you."

His eyes grew shuttered. "Every day. What about you?"

"An orphan." She said the word lightly, the way she always did when anyone asked, but it felt lumpy.

"I thought Bert only married Vegas showgirls." The way his eyes swept from her crimson hair to linger on her modest chest told her he didn't believe she could have sequins in her gene pool.

"My mother was in the chorus at The Sands. She was Bert's third wife, and she died when I was two. She was flying to Aspen to celebrate her divorce."

"You and Phoebe didn't have the same mother?"

"No. Phoebe's mother was his first wife. She was in the chorus at The Flamingo."

"I never met Bert Somerville, but from what I've heard, he wasn't an easy man to live with."

"Fortunately, he sent me off to boarding school when I was five. Before that, I remember a stream of very attractive nannies."

"Interesting." He dropped his feet from the coffee table and picked up the pair of silver-framed Rēvo sunglasses he'd left there. Molly gazed at them with envy. Two hundred and seventy dollars at Marshall Field's.

Daphne set the sunglasses that had fallen from Benny's pocket on her own nose and bent over to admire her reflection in the pond. *Parfait!* (She believed French was the best language for contemplating personal appearance.)

"Hey!" Benny called out from behind her.

Plop! The sunglasses slid from her nose into the pond.

Kevin rose from the couch, and she could feel his energy filling the room. "Where are you going?" she asked.

"Out for a while. I need some fresh air."

"Out where?"

He folded in the stems of his sunglasses, the motion deliberate. "It's been nice talking to you, but I think I've had enough questions from management for now."

"I told you. I'm not management."

"You've got a financial stake in the Stars. In my book that makes you management."

"Okay. So management wants to know where you're going."

"Skiing. Do you have a problem with that?"

No, but she was fairly sure Dan would. "There's just one alpine ski area around here, and the drop is only a hundred and twenty feet. That's not enough challenge for you."

"Damn."

She concealed her amusement.

"I'll go cross-country, then," he said. "I've heard there are some world class trails up here."

"Not enough snow."

"I'm going to find that *airfield*!" He shot toward the coat closet.

"No! We'll—we'll hike."

"Hike?" He looked as if she'd suggested bird-watching.

She thought fast. "There's a really treacherous path along the bluffs. It's so dangerous that it's closed off when there's wind or even a hint of snow, but I know a back way to get to it. Except you need to be really sure you want to do this. It's narrow and icy, and the slightest misstep could send you plunging to your death."

"You're making this up."

"I don't have that much imagination."

"You're a writer."

"Children's books. They're completely nonviolent. Now, if you want to stand around and talk all morning, that's up to you. But I'd like a little adventure."

She'd finally caught his interest.

"Let's get to it, then."

They had a good time on their hike, even though Molly never quite managed to locate the treacherous path she'd promised Kevin—maybe because she'd invented it. Still, the bluff they crossed was bitterly cold and windy, so he didn't complain too much. He even reached out to take her hand on an icy stretch, but she wasn't that foolish. Instead, she gave him a snooty look and told him he'd have to manage on his own because she wasn't going to prop him up every time he saw a little ice and got scared.

He'd laughed and climbed up on a slippery pile of rocks. The sight of him facing the winter-gray water, head thrown back, wind tearing through that dark blond hair had stolen her breath.

For the rest of their walk she'd forgotten to be obnoxious, and they had far too much fun. By the time they returned to the house, her teeth were chattering from the cold, but every womanly part of her burned.

He shrugged out of his coat and rubbed his hands. "I wouldn't mind using your hot tub."

And she wouldn't mind using his hot body. "Go ahead. I have to get back to work." As Molly rushed toward the loft, she found herself remembering what Phoebe had once said to her.

When you're raised as we were, Moll, casual sex is a snake pit. We need a love that's soul-deep, and I'm here to testify that you don't find it by bed-hopping.

Although Molly had never bed-hopped, she knew that

Phoebe was right. Except what was a twenty-seven-year-old woman with a healthy body, but no soul-deep love, supposed to do? If only Kevin had acted shallow and stupid on their walk . . . but he hadn't talked about football once. Instead, they'd talked about books, living in Chicago, and their mutual passion for *This Is Spinal Tap.*

She couldn't concentrate on Daphne, so she flipped open her laptop to work on "Making Out—How Far to Go?" The subject depressed her even more.

By her junior year at Northwestern she'd grown sick of waiting for her Great Love Story to come along, so she'd decided to forget about soul-deep love and settle for soul-deep caring with a boy she'd been dating for a month. But losing her virginity had been a mistake. The affair had left her depressed, and she knew that Phoebe had been right. She wasn't made for casual sex.

A few years later she'd convinced herself she finally cared enough about a man to try again. He'd been intelligent and charming, but the wrenching sadness following the affair had taken months to fade.

She'd had a number of boyfriends since then, but no lovers, and she'd done her best to sublimate her sex drive with hard work and good friends. Chastity might be old-fashioned, but sex was an emotional quagmire for a woman who hadn't known love until she was fifteen. So why did she keep thinking about it, especially with Kevin Tucker in the house?

Because she was only human, and the Stars quarterback was a delectable piece of body candy, a walking aphrodisiac, a grown-up toy boy. She moaned, glared at her keyboard, and forced herself to concentrate.

At five she heard him leave the house. By seven "Making Out—How Far to Go?" was nearly done. Unfortunately, the subject had left her edgy and more than a little aroused. She called Janine, but her friend wasn't home, so she went downstairs and stared at herself in the small kitchen mirror. It was too late for the stores to be open, or she could have run out for hair color. Maybe she'd just cut it. That crew cut a few years ago hadn't been so bad.

She was lying to herself. It had been horrible.

She grabbed a Lean Cuisine instead of the scissors and ate at the kitchen counter. Afterward she dug the marshmallows out of a carton of Rocky Road ice cream. Finally she grabbed her drawing pad and settled in front of the fireplace to sketch. But she hadn't slept well, and before long her lids grew heavy. Kevin's arrival sometime after midnight made her bolt up.

"Hey, Daphne."

She rubbed her eyes. "Hello, Karl."

He hung his coat on the back of a chair. It reeked of perfume. "This thing needs to air out."

"I'll say." Jealousy gnawed at her. While she'd been drooling over Kevin's body and obsessing about her own hangups, she'd ignored one important fact: He hadn't shown the slightest interest in her. "You must have been busy," she said. "It smells like more than one brand. All of them domestic, or did you find an au pair somewhere?"

"I wasn't that lucky. The women were unfortunately American, and they all talked too much." His pointed look said she did, too.

"And I'll bet lots of the words had more than one syllable, so you probably have a headache." She needed to stop this. He wasn't nearly as dumb as she wanted him to be, and if she didn't watch herself, he was going to figure out exactly how much interest she took in his personal life.

He looked more aggravated than angry. "I happen to like to relax when I'm on a date. I don't want to debate world politics or discuss global warming or be forced to listen to people with unpredictable personal hygiene recite bad poetry."

"Gee, and those are all my favorite things."

He shook his head, then rose and stretched, lengthening that lean body vertebra by vertebra. He was already bored with her. Probably because she hadn't entertained him by reciting his career statistics.

"I'd better turn in," he said. "I'm taking off first thing tomorrow, so if I don't see you, thanks for the hospitality."

She managed a yawn. "*Ciao,* babycakes." She knew he had to get back for practice, but that didn't ease her disappointment.

He smiled. "Night, Daphne."

She watched him mount the stairs, the denim tightening around those lean legs, molding his narrow hips, muscles rippling beneath his T-shirt.

Oh, God, she was drooling! And she was Phi Beta Kappa!

She was also aching and restless, blazingly dissatisfied with everything in her life.

"Damn it!" She knocked her sketch pad to the floor, jumped to her feet, and made a beeline for the bathroom to stare at her hair. She was going to shave it off!

No! She didn't want to be bald, and this time she wouldn't let herself act crazy.

She moved purposefully to the video center and pulled out the remake of *The Parent Trap.* Her inner child loved watching the twins get their parents back together, and her outer child loved Dennis Quaid's smile.

Kevin had that same crooked smile.

Resolutely, she took his game film from the VCR, put in *The Parent Trap,* and settled back to watch.

By two o'clock in the morning, Hallie and Annie had reunited their parents, but Molly was more restless than ever. She began surfing through old movies and infomercials, only to pause as she heard the familiar theme song of the old show, *Lace, Inc.*

"*Lace is on the case, oh yeah . . . Lace can solve the case, oh yeah . . .* " Two beautiful women ran across the screen, the sexy detectives Sable Drake and Ginger Hill.

Lace, Inc. had been one of Molly's favorite shows as a child. She'd wanted to be Sable, the smart brunette, played by actress Mallory McCoy. Ginger was the redheaded sexpot karate expert. *Lace, Inc.* had been a jiggle show, but Molly hadn't cared about that. She'd simply enjoyed watching women beat up the bad guys for a change.

The opening credits showed Mallory McCoy first, then Lilly Sherman, who'd played Ginger Hill. Molly sat up straighter as she remembered a fragment of conversation she'd once overheard at Stars headquarters indicating that Lilly Sherman had some sort of connection with Kevin. She hadn't wanted anyone to know she was interested, so she didn't ask any questions. She studied the actress more carefully.

She wore her trademark tight pants, tube top, and high heels. Her long red hair curled around her shoulders, and her eyes batted seductively at the camera. Even with a dated hairstyle and big gold hoop earrings, she was a knockout.

Sherman must be in her forties by now, surely a little old to be one of Kevin's women, so what was their connection? A photograph she'd seen of the actress a few years ago showed that she'd gained weight since the television show. She was still a beautiful woman, though, so it was possible they'd had a fling.

Molly stabbed the remote, and a cosmetics commercial came on. Maybe that's what she needed. A complete makeover.

She flipped off the TV and headed upstairs. Somehow she didn't think a makeover would fix what was wrong with her.

After a hot shower she slipped into one of the Irish linen nightgowns she'd bought when she was rich. It still made her feel like a heroine in a Georgette Heyer novel. She carried her notepad to bed so she could think more about Daphne, but the surge of creativity she'd experienced that afternoon had vanished.

Roo snored softly at the foot of the bed. Molly told herself she was getting sleepy. She wasn't.

Maybe she could finish polishing her article, but as she made her way to the loft to get her laptop, she glanced into the guest bathroom. It had two doors—the one she was standing in and a second one across from it that led directly into the bedroom where he slept. That door was ajar.

Her restless, twitchy legs carried her onto the tile.

She saw a Louis Vuitton shaving kit sitting on the counter. She couldn't imagine Kevin buying it for himself, so it must have been a gift from one of his international beauties. She moved closer and saw a red toothbrush with crisp white bristles. He'd put the cap back on the tube of Aquafresh.

She brushed her fingertip over the lid of a column of deodorant, then reached for a frosted glass bottle of very expensive aftershave. She unscrewed the stopper and drew it to her nose. Did it smell like Kevin? He wasn't one of those men who drowned himself in cologne, and she hadn't gotten close enough to know for sure, but something familiar about the scent made her close her eyes and inhale more deeply. She shivered and set it down, then glanced into the open shaving kit.

Lying next to a bottle of ibuprofen and a tube of Neosporin was Kevin's Super Bowl ring. She knew he'd earned it in the early days of his career as Cal Bonner's backup. It surprised her to see a championship ring tossed so carelessly in the bottom of a shaving kit, but then everything she knew about Kevin said he wouldn't want to wear a ring that had been earned when someone else was in charge.

She began to move away, only to pause as she saw what else lay in the shaving kit.

A condom.

No big deal. Of course he'd carry condoms with him. He

probably had a whole crate of them. She picked it up and studied it. It seemed to be an ordinary condom. So why was she staring at it?

This was insane! All day she'd been acting like a woman obsessed. If she didn't pull herself together, she'd be boiling a bunny just like crazy Glenn Close.

She winced. *Sorry, Daphne.*

One peek. That was it. She'd just take one peek at him sleeping and then she'd leave.

She moved toward the bedroom door and slowly pushed it open.

Chapter 3

Late that night Daphne sneaked into Benny's badger den with the scary Halloween mask fastened around her head . . .

Daphne Plants a Pumpkin Patch

A DIM WEDGE OF LIGHT FROM THE HALLWAY FELL ACROSS THE CAR-pet. Molly could make out a large shape beneath the bedcovers. Her heart hammered with the excitement of the forbidden. She took a tentative step inside.

The same dangerous energy shot through her that she'd felt when she was seventeen, right before she'd pulled the fire alarm. She moved closer. Just one look and then she'd leave.

He lay on his side, turned away from her. The sound of his breathing was deep and slow. She remembered old Westerns where the gunslinger woke up at the slightest sound, and she envisioned a rumple-haired Kevin pointing a Colt .45 at her belly.

She'd pretend she was sleepwalking.

He'd left his shoes on the floor, and she pushed one of them aside with her foot. It made a slight rustle as it brushed over the carpet, but he didn't move. She pushed aside its mate, but he didn't react to that either. So much for the Colt .45.

Her palms grew damp. She rubbed them on her gown. Then she bumped ever so gently against the end of the bed.

He was dead to the world.

Now that she knew what he looked like asleep, she'd leave.

She tried to, but her feet took her to the other side of the bed instead, where she could see his face.

Andrew slept like this. Fireworks could explode next to her nephew, and he wouldn't stir. But Kevin Tucker didn't look at all like Andrew. She took in his amazing profile—strong forehead, angled cheekbones, and straight, perfectly proportioned nose. He was a football player, so he must have broken it a few times, but there was no bump.

This was a terrible invasion of his privacy. Inexcusable. But as she gazed down at his rumpled dark blond hair, she could barely resist brushing it back from his brow.

One perfectly sculpted shoulder rose above the covers. She wanted to lick it.

That's it! She'd lost her mind. And she didn't care.

The condom was still in her hand and Kevin Tucker lay under the blankets—naked, if that bare shoulder was any indication. What if she crawled in with him?

It was unthinkable.

But who would know? He might not even wake up. And if he did? He'd be the last person to tell the world he'd been with the owner's oversexed sister.

Her heart was beating so fast she was lightheaded. Was she really thinking about doing this?

There'd be no emotional aftermath. How could there be when she didn't harbor even the illusion of a soul-deep love? As for what he'd think of her . . . He was used to having women throw themselves at him, so he'd hardly be surprised.

She could see the fire alarm hanging on the wall right in front of her, and she told herself not to touch it. But her hands tingled, and her breath came fast and shallow. She'd run out of willpower. She was tired of her restlessness, her twitchy feet. Tired of mutilating her hair because she didn't know how to fix herself. Fed up from too many years trying to be perfect. Her skin was damp with desire and a growing sense of horror as she watched herself slide off her bunny slippers.

Put those right back on!

But she didn't. And the fire alarm clanged in her head.

She reached for the hem of her nightgown . . . pulled it over her head . . . stood naked and trembling. Appalled, she watched her fingers curl around the covers and tug. Even as the blankets fell back, she told herself she wasn't going to do it. But her breasts were tingling, her body crying out with need.

She set her hip on the mattress, then slowly slipped her legs beneath the covers. Oh, God, she was really doing this. She was naked, and she'd climbed into bed with Kevin Tucker.

Who let out a soft snore and rolled over, taking most of the covers with him.

She stared at his back and knew she'd just been given a divine sign telling her to leave. She had to get out of his bed right this minute!

Instead, she curled around him, pressed her breasts against his back, breathed him in. There . . . that whiff of musky aftershave. It had been so long since she'd touched a man like this.

He stirred, shifted, muttered something as if he were dreaming.

The shriek of the fire alarm grew louder. She slid her arm around him and stroked his chest.

Only for a minute, she told herself. And then she'd leave.

Kevin felt his old girlfriend Katya's hand on his chest. He'd been standing in his garage with the first car he'd ever owned and Eric Clapton. Eric had been giving him a guitar lesson, but instead of a guitar, Kevin kept trying to play a leaf rake.

Then he looked up, and Eric was gone. He was in this weird log room with Katya.

She kept stroking his chest, and he realized that she was naked. He forgot about Eric's guitar lesson as blood rushed to his groin.

He'd broken it off with Katya months ago, but now he had to have her. She used to wear bad perfume. Too strong. It was a stupid reason to break up with a woman, because now she smelled like cinnamon rolls.

Good smell. Sexy smell. Made him sweat. He couldn't remember being this turned on by her when they were together. No sense of humor. Too much time putting on makeup. But now he needed her right away. Right that moment.

He rolled toward her. Curled his hand around her bottom. It felt different. Fleshier. More to squeeze.

He ached, and she smelled so good. Like oranges now. And her breasts were full against his chest—warm, soft, juicy oranges—and her mouth was on his, and her hands were all over him. Playing. Stroking. Finding their way to his cock.

He groaned as she caressed him. He smelled her woman's smell and knew he wouldn't last long. His arm didn't want to move, but he had to feel her.

She was slick, wet honey.

He moaned and rolled over. On top of her. Pushed inside her. It didn't happen easily. Strange.

The dream began to fade, but not his lust. He was feverish with it. The smell of soap, shampoo, and woman enflamed him. He thrust again and again, dragged open his eyes, and . . . couldn't believe what he saw!

He was buried inside Daphne Somerville.

He tried to say something, but he was long past talking. His blood pounded, his heart raced. There was a roaring in his head. He exploded.

At that moment everything inside Molly went cold. *No! Not yet!*

She felt his shudder. His weight crushed her, driving her into the mattress. Much too late, her sanity returned.

He went slack. Dead weight on top of her. Useless dead weight.

It was over. *Already!* And she couldn't even blame him for being the worst lover in history because she'd gotten exactly what she deserved. Nothing at all.

He jerked his head to clear it, then pulled out of her and erupted from the covers. *"What in the hell are you doing?"*

She wanted to yell at him for being such a disappointment, wanted to yell at herself even more. Once again she'd been caught pulling the fire alarm, but she wasn't seventeen any longer. She felt old and defeated.

Humiliation burned through her. "S-s-sleepwalking?"

"Sleepwalking, *my ass!*" He vaulted out of bed and stalked toward the bathroom. "Don't you dare move!"

Too late she remembered that Kevin had a reputation for holding grudges. Last year it had turned a rematch against the Steelers into a bloodbath, and the year before that he'd gone after a three-hundred-pound Viking defensive tackle. She scrambled from the bed and looked frantically for her nightgown.

A stream of obscenities erupted from the bathroom.

Where was her gown?

He shot back out, naked and furious. "Where the hell did you get that condom?"

"From your—your shaving kit." She spotted her linen gown, snatched it up, and clutched it to her breasts.

"My shaving kit?" He rushed back into the bathroom. "You pulled it from my— Shit!"

"It was . . . an impulse. A—a sleepwalking accident." She edged toward the hall door, but he reappeared before she could get there, charging across the carpet and grabbing her arm, giving her a shake.

"Do you know how long that thing was in there?"

Not nearly long enough! And then she realized he was talking about the condom. "What are you trying to say?"

He dropped her arm and pointed toward the bathroom. "I'm trying to say that it's been in there forever, and the son of a bitch *broke!*"

Exactly three seconds ticked by. Then her knees gave out. She sagged into the chair across from the bed.

"Well?" he barked.

Her fuzzy brain started working again. "Don't worry about it." Too late she grew conscious of the dampness between her thighs. "It's the wrong time of the month."

"There isn't any wrong time of the month." He flipped on the floor lamp, exposing more than she wanted him to see of her very ordinary, very naked body.

"There is for me. I'm as regular as a clock." She didn't want to talk to him about her period. She clutched her nightgown and tried to figure out how to get it back on without showing more of herself than she already had.

He didn't seem the slightest bit interested in either her nudity or his. "What the hell were you doing poking around in my shaving kit?"

"It, uh, was open, and I just happened to look in, and . . . " She cleared her throat. "If it was so old, why were you still carrying it around?"

"I forgot about it!"

"That's a stupid reason."

Those Astroturf-green eyes were murderous. "Are you trying to blame this on me?"

She drew a deep breath. "No. No, I'm not." It was time to stop acting like a coward and face the music. She stood up and pulled the nightgown over her head. "I'm sorry, Kevin. Really. I've been acting crazy lately."

"You're not telling me a damn thing."

"I apologize. I'm embarrassed." Her voice quivered. "Actually, I'm beyond embarrassment. I'm completely humiliated. I—I hope you can forget about this."

"Not likely." He grabbed a pair of dark green boxers from the floor and shoved his legs in.

"I'm sorry." She deserved to grovel, but since that didn't appear to be working, she reverted to being the world-weary, spoiled heiress. "The truth is, I was lonesome and you were available. You have a—reputation as a playboy. I didn't think you'd mind."

"I was *available*?" The air crackled. "Let's think about this. Let's think about what this would be called if the situation was reversed?"

"I don't know what you're talking about."

"What would this situation be called, for example, if I'd decided to crawl in bed with you—a nonconsenting female!"

"It's—" Her fingers fidgeted with the skirt of her nightgown. "Uh, yes, I see what you mean."

His eyes narrowed, and his voice grew low and dangerous. "It would be called rape."

"You're not seriously trying to say that I—I raped you?"

He regarded her coldly. "Yeah, I think I am."

This was far worse than she'd imagined. "That's ridiculous. You—you weren't nonconsenting!"

"Only because I was asleep and I thought you were someone else."

That stung. "I see."

He didn't back off. If anything, his jaw hardened. "Contrary to what you seem to think, I like having a relationship before I have sex. And I don't let anybody use me."

Which was exactly what she'd done. She wanted to cry. "I'm sorry, Kevin. Both of us know my behavior was outrageous. Could we forget about this?"

"I don't have much choice." He bit off his words. "It's not something I want to read about in the papers."

She backed toward the door. "I hope you realize I'll never say anything."

He regarded her with disgust.

Her face crumpled. "I'm sorry. Really."

Chapter 4

Daphne jumped off her skateboard and crouched down in the long weeds so she could peer into the nest.

Daphne Finds a Baby Rabbit
(preliminary notes)

KEVIN DROPPED BACK INTO THE POCKET. SIXTY-FIVE THOUSAND screaming fans were on their feet, but a perfect stillness cocooned him. He didn't think about the fans, the TV cameras, about the *Monday Night Football* crew in the booth. He didn't think about anything except what he'd been born to do—play the game that had been invented just for him.

Leon Tippett, his favorite receiver, ran the pattern perfectly and broke free, ready for that sweet moment when Kevin would drill the ball into his hands.

Then, in an instant, the play turned to crap. Their safety came out of nowhere, ready to pick off the pass.

Adrenaline flooded Kevin's body. He was deep behind the line of scrimmage, and he needed another receiver, but Jamal was down, and Stubs had double coverage.

Briggs and Washington broke through the Stars' line and bore down. Those same fire-breathing monsters, disguised as Tampa Bay defensive ends, had dislocated his shoulder last year, but Kevin wasn't about to throw the ball away. With the recklessness that had been causing him so much trouble lately, he looked to the left . . . and then made a sharp, blind, *insane* cut to the right. He needed a hole in that wall of white jerseys. He willed it to be there. And found it.

With the agility that had become his trademark, he slipped through, leaving Briggs and Washington grabbing air. He spun and shook off a defender who outweighed him by eighty pounds.

Another cut. A jitterbug. Then he put on the steam.

Off the field he was a big man, six feet two and 193 pounds of muscle, but here in the Land of Mutant Giants he was small, graceful, and very fast. His feet conquered the artificial turf. The lights in the dome turned his gold helmet into a meteor, his aqua jersey into a banner woven from the heavens. Human poetry. God-kissed. Blessed among men. He carried the ball across the goal line into the end zone.

And when the official signaled the touchdown, Kevin was still standing.

The postgame party was at Kinney's house, and from the moment Kevin walked in the door, women started to grab him.

"Fabulous game, Kevin."

"Kevin, *querido,* over here!"

"You were awesome! I'm hoarse from screaming!"

"Were you excited when you took it in? God, I know you were excited, but how did it really feel?"

"*¡Felicitación!*"

"Kevin, *chéri!*"

Charm came easily to Kevin, and he flashed his smile while he untangled himself from all but two of the most persistent.

"You like your women beautiful and silent," his best friend's wife had said the last time they'd talked. "But most women aren't silent, so you home in on foreign babes with limited English. A classic case of intimacy avoidance."

Kevin remembered giving her a lazy once-over. "Is that

so? Well, listen up, Dr. Jane Darlington Bonner. I'll be intimate with you anytime you want."

"Over my dead body," her husband, Cal, had responded
from across the dinner table.

Even though Cal was his best friend, Kevin enjoyed giving
him a hard time. It had been that way since the days he'd
been the old man's resentful backup. Now, however, Cal was
retired from football and beginning his residency in internal
medicine at a hospital in North Carolina.

Kevin couldn't resist needling him. "It's a matter of principle, old man. I need to prove a point."

"Yeah, well, prove it with your own woman, and leave
mine alone."

Jane had laughed, kissed her husband, given their daughter, Rosie, a napkin, and picked up their new son, Tyler.
Kevin smiled as he remembered Cal's response when he'd
asked about the Post-it notes he kept seeing on Ty's diapers.

"It's because I won't let her write on his legs anymore."

"Still at it, is she?"

"Arms, legs—the poor kid was turning into a walking scientific notebook. But it's gotten better since I started tucking
Post-its in all her pockets."

Jane's habit of absentmindedly jotting down complex
equations on unorthodox surfaces was well known, and
Rosie Bonner piped up.

"Once she wrote on my foot. Didn't you, Mommy? And
another time—"

Dr. Jane pushed a drumstick into her daughter's mouth.

Kevin smiled at the memory, only to be interrupted as the
beautiful Frenchwoman on his right shouted over the music.
"Tu es fatigué, chéri?"

Kevin had a facility with languages, but he'd learned to
keep it hidden. "Thanks, but I don't want anything to eat
right now. Hey, let me introduce you to Stubs Brady. I think
you two might have a lot in common. And—Heather, is it?—

my buddy Leon has been watching you with lascivious intent all evening."

"What kind of tent?"

Definitely time to shed a few females.

He'd never admit to Jane that she was right about his preference in women. But unlike some of his teammates, who paid lip service to the notion of giving all they had to the game, Kevin really did. Not only his body and mind but his heart as well, and you couldn't do that with a high-maintenance female in your life. Beautiful and undemanding, that's what he wanted, and foreign women fit the bill.

Playing for the Stars was everything that mattered to him, and he wouldn't let anybody get in the way of that. He loved wearing the aqua and gold uniform, taking the field in the Midwest Sports Dome, and most of all, working for Phoebe and Dan Calebow. Maybe it was the result of a childhood spent as a preacher's kid, but there was honor in being a Chicago Star, something that couldn't be said for every NFL team.

When you played for the Calebows, respect for the game was more important than the bottom line. The Stars weren't the team for thugs or prima donnas, and during the course of his career Kevin had seen some brilliant talent traded because those players hadn't measured up to Phoebe and Dan's standards of character. Kevin couldn't imagine playing for anyone else, and when he no longer got the job done for the Stars on the field, then he'd retire to coaching.

Coaching the Stars.

But two things had happened this season to jeopardize his dreams. One was his own fault—the crazy recklessness that had hit him right after training camp. He'd always had a reckless streak but, until now, he'd restricted it to off-season. The other was Daphne Somerville's midnight visit to his bedroom. That had done more to jeopardize his career than all the skydiving and dirt-bike racing in the world.

He was a sound sleeper, and it hadn't been the first time he'd awakened in the middle of making love, but up until then he'd always chosen his partners. Ironically, if it hadn't been for her family connections, he might have thought about choosing her. Maybe it was the appeal of forbidden fruit, but he'd had a great time with her. She'd kept him on his toes and made him laugh. Although he'd been careful not to let her see it, he'd found himself watching her. She moved with a rich girl's confidence he'd found sexy. Her body might not be flashy, but everything was in the right place, and he'd definitely noticed.

Even so, he'd kept his distance. She was the boss's sister, and he never fraternized with women connected with the team—no coaches' daughters, front-office secretaries, or even teammates' cousins. Despite that, look what had happened.

Just thinking about it made him angry all over again. Not even a hotshot quarterback was more important to the Calebows than family, and if they ever found out what had happened, he was the one they'd be coming after for explanations.

His conscience was going to force him to call her soon. Just once to make certain there hadn't been any consequences. There wouldn't be, he told himself, and he wasn't going to worry about it, especially now, when he couldn't afford any distractions. On Sunday, they were playing in the AFC Championship, and his game had to be flawless. Then his ultimate dream would come true. He'd be taking the Stars to the Super Bowl.

But six days later his dream was snatched away. And he had no one to blame but himself.

By working day and night, Molly finished *Daphne Takes a Tumble* and put it in the mail the same week the Stars lost the

AFC Championship. With fifteen seconds left on the clock, Kevin Tucker had refused to play it safe and thrown into double coverage. His pass was intercepted, and the Stars had lost by a field goal.

Molly fixed herself a cup of tea to ward off the chill of the January evening and took it over to her worktable. She had an article due for *Chik,* but instead of turning on her laptop, she picked up the legal pad she'd left on the couch to jot down some ideas she had for a new book, *Daphne Finds a Baby Rabbit.*

The telephone rang just as she sat down. "Hello."

"Daphne? It's Kevin Tucker."

Tea splashed into the saucer, and the breath went out of her. Once she'd had a crush on this man. Now just the sound of his voice terrified her.

She forced in air. Since he was still calling her Daphne, he must not have talked to anyone about her. That was good. She didn't want him talking about her, didn't even want him to think of her. "How did you get my number?"

"I made you give it to me."

She'd managed to forget. "I, uh . . . What can I do for you?"

"With the season over, I'm getting ready to leave town for a while. I wanted to be sure there weren't any . . . unfortunate consequences from . . . what happened."

"No! No consequences at all. Of course not."

"That's good."

Beneath his chilly response, she heard relief. At the same time she saw a way to make things easier, and she jumped at it. "I'm coming, darling!" she called out to an imaginary person.

"I take it you're not alone."

"No, I'm not." Again the raised voice. "I'm on the phone, Benny! I'll be there in a moment, sweetheart." She winced. Couldn't she have thought of a better name?

Roo trotted in from the kitchen to see what was up. She

clutched the receiver tighter. "I appreciate your call, Kevin, but there was no need."

"As long as everything's—"

"Everything's wonderful, but I have to go. Sorry about the game. And thanks for calling." Her hand was still trembling when she disconnected.

She had just talked with the father of her unborn baby.

Her palm settled over her flat abdomen. She still hadn't completely absorbed the fact that she was pregnant. When her period hadn't arrived on schedule, she'd convinced herself that stress was the cause. But her breasts had grown increasingly tender, she'd begun to feel nauseated, and two days ago, she'd finally bought a home pregnancy test. The result had left her so panic-stricken she'd rushed out and bought another one.

There was no mistake. She was going to have Kevin Tucker's baby.

But her first thoughts hadn't been of him. They'd been of Dan and Phoebe. Family was the center of their existence, and neither of them would be able to imagine raising a child without the other. This was going to devastate them.

When she'd finally considered Kevin, she'd known she had to make certain he never found out. He'd been her unwilling victim, and she would bear the consequences alone.

It wouldn't be all that difficult to keep him in the dark. With the season over, there was little chance she'd run into him, and she'd simply stay away from Stars headquarters when they started practice in the summer. Except for a few of Dan and Phoebe's team parties, she'd never socialized much with the players. Eventually Kevin might hear that she'd had a baby, but this morning's phone call would make him believe there had been another man in her life.

She gazed through the windows of her loft into the winter sky. Although it wasn't even six o'clock, it was already dark. She stretched out on the couch.

Until two days ago she'd never considered single motherhood. She hadn't thought much about motherhood at all. Now she couldn't think of anything else. The restlessness that had always seemed like a backbeat to her life had vanished, leaving her with the unfamiliar feeling that everything was exactly as it should be. She'd finally have a family of her own.

Roo licked the hand she was dangling over the side of the couch. She closed her eyes and wove the daydreams that had taken over her imagination now that her initial shock had worn off. A little boy? A girl? It didn't matter. She'd spent enough time with her nieces and nephew to know that she'd be a good mother regardless, and she'd love this baby enough for two parents.

Her baby. Her family.

Finally.

She stretched, content to the tips of her toes. This was what she'd been searching for all these years, a family of her very own. She couldn't remember ever feeling so peaceful. Even her hair was peaceful, no longer brutally short and back to its natural dark brown color. Just right for her.

Roo nudged her hand with his wet nose.

"Hungry, buddy?" She rose and was on her way to the kitchen to feed him when the phone rang again. Her pulse raced, but it was only Phoebe.

"Dan and I had a meeting in Lake Forest. We're on the Edens now, and he's hungry. Want to go to Yoshi's with us for dinner?"

"I'd love to."

"Great. See you in about half an hour."

As Molly hung up, the knowledge of how much she was going to hurt them hit hard. They wanted her to have exactly what they did—a deep, unconditional love that formed the foundation of both their lives. But most people weren't that lucky.

She slipped into her threadbare Dolce & Gabbana sweater and a skinny, ankle-length charcoal skirt she'd bought last spring for half off at Field's. Kevin's phone call had unsettled her, so she flipped on the television. Lately she'd gotten into the habit of watching reruns of *Lace, Inc.* The show was nostalgic for her, a link to one of the few pleasant parts of her childhood.

She still wondered about Kevin's connection to Lilly Sherman. Phoebe might know, but Molly was afraid to mention his name, even though Phoebe had no idea Molly had been with him at the Door County house.

"Lace is on the case, oh yeah . . . Lace can solve the case, oh yeah . . . "

Commercials followed the credits, and then Lilly Sherman as Ginger Hill bounced across the screen in a pair of tight white shorts, her breasts overflowing a bright green bikini top. Auburn hair billowed around her face, gold hoops brushed her cheekbones, and her seductive smile promised untold sensual delights.

The camera angle widened to show both detectives at the beach. In contrast to Ginger's skimpier apparel, Sable wore a high-cut maillot. Molly remembered there'd been an off-screen friendship between the two actresses.

The buzzer from the lobby sounded. She turned off the television and, a few minutes later, opened the door for her sister and brother-in-law.

Phoebe kissed her cheek. "You look pale. Are you all right?"

"It's January in Chicago. Everybody's pale." Molly squeezed her a moment longer than necessary. Celia the Hen, a motherly resident of Nightingale Woods who clucked over Daphne, had been created just for her sister.

"Hey, Miz Molly. We've missed you." Dan gave her his customary rib-crushing bear hug.

As she hugged him back, she thought how lucky she was to have them both. "It's only been two weeks since New Year's."

"And two weeks since you've been home. Phoebe gets cranky." He tossed his jacket over the back of the couch.

As Molly took Phoebe's coat, she smiled. Dan still considered their house Molly's real home. He didn't understand how she felt about her condo. "Dan, do you remember the first time we met? I tried to convince you Phoebe was beating me."

"Hard to forget something like that. I still remember what you told me. You said she wasn't entirely evil, just mildly twisted."

Phoebe laughed. "The good old days."

Molly gazed fondly at her sister. "I was such a little prig, it's a wonder you *didn't* beat me."

"Somerville girls had to find their own ways to survive."

One of us still does, Molly thought.

Roo adored Phoebe and pounced into her lap the moment she sat. "I'm so glad I got to see the illustrations for *Daphne Takes a Tumble* before you sent them off. The expression on Benny's face when his mountain bike slips in the rain puddle is priceless. Any ideas for a new book?"

She hesitated. "Still in the thinking stages."

"Hannah was delirious when Daphne bandaged Benny's paw. I don't think she expected Daphne to forgive him."

"Daphne is a very forgiving rabbit. Although she did use a pink lace ribbon for his bandage."

Phoebe laughed. "Benny needs to be more in touch with his feminine side. It's a wonderful book, Moll. You always manage to stick in one of life's important lessons and still be funny. I'm so glad you're writing."

"It's exactly what I always wanted to do. I just didn't know it."

"Speaking of that . . . Dan, did you remember—" Phoebe broke off as she realized Dan wasn't there. "He must have gone to the bathroom."

"I haven't cleaned in there for a couple of days. I hope it's not too—" Molly sucked in her breath and whirled around.

But it was too late. Dan was walking back in with the two empty boxes he'd seen in the wastebasket. The pregnancy test kits looked like loaded grenades in his big hands.

Molly bit her lip. She hadn't wanted to tell them yet. They were still dealing with the loss of the AFC Championship, and they didn't need another disappointment.

Phoebe couldn't see what her husband was holding until he dropped one of the boxes into her lap. She slowly picked it up. Her hand traveled to her cheek. "Molly?"

"I know you're twenty-seven years old," Dan said, "and we both try to respect your privacy, but I've got to ask about this."

He looked so upset that Molly couldn't bear it. He loved being a father, and he was going to have a harder time accepting this than Phoebe would.

Molly took the boxes and set them aside. "Why don't you sit down?"

He slowly folded his big body onto the couch next to his wife. Phoebe's hand instinctively crept into his. The two of them together against the world. Sometimes watching the love they had for each other made Molly feel lonely to the bottom of her soul.

She took the chair across from them and managed a shaky smile. "There's no easy way to tell you this. I'm going to have a baby."

Dan flinched, and Phoebe leaned against him.

"I know it's a shock, and I'm sorry for that. But I'm not sorry about the baby."

"Tell me there's going to be a wedding first."

Dan's lips had barely moved, and she was once again reminded of exactly how unbending he could be. If she didn't hold her ground now, he'd never give her any peace. "No wedding. And no daddy. That's not going to change, so you need to make peace with it."

Phoebe looked even more distressed. "I—I didn't know you were seeing anyone special. You usually tell me."

Molly couldn't let her probe too deeply. "I share a lot with you, Phoeb, but not everything."

A muscle had started to tic in Dan's jaw, definitely a bad sign. "Who is he?"

"I'm not going to tell you," she said quietly. "This was my doing, not his. I don't want him in my life."

"You damn well wanted him in your life long enough to get pregnant!"

"Dan, don't." Phoebe had never been intimidated by Dan's hot temper, and she looked far more concerned about Molly. "Don't make a decision too quickly, Moll. How far along are you?"

"Only six weeks. And I'm not going to change my mind. There'll be just the baby and me. And both of you, I hope."

Dan shot up and began to pace. "You have no idea what you're getting yourself into."

She could have pointed out that thousands of single women had babies every year and that he was a bit old-fashioned in his outlook, but she knew him too well to waste her breath. Instead, she concentrated on practicalities.

"I can't stop either of you from worrying, but you need to remember that I'm better equipped than most single women to have a child. I'm nearly thirty, I love children, and I'm emotionally stable." For the first time in her life she felt as if that might be true.

"You're also broke most of the time." Dan's lips were tight.

"Daphne sales are going up slowly."

"Very slowly," he said.

"And I can do more freelancing. I won't even have to pay for child care because I work at home."

He regarded her stubbornly. "Children need a father."

She rose and walked to him. "They need a good man in

their life, and I hope you'll be there for this baby because you're the best there is."

That got to him, and he hugged her. "We just want you to be happy."

"I know. That's why I love you both so much."

"I just want her to be happy," Dan repeated to Phoebe as the two of them drove home that night after a strained dinner.

"We both do. But she's an independent woman, and she's made up her mind." Her brow knit with worry. "I suppose all we can do now is support her."

"It happened sometime around the beginning of December." Dan's eyes narrowed. "I promise you one thing, Phoebe. I'm going to find the son of a bitch who did this to her, and then I'm going to take his head off."

But finding him was easier said than done, and as one week slipped into another, Dan came no closer to discovering the truth. He made up excuses to phone Molly's friends and shamelessly pumped them for information, but no one remembered her dating anyone at the time. He pumped his own children with no more success. Out of desperation he finally hired a detective, a fact he neglected to mention to his wife, who would have ordered him to mind his own business. All he ended up with was a big bill and nothing he didn't already know.

In mid-February Dan and Phoebe took the kids to the Door County house for a long weekend of snowmobiling. They invited Molly to come along, but she said she was on deadline for *Chik* and couldn't stop work. He knew the real reason was that she didn't want any more lectures from him.

On Saturday afternoon he'd just brought Andrew inside to warm up from snowmobiling when Phoebe found him in the mudroom where they were taking off their boots.

"Have fun, pookie?"

"Yes!"

Dan grinned as Andrew flew across the wet floor in his socks and threw himself into her arms, something he generally did when he was separated from either one of them for more than an hour.

"I'm glad." She buried her lips in his hair, then gave him a nudge toward the kitchen. "Get your snack. The cider's hot, so let Tess pour it for you."

As Andrew ran off, Dan decided Phoebe looked particularly delectable in a pair of gold jeans with a soft brown sweater. He was just starting to reach for her when she held out a yellow credit card receipt. "I found this upstairs."

He glanced at it and saw Molly's name.

"It's a receipt from the little drugstore in town," Phoebe said. "Look at the date at the top."

He found it, but he still didn't understand why she seemed upset. "So what?"

She sagged against the washer. "Dan, that's when Kevin stayed here."

Kevin left the sidewalk café and began walking along the Cairns Esplanade toward his hotel. Palm trees swayed in the sunny February breeze, and boats bobbed in the harbor. After spending five days diving in the Coral Sea with the sharks that swam near the North Horn site of Australia's Great Barrier Reef, it was nice being back in civilization.

The city of Cairns on the northeastern coast of Queensland was the diving expedition's home port. Since the town had good restaurants and a couple of five-star hotels, Kevin had decided to stay around for a while. The city was far enough from Chicago that he wasn't in much danger of running into a Stars fan who wanted to know why he threw into double coverage late in the fourth quarter of the AFC Championship. Instead of giving the Stars the victory that would have taken them to the Super Bowl, he'd let his teammates down, and even swimming with a school of hammerheads wasn't making him forget that.

An Aussie hottie in a halter top and tight white shorts gave him the twice-over, followed by an inviting smile. "Need a tour guide, Yank?"

"Thanks, not today."

She looked disappointed. He probably should take her up on her invitation, but he couldn't work up enough interest. He'd also ignored the seductive overtures of the sexy blond doctoral candidate who'd cooked on the dive boat, but that had been more understandable. She was one of the smart, high-maintenance women.

This was the heart of Queensland's monsoon season, and a splatter of raindrops hit him. He decided to work out at the hotel health club for a while, then head over to the casino for a few games of blackjack.

He'd just changed into his gym clothes when a sharp knock sounded at the door. He walked over and opened it. "Dan? What are you doing—"

That was as far as he got before Dan Calebow's fist came up to meet him.

Kevin staggered backward, caught the corner of the couch, and fell.

Adrenaline rushed through him, hot and fast. He shot back up, ready to take Dan apart. Then he hesitated, not because Dan was his boss but because the raw fury in his expression indicated that something was drastically wrong. Since Dan had been more understanding than Kevin had deserved about the game, Kevin knew it didn't have anything to do with that ill-advised pass.

It went against his grain not to fight back, but he forced himself to lower his fists. "You'd better have a good reason for that."

"You son of a bitch. Did you really think you were going to walk away?"

Seeing such contempt on the face of a man he respected made his gut clench. "Walk away from what?"

"It didn't mean anything to you, did it?" Dan sneered.

Kevin waited him out.

Dan came forward, his lip curled. "Why didn't you tell me you weren't alone when you stayed at my house in December?"

The hair on the back of Kevin's neck prickled. He chose his words carefully. "I didn't think it was up to me. I thought it was Daphne's business to tell you she'd been there."

"*Daphne?*"

Enough was enough, and Kevin's own temper snapped. "It wasn't my fault your nutcase of a sister-in-law showed up!"

"You don't even know her fucking *name*?"

Dan looked as if he was getting ready to spring again, and Kevin was angry enough to hope he would. "Stop right there! She told me her name was Daphne."

"Yeah, right," Dan scoffed. "Well, her name is Molly, you son of a bitch, and she's pregnant with your baby!"

Kevin felt as if he'd taken the sack of his life. "What are you talking about?"

"I'm talking about the fact that I've had a stomachful of high-priced athletes who think they have a God-given right to scatter illegitimate kids around like so much trash."

Kevin felt sick. She'd told him there hadn't been any consequences when he'd called. She'd even had her boyfriend with her.

"You could at least have had the decency to use a goddamn rubber!"

His brain started working again, and there was no way he'd take the blame for this. "I talked to Daph—to your sister-in-law before I left Chicago, and she said everything was fine. Maybe you'd better have this conversation with her boyfriend."

"She's a little preoccupied to have a boyfriend right now."

"She's holding out on you," he said carefully. "You made this trip for nothing. She's going with a guy named Benny."

"Benny?"

"I don't know how long they've been together, but I'm guessing he's the one responsible for her current condition."

"Benny's not her boyfriend, you arrogant son of a bitch! He's a fricking *badger!*"

Kevin stared at him, then headed for the wet bar. "Maybe we'd better start over from the beginning."

Molly parked her Beetle behind Phoebe's BMW. As she got out of the car, she dodged a mound of dingy, ice-crusted snow. Northern Illinois was in the grip of a frigid spell that showed every sign of lingering, but she didn't mind. February was the best time of year for curling up with a warm computer and a sketchbook, or just for daydreaming.

> Daphne couldn't wait until the baby rabbit was big enough to play with. They'd dress up in skirts with sparkly beads and say, "Oo-la-la! You look divine!" Then they'd drop water balloons on Benny and his friends.

Molly was glad her speech at the literacy luncheon was over and that Phoebe had come along for moral support. Although she loved visiting schools to read to children, giving speeches to adults made her nervous, especially with an unpredictable stomach.

A month had passed since she'd discovered she was pregnant, and every day the baby became more real to her. She hadn't been able to resist buying a tiny pair of unisex denim overalls, and she couldn't wait to start wearing maternity clothes, although, since she was only two and a half months along, that wasn't necessary yet.

She followed her sister inside the rambling stone farmhouse. It had been Dan's before he and Phoebe were married, and he hadn't uttered a word of complaint when Molly had moved in along with his new bride.

Roo raced out to growl hello, while his more mannerly sister, Kanga, trotted behind. Molly had left him here while she was at the luncheon, and as soon as she hung up her coat, she leaned over to greet both dogs. "Hey, Roo. Hello, Kanga, sweetie."

Both poodles rolled over to get their tummies scratched.

As Molly complied, she watched Phoebe slip the Hermès scarf she'd been wearing into the pocket of Andrew's jacket.

"What's with you?" Molly asked. "All afternoon you've been distracted."

"Distracted? What do you mean?"

Molly retrieved the scarf and held it out to her sister. "Andrew gave up cross-dressing when he turned four."

"Oh, dear. I guess—" She broke off as Dan appeared from the back of the house.

"What are you doing here?" Molly asked. "Phoebe told me you were traveling."

"I was." He kissed his wife. "Just got back."

"Did you sleep in those clothes? You look awful."

"It was a long flight. Come in the family room, will you, Molly?"

"Sure."

The dogs trailed behind her as she made her way toward the back of the house. The family room was part of the addition that had been built as the Calebow family had grown. It had lots of glass and comfortable seating areas, some with armchairs for reading, another with a table for doing homework or playing games. A state-of-the-art stereo system held everything from Raffi to Rachmaninoff.

"So where did you go anyway? I thought you were—" Molly's words died as she saw the large man with dark blond hair standing in the corner of the room. The green eyes she'd once found so alluring regarded her with undiluted hostility.

Her heart began to hammer. His clothes were as wrinkled as Dan's, and stubble covered his jaw. Although he had a fresh suntan, he didn't look like someone who'd come off a relaxing vacation. Instead, he looked dangerously wired and ready to detonate.

Molly remembered Phoebe's distraction that afternoon, her furtive expression when she'd slipped into the back of the room right after Molly's speech to take a call on her cell phone. There was nothing coincidental about this meeting. Somehow Phoebe and Dan had unearthed the truth.

Phoebe spoke with quiet determination. "Let's all sit down."

"I'll stand," Kevin said, his lips barely moving.

Molly felt sick and angry and panicked. "I don't know what's going on here, but I won't have any part of it." She spun around, only to have Kevin step forward and block her way.

"Don't even think about it."

"This has nothing to do with you."

"That's not what I hear." His cold eyes cut into hers like shards of green ice.

"You heard wrong."

"Molly, let's sit down so we can discuss this," Phoebe said. "Dan flew all the way to Australia to find Kevin, and the least you—"

Molly whirled toward her brother-in-law. "You flew to Australia?"

He gave her the same stubborn look she'd seen on his face when he'd refused to let her go to a co-ed sleepover after her high school prom. The same look she'd seen when he wouldn't let her postpone college to backpack through Europe. But she hadn't been a teenager for years, and something inside her snapped.

"You had no right!" Without planning it, she found herself hurtling across the room to get to him.

She wasn't a violent person. She wasn't even hot-tempered. She liked rabbits and fairy tale forests, china teapots and linen nightgowns. She'd never struck anyone, let alone someone she loved. Even so, she felt her hand curling into a fist and flying toward her brother-in-law.

"How could you?" She caught Dan in the chest.

"Molly!" her sister cried.

Dan's eyes widened in astonishment. Roo began to bark.

Guilt, anger, and fear coalesced into an ugly ball inside Molly. Dan backed away, but she went after him and landed another blow. "This isn't your business!"

"Molly, stop it!" Phoebe exclaimed.

"I'll never forgive you." She swung again.

"Molly!"

"It's my life!" she cried over Roo's frenzied barks and her sister's protests. "Why couldn't you stay out of it!"

A strong arm caught her around the waist before she could land another blow. Roo howled. Kevin drew her back against his chest. "Maybe you'd better calm down."

"Let me go!" She jabbed him with her elbow.

He grunted but didn't release her.

Roo clamped on to his ankle.

Kevin yelped, and Molly jabbed him again.

Kevin started to swear.

Dan joined in.

"Oh, for Pete's sake!" A shrill noise split the air.

Chapter 5

Sometimes you need a friend really badly, but everyone's gone away for the day.

Daphne's Lonesome Day

MOLLY'S EARDRUMS RANG FROM THE BLAST OF THE TOY WHISTLE clamped between Phoebe's teeth.

"That's enough!" Her sister marched forward. "Molly, you are offside! Roo, let go! Kevin, get your hands off her. Now, everybody *sit down*!"

Kevin dropped his arm. Dan rubbed his chest. Roo released Kevin's pant leg.

Molly felt sick. Exactly what had she hoped to accomplish? She couldn't bear looking at anyone. The idea that her sister and brother-in-law must know by now how she'd attacked Kevin while he slept was beyond humiliating.

But she was accountable for what had happened, and she couldn't run away. Taking a cue from Daphne's fans, she grabbed her lovey for comfort and carried him to an armchair as far away from the rest of them as she could get. He gave her a sympathetic lick on the chin.

Dan took a seat on the couch. He wore the same stubborn expression that had unglued her. Phoebe perched next to him looking like a worried Vegas showgirl wearing mommy clothes. And Kevin . . .

His anger filled the room. He stood next to the fireplace, arms crossed over his chest, hands locked beneath his armpits, as if he didn't trust himself not to use them on her. How could she ever have had a crush on someone who was so dangerous?

That's when it sank in. Phoebe, Dan, Kevin . . . and her. The creator of Daphne the Bunny was up against the NFL.

Her only strategy lay in a strong offense. She'd look like a bitch, but it was the kindest thing she could do for Kevin. "Let's make it snappy. I have things to do, and this is just too boring for words."

A dark blond eyebrow shot to the middle of his forehead.

Phoebe sighed. "It's not going to work, Molly. He's too tough to scare off. We know Kevin is the father of your baby, and he's here to talk about the future."

She whirled toward Kevin. He hadn't told them! Phoebe would never be talking like this if she knew what Molly had done.

His eyes gave nothing away.

Why had he kept silent? Once Phoebe and Dan knew the truth, he'd be off the hook.

She turned toward her sister. "The future doesn't involve him. The truth is, I—"

Kevin sprang away from the fireplace. "Get your coat," he snapped. "We're going for a walk."

"I don't really—"

"Now!"

As much as she hated facing him, talking with Kevin alone would be easier than dealing with him in front of the Calebow Mafia. She set her lovey on the carpet and rose. "Stay here, Roo."

Phoebe picked up the poodle as he began to whine.

With her spine ramrod straight, Molly marched out of the room. Kevin caught up with her in the kitchen, gripped her arm, and hauled her into the laundry room. There he shoved Julie's pink and lavender ski jacket at her and snagged Dan's brown duffel coat from a hook for himself. He threw open the back door and gave her a none-too-gentle nudge outside.

Molly pulled on the coat and tugged at the zipper, but it didn't come close to meeting in the front, and the wind cut through her silk blouse. Kevin didn't bother fastening Dan's coat, even though he only wore a summer weight knit shirt and khakis. The heat of his fury was keeping him warm.

She reached nervously into Julie's pocket and found an old knit cap with a faded Barbie patch. The remnants of a glittery silver pompon hung by a few threads at the top. She yanked it on over her hair. He pulled her to a flagstone path that led to the woods. She could feel the anger rolling off him.

"You weren't going to tell me," he said.

"There was no need. But I'm going to tell *them*! You should have done that when Dan showed up and spared yourself a long trip."

"I can just imagine his reaction. This isn't my fault, Dan. Your perfect little sister-in-law raped me. I'm sure he'd have believed that."

"He'll believe it now. I'm sorry you had to be . . . inconvenienced this way."

"Inconvenienced?" The word was a whiplash to her. "This is a hell of a lot more than an inconvenience!"

"I know that. I—"

"This might be an *inconvenience* in your rich-girl's life, but in the real world—"

"I understand! You were a victim." She hunched her shoulders against the cold and tried to fit her hands into the pockets. "This is my situation to deal with, not yours."

"I'm not anybody's victim," he snarled.

"You were mine, and that makes me responsible for the consequences."

"The consequences, as you call them, add up to a human life."

She stopped walking and looked up at him. The wind snatched a lock of his hair and slapped it against his forehead. His face was rigid, his too-handsome features uncompromising.

"I know that," she said. "And you have to believe that I didn't plan any of this. But now that I'm pregnant, I want this baby very much."

"I don't."

She winced. Logically, she understood. Of course he wouldn't want a baby. But his anger was so fierce that she crossed her arms protectively over her waist. "Then we haven't got a problem. I don't need you, Kevin. Really. And I'd very much appreciate it if you'd forget all about this."

"Do you really think I'm going to do that?"

To her this was personal, but she had to remember this was a professional crisis for him. Kevin's passion for the Stars was well known. Phoebe and Dan were his bosses and two of the most powerful people in the NFL.

"As soon as I tell my sister and Dan what I did, you'll be off the hook. This won't affect your career at all."

His eyes narrowed. "You aren't telling them anything."

"Of course I am!"

"Keep your mouth shut."

"Is this your pride talking? You don't want anyone to know you were a victim? Or are you that afraid of them?"

His lips barely moved. "You don't know anything about me."

"I know the difference between right and wrong! What I did was wrong, and I won't compound it by bringing you any further into this. I'm going back inside, and—"

He caught her arm and gave her a shake. "Listen up, because I'm jet-lagged and I don't want to have to say this more than once. I've been guilty of a lot of things in my life, but

I've never left behind an illegitimate kid, and I don't intend to start now."

She drew away and clutched herself tighter. "I'm not getting rid of this baby, so don't even suggest it."

"I'm not." His lips tightened into a bitter line. "We're getting married."

She was flabbergasted. "I don't want to get married."

"That makes two of us, and we won't stay that way for long."

"I won't—"

"Don't waste your breath. You screwed me over, lady, and now I'm making the calls."

Normally Kevin enjoyed the dance club, but now he wished he hadn't come. Even though his confrontation with the Calebow clan had taken place yesterday afternoon, he still wasn't fit to be around other people.

"Kevin! Over here!"

A girl with glitter on her eyelids and a cellophane dress called to him above the noise. They'd dated for a couple of weeks last summer. Nina? Nita? He no longer remembered or cared.

"Kevin! Hey, buddy, come on over here and let me buy you a drink!"

He pretended he didn't hear either of them and made his way back through the crowd in the direction he'd just come. This had been a mistake. He couldn't deal with friends now, let alone fans eager to talk about the championship game he'd lost.

He claimed his coat but didn't button it, and the cold air of Dearborn Street hit him like a fist. On his drive into the city, the car radio had announced that the mercury had dipped to three below. Winter in Chicago. The valet spotted him and went to get his car, which was parked in a prominent space less than twenty feet away.

In another week he'd be a married man. So much for keeping his personal life separate from his career. He handed the valet a fifty, then slid behind the wheel of his Spider and pulled away.

You have to set an example, Kevin. People expect the children of clergy to do the right thing.

He shook off the voice of the good Reverend John Tucker. Kevin was doing this to protect his career. Okay, so the idea of an illegitimate child made his skin crawl, but that would bother anybody. This sure as hell wasn't some leftover preacher's kid thing. It was all about the game.

Phoebe and Dan weren't expecting a love match, and the fact that the marriage wasn't going to last long wouldn't surprise them. At the same time, he'd be able to hold up his head around them. As for Molly Somerville, with her important connections and her careless morality, he'd never hated anyone more. So much for marrying the silent, undemanding woman Jane Bonner loved to taunt him about. Instead, he had a snooty egghead who'd take big bites out of him if he gave her the chance. Luckily, he didn't intend to give her one.

Kevin, there's right and there's wrong. You can either walk through your life in the shadows or you can stay in the light.

He ignored John Tucker and accelerated onto Lake Shore Drive. This had nothing to do with right and wrong. It was career damage control.

Not quite, a small voice whispered inside him. He shot into the left lane, then the right, then the left again. He needed speed and danger, but he wasn't going to get either on Lake Shore Drive.

A few days after Phoebe and Dan's ambush, Molly met Kevin to take care of the wedding license. Afterward, they drove separately downtown to the Hancock Building where they signed the legal papers that would separate their finances.

Kevin didn't know that Molly had no finances to separate, and she didn't tell him. It would only make her look loonier than he already thought she was.

Molly tuned out as the attorney explained the documents. She and Kevin hadn't said a word about what role he'd take in her child's life, and she was too dispirited to bring it up. One more thing they needed to work out.

Leaving the office, Molly gathered her courage and tried once more to talk to him. "Kevin, this is crazy. At least let me tell Dan and Phoebe the truth."

"You swore to me you'd keep your mouth shut."

"I know, but—"

His green eyes chilled her to the bone. "I'd like to believe you can be honorable about something."

She looked away, wishing she hadn't given him her word. "These aren't the 1950s. I don't need marriage to raise this child. Single women do it all the time."

"Getting married won't be anything more than a minor inconvenience for either one of us. Are you so self-centered you can't give up a few weeks of your life to try to set this straight?"

She didn't like the contempt in his voice or being called self-centered, especially when she knew he was doing this only to keep himself on good terms with Dan and Phoebe, but he walked away before she could respond. She finally gave up. She could fight one of them, but not all three.

The wedding took place a few days later in the Calebow living room. Molly wore the winter-white midcalf dress her sister had bought her. Kevin wore a deep charcoal suit with a matching tie. Molly thought it made him look like a gorgeous mortician.

They'd both refused to invite any of their friends to the ceremony, so only Dan, Phoebe, the children, and the dogs were there. The girls had decorated the living room with white crepe-paper streamers and tied bows on the dogs. Roo wore his around his collar, and Kanga's perched crookedly on her topknot. She flirted shamelessly with Kevin, shaking her topknot to get his attention and batting her tail. Kevin ignored her just as he ignored Roo's growling, so Molly knew he was one of those men who believed that a poodle threatened his masculinity. Why hadn't she considered that in Door County instead of looking for burps, gold chains, and "You duh man"?

Hannah's eyes shone, and she gazed at Kevin and Molly as if they were the central figures in a fairy tale. Because of her, Molly pretended to be happy when all she wanted to do was throw up.

"You look so beautiful." Hannah sighed. Then she turned to Kevin, her heart in her eyes. "You look beautiful, too. Like a prince."

Tess and Julie let out whoops of laughter. Hannah turned crimson.

But Kevin didn't laugh. He smiled instead and squeezed her shoulder. "Thanks, kiddo."

Molly blinked her eyes and looked away.

The judge conducting the ceremony stepped forward. "Let's begin."

Molly and Kevin moved toward him as if they were passing through a force field.

"Dearly beloved . . . "

Andrew wiggled loose from his mother's side and shot forward to wedge himself between the bride and groom.

"Andrew, come back here." Dan reached out to retrieve him, but Kevin and Molly simultaneously snatched his sticky little hands to keep him right where he was.

And that was how they got married—underneath a makeshift bower of mismatched crepe-paper streamers with a five-year-old planted firmly between them and a gray poodle glaring at the groom.

Not once did Molly and Kevin look at each other, not even during the kiss, which was dry, fast, and closemouthed.

Andrew looked up at them and grimaced. "Yucky, mush, mush."

"They're supposed to kiss, you baby," Tess said from behind.

"I'm not a baby!"

Molly leaned down to hug him before he could get worked up. Out of the corner of her eye she saw Dan shake Kevin's hand and Phoebe give him a quick embrace. It was awkward and awful, and Molly couldn't wait to get away. Except that was a problem all in itself.

They made a play of sipping a few drops of champagne, but neither of them managed to eat more than a bite of the small white wedding cake. "Let's get out of here," Kevin finally growled in her ear.

Molly didn't have to fabricate a headache. She'd been feeling increasingly ill all afternoon. "All right."

Kevin murmured something about getting on the road before it snowed.

"A good idea," Phoebe said. "I'm glad you're taking us up on our offer."

Molly tried to look as if the prospect of spending a few days in Door County with Kevin weren't her worst nightmare.

"It's the best thing to do," Dan agreed. "The house is far enough away that you'll avoid the worst of the media stir when we make the announcement."

"Besides," Phoebe said with phony cheer, "it'll give you a chance to get to know each other better."

"Can't wait for that," Kevin muttered.

They didn't bother changing their clothes, and ten minutes later Molly was kissing Roo good-bye. Under the circumstances she thought it best to leave her dog with her sister.

As Molly and Kevin drove off in his Ferrari, Tess and Julie wrapped crepe-paper streamers around Andrew while Hannah cuddled up to her father.

"My car's at an Exxon station a couple of miles from here. Turn left when you get to the highway." The idea of being closed up together for the seven-and-a-half-hour trip to northern Wisconsin had been more than her nerves could handle.

Kevin slipped on his silver-framed Rēvos. "I thought we'd agreed on the Door County plan."

"I'll drive there in my own car."

"Suits me."

Kevin followed her directions and pulled into the service station a few minutes later. His arm pressed her waist as he leaned across her to open the passenger door. Molly took the keys from her purse and climbed out.

He roared off without a word.

She cried all the way to the Wisconsin border.

Kevin made a detour to his home in one of Oak Brook's gated communities, where he changed into jeans and a flannel shirt. He picked up a couple of CDs by a Chicago jazz group he liked, along with a book about climbing Everest that he'd forgotten to stick in his suitcase. He thought about fixing himself something to eat since he wasn't in any hurry to get back on the road, but he'd lost his appetite along with his freedom.

As he headed north into Wisconsin on I-94, he tried to remember the way he'd felt when he'd swum with the reef sharks only a little over a week ago, but he couldn't recapture the sensation. Rich athletes were a target for predatory women, and the notion that she might have gotten pregnant on purpose had occurred to him. But Molly didn't need the money. No, she'd been after kicks instead, and she hadn't bothered to consider the consequences.

North of Sheboygan his cell phone rang. When he answered, he heard the voice of Charlotte Long, a woman who'd been his parents' friend for as long as he could remember. Like his parents, she'd spent her summers at his family's campground in northern Michigan, and she still returned there every June. He'd been out of contact with her until his mother's death.

"Kevin, your Aunt Judith's attorney just called me again."

"Terrific," he muttered. He remembered Charlotte talking with his father and mother after the daily service in the Tabernacle. Even in his earliest memories they'd all seemed ancient.

At the time of his birth his parents' well-ordered lives had centered on the Grand Rapids church where his father had been pastor, the books they'd loved, and their scholarly hobbies. They had no other children, and they didn't have a clue what to do with a lively little boy they loved with all their hearts but didn't understand.

Please try to sit still, sweetheart.

How did you get so dirty?

How did you get so sweaty?

Not so fast.

Not so loud.

Not so fierce.

Football, son? I believe my old tennis racket is stored in the attic. Let's try that instead?

Even so, they'd attended his games because that's what good parents did in Grand Rapids. He still remembered looking up into the stands and catching sight of their anxious, mystified faces.

They must have wondered how they hatched you.

That's what Molly had said when he'd told her about them. She might be wrong about everything else, but she sure had been right about that.

"He said you haven't called him." The note of accusation was strong in Charlotte's voice.

"Who?"

"Your Aunt Judith's attorney. Pay attention, Kevin. He wants to talk about the campground."

Even though Kevin had known what Charlotte was going to say, his hands tightened on the steering wheel. Conversations about the Wind Lake Campground always made him tense, which was why he avoided them. It was the place where the gap between himself and his parents had been the most painful.

The campground had been established by his great-grandfather on some land he'd bartered for in remote northeastern Michigan during the late 1800s. From the beginning it had served as a summer gathering place for Methodist religious revivals. Since it was located on an inland lake instead of on the ocean, it never acquired the fame of campgrounds like Ocean Grove, New Jersey, or Oak Bluffs on Martha's Vineyard, but it had the same gingerbread cottages, as well as a central Tabernacle where services had been held.

Growing up, Kevin had been forced to spend summers there as his father conducted daily services for the dwindling number of elderly people who came back each year. Kevin was always the only child.

"You realize the campground is yours now that Judith has died," Charlotte said unnecessarily.

"I don't want it."

"Of course you do. It's been passed down through the Tucker family for over a hundred years. It's an institution, and you certainly don't want to be the one to end that."

Oh, yes, he did. "Charlotte, the place is a sinkhole for money. With Aunt Judith dead, there's no one to look after it."

"You're going to look after it. She's taken good care of everything. You can hire someone to run it."

"I'm selling it. I have a career to concentrate on."

"You can't! Really, Kevin, it's part of your family history. Besides, people still come back every year."

"I'll bet that makes the local undertaker happy."

"What was that? Oh, dear . . . I have to go or I'll be late to my watercolor class."

She hung up before he could tell her about his marriage. Just as well. Talking about the campground darkened an already black mood.

God, those summers had been agonizing. While his friends at home played baseball and hung out, he was stuck with a bunch of old people and a million rules.

Not so much splashing when you're in the water, dear. The ladies don't like getting their hair wet.

Worship starts in half an hour, son. Get cleaned up.

Were you throwing your ball against the Tabernacle again? There are marks all over the paint.

When he'd turned fifteen, he'd finally rebelled and nearly broken their hearts.

I'm not going back, and you can't make me! It's so damn boring there! I hate it! I'll run away if you try to make me go back! I mean it!

They'd given in, and he'd spent the next three summers in Grand Rapids with his friend Matt. Matt's dad was young and tough. He'd played college football for the Spartans, and every evening he threw the ball around with them. Kevin had worshipped him.

Eventually John Tucker had grown too old to minister, the Tabernacle had burned down, and the religious purpose of the campgrounds had come to an end. His Aunt Judith had moved into the bleak old house on the grounds where Kevin and his parents used to stay, and she'd continued to rent out the cottages in the summer. Kevin had never returned.

He didn't want to think anymore about those endless, boring summers filled with old people shushing him, so he cranked up the volume on his new CD. But just as he left the interstate behind, he spotted a familiar chartreuse Beetle on the shoulder of the road. Gravel clicked against the undercarriage as he pulled over. It was Molly's car, all right. She was leaning against the steering wheel.

Great. Just what he needed. A hysterical female. What right did she have to be hysterical? He was the one who should be howling.

He debated driving away, but she'd probably already spotted him, so he got out and walked toward the car.

The pain stole her breath, or maybe it was the fear. Molly knew she had to get to a hospital, but she was afraid to move. Afraid if she moved, the hot, sticky wetness that had already seeped through the skirt of her white woolen wedding dress would become a flood that would sweep away her baby.

She'd attributed the first cramps to hunger pangs from forgetting to eat all day. Then a spasm had gripped her that was so strong she'd barely been able to pull the car over.

She folded her hands over her stomach and curled in on herself. *Please don't let me lose this baby. Please, God.*

"Molly?"

Through the haze of her tears, she saw Kevin peering through the car window. When she didn't move, he rapped on the glass. "Molly, what's wrong?"

She tried to respond but couldn't.

He jiggled the handle. "Unlock the door."

She began to reach for it, but another cramp hit. She whimpered and wrapped her arms around her thighs to hold them together.

He rapped again, harder this time. "Hit the lock! Just hit it!"

Somehow she managed to do as he asked.

A wave of bitterly cold air struck her as he jerked open the door, and his breath made a frosty cloud in the air. "What's wrong?"

Fear clogged her throat. All she could do was bite her lip and squeeze her thighs more tightly.

"Is it the baby?"

She managed a jerky nod.

"Do you think you're having a miscarriage?"

"*No!*" She fought the pain and tried to speak more calmly. "No, it's not a miscarriage. Just—just some cramps."

She could see that he didn't believe her, and she hated him for it.

"Let's get you to a hospital."

He ran to the other side of the car, opened the door, and reached through to shift her into the passenger seat, but she couldn't let him do that. If she moved . . . "No! Don't . . . don't move me!"

"I have to. I won't hurt you. I promise."

He didn't understand. It wasn't she who'd be hurt. "No . . . "

But he didn't listen. She gripped her thighs tighter as he reached beneath her and awkwardly shifted her into the other seat. The effort left her gasping.

He raced back to his car and returned moments later with his cell phone and a wool stadium blanket that he tossed over her. Before he slid behind the wheel, he threw a jacket on the seat. Covering up her blood.

As he pulled back onto the highway, she willed her arms to keep their strength as she clamped her legs together. He was talking to someone on the phone . . . locating a hospital. The tires on her tiny Bug squealed as they hurtled down the highway and around a bend. Reckless, daredevil driving. *Please, God . . .*

She had no idea how long it took to reach the hospital. She knew only that he was opening the door next to her and getting ready to pick her up again.

She tried to blink away her tears as she gazed up at him. "Please . . . I know you hate me, but . . . " She gasped against another cramp. "My legs . . . I have to keep my legs together."

He studied her for a moment, then slowly nodded.

She felt as though she weighed nothing as he slipped his

arms beneath the skirt of her wedding dress and lifted her so effortlessly. He pressed her thighs tightly against his body and carried her through the door.

Someone came forward with a wheelchair, and he hurried toward it.

"No . . . " She tried to grip his arm, but she was too weak. "My legs . . . If you set me down . . . "

"Right here, sir," the attendant called out.

"Just show me where to take her," Kevin said.

"I'm sorry, sir, but—"

"Get moving!"

She rested her cheek against his chest and for a moment felt as if she and her baby were safe. The moment evaporated as he carried her into a curtained cubicle and carefully set her on the table.

"We'll take care of her while you go to registration, sir," the nurse said.

He squeezed Molly's hand. For the first time since he'd come back from Australia, he looked concerned instead of hostile. "I'll be right back."

As she gazed into the flickering fluorescent light above her, she wondered how he'd fill out the paperwork. He didn't know her birthday or her middle name. He knew nothing about her.

The nurse was young, with a soft, sweet face. But when she tried to help Molly off with her bloody panties, Molly refused. She'd have to ease open her legs to do that.

The nurse stroked her arm. "I'll be very careful."

But in the end it didn't do any good. By the time the emergency room doctor arrived to examine her, Molly had already lost her baby.

Kevin refused to let them dismiss her until the next day, and because he was a celebrity, he got his wish. Through the window of the private room she saw a parking lot and a line of barren trees. She shut her eyes against the voices.

One of the doctors was talking to Kevin, using the deferential tone people adopted when they spoke with someone famous. "Your wife is young and healthy, Mr. Tucker. She'll need to be checked by her own physician, but I don't see any reason why the two of you won't be able to have another child."

Molly saw a reason.

Someone took her hand. She didn't know if it was a nurse, the doctor, or Kevin. She didn't care. She pulled her hand away.

"How are you feeling?" Kevin whispered.

She pretended to be asleep.

He stayed in her room for a long time. When he finally left, she rolled over and reached for the telephone.

Her head was fuzzy from the pills they'd given her, and she had to dial twice before she finally got through. When Phoebe answered, Molly started to cry. "Come get me. Please . . . "

Dan and Phoebe appeared in her room sometime after midnight. Molly thought Kevin had left, but he must have been sleeping in the lounge because she heard him talking to Dan.

Phoebe stroked her cheek. Fertile Phoebe, who'd given birth to four children without mishap. One of her tears dropped onto Molly's arm. "Oh, Moll . . . I'm so sorry."

When Phoebe left her bedside to talk to the nurse, Kevin took her place. Why wouldn't he go away? He was a stranger, and no one wanted a stranger around when her life was falling apart. Molly turned her head into the pillow.

"You didn't need to call them," he said quietly. "I would have driven you back."

"I know."

He'd been kind to her, so she made herself look at him. She saw concern in his eyes, as well as fatigue, but she couldn't see even the smallest shadow of grief.

As soon as she got back home, she tore up *Daphne Finds a Baby Rabbit* and carried it out to the trash.

The next morning the story of her marriage hit the news-papers.

Chapter 6

Melissa the Wood Frog was Daphne's best friend.
Most days she liked to dress in pearls and or-
gandy. But every Saturday she added a shawl and
pretended she was a movie star.

Daphne Gets Lost

*"OUR CHICAGO CELEBRITY OF THE WEEK SPOTLIGHT TURNS TO
wealthy football heiress Molly Somerville. Unlike her flamboy-
ant sister, Chicago Stars owner Phoebe Calebow, Molly
Somerville has kept a low profile. But while no one was looking,
sly Miss Molly, who dabbles at writing children's books, scooped
up Chicago's most eligible bachelor, the delectable Stars quarterback Kevin Tucker. Even close friends were shocked when the
couple was married in a very private ceremony at the Calebow
home just last week."*

The gossip reporter rearranged her plastic expression into
a look of deep concern. *"But it looks like there's no happy ending for the newlyweds. Sources now report the couple suffered a
miscarriage almost immediately after the wedding ceremony,
and they've since separated. A spokesman for the Stars would
say only that the couple was working through their troubles
privately and would make no comments to the media."*

Lilly Sherman snapped off the Chicago television station,
then took a deep breath. Kevin had married a spoiled Mid-
western heiress. Her hands trembled as she closed the French
doors that looked out over the garden of her Brentwood

home, then picked up the coffee-colored pashmina shawl that lay at the foot of her bed. Somehow she had to steady herself before she reached the restaurant. Although Mallory McCoy was her best friend, this secret was Lilly's own.

She tossed the pashmina over the shoulders of her latest St. John knit, a creamy suit with gold buttons and exquisite braided trim. Then she picked up a brightly wrapped gift bag and set off for one of Beverly Hills' newest restaurants. After she'd been shown to her table, she ordered a blackberry kir. Ignoring the curious gazes of a couple at the next table, she studied the décor.

Subdued lighting glazed the oyster-white walls and illuminated the restaurant's small but fine display of original art. The carpet was aubergine, the linens crisp and white, the silver a sleek Art Deco design. A perfect place to celebrate an unwelcome birthday. Her fiftieth. Not that anyone knew. Even Mallory McCoy thought they were celebrating Lilly's forty-seventh.

Lilly hadn't been given the room's best table, but she'd grown so accustomed to playing the diva that no one would have known it. Two of the top men at ICM occupied the prime spot, and she momentarily contemplated walking over and introducing herself. They would know who she was, of course. Only a rare man didn't remember Ginger Hill from *Lace, Inc.* But nothing was less welcome in this town than an overweight former sex kitten celebrating a fiftieth birthday.

She reminded herself that she didn't look her age. Her eyes were the same brilliant green the camera had always loved, and although she wore her auburn hair shorter now, Beverly Hills' top colorist made certain it hadn't lost any of its luster. Her face was barely lined, her skin still smooth, thanks to Craig, who wouldn't let her lie in the sun when she was younger.

The twenty-five-year age difference between her husband

and herself, along with Craig's good looks and his role as her manager, had invited inevitable comparisons to Ann-Margret and Roger Smith, as well as to Bo and John Derek. And it was true that Craig had been her Svengali. When she'd arrived in L.A. over thirty years ago, she hadn't even possessed a high school diploma, and he'd taught her how to dress, walk, and speak. He'd exposed her to culture and transformed her from an awkward teenager into one of the eighties' hottest sex symbols. Because of Craig, she was well read and culturally literate, with a particular passion for art.

Craig had done everything for her. Too much. Sometimes she'd felt as if she'd been swallowed up by the demanding force of his personality. Even when he was dying, he'd been dictatorial. Still, he'd truly loved her, and she only wished, at the end, that she'd been able to love him more.

She distracted herself with the paintings on the restaurant's walls. Her eyes drifted past a Julian Schnabel and a Keith Haring to take in an exquisite Liam Jenner oil. He was one of her favorite artists, and just looking at the painting calmed her.

She glanced at her watch and saw that Mallory was late as usual. During the six years they'd filmed *Lace, Inc.,* Mallory had always been the last to arrive on the set. Normally Lilly didn't mind, but now it gave her too much time to think about Kevin and the fact that he'd separated from his heiress wife before the ink was dry on the wedding license. The reporter said Molly Somerville had suffered a miscarriage. Lilly wondered how Kevin had felt about that, or even if the baby had been his. Famous athletes were prime targets for unscrupulous women, including rich ones.

Mallory came dashing toward the table. She was still the same size four she'd been during their days on *Lace, Inc.,* and unlike Lilly, she'd been able to keep her career alive by becoming the queen of the miniseries. Even so, Mallory didn't have Lilly's presence in person, and no one took note of her arrival. Lilly had nagged her about this countless times, *Attitude, Mallory! Walk like you're getting twenty mil a picture.*

"Sorry I'm late," Mallory chirped. "Happy, happy, you adorable person! Present later."

They exchanged social kisses just as if Mallory hadn't held Lilly in her arms more than once through the ordeal of Craig's long illness and death two years ago.

"Do you hate me for being late for your birthday dinner?"

Lilly smiled. "I know you'll be surprised to hear this, but after twenty years of friendship I've gotten used to it."

Mallory sighed. "We've been together longer than either of my marriages lasted."

"That's because I'm nicer than your ex-husbands."

Mallory laughed. The waiter appeared to take her drink order, then pressed them to try an *amuse-bouche* of ratatouille tart with goat cheese while they contemplated the menu. Lilly briefly considered the calories before she agreed to the tart. It was her birthday, after all.

"Do you miss it a lot?" Mallory inquired when the waiter left.

Lilly didn't have to ask what Mallory meant, and she shrugged. "When Craig was sick, caring for him took so much of my energy that I didn't think about sex. Since he died, there's been too much to do." *And I'm so fat I'd never let any man see my body.*

"You're so independent now. Two years ago you didn't have a clue what was in your financial portfolio, let alone know how to manage it. I can't tell you how much I admire the way you've taken charge."

"I didn't have any choice." Craig's financial planning had left her wealthy enough that she no longer needed work to support herself, only to give her life purpose. In the past year she'd had a small part as the sexy mother of the male star in a halfway decent movie. She'd been able to carry it off because she was a pro, but the whole time they were filming, she'd had to struggle against a sense of the ridiculous. For a woman of her size and age still to be playing sexpots, even aging ones, seemed somehow absurd.

She didn't like having her sense of identity wrapped up in a profession for which she no longer had a passion, but acting was all she knew, and with Craig's death she needed to keep busy or she'd think too much about the mistakes she'd made. If only she could peel away the years and go back in time to that crucial point where she'd lost her way.

The waiter returned with Mallory's drink, the *amuse-bouche,* and a lengthy explanation of the menu's many courses. After they'd made their selections, Mallory lifted her champagne flute. "To my dearest friend. Happy birthday, and I'll kill you if you don't love your present."

"Gracious as always."

Mallory laughed and pulled a flat, rectangular box from the tote she'd set at the side of her chair. The package was professionally wrapped in paisley paper tied with a burgundy bow. Lilly opened it to find an exquisite antique shawl of gold lace.

Her eyes stung with sentimental tears. "It's beautiful. Where ever did you find it?"

"A friend of a friend who deals in rare textiles. It's Spanish. Late nineteenth century."

The symbolism of the lace made it hard for her to speak, but there was something she needed to say, and she reached across the table to touch her friend's hand. "Have I ever told you how dear you are to me?"

"Ditto, sweetie. I've got a long memory. You held me together through my first divorce, through those awful years with Michael . . . "

"Don't forget your face-lift."

"Hey! I seem to remember a little eye job you had a few years ago."

"I have no idea what you're talking about."

They exchanged smiles. Plastic surgery might seem vain to much of the world, but it was a necessity for actresses who'd built their reputations on sex appeal. Although Lilly wondered why she'd bothered with an eye job when she couldn't manage to lose even twenty pounds.

The waiter set a gold-rimmed Versace plate in front of Lilly with a tiny square of aspic containing slivers of poached lobster surrounded by a trail of saffron sauce that had been whipped into a creamy froth. Mallory's plate held a wafer-thin slice of salmon accented with capers and a few transparent slices of julienned apple. Lilly mentally compared calories.

"Stop obsessing. You worry so much about your weight that you've lost sight of how gorgeous you still are."

Lilly deflected the well-meaning lecture she'd heard before by reaching behind her chair and coming up with the gift bag. The waterfall of French ribbon she'd tied around the handles brushed her wrist as she handed it over.

Mallory's eyes lit up with delight. "It's *your* birthday, Lilly. Why are you giving me a present?"

"Coincidence. I finished it this morning, and I couldn't wait any longer."

Mallory tore at the ribbons. Lilly sipped her kir as she watched, trying not to show how much Mallory's opinion meant.

Her friend pulled out the quilted pillow. "Oh, sweetie . . . "

"The design might be too strange," Lilly said quickly. "It's just an experiment."

She'd taken up quilting during Craig's illness, but the traditional patterns hadn't satisfied her for long, and she'd begun to experiment with designs of her own. The pillow she'd made for Mallory had a dozen shades and patterns of blue swirling together in an intricate design, while a trail of delicate gold stars peeped out from unexpected places.

"It's not strange at all." Mallory smiled at her. "I think it's the most beautiful thing you've done so far, and I'll always treasure it."

"Really?"

"You've become an artist."

"Don't be silly. It's just something to do with my hands."

"You keep telling yourself that." Mallory grinned. "Is it coincidence that you used the colors of your favorite football team?"

Lilly hadn't even realized it. Maybe it was a coincidence.

"I've never understood how you turned into such a sports fan," Mallory said. "And not even a West Coast team."

"I like the uniforms."

Lilly managed a shrug and turned the conversation in another direction. Her thoughts, however, remained stuck.

Kevin, what have you done?

Chef Rick Bayless's cutting-edge Mexican cuisine made the Frontera Grill one of Chicago's favorite spots for lunch, and before Molly had given away her money, she'd frequently eaten here. Now she ate at this North Clark Street restaurant only when someone else was picking up the check, in this case Helen Kennedy Schott, her editor at Birdcage Press.

" . . . we're all very committed to the Daphne books, but we do have some concerns."

Molly knew what was coming. She'd submitted *Daphne Takes a Tumble* in mid-January, and she should have given Helen at least an idea about her next book by now. But *Daphne Finds a Baby Rabbit* had gone into the trash, and Molly had a devastating case of writer's block.

In the two months since her miscarriage she hadn't been able to write a word, not even for *Chik*. Instead, she'd kept busy with school book talks and a local tutoring program for preschoolers, forcing herself to focus on the needs of living children instead of the baby she'd lost. Unlike the adults

Molly met, the children didn't care that she was the about-to-be-ex-wife of the city's most famous quarterback.

Just last week the town's favorite gossip column had once again turned the media spotlight on her:

> Heiress Molly Somerville, the estranged wife of Stars Quarterback Kevin Tucker, has been keeping a low profile in the Windy City. Has it been boredom or a broken heart over her failed marriage to Mr. Football? No one has seen her at any of the city's nightspots, where Tucker still shows up with his foreign lovelies in tow.

At least the column hadn't said Molly "dabbled at writing children's books." That had stung, although lately she hadn't even been able to dabble. Every morning she told herself this would be the day she'd come up with an idea for a new Daphne book or even an article for *Chik,* and every morning she'd find herself staring at a blank piece of paper. In the meantime her financial situation was deteriorating. She desperately needed the second part of the advance payment she was due to receive for *Daphne Takes a Tumble,* but Helen still hadn't approved it.

The restaurant's colorful décor suddenly seemed too bright, and the lively chatter jangled her nerves. She'd told no one about her block, especially not the woman sitting across from her. Now she spoke carefully. "I want this next book to be really special. I've been tossing around a number of ideas, but—"

"No, no." Helen held up her hand. "Take your time. We understand. You've been through a lot lately."

If her editor wasn't concerned about not getting a manuscript, why had she invited her to lunch? Molly rearranged one of the tiny corn masa boats on her plate. She'd always loved them, but she'd been having trouble eating since the miscarriage.

Helen touched the rim of her margarita glass. "You should know that we've had some inquiries from SKIFSA about the Daphne books."

Helen mistook Molly's stunned expression. "Straight Kids for a Straight America. They're an antigay organization."

"I know what SKIFSA is. But why are they interested in the Daphne books?"

"I don't think they would have looked at them if there hadn't been so much press about you. The news reports apparently caught their attention, and they called me several weeks ago with some concerns."

"How could they have concerns? Daphne doesn't have a sex life!"

"Yes, well, that didn't stop Jerry Falwell from outing Tinky Winky on the *Teletubbies* for being purple and carrying a purse."

"Daphne's allowed to carry a purse. She's a girl."

Helen's smile seemed forced. "I don't think the purse is the issue. They're . . . concerned about possible homosexual overtones."

It was a good thing Molly hadn't been eating, because she would have choked. "In my books?"

"I'm afraid so, although there haven't been any accusations yet. As I said, I think your marriage caught their attention, and they saw a chance for publicity. They asked for an advance look at *Daphne Takes a Tumble,* and since we didn't foresee any problems, we sent them a copy of the mock-up. Unfortunately, that was a mistake."

Molly's head was beginning to ache. "What possible concerns could they have?"

"Well . . . they mentioned that you use a lot of rainbows in all of your books. Since that's a symbol for gay pride . . . "

"It's become a crime to use rainbows?"

"These days it seems to be," Helen said dryly. "There are a few other things. They're all ridiculous, of course. For example, you've drawn Daphne giving Melissa a kiss in at least three different books, including *Tumble*."

"They're best friends!"

"Yes, well . . . " Like Molly, Helen had given up any pretense of eating, and she crossed her arms on the edge of the table. "Also, Daphne and Melissa are holding hands and skipping down Periwinkle Path. There's some dialogue."

"A song. They're singing a song."

"That's right. The lyrics are 'It's spring! It's spring! We're gay! We're gay!' "

Molly laughed for what seemed the first time in two months, but her editor's tight-lipped smile sobered her. "Helen, you're not seriously telling me they think Daphne and Melissa are getting it on?"

"It's not just Daphne and Melissa. Benny—"

"Hold it right there! Even the most paranoid person couldn't accuse Benny of being gay. He's so macho that he—"

"They've pointed out that he borrows a lipstick in *Daphne Plants a Pumpkin Patch*."

"He uses it to make his face scary so he can frighten Daphne! This is so ludicrous it doesn't even deserve a response."

"We agree. On the other hand, I'd be less than truthful if I didn't admit we're a little edgy about this. We think SKIFSA wants to use you to raise their profile, and they're going to do it by zeroing in on *Daphne Takes a Tumble*."

"So what? When the fringe groups started accusing J. K. Rowling of Satanism in the Harry Potter books, her publisher ignored it."

"Forgive me, Molly, but Daphne isn't quite as well known as Harry Potter."

And Molly didn't have either J. K. Rowling's clout or her money. The possibility of Helen's authorizing the rest of her advance seemed to be growing more remote by the minute.

"Look, Molly, I know this is ridiculous, and Birdcage is

standing behind the Daphne books one hundred percent—
there's no question about that. But we're a small company,
and I thought it was only fair to tell you that we're getting a
fair amount of pressure about *Daphne Takes a Tumble.*"

"I'm sure it'll disappear as soon as the press lets go of the
story about . . . about my marriage."

"That may take a while. There's been so much speculation . . . " She let her words trail off, subtly hinting for details.

Molly knew it was the air of mystery around her marriage
that was keeping the press interested, but she refused to
comment on it, and so did Kevin. His courteous, formal calls
to check up on her had finally stopped at her insistence.
From the time he'd learned of her pregnancy right through
her miscarriage, his behavior had been faultless, and the resentment she felt whenever she thought of him made her
ashamed, so she stopped thinking about him.

"We think it's a good idea to be cautious now." Her editor
slipped an envelope from the folder she had at her side and
passed it across the table. Unfortunately, it was too large to
contain a check.

"Luckily, *Daphne Takes a Tumble* hasn't gone into final
production yet, and that gives us a chance to make a few of
the changes they're suggesting. Just to avoid any misunderstanding."

"I don't want to make changes." The muscles tightened in
a painful band around Molly's shoulders.

"I understand, but we think—"

"You told me you loved the book."

"And we're totally committed. The changes I'm suggesting are very minor. Just look through them and think about
it. We can talk more next week."

Molly was furious when she left the restaurant. By the
time she got home, however, her anger had faded, and the
bleak sense of emptiness she couldn't shake off settled over

her once again. She tossed aside the envelope with Helen's suggestions and went to bed.

Lilly wore the shawl Mallory had given her to the J. Paul Getty Museum. She stood on one of the curved balconies that made the museum so wonderful and gazed out over the hills of Los Angeles. The May day was sunny, and if she turned her head a bit, she could see Brentwood. She could even make out the tile roof of her house. She'd loved the house when she and Craig first found it, but now all the walls seemed to be closing in on her. Like so much else in her life, it was more Craig's than hers.

She slipped back inside the museum, but she paid little attention to the old masters on the wall. It was the Getty itself she loved. The cluster of ultramodern buildings with their wonderful balconies and unpredictable angles formed a work of art that pleased her far more than the precious objects inside. A dozen times since Craig's death she'd ridden the sleek white tram that carried visitors to the hilltop museum. The way the buildings enfolded her made her feel as if she'd become part of the art—frozen in time at the moment of perfection.

People magazine had showed up on the stands today with a two-page story about Kevin and his mystery marriage. She'd fled here to escape a nearly overwhelming urge to pick up the phone and call Charlotte Long, the woman who was her only inside source of information about Kevin. It was May, and the marriage and separation had taken place three months ago, but she didn't know anything more now than she had then. If only she could call Charlotte Long without worrying that she'd tell Kevin.

As she headed down the staircase and into the courtyard, she tried to figure out how to keep herself busy for the rest of the day. No one was banging on her door begging her to star in a new film. She didn't want to start another quilting project because it would give her too much time to think, and she'd had more than enough of that lately. The breeze loosened a lock of hair and whipped it against her cheek. Maybe she should stop worrying about the consequences and just give in to the urge to call Charlotte Long. But how much pain did she want to put herself through when she couldn't see any possibility of a happy ending?

If only she could see him.

Chapter 7

Should I overdose on pills? Daphne asked herself. Or jump from the top of a very tall tree? Oh, where was that handy carbon monoxide leak when a girl needed it?

Daphne's Nervous Breakdown
(notes for a never-to-be-
published manuscript)

"I'M FINE," MOLLY TOLD HER SISTER EVERY TIME THEY TALKED.

"Why don't you come out to the house this weekend? I promise, you won't find a single copy of *People* around. The irises are beautiful, and I know how much you love May."

"This weekend's not good. Maybe next."

"That's what you said the last time we talked."

"Soon, I promise. It's just that I've got so many things going right now."

It was true. Molly had painted her closets, pasted photos in albums, cleaned out files, and groomed her sleepy poodle. She did everything but work on the revisions she'd finally been forced to agree to do because she needed the rest of her advance money.

Helen wanted some dialogue changed in *Daphne Takes a Tumble* as well as three new drawings. Two would show Daphne and Melissa standing farther apart, and in the third, Benny and his friends were to be eating cheese sandwiches instead of hot dogs. Everyone had scoured Daphne with the most lascivious of adult minds. Helen had also asked Molly to make changes in the text of two older Daphne books that were going back to press. But Molly had done none of it, not out of principle, although she wished that were the case, but because she couldn't concentrate.

Her friend Janine, who was still stung over SKIFSA'S condemnation of her own book, was upset that Molly hadn't told Birdcage to go to hell, but Janine had a husband who made their mortgage payment every month.

"The kids miss you," Phoebe said.

"I'll call them tonight. I promise."

She did call them, and she managed to do all right with the twins and Andrew. But Hannah broke her heart.

"It's because of me, isn't it, Aunt Molly?" she whispered. "That's why you don't want to come over anymore. It's because the last time you were here, I said I was sad that your baby died."

"Oh, sweetheart . . . "

"I didn't know I wasn't supposed to talk about the baby. I promise, I won't ever, ever say anything again."

"You didn't do anything wrong, love. I'll come over this weekend. We'll have a great time."

But the trip only made her feel worse. She hated being responsible for the worry that clouded Phoebe's face, and she couldn't bear the soft, considerate way Dan spoke to her, as if he were afraid she would shatter. Being with the children was even more painful. As they looped their arms around her waist and demanded she come with them to see their newest projects, she could barely breathe.

The family was tearing her apart with their love. She left as soon as she could.

May slid into June. Molly sat down a dozen times to work on the drawings, but her normally agile pen refused to move. She tried to come up with an idea for a *Chik* article, but her mind was as empty as her bank account. She could make her mortgage payments through July, but that was all.

As one June day slipped into the next, little things began

to get away from her. One of her neighbors set a sack of mail he'd pulled from her overflowing mailbox outside her door. Her laundry piled up, and dust settled over her normally tidy condo. She got a cold and had trouble shaking it off.

One Friday morning her head ached so badly she called in sick for her volunteer tutoring and went to bed. Other than dragging herself outside long enough for Roo to do his business and occasionally forcing down a piece of toast, she slept all weekend.

When Monday came, her headache was gone, but the aftereffects of the cold had sapped her energy, so she phoned in sick again. Her bread box was empty, and she was out of cereal. She found some canned fruit in the cupboard.

On Tuesday morning as she dozed in bed, her sleep was disturbed by the buzzer from the lobby. Roo hopped to attention. Molly burrowed deeper into her covers, but just when she was falling back asleep, someone began pounding on her door. She pulled a pillow over her head, but it didn't block out the deep, familiar voice clearly audible over the sound of Roo's yips.

"Open up! I know you're in there!"

That awful Kevin Tucker.

She sneezed and stuck her fingers in her ears, but Roo kept barking and Kevin kept banging. Miserable dog. Reckless, scary quarterback. Everyone in the building was going to complain. Cursing, she dragged herself out of bed.

"What do you want?" Her voice sounded creaky from lack of use.

"I want you to open the door."

"Why?"

"Because I need to talk to you."

"I don't want to talk." She grabbed a tissue and blew her nose.

"Tough. Unless you'd like everyone in this building to know your private business, I suggest you open up."

Reluctantly, she flipped the lock. As she opened the door, she wished she were armed.

Kevin stood on the other side, dazzling and perfect with his healthy body, gleaming blond hair, and blazing green eyes. Her head pounded. She wanted to hide behind dark glasses.

He pushed his way past her snarling poodle and shut the door. "You look like hell."

She stumbled over to the couch. "Roo, be quiet."

The dog gave Molly an offended sniff as she lay down.

"Have you seen a doctor?"

"I don't need a doctor. My cold is almost gone."

"How about a shrink?" He walked over to the windows and began opening them.

"Stop that." It was bad enough that she had to endure his arrogance and the threatening glare of his good looks. She didn't have to tolerate fresh air, too. "Will you go away?"

As he gazed around at her condo, she noticed the dirty dishes littering the kitchen counter, the bathrobe hanging over the end of the couch, and the dusty tabletops. He was an uninvited guest, and she didn't care.

"You blew off the appointment with the attorney yesterday."

"What appointment?" She shoved a hand into her ratty hair, then winced as it caught on a snarl. Half an hour ago she'd stumbled into the bathroom to brush her teeth, but she couldn't remember taking a shower. And her shabby gray Northwestern nightshirt smelled like poodle.

"The annulment?" He glanced toward the pile of unopened mail spilling out of the white Crate & Barrel shopping bag next to the door and said sarcastically, "I guess you didn't get the letter."

"I guess. You'd better leave. I might still be contagious."

"I'll take my chances." He wandered over to the windows and gazed down at the parking lot. "Nice view."

She closed her eyes to sneak in a nap.

* * *

Kevin didn't think he'd ever seen anyone more pathetic. This pasty-faced, stringy-haired, musty-smelling, sniffling, sad-eyed female was his wife. Hard to believe she was the daughter of a showgirl. He should have let his attorney take care of this, but he kept seeing the raw desperation in her eyes when she'd begged him to hold her legs together, as if brute strength alone could keep that baby inside her.

I know you hate me, but . . .

He couldn't quite hate her any longer, not after he'd watched her fruitless struggle to hold on to that baby. But he did hate the way he felt, as if he had some sort of responsibility for her. Training camp started in less than two months. He needed to be focusing all his energy on getting ready for next season. He gazed at her resentfully.

You have to set an example, Kevin. Do the right thing.

He moved away from the windows and stepped over her worthless, pampered dog. Why did someone with her millions live in such a small place? Convenience, maybe. She probably had at least three other addresses, all of them in warm climates.

He sank down on the sectional couch at the opposite end from where she was lying and studied her critically. She must have dropped ten pounds since the miscarriage. Her hair had grown longer, nearly to her jawline, and it had lost that silky sheen he remembered from their wedding day. She hadn't bothered with makeup, and the deep bruises under those exotic eyes made her look as if she'd been somebody's punching bag.

"I had an interesting conversation with one of your neighbors."

She settled her wrist over her eyes. "I promise I'll call your attorney first thing in the morning if you'll just leave."

"The guy recognized me right away."

"Of course he did."

She wasn't too tired for sarcasm, he noticed. His resentment simmered.

"He was more than happy to gossip about you. Apparently you stopped emptying your mailbox a few weeks ago."

"Nobody sends me anything interesting."

"And the only time you've left your apartment since Thursday night is to take out your pit bull."

"Stop calling him that. I'm recovering from a cold, that's all."

He could see her red nose, but somehow he didn't think a cold was the only thing wrong with her. He rose. "Come on, Molly. Holing up like this isn't normal."

She peered at him from beneath her wrist. "Like you're an expert on normal behavior? I heard you were swimming with sharks when Dan found you in Australia."

"Maybe it's depression."

"Thank you, Dr. Tucker. Now, get out."

"You lost a baby, Molly."

He'd made a statement of fact, but it was as if he'd shot her. She sprang up from the couch, and the way her expression turned feral told him more than he wanted to know.

"Get out of here before I call the police!"

All he had to do was walk through the door. God knew he had enough aggravation on his plate right now with the publicity the *People* article had kicked up. And just being with her was making his gut churn. If only he could forget the way she'd looked when she'd been trying to hold on to that baby.

Even as the words were coming out of his mouth, he tried to cut them off. "Get dressed. You're coming with me."

Her rage seemed to frighten her, and he watched her struggle to make light of it. The best she could manage was a pitiful croak. "Been smoking a little too much weed, have you?"

Furious with himself, he stomped up the five steps that

led to her bedroom loft. Her pit bull shadowed him to make sure he didn't steal the jewelry. He looked down at her from over the top of the kitchen cabinets. God, he hated this. "You can either get yourself dressed or go with me the way you are. Which will probably get you quarantined by the Health Department."

She lay back on the couch. "You're so wasting your breath."

It would be for only a few days, he told himself. He was already in a foul mood about being forced to drive up to the Wind Lake Campground. Why not make himself completely miserable by bringing her along?

He'd never intended to go back there, but he couldn't avoid it. For weeks he'd been telling himself he could sell off the property without seeing it again. But when he couldn't answer any of the questions his business manager had posed, he'd known he had to bite the bullet and see exactly how run-down it had become.

At least he'd be getting rid of two ugly duties at the same time. He'd settle the campground and badger Molly into getting her butt moving again. Whether it worked or not would be up to her, but at least his conscience would be clean.

He unearthed a suitcase from the back of her closet and yanked open her drawers. Unlike her messy kitchen, here everything was neatly arranged. He tossed shorts and tops in the suitcase, then threw in some underwear. He found jeans along with sandals and a pair of sneakers. A couple of sundresses caught his eye. He threw them on top. Better to take too much than have her sulk because she didn't have what she wanted.

The suitcase was full, so he grabbed what looked like her old college backpack and glanced around for the bathroom. He found it downstairs, near the front door, and began dumping in various cosmetics and toiletries. Succumbing to the inevitable, he headed for the kitchen and loaded up on dog food.

"I hope you're planning to put all that back." She was standing by the refrigerator, the pit bull in her arms, her rich-girl's eyes weary.

He'd like nothing better than to put it back, but she looked too damn pathetic. "You want to take a shower first, or do we drive with the windows down?"

"Are you deaf? I'm not some rookie you can order around."

He propped one hand on the edge of the sink and gave her the same stony look he used on those rookies. "You've got two choices. Either you can go with me right now, or I'm taking you over to your sister's house. Somehow I don't think she'll like what she sees."

Her expression told him he'd just thrown a Hail Mary.

"Please leave me alone," she whispered.

"I'll look through your bookshelves while you take a shower."

Chapter 8

A smart girl never accepts a ride from a stranger, even if he is a hottie.

"Hitchhiking Hell"
article for Chik magazine

MOLLY CRAWLED WITH ROO INTO THE BACKSEAT OF THE SNAPPY SUV Kevin was driving instead of his Ferrari. She propped up the pillow she'd brought along and tried to go to sleep, but it wasn't possible. As they sped east past the urban blight of Gary, then took I-94 toward Michigan City, she kept asking herself why she hadn't opened her mail. All she'd needed to do was show up at the attorney's office. Then she wouldn't have been body-snatched by a mean-tempered quarterback.

Her refusal to talk to him was beginning to seem childish. Besides, her headache was better, and she wanted to know where they were going. She stroked Roo. "Do you have a destination in mind, or is this a make-it-up-as-you-go kidnapping?"

He ignored her.

They drove for another hour in silence before he pulled over for gas near Benton Harbor. While he was filling the tank, a fan spotted him and asked for an autograph. She clipped a leash on Roo and took him into the grass, then slipped into the bathroom. As she washed her hands, she caught a glimpse of herself in the mirror. He was right. She did look like hell. She'd washed her hair, but she hadn't done anything more than drag her fingers through it afterward. Her skin was ashen, her eyes sunken.

She began to reach into her purse for a lipstick, then decided it took too much effort. She thought about phoning one of her friends to come get her, but Kevin's implied threat to talk to Phoebe and Dan about her physical condition made her hesitate. She couldn't stand causing them more worry than she already had. Better to go along with him for now.

He wasn't in the car when she returned. She debated getting into the backseat again, but doubted he'd talk to her unless she was in his face, so she put Roo there instead and climbed in the front. He emerged from the service station with a plastic bag and a Styrofoam coffee cup. After he got inside, he stuck the coffee in the cup holder, then pulled a bottle of orange juice from the sack and handed it to her.

"I'd rather have coffee."

"Too bad."

The cold bottle felt good in her hands, and she realized she was thirsty, but when she tried to open it, she discovered she was too weak. Her eyes filled unexpectedly with tears.

He took it without comment, unscrewed the lid, and returned it to her.

As he pulled away from the pump, she choked back the tightness in her throat. "At least you muscle boys are good for something."

"Be sure to let me know if you want any beer cans crushed."

She was startled to hear herself laugh. The orange juice slid in a cool, sweet trickle down her throat.

He pulled out onto the interstate. Sand dunes stretched on their left. She couldn't see the water, but she knew there would be cruisers on the lake, probably some freighters on their way to Chicago or Ludington. "Would you mind telling me where we're going?"

"Northeast Michigan. A hole called Wind Lake."

"There goes my fantasy of a Caribbean cruise."

"The campground I told you about."

"The place where you told me you spent your summers when you were a kid?"

"Yeah. My aunt inherited it from my father, but she died a few months back, and I was unlucky enough to end up with it. I'm going to sell it, but I have to check out the condition first."

"I can't go to a camp. You'll have to turn around and take me home."

"Believe me, we won't be there for long. Two days at the most."

"Doesn't matter. I don't do camp anymore. I had to go every summer when I was a kid, and I promised myself I'd never go back."

"What was so bad about camp?"

"All that organized activity. Sports." She blew her nose. "There was no time to read, no time to be alone with your thoughts."

"Not much of an athlete?"

One summer she'd sneaked out of her cabin in the middle of the night and gathered up every ball in the equipment shed—volleyballs, soccer, tennis, softballs. It had taken her half a dozen trips to carry them all to the lake and throw them in the water. The counselors had never discovered the culprit. Certainly no one had suspected quiet, brainy Molly Somerville, who'd been named Most Cooperative despite spraying her bangs green.

"I'm a better athlete than Phoebe," she said.

Kevin shuddered. "The guys are still talking about the last time she played softball at the Stars picnic."

Molly hadn't been there, but she could imagine.

He swung into the left lane and said, with an edge, "I wouldn't think spending a few weeks every summer at some rich-kid's camp damaged you too much."

"I suppose you're right."

Except she never went for a few weeks. She went all summer, every summer, from the time she was six.

When she'd been eleven, there was a measles outbreak and all the campers were sent home. Her father had been furious. He couldn't find anyone to stay with her, so he'd been forced to take her with him to Vegas, where he'd set her up in a suite separate from his own with a change girl as a babysitter, even though Molly kept telling him she was too old for one. During the day the girl watched the soaps, and at night she crossed the hall to sleep with Bert.

They'd been the best two weeks of Molly's childhood. She'd read the complete works of Mary Stewart, ordered cherry cheesecake from room service, and made friends with the Spanish-speaking maids. Sometimes she'd announce to her sitter that she was going down to the pool, but instead, she'd wander around near the casino until she found a family with a lot of kids. Then she'd stay as close as she could and pretend she belonged to them.

Normally, the memories of her childish attempts to create a family made her smile, but now she felt another prickle of tears and swallowed. "Have you noticed there's a speed limit?"

"Making you nervous?"

"You should be, but I'm numb from too many years of riding with Dan." Besides, she didn't care that much. It shocked her—the realization that she had no interest in the future. She couldn't even muster the energy to worry about her finances or the fact that her editor at *Chik* had stopped calling.

He backed off on the accelerator. "Just so you know, the campground is in the middle of nowhere, the cottages are so old they're probably in ruins by now, and the place is more boring than elevator music because nobody under the age of seventy ever goes there." He tilted his head toward the sack of food he'd picked up at the service station. "If you're done with that orange juice, there are some cheese crackers inside."

"Yummy, but I think I'll pass."

"You seem to have passed on a lot of meals lately."

"Thanks for noticing. I figure if I lose another sixty pounds, I might be as skinny as some of your *chères amies*."

"Feel free to concentrate on that nervous breakdown of yours. At least it'll keep you quiet."

She smiled. One thing she'd say for Kevin, he didn't handle her with kid gloves like Phoebe and Dan. It was nice to be treated as an adult. "Maybe I'll just take a nap instead."

"You do that."

But she didn't sleep. Instead, she closed her eyes and tried to make herself think about her next book, but her mind refused to take a single step into the cozy byways of Nightingale Woods.

After they got off the interstate, Kevin stopped at a roadside store with a smokehouse attached and returned carrying a brown paper bag that he tossed into her lap. "Michigan lunch. Do you think you can make some sandwiches?"

"Maybe if I concentrate."

Inside she found a generous piece of smoked whitefish, a hunk of sharp cheddar cheese, and a loaf of dark pumpernickel bread, along with a plastic knife and a few paper napkins. She mustered enough energy to put together two crude, open-faced sandwiches for him and a smaller one for herself, all but a few bites of which she ended up feeding to Roo.

They headed east toward the middle of the state. Through half-closed eyes she saw orchards coming into bloom and neat farms with silos. Then, as the afternoon light began to fade, they made their way north toward I-75, which stretched all the way to Sault Ste. Marie.

They didn't talk much. Kevin listened to the CDs he'd

brought with him. He liked jazz, she discovered, everything from forties bebop to fusion. Unfortunately, he also liked rap, and after fifteen minutes of trying to ignore Tupac's views of women, she hit the eject button, grabbed the disk, and tossed it out the car window.

His ears turned red, she discovered, when he yelled.

It was getting dark when they reached the northern part of the state. Just beyond the pretty town of Grayling they left the freeway for a two-lane highway that seemed to lead nowhere. Before long they were driving through dense woods.

"Northeastern Michigan was nearly stripped of timber by the lumber industry during the 1800s," he said. "What you're seeing now is second- and third-growth forest. Some of it is pretty wild. Towns in this area are small and scattered."

"How much farther?"

"Only a little over an hour, but the place is run-down, so I don't want to get there after dark. There's supposed to be a motel not far from here, but don't expect the Ritz."

Since she couldn't imagine him worrying about the dark, she suspected he was stalling, and she curled deeper into the seat. The headlights of an occasional oncoming car flickered across his features, casting dangerous shadows beneath those male underwear model cheekbones. She felt a shiver of foreboding, so she closed her eyes and pretended she was alone.

She didn't open them again until he pulled up in front of an eight-unit roadside motel made of white aluminum siding and fake brick. As he got out of the car to register, she thought about making sure he understood that she wanted a separate unit, but common sense intervened.

Sure enough, he returned from the office with two keys. His unit, she noticed, was at the opposite end from hers.

*   *   *

Early the next morning she awakened to door pounding and poodle barking. "Slytherins," she grumbled. "This is getting to be a bad habit."

"We're leaving in half an hour," Kevin called from the other side. "Get the lead out."

"Hut, hut," she muttered into her pillow.

She dragged herself into the cramped shower and even managed to run a comb through her hair. Lipstick, however, was beyond her. She felt as if she had a colossal hangover.

When she finally emerged, he was pacing near the car. The lemony patch of sunlight that splashed over him revealed a grim mouth and unfriendly expression. As Roo took advantage of the shrubbery, Kevin grabbed her suitcase and tossed it into the back of the car.

Today he'd decorated his muscles with an aqua Stars T-shirt and light gray shorts. They were ordinary clothes, but he wore them with the confidence of those who were born beautiful.

She fumbled in her purse for her sunglasses, then glared at him resentfully. "Don't you ever turn it off?"

"Turn what off?"

"Your basic ugliness," she muttered.

"Maybe I should just drop you off at a funny farm instead of taking you to Wind Lake."

"Whatever. Is coffee too much to hope for?" She shoved on her glasses, but they didn't do a whole lot to shut out the blinding glare of his irritating beauty.

"It's in the car, but it took you so long to get ready that it's probably cold by now."

It was piping hot, and as they pulled back out onto the road, she took a long, slow sip.

"Fruit and doughnuts were the best I could do for breakfast. They're in that bag." He sounded as grouchy as she felt. She wasn't hungry, and she concentrated on the scenery.

They might have been in the wilds of the Yukon instead of

a state that made Chevrolets, Sugar Pops, and soul music. From a bridge crossing the Au Sable River she saw rocky cliffs rising on one shore and dense woods stretching on the other. An osprey soared down over the water. Everything seemed wild and remote.

Occasionally they passed a farm, but this was clearly timber country. Maple and oak competed with pine, birch, and cedar. Here and there, golden straws of sunlight penetrated the canopy formed by the trees. It was wonderfully serene, and she tried to feel peaceful, but she was out of practice.

Kevin swore and jerked the wheel to avoid a squirrel. Getting closer to their destination definitely hadn't improved his mood. She spotted a metal highway sign that indicated the turnoff for Wind Lake, but he flew past it. "That's the town," he grunted. "The campground is on the far side of the lake."

They drove for another few miles before a decorative green-and-white sign with a Chippendale top edged in gilt came into sight.

Wind Lake Cottages
BED & BREAKFAST
ESTABLISHED 1894

Kevin frowned. "That sign looks new. And nobody said anything to me about a bed-and-breakfast. She must have used the old house to take in guests."

"Is that bad?"

"The place is musty and dark as sin. I can't believe anybody would want to stay there." He turned onto a gravel lane that wound through the trees for about half a mile before the campground emerged.

He stopped the car, and Molly caught her breath. She'd expected to see rough cabins decaying on their foundations. Instead, they'd driven into a storybook village.

A shady rectangular Common sat at the center, surrounded by small gingerbread cottages painted in colors that could have spilled from a box of bonbons: mint with tangerine and toffee, mocha touched with lemon and cranberry, peach with blueberry and brown sugar. Wooden lace dripped from tiny eaves, and fanciful spindles bordered front porches no larger than a trundle bed. At one end of the Common sat a charming gazebo.

A closer inspection showed that the flower beds in the Common were overgrown, and the loop of road that surrounded it needed fresh gravel. Everything bore an air of neglect, but it seemed recent rather than long-term. Most of the cottages were tightly shuttered, although a few had been opened up. An elderly couple emerged from one of them, and Molly spotted a man with a cane walking near the gazebo.

"These people shouldn't be here! I had all the summer rentals canceled."

"They must not have gotten the word." As Molly gazed around, she experienced the oddest sense of familiarity. Since she'd never been anywhere like this, she couldn't explain it.

Across the road from the center of the Common was a small picnic area with a sandy, crescent-shaped beach directly behind it and, beyond that, a sliver of the blue-gray water of Wind Lake against the backdrop of a tree-lined shore. Several canoes and a few rowboats were overturned near a weathered dock.

She wasn't surprised that the beach was deserted. Although the early-June morning was sunny, this was a North Woods lake, and the water would still be too chilly for all but the hardiest swimmers.

"Notice the complete absence of anyone under the age of seventy!" Kevin exclaimed as he stepped on the accelerator.

"It's early. A lot of schools aren't out yet."

"It'll look this way at the end of July. Welcome to my

childhood." He swung away from the Common onto a narrower lane that ran parallel to the lake. She saw more cottages, all of them built in the same Carpenter Gothic style.
Presiding over them was a beautiful two-story Queen Anne.

This couldn't be the dark, musty place he'd described.
The house was painted a light cocoa with salmon, maize, and
moss green accents decorating the gingerbread trim above
the porch, over the gables, and on the porch spindles. A
round turret curved on the left of the house, and the broad
porch extended around two sides. Petunias bloomed in clay
pots by the double front doors, which held matching panels
of frosted glass etched with a design of vines and flowers.
Ferns spilled over brown wicker stands, and old-fashioned
wooden rockers held cheery checked pillows in colors that
matched the trim. Once again she had the sense of being
plunged into an earlier time.

"I don't frickin' believe this!" Kevin vaulted out of the car.
"This place was a wreck the last time I saw it."

"It sure isn't a wreck now. It's beautiful."

She winced as he slammed the door, then got out herself.
Roo broke free and headed for the shrubs. Kevin gazed up at
the house, his hands planted on his hips.

"When the hell did she turn this into a bed-and-
breakfast?"

Just then the front door opened, and a woman who appeared to be in her late sixties emerged. She had faded
blond-and-gray hair caught up in a clip with strands escaping here and there. She was tall and big-boned, and her
mouth was wide, topped by prominent cheekbones and
bright blue eyes. A flour-dusted blue apron protected her
khaki slacks and short-sleeved white blouse.

"Kevin!" She hurried down the steps and gave him a vigorous hug. "You sweet boy! I knew you'd come!"

To Molly, Kevin's hug in return seemed perfunctory.

The woman gave her an assessing look. "I'm Charlotte

Long. My husband and I came here every summer. He died eight years ago, but I still stay in Loaves and Fishes. Kevin was always losing balls in my rosebushes."

"Mrs. Long was a good friend of my parents and my aunt," Kevin said.

"My, I miss Judith. We met when my family first came here." Her sharp blue eyes returned to Molly. "And who's this?"

Molly extended her hand. "Molly Somerville."

"Well, now . . . " Her lips pursed as she turned back to Kevin. "You can't read a magazine without hearing about that marriage of yours. Isn't it a little early to be seeing someone else? I'm sure Pastor Tucker would be disappointed that you aren't trying harder to make things work with your wife."

"Uh, Molly is my . . . " The word seemed to stick in his throat. Molly sympathized, but she wasn't going to be the one to say it.

"Molly's my . . . wife." He finally managed to get it out.

Once again Molly found herself under the scrutiny of those blue eyes. "Well, that's good, then. But why are you calling yourself Somerville? Tucker's a good, proud name. Pastor Tucker, Kevin's father, was one of the finest men I ever knew."

"I'm sure he was." She'd never liked disappointing people. "Somerville's also my professional name. I write children's books."

Her disapproval vanished. "I've always wanted to write a children's book. Well, now, isn't this nice? You know, when Kevin's mother was alive, she was afraid he'd marry one of those supermodels who go around smoking dope and having sexual relations with everybody."

Kevin choked.

"Here now, pup, you get out of Judith's lobelia." Charlotte patted her thigh, and Roo abandoned the flowers to trot over. Charlotte reached down to chuck his chin. "Better keep an eye on him. We've got some coyotes around here."

Kevin's expression turned calculating. "Big ones?"

Molly gave him a reproachful gaze. "Roo sticks close to home."

"Too bad."

"Well, I'm off! There's a list of guests and dates on Judith's computer. The Pearsons should be here any time. They're bird-watchers."

Kevin turned pale beneath his tan. "Guests? What do you—"

"I had Amy freshen up Judith's old room for you, the one your parents used. The other bedrooms are rented."

"Amy? Wait a—"

"Amy and Troy Anderson, he's the handyman. They just got married, even though she's only nineteen and he's twenty. I don't know why they were in such a hurry." Charlotte reached back to untie the apron. "Amy's supposed to take care of the cleaning, but they're so gaga over each other that they're worthless. You'll have to keep after them." She handed the apron to Molly. "It's a good thing you're here, Molly. I never was much of a cook, and the guests are complaining."

Molly stared down at the apron. Kevin shot forward as the older woman began to walk away. "Wait a minute! The campground's closed. All the reservations were canceled."

She regarded him with disapproval. "How could you even think to do that, Kevin? Some of these people have been coming here for forty years. And Judith spent every penny she had sprucing up the cottages and turning the house into a bed-and-breakfast. Do you have any idea how much it costs to advertise in *Victoria* magazine? And that Collins boy in town charged her almost a thousand dollars to set up a Web site."

"A *Web site*?"

"If you're not familiar with the Internet, I suggest you look into it. It's a wonderful thing. Except for all that porno."

"I'm familiar with the Internet!" Kevin exclaimed. "Now, tell me why people are still coming here after I closed the place down."

"Why, because I told them to. Judith would have wanted it. I kept trying to explain that to you. Do you know that it took me nearly a week to get hold of everyone?"

"You called them?"

"I used that E-mail, too," she said proudly. "It didn't take me long to get the hang of it." She patted his arm. "Don't be nervous, Kevin. You and your wife will do just fine. As long as you put out a nice, big breakfast, most people are happy. The menus and recipes are in Judith's blue notebook in the kitchen. Oh, and get Troy to look at the toilet in Green Pastures. It's leaking."

She headed off down the lane.

Kevin looked sick. "Tell me this is a bad dream."

As Mrs. Long disappeared, Molly watched a late-model Honda Accord turn into the lane and head toward the B&B. "As a matter of fact, I think you're wide awake."

Kevin followed the direction of her gaze and swore as the car stopped in front of the B&B. Molly was too tired to stand any longer, so she sank down on the top step to watch the entertainment. Roo yipped a greeting at the couple who came up the sidewalk.

"We're the Pearsons," a thin, round-faced, sixtyish woman said. "I'm Betty and this is my husband, John."

Kevin looked as if he'd taken a direct hit to the head, so Molly replied for him. "Molly Somerville. This is Kevin, the new owner."

"Oh, yes. We heard about you. You play baseball, don't you?"

Kevin sagged against the gas lamppost.

"Basketball," Molly said. "But he's really too short for the NBA, so they're cutting him."

"My husband and I aren't much for sports. We were sorry to hear about Judith. Lovely woman. Very knowledgeable about the local bird population. We're on the trail of Kirtland's warbler."

John Pearson outweighed his wife by nearly two hundred pounds, and his double chins wiggled. "We hope you're not planning on making too many changes in the food. Judith's breakfast spread is famous. And her cherry chocolate cake . . . " He paused, and Molly half expected him to kiss his fingertips. "Is afternoon tea still at five o'clock?"

Molly waited for Kevin to respond, but he seemed to have lost the power of speech. She cocked her head at them. "I have a feeling tea might be a little late today."

Chapter 9

Daphne lived in the prettiest cottage in Nightingale Woods. It sat off by itself in a great grove of trees, which meant she could play her electric guitar whenever she wanted and no one complained.

Daphne Gets Lost

KEVIN HAD HIS CELL PHONE PRESSED TO ONE EAR, THE B&B'S PHONE pressed to the other as he paced the entrance hall barking orders to his business manager and somebody who was either a secretary or a housekeeper. Behind him an imposing walnut staircase rose half a flight, then turned at a right angle. The spindles were dusty, and the richly patterned carpet on the treads needed vacuuming. An urn filled with drooping peacock feathers topped a pilaster on the landing.

His pacing was wearing her out, so Molly decided to explore while he talked. With Roo trotting after her, she moved slowly into the front parlor. The pincushion settee and pleasing jumble of chairs were upholstered in pretty buttercup and rose fabrics. Botanical prints and pastoral scenes hung in gilded frames on the cream-colored walls, while lace curtains framed the windows. Brass candlesticks, a Chinese jardiniere, and some crystal boxes ornamented the mantel above the fireplace. Unfortunately, the brass was tarnished, the crystal dull, and the tabletops dusty. A lint-flecked Oriental carpet contributed to the overall air of neglect.

The same was true of the music room, where the traditional pineapple-patterned wallpaper served as a background for rose-patterned reading chairs and a spinet piano. A writing desk in the corner held ivory stationery, along with an old-fashioned fountain pen and a bottle of ink. A pair of tarnished silver candlesticks sat on top, near an old toby jug.

A Queen Anne table and ten matching high-backed chairs graced the dining room across the hallway. The room's dominant feature was a square, cutaway bay window that provided a generous view of lake and woods. Molly suspected that the tall crystal vases on the sideboard had held fresh flowers when his Aunt Judith was alive, but now the marble top was cluttered with the remains of breakfast serving dishes.

She walked through a door at the back into an old-fashioned country kitchen warmed by blue-and-white tiles as well as wooden cabinets topped with a collection of chintzwear china pitchers. In the center a sturdy farm table with a marble slab served as a workspace, but now dirty mixing bowls, eggshells, measuring cups, and an open jar of dried cranberries littered the surface. The very modern restaurant-size stove needed cleaning, and the dishwasher door hung open.

A round oak table for informal dining sat in front of the windows. Printed pillows covered the seats of the farmhouse chairs, and a punched-tin chandelier hung above. Behind the house the yard sloped down to the lake, with woods on each side.

She peeked into a large, well-stocked pantry that smelled of baking spices, then entered a small connecting room, where the very modern computer resting on an old tavern table signaled that this was the office. She was tired of walking, so she sat down and booted it up. Twenty minutes later she heard Kevin.

"Molly! Where the hell are you?"

Slytherin rudeness didn't deserve a response, so she ignored him and opened another file.

For a normally graceful man, he had an unusually heavy step that morning, and she heard his approach long before he located her. "Why didn't you answer me?"

She repositioned the mouse as he came up behind her, deciding it was time to face up to him. "I don't answer roars."

"I wasn't roaring! I was—"

When he didn't finish, she looked up to see what had distracted him. Outside the window a very young woman in skimpy black shorts and a tight, scoop-neck top flew across the garden, followed by an equally young man. She turned and ran backward, laughing and taunting him. He called out something to her. She grabbed the hem of her top and tugged it up, flashing her bare breasts.

"Whoa . . . " Kevin said.

Molly felt her skin grow hot.

The man caught her around the waist and dragged her into the woods so that they weren't visible from the road, although Kevin and Molly could see them clearly. He leaned against the trunk of an old maple. She immediately jumped on him and wrapped her legs around his waist.

Molly felt the slow pulse of dormant blood stirring as she watched the young lovers begin to devour each other. He cupped her bottom. She pressed her breasts to his chest, then, resting her elbows on his shoulders, caught his head to steady it, as if she weren't already kissing him deeply enough.

Molly heard Kevin move behind her, and her body gave a sluggish throb. She could feel his height looming over her, his warmth penetrating her thin top. How could someone who made his living with sweat smell so clean?

The young man turned his lover so that her back was against the tree. He pushed a hand under her T-shirt and covered her breast.

Molly's own breasts tingled. She wanted to look away, but she couldn't manage it. Apparently Kevin couldn't either, because he didn't move, and his voice sounded vaguely husky.

"I think we've just caught our first glimpse of Amy and Troy Anderson."

The young woman dropped to the ground. She was petite but leggy, with dishwater-blond hair pulled up in a purple scrunchy. His hair was darker and cut close to his head. He was thin and quite a bit taller than the girl.

Her hands slipped between their bodies. It took Molly only a moment to realize what she was doing.

Unzipping his jeans.

"They're going to do it right in front of us," Kevin said softly.

His comment jerked Molly out of her trance. She bolted up from the computer and turned her back to the window. "Not in front of me."

His eyes drifted from the window to her, and for a moment he didn't say anything. He just gazed at her. Again that sluggish pulsing in her bloodstream. It reminded her that even though they'd been intimate, she didn't know him.

"Getting a little hot for you?"

She was definitely warmer than she wanted to be. "Voyeurism isn't my thing."

"Now, that surprises me. This should be right up your alley, since you seem to like preying on the unsuspecting."

Time hadn't diminished the embarrassment she felt. She opened her mouth to apologize once again, only to have something calculating in his expression stop her. With a shock she realized that Kevin wasn't interested in groveling. He wanted to be entertained with an argument.

He deserved her very best, but her brain had been inactive for so long, it was hard to come up with a response. "Only when I'm drunk."

"Are you saying you were drunk that night?" He glanced out the window, then back at her.

"Totally wasted. Stoli on ice. Why else do you think I behaved like that?"

Another look out the window, this one lasting a bit longer. "I don't remember you being drunk."

"You were asleep."

"What I remember is that you told me you were sleepwalking."

She managed a huffy sniff. "Well, I hardly wanted to confess that I had a problem with alcohol."

"Recovered now, are you?" Those green eyes were much too perceptive.

"Even the thought of Stoli makes me nauseous."

His gaze raked a slow, steady path over her body. "You know what I think?"

She swallowed. "I'm not interested."

"I think I was just irresistible to you."

She searched her imaginative brain for a scorching comeback, but the best she could come up with was a rather pitiful "Whatever makes you happy."

He shifted his position to get a better view of the scene outside. Then he winced. "That's got to hurt."

She wanted to look so badly she could barely stand it. "That's sick. Don't watch them."

"It's interesting." He tilted his head slightly. "Now, that's a new way to go about it."

"Stop it!"

"And I don't even think *that's* legal."

She couldn't stand it any longer, and she whirled around, only to realize that the lovers had vanished.

His chuckle had an evil edge. "If you run outside, you might be able to catch them before they're done."

"You think you're funny."

"Fairly amusing."

"Well, then, this should really entertain you. I dipped into Aunt Judith's computer records, and the B&B seems to be booked solid into September. Most of the cottages, too. You won't believe how much people are willing to pay to stay here."

"Let me see that." He pushed past her to get to the computer.

"Enjoy yourself. I'm going to find someplace to stay."

He was busy scanning the screen, and he didn't respond, not even when she reached over him to pick up the piece of notepaper she'd used to jot down the names of the vacant cottages.

A pegboard hung on the wall next to the desk. She found the appropriate keys, stuck them in her pocket, and made her way through the kitchen. She hadn't eaten that day, and on the way she picked up a leftover slice of Charlotte Long's cranberry bread. The first bite told her that Mrs. Long had been right when she'd said she wasn't much of a cook, and she dropped it in the trash.

When she reached the hallway, curiosity won out over her fatigue, and she climbed the steps to see the rest of the house. Roo trotted at her side as she peered into the guest rooms, each of which had been individually decorated. There were book-filled nooks, pretty views from the windows, and the homey decorating touches people expected at an upscale B&B.

She spotted a bird's nest filled with antique glass marbles on top of a stack of vintage hatboxes. An arrangement of apothecary bottles sat near a wire birdcage. Pieces of embroidery in oval frames, old wooden signs, and wonderful stoneware vases that should have held fresh flowers were tucked here and there. She also saw unmade beds, overflowing trash cans, and grubby bathtubs draped with discarded towels. Clearly Amy Anderson would rather cavort in the trees with her new husband than clean.

At the end of the hallway she opened the door into the only room that hadn't been rented out. She knew because it was tidy. Judging from the family photos propped on the dressing table, the room had belonged to Judith Tucker. It occupied the corner of the house, including the turret. She visualized Kevin sleeping beneath the carved headboard. He was so tall, he'd have to lie across the mattress.

An image of the way he'd looked the night she'd slipped into his bed came back to her. She shook it off and made her way downstairs. As she stepped out onto the front porch, she smelled pine, petunias, and the lake. Roo stuck his nose in a flowerpot.

She wanted nothing more than to sink into one of the rockers and take a nap, but since she wasn't going to join Kevin in Aunt Judith's bedroom, she needed to find a place to stay. "Come on, Roo. Let's go visit the empty cottages."

One of the computer files had contained a diagram that marked the location of each cottage. As she approached the Common, she noticed the small, hand-painted signs near the front doors: GABRIEL'S TRUMPET, MILK AND HONEY, GREEN PASTURES, GOOD NEWS.

As she passed Jacob's Ladder, a handsome, rawboned man came through the woods. He looked as if he was in his early to mid-fifties, significantly younger than the other residents she'd spotted. She nodded and received a brusque nod in response.

She headed in the opposite direction, toward Tree of Life, a coral cottage with plum and lavender trim. It was empty, as was Lamb of God. They were both charming, but she decided she'd like more privacy than the cottages on the Common afforded, so she turned away and walked back toward the more isolated ones that perched along the lane that paralleled the lake.

An odd sense of déjà vu came over her. Why did this place seem so familiar? As she passed the B&B, Roo pranced ahead of her, stopping to sniff at a clump of chickweed, then discovering an alluring patch of grass. When she came to the end of the lane, she saw exactly what she wanted nestled in the trees. Lilies of the Field.

The tiny cottage had been freshly painted the softest of creamy yellows with its spindles and lacy wooden trim accented in palest blue and the same dusty pink as the inside of a seashell. Her chest ached. The cottage looked like a nursery.

She mounted the steps and discovered that the screen door squeaked, just as it should. She found the proper key in her pocket and turned it in the lock. Then she stepped inside.

The cottage was decorated in authentic shabby chic instead of the kind that was trendy. The white-painted walls were old and wonderful. Underneath a dustcover she found a couch upholstered in a faded print. The battered wooden trunk in front of it served as a coffee table. A scrubbed pine chest sat along one wall, a brass swing-arm lamp next to it. Despite the musty smell, the cottage's white walls and lace curtains made everything feel airy.

Off to the left, the tiny kitchen held an old-fashioned gas stove and a small drop-leaf table with two farmhouse chairs similar to the ones she'd seen in the B&B's kitchen. A glance inside the painted wooden cupboard showed wonderfully mismatched pottery and china plates, more pressed glass, and sponge-painted mugs. Something ached inside her as she spotted a child's set of Peter Rabbit dishes, and she turned away.

The bathroom had a claw-foot tub along with an ancient pedestal sink. A rag rug covered the rough-planked floor in front of the tub, and someone had stenciled a chain of vines near the ceiling.

Two bedrooms occupied the back, one tiny and the other large enough for a double bed and a painted chest of drawers. The bed, covered in a faded quilt, had a curved iron headboard painted a soft yellow with a flower basket motif worked in the center. A small milk-glass lamp rested on the bedside table.

In the back of the cottage, nestling into the woods, was a screened porch. Bent-willow chairs leaned against the wall, and a hammock hung across one corner. She'd done more today than she'd done in weeks, and just looking at the hammock made her realize how tired she was.

She lowered herself into it. Above her the beaded-board ceiling was painted the same creamy yellow as the exterior of the house, with subtle dusty pink and blue accents along the moldings. What a wonderful place. Just like a nursery.

She closed her eyes. The hammock rocked her like a cradle. She was asleep almost instantly.

The Klingon greeted Kevin at the cottage door with a growl and bared teeth. "Don't start. I'm not in the mood."

He walked past the dog to the bedroom and set down Molly's suitcase, then made his way to the kitchen. She wasn't there, but Charlotte Long had seen her disappear inside, and he found her on the porch, asleep in the hammock. Her watchdog scampered past him to do guard duty. Kevin gazed down at her.

She looked small and defenseless. One hand curled under her chin, and a lock of dark brown hair fell over her cheek. Her lashes were thick, but not thick enough to hide the shadows under her eyes, and he felt guilty for the way he'd been bullying her. At the same time, something told him she wouldn't react well to coddling. Not that he could have coddled her anyway. He still had too much resentment.

His eyes skimmed along her body, then lingered. She wore bright red capri jeans and a rumpled yellow sleeveless blouse with one of those Chinese collars. When she was awake and being her normal smart-ass self, it was hard to see her showgirl ancestry, but asleep it was a different story. Her ankles were trim, her legs slim, and her hips had a nice soft curve. Beneath her blouse, her breasts rose and fell, and, through the open V, he caught a glimpse of black lace. His hand itched to pop open the buttons and see more.

His reaction disgusted him. As soon as he got back to Chicago, he'd better call an old girlfriend because it had clearly been too long since he'd had sex.

The Klingon must have been reading his mind because he started to growl at him, then barked.

Roo awakened her. Molly eased her eyes open, then sucked in her breath as she saw the shadow of a man looming over her. She tried to sit up too quickly, and the hammock tipped.

Kevin caught her before she could fall and set her on her feet. "Don't you ever think first?"

She brushed the hair from her eyes and tried to blink herself awake. "What do you want?"

"Next time tell me when you're going to disappear."

"I did." She yawned. "But you were too busy gaping at Mrs. Anderson's breasts to pay attention."

He pulled a bent-willow chair away from the wall and sat down on it. "That couple is completely worthless. The minute you turn your back on them, they're climbing all over each other."

"They're newlyweds."

"Yeah, well, so are we."

There was nothing she could say to that. She sank down on the metal glider, which was missing its cushions and very uncomfortable.

His expression grew calculating. "One thing I'll say about Amy, at least she supports her husband."

"The way he was holding her against the tree—"

"It's the two of them against the world. Working side by side. Helping each other out. A team."

"If you think you're being subtle, you're not."

"I need some help."

"I can't hear a word you're saying."

"Apparently I'm stuck with this place for the summer. I'll get somebody in here to run it as soon as I can, but until then . . . "

"Until then nothing." She rose from the glider. "I'm not doing it. The sex-crazy newlyweds can help you. And what about Charlotte Long?"

"She says she hates to cook, and she was only doing it because of Judith. Besides, a couple of the guests came looking for me, and all of them take a dim view of her efforts." He rose and started to pace, his restless energy buzzing like a bug zapper. "I offered them a refund, but when it comes to their vacations, people are completely unreasonable. They want the refund plus everything they were promised in that *Virginia* magazine."

"*Victoria.*"

"Whatever. The point is, we're going to have to stay in this godforsaken place a little longer than I planned."

It wasn't godforsaken to her. It was charming, and she tried to make herself feel happy that they'd be here longer, but all she felt was empty.

"While you were taking your beauty rest, I went into town to put a Help Wanted ad in the local paper. I find out the place is so damn small the paper's a weekly, and it just came out today, so the next issue is seven days off! I put out the word with some of the locals, but I don't know how effective that's going to be."

"You think we'll be here a week?"

"No, I'll talk to people." He looked ready to take a bite out of something. "But I guess there's a chance if I can't find anyone until the ad's out. Not a big chance, but I suppose it could happen."

She sat on the glider. "I guess you'll be running a B&B until then."

He narrowed his eyes. "You seem to have forgotten that you took a vow to support me."

"I did not!"

"Did you pay any attention to those wedding vows you were saying?"

"I tried not to," she admitted. "I'm not in the habit of making promises I know I'm not going to keep."

"Neither am I, and so far I've kept my word."

"To love, honor, and obey? I don't think so."

"Those weren't the vows we took." He tucked his hands under his arms and watched her.

She tried to figure out what he was talking about, but her only memories of the ceremony were of the poodles and the way she'd held on to Andrew's sticky little hand for dear life. A sense of uneasiness crept through her. "Maybe you'd better refresh my memory."

"I'm talking about the vows Phoebe wrote for us," he said quietly. "Are you sure she didn't mention it to you?"

She'd mentioned it, but Molly'd been so miserable she hadn't paid attention. "I guess I wasn't listening."

"Well, I was. I even fixed a couple of the sentences to make them more realistic. Now, I might not have this exactly right—you can call your sister to verify—but the gist of it is that you, Molly, promised to accept me, Kevin, as your husband, at least for a while. You promised to give me your respect and consideration from that day forward. Notice there was no mention of love and honor. You promised not to speak badly of me to others." He eyed her. "And to support me in everything we share together."

Molly bit her lip. It was just like Phoebe to have written something like that. Of course she'd done it to protect the baby.

She pulled herself together. "Okay, you're a great quarterback. I can do the respect part. And if you don't count Phoebe, Dan, and Roo, I never speak badly of you to others."

"My eyes are tearing up from emotion. How about the other part? That 'support' thing?"

"That was supposed to be about— You know what it was about." She blinked her eyes and took a deep breath. "Phoebe certainly wasn't trying to force me into helping you run a B&B."

"Don't forget the cottages, and a sacred vow is just that."

"You kidnapped me yesterday, and now you're trying to manipulate me into forced labor!"

"It'll only be for a couple of days. A week at the most. Or maybe that's too much to ask from a rich girl."

"This is your problem, not mine."

He stared at her for a long moment, then that cold look settled over his face. "Yeah, I guess it is."

Kevin wasn't someone who asked for help easily, and she regretted her peevishness, but she couldn't be around people now. Still, she should have been more tactful about refusing him. "I just—I haven't been in great shape lately, and—"

"Forget it," he snapped. "I'll manage on my own." He stalked across the porch and out through the back door.

She stomped around the cottage for a while, feeling ugly and out of sorts. He'd brought in her suitcase. She unzipped it, only to go back out on the porch and stare at the lake.

Those wedding vows . . . She'd been prepared to break the traditional ones. Even couples who loved each other had a hard time living up to those. But these vows—the ones Phoebe had written—were different. These were vows that an honorable person should be able to keep.

Kevin had.

"Damn."

Roo looked up.

"I don't want to be with a lot of people now, that's all."

But she wasn't telling herself the whole truth. She mainly didn't want to be around *him*.

She glanced at her watch and saw that it was five o'clock.

With a grimace she gazed down at her poodle. "I'm afraid we have some personal character building to do."

Ten guests had gathered in the buttercup and rose parlor for afternoon tea, but somehow Molly couldn't imagine *Victoria* magazine giving the occasion its seal of approval. The inlaid table at the side of the room held an open bag of Oreos, a can of grape Hi-C, a coffeepot, Styrofoam cups, and a jar that looked as if it contained powdered tea. Despite the fare, the guests seemed to be enjoying themselves.

The bird-watching Pearsons stood behind a pair of elderly women perched on the pincushion settee. Across the room two white-haired couples chatted. The women's gnarled fingers flashed with old diamonds and newer anniversary rings. One of the men had a walrus mustache, the other lime green golf slacks with white patent leather shoes. Another couple was younger, in their early fifties perhaps, prosperous baby boomers who could have stepped out of a Ralph Lauren ad. It was Kevin, however, who dominated the room. As he stood by the fireplace, he looked so much like the lord of the manor that his shorts and Stars T-shirt might have been jodhpurs and a riding jacket.

" . . . so the president of the United States is sitting on the fifty-yard line, the Stars are down by four points, there are only seven seconds left on the clock, and I'm pretty sure I just sprained the heck out of my knee."

"That must have been painful," the boomer woman cooed.

"You don't notice the pain until later."

"I remember this game!" her husband exclaimed. "You hit Tippett on a fifty-yard post pattern, and the Stars won by three."

Kevin shook his head modestly. "I got lucky, Chet."

Molly rolled her eyes. Nobody made it to the top of the NFL trusting in luck. Kevin had gotten where he was by being the best. His good ol' boy act might charm the guests, but she knew the truth.

Still, as she watched him she knew she was seeing self-discipline in action, and she begrudgingly gave him her respect. No one suspected he hated being here. She'd forgotten that he was a minister's son, but she shouldn't have. Kevin was a man who did his duty, even though he hated it. Just as he'd done when he'd married her.

"I can't believe it," Mrs. Chet cooed. "When we chose a bed-and-breakfast in the wilds of northeastern Michigan, we never imagined our host would be the famous Kevin Tucker."

Kevin graced her with his aw-shucks expression. Molly wanted to tell her not to bother flirting with him, since she didn't have a foreign accent.

"I'd love to hear your take on the draft." Chet readjusted the navy cotton sweater he'd tossed around the shoulders of his kelly green polo shirt.

"How about the two of us share a beer out on the front porch later on tonight?"

"I wouldn't mind joining you," walrus mustache interjected, while lime green pants nodded in agreement.

"We'll all do it," Kevin said graciously.

John Pearson polished off the last of the Oreos. "Now that Betty and I know you personally, we'll have to start following the Stars. You, uh, wouldn't happen to have located one of Judith's lemon–poppy seed cakes in the freezer, would you?"

"I have no idea," Kevin said. "And that reminds me, I'd better apologize in advance for tomorrow's breakfast. Pancakes from a mix is the best I can do, so if you decide to leave, I'll understand. That offer for double your refund still stands."

"We wouldn't think about leaving such a charming place." Mrs. Chet gave Kevin a look that had adultery written all over it. "And don't worry about breakfast. I'll be glad to pitch in."

Molly did her part to protect the Ten Commandments by forcing herself out of the doorway and into the room. "That won't be necessary. I know Kevin wants you to relax while you're here, and I think I can promise that the food will be a little better tomorrow."

Kevin's eyes flickered, but if she expected him to fall at her feet from gratitude, he quickly disabused her of the notion with his introduction. "This is my estranged wife, Molly."

"She doesn't look strange," walrus mustache's wife said in a too-loud whisper to her friend.

"That's because you don't know her," Kevin murmured.

"My wife's a bit hard of hearing." Like the others, Mr. Mustache was obviously taken aback by Kevin's introduction. Several of those in the room regarded her curiously. The *People* spread . . .

Molly tried to be annoyed, but it was a relief not having to pretend they were a happily married couple.

John Pearson stepped forward hastily. "Your husband has quite a sense of humor. We're delighted you'll be cooking for us, Mrs. Tucker."

"Please call me Molly. Now, if you'll excuse me, I need to check the supplies in the kitchen. And I know your rooms aren't as orderly as they should be, but Kevin will clean them up himself before bedtime." As she headed down the hallway, she decided Mr. Tough Guy didn't always have to have the last word.

Her satisfaction faded the moment she opened the kitchen door and saw the young lovers having sex against Aunt Judith's refrigerator. She stepped backward only to bump into Kevin's chest.

He peered over her head. "Awww, for Pete's sake."

The lovers sprang apart. Molly was ready to avert her eyes, but Kevin stalked into the kitchen. He glared at Amy, whose scrunchy had come out of her hair and who was doing up her buttons wrong. "I thought I asked you to get those dishes cleaned up."

"Yeah, well, uh . . . "

"Troy, you're supposed to be mowing the Common."

He struggled with his zipper. "I was just getting ready to—"

"I know exactly what you were getting ready to do, and believe me, that won't get the grass cut!"

Troy looked sulky and muttered under his breath.

"Did you say something?" Kevin's bark must be the same one he used on rookies.

Troy's Adam's apple worked. "There's, uh, too much work to do around here for what we're getting paid."

"And what's that?"

Troy told him, and Kevin doubled it on the spot. Troy's eyes gleamed. "Cool."

"But there's a catch," Kevin said smoothly. "You're going to have to actually do some work for that money. Amy, sweetheart, don't even think about leaving tonight until those guest rooms are spick-and-span. And, Troy, you've got an appointment with the lawn mower. Any questions?"

As they shook their heads warily, Molly saw matching hickeys on their necks. Something uncomfortable stirred in the pit of her stomach.

Troy moved toward the door, and Amy's longing gaze reminded Molly of Ingrid Bergman bidding Humphrey Bogart a final farewell on that Casablanca runway.

What would it feel like to be that much in love? Again she felt that unpleasant quivering in her stomach. Only after the lovers had parted did she realize it was jealousy. They had something she seemed destined never to experience.

Chapter 10

"It's much too dangerous," said Daphne.
"That's what makes it fun," Benny replied.

Daphne Gets Lost

A FEW HOURS LATER MOLLY STEPPED BACK TO ADMIRE THE HOMEY space she'd created for herself on the nursery cottage's screened porch. She'd put the blue-and-yellow striped cushions on the glider and the chintz-patterned ones on the bent-willow chairs. The small, drop-leaf kitchen table with its chipped white paint now sat against one side of the screen with two of the unmatched farmhouse chairs. Tomorrow she'd find some flowers to put in the old copper watering can she'd stuck on top.

With some of the essentials she'd transferred from the B&B to the cottage, she fixed toast and a scrambled egg and carried them out to the table. While Roo snoozed nearby, she watched daylight begin to fade over the wedge of lake visible through the trees. Everything smelled of pine and the dank, distant scent of the water. She heard something that sounded distinctly human rustling outside. At home she would have been alarmed. Here she settled back in the chair and waited to see who would appear. Unfortunately, it was Kevin.

She hadn't thrown the latch on the screen door, and she wasn't surprised when he walked inside without an invitation. "The brochure says breakfast is from seven to nine. What kind of people want to eat that early when they're on vacation?" He set an alarm clock on the table, then glanced at the remnants of her scrambled egg. "You could have gone into town with me and had a burger," he said begrudgingly.

"Thanks, but I don't do burgers."

"So you're a vegetarian like your sister?"

"I'm not as strict. She won't eat anything with a face. I won't eat anything with a cute face."

"This I've got to hear."

"Actually, it's a pretty good system for healthy eating."

"I take it you think cows are cute." He couldn't have sounded more skeptical.

"I love cows. Definitely cute."

"How about pigs?"

"Does the movie *Babe* ring a bell?"

"I won't even ask about lamb."

"I'd appreciate it if you didn't. Or rabbit." She shuddered. "I'm not too attracted to chickens and turkey, so I do occasionally indulge. I also eat fish since I can avoid my favorite."

"Dolphin, I'll bet." He settled into the old wooden chair across from her and gazed down at Roo, who'd stirred enough to snarl. "You might have latched on to something here that I could get into. There are certain animals, for example, I find positively repulsive."

She gave him her silkiest smile. "It's well known that men who don't like poodles are the same ones who grind up human body parts in garbage disposals."

"Only if I'm bored."

She laughed, then caught herself as she realized he'd turned the charm-thing on her, and she'd nearly gotten caught up in it. Was this supposed to be her reward for agreeing to help him out? "I don't understand why you dislike it here so much. The lake is beautiful. There's swimming, boating, hiking. What's so bad about that?"

"When you're the only kid, and you have to go to a church service every day, it loses its charm. Besides, there's a limit to the size motor you can put on a boat, so there's no water skiing."

"Or Jet Skis."

"What?"

"Nothing. Weren't there ever other children around?"

"Sometimes a grandkid would show up for a few days. That was the highlight of my summer." He grimaced. "Of course, half the time that grandkid was a girl."

"Life's a bitch."

He leaned back in his chair until it rested on two legs. She waited for it to tilt over, but he was too well coordinated for that to happen. "Do you really know how to cook, or were you just winging it in front of the guests?"

"I was winging it." She lied hoping to make him nervous. Her everyday cooking might leave something to be desired, but she loved to bake, especially for her nieces and nephews. Sugar cookies with bunny ears were her specialty.

"Terrific." The legs of the chair banged to the floor. "God, this place is boring. Let's take a walk along the lake before it gets dark."

"I'm too tired."

"You haven't done enough today to make yourself tired." He was full of restless energy with no place to go, so she shouldn't have been startled when he grabbed her wrist and tugged her from her seat. "Come on, I haven't been able to work out for two days. I'm going stir crazy."

She pulled away. "Go work out now. Nobody's stopping you."

"I have to meet my fan club on the front porch soon. You need the exercise, so stop being stubborn. Stay here, Godzilla." He opened the screen and gave Molly a gentle push, then firmly closed in a yapping Roo.

She didn't offer any real resistance, even though she was

exhausted and she knew it wasn't a good idea to be alone with him. "I'm not in the mood, and I want my dog."

"If I said grass was green, you'd argue with me." He tugged her along the path.

"I refuse to be nice to my kidnapper."

"For somebody who was kidnapped, you're not trying too hard to get away."

"I like it here."

He glanced back at the cozy nest she'd made for herself on the porch. "Next thing you'll be hiring a decorator."

"We rich girls like our comforts, even if it's only for a few days."

"I guess."

The path widened as it got closer to the lake, then wound along the shore for a while before narrowing again and making a sharp incline up a rocky bluff that overlooked the water. Kevin pointed in the opposite direction. "There are some wetlands over there, and behind the campgrounds there's a meadow with a brook."

"Bobolink Meadow."

"What?"

"It's a— Nothing." It was the name of the meadow on the edge of Nightingale Woods.

"You can get a good view of the town from that bluff."

She gazed up the steep path. "I don't have enough energy for the climb."

"Then we won't go all the way."

She knew he was lying. Still, her legs didn't feel as wobbly as they'd been yesterday, so she set off with him. "How do the people in the town support themselves?"

"Tourism mainly. The lake has good fishing, but it's so isolated that it hasn't been overdeveloped like a lot of other places. There's a decent golf course, and the area has some of the best cross-country trails in the state."

"I'm glad nobody's spoiled it with a big resort."

The path was beginning to angle uphill, and she needed all her breath for the climb. She wasn't surprised when he left her behind. What surprised her was the fact that she kept on going.

He called down to her from the top of the bluff. "Not exactly a walking advertisement for physical fitness, are you?"

"Just skipped a few"—she gasped—"Tae-Bo classes."

"You want me to find an oxygen tank?"

She was breathing too hard to respond.

She was glad she'd made the effort when she caught the view from the top. There was still enough light to see the town at the far end of the lake. It looked quaint and rustic. Boats bobbed in the harbor, and a church steeple peeked through the trees against a rainbow candy sky.

Kevin pointed toward a cluster of luxury houses closer to the bluff. "Those are vacation homes. The last time I was here, that was all woods, but nothing else seems to have changed much."

She took in the vista. "It's so pretty."

"I guess." He'd moved toward the edge of the bluff, where he gazed down at the water. "I used to dive off here in the summer."

"A little dangerous for a kid by himself, wasn't it?"

"That's what made it fun."

"Your parents must have been saints. I can't imagine how many gray hairs you—" She stopped as she realized he was kicking off his shoes instead of paying attention to her.

Pure instinct made her take a quick step forward, but she was too late. He threw himself into space, clothes and all.

She gasped and rushed to the edge just in time to watch the sharp, clean line of his body hit the water. There was barely a splash.

She waited, but he didn't come up. Her hand flew to her mouth. She searched the water but couldn't spot him. "Kevin!"

Then the surface rippled, and his head emerged. She released her breath, then caught it again as he turned his face to the evening sky. Water ran in rivulets over those clean planes, and something triumphant shone in his expression.

She clenched her fists and shouted down at him. "*You idiot!* Are you completely crazy?"

Treading water, he looked up at her, his teeth gleaming. "Are you going to tattle to your big sister?"

She was shaking so much that she stomped her foot. "You had no idea whether that water was deep enough for diving!"

"It was deep enough the last time I dove in."

"And how long ago was that?"

"About seventeen years." He flipped to his back. "But there's been a lot of rain."

"You're a moron! Have all those concussions scrambled your brain cells?"

"I'm alive, aren't I?" He flashed a daredevil grin. "Come on in, bunny lady. The water's real warm."

"Are you out of your mind? I'm not diving off this cliff!"

He flipped to his side, took a few lazy strokes. "Don't you know how to dive?"

"Of course I do. I went to summer camp for *nine* years!"

His voice lapped at her, a low, lazy taunt. "I'll bet you stink."

"I do not!"

"Then are you chicken, bunny lady?"

Oh, God. It was as if a fire alarm had gone off inside her head, and she didn't even kick off her sandals. She just curled the toes over the edge of the rock and threw herself off the bluff, following him into insanity.

All the way down she tried to scream.

She hit harder than he had and there was a lot more splash. When she came up, water dripped over the stunned expression on his face.

"Jesus." He spoke on a softly expelled breath that sounded more like a prayer than a curse. And then he started to yell. "*What the hell do you think you're doing?*"

The water was so cold she couldn't catch her breath. Even her bones were shriveling. "It's *freezing*! You lied to me!"

"If you ever do anything like that again . . . "

"You dared me!"

"If I'd dared you to drink poison, would you have been stupid enough to do that, too?"

She didn't know if she was angrier with him for goading her into being so reckless or at herself for taking the bait. Water flew as she slapped it with her arm. "Look at me! I act like a normal person when I'm around other people!"

"Normal?" He blinked the splash from his eyes. "Is that why I found you holed up in your apartment looking like spoiled shrimp?"

"At least I was safe there, instead of catching pneumonia here!" Her teeth began to chatter, and her icy, waterlogged clothes pulled at her. "Or maybe making me jump off a cliff is your idea of therapy?"

"I didn't think you'd do it!"

"I'm nuts, remember?"

"Molly . . . "

"Crazy Molly!"

"I didn't say—"

"That's what you're thinking. Molly the fruitcake! Molly the lunatic! Off her rocker! Certifiable! The tiniest little miscarriage, and she flips out!"

She choked. She hadn't meant to say that, hadn't ever intended to mention it again. But the same force that had made her jump off the cliff had pushed out the words.

A thick, heavy silence fell between them. When he finally broke it, she heard his pity. "Let's go in now so you can get warmed up." He turned away and began swimming toward the shore.

She had started to cry, so she stayed where she was.

He reached the bank, but he didn't try to climb out. Instead, he looked back at her. The water lapped at his waist, and his voice was a gentle ripple. "You need to get out. It'll be dark soon."

The cold had numbed her limbs, but it hadn't numbed her heart. Grief overwhelmed her. She wanted to sink under the surface and never come up. She gulped for air and whispered words she'd never intended to say. "You don't care, do you?"

"You're just trying to pick a fight," he said softly. "Come on. Your teeth are chattering."

Words slid through the tightness in her throat. "I know you don't care. I even understand."

"Molly, don't do this to yourself."

"We had a little girl," she whispered. "I made them find out and tell me."

The water lapped the bank. His hushed words drifted across the smooth surface. "I didn't know."

"I named her Sarah."

"You're tired. This isn't a good time."

She shook her head. Looked up into the sky. Spoke the truth, not to condemn him, just to point out why he could never understand how she felt. "Losing her didn't mean anything to you."

"I haven't thought about it. The baby wasn't real to me like it was to you."

"*She!* The baby was a *she,* not an *it!*"

"I'm sorry."

The unfairness of attacking him silenced her. It was wrong to condemn him for not sharing her suffering. Of course the baby hadn't been real to him. He hadn't invited Molly into his bed, hadn't wanted a child, hadn't carried the baby inside him.

"I'm the one who's sorry. I didn't mean to yell. My emotions keep getting away from me." Her hand trembled as she pushed a strand of wet hair from her eyes. "I won't bring this up again. I promise you."

"Come on out now," he said quietly.

Her limbs were clumsy from the cold, and her clothes heavy as she swam toward the bank. By the time she got there, he'd climbed out onto a low, flat rock.

He crouched down and pulled her up beside him. She landed on her knees, a cold, dripping, miserable wreck.

He tried to lighten the mood. "At least I kicked off my shoes before I dove in. Yours flew off when you hit the water. I'd have gone after them, but I was in shock."

The rock had retained some of the day's heat, and a little of it seeped through her clammy shorts. "It doesn't matter. They were my oldest sandals." Her last pair of Manolo Blahniks. Given the current state of her finances, she'd have to replace them with rubber shower thongs.

"You can pick up another pair in town tomorrow." He rose. "We'd better head back before you get sick. Why don't you start walking? I'll catch up with you as soon as I rescue my own shoes."

He headed back up the path. She hugged herself against the evening chill and put one foot in front of the other, trying not to think. She hadn't gone far before he came up next to her, T-shirt and shorts sticking to his body. They walked in silence for a while.

"The thing is . . . "

When he didn't go on, she looked up at him. "What?"

He looked troubled. "Forget it."

The woods rustled around them with evening sounds. "All right."

He shifted his shoes from one hand to the other. "After it was over . . . I just . . . I didn't let myself think about her."

She understood, but it made her feel even lonelier.

He hesitated. She wasn't used to that. He always seemed so certain. "What do you think she—" He cleared his throat. "What do you think Sarah would have been like?"

Her heart constricted. A fresh wave of pain swept over

her, but it didn't throb in the same way as her old pain. Instead, it stung like antiseptic on a cut.

Her lungs expanded, contracted, expanded again. She was startled to realize she could still breathe, that her legs could still move. She heard the crickets begin their evening jam. A squirrel scuffled in the leaves.

"Well . . . " She was trembling, and she wasn't sure whether the sound that slipped from her was a choked laugh or a leftover sob. "Gorgeous, if she took after you." Her chest ached, but instead of fighting the pain, she embraced it, absorbed it, let it become part of her. "Extremely smart, if she took after me."

"And reckless. I think today pretty much proves that. Gorgeous, huh? Thanks for the compliment."

"Like you don't know." Her heart felt a little lighter. She wiped at her runny nose with the back of her hand.

"So how come you think you're so smart?"

"Summa cum laude. Northwestern. What about you?"

"I graduated."

She smiled, but she wasn't ready to stop talking about Sarah. "I'd never have sent her to summer camp."

He nodded. "I'd never have made her go to church every day during the summer."

"That's a lot of church."

"Nine years is a lot of summer camp."

"She might have been clumsy and a slow learner."

"Not Sarah."

A little capsule of warmth encircled her heart.

He slowed. Looked up into the trees. Slipped one hand into his pocket. "I guess it just wasn't her time to be born."

Molly took a breath and whispered back, "I guess not."

Chapter 11

"Company's coming!" Celia the Hen clucked.
"We'll bake cakes and tarts and custard pies!"

Daphne Makes a Mess

MOLLY SET THE ALARM CLOCK KEVIN HAD LEFT FOR FIVE-THIRTY, and by seven o'clock the smell of blueberry muffins filled the downstairs of the B&B. In the dining room, the sideboard held a stack of pale yellow china plates with a ginkgo leaf at each center. Dark green napkins, pressed-glass water goblets, and pleasantly mismatched sterling completed the setting. A pan of sticky buns from the freezer baked in the oven while the marble slab on the worktable held a brown pottery baking dish filled with thick slices of bread soaking in an egg batter fragrant with vanilla and cinnamon.

For the first time in months Molly was ravenous, but she hadn't found time to eat. Preparing breakfast for a house full of paying guests was a lot more challenging than making smiley-face pancakes for the Calebow kids. As she moved Aunt Judith's recipe notebook away from the French toast batter, she tried to work up some resentment against Kevin, who was still asleep upstairs, but she couldn't. By acknowledging the baby last night, he'd given her a gift.

The burden of the miscarriage no longer felt as if it were hers alone to bear, and her pillow hadn't been tear-soaked when she'd awakened. Her depression wasn't going to vanish instantly, but she was ready to entertain the possibility of being happy again.

Kevin straggled in after she'd given John Pearson his second serving of French toast. His eyes were bleary, and he bore the look of a man suffering from a lethal hangover. "Your pit bull tried to corner me in the hallway."

"He doesn't like you."

"So I've noticed."

She realized something was missing, but it took her a moment to figure out what it was. His hostility. The anger Kevin had been holding against her finally seemed to have faded.

"Sorry I overslept," he said. "I told you last night to kick me out of bed if I wasn't up when you got here."

Not in a million years. Nothing would make her enter Kevin Tucker's bedroom, especially now that he was no longer looking at her as if she were his mortal enemy. She tilted her head toward the empty liquor bottles in the trash. "It must have been quite a party last night."

"They all wanted to talk about the draft, and one topic led to another. I'll say one thing for that generation, they sure know how to drink."

"It didn't affect Mr. Pearson's appetite."

He gazed at the French toast that was turning golden brown on the griddle. "I thought you didn't know how to cook."

"I phoned Martha Stewart. If people want bacon or sausage, you'll have to fry it."

"The *Babe* thing?"

"And proud of it. You're also waiting tables." She shoved the coffeepot at him, then turned the French toast.

He gazed at the coffeepot. "Ten years in the NFL, and this is what it all comes down to."

Despite his complaints, Kevin was surprised how quickly the next hour passed. He poured coffee, carried food back and forth, entertained the guests, and swiped some of Molly's pancakes for himself. She was a great cook, and he got sparks out of her by telling her he'd decided he'd let her keep the job.

Seeing those eyes flash felt good. Last night's confrontation seemed to have lifted some of her depression, and she had a little of the sparkle back that he remembered from Door County. He, on the other hand, had stared at the bedroom ceiling until dawn. Never again would he be able to think about the baby as an abstraction. Last night had given her a name. *Sarah.*

He blinked and grabbed the coffeepot for another round of refills.

Charlotte Long peeked in to see how Molly was doing and ended up eating two muffins. The sticky buns had gotten a little burned at the corners, but the French toast was good, and Molly didn't hear any complaints. She'd just downed her own breakfast standing up when Amy appeared.

"Sorry I'm late," she muttered. "I didn't get out of here until like eleven last night."

Molly spotted a fresh hickey on her neck, this one just above her collarbone. She was ashamed to feel another pang of jealousy. "You did a good job. The house already looks better. Why don't you get started on those dishes?"

Amy wandered over to the sink and began loading the dishwasher. Clips with tiny pink starfish on them held her hair away from her face. She'd outlined, shadowed, and mascaraed her eyes, but either she hadn't bothered with lipstick or Troy had already eaten it off.

"Your husband's really cute. I don't watch football, but even I know who he is. That's so cool. Troy says he's like the third-best quarterback in the NFL."

"First-best. He just needs to control his talent better."

Amy stretched, hiking her purple top above her navel and

forcing her shorts even lower on her hipbones. "I heard you just got married, too. Isn't it great?"

"A dream come true," Molly said dryly. Apparently Amy didn't read *People*.

"We've been married like three and a half months."

Just about the same as Kevin and Molly. Except Kevin and Molly weren't having any trouble keeping their hands off each other.

Amy resumed loading the dishwasher. "Everybody said we were too young—I'm nineteen and Troy's twenty—but we couldn't wait any longer. Me and Troy are Christians. We don't believe in sex before marriage."

"So now you're making up for lost time?"

"It's so cool." Amy grinned, and Molly smiled back.

"It might be better if you didn't try to make up for any more of that lost time during working hours."

Amy rinsed out a mixing bowl. "I guess. It's just so hard."

"The slave driver will probably be checking up on you today, so why don't you get the bedrooms done as soon as you're finished here?"

"Yeah . . . " She sighed. "If you see Troy outside, will you like tell him I love him and everything?"

"I don't think so."

"Yeah, I guess that's immature. My sister says I should be a little more standoffish or he'll take me for granted."

Molly remembered the adoration on Troy's youthful face. "I don't think you have to worry about that yet."

Kevin had disappeared by the time Molly was done in the kitchen, probably tending to his hangover. She made iced tea, then phoned Phoebe to tell her where she was. Her sister's confusion didn't surprise her, but she couldn't explain how Kevin had blackmailed her into going with him without revealing too much about her physical and emotional condition. Instead, she just said that Kevin needed some help and she'd wanted to get away from the city. Phoebe started clucking just like Celia the Hen, and Molly got off the phone as quickly as possible.

She was tired by the time she finished baking Aunt Judith's citrus Bundt cake for afternoon tea, but she couldn't resist sprucing up the parlor a little. As she filled a cut-glass bowl with potpourri, Roo began barking. She went outside to investigate and saw a woman emerge from a dusty burgundy Lexus and turn to gaze out over the Common. Molly wondered if Kevin had checked the computer to see if any new guests were arriving. They needed to get better organized.

Molly took in the woman's oyster-white tunic, bronze capris, and sculpted sandals. Everything about her was stylish and expensive. She turned, and Molly immediately recognized her: Lilly Sherman.

Molly had met a lot of celebrities over the years, so she was seldom awed by famous people, but Lilly Sherman made her feel starstruck. Everything about her radiated glamour. This was a woman accustomed to snarling traffic, and Molly half expected some paparazzi to jump out of the pine trees.

The stylish sunglasses on top of her head held the rich auburn hair that had been her trademark away from her face. Her hair was shorter than it had been in her days as Ginger Hill, but it still had a sexy, tumbled look. Her complexion was pale and porcelain-smooth, her figure voluptuous. Molly thought of all the girls she'd known with eating disorders that had left them cadaverously thin. In earlier times women had aspired toward Lilly's figure, and they'd probably been better for it.

As Lilly headed up the path toward the house, Molly saw that her eyes were an unusually vibrant shade of green, even more vivid than on television. A faint web of lines fishtailed from the corners, but she looked barely forty. The large diamond on her left hand sparkled as she bent down to greet Roo. It took Molly a few moments to accept the fact that her poodle's stomach was being rubbed by Lilly Sherman.

"This place is a bitch to get to." Lilly's voice had the same husky quality Molly remembered from her days as Ginger Hill, but now it was a shade more sultry.

"It's a little isolated."

Lilly straightened and came closer, regarding Molly with the neutral politeness celebrities adopted to keep people at a distance. Then her attention sharpened, and her eyes frosted. "I'm Lilly Sherman. Would you have someone bring in my suitcases?"

Uh-oh. She'd recognized Molly from the *People* article. This woman wasn't her friend.

Molly stepped aside as Lilly climbed the steps to the porch. "We're sort of reorganizing at the moment. Do you happen to have a reservation?"

"I'd hardly come all this way without one. I spoke with Mrs. Long two days ago, and she said you had a room."

"Yes, we probably do. I'm just not exactly sure where. I'm a big fan, by the way."

"Thank you." Her reply was so cool that Molly wished she hadn't mentioned it.

Lilly gazed at Roo, who was trying to impress her with his Bruce Willis sneer. "My cat's in the car. Mrs. Long said it wouldn't be a problem to bring her, but your dog seems a little fierce."

"It's all show. Roo might not like having a cat around, but he won't hurt her. Introduce them if you like while I go inside to check on your room."

Lilly Sherman's star might have faded, but she was still a star, and Molly expected her to object to being kept waiting, but she said nothing.

As Molly headed inside, she wondered if Kevin knew about this. Had they been lovers? Lilly seemed too intelligent, not to mention that she spoke flawless English. Still . . .

Molly hurried upstairs and found Amy bent over one of

the tubs, her tight black shorts forming a world-class wedgie.

"A guest just arrived, and I don't know where to put her. Is anybody leaving?"

Amy straightened and gazed at Molly strangely. "No, but there's the attic. No one's stayed up there this season."

"The attic?"

"It's pretty nice."

Molly couldn't imagine sticking Lilly Sherman in an attic.

Amy settled back on her heels. "Uh, Molly, if you ever want to talk about, you know, things with me, you can . . . "

"Things?"

"I mean, I noticed when I cleaned Kevin's room that you didn't sleep there last night."

Molly found it irritating to be pitied by someone with connect-the-dots hickeys. "We're estranged, Amy. Nothing for you to worry about."

"I'm really sorry. I mean, like, if it's about sex or anything, I could maybe answer any questions or, you know, give you some advice."

Molly had become an object of pity for a nineteen-year-old Dr. Ruth. "Not necessary."

She hurried upstairs to the attic and found the room surprisingly spacious, despite its sloping ceiling and dormers. The antique furniture was homey and the four poster double bed seemed to have a comfortable mattress. A large window had been added at one end to give more light. Molly threw it open for fresh air, then investigated the tiny, old-fashioned bathroom at the opposite end. Barely adequate, but at least it was private, and if Lilly Sherman didn't like it, she could leave.

Just the thought of it raised her spirits.

She asked Amy to get the room ready, then rushed downstairs. There was still no sign of Kevin. She returned to the front porch.

Lilly stood near the railing stroking the enormous marmalade cat in her arms while Roo sulked beneath one of the wooden rockers. He hopped up as Molly opened the front door, gave her an injured look, and scurried inside. She arranged her face in a pleasant expression. "I hope your cat will be gentle with him."

"They kept their distance." Lilly rubbed her thumb over the cat's chin. "This is Marmalade, commonly known as Marmie."

The longhaired cat was nearly the size of a raccoon, with gold eyes, enormous paws, and a large head. "Hey, Marmie. Go easy on Roo, will you?" The cat meowed.

"I'm afraid the only empty room is the attic. It's nice, but it's still an attic, and the bathroom leaves something to be desired. You may want to reconsider staying or maybe you'd rather take one of the cottages. They're not all filled yet."

"I prefer the house, and I'm sure this will be fine."

Since Lilly had Four Seasons written all over her, Molly couldn't imagine anything about it would be fine. Still, manners were manners. "I'm Molly Somerville."

"Yes, I recognized you," she said coldly. "You're Kevin's wife."

"We're estranged. I'm just helping him out for a few days."

"I see." Her expression said she didn't see at all.

"I'll get you some iced tea while you're waiting."

Molly raced through her preparations and was just returning to the porch when she spotted Kevin crossing the Common toward the house. Since breakfast he'd changed into faded jeans, a pair of battered sneakers, and an old black T-shirt with the sleeves ripped out so that ravelings draped his biceps. The hammer protruding from his pocket indicated either that he'd recovered from his hangover or had a high tolerance for pain. Remembering the hits he'd taken over the years, she suspected it was the latter. Since he disliked the place so much, she wondered why he was putting himself out to do repairs. Boredom, she suspected, or maybe that preacher's kid's sense of duty that kept complicating his life.

"Hey, Daphne! You want to go into town with me to pick up some supplies?"

She smiled to hear him call her Daphne again. "We have a new guest."

"That's great," he said unenthusiastically. "Just what we need."

The rocker banged against the wall, and she turned to see Lilly stand up. The diva had disappeared, and in her place was a vulnerable, ashen-faced woman. Molly set down the iced tea tumbler. "Are you all right?"

In a barely perceptible motion she shook her head.

Kevin's foot hit the bottom porch step, and he looked up. "I thought we might—" He froze.

They'd had a love affair. Now Molly was certain of it. Despite the age disparity, Lilly was a beautiful woman—her hair, those green eyes, that voluptuous body. She'd come to find Kevin because she wanted him back. And Molly wasn't ready to give him away. The idea shocked her. Was her old crush sneaking back?

He stayed where he was. "What are you doing here?"

Lilly didn't flinch from his rudeness. She almost seemed to be expecting it. "Hello, Kevin." Her arm fluttered at her side, as if she wanted to touch him but couldn't. Her eyes drank in his face.

"I'm here on vacation." Her throaty voice sounded breathless and very uncertain.

"Forget it."

Molly watched as Lilly pulled herself together. "I have a reservation. I'm staying."

Kevin turned on his heel and stalked from the house.

Lilly pressed her fingers to her mouth, smearing her soft taupe lipstick. Her eyes shimmered with tears. Pity stirred inside Molly, but Lilly wouldn't tolerate it, and she rounded on her with a hiss. "I'm staying!"

Molly gazed uncertainly toward the Common, but Kevin had disappeared. "All right." She had to know if they'd been lovers, but she couldn't just blurt out something like that. "You and Kevin seem to have a history."

Lilly sank back down in the rocker, and the cat jumped into her lap. "I'm his aunt."

Molly's relief was followed almost immediately by a weird sense of protectiveness toward Kevin. "Your relationship seems to leave something to be desired."

"He hates me." Lilly suddenly looked too fragile to be a star. "He hates me, and I love him more than anyone on earth." She seemed to pick up the iced tea tumbler as a distraction. "His mother, Maida, was my older sister."

The intensity in her voice made the small of Molly's back tingle. "Kevin told me his parents were elderly."

"Yes. Maida married John Tucker the same year I was born."

"A big age difference."

"She was like a second mother to me. We lived in the same town when I was growing up, practically next door."

Molly had the sense that Lilly was telling her this not because she wanted Molly to know but simply to keep from falling apart. Her curiosity made her take advantage of it. "I remember reading you were very young when you went to Hollywood."

"Maida moved when John was assigned to a church in Grand Rapids. My mother and I didn't get along, and things went downhill fast, so I ran away and ended up in Hollywood."

She fell silent.

Molly had to know more. "You did very well for yourself."

"It took a while. I was wild, and I made a lot of mistakes." She leaned back in the rocker. "Some of them can't be undone."

"My older sister raised me, too, but she didn't come into my life until I was fifteen."

"Maybe it would have been better for me that way. I don't know. I guess some of us were just born to raise hell."

Molly wanted to know why Kevin was so hostile, but Lilly had turned her head away, and just then Amy popped out onto the porch. She was either too young or too self-absorbed to recognize their celebrity guest. "The room's ready."

"I'll show you upstairs. Amy, would you get Miss Sherman's suitcase from her car?"

When Molly let Lilly into the attic, she expected her to object to such humble quarters, but Lilly said nothing. Molly pointed out the general direction of the beach from the window. "There's a nice walk along the lake, but maybe you know all this. Have you been here before?"

Lilly set her purse on the bed. "I wasn't invited."

The uncomfortable prickling Molly had been feeling at the back of her neck intensified. As soon as Amy appeared with the suitcase, Molly excused herself.

Instead of heading back to the cottage for a nap, she wandered into the music room. She touched the old fountain pen at the desk, then the ink bottle, then the ivory and rose stationery with WIND LAKE BED & BREAKFAST engraved at the top. Finally she stopped fidgeting and sat down to think.

By the time the small gold anniversary clock chimed the hour, she'd made up her mind to find Kevin.

She started her search at the beach, where she found Troy repairing some boards that had come loose on the dock. When she asked him about Kevin, he shook his head and adopted the same pitiful expression Roo had just used when Molly had left the house without him. "He hasn't been around for a while. Have you seen Amy?"

"She's finishing the bedrooms."

"We're, uh, trying to get everything done so we can go home early."

Where you'll rip off each other's clothes and fall into bed. "I'm sure that'll be fine."

Troy looked as grateful as if she'd scratched him under the chin.

Molly headed for the Common, then followed the sound of an angry hammer to the rear of a cottage named Paradise. Kevin was crouched on the roof taking out his frustration on a new set of shingles.

She tucked her thumbs in the back pockets of her shorts and tried to figure out how to go about this. "Are you still planning a trip into town?"

"Maybe later." He stopped hammering. "Did she leave?"

"No."

His hammer thwacked the shingles. "She can't stay here."

"She had a reservation. I couldn't really kick her out."

"Damn it, Molly!" *Thwack!* "I want you to . . . " *Thwack!* " . . . get rid of her!" *Thwack!*

She didn't appreciate being thwacked at, but she still had enough warm feelings left over from last night to treat him gently. "Would you come down for a minute?"

Thwack! "Why?"

"Because it's hurting my neck to look up at you, and I'd like to talk."

"Don't look up!" *Thwack! Thwack!* "Or don't talk!"

She sat on a stack of shingles, letting him know she wasn't going anywhere. He tried to ignore her, but he finally blasted out an obscenity and put aside his hammer.

She watched him come down the ladder. Lean, muscular legs. Great butt. What was it about men and their butts that was so enticing? He glared at her when he reached the ground, but it was more annoyance than hostility. "Well?"

"Would you tell me about Lilly?"

He narrowed those green eyes. "I don't like her."

"So I gathered." The suspicion that had been eating at her wouldn't go away. "Did she forget to send you a Christmas present when you were growing up?"

"I don't want her here, that's all."

"She doesn't look like she's going anywhere."

He braced his hands on his hips, his elbows jutting out in angry wings. "That's her problem."

"Since you don't want her here, it seems to be yours, too."

He headed back to the ladder. "Can you handle that damned tea by yourself today?"

Once again the base of her neck prickled. Something was very wrong. "Kevin, wait."

He turned to look at her, his expression impatient.

She told herself this wasn't any of her business, but she couldn't let it go. "Lilly said she's your aunt."

"Yeah, so what?"

"When she looked at you, I got this strange feeling."

"Spit it out, Molly. I've got things to do."

"Her heart was in her eyes."

"I seriously doubt that."

"She loves you."

"She doesn't even know me."

"I've got this weird feeling about why you're so upset." She bit her lip and wished she hadn't started this, but some powerful instinct wouldn't let her back off. "I don't think Lilly's your aunt, Kevin. I think she's your mother."

Chapter 12

"Fudge!" Benny smacked his lips. "I love fudge!"

Daphne Says Hello

KEVIN LOOKED AS THOUGH SHE'D PUNCHED HIM. "HOW DID YOU know? *Nobody* knows that!"

"I guessed."

"I don't believe you. She told you. Damn her!"

"She didn't say a thing. But the only other person I've seen with eyes that exact color of green is you."

"You knew just by looking at her eyes?"

"There were a couple of other things." The longing Molly had witnessed on Lilly's face when she gazed at Kevin had been too intense for an aunt. And Lilly had given her clues.

"She told me how young she was when she left home, and she said she'd gotten into trouble. I knew your parents were older. It was just a hunch."

"A damn good hunch."

"I'm a writer. Or at least I used to be. We tend to be fairly intuitive."

He flung down his hammer. "I'm getting out of here."

And she was going with him. He hadn't abandoned her last night, and she wouldn't abandon him now. "Let's go cliff diving," she blurted out.

He stopped and stared at her. "You want to go cliff diving?"

No, I don't want to go cliff diving! Do you think I'm an idiot? "Why not?"

He gazed at her for a long moment. "Okay, you're on."

Exactly what she'd been afraid of, but it was too late to back out now. If she tried, he'd just call her "bunny lady" again. That was what the kindergarten children called her when she read them her stories, but, from him, it didn't sound as innocent.

An hour and a half later she lay on a flat rock near the edge of the bluff trying to catch her breath. As the heat from the rocks seeped through her wet clothes, she decided the diving hadn't been the worst part. She was a good diver, and it had even been sort of fun. The worst part was hauling her body back up that path so she could throw herself off again.

She heard him coming up the path, but unlike her, he wasn't breathing hard. She shut her eyes. If she opened them, she'd just see what she already knew, that he'd stripped down to a pair of navy blue boxers before his first dive. It was painful to look at him—all those ripples, planes, and smooth long muscles. She'd been terrified—hopeful?—the boxers would come off in the dive, but he'd somehow managed to keep them on.

She reined in her imagination. This was exactly the kind of fantasizing that had gotten her in such terrible trouble. And maybe it was time she reminded herself that Kevin hadn't exactly been the most memorable lover. In point of fact, he'd been a dud.

That wasn't fair. He'd been operating under a double disadvantage. He'd been sound asleep, and he wasn't attracted to her.

Some things hadn't changed. Although he seemed to have worked past his contempt for her, he hadn't sent out any signals that he found her sexually irresistible—or even remotely appealing.

The fact that she could think about sex was upsetting but also encouraging. The first crocus seemed to have popped up in the dark winter of her soul.

He flopped down next to her and stretched out on his back. She smelled heat, lake, and devil man.

"No more somersaults, Molly. I mean it. You were too close to the rocks."

"I only did one, and I knew exactly where the edge was."

"You heard me."

"Jeez, you sound like Dan."

"I'm not even going to think about what he'd say if he saw you do that."

They lay there for a while in silence that was surprisingly companionable. Every one of her muscles felt achy but relaxed.

Daphne lay sunning herself on a rock when Benny came racing up the path. He was crying.
    "What's the matter, Benny?"
    "Nothing. Go away!"

Her eyes flicked open. It had been nearly four months since Daphne and Benny had held an imaginary conversation in her head. Probably just a fluke. She rolled toward Kevin. Although she didn't want to ruin the good time they'd been having, he needed help dealing with Lilly just as she needed help dealing with the loss of Sarah.

His eyes were closed. She noticed that his lashes were darker than his hair, which was already drying at the temples. She rested her chin on her hand. "Did you always know that Lilly was your birth mother?"

He didn't open his eyes. "My parents told me when I was six."

"They did the right thing not trying to keep it a secret." She waited, but he didn't say anything more. "She must have been very young. She hardly looks forty now."

"She's fifty."

"Wow."

"She's a Hollywood type. A ton of plastic surgery."

"Did you get to see her a lot when you were young?"

"On television."

"But not in person?" A woodpecker drummed not far away, and a hawk soared above the lake. She watched the rise and fall of his chest.

"She showed up once when I was sixteen. Must have been a slow time in Tinsel Town." He opened his eyes and sat up. Molly expected him to get up and walk away, but he gazed out at the lake. "As far as I'm concerned, I had one mother, Maida Tucker. I don't know what game the bimbo queen thinks she's playing by coming here, but I'm not playing it with her."

The word "bimbo" stirred old memories inside Molly. That used to be what people thought of Phoebe. Molly remembered what her sister had told her years ago. *Sometimes I think "bimbo" is a word men made up so they could feel superior to women who are better at survival than they are.*

"The best thing might be to talk to her," Molly said now. "Then you can find out what she wants."

"I don't care." He rose, grabbed his jeans, and shoved his legs in. "What a shitty week this is turning out to be."

Maybe for him, but not for her. This was turning out to be the best week she'd had in months.

He pushed his fingers through his damp hair and spoke more gently. "Do you still want to go into town?"

"Sure."

"If we go now, we can make it back by five o'clock. You'll take care of tea for me, won't you?"

"Yes, but you know you'll have to deal with her sooner or later."

She watched the play of hard emotion over his face. "I'll deal with her, but I'm choosing the time and the place."

Lilly stood at the attic window and watched Kevin drive away with the football heiress. Her throat tightened as she remembered his contempt. Her baby boy . . . The child she'd given birth to when she was barely more than a child herself. The son she'd handed over to her sister to raise as her own.

She knew it had been the right thing to do—the unselfish thing—and the success he'd made of his life proved that. What chance would he have had as the child of an undereducated, screwed-up seventeen-year-old who dreamed of being a star?

She let go of the curtain and sat on the edge of the bed. She'd met the boy the same day she'd gotten off the bus in L.A. He was a teenager fresh from an Oklahoma ranch and looking for stunt work. They'd shared a room in a fleabag hotel to save money. They'd been young and randy, hiding their fear of a dangerous city behind fumbling sex and tough talk. He'd disappeared before he knew she was pregnant.

She'd been lucky to find work waiting tables. One of the older waitresses, a woman named Becky, had taken pity on her and let her sleep on her couch. Becky had been a single mother with no patience left at the end of a long workday for the demands of her three-year-old child. Watching the little girl cringe from her mother's harsh words and occasional slaps had been a cold dose of reality. Two weeks before Kevin was born, Lilly had called Maida and told her about the baby. Her sister and John Tucker immediately drove to L.A.

They'd stayed with her through Kevin's birth and even told her she could return to Michigan with them. But she couldn't go back, and she knew by the way they looked at each other that they didn't want her to.

At the hospital, Lilly held her baby boy every chance she

got and tried to whisper a lifetime of love to him. She watched the love blossoming on her sister's face whenever she picked him up, and saw John's expression soften with longing. Their absolute worthiness to raise her child couldn't have been more apparent, and she'd loved and hated them for it. Watching them drive away with her baby boy had been the worst moment of her life. Two weeks later, she'd met Craig.

Lilly knew she'd done the right thing by giving Kevin up, but the price had still been too high. For thirty-two years she'd lived with a gaping hole in her heart that neither her career nor her marriage could fill. Even if she'd been able to have more children, that hole would still have been there. Now she wanted to heal it.

When she'd been seventeen, the only way she could fight for her son was to give him up. But she wasn't seventeen anymore, and it was time to find out, once and for all, if she could ever have a place in his life. She'd take whatever he'd give her. A Christmas card once a year. A smile. Something to tell her he'd stopped hating her. The fact that he didn't want her near him had been brutally apparent each time she'd tried to contact him since Maida's death, and it had been even more apparent today. But maybe she just hadn't tried hard enough.

She thought of Molly and felt a chill. Lilly had no respect for females who preyed on famous men. She'd seen it happen dozens of times in Hollywood. Bored, wealthy young things with no life of their own tried to define themselves by snaring famous men. Molly had trapped him with her pregnancy and her position as the sister of Phoebe Calebow.

Lilly got up from the bed. During Kevin's growing up years, she hadn't been able to protect him when he needed it, but now she had a chance to make up for that.

*   *   *

Wind Lake was a typical resort village—quaint at its center and a bit shabby at the edges. The main street ran along the lake and featured a few restaurants and gift shops, a marina, an upscale clothing boutique for the tourists, and the Wind Lake Inn.

Kevin parked and Molly got out of the car. Before they'd left the campground, she'd showered, conditioned her hair, used a little eye makeup and her M.A.C. Spice lipstick. Since she only had sneakers, her sundress wasn't an option, so she'd slipped into light gray drawstring shorts and a black cropped top, then consoled herself by noticing that she'd lost enough weight to let the shorts ride below her belly button.

As he came around the front of the car, his eyes skimmed over her, then studied her more closely. She felt an unwelcome tingle and wondered if he liked what he saw, or if he was making an unfavorable comparison with his United Nations companions.

So what if he was? She liked her body and her face. They might not be memorable to him, but she was happy with them. Besides, she didn't care what he thought.

He gestured toward the boutique. "They should have sandals in there if you want to replace the ones you lost in the lake."

Boutique sandals were way out of her price range. "I'll try the beach shop instead."

"Their stuff is pretty cheap."

She pushed her sunglasses higher on her nose. Unlike his Rēvos, hers had cost nine dollars at Marshall's. "I have simple tastes."

He regarded her curiously. "You're not one of those penny-pinching multimillionaires, are you?"

She thought for a moment, then decided not to play any more games with him about this. It was time for him to see who she was, insanity and all. "I'm not actually a multimillionaire."

"It's fairly common knowledge that you're an heiress."

"Yes, well . . . " She bit her lip.

He sighed. "Why do I think I'm going to hear something really wacky?"

"I guess that depends on your perspective."

"Go on. I'm still listening."

"I'm broke, okay?"

"Broke?"

"Never mind. You wouldn't understand in a million years." She walked away from him.

As she crossed the street toward the beach shop, he came up next to her. It irritated her to see that he looked disapproving, although she should have expected it from Mr. I'll-Take-the-High-Road, who could be the poster boy for grown-up preachers' kids, even though he was in denial about it.

"You blew all that money the first chance you got, didn't you? That's why you live in such a small place."

She turned on him in the middle of the street. "No, I didn't blow it. I splurged a little the first year, but believe me, there was plenty left."

He took her arm and pulled her out of the traffic onto the curb. "Then what happened?"

"Don't you have something better to do than harass me?"

"Not really. Bad investments? Did you put everything you had in vegetarian crocodile meat?"

"Very funny."

"You cornered the market in bunny slippers?"

"How about this?" She stopped in front of the beach shop. "I bet everything I had on the Stars in the last game, and some dickhead threw into double coverage."

"That was low."

She took a deep breath and pushed her sunglasses to the top of her head. "Actually, I gave it all away a few years ago. And I'm not sorry."

He blinked, then laughed. "You gave it away?"

"Having trouble with your hearing?"

"No, really. Tell me the truth."

She glared at him and went inside the shop.

"I don't believe this. You really did." He came up behind her. "How much was there?"

"A lot more than you have in your portfolio, sonny boy."

He grinned. "Come on. You can tell me."

She headed for a bin of footwear, then wished she hadn't, since it was filled with neon plastic sandals.

"More than three million?"

She ignored him and reached for the plainest ones, a disgusting pair with silver glitter imbedded in the vamp.

"Less than three?"

"I'm not saying. Now, go away and don't bother me."

"If you tell me, I'll take you over to that boutique, and you can put whatever you want on my credit card."

"You're on." She threw down the silver glitter sandals and made for the door.

He moved ahead of her to open it. "Don't you want me to twist your arm a little so you can hold on to your pride?"

"Did you see how ugly those sandals were? Besides, I know how much you earned last season."

"I'm glad we signed that prenuptial agreement. Here I thought we were protecting your fortune, but son of a gun, in one of those ironic twists life sometimes throws at you, it turns out we were really protecting mine." His grin grew bigger. "Who'd have figured?"

He was enjoying himself way too much, so she picked up her stride. "I'll bet I can max out your credit card in half an hour."

"Was it more than three million?"

"I'll tell you *after* I've finished shopping." She smiled at an elderly couple.

"If you lie, I'm taking everything back."

"Isn't there a mirror someplace where you can go admire yourself?"

"I never knew a woman so hung up on my good looks."

"*All* your women are hung up on your good looks. They just *pretend* it's your personality."

"I swear, somebody needs to spank you."

"You are, like, so not the man to do it."

"You are, like, such a damned brat."

She smiled and headed into the boutique. Fifteen minutes later she emerged with two pairs of sandals. Only as she put her sunglasses back on did she notice that Kevin also carried a shopping bag. "What did you buy?"

"You need a bathing suit."

"You bought me one?"

"I guessed at the size."

"What kind of bathing suit?"

"Jeez, if somebody bought me a present, I'd be happy about it instead of acting so suspicious."

"If it's a thong, it goes back."

"Now, would I insult you that way?" They began wandering down the street.

"A thong is probably the only kind of suit you know exists. I'm sure that's what all your girlfriends wear."

"You think you can distract me, but it's not going to work." They passed a sweet shop called Say Fudge. Next to it was a tiny public garden, little more than a few hydrangea bushes and a pair of benches. "It's reckoning time, Daphne." He indicated one of the benches, then settled beside her. His arm brushed her shoulder as he propped it along the back. "Tell me all about the money. Didn't you have to wait till you were twenty-one to get your hands on it?"

"Yes, but I was still in school, and Phoebe wouldn't let me touch a penny. She said if I wanted into the accounts before I graduated, I'd have to sue her."

"Smart lady."

"She and Dan kept me on a pretty tight leash, so once I graduated and she finally handed it over, I did everything you'd expect. I bought a car, moved into a luxury apartment, bought loads of clothes—I do miss those clothes. But after a while the life of a trust-fund baby lost its luster."

"Why didn't you just get a job?"

"I did, but the money kept hanging over me. I hadn't earned a penny of it. Maybe if it had come from someone other than Bert Somerville, I wouldn't have had such a hard time with it, but it felt as if he'd poked his nasty head back in my life, and I didn't like it. Finally I decided to set up a foundation and give it all away. And if you tell anybody, I swear I'll make you regret it."

"You gave away all of it?"

"Every penny."

"How much?"

She fiddled with the drawstring on her shorts. "I don't want to tell you. You already think I'm nuts."

"It's going to be so easy for me to return those sandals."

"Fifteen million, all right!"

He looked as if he'd been face-masked. "You gave away fifteen million dollars!"

She nodded.

He threw back his head and laughed. "You *are* nuts!"

She remembered the somersault dive she'd made off the cliff. "Probably. But I haven't regretted it for a moment." Although now she wouldn't mind having some of it back so she could keep paying her mortgage.

"You really don't miss it?"

"No. Except for the clothes, which I believe I already mentioned. And thank you for the sandals, by the way. I love them."

"My pleasure. Matter of fact, I've enjoyed your story so much, I'll add a new outfit the next time you're in town."

"Done!"

"God, it's heartbreaking to see a woman fight so hard to hang tough."

She laughed.

"Kevin! Hello!"

Molly heard a distinctly Germanic accent and looked up to see a willowy blonde hurrying toward them with a small white box in her hand. The woman wore a blue-and-white-striped apron over black slacks and a V-neck top. She was pretty. Lots of hair, brown eyes, good makeup. She was probably a couple of years older than Molly, nearer Kevin's age.

"Hey, there, Christina." Kevin gave the woman a smile that was way too sexy as he rose to greet her.

She extended the white cardboard box, and Molly spotted a blue seal on the side with SAY FUDGE embossed on it. "You seemed to enjoy the fudge last night, *ja*? This is a small present to welcome you to Wind Lake. Our sample box."

"Thanks a lot." He looked so pleased that Molly wanted to remind him it was just candy, not a Super Bowl ring! "Christina, this is Molly. Christina owns that fudge shop over there. I met her yesterday when I came into town to grab a burger."

Christina was more slender than a woman who owned a fudge shop should be. That struck Molly as a crime against nature.

"Pleasure to meet you, Molly."

"Nice meeting you, too." Molly could have ignored the curiosity in her expression, but she wasn't that good a person. "I'm Kevin's wife."

"Oh." Her disappointment was just as blatant as her mission with the fudge box.

"Estranged wife," Kevin cut in. "Molly writes children's books."

"*Ach so?* I've always wanted to write a children's book. Maybe you could give me a few suggestions sometime."

Molly kept her expression pleasant but noncommittal.

Just once she'd like to meet someone who *didn't* want to write a children's book. People assumed they were easy to write because they were short. They had no idea what went into writing a successful book, one that children genuinely enjoyed and learned from, not just something adults had decided a child should enjoy.

"I'm sorry you're going to sell the campground, Kevin. We'll miss you." Before Christina could drool over him any more, she spotted a woman heading into the fudge shop. "I have to go. Stop by the next time you're in town so you can sample my cherry chocolate."

The minute she was out of earshot, Molly turned on him. "You can't sell the campground!"

"I told you from the beginning that's what I was doing."

True, but it hadn't meant anything at the time. Now she couldn't bear the idea that he would throw it away. The campground was a permanent part of him, part of his family, and in a strange way she couldn't analyze, it was beginning to feel like part of her.

He misunderstood her silence. "Don't worry. We won't have to stay around that long. The minute I find someone to take over, we're out of here."

All the way back to the campground, Molly tried to sort out her thoughts. The only deep roots Kevin had left were here. He'd lost his parents, he had no siblings, and he didn't seem inclined to let Lilly into his life. The house where he'd grown up belonged to the church. He had nothing to connect him with his past except the campground. It would be wrong to give that up.

The Common came into sight, and her jumbled thoughts gave way to a feeling of peace. Charlotte Long was sweeping her front porch, an elderly man rode by on a three-wheel bike, and a couple chatted on a bench. Molly drank in the storybook cottages and shady trees.

No wonder she'd experienced a sense of familiarity the

moment she'd arrived here. She'd stepped through the pages of her books right into Nightingale Woods.

Instead of heading along the lake where she might meet someone, Lilly followed a narrow path that led into the woods beyond the Common. She'd changed into a pair of slacks and a square-neck, tobacco-brown top, but she was still hot, and she wished she were thin enough to wear shorts. Those little white ones that had been a permanent part of her wardrobe on *Lace, Inc.* They'd barely covered her bottom.

Weeds brushed her legs as the trees opened into a meadow. Her toes felt pleasantly gritty inside her sandals, and some of the tension she'd been carrying all day began to ease. She heard running water from a stream and turned to look for it, only to see something so out of place that she blinked.

A chrome diner's chair with a red vinyl seat.

Lilly couldn't imagine what it was doing in the middle of the meadow. As she began to walk toward it, she saw a creek with ferns growing among the reeds and mossy rocks. The chair sat on a lichen-encrusted boulder. Its red vinyl seat sparkled in the sunlight, and there was no visible rust, so it had been put there recently. But why? Its perch was precarious, and it wobbled as she touched it.

"Leave that alone!"

She spun around to see a big bear of a man crouched in bars of sunlight at the edge of the meadow.

Her hand flew to her throat.

Behind her the chair splashed into the creek.

"Damn it!" The man jumped to his feet.

He was huge, with shoulders as wide as twelve lanes of L.A. freeway and a scowling, rough-hewn face that belonged on the villain in an old B Western. *I got ways of makin' a woman like you talk.* The only thing missing was a week's worth of stubble on that grim jaw.

His hair was a Hollywood stylist's nightmare or day-dream, she wasn't sure which. Thick and graying at the temples, it grew too long at the collar, where it looked as if he might have swiped at it with the knife he undoubtedly kept in his boot. Except he wore a pair of battered running shoes instead, with socks that slouched around his ankles. And his eyes—mysteriously dark in that deeply tanned, dangerously lined face.

Every casting agent in Hollywood would salivate over him.

All those thoughts were scrambling through Lilly's head instead of the one thought that should have been there: *Run!*

He strode toward her. Beneath his khaki shorts his legs were brown and strong. He wore an old blue denim work shirt with the sleeves rolled up to reveal muscular forearms dusted with dark hair. "Do you know how long it took me to get that chair right where I wanted it?"

She backed away from him. "Maybe you have too much leisure time."

"Do you think that's funny?"

"Oh, no." She kept backing. "Not funny. Definitely not."

"Does it amuse you to spoil a whole day's work?"

"Work?"

His eyebrows shot together. "What are you doing?"

"Doing?"

"Stand still, damn it, and stop cowering!"

"I'm not cowering!"

"For God's sake, I'm not going to hurt you!" Grumbling under his breath, he stalked back to where he'd been sitting and picked up something off the ground. She took advantage of his distraction to edge closer to the path.

"I told you not to move!"

He was holding some kind of notebook, and he no longer seemed sinister, just incredibly impolite. She regarded him with all the imperiousness of Hollywood royalty. "Someone's forgotten his manners."

"Waste of energy. I come here for privacy. Is that too much to ask?"

"Not at all. I'm leaving right now."

"Over there!" He pointed an angry finger toward the creek.

"Pardon me?"

"Sit over there."

She was no longer frightened, just annoyed. "I don't think so."

"You ruined an afternoon's work. Sitting for me is the least you can do to make up for it."

He was holding a sketch pad, she realized, not a notebook. He was an artist. "Why don't I just leave instead?"

"I told you to sit!"

"Has anyone ever mentioned that you're rude?"

"I work hard at it. Sit on that boulder and face the sun."

"Thanks, but I don't do sun. Bad for the complexion."

"Just once I'd like to meet a beautiful woman who isn't vain."

"I appreciate the compliment," she said dryly, "but I passed the beautiful woman mark a good ten years and forty pounds ago."

"Don't be infantile." He whipped a pencil from his shirt pocket and began to sketch, not bothering to argue with her any longer, or even to sit down on the small camp stool she spotted a few feet away. "Tilt your chin. God, you really are beautiful."

He uttered the compliment so dispassionately that it didn't seem flattering. She resisted the urge to tell him he should have seen her in her prime. "You're right about my vanity," she said, just to needle him. "Which is why I'm not going to stand here in the sun any longer."

The pencil continued to fly over his sketch pad. "I don't like models talking when I'm working."

"I'm not your model."

Just as she was about to turn away for the last time, he

jabbed his pencil in the pocket of his work shirt. "How do you expect me to concentrate when you won't stand still?"

"Pay attention: I don't care whether you concentrate or not."

His brow furrowed, and she had the feeling he was trying to make up his mind whether he could bully her into staying. Finally he flipped his sketch pad shut. "We'll meet here tomorrow morning then. Let's say seven. That way the sun won't be too hot for you."

Her irritation turned to amusement. "Why not make it six-thirty?"

His eyes narrowed. "You're patronizing me, aren't you?"

"Rude and astute. A fascinating combination."

"I'll pay you."

"You couldn't afford me."

"I seriously doubt that."

She smiled and turned onto the path.

"Do you know who I am?" he called out.

She glanced back. His expression couldn't have been more threatening. "Should I?"

"I'm Liam Jenner, damn it!"

She sucked in her breath. Liam Jenner. The J. D. Salinger of American painters. My God . . . What was he doing here?

He could see that she knew exactly who he was, and his scowl turned smug. "We'll compromise on seven then."

"I—" *Liam Jenner!* "I'll think about it."

"You do that."

What an obnoxious man! He'd done the world a favor by being so reclusive. But still . . .

Liam Jenner, one of the most famous painters in America, wanted her to sit for him. If only she were twenty and beautiful again.

Chapter 13

Daphne put down her hammer and hopped back to admire the sign she'd nailed to her front door. It read NO BADGERS ALLOWED (AND THIS MEANS VOUS!). She'd painted it herself just that morning.

Daphne's Lonesome Day

"USE THE STEPSTOOL TO CHECK THAT TOP SHELF, WILL YOU, AMY?" Kevin said from the pantry. "I'm going to move these boxes out of the way."

As soon as they'd returned from town, Kevin had enlisted Amy's help taking inventory of their food supplies. For the past ten minutes she'd been darting assessing glances between the pantry where he was working and the kitchen counter where Molly was preparing for the tea. Finally, she couldn't hold back any longer.

"It's sort of interesting, isn't it, that you and Molly got married about the same time as me and Troy."

Molly set the first slice of Bundt cake on the Victorian cake platter and listened to Kevin dodge. "Molly said she was going to need more brown sugar. Anything up there?"

"I see two bags. There's this book I read about marriage . . . "

"What else?"

"Some raisin boxes and a thingy of baking powder. Anyway, this book said that sometimes couples who, like, have just got married have a hard time adjusting and everything. Because it's such a big change."

"Is there any oatmeal? She said she needed that, too."

"There's a box, but it's not a big one. Troy, like, thinks being married is awesome."

"What else?"

"Pans and stuff. No more food. But if you're having trouble adjusting or anything, I mean, you could talk to Troy."

Molly smiled at the long silence that followed. Eventually, Kevin said, "Maybe you'd better see what's left in the freezer."

Amy emerged from the pantry and gave Molly a pitying glance. There was something about the teenager's sympathy and those hickeys that was getting under her skin.

Tea wasn't nearly as much fun without Kevin. Mrs. Chet—actually Gwen—didn't try to hide her disappointment when Molly said he had another commitment. She might have cheered up if she'd known that Lilly Sherman was staying there, but Lilly didn't appear, and Molly wasn't going to announce her presence.

She was setting out the pottery mixing bowls so she'd be ready for breakfast the next morning when Kevin came in through the back carrying groceries. He dodged Roo, who was trying to make a meal of his ankles, and set the bags on the counter. "Why are you doing that? Where's Amy?"

"Stop it, Roo. I just let her go. She was starting to whimper from Troy-deprivation."

No sooner had she said it than she spotted Amy flying across the yard toward her husband, who must have sniffed her on the wind, because he'd appeared out of nowhere.

"There they go again," Kevin said.

Their reunion was more passionate than a perfume commercial. Molly watched Troy dip his mouth to the top of Amy's exposed breast. She threw back her head. Arched her neck.

Another hickey.

Molly smacked a Tupperware lid back on its container. "She's going to end up needing a blood transfusion if he doesn't stop that."

"She doesn't seem to mind it too much. Some women like it when a man puts his mark on them."

Something in the way he looked at her made her breasts prickle. She didn't like her reaction. "And some women see it for what it is—the pathetic attempt of an insecure man to dominate a woman."

"Yeah, there's always that." He gave her a lazy smile and headed back out the side door for the rest of the groceries.

While he unloaded, he asked Molly if she wanted to go into town for dinner, but she declined. There was only so much Kevin temptation she wanted to expose herself to at one time. She headed back to the cottage, feeling good about her self-discipline.

The sun looked like a big lemon cookie in the sky, which made Daphne hungry. Green beans! she thought. With a nice topping of dandelion leaves. And strawberry cheese-cake for dessert.

This was the second time today the critters had popped into her head. Maybe she was finally ready to get back to work—if not to write, then at least to do the drawings Helen wanted and free up the rest of her advance.

She let herself into the cottage and found a well-stocked refrigerator and a cupboard stacked with supplies. She had to give Kevin credit. He was doing his best to be considerate. She wasn't crazy about the fact that she was starting to like him so much, and she tried to work up some anger by reminding herself he was a shallow, egotistical, overpriced, Ferrari-driving, kidnapping, poodle-hating womanizer. Except she hadn't seen any evidence of womanizing. None at all.

Because he didn't find her attractive.

She grabbed her hair and let out a muffled scream at her

own utter patheticness. Then she fixed a huge dinner and ate every bite.

That evening she sat on the porch gazing down at the pad of paper she'd found in a drawer. Would it hurt to move Daphne and Melissa just a little farther apart? After all, it was only a children's book. It wasn't as if America's civil liberties rested on how close Daphne and Melissa were standing to each other.

Her pencil began to move, at first hesitantly, and then more quickly. But the sketch that appeared wasn't the one she'd planned. Instead, she found herself drawing Benny in the water, fur dripping into his eyes, his mouth agape, as he looked up at Daphne, who was diving off the top of a cliff. Her ears streamed behind her, the beaded collar of her denim jacket flapped open, and a pair of very stylish Manolo Blahniks flew from her paws.

She frowned and thought of all the accounts she'd read of young people being permanently paralyzed from diving into unfamiliar water. What kind of safety message would this send small children?

She ripped the paper from the pad and crumpled it. This was the sort of problem all those people who wanted to write a children's book never considered.

Her brain had dried up again. Instead of thinking about Daphne and Benny, she found herself thinking about Kevin and the campground. This was his heritage, and he should never sell it. He said he'd been bored here as a child, but he didn't have to be bored now. Maybe he just needed a playmate. Her brain skittered away from thinking about exactly what playing with Kevin would involve.

She decided to walk to the Common. Maybe she'd sketch some of the cottages just for fun. On the way there, Roo trotted over to greet Charlotte Long and impress her with his dead dog imitation. Although fewer than half the cottages were occupied, most of the residents seemed to be out for an evening stroll, and long, cool shadows fell like whispers across the grass. Life passed more slowly here in Nightingale Woods . . .

The gazebo caught Molly's attention.

I'll have a tea party! I'll invite my friends, and we'll wear fabulous hats and eat chocolate frosting and say, "*Ma chère*, have you ever seen such a bee-you-tee-ful day?"

She settled cross-legged on the beach towel she'd brought with her and began to sketch. Several couples strolled by and stopped to observe, but they were members of the last generation with manners, and they didn't interrupt her. As she drew, she found herself thinking about all her years at summer camp. The frailest thread of an idea began to form in her mind, not about a tea party but about—

She closed her notebook. What was the use of thinking so far ahead? Birdcage had contractual rights to two more Daphne books, neither of which they'd accept until she'd made the revisions they'd demanded of *Daphne Takes a Tumble.*

The lights were on when she returned to the cottage. She hadn't left them that way, but she wasn't too worried.

Roo immediately started barking and made a dash for the bathroom door. It wasn't latched, and the dog bumped it open a few inches with his head.

"Calm down, poochy." Molly pushed it open the rest of the way and saw Kevin, all bare-naked beautiful, stretched out in the old-fashioned tub, legs crossed and propped on the rim, a book in his hands, and a small cigar clamped in the corner of his mouth.

"What are you doing in my bathtub?" Although the water came all the way to the top, there weren't any soap bubbles to hide him, so she didn't go closer.

He pulled the cigar from the corner of his mouth. No smoke curled from it, and she realized it wasn't a cigar but a stick of candy—chocolate or root beer.

He had the gall to sound irritated. "Now, what do you think I'm doing? And would you mind knocking before you barge in?"

"Roo barged in, not me." The dog ambled out, his job done, and headed for his water bowl. "Why aren't you using your own tub?"

"I don't like sharing a bathroom."

She didn't point out what had to be obvious—that he seemed to be sharing this one with her. She noticed that his chest looked just as good wet as it did dry. Even better. Something about the way he was watching her made her feel edgy. "Where did you get that candy?"

"In town. And I only bought one."

"Nice going."

"All you had to do was ask."

"Like I knew you were going to buy candy? And I'll just bet there's a box of the beautiful fräulein's fudge tucked away somewhere."

"Close the door on your way out. Unless you want to get naked and climb in here with me?"

"Thanks so much, but it looks a little small."

"Small? I don't think so, sweetheart."

"Oh, grow up!"

His chuckle followed her as she spun around and slammed the door. *Slytherin!* She headed for the small bedroom. Sure enough, his suitcase was there. She sighed and pressed her fingers to her temple. Her old headache was coming back.

Daphne put down her electric guitar and opened her door. Benny stood on the other side.

"Can I use your bathtub, Daphne?"

"Why do you want to?"
He looked scared. "I just do."

She poured herself a glass of sauvignon blanc from the bottle she found chilling in the refrigerator, then carried it out to the porch. Her black cropped top wasn't warm enough for the evening chill, but she didn't bother going inside to get a sweater.

She was rocking in the glider when he appeared. He wore a pair of gray sweat socks with a silky-looking robe that had dark maroon and black vertical stripes. It was the kind of robe a woman would buy for a man she loved sleeping with. Molly hated it.

"Let's host a tea in the gazebo before we leave," she said. "We'll make an event of it and invite everyone in the cottages."

"Why would we want to do that?"

"For fun."

"Sounds like a real thrill ride." He sat on the chair next to her and stretched his legs. The hair on his calves lay damp against his skin. He smelled like Safeguard and something expensive—a Brinks truckload of broken female hearts.

"I'd rather you didn't stay here, Kevin."

"I'd rather I did." He took a sip of wine from the glass he'd brought out with him.

"Can I sleep at your house, Daphne?"
    "I guess. But why do you want to?"
    "Because mine has a ghost."

"You can't hide from Lilly forever," she said.

"I'm not hiding. Just picking my own time."

"I don't know much about getting annulments, but it seems as though this might compromise ours."

"It was compromised from the beginning," he said. "The

way my attorney explained it, the grounds for a legal annulment are misrepresentation or duress. I figured you could claim duress. I sure wasn't going to argue."

"But the fact that we're together now makes that doubtful."

"Big deal. We'll get a divorce instead. It might take a little longer, but it'll accomplish the same thing."

She rose from the glider. "I still don't want you to stay here."

"It's my cottage."

"I have renter's rights."

His voice slid over her, soft and sexy. "I think being around me just makes you nervous."

"Yeah, right." She managed a yawn.

Amused, he nodded toward her wineglass. "You're drinking. Aren't you afraid you'll attack me again in my sleep?"

"Oops. Relapse. And I didn't even realize it."

"Or maybe you're afraid I'll attack you."

Something licked at her deep inside, but she played Ms. Cool, wandering over to the table to wipe up a few bread crumbs with the napkin she'd left there. "Why should I be? You're not attracted to me."

He waited just long enough before he replied to make her nervous. "How do you know who I'm attracted to?"

Her heart did a provoking little skipper-dee. "Oh, my gosh! And here I thought my command of the English language would drive us apart."

"You're such a wise-ass."

"Sorry, but I like my men with more depth of character."

"Are you trying to say you think I'm shallow?"

"As a sidewalk puddle. But you're rich and gorgeous, so it's okay."

"I am not shallow!"

"Fill in the blank: The most important thing in Kevin Tucker's life is—"

"Football is my career. That hardly makes me shallow."

"The second, third, and fourth most important things in Kevin Tucker's life are football, football, and oh my god, football."

"I'm the best at what I do, and I'm not apologizing."

"The fifth most important thing in Kevin Tucker's life is— Oh, wait now, that would be women, wouldn't it?"

"Quiet ones, so that leaves you out!"

She was halfway to a great comeback when it hit her. "I get it. All the foreign women . . . " He looked wary. "You don't want someone you can truly communicate with. That might get in the way of your primary obsession."

"You have no idea what you're talking about. I keep telling you: I date lots of American women."

"And I'll bet they're interchangeable. Beautiful, not too bright, and—as soon as they turn demanding—out the door."

"The good old days."

"I insulted you, in case you didn't realize it."

"I insulted you back, in case you didn't realize it."

She smiled. "I'm sure you don't want to stay under the same roof with someone who's so demanding."

"You're not getting rid of me that easily. As a matter of fact, living together could have some advantages." He rose from the glider and gazed at her with an expression that conjured up images of sweaty bodies and messy sheets. Then he reached into the pocket of his robe, breaking the spell which had probably all been in her imagination anyway.

He pulled out a crumpled sheet of paper. It took her only a moment to recognize the drawing she'd made of Daphne diving into the water.

"I found this in the trash." He smoothed it out as he came toward her, then pointed down at Benny. "This guy? He's the badger?"

She nodded slowly, wishing she hadn't discarded the drawing where he could find it.

"So why did you throw it away?"

"Safety issues."

"Uhm . . . "

"Sometimes I use incidents in my own life for inspiration."

His mouth quirked. "I can see that."

"I'm really more a cartoonist than an artist."

"This is a little too detailed for a cartoon."

She shrugged and held out her hand to take it back, but he shook his head. "It's mine now. I like it." He slipped it in his pocket, then turned back toward the kitchen door. "I'd better get dressed."

"Good, because staying here won't work."

"Oh, I'm staying here. I'm just going into town for a while." He paused and gave her a crooked smile. "You can come along if you'd like."

Her brain sounded a warning. "Thanks anyway, but my German's rusty, and too much chocolate makes my skin break out."

"If I didn't know better, I'd say you were jealous."

"Just remember, *liebling,* the alarm goes off at five-thirty tomorrow morning."

She heard him come in sometime after one, so it was a pleasure banging on his bedroom door at dawn. There had been rain overnight, but as they walked silently down the lane, they were both too groggy to appreciate the freshly washed, rosy-gray sky. While Kevin yawned, she concentrated on putting one foot in front of the other and avoiding puddles. Only Roo was happy to be up and about.

Molly fixed blueberry pancakes, and Kevin sliced uneven chunks of fruit into a blue pottery bowl. As he worked, he grumbled that someone with a 65-percent pass completion record shouldn't have to do kitchen duty. His complaining stopped, however, when Marmie strolled in.

"Where did that cat come from?"

Molly dodged his question. "She showed up yesterday. That's Marmie."

Roo whimpered and crawled under the table. Kevin grabbed a tea towel to dry his hands. "Hey, girl." He knelt and stroked the animal. Marmie immediately curled against him.

"I thought you didn't like animals."

"I love animals. Where did you get that idea?" Marmie put her paws on his leg, and he picked her up.

"From my dog?"

"That's a dog? Jeez, I'm sorry. I thought it was an industrial-waste accident." His long, lean fingers slid through the cat's fur.

"Slytherin." She slapped the lid back onto the flour container. What kind of man liked a cat more than he liked an exceptionally fine French poodle?

"What did you call me?"

"It's a literary reference. You wouldn't understand."

"Harry Potter. And I don't appreciate name calling."

His reply irritated her. It was getting harder and harder to convince herself he was just a pretty face.

The Pearsons were their first customers. John Pearson consumed half a dozen pancakes and a serving of scrambled eggs while he updated Kevin on the couple's so-far-fruitless search for Kirtland's warbler. Chet and Gwen were leaving that day, and when Molly peered into the dining room, she saw Gwen casting come-hither glances at Kevin. A little later she heard a commotion from the front of the house. She turned off the heat and rushed into the foyer, where the forbidding man she'd seen on the Common the day she'd arrived was growling at Kevin.

"She's a redhead. Tall—five feet nine. And beautiful. Somebody said they saw her here yesterday afternoon."

"What do you want with her?" Kevin asked.

"We had an appointment."

"What kind of an appointment?"

"Is she here or not?"

"I thought I recognized that snarl." Lilly appeared at the top of the stairs. Somehow she managed to make her simple periwinkle linen camp shirt and matching walking shorts look glamorous. She began to descend, every inch the queen of the screen, then stalled awkwardly as she spotted Kevin. "Good morning."

He gave her a brusque nod and disappeared into the dining room.

Lilly retained her composure. The man who'd come to see her stared toward the dining room, and Molly realized he was the one she'd passed coming out of the woods her first day here. How did Lilly know him?

"It's eight-thirty," he grumbled. "We were supposed to meet at seven."

"I mulled it over for a few seconds and decided I'd rather sleep in."

He glared at her like a surly lion. "Let's get going. I'm losing the light."

"If you search hard enough, I'm sure you'll be able to find it. In the meantime I'm eating breakfast."

His brow furrowed.

Lilly turned to Molly, her expression frosty. "Would it be possible for me to eat in the kitchen instead of the dining room?"

Molly told herself to rise above Lilly's hostility, then decided the heck with it. Two could play this game. "Of course. Maybe you'd *both* like to eat there. I've made blueberry pancakes."

Lilly looked miffed.

"Do you have coffee?" he barked.

Molly had always been drawn to individuals who didn't care about earning the approval of others—probably because she'd spent so much time trying to earn her father's.

This man's outrageous crankiness fascinated her. She also noticed that he was very sexy for someone his age. "All the coffee you can drink."

"Well, all right then."

Molly felt a little guilty and returned her attention to Lilly. "Feel free to use the kitchen anytime you want. I'm sure you'd rather avoid facing your fans first thing in the morning."

"What kind of fans?" he demanded.

"I'm fairly well known," Lilly said.

"Oh." He dismissed her celebrity. "If you insist on eating, could you hurry up about it?"

Lilly addressed Molly, but only to aggravate him, she was certain. "This unbelievably self-absorbed man is Liam Jenner. Mr. Jenner, this is Molly, my . . . nephew's wife."

For the second time in two days Molly found herself starstruck. "Mr. Jenner?" She gulped. "I can't tell you what a pleasure this is. I've admired your work for years. I can't believe you're here! I just— You have long hair in that photograph they always print of you. I know it was taken years ago, but— I'm sorry. I'm babbling. It's just that your work has meant a lot to me."

Jenner glowered at Lilly. "If I'd wanted her to know my name, I'd have told her myself."

"Lucky us," Lilly said to Molly. "We finally have a winner for our Mr. Charm pageant."

Molly tried to catch her breath. "That's all right. I understand. I'm sure lots of people try to violate your privacy, but—"

"Maybe you could skip the adulation and just lead the way to those pancakes."

She gulped some air. "Right this way. Sir."

"Perhaps you should fix crab cakes instead," Lilly said.

"I heard that," he muttered.

In the kitchen Molly pulled herself together enough to direct Lilly and Liam Jenner to the round table that sat in the bay. She raced to rescue the scrambled eggs she'd abandoned and toss them on a plate.

Kevin came through the door and glanced toward Lilly and Jenner but apparently decided not to ask any questions. "Are those eggs ready yet?"

She handed him the plates. "They're overdone. If Mrs. Pearson complains, charm her out of it. Would you bring in some coffee? We have kitchen guests. This is Liam Jenner."

Kevin nodded at the artist. "I heard in town that you had a house on the lake."

"And you're Kevin Tucker." For the first time Jenner smiled, and Molly was startled by the transformation of those craggy features. Very sexy indeed. Lilly noticed, too, although she didn't seem as impressed as Molly.

He stood and extended his hand. "I should have recognized you right away. I've been following the Stars for years."

As the two men shook, Molly watched the temperamental artist turn into a football fan. "You had a pretty good season."

"Could have been better."

"I guess you can't win them all."

As the conversation turned to the Stars, Molly gazed at the three of them. What an odd group of people to have come together in this isolated place. A football player, an artist, and a movie star.

Here on Gilligan's Isle.

She smiled and took the plates from Kevin, who seemed to be enjoying the conversation, then plopped them on a tray and delivered them to the dining room. Luckily there were no complaints about the eggs. She filled two mugs from the coffee urn, picked up an extra cream and sugar, and carried it all back to the kitchen.

Kevin was leaning against the pantry door ignoring Lilly while he spoke to Jenner. " . . . heard in town that lots of people are visiting Wind Lake hoping to catch a glimpse of you.

Apparently you've been a boon to local tourism."

"Not by choice." Jenner took the coffee Molly set in front of him and leaned back in his chair. He looked easy in his skin, she thought. Solidly built, a little grizzled, an artist disguised as a rugged outdoorsman. "As soon as word got around that I'd built a house here, all kinds of idiots started showing up."

Lilly accepted the spoon Molly handed her and began stirring her coffee. "You don't seem to think much of your admirers, Mr. Jenner."

"They're impressed by my fame, not my work. They start babbling about how they're so honored to meet me, but three-quarters of them wouldn't know one of my paintings if it bit 'em on the ass."

As one who'd babbled, Molly couldn't let that pass. "*Mamie in Earnest*, painted in 1968, a very early watercolor." She poured out the batter onto the griddle. "An emotionally complex work with a deceptive simplicity of line. *Tokens*, painted around 1971, a dry brush watercolor. The critics hated it, but they were wrong. From 1996 to 1998 you concentrated on acrylics with the *Desert Series*. Stylistically, those paintings are a pastiche—postmodern eclecticism, classicism, with a nod toward the Impressionists that only you could have pulled off."

Kevin smiled. "Molly's summa cum laude. Northwestern. She writes bunny books. My personal favorite of your paintings is a landscape—don't have a clue when you painted it or what the critics had to say about it—but there's this kid in the distance and I like it."

"I love *Street Girl*," Lilly said. "A solitary female figure on an urban street, worn-down red shoes, a hopeless expression on her face. Ten years ago it sold for twenty-two thousand dollars."

"Twenty-four."

"Twenty-two," she said smoothly. "I bought it."

For the first time Liam Jenner seemed to be at a loss for words. But not for long. "What do you do for a living?"

Lilly took a sip of coffee before she spoke. "I used to solve crimes."

Molly briefly debated letting Lilly's evasion go, but she was too curious to see what would happen. "This is Lilly Sherman, Mr. Jenner. She's quite a famous actress."

He leaned back in his chair and studied her before he finally murmured, "That silly poster. Now I remember. You were wearing a yellow bikini."

"Yes, well, the poster days are obviously long behind me."

"Praise God for that. The bikini was obscene."

Lilly looked surprised, then indignant. "There was nothing obscene about it. Compared to today it was modest."

His heavy brows drew together. "Covering your body with anything was obscene. You should have been nude."

"I'm outta here." Kevin headed back to the dining room.

Wild horses couldn't have dragged Molly from that kitchen, and she slipped a plate of pancakes in front of each of them.

"Nude?" Lilly's cup clattered into the saucer. "Not in this lifetime. I once passed up a fortune to pose for *Playboy*."

"What does *Playboy* have to do with it? I'm talking about art, not titillation." He tucked into the pancakes. "Excellent breakfast, Molly. Leave here and come cook for me."

"I'm actually a writer, not a cook."

"The children's books." His fork paused in midair. "I've thought about writing a children's book . . . " He speared one of Lilly's uneaten pancakes from her plate. "Probably not much of a market for my ideas."

Lilly sniffed. "Not if they involve nudes."

Molly giggled.

Jenner shot her a quelling gaze.

"Sorry." Molly bit her lip, then gave an unladylike snort.

Jenner's frown grew more ferocious. She was ready to

apologize again when she spotted a small quiver at the corner of his mouth. So Liam Jenner wasn't quite the curmudgeon he pretended to be. This was getting more and more interesting.

He gestured toward Lilly's half-filled mug. "You can take that with you. What's left of your breakfast, too. We need to go."

"I never said I'd sit for you. I don't like you."

• "Nobody does. And of course you'll sit for me." His voice deepened with sarcasm. "People stand in line for the honor."

"Paint Molly. Just look at those eyes."

Jenner studied her. Molly blinked self-consciously. "They're quite extraordinary," he said. "Her face is becoming interesting, but she hasn't lived in it long enough for it to be really fascinating."

"Hey, don't talk about me when I'm listening."

He lifted a dark eyebrow at Molly, then returned his attention to Lilly. "Is it just me, or are you this stubborn with everyone?"

"I'm not being stubborn. I'm simply protecting your reputation for artistic infallibility. Perhaps if I were twenty again, I'd pose for you, but—"

"Why would I be interested in painting you when you were twenty?" He seemed genuinely perplexed.

"Oh, I think that's obvious," Lilly said lightly.

He studied her for a moment, his expression difficult to read. Then he shook his head. "Of course. Our national obsession with emaciation. Aren't you a little old to be still buying into that?"

Lilly planted a perfect smile on her face as she got up from her chair. "Of course. Thank you for breakfast, Molly. Goodbye, Mr. Jenner."

His gaze followed her as she swept from the kitchen. Molly wondered if he noticed the tension she was carrying in her shoulders.

She left him to his own thoughts while he finished his coffee. Finally he picked up the plates from the table and carried them over to the sink. "Those were the best pancakes I've had in years. Tell me what I owe you."

"Owe me?"

"This is a commercial establishment," he reminded her.

"Oh, yeah. But there's absolutely no charge. It was my pleasure."

"I appreciate it." He turned to leave.

"Mr. Jenner."

"Just Liam."

She smiled. "Come for breakfast anytime you want. You can slip in through the kitchen."

He nodded slowly. "Thanks. I just might do that."

Chapter 14

"Come closer to the water, Daphne," Benny said.
"I won't get you wet."

Daphne Makes a Mess

"ANY IDEAS FOR A NEW BOOK?" PHOEBE ASKED EARLY THE NEXT afternoon over the phone.

An unwelcome subject, but since Molly had spent the first ten minutes of their conversation dodging Celia the Hen's nosy questions about Kevin, anything was an improvement. "A few. But remember that *Daphne Takes a Tumble* is the first book on a three-book contract. Birdcage won't accept another manuscript until I finish making the changes they want." No need to tell her sister she still hadn't started on those changes, although she'd borrowed Kevin's car after breakfast and gone into town to buy some art supplies.

"SKIFSA is a joke."

"Not a very funny one. I don't have a TV in the cottage. Have they popped up lately?"

"Last night. The new gay rights legislation in Congress has bought them a lot of local airtime." Phoebe's hesitation wasn't a good sign. "Moll, they mentioned Daphne again."

"I can't believe it! Why are they doing this? It's not like I'm a big-time children's author."

"This is Chicago, and you're the wife of the city's most famous quarterback. They're using that connection to get airtime. You *are* still Kevin's wife, aren't you?"

Molly didn't want to get into that discussion again. "Temporarily. Next time remind me to find a publisher with a little backbone." She wished she hadn't said that, since her publisher wasn't the only one who needed some backbone. Once again she reminded herself that she didn't have any choice, not if she wanted to pay her bills.

As if Phoebe had read her mind, she said, "How are you doing for money? I know you haven't—"

"I'm doing fine. No problem." As much as Molly loved her sister, she sometimes wished that everything Phoebe touched hadn't turned to gold. It made Molly feel so inadequate. Phoebe was wealthy, beautiful, and emotionally stable. Molly was poor, merely attractive, and she'd been a lot closer to a nervous breakdown than she'd ever admit. Phoebe had overcome enormous odds to become one of the most powerful owners in the NFL, but Molly couldn't even defend her fictional bunny from a real-life attack.

After she hung up, she chatted with some of the guests, then put fresh towels in the bathrooms while Kevin checked a retired couple from Cleveland into one of the cottages. Afterward she headed to her own cottage so she could change into the red suit he'd bought her and go for a swim.

As she pulled the two-piece suit from the bag, she discovered that the bottom wasn't quite a thong, but since it was held together by only a narrow tie on each side, it was a little skimpier than she liked. The top, however, had an underwire that pushed her up in all the right places, and Roo seemed to approve.

Although the air temperature was in the low eighties, the lake still hadn't warmed up, and the beach was deserted when she got there. She hissed against the cold as she waded in. Roo got his paws wet, then backed off and chased the herons instead. When she couldn't stand the torture any longer, she dove under.

She came up gasping, then began a vigorous sidestroke to keep warm as she caught sight of Kevin standing on the Common. Nine years of summer camp had taught her the importance of the buddy system, but he was near enough that he'd hear her yell if she started to drown.

She flipped to her back and swam for a while, avoiding the deeper water because, no matter what Kevin said, she was an extremely sensible person when it came to water safety. The next time she looked toward the Common, he was standing exactly where he'd been before.

He looked bored.

She waved her arm to catch his attention. He gave her a desultory wave back.

This wasn't good. This wasn't good at all.

She dove under and began to think.

Kevin watched Molly in the water while he waited for the garbage company to show up with the new Dumpster. He spotted a flash of crimson as she jackknifed, then dove beneath the surface. Buying that particular swimsuit for her had been a big mistake. It showed way too much of the tempting little body he was having an increasingly hard time ignoring. But the suit's color had caught his eye yesterday in the boutique because it was almost the same shade her hair had been the first time they'd met.

Her hair didn't look that way now. It had only been four days, but she was taking care of herself again, and her hair was the same rich color as the maple syrup he'd poured over the pancakes she'd made. He felt as if he were watching her come back to life. Her skin had lost its pasty look, and her eyes had begun to sparkle, especially when she wanted to give him a hard time.

Those eyes . . . That wicked slant shouted to the world that she was up to no good, but he seemed to be the only one who got the message. Phoebe and Dan saw brainy Molly, the lover of children, bunnies, and ridiculous dogs. Only he seemed to understand that Molly Somerville's veins had trouble rushing through them instead of blood.

On the flight back to Chicago, Dan had lectured him about how seriously she'd always taken everything. How as a kid she never did anything wrong. What a good student she'd been, a model citizen. He'd said that Molly was twenty-seven going on forty. Twenty-seven going on *seven* was more like it. No wonder she'd made a career as a children's book author. She was entertaining her peer group!

It galled him that she had the audacity to call him reckless. He'd never have given away fifteen million dollars. As far as he could tell, she didn't know anything about playing it safe.

He saw another flash of red in the water. All those years of summer camp had made her a good swimmer with a steady, graceful stroke. And a nice, neat body . . . But the last thing he wanted to do was start thinking about her body again, so he thought about the way she made him laugh.

Which didn't mean she wasn't a pain in the butt. She had a lot of nerve trying to poke around in his head, since it was screwed on a lot tighter than hers ever would be.

His eyes flicked back over the lake, but he couldn't see her. He waited for a flash of red. And waited . . . His shoulders grew tense as the surface remained smooth. He took a step forward. Then her head bobbed up, little more than a dot in the distance. Just before it disappeared again, she managed to shout one faint word.

"*Help!*"

He started to run.

Molly held her breath as long as she could, then resurfaced to fill her lungs. Sure enough, he'd just thrown himself into the water with a very nice racing dive.

This should get his adrenaline pumping.

She flailed around until she was sure he'd spotted her, then went under again, diving deep and swimming off to her right. It was a rotten thing to do, but it was for the greater good. A bored Kevin was an unhappy Kevin, and it was long past time he had some fun at the Wind Lake Campground. Maybe then he wouldn't be so anxious to sell it.

She surfaced again. Thanks to her crafty underwater change of direction, he was heading too far to the left. She caught another breath and went back under.

As Daphne went under for the third time, Benny swam—

Delete that.

As Benny went under for the third time, Daphne swam faster and faster . . .

Being rescued by Daphne would serve Benny right, Molly thought virtuously. He shouldn't have gone swimming without a buddy.

She opened her eyes underwater, but the lake was murky from all the rain, and she couldn't see much. She remembered how squeamish some of her campmates used to be about swimming in a lake instead of a pool—*What if a fish bites me?*—but Molly had grown used to it after her first summer, and she felt right at home.

Her lungs were starting to burn, and she came up for more air. He was about fifteen yards to her left. She refused to think about the boy and the wolf as she made her next move. *"Help!"*

He pivoted in the water, wet blond hair sticking to that superb forehead. "Hold on, Molly!"

"Hurry! I've got a"—*hole in my head*—"a cramp!" Down she went.

She cut to the right, swam the pattern, headed for the sideline—made ol' Number Eleven work for it.

Her lungs were burning again. Time to resurface near the goal line.

He'd spent two decades picking out receivers in a crowd, and he spotted her instantly. His stroke was powerful, and she got so caught up watching the way he churned through the water that she nearly forgot to go under again.

His hand brushed her thigh, then fastened around the skimpy bottom of her bathing suit.

His hand. On her butt. She should have thought further ahead.

He jerked hard on the suit to pull her to him, and the skimpy pair of ties that were holding it on snapped. He clamped his arm around her and pulled her to the surface.

The bottom part of the suit didn't come along.

As it trailed away in the water, she could only wonder how she'd gotten herself into this situation. Was this going to be her reward for doing a little good in the world?

"Are you all right?"

She glimpsed his face just before he started hauling her toward the shore. She'd really scared him. Part of her felt guilty, but she still remembered to cough and gasp for air as he dragged her through the water. At the same time she struggled with her modesty.

He wasn't even breathing heavily, and for a moment she let herself relax against him and enjoy the sensation of his body doing the work for hers. But it was hard to be both relaxed and bare-butt naked. "I—I had a cramp."

"Which leg is it?" His own leg brushed her hip, but he didn't seem to notice anything was missing.

"Stop—stop for a minute, will you?"

He slowed in the water and turned her in his arms without letting her go. She saw that anger had replaced his concern. "You shouldn't have been in the water by yourself! You could have drowned."

"It was . . . stupid."

"Which leg?"

"My . . . left. But it's better. I can move it now."

He let go of one arm to reach for her leg.

"No!" she squeaked, afraid of what he'd encounter on the way.

"Is it cramping again?"

"Not . . . exactly."

"Let's get to shore. I'll look at it there."

"I'm fine now. I can—"

He didn't pay any attention. Instead, he started hauling her toward the beach again.

"Uh, Kevin . . . " She coughed as she caught a mouthful.

"Keep still, damn it!"

Nice way for a PK to talk, especially to a drowning victim. She did her best to keep her lower half away from his lower half, but he kept sliding against her. Slip sliding . . . slip sliding . . . She groaned against a rush of sensation.

His rhythm changed, and she realized he'd touched bottom. She tried to disengage herself. "Let me go. I can walk now."

He swam farther in before he loosened his grip and stood. She dropped her feet.

The water came to her chin, but it was below his shoulders. Wet strands of hair plastered his forehead, and he looked grumpy. "You could be a tad more grateful, you know. I just saved your annoying life."

At least he didn't looked bored any longer. "Thank you."

He still had her arm, and he began moving toward the shore. "Have you ever had a cramp like this before?"

"Never. It took me completely by surprise."

"Why are you dragging your feet?"

"I'm cold. Probably a little shocky. Would you lend me your T-shirt?"

"Sure." He kept heading toward the beach.

She dragged her heels. "Could I have it now, please?"

"Now?" He stopped. The water lapped at her breasts. The red top had pushed them up quite nicely, and his gaze lingered. She noticed that his lashes had formed aggressive little spikes over those sharp green eyes, and she fought a sudden wobbliness in her knees.

"I'd like to put it on before we get out of the water," she said as pleasantly as she could.

He pulled his gaze from her breasts and started moving again. "It'll be easier to get you warm on the beach."

"Stop! Will you just stop!"

He did, but he was looking at her as if she'd sprung a fresh leak in the head.

She took a nibble out of her bottom lip. No good deed went unpunished, and she was going to have to tell him. "I have a slight problem . . . "

"I'll say. You don't have any sense. That Northwestern diploma you're so proud of should have read 'summa cum loony.'"

"Just give me your T-shirt. Please."

He made no move to take it off. Instead, he grew suspicious. "What kind of problem?"

"I seem to have . . . I'm really cold. Aren't you cold?"

He waited, that stubborn expression clearly indicating he wasn't going anywhere until she'd 'fessed up. She mustered her dignity. "I seem to have . . . " She cleared her throat. "Left the bottom half of my swimsuit . . . on the bottom."

Naturally, the first thing he did was stare straight down into the murky water.

"Stop that!"

As he gazed back up at her, his eyes looked less like jade daggers and more like happy green jelly beans. "How did you do that?"

"*I* didn't do it. *You* did. When you rescued me."

"I pulled off your suit?"

"You did."

He grinned. "I've always been damn good with women."

"Never mind. Just give me your stupid T-shirt!"

Was it accidental that his thigh brushed her hip? He gazed down into the water again, and she was possessed with a sudden crazy wish for all the murkiness to clear away. She heard something husky and seductive in his voice.

"So what you're telling me is that you're bare-ass naked under the water."

"You know exactly what I'm telling you."

"Now, this makes for an interesting dilemma."

"There's no dilemma."

He stroked the corner of his mouth with his thumb, and his smile was as soft as smoke. "We're up against the essence of true capitalism right here, right now, you and me, God bless America for the great country it is."

"What are you—"

"Pure capitalism. I have a commodity that you want—"

"My leg is starting to cramp again."

"The question is"—he lingered over his words, his eyes grazing her breasts—"what are you going to give me for that commodity?"

"I've been giving you my services as a cook," she said quickly.

"I don't know. Those sandals yesterday were pretty expensive. I think I've already paid for at least three days of cooking."

He was making her insides purr, and she didn't like it. "I won't be around for another day if you don't take that stupid shirt off your stupid overdeveloped chest right this second!"

"I never met such an ungrateful woman in my life." He started to pull it off, stalled to rub his arm, tugged on it again, inched it over his chest, flexed his gorgeous muscles . . .

"That's twenty yards for delay of game!"

"It's a five-yard penalty," he pointed out from under the T-shirt.

"Not today!"

He finally got it off, and she snatched it from him before he took it into his head to play keep-away, a game she was fairly certain an NFL quarterback could win against a bunny-book author.

"Bare-ass naked . . . " His smile grew broader.

She ignored him and struggled to put on the shirt, but handling all that wet cotton in bust-deep frigid water wasn't exactly easy. Naturally, he didn't help.

"Maybe it would work better if you climbed out of the water before you did that."

His humor was too infantile to merit a response. She finally got the T-shirt on inside out, but a huge air pocket left it billowing around her. She pushed it down and marched toward the shore, which was mercifully empty of guests.

Kevin stayed where he was and watched Molly emerge from the water. The view from behind was making it hard for him to take a good solid breath. It didn't seem to have occurred to her that white T-shirts pretty much turned to tissue paper when they got wet. First that trim little waist emerged, then curvy hips, then her legs, as sturdy and pretty as any he'd ever seen.

He swallowed hard at the sight of that sweet little bottom. The glaze of white T-shirt made it look as if it had been sponged with wet sugar.

He licked his lips. It was a good thing the water was cold enough for an iceberg, because the sight of her striding toward the beach had set him on fire. That small round bottom . . . the dark, seductive crevice. And he hadn't even caught the view from the front.

A circumstance he was about to change.

Molly heard Kevin splashing behind her. Then he was next to her, taking giant steps in the water. He pulled ahead, back muscles rippling as he pumped his arms. He hit the beach and turned around to face her.

Exactly what did he think was so interesting?

She began to feel nervous. One of his hands moved. He tugged absentmindedly on the front of his wet, low-riding jeans. "Maybe it's not so hard to believe your mother was a showgirl after all."

She glanced down at herself and yelped. Then she grabbed the T-shirt fabric, pulled it away from her body, and turned to rush back to the cottage.

"Uh . . . Molly? The view's pretty interesting from the back, too. And we've got company coming."

Sure enough, the Pearsons were approaching in the distance. They were barely visible behind beach chairs, tote bags, and a cooler.

Molly wasn't going to rely on Kevin's cooperation to get back to the cottage, so she headed toward the woods, holding the T-shirt away from her body in the front and back, while she stretched it to make it longer.

"If anybody throws you a fish," he called after her, "it's because you're waddling like a penguin."

"If anybody asks you to bray, it's because you're acting like an—"

"Save your sweet talk for later, Daphne. The garbage guys just drove up with the new Dumpster."

"Shut the lid after you climb in." She picked up her waddle and somehow managed to reach the cottage without further mishap. Once inside, she pressed her hands to her hot cheeks and laughed.

But Kevin wasn't laughing. As he stood on the Common gazing in the direction of the cottage, he knew he couldn't keep going on like this. It was ironic. He was a married man, but he wasn't taking advantage of the principal advantage marriage offered.

The question was, what did he intend to do about it?

Chapter 15

Daphne sprayed her favorite perfume, Eau de Strawberry Shortcake, in a big squirty puff around her head. Then she fluffed her ears, straightened her whiskers, and put on her brand-new tiara.

Daphne Plants a Pumpkin Patch

AFTER HER DIP IN THE LAKE, MOLLY SHOWERED AND CHANGED, then found herself walking out to the porch and gazing toward the table where she'd left the sack of art supplies she'd bought in town that morning. It was long past time to start work on the drawings.

Instead of settling at the table, however, she sat on the glider and picked up the pad she'd used yesterday to sketch Daphne diving off the cliff. She gazed off into the distance. Finally she began to write.

"Mrs. Mallard is building a summer camp on the other side of Nightingale Woods," Daphne announced one afternoon to Benny, Melissa, Celia the Hen, and Benny's pal Corky the Raccoon. "And we all get to go!"

"I don't like summer camp," Benny grumbled.

"Can I wear my movie-star sunglasses?" Melissa asked.

"What if it rains?" Celia clucked.

By the time Molly set aside the notepad, she'd written the beginning of *Daphne Goes to Summer Camp*. Never mind that she'd barely covered two pages, and never mind that her brain might dry up at any minute or that her publisher wouldn't buy this book until she did what they wanted to *Daphne Takes a Tumble*. At least she'd written, and for now she was happy.

The scent of lemon furniture polish greeted her as she walked into the B&B. The rugs had been vacuumed, the windows gleamed, and the tea table in the sitting room held a stack of Dresden rose china dessert plates with matching cups and saucers. Kevin's strategy of keeping the lovers separated until they'd finished their work seemed to be effective.

Amy emerged from the back with a pile of fresh white towels and took in the inexpensive canary-yellow sundress Molly had customized with four rows of colorful ribbon trim at the hem. "Wow! You look really cool. Nice makeup. I bet this'll get Kevin's attention."

"I'm not trying to get Kevin's attention."

Amy caressed the luscious little bruise at the base of her throat. "I've got this new perfume in my purse. It drives Troy nuts if I dab a little on my . . . well, you know. Do you want to borrow some?"

Molly avoided strangling her by making a dash for the kitchen.

It was too early to put out the apricot scones and oatmeal-butterscotch bread she'd made that morning, so she picked up her lovey and settled down with him on one of the kitchen chairs near the bay window. He tucked his topknot under her chin and rested his paw on her arm. She drew him closer. "Do you like it here as much as I do, pooch?"

He gave her an affirmative lick.

She gazed down the sloping yard toward the lake. These past few days in what she now thought of as Nightingale Woods had brought her back to life. She stroked Roo's warm belly and admitted that being with Kevin was a big part of it.

He was stubborn and cocky—maddening beyond belief—but he'd made her feel alive again.

For all his talk about how smart *she* was, he didn't have any trouble keeping up with her. Like a few other jocks she knew—Dan sprang to mind, along with Cal Bonner and Bobby Tom Denton—Kevin's passion for athletics ran side by side with a keen intellect that his doofus behavior couldn't hide.

Not that she'd ever compare Kevin with Dan. Look at the way Dan loved dogs, for example. And kids. And most of all, look at the way Dan loved Phoebe.

She sighed again and let her gaze wander toward the gardens in the back, where Troy had finally cleared away the winter debris. The lilacs were in bloom, and a few irises displayed their purple ruffles, while a peony bush prepared to open.

A flicker of movement caught Molly's eye, and she saw Lilly sitting off to the side on an iron bench. At first Molly thought she was reading, but then she realized she was sewing instead. She thought about Lilly's coolness toward her and wondered if she were reacting personally or to the bad publicity from the wedding? . . . *the Chicago Stars football heiress who dabbles in writing children's books* . . . Molly hesitated, then rose and let herself out the back door.

Lilly sat near a small herb garden. Molly found it odd that someone who played the diva so convincingly hadn't objected to being stuck away in an attic. And despite that Armani sweater tossed so casually around her shoulders, she seemed remarkably content simply sitting by an overgrown garden and sewing. She was a puzzle. It was hard for Molly to warm up to someone who was so cold to her, but she couldn't quite dislike Lilly and not just because of her old affection for *Lace, Inc.* It took courage to stick around in the face of Kevin's hostility.

Marmie lay at Lilly's feet next to a large sewing basket. Roo ignored the cat to trot over and greet her owner, who leaned down to pat him. Molly realized she was working on a piece of a quilt, but it didn't look like anything she'd ever seen. The design wasn't a neatly arranged geometric, but a subtly shaded medley of curves and swirls in various patterns and shades of green, with touches of lavender and a surprising dab of sky blue.

"That's beautiful. I didn't know you were an artist."

The familiar hostility that formed in Lilly's eyes gave the summer afternoon a January chill. "This is just a hobby."

Molly decided to ignore the freeze-out. "You're very good. What's it going to be?"

"Probably a real quilt," she said reluctantly. "Usually I do smaller pieces like pillows, but this garden seems to demand something more dramatic."

"You're doing a quilt of the garden?"

Lilly's inherent good manners forced her to respond. "Just the herb garden. I started experimenting with it yesterday."

"Do you work from a drawing?"

Lilly shook her head, attempting to put an end to the conversation. Molly considered letting her do it, but she didn't want to. "How can you make something this complicated without a drawing?"

Lilly took her time responding. "I start putting scraps together that appeal to me, and then I pull out my scissors and see what happens. Sometimes the results are disastrous."

Molly understood. She created from bits and pieces, too—a few lines of dialogue, random sketches. She never knew what her books were about until she was well into them. "Where do you get your fabrics?"

Roo had propped his chin on one of Lilly's pricey Kate Spade sandals, but Molly's persistence seemed to bother her more. "I always have a box of scraps in my trunk," she said brusquely. "I buy a lot of remnants, but this project needs fabrics with some history. I'll probably try to find an antique store that sells vintage clothing."

Molly gazed back at the herb garden. "Tell me what you see."

She expected a rebuff, but, again, Lilly's good manners won out. "I was drawn to the lavender first. It's one of my favorite plants. And I love the silver of that sage behind it." Lilly's enthusiasm for her project began to overcome her personal dislike. "The spearmint needs to be weeded out. It's greedy, and it'll take over. That little tuft of thyme is fighting to survive against it."

"Which one is the thyme?"

"Those tiny leaves. It's vulnerable now, but it can be as aggressive as spearmint. It just goes about it more subtly." Lilly lifted her eyes, and her gaze held Molly's for a moment.

Molly got the message. "You think the thyme and I have something in common?"

"Do you?" she asked coolly.

"I have a lot of faults, but subtlety isn't one of them."

"I suppose that remains to be seen."

Molly wandered to the edge of the garden. "I'm trying hard to dislike you as much as you seem to dislike me, but it's tough. You were my heroine when I was a little girl."

"How nice." Icicles dripped.

"Besides, you like my dog. And I have a feeling that your attitude has less to do with my personality than it has to do with your concerns about my marriage."

Lilly stiffened.

Molly decided she had nothing to lose by being blunt. "I know about your real relationship with Kevin."

Lilly's fingers stalled on her needle. "I'm surprised he told you. Maida said he never spoke about it."

"He didn't. I guessed."

"You're very astute."

"You've taken a long time to come see him."

"After abandoning him, you mean?" Her voice had a bitter edge.

"I didn't say that."

"You were thinking it. What kind of woman abandons her child then tries to worm her way back into his life?"

Molly spoke carefully. "I doubt that you abandoned him. You seem to have found him a good home."

She gazed at the garden, but Molly suspected the peace she'd felt here earlier had vanished. "Maida and John had always wanted a child, and they loved him from the day he was born. But as torturous as it was to make my decision, I still gave him up too easily."

"Hey, Molly!"

Lilly tensed as Kevin came around the corner with Marmie lolling fat and happy in his arms. He stopped abruptly when he saw Lilly, and, as Molly watched, the charmer gave way to a hard-eyed man with a grudge.

He approached Molly as if she were alone in the garden. "Somebody let her out."

"I did," Lilly said. "She was with me until a few minutes ago. She must have heard you coming."

"This is your cat?"

"Yes."

He put her on the ground, almost as if she'd gone radioactive, then turned to walk away.

Lilly came up off the bench. Molly saw something both desperate and touching in her expression. "Do you want to know about your father?" Lilly blurted out.

Kevin stiffened. Molly's heart went out to him as she thought of all the questions she'd had over the years about her own mother. Slowly he turned.

Lilly clutched her hands. She sounded breathless, as if she'd just run a long distance. "His name was Dooley Price. I don't think that was his real first name, but it was all I knew. He was eighteen, a tall, skinny farm kid from Oklahoma. We met at the bus station the day we arrived in L.A." She drank in Kevin's face. "His hair was as light as yours, but his features were broader. You look more like me." She dipped her head. "I'm sure you don't want to hear that. Dooley was athletic. He'd ridden in rodeos—earned some prize money, I think—and he was convinced he could get rich doing stunts in the movies. I don't remember any more about him—another black mark you can chalk up against me. I think he smoked Marlboros and loved candy bars, but it was a long time ago, and that could have been someone else. We'd broken up by the time I discovered I was pregnant, and I didn't know how to find him." She paused and seemed to brace herself. "A few years later I read in the paper that he'd been killed doing some kind of stunt with a car."

Kevin's expression remained stony. He wouldn't let anyone see that this meant anything to him. Oh, Molly understood all about that.

Roo was sensitive to people's distress. He got up and rubbed against Kevin's ankles.

"Do you have a picture of him?" Molly asked because she knew Kevin wouldn't. The only photograph she had of her mother was her most treasured possession.

Lilly made a helpless gesture and shook her head. "We were only kids—two screwed-up teenagers. Kevin, I'm sorry."

He regarded her coldly. "There's no place for you in my life. I don't know how I can make that any clearer. I want you to leave."

"I know you do."

Both animals got up and followed him as he walked away.

Lilly's eyes glistened with fierce tears as she spun on Molly. "I'm not leaving!"

"I don't think you should," Molly replied.

Their eyes locked, and Molly thought she saw a faint crack forming in the wall between them.

*   *   *

Half an hour later, as Molly slipped the last of her apricot scones into a wicker basket, Amy appeared to announce that she and Troy would be staying in the upstairs bedroom Kevin had abandoned when he'd moved into Molly's cottage. "Somebody has to sleep here at night," Amy explained, "and Kevin said he'd pay us extra to do it. Isn't that cool?"

"That's great."

"I mean, we won't be able to make noise, but—"

"Get the jam, will you?" Molly couldn't bear hearing any more details of Amy and Troy's Super Bowl sex life.

But Amy wouldn't give up, and the buttery late-afternoon sunlight splashed her love-bitten neck as she regarded Molly earnestly. "It looks like things with you and Kevin could still work out if you just, maybe, tried a little harder. I'm serious about the perfume. Sex is real important to men, and if you'd just use a little—"

Molly shoved the scones at her and made a dash for the sitting room.

Later, when she got back to the cottage, Kevin was already there. He sat on the droopy old couch in the front room with Roo lolling on the cushion next to him. His feet were propped up, and a book lay open in his lap. Although he looked as if he didn't have a care in the world, Molly knew better.

He glanced up at her. "I like this Benny guy."

Her heart sank as she realized he was reading *Daphne Says Hello*. The other four books in the series lay nearby.

"Where did you get those?"

"Last night when I went into town. There's a kids' store— mainly clothes, but the owner sells some books and toys, too. She had these in the window. When I told her you were here, she got pretty excited about it." He tapped the page with his index finger. "This Benny character—"

"Those are children's books. I can't imagine why you'd bother reading them."

"Curiosity. You know, there are a couple of things about Benny that seem kind of familiar. For example—"

"Really? Well, thank you. He's entirely imaginary, but I do try to give all my characters qualities that readers can identify with."

"Yeah, well, I can identify with Benny, all right." He gazed down at a drawing of Benny wearing sunglasses that looked very much like his silver-rimmed Rēvos. "One thing I don't understand . . . The store owner said she'd gotten some pressure from one of her customers to take the books off the shelf because they were pornographic. Tell me what I'm missing."

Roo finally hopped off the couch and came over to greet her. She leaned down to pat him. "Have you ever heard of SKIFSA? Straight Kids for a Straight America?"

"Sure. They get their kicks going after gays and lesbians. The women all have big hair, and the men show too much teeth when they smile."

"Exactly. And right now they're after my bunny."

"What do you mean?" Roo trotted back to Kevin.

"They're attacking the Daphne series as homosexual propaganda."

Kevin started to laugh.

"I'm not kidding. They hadn't paid any attention to my books until we got married, but after all the stories about us appeared in the press, they decided to jump on the publicity bandwagon and go after me." She found herself telling him about her conversation with Helen and the changes Birdcage wanted in the Daphne books.

"I hope you told her exactly what she could do with her changes."

"It's not that easy. I have a contract, and they're keeping

Daphne Takes a Tumble off the publication schedule until I send them the new illustrations." She didn't mention the rest of the advance money they owed her. "Besides, it's not as if moving Daphne and Melissa a few inches farther apart affects the story."

"Then why haven't you done the drawings?"

"I've had some troubles with . . . with writer's block. But it's gotten a lot better since I've been here."

"So now you're going to do them?"

She didn't like the disapproval she detected in his voice. "It's easy to stand on principle when you have a few million dollars in the bank, but I don't."

"I guess."

She got up and headed into the kitchen. As she pulled out a bottle of wine, Roo rubbed against her ankles. She heard Kevin come up behind her.

"We're drinking again, are we?"

"You're strong enough to fight me off if I get out of hand."

"Just don't make me hurt my passing arm."

She smiled and poured. He took the glass she handed him, and by unspoken agreement they walked together out onto the porch. The glider squeaked as he eased down next to her and took a sip of wine.

"You're a good writer, Molly. I can see why kids like your books. When you were drawing Benny, did you happen to notice how much—"

"What's with you and my pooch?"

"Damned if I know." He glared down at the poodle, who'd collapsed over one of his feet. "He followed me back here from the B&B. Believe me, I didn't encourage it."

Molly remembered the way Roo had picked up on Kevin's distress in the garden with Lilly. Apparently they had bonded, only Kevin didn't know it yet.

"How's your leg?" he asked.

"Leg?"

"Any aftereffects from that cramp?"

"It's . . . a little sore. Very sore. Sort of this dull throb. Pretty painful, actually. I'll have to take some Tylenol. But I'm sure it'll be better by tomorrow."

"No more swimming alone, okay? I'm serious. It was a stupid thing to do." He propped his arm along the back of the cushions and gave her his I-mean-business-you-lowlife-rookie look. "And while we're at it, don't get too cozy with Lilly."

"I don't think you have to worry about that. In case you didn't notice, she's not too fond of me. Still, I think you need to hear her out."

"That's not going to happen. This is my life, Molly, and you don't understand anything about it."

"That's not exactly true," she said carefully. "I'm an orphan, too."

He withdrew his arm. "You don't get to call yourself an orphan if you're over twenty-one."

"The point is, my mother died when I was two, so I know something about feeling disconnected from your roots."

"Our circumstances aren't anything alike, so don't try to make comparisons." He gazed out into the woods. "I had two great parents. You didn't have any."

"I had Phoebe and Dan."

"You were a teenager by then. Before that, you seem to have raised yourself."

He was deliberately turning the conversation away from himself. She understood that, too, and she let him do it. "Me and Danielle Steel."

"What are you talking about?"

"I was a fan, and I knew she had lots of kids. I used to pretend I was one of them." She smiled at his amusement. "Now, some might find that pathetic, but I think it was pretty creative."

"It's definitely original."

"Then I'd fantasize a mercifully painless death for Bert, at which point it would be magically revealed that he wasn't my father at all. My real father was—"

"Let me guess. Bill Cosby."

"I wasn't that well adjusted. It was Bruce Springsteen. And no comments, okay?"

"Why should I comment when Freud already did the job?"

Molly wrinkled her nose at him. They sat in surprisingly companionable silence, broken only by Roo's rhythmic snores. But Molly'd never been good at leaving well enough alone. "I still think you need to hear her out."

"I can't come up with a single reason why."

"Because she won't go away until you do. And because this will keep hovering over you for the rest of your life."

He set down his glass. "Maybe the reason you're so obsessed with analyzing my life is so you won't get depressed thinking about your own neuroses."

"Probably."

He rose from the glider. "What do you say we go into town for some dinner?"

She'd already spent far too much time with him today, but she couldn't stand the idea of staying here alone tonight while he painted the town German chocolate. "I suppose. Let me get a sweater."

As she headed back to her bedroom, she told herself what she already knew. Going out to dinner with him was a lousy idea, just as lousy as the two of them sitting around on the porch drinking wine together. Almost as lousy as not insisting he sleep under another roof.

Even though she didn't care about impressing him, she decided a shawl would make a better fashion statement with her sundress than a sweater, and she whipped out the bright red tablecloth she'd discovered in the bottom drawer of the dresser. As she unfolded it, she spotted something strange on the table next to her bed, something that hadn't been there earlier and that definitely didn't belong to her. *"Aarrrggghhhh!"*

Kevin shot into the room. "What's wrong?"

"Look at that!" She pointed at the small bottle of drug-store perfume. "That meddling little . . . *trollop!*"

"What are you talking about?"

"Amy stuck that perfume there!" She rounded on him. "Bite me!"

"Why are you mad at me? I didn't do it."

"No! Bite me. Give me a hickey right here." She jabbed her finger at a spot a few inches above her collarbone.

"You want me to give you a hickey?"

"Are you deaf?"

"Just thunderstruck."

"There's no one else I can ask, and I can't stand spending another day getting marital advice from a nineteen-year-old nymphomaniac. This'll put a stop to it."

"Did anybody ever mention you might be a few french fries short of a Happy Meal?"

"Go ahead. Make fun of me. She doesn't condescend to you the same way she does to me."

"Forget it. I'm not giving you a hickey."

"Fine. I'll get someone else to do it."

"You will not!"

"Desperate times call for desperate measures. I'll ask Charlotte Long."

"That's disgusting."

"She knows how the lovebirds behave. She'll understand."

"The image of that woman chomping on your neck just took away my appetite. And don't you think it'll be a little embarrassing showing off your bruise when other people are around?"

"I'll wear something with a collar, and I'll flip it up."

"Then push it right back down when you see Amy."

"Okay, I'm not proud of myself. But if I don't do something, I'm going to strangle her."

"She's just a teenager. Why do you care?"

"Fine. Forget it."

"And have you run off to Charlotte Long?" His voice dropped a husky note. "I don't think so."

She swallowed. "You'll do it?"

"I guess I have to."

Oh, boy . . . She squeezed her eyes shut and tilted her neck toward him. Her heart started to pound. What did she think she was doing?

Not a thing, apparently, because he didn't touch her.

She opened her eyes and blinked. "Could you, uh, hurry up?"

He didn't touch her, but neither did he move away. Oh, God, why did he have to be so gorgeous? Why couldn't he have wrinkly skin and a big potbelly instead of being a walking advertisement for hard bodies? "What are you waiting for?"

"I haven't given a girl a hickey since I was fourteen."

"I'm sure it'll come back if you concentrate."

"Concentration isn't my problem."

The gleam in those smoky green eyes indicated that her behavior had put her right on the border between eccentric and insane. Her burst of temper had faded. She had to extricate herself. "Oh, never mind."

She spun around to leave, but he caught her arm. The feel of his fingers on her skin made her shiver. "I didn't say I wouldn't. I just need to warm up a little."

Even if her feet had caught fire, she couldn't have moved.

"I can't just lunge and bite." His thumb stroked her arm. "It's not in my nature." Goose bumps quivered over her skin as he lifted his hand and trailed a finger over the curve of her neck.

Her voice developed a really annoying rasp. "It's all right. Go ahead and lunge."

"I'm a professional athlete." His words were a seductive caress as he traced a lazy S to the base of her throat. "Lack of a proper warm-up leads to injuries."

"That's the point, isn't it? An . . . injury?"

He didn't reply, and she stopped breathing as his mouth came closer. She felt a shock when his lips brushed the corner of hers.

He hadn't even made a direct hit, but her bones melted. She heard a soft, indecipherable sound and realized it had come from her, the easiest woman on planet earth.

He pulled her against him, a gentle movement, but the contact sizzled. Hard bone and warm flesh. She wanted all of his mouth, and she turned her head to find it, but he altered course. Instead of giving her the kiss she yearned for, he touched the opposite corner of her mouth.

Her blood pounded. His lips trailed from her jaw to her neck. Then he got ready to do exactly as she'd asked.

I've changed my mind! Please don't bite!

He didn't. He played at her throat until her breathing came fast and shallow. She hated him for teasing her, but couldn't make herself push away. And then he put an end to the game and kissed her for real.

The world spun, and everything turned upside down. His arms cradled her as if she really belonged inside them. She didn't know whose lips parted first, but their tongues touched.

It was a kiss made in lonely dreams. A kiss that took its time. A kiss that felt so right she couldn't remember all the reasons it was wrong.

His hand plowed through her hair, and those hard hips pressed against hers. She felt what she'd done to him and loved it. Her breast tingled as he covered it with his palm.

He yelped and snatched his hand away. "Damn it!"

She sprang back and instinctively checked to see if her

breast had grown teeth. But it wasn't her breast.

He glared down at Roo, whose sharp, canine nails were digging into his leg. "Go away, mutt!"

Reality crashed back in on her. Just what did she think she was doing playing kissy-face with Mr. I'm Too Sexy? And she couldn't even blame him for letting things get out of hand because she was the one who'd started it.

"Stop it, Roo." Shaken, she pulled the dog away.

"Don't you ever trim the Klingon's toenails?"

"He wasn't attacking you. He just wanted to play."

"Yeah? Well, so did I!"

A long silence quivered between them.

She wanted him to be the first to look away, but he didn't, so she looked right back. It was unnerving. While she felt like hiding under the bed, he seemed perfectly willing to stand there all evening and think things over. The breast he'd touched still felt warm.

"This is getting complicated," he finally said.

She was messing with the NFL, so she ignored her rubbery legs. "Not for me. You're an okay kisser, by the way. So many athletes gnaw."

The corners of his eyes crinkled. "You just keep fighting, Daphne. Now, are we going to get dinner, or should we get back to work on that hickey you want so bad?"

"Forget the hickey. Sometimes the cure is worse than the disease."

"And sometimes bunny ladies turn into chickens."

She wasn't going to win this game, so she stuck her nose in the air like the rich heiress she wasn't, then grabbed the red tablecloth and swirled it around her shoulders.

The North Woods décor made the dining room of the Wind Lake Inn feel like an old hunting lodge. Indian-blanket-print curtains hung at the long, narrow windows, and the rustic walls displayed a collection of snowshoes and antique animal traps, along with the mounted heads of deer and elk. Molly focused on the birchbark canoe hanging from the rafters instead of those staring glass eyes.

Kevin was getting good at reading her mind, and he nodded toward the dead animals. "There used to be this restaurant in New York that specialized in exotic game—kangaroo, tiger, elephant steaks. One time some friends took me there for lionburgers."

"That's revolting! What kind of sick person would eat Simba?"

He chuckled and returned to his trout. "Not me. I had hash browns and pecan pie instead."

"You're messing with me. Stop it."

His eyes took a few lazy tango steps over her body. "You didn't mind earlier."

She toyed with the stem of her wineglass. "It was the alcohol."

"It was the sex we're not having."

She opened her mouth to cut him off at the knees, but he cut her off first. "Save your breath, Daph. It's time you faced a few important facts. Number one, we're married. Number two, we're living under the same roof—"

"Not by my choice."

"And number three, we're both celibate at the moment."

"You can't be celibate for a moment. It's a long-term lifestyle. Believe me, I know." She hadn't meant to say the last part out loud. Or maybe she had. She speared a carrot coin she didn't want to eat.

He set down his fork to study her more closely. "You're kidding, aren't you?"

"Of course I'm kidding." She gobbled up the carrot. "Did you think I was serious?"

He rubbed his chin. "You aren't kidding."

"Do you see the waiter? I think I'm ready for dessert."

"Care to elaborate?"

"No."

He bided his time.

She fiddled with another piece of carrot, then shrugged. "I've got issues."

"So does *Time* magazine. Stop hedging."

"First tell me where you think this conversation is going."

"You know where. Straight to the bedroom."

"Bedrooms," she emphasized, wishing he didn't look so grim about it. "His and hers. And it has to stay that way."

"A couple of days ago I'd have agreed with you. But both of us know that if it hadn't been for Godzilla's toenails, we'd be naked right now."

She shivered. "You don't know that for a fact."

"Listen, Molly, the newspaper ad doesn't come out until next Thursday. Today's only Saturday. It'll take another couple of days for interviews. Then another day or so to train whoever I hire. That's a lot of nights."

She'd wimped around long enough, and she abandoned all pretense of eating. "Kevin, I don't do casual sex."

"Now, that's weird. I seem to remember a night last February . . . "

"I had a crush on you, all right? A stupid crush that got out of hand."

"A crush?" He leaned back in the chair, beginning to enjoy himself. "What are you, twelve?"

"Stop being a jerk."

"So you had a crush on me?"

His crooked smile looked exactly like Benny's when he thought he had Daphne right where he wanted her. The bunny didn't like it, and neither did Molly.

"I had crushes on you and Alan Greenspan both at the same time. I can't imagine what I was thinking of. Although the crush I had on Greenspan was a lot worse. Thank God I didn't run into him with that sexy briefcase."

He ignored that bit of folderol. "Interesting that Daphne seems to have a crush on Benny, too."

"She does not! He's horrible to her."

"Maybe if she'd put out, he'd be nicer."

"That's more disgusting than me and Charlotte Long!" She needed to sidetrack this conversation. "You can get sex anywhere, but we have a friendship, and that's more important."

"A friendship?"

She nodded.

"Yeah, I guess we do. Maybe that's what makes this exciting. I've never had sex with a friend before."

"It's nothing more than a fascination with the forbidden."

"I don't see why it's forbidden to you." He frowned. "I have a lot more to lose."

"Exactly how do you figure that?"

"Come on. You know how I feel about my career. Your closest family members happen to be my employers, and I'm on shaky ground with them at the moment. This is exactly why I always keep my female relationships separate from the team. I've never even dated one of the Star Girl cheerleaders."

"Yet here you are, all ready to get jiggy with the boss's sister."

"I've got everything to lose. You don't have anything."

Just this fragile little heart of mine.

He ran his thumb along the stem of his wineglass. "The truth is, a few nights of sexual dalliance might help your writing career."

"I can't wait to hear this."

"It'll reprogram your subconscious so you don't send out any more secret homosexual messages in your books."

She rolled her eyes.

He grinned.

"Give me a break, Kevin. If we were back in Chicago, it wouldn't occur to you to even think about having sex with me. How flattering is that?"

"It sure as hell would occur to me if we were together all the time like we are here."

He was deliberately missing the point, but before she could tell him that, the waitress appeared to see if there was anything wrong with the meals they weren't eating.

Kevin assured her there wasn't. She gave him a full-blast smile and began chatting with him as if he were her best friend. Since people reacted the same way to Dan and Phoebe, Molly was used to this kind of interruption, but the waitress was cute and curvy, so she found it annoying.

When the woman finally left, Kevin settled back in his chair and picked up the one part of their conversation she most wished he'd forgotten. "This celibacy thing . . . how long has that been going on?"

She took her time cutting a small piece of chicken. "A while."

"Any particular reason?"

She chewed slowly, as if she were thinking over his question instead of trying to find a way out. There wasn't any, so she attempted to sound grand and mysterious. "A choice I made."

"Is this one more part of that good girl thing everybody in the world believes about you except me?"

"I am a good girl!"

"You're a brat."

She sniffed, a little pleased, but not letting on. "Why should a virtuous woman have to justify herself? Or semivirtuous anyway, so don't think I was a virgin before I lost my mind with you." But in some ways she was a virgin. Although she knew about sex, neither of her two affairs had taught her anything about making love, and neither had that awful night with Kevin.

"Because we're friends, remember? Friends tell each other things. You already know a lot more about me than almost anybody."

She didn't like being more embarrassed about this disclosure than she'd been when she told him she'd given away her inheritance, so she tried her best to look pious by putting her elbows on the table and making little prayer hands. "Being sexually discriminating is nothing to be ashamed about."

In some ways he understood her better than her own family, and his raised eyebrow told her she hadn't impressed him.

"I'm just—I know a lot of people treat sex casually, but I can't do that. I think it's too important."

"I'm not going to argue with you."

"Well, then, that's it."

"I'm glad."

Was it her imagination, or did she detect a little smugness in his expression?

"You're glad about what? That you've had a stadium full of easy women while I've been keeping my legs crossed? Talk about a double standard."

"Hey, I'm not proud of it. It's programmed in those X chromosomes. And it hasn't been a stadium full."

"Let me put it like this: Some people can handle sex without commitment, but it turns out that I'm not one of them, so it would be better if you'd move back into the house."

"Technically speaking, Daph, I've made a pretty big commitment to you, and I'm thinking it's payback time."

"Sex is not a commodity. You can't bargain with it."

"Who says?" His smile turned positively diabolical. "There were lots of nice-looking clothes at that boutique in town, and I can be real free with my credit card."

"What a proud moment this is for me. Bunny-book author turned hooker in one easy step."

He liked that, but his rumble of laughter was interrupted by a couple approaching from the other side of the dining room. "Excuse me, but aren't you Kevin Tucker? Hey, my wife and I are big fans . . . "

Molly settled back and sipped her coffee while Kevin dealt with his admirers. The man made her melt, and there was no use pretending otherwise. If it were just his good looks that attracted her, he wouldn't be so dangerous, but that cocky charm was chipping away at her defenses. As for the kiss they'd shared . . .

Stop right there! Just because their kiss had knocked her off her feet didn't mean she was going to act on it. She'd only begun to pull out of her emotional tailspin, and she wasn't self-destructive enough to throw herself back into it. She simply needed to keep reminding herself that Kevin was bored, and he wanted a little hanky-panky. The grim truth was that any woman would do, and she happened to be handy. Still, she could no longer deny that her old crush was back.

Some women were too dumb to draw breath.

Kevin tossed down the last of the Daphne books Molly had tried unsuccessfully to hide when they returned to the cottage. He couldn't believe it! Half of his recent life lay on the pages she'd written. Expurgated, of course. But still . . .

He was Benny the Badger! His red Harley . . . His Jet Ski . . . That very minor skydiving incident blown *way* out of proportion . . . And Benny snowboarding down Old Cold Mountain wearing a pair of silver Rēvos. He should sue!

Except he was flattered. She was a terrific writer, and the stories were great—kid-hip and funny. Although there was one thing he didn't like about the Daphne books—the bunny generally ended up getting the upper hand over the badger. What kind of message was that to send to little boys? Or big ones, for that matter?

He leaned back on the saggy excuse for a couch and glared toward the bedroom door she'd shut behind her. His good mood from dinner had faded. He'd have to be blind not to know that she was attracted to him. So what was the point?

She wanted to jerk his chain, that was the point. She wanted to make him beg so she could feel like she had her pride back. This whole thing was some kind of power trip for her. She was getting off on being cute and funny around him, making him enjoy her company, fluffing her hair, wearing funky clothes designed just so he'd itch to pull them off her. Then, when it was time to do exactly that, she jumped back and said she didn't believe in sex without *commitment*. Bull.

He needed a shower—a cold one—but there was only that pint-size bathtub. God, he hated it here. Why was she making such a big frickin' deal out of this? She might have said no at dinner, but when he'd kissed her, that sweet little body sure had been saying yes. They were *married*! He was the one who had to compromise himself, not her!

His policy of never mixing business with pleasure had blown up in his face. The trouble he was having keeping his eyes off the bedroom door filled him with self-disgust. He was Kevin Tucker, damn it, and he didn't have to beg for any woman's affections, not when there were so many others standing in line trying to catch his attention.

Well, he'd had enough. From now on he was going to be all business. He'd take care of the campground and step up his workouts so he was in top shape when training camp started. As for that irritating little brat who happened to be his wife . . . Until they got back to Chicago, it was strictly hands off.

Chapter 16

"My boyfriend's parents were gone for the night,
and he invited me over. As soon as I walked in the
door, I knew what was going to happen . . . "

"My Boyfriend's Bedroom"
for Chik

LILLY HATED HERSELF FOR SAYING YES, BUT WHAT ART LOVER COULD
turn down an invitation to visit Liam Jenner's house and
see his private collection? Not that the invitation had been
issued graciously. Lilly had just come in from a Sunday-
morning walk when Amy handed her the telephone.

"If you want to see my paintings, come to my house this
afternoon at two," he'd barked. "No earlier. I'm working, and
I won't answer the bell."

She'd definitely been in L.A. too long, because she almost
found his rudeness refreshing. As she turned off the highway
and onto the side road he'd indicated, she realized how accustomed she'd grown to meaningless compliments and
empty flattery. She'd nearly forgotten that people still existed
who said exactly what was on their minds.

She spotted the weather-beaten turquoise mailbox he'd
told her to look for. It perched crookedly on a battered metal
pole set in a tractor tire filled with cement. The ditch behind
the tire held rusted bedsprings and a twisted sheet of corru-
gated tin, which made the NO TRESPASSING sign at the top of
the rutted, overgrown lane seem superfluous.

She turned in and slowed to a crawl. Even so, her car lurched alarmingly in the ruts. She'd just decided to abandon it and walk the rest of the way when the overgrowth disappeared and fresh gravel smoothed the bumpy road surface. Moments later she caught her breath as the house came into view.

It was a sleekly modern structure with white concrete parapets, stone ledges, and glass. Everything about the design bore Liam Jenner's signature. As she got out of the car and made her way toward the niche that held the front door, she wondered where he'd found an architect saintly enough to work with him.

She glanced down at her watch and saw that she was exactly half an hour late for this command performance. Just as she'd intended.

The door swung open. She waited for him to bark at her for not being on time and was disappointed when he merely nodded, then stepped back to let her in.

She caught her breath. The glass wall opposite the entrance had been constructed in irregular sections bisected by a narrow iron catwalk some ten feet from the ground floor. Through the glass she could see the sweeping vista of lake, cliffs, and trees.

"What an amazing house."

"Thanks. Would you like something to drink?"

His request sounded cordial, but she was even more impressed that he'd traded in his paint-stained denim shirt and shorts for a black silk shirt and light gray slacks. Ironically, his civilized clothes only emphasized the Sturm und Drang of that rugged face.

She declined his offer for a drink. "I'd love a tour, though."

"All right."

The house hugged the terrain in two uneven sections, the larger of which held an open living area, kitchen, library, and cantilevered dining room, with several smaller bedrooms tucked into lower levels. The catwalk she'd seen when she'd entered led to a glass-enclosed tower that Liam told her held his studio. She hoped he'd let her see it, but he showed her only the master bedroom below, a space designed with an almost monastic simplicity.

Magnificent works of art were on display everywhere, and Liam talked about them with passion and discernment. An enormous Jasper Johns canvas hung not far from a contemplative composition in blues and beige by Agnes Martin. One of Bruce Nauman's neon sculptures flickered near the library archway. Across from it hung a work by David Hockney, then a portrait of Liam done by Chuck Close. An imposing Helen Frankenthaler canvas occupied one long wall of the living area, and a totemlike stone-and-wood sculpture dominated a hallway. The very best of the world's contemporary artists were represented in this house. All except Liam Jenner.

Lilly waited until the tour was over and they'd returned to the central living area before she asked about it. "Why haven't you hung any of your own paintings?"

"Looking at my work when I'm not in the studio feels too much like a busman's holiday."

"I suppose. But they'd be so joyous in this house."

He stared at her for a long moment. Then the craggy lines of his face softened in a smile. "You really are a fan, aren't you?"

"I'm afraid so. I bid on one of your paintings a few months ago—*Composition #3*. My business manager forced me to drop out at two hundred and fifty thousand."

"Obscene, isn't it?"

He looked so pleased that she laughed. "You should be ashamed of yourself. It wasn't worth a penny over two hundred thousand. And I'm just beginning to realize how much I hate giving you compliments. You truly are the most overbearing man."

"It makes life easier."

"Keeps the masses at a distance?"

"I value my privacy."

"Which explains why you've built such an extraordinary house in the wilds of northern Michigan instead of Big Sur or Cap d'Antibes."

"Already you know me well."

"You're such a diva. I'm certain I've had my privacy invaded far more than you have, but it hasn't turned me into a hermit. Do you know that I still can't go anywhere without people recognizing me?"

"My nightmare."

"Why is it such a big deal to you?"

"Old baggage."

"Tell me."

"It's an incredibly boring story. You don't want to hear it."

"Believe me, I do." She sat on the couch to encourage him. "I love hearing people's stories."

He gazed at her, then sighed. "The critics discovered me just before my twenty-sixth birthday. Are you sure you want to hear this?"

"Definitely."

He stuck his hands in his pockets and wandered toward the windows. "I became the proverbial overnight sensation—on everybody's guest list, the subject of national magazine articles. I had people throwing money at me."

"I remember what that was like."

The fact that she understood what he'd gone through in ways most people couldn't seemed to relax him. He left the windows to sprawl down across from her, dominating the chair he'd chosen in the same way he dominated every space he occupied. She felt a moment of uneasiness. Craig had been overpowering like that.

"It went to my head," he said, "and I started believing all the hype. Do you remember that, too?"

"I was lucky. My husband kept me grounded in reality." Too grounded, she thought now. Craig never understood that she'd needed his praise more than his criticism.

"I wasn't lucky. I forgot that it was about the work, not about the artist. I partied instead of painted. I drank too much. I developed a taste for nose candy and free sex."

"Except sex never is free, is it?"

"Not when you're married to a woman you love. Ah, but I justified my behavior, you see, because *she* was my *true* love and all that other sex was meaningless. I justified it because she was having a tough pregnancy, and the doctor had told me to leave her alone until after the baby was born."

Lilly heard his self-contempt. This was a man who judged himself even more harshly than he judged others.

"My wife found out, of course, and did the right thing by walking out on me. A week later she went into labor, but the baby was born dead."

"Oh, Liam . . ."

He turned away her sympathy with an arch twist of his mouth. "There's a happy ending. She married a magazine editor and went on to have three healthy, well-adjusted children. As for me . . . I learned an important lesson about what is important and what isn't."

"And you've lived in lonely isolation ever since?"

He smiled. "Hardly that. I do have friends, Lilly. Genuine ones."

"People you've known for a hundred years," she guessed. "Newcomers need not apply."

"I think all of us get set in our friendships as we grow older. Haven't you?"

"I suppose." She started to ask why he'd invited her here, since she was definitely a newcomer, but a more important question was on her mind. "Am I mistaken, or didn't you leave something important out of the house tour?"

He sank deeper into his chair and looked annoyed. "You want to see my studio."

"I'm sure you don't make a habit of opening it up to everyone, but—"

"No one goes in there but me and an occasional model."

"Perfectly understandable," she said smoothly. "Still, I'd be grateful if I could just have a peek."

A calculating glint appeared in his eyes. "How grateful?"

"What do you mean?"

"Grateful enough to pose for me?"

"You don't give up, do you?"

"It's part of my charm."

If they'd been at the B&B or by the stream in the meadow, she might have been able to refuse, but not here. That mysterious space where he created some of the world's most beautiful art was too near. "I can't imagine why you'd want to sketch a fat, over-the-hill, forty-five-year-old woman, but if that's what it takes to see your studio, then, yes, I'll pose for you."

"Good. Follow me." He vaulted from his chair and headed for a set of stone steps that led to the catwalk. As he reached it, he glanced back at her. "You're not fat. And you're older than forty-five."

"I am not!"

"You've had work done around your eyes, but no plastic surgeon can cut away the life experience behind them. You're closer to fifty."

"I'm forty-seven."

He gazed down at her from the catwalk. "You're making me lose patience."

"Air could make you lose patience," she grumbled.

The corner of his mouth curled. "Do you want to see my studio or not?"

"Oh, I suppose." Frowning, she swept up the steps, then followed him across the narrow, open structure. She glanced uneasily down at the living area below. "I feel as if I'm walking the plank."

"You'll get used to it."

His statement implied she'd be coming back, an impression she immediately corrected. "I'll pose for you today, but that's all."

"Stop irritating me." He'd reached the end of the catwalk, and he turned toward her so he stood silhouetted against the stone arch. She felt a tiny erotic thrill as he watched her approach with his legs braced and his arms crossed over his chest like an ancient warrior.

She gave him her diva's gaze. "Remind me again why I even wanted to see it."

"Because I'm a genius. Just ask me."

"Shut up and get out of my way."

His laugh held a deep, pleasing resonance. He turned away and led her around a curve of wall into his studio.

"Oh, Liam . . . " She pressed her fingertips to her lips.

The studio sat suspended above the trees in its own private universe. It was oddly shaped with three of its five sides curved. Late-afternoon light glowed through the northern wall, which was constructed entirely of glass. Overhead, the various skylights had shades that could be adjusted according to the time of day. The layers of colorful paint splatters on the rough walls, the furniture, and the limestone floor had turned the studio into a work of modern art all its own. She had the same sensation she experienced when she stood inside the Getty.

Half-finished canvases sat on easels while others leaned against the walls. Several large canvases hung on special frames. Her mind whirled as she tried to take it all in. She might not have had much formal education, but she'd studied art on her own for several decades, and she wasn't a novice. Still, she found his mature work difficult to categorize. All the influences were evident—the teeth-gnashing of the Abstract Expressionists, the studied cool of Pop, the starkness of the Minimalists. But only Liam Jenner had the audacity to superimpose the sentimental over those decidedly unsentimental styles.

Her eyes drank in the monumental, unfinished Madonna and Child that occupied most of one wall. Of all the great contemporary artists, only Liam Jenner could paint a Madonna and Child without using cow dung as his medium, or smearing an obscenity over her forehead, or adding a flashing Coca-Cola sign in place of a star. Only Liam Jenner had the absolute self-confidence to show the cynical deconstructionists who populated the world of contemporary art the meaning of unabashed reverence.

Her heart filled with tears she couldn't let herself shed. Tears of loss for the way she'd let her identity get swallowed up by Craig's expectations, tears of loss for the son she'd given away. Gazing at the painting, she realized how careless she'd been with what she should have held sacred.

His hand curled around her shoulder in a gesture as gentle as the wisps of blue-gold paint softening the Madonna's hair. His touch seemed both natural and necessary, and as she swallowed her tears, she had to resist the urge to curl into his chest.

"My poor Lilly," he said softly. "You've made your life even harder for yourself than I have mine."

She didn't question how he knew, but as she stood before that miraculous, unfinished painting and felt the comforting hand on her shoulder, she understood that all these canvases were reflections of the man—his angry intensity, his intelligence, his severity, and the sentiment he worked so hard to hide. Unlike her, Liam Jenner was one with his work.

"Sit," he murmured. "Just as you are." She let him lead her to a simple wooden chair across the room. He caressed her shoulder, then stepped back and reached for one of the blank canvases near his worktable. If he had been any other man, she would have felt manipulated, but manipulation wouldn't oc-cur to him. He had simply been overcome with the need to cre-ate, and for a reason she couldn't fathom, that involved her.

She no longer cared. Instead, she gazed at the Madonna and Child and thought about her life, richly blessed in so many ways but barren in others. Instead of concentrating on her losses—her son, her identity, the husband she'd both loved and resented—she thought of all she'd been granted. She'd been blessed with a good brain and the intellectual cu-riosity to challenge it. She'd been given a beautiful face and body when she'd needed them most. So what if that beauty had faded? Here beside this lake in northern Michigan, it didn't seem quite so important.

As she gazed at the Madonna, something began to hap-pen. She saw her herb-garden quilt instead of Liam's paint-ing, and she began to understand what had eluded her. The herb garden was a metaphor for the woman who now lived inside her—a more mature woman, one who wanted to heal and nurture instead of seduce, a woman with subtle nuances instead of splashy beauty. She was no longer the person she'd been, but she didn't yet understand the person she'd become. Somehow the quilt held the answer.

Her fingers twitched in her lap as a rush of energy shot through her. She needed her sewing basket and her box of fabrics. She needed them now. If she had them—if she had them right now!—she could find the path that would unlock who she was. She jumped up from the chair. "I have to go."

He'd been completely absorbed in his work, and for a moment he didn't seem to comprehend what she'd said. Then something that almost looked like pain twisted those craggy features. "Oh, God, you can't."

"Please. I'm not being difficult. I have to—I'll come right back. I just need to get something from my car."

He stepped away from the canvas. Left a smudge on his

forehead as he shoved a hand through his hair. "I'll get it for you."

"There's a basket in my trunk. No, I need the box that's with it. I need— We'll go together."

They ran across the catwalk, both of them on fire to get this done so they could return to what was essential. Her breath came in little gasps as she raced down the steps. She looked for the purse that held her keys but couldn't find it.

"Why the hell did you lock your car!" he roared. "We're in the middle of godforsaken nowhere!"

"I live in L.A.!" she shouted back.

"Here!" He snatched the purse from beneath one of the tables and began rummaging through it.

"Give it to me!" She grabbed it away and dug herself.

"Hurry up!" He seized her at the elbow, shoved her toward the front door and down the steps. On the way she found the keys. She broke away from him and flicked the remote that opened the trunk.

She nearly sobbed with relief as she grabbed her sewing basket and pushed the box of fabrics at him. He barely glanced at it.

They fled inside again, rushed up the stairs, raced across the catwalk. By the time they got to the studio, they were both struggling to breathe, more from emotion than exertion. She collapsed into the chair. He rushed toward the canvas. They gazed at each other. And both of them smiled.

It was an exquisite moment. One of perfect communication. He hadn't questioned her urgency, hadn't shown the slightest disdain when he'd seen it was only a woman's sewing basket that had made her so frantic. Somehow he understood her need to create, just as she understood his.

Content, she bent to her work.

Gradually it grew dark outside. The studio's interior lights came on, each one exquisitely placed to provide illumination without shadow. Her scissors snipped. Her needle flew in the broad basting stitches that would hold the fabric together until she could get to her sewing machine. Seam met seam. Colors blended. Patterns overlapped.

His fingers brushed her neck. She hadn't realized he'd left his canvas. A streak of scarlet smeared his black silk shirt, and a smear of orange clung to his expensive slacks. His crisp, graying hair was rumpled, and more paint smudged his hairline.

Her skin prickled as he touched the top button on her gauzy, tangerine blouse. Gazing into her eyes, he slipped it free of its buttonhole. Then he opened the next one.

"Please," he said.

She didn't try to stop him, not even when he slipped one side of the blouse down. Not even when his square, paint-smeared fingers brushed the front clasp of her bra. Instead, she bent her head to her sewing and let him unfasten it.

Her breasts spilled free, so much heavier than they'd been when she was younger. She allowed him to arrange the gauzy fabric of her blouse as he wished. He slipped one sleeve down her arm until it caught at the crook. Then the other. Her breasts rested in the nest of fabric like plump hens.

His footsteps tapped the limestone floor as he returned to his canvas.

Bare-breasted, she kept to her sewing.

Earlier she'd believed that her quilt would be about nurture instead of seduction, but now the astonishing fact that she'd allowed him to do this told her the meaning was more complex. She'd thought the sexual part of her had died. Now the hot ache in her body made her understand this wasn't true. The quilt had just unlocked one secret of her new identity.

Without disturbing the drape of fabric at the crook of her arms, she dipped into the box at her side and found a soft piece of old velvet. It was a deep, sensual crimson shaded with darker hues. The color of dark opal basil. The secret color of a woman's body. Her fingers trembled as she rounded the corners. The fabric brushed her nipples as she worked it, making them tighten and bead. She dipped into the box again and found an even deeper hue to serve as the secret heart.

She would add tiny crystals of dew.

A muffled curse made her look up. Liam stared at her, perspiration glistening on the rugged planes of his face. His paint-streaked arms hung slack at his sides, and a brush lay at his feet where he'd dropped it. "I've painted a hundred nudes. This is the first time . . . " He shook his head, looking momentarily bewildered. "I can't do this."

A rush of shame filled her. Her quilt piece fell to the floor as she leaped up, grabbed her blouse, pulled it closed.

"No." He came toward her. "Oh, no, not that."

The fire in his eyes stunned her. His legs brushed her skirt, and he plunged his hands inside the blouse she'd just drawn closed. Gathering her breasts in his hands, he buried his face in the swells. She clutched his arms as his lips closed around a nipple.

Their explosion of passion should have been reserved for youth, but neither of them was young. She felt his hard, thick length. He reached for the waistband of her skirt. Sanity returned, and she pushed his hands away. She wanted him to see her naked as she'd once been, not as she was now.

"Lilly . . . " He breathed her name in protest.

"I'm sorry . . . "

He had no patience for cowardice. He reached beneath her skirt and snagged her panties, then dropped to his knees and drew them off. He pressed his face into her skirt, against her . . . His warm breath seeped between her legs. It felt so good. She separated them, just a few inches, and let his breath touch her secret heart.

He pulled her down beside him on that hard limestone

floor. Cupping her face in his hands, he kissed her. The deep, experienced kiss of a man who knew women well.

Together they fell back. Her skirt tangled at her waist. He ran his hands along her legs and pushed them far apart. Then he buried his face between them.

She drew up her ankles, let her knees fall open, and reveled in his lusty, vigorous feasting. Her orgasm was fierce and strong, taking her by surprise. By the time she'd recovered, he was naked.

His body was powerful and fine. She opened her arms, and he plunged inside her. With her fingers curled into his hair, she took his deepest kiss, wrapped her legs around him. Her spine dug into the hard floor beneath. She winced as he plunged again.

He stopped, stroked more gently, then turned them so his body took the punishment of the floor. "Better?" He reached up to cup her breasts as they swung before him.

"Better," she replied, finding a rhythm that pleased them both.

As they moved, the paints on the canvases seemed to swirl around them, the colors growing brighter, turning liquid. Their bodies worked together, awash in hot sensation. Finally neither of them could bear it any longer, and all the colors of the universe shattered in an explosion of bright, white light.

She came back to herself slowly. She was lying on top of him, her blouse and skirt bunched at her waist. She'd fallen under a spell. The man had cast a spell over her as surely as his paintings had.

He groaned. "I'm too old for floors."

She leaped off him, scrambling awkwardly to cover herself. "I'm sorry. I'm—I'm so heavy. I must have crushed you."

"Not this again." He rolled to his side, winced, and slowly rose to his feet. Unlike her, he didn't seem to be in any hurry to get his clothes back on. She refused to look. Instead, she pushed her crumpled skirt down, noticing at the same time that her panties lay on the floor at his feet. She couldn't manage her bra, so she pulled the front of her blouse together, only to have him catch her hands and still them over the buttons.

"You listen to me, Lilly Sherman. I've worked with hundreds of models over the years, but I've never had to stop painting to seduce one of them."

She started to say that she didn't believe him, but this was Liam Jenner, a man with no patience for niceties. "It's—it was crazy."

His expression grew fierce. "Your body is magnificent. It's lush and extravagant, exactly the way a woman's body should be. Did you see the way the light fell on your skin? On your breasts? They're outrageous, Lilly. Big. Fleshy. Bountiful. I couldn't ever get enough of painting them. Your nipples . . . " He settled his thumbs over them, rubbed, and his eyes burned with the same passion she'd seen when he painted. "They make me think of showers. Showers of rich, golden milk." She shivered at the intensity she heard in his husky whisper. "Spilling to the ground . . . turning into rivers . . . sparkling, golden rivers flowing to nourish continents of parched land."

Such an outlandish, excessive man. She didn't know what to do with a vision so outrageous.

"Your body, Lilly . . . don't you see? This is the body that gave birth to the human race."

His words ran counter to everything that the world she lived in preached. Diets. Denial. An obsession with female bone instead of female flesh. The culture of youth and thinness.

Of stinginess.

Of disfigurement.

Of fear.

For a fraction of a moment she glimpsed the truth. She

saw a world so terrified of Woman's mystical power that nothing would do but to obliterate the very source of that power—the natural shape of her body.

The vision was too foreign to her experience, and it faded. "I—I have to go." Her heart hammered in her chest. She leaned down and grabbed her panties, threw them into her sewing basket, snatched up her quilt pieces. "This was . . . this was so irresponsible."

He smiled. "Am I likely to get you pregnant?"

"No. But there are other things."

"Neither of us is promiscuous. We've both learned the hard way that sex is too important."

"What do you call *that*?" She jabbed her hand toward the floor.

"Passion." He nodded toward the quilt pieces spilling from her basket. "Let me see what you're working on."

She couldn't imagine permitting a genius like Liam Jenner to see her simple craft project. Shaking her head, she made her way toward the door, but just before she got there, something made her stop and turn back.

He stood watching her. A smudge of blue paint marked his thigh near his groin. He was naked and magnificent.

"You were right," she said. "I'm fifty!"

His soft reply followed her out of the house and down the road.

"Too old to be such a coward."

Chapter 17

Daphne packed her most necessary things: sun-block, a pair of lollipop-red water wings, a box of Band-Aids (because Benny was going to camp, too), her favorite crunchy cereal, a very loud whistle (because Benny was going to camp, too), crayons, one book for every day she'd be gone, opera glasses (because you never knew what you might want to see), a beach ball that said FORT LAUDERDALE, her plastic bucket and shovel, and a great big sheet of bubble wrap to pop if she got bored.

Daphne Goes to Summer Camp

BY TUESDAY, MOLLY WAS WORN OUT FROM THE UPS AND DOWNS OF working on *Daphne Goes to Summer Camp* as well as trying to keep Kevin entertained. Not that he'd asked to be entertained. In fact, he'd turned surly after their Saturday-night dinner and gone out of his way to avoid her. He even had the gall to behave as if *she* were imposing on *him*. She'd had to threaten to go on strike to get him to come with her today.

She should have left him alone, but she couldn't. The only way she could make him change his mind about selling the Wind Lake Campground was to convince him that this was no longer the boring place of his childhood. Unfortunately, she hadn't been able to convince him of a thing so far, which meant it was time to make her next move. Resigned, she forced herself to her feet.

"Look, Kevin! In the trees over there!"

"What are you doing, Molly? Sit down!"

She gave a jump of excitement. "Isn't that a Kirtland's warbler?"

"Stop!"

All it took was one more small jump and the canoe tipped.

"Aw, *shit!*"

They tumbled into the lake.

As she went under, she thought about the earth-shattering kiss they'd exchanged three days ago. Ever since then he'd kept his distance, and the few times they'd been together, he was barely civil. Once she'd told him she wouldn't sleep with him, he'd lost interest in her. If only . . .

If only what, you dope? If only he were banging his fists on your bedroom door every night begging you to change your mind and let him in? Like that would ever happen.

But couldn't he look as if he were suffering from a little of the lust that had her tossing in her bed the last three nights until she thought she'd scream? It had even affected her writing. This morning Daphne had told her best friend Melissa the Wood Frog that Benny was looking particularly sexy that day! Molly had thrown down her notebook in disgust.

She felt above her head for the capsized canoe's gunwale, then swam beneath it. With a kick she came up into the air pocket beneath the hull, which was just big enough for her head. This drowning thing was going to turn her into a prune.

She knew it would be easy to regain his attention. All she had to do was undress. But she wanted to be something more to him than another sexual fling. She wanted to be . . .

Her mind balked, but only for a moment. A *friend,* that was it. She'd just begun to value their friendship when he'd grown surly. There wouldn't be any chance of reestablishing that relationship if they went to bed together.

Once again she forced herself to remember that Kevin

wouldn't be much of a lover. Yes, he was a great kisser, and yes, he'd been asleep during their brief, ill-fated sexual encounter, but she'd already observed that he wasn't really a sensualist. He never lingered over his food. He didn't savor the wine or take the time to appreciate the presentation of the meal on his plate. He ate efficiently and his table manners were flawless, but food wasn't anything more than body fuel to him. Besides, how much energy did a gorgeous multimillionaire pro athlete really need to invest into developing his skills as a lover? Women lined up to please him, not the other way around.

Face it: The sex she wanted to have with him was romantic fantasy sex, and she wasn't willing to sell her soul for that. Despite three nights of tossing and turning, despite the embarrassing heat that made her knees turn goofy at the most inopportune moments, she didn't want an affair. She wanted a real relationship. A *friendship,* she reminded herself.

She'd just begun to imagine how a pair of dripping bunny ears would look peeking out from beneath a capsized canoe when Kevin's head surfaced next to her. It was too dark beneath the hull to see his expression, but the anger in his voice came through loud and clear.

"Why did I know I'd find you here?"

"I got disoriented."

"I swear, you're the most uncoordinated person I've ever met!" He rudely grabbed her arm and yanked on it, pulling her back underwater. They resurfaced in the daylight.

It was a beautiful afternoon on Wind Lake. The sun shone, and the gem-blue water mirrored a single fluffy cloud floating in the sky above like one of Molly's meringue cookies that hadn't gotten burned on the bottom. Kevin, however, looked more than a little stormy.

"What the hell were you thinking of? When you blackmailed me into coming out here, you told me you knew all about canoeing!"

As she treaded water, she was glad she'd remembered to leave her sneakers at the dock, which was more than he'd done. But then, he hadn't possessed her insider's knowledge of where they'd end up.

"I do know about canoeing. My last summer at camp I was in charge of taking out the six-year-olds."

"Are any of them still *alive*?"

"I don't know why you're being so grouchy. You like to swim."

"Not when I'm wearing a Rolex!"

"I'll buy you a new one."

"Yeah, right. The point is, I didn't want to come canoeing today. I had work to do. But all weekend, whenever I tried to get something done, you'd decide a burglar was trying to break into the cottage, or you couldn't concentrate on cooking unless you went cliff diving. This morning you nagged me into playing catch with your *poodle*!"

"Roo needs exercise." And Kevin needed someone to play with.

He hadn't been able to sit still all weekend. Instead of giving in to the spell of Wind Lake and reconnecting with his heritage, he was working out or trying to pound away his restlessness with hammer and nails. Any moment she expected him to hop into his car and drive off forever.

Just the thought of it depressed her. She couldn't leave here, not yet. There was something magical about the campground. Possibilities seemed to shimmer in the air. It felt almost enchanted.

Now he swam toward the stern of the capsized canoe. "What are we supposed to do with this thing now?"

"Can you touch bottom?"

"We're in the middle of a frickin' lake! Of course I can't touch bottom."

She ignored his surliness. "Well, our instructor once

taught us a technique to turn over a canoe. It's called the Capistrano Flip, but—"

"How do you do it?"

"I was fourteen. I can't remember."

"Then why did you mention it?"

"I was thinking out loud. Come on, I'm sure we can manage."

They finally righted the canoe, but their technique, which was based mostly on Kevin's brute strength, left the hull full of water and partially submerged. With nothing to use as a bailer, they were forced to paddle back that way, and Molly was gasping for breath by the time she'd finished helping him haul it up onto the beach. She'd never been a quitter, though.

"Look over to the right, Kevin! Mr. Morgan's here!" She hooked a lock of wet hair behind her ear and gestured toward the slightly built, bespectacled accountant setting up a chair in the sand.

"Not this again."

"Really, I think you should follow him—"

"I don't care what you say. He does *not* look like a serial killer!" He yanked off his sodden T-shirt.

"I'm very intuitive, and he has shifty eyes."

"I think you've lost your mind," he muttered. "I really do. And I have no idea how I'm going to explain that to your sister—a woman who happens to be my boss."

"You worry too much."

He spun on her. She saw fire in those green eyes and knew she'd pushed him too far.

"You listen to me, Molly! Fun and games are over. I've got better things to do than waste my time like this."

"This isn't a waste of time. It's—"

"I'm not going to be your *pal*! Can you understand that? You want our relationship to stay out of the bedroom? Fine. That's your prerogative. But don't expect me to be your buddy. From now on you entertain yourself and stay the hell away from me!"

She watched him stomp off. Even though she probably deserved a little of his anger, she still felt disappointed with him.

Summer camp was supposed to be fun, but Daphne was sad. Ever since she'd capsized their canoe, Benny had been mad at her. Now he didn't ask her to spin around in circles until they got dizzy. He didn't notice that she'd painted each of her toenails a different color so they looked like they'd been dipped in a puddle of rainbows. He didn't squish his nose and stick out his tongue to get her attention or burp really loud. Instead, she saw him making stupid faces at Cicely, a bunny from Berlin, who gave him chocolate rabbits and had no flair for fashion.

Molly set aside her notebook and made her way to the sitting room, taking along the newest box of Say Fudge. She dumped it into a milk-glass bowl that still held crumbs from yesterday's fudge. It had been four days since she'd overturned the canoe, and each morning since then she'd found a fresh box sitting on the kitchen counter in the cottage. It sure eliminated any mystery about where Kevin had been the night before. *Slytherin!*

He'd done everything possible to get away from her except the one thing he should do—move back into the B&B. But his aversion to being around Lilly was worse than his aversion to being around her. Not that it mattered much, since they were hardly ever in the cottage at the same time.

Depressed, she shoved a piece of fudge into her mouth. It was Saturday, and the B&B was full for the weekend. She wandered into the foyer and straightened the pile of brochures on the hall console. The job ad had appeared in the paper, and Kevin had spent the morning interviewing the two best candidates, while Molly had shown the B&B guests to their rooms and helped Troy with the new cottage rentals. Now it was early afternoon, and she needed a writing break.

She stepped onto the front porch and saw Lilly kneeling in the shade at the side of the front yard, planting the last of the pink and lavender impatiens she'd bought to go in the empty beds. Even wearing gardening gloves and kneeling in the grass, she managed to look glamorous. Molly didn't bother reminding her she was a guest. She'd tried that a few days ago when Lilly had appeared with a trunk full of annuals. Lilly had said she enjoyed gardening, that it relaxed her, and Molly had to agree that she appeared less tense, even though Kevin continued to ignore her.

As Molly reached the bottom of the stairs, Marmie lifted her head and blinked her big golden eyes. Since Roo was safely inside with Amy, the cat rose and walked over to rub against Molly's ankles. Although Molly wasn't a cat person like Kevin, Marmie was a winning feline, and the two of them had developed a distant fondness. She loved to be held, and Molly bent down to pick her up.

Lilly gave the earth around the seedling a sharp little slap. "I wish you wouldn't encourage Liam to keep showing up for breakfast every morning."

"I like him." *And you do, too,* Molly thought.

"I don't know how you could. He's rude, arrogant, and egotistical."

"Also amusing, intelligent, and very sexy."

"I hadn't noticed."

"I believe you."

Lilly lifted a diva's eyebrow at her, but Molly wasn't intimidated. Lately, Lilly sometimes seemed to forget Molly was the enemy. Maybe the sight of her working around the B&B didn't fit the actress's image of a spoiled football heiress. Molly thought about confronting her again as she'd done in the herb garden over a week ago, but she didn't feel like defending herself.

Each morning, Liam Jenner appeared in the kitchen to have breakfast with Lilly. They bickered while they ate, but they seemed to argue more to prolong their time together than for any other reason. When they weren't bickering, their conversations ranged from art and their travels to their observations about human nature. They had everything in common, and it was obvious they were attracted. Just as obvious that Lilly was fighting it.

Molly learned that Lilly had been to his house once and that he'd started a portrait of her, but Lilly refused his repeated requests to return and sit for him. Molly wondered what had happened at the house that day.

She carried Marmie over to the shade of a big linden tree near where Lilly was planting. Just to be perverse, she said, "I'll bet he looks great naked."

"Molly!"

Molly's devilry faded as she saw Kevin jogging toward the Common from the highway. As soon as he'd finished his interviews, he'd changed into a T-shirt and his gray athletic shorts, then taken off. Even when they served breakfast together, he barely spoke to her. As Amy felt duty-bound to point out, he spent more time talking to Charlotte Long than he spent talking to Molly.

All week he'd been killing Lilly with cool politeness, and Lilly had been letting him get away with it. Now, however, she jabbed her trowel in the ground. "You know, Molly, I've just about run out of patience with your husband."

That made two of them.

Molly watched as he slowed to cool off. He bent his head and rested the palms of his hands on the small of his back. Marmie spotted him and stirred in her arms. Molly gazed at the cat resentfully. She was jealous. Jealous of Kevin's affection for a cat. She remembered the way he stroked Marmie's fur, those long fingers sinking deep . . . sliding down her spine . . . It gave Molly goose bumps.

She realized she was blindly, utterly furious with him! She hated the fact that he'd spent the morning interviewing strangers to take over the campground. And what right did he have to act as if they had a genuine friendship, then dismiss her just because she'd refused to go to bed with him? He might pretend he was angry because of the incident with the canoe, but both of them knew that was a lie.

Impulsively, she turned around and set the cat against the trunk of the linden tree they'd been standing beneath. A squirrel stirred in the branches above. Marmie flicked her tail and began to climb.

Lilly caught the action out of the corner of her eye and spun around. "What are you—"

"You're not the only one running out of patience!" Molly glanced up to see Marmie scramble higher. Then she called out. "*Kevin!*"

He looked over.

"We need your help! It's Marmie!"

He picked up his stride and hurried toward them. "What's wrong with her?"

She pointed into the linden tree, where Marmie had climbed out on a branch high above the ground. The cat yowled her displeasure as the squirrel scampered from sight.

"She's stuck and we can't get her down. The poor thing is terrified."

Lilly rolled her eyes, but she didn't say anything.

Kevin gazed up into the tree. "Hey, girl. Come on down." He extended his arms. "Come here."

"We've been doing that for ages." Molly eyed his sweat-soaked T-shirt and running shorts. The hair on his bare legs was matted. How could he still look so gorgeous? "I'm afraid you'll have to climb up after her." She paused. "Unless you want me to do it."

"Of course not." He grabbed one of the lower branches and pulled himself up.

She couldn't quite contain her relish. "Your legs are going to get ripped to shreds."

He shimmied higher.

"If you slip, you could break your passing arm. This might end your whole career."

He was disappearing into the branches now, and she raised her voice. "Please come down! It's too dangerous."

"You're making more noise than the cat!"

"Let me get Troy."

"Great idea. The last time I saw him, he was down at the dock. And take your time."

"Do you think there are any tree snakes up there?"

"I don't know, but I'll bet you can find some in the woods. Go look." The branches rustled. "Come here, Marmie. Here, girl."

The limb where the yowling cat crouched was fairly thick, but he was a large man. What if it snapped and he really did injure himself? For the first time Molly's warning was genuine. "Don't climb out on that, Kevin. You're too big."

"Would you be quiet!"

Molly held her breath as he threw his leg over the limb about eight feet from where Marmie crouched. He scooted forward, making soothing noises to the cat. He'd just about reached her when Marmie stuck her nose in the air, hopped delicately to a lower branch, then proceeded to pick her way down the tree.

Molly watched in disgust as the traitorous cat reached the ground, then shot toward Lilly, who scooped her up and gave Molly a pointed look. She didn't say anything to Kevin, however, who was climbing back down.

"How long did you tell me she was stuck up there?" he asked as he dropped.

"It's, uh, tough to keep track of time when you're terrified."

He studied Molly, his expression suspicious, then bent to examine a nasty scrape on the inside of his calf.

"I've got some ointment in the kitchen," she said.

Lilly stepped forward. "I'll get it."

"Don't do me any favors," Kevin snapped.

Lilly clenched her teeth. "You know, I'm getting really sick of your attitude. And I'm tired of biding my time. We're going to talk right *now*." She set down the cat.

Kevin was taken aback. He'd grown accustomed to the way she hadn't pressed him, and he didn't seem to know how to respond.

She jabbed her finger toward the side of the house. "We've postponed this long enough. Follow me! Or maybe you don't have the guts."

She'd waved a red flag in his face, and Kevin was quick to respond. "We'll see who has guts," he growled.

Lilly charged toward the woods.

Molly wanted to applaud, but she was glad she didn't because Lilly spun around to glare at her. "Don't touch my cat!"

"Yes, ma'am."

Lilly and Kevin headed off together.

Lilly heard the sounds of Kevin's footsteps rustling in the pine needles strewn over the path. At least he was following her. Three decades of guilt began to snuff out the temper that had finally given her the courage to force this confrontation. She was so sick of that guilt. All it had done was paralyze her, and she couldn't stand it any longer. Liam tormented her by appearing every morning for a breakfast she never felt like eating but couldn't seem to avoid. Molly wouldn't fit into the pigeonhole Lilly had assigned her. Kevin looked at her as if she were his worst enemy. It was too much.

In the distance ahead, the trees gave way to the lake. She marched toward it, silently daring him not to follow. When she couldn't stand it any longer, she turned to confront him, not knowing until she spoke what she was going to say.

"I won't apologize for giving you up!"

"Why am I not surprised?"

"Sneer all you want, but have you once asked yourself where you'd be today if I'd kept you? What chance do you think you'd have had living in a roach-infested apartment with an immature teenager who had big dreams and no idea how to make them come true?"

"No chance at all," he said stonily. "You did the right thing."

"You're damn right I did. I made sure you had two parents who doted on you from the day you were born. I made sure you lived in a nice house where there was plenty to eat and a backyard to play in."

He gazed out at the lake, looking bored. "I'm not arguing. Are you about done with this, because I have things to do."

"Don't you understand? I couldn't come to see you!"

"It's not important."

She started to move closer, then stopped herself. "Yes, it is. And I know that's why you hate me so much. Not because I gave you away, but because I never answered your letters begging me to come to see you."

"I hardly remember. I was—what—six years old? You think something like that is still bothering me?" His air of studied indifference developed a bitter edge. "I don't hate you, Lilly. I don't care that much."

"I still have those letters. Every one you wrote. And they're soaked with more tears than you can imagine."

"You're breakin' my heart."

"Don't you understand? There was nothing I wanted to do more, but it wasn't allowed."

"This I've got to hear."

She finally had his attention. He came closer and stopped near the base of an old gnarled oak.

"You weren't six. The letters started when you were seven. The first was printed in block letters on yellow lined paper. I

still have it." She'd read it so many times the paper had
grown limp.

Dear Ant Lilly,

*I know your my real mom and I love you very much.
Could you come see me. I have a cat. His name is Spike.
He is 7 to.*

Love,

Kevin

Please dont tell my mom I wrote this leter. She mite cry.

"You wrote me eighteen letters over four years."
"I really don't remember."
She risked taking a few steps toward him. "Maida and I
had an agreement."
"What kind of agreement?"
"I didn't give you to them casually. You can't believe that.
We talked everything through. And I made long lists." She realized she was twisting her hands, and she let them fall to her
sides. "They had to promise never to spank you, not that they
would have anyway. I told them they couldn't criticize your
music when you got to be a teenager, and they had to let you
wear your hair however you wanted. Remember, I'd just
turned eighteen." She gave him a rueful smile. "I even tried to
make them promise to buy you a red convertible for your
sixteenth birthday, but they wisely refused."
For the first time he smiled back at her. The movement
was small, the slightest twitch at the corner of his mouth, but
at least it was there.
She blinked, determined to get through this without
shedding a tear. "One thing I didn't back down on, though—
I made them promise to always let you follow your dreams,
even if they weren't the same dreams they had for you."

He cocked his head, all pretense of indifference gone.

"They hated letting you play football. They were so terrified that you'd get hurt. But I held them to their promise, and they never tried to stop you." She could no longer meet his eyes. "All I had to do was give them one thing in exchange . . . "

She heard him move closer, and she looked up to see him step into a narrow shaft of sunlight.

"What was that?"

She could hear in his voice that he already knew. "I had to agree never to see you."

She couldn't look at him, and she bit her lip. "Open adoption didn't exist then, or if it did, I didn't know about it. They explained to me how easily confused children can get, and I believed them. They agreed to tell you who your birth mother was as soon as you were old enough to understand, and they sent me a hundred pictures over the years, but I could never visit you. As long as Maida and John were alive, you were to have just one mother."

"You broke your promise once." His lips barely moved. "When I was sixteen."

"It was an accident." She wandered toward a boulder protruding from the sandy soil. "When you started playing high school football, I realized I finally had a chance to see you without breaking my promise. I started flying into Grand Rapids on Fridays to watch the games. I'd strip off my makeup and wrap this old scarf around my head, put on nondescript clothes so no one would recognize me. Then I'd sit in the visitors' stands. I had this little pair of opera glasses I'd train on you for the whole game. I lived for the times you'd take off your helmet. You'll never know how much I grew to hate that thing."

The day was warm, but she felt chilled, and she rubbed her arms. "Everything went fine until you were a junior. It was the last game of the season, and I knew it would be nearly a year before I could see you again. I convinced myself there wouldn't be any harm in driving by the house."

"I was mowing the grass in the front yard."

She nodded. "It was one of those Indian summer days, and you were sweaty, just like you are now. I was so busy looking at you that I didn't see your neighbor's car parked on the street."

"You scraped the side."

"And you came running over to help." She hugged herself. "When you realized who I was, you looked at me like you hated me."

"I couldn't believe it was you."

"Maida never confronted me about it, so I knew you hadn't told them." She tried to read his expression, but he wasn't giving anything away. He nudged aside a fallen branch with the toe of his running shoe.

"She died a year ago. Why did you wait until now to tell me all this?"

She stared at him and shook her head. "How many times did I call and try to talk to you? You refused, Kevin. Every time."

He gazed at her. "They should have told me they wouldn't let you see me."

"Did you ever ask them about it?"

He shrugged, and she knew he hadn't.

"I think John might have said something, but Maida would never have allowed it. We talked about it over the phone. You have to remember that she was older than all your friends' mothers, and she knew she wasn't one of those fun moms every kid wants. It made her insecure. Besides, you were a headstrong kid. Do you really think you'd have shrugged it off and gone about your business if you'd known how much I wanted to see you?"

"I'd have been on the first bus to L.A.," he said flatly.

"And that would have broken her heart."

She waited, hoping he'd come nearer. She fantasized that he'd let her put her arms around him and all the lost years would vanish. Instead, he bent to pick up one of the pinecones lying on the ground.

"We had a TV in the basement. I went down there every week to watch your show. I always turned the volume low, but they knew what I was doing. They never said a word about it."

"I don't suppose they would have."

He rubbed his thumb over the scales. His hostility was gone, but not his tension, and she knew the reunion she'd dreamed of wasn't going to happen.

"So what am I supposed to do about all this now?"

The fact that he had to ask the question showed that he wasn't ready to give her anything. She couldn't touch him, couldn't tell him she'd loved him from the moment of his birth and had never stopped. Instead, she only said, "I guess that'll be up to you."

He nodded slowly, then dropped the pinecone. "Now that you've told me, are you going to leave?"

Neither his expression nor his tone gave her a cue how he wanted her to respond, and she wouldn't ask. "I'm going to finish planting the annuals I bought. A few more days."

It was a lame excuse, but he nodded and turned toward the path. "I need to take a shower."

He hadn't ordered her to leave. He hadn't told her this had come too late. She decided it was enough for now.

Kevin found Molly perched in her favorite spot, the glider on the back porch of the cottage, a notebook on her thighs. It hurt too much to think about Lilly's earthshaking revelations, so he stood in the doorway gazing at Molly instead. She must not have heard him come in because she didn't look up. On the other hand, he'd been acting like such a jerk there was a good chance she was ignoring him, but how was he supposed to behave when Molly kept hatching up all these zany adventures without a clue how being near her affected him?

Did she think it was easy watching her splash around in that skimpy one-piece black bathing suit he'd had to buy her to replace the red one? Did she ever once glance down to see what happened to her breasts when she got *cold*? The legs of the suit were cut so high they practically begged him to slip his hands underneath so he could cup those round little cheeks. And she had the gall to be mad at him because he'd been ignoring her! Didn't she understand he couldn't ignore her?

He wanted to push aside the notebook she was writing in, toss her over his shoulder, and carry her straight to the bedroom. Instead, he headed for the bathroom and filled the tub with very cold water, once again cursing the lack of a shower. He washed himself quickly and slipped into clean clothes. All week he'd been driving himself, but it hadn't done a damn bit of good. Despite the carpentry and painting, despite the daily workouts and the miles he'd added to his run, he wanted her more than ever. Even the game films he'd started watching on the TV in the office couldn't hold his attention. He should have moved back into the B&B, but Lilly was there.

A stab of pain shot through him. He couldn't think about her now. Maybe he'd drive into town for another workout in the tiny health club at the inn.

But no, he found himself moving toward the porch, all his vows to stay away from Molly evaporating. As he stepped through the doorway, he realized he was in the only place he could possibly be right now, in the presence of the only person who might understand his confusion over what had just happened.

She gazed up at him, her eyes full of that generous concern she showed for anyone she thought might have a problem. He couldn't spot even a hint of censure toward him for being so surly, although he knew she'd get around to putting him in his place sooner or later.

"Is everything all right?"

He shrugged, not giving away a thing. "We talked."

But she wasn't impressed by his tough-guy act. "Were you your normal repugnant self?"

"I listened to her, if that's what you mean." He knew exactly what she meant, but he wanted her to pull the story out of him. Maybe because he didn't know what she'd find when she did.

She waited.

He wandered toward the screen. The plant she'd hung from a hook brushed against his shoulder. "She told me some things . . . I don't know . . . It wasn't exactly the way I thought."

"What way was it?" she asked quietly.

So he told her. Leaving out how muddled his feelings were. Just giving her the facts.

When he was done, she nodded slowly. "I see."

If only he did.

"Now you have to adjust to knowing that what you believed about her wasn't true."

"I thinks she wants . . . " He shoved his hands into his pockets. "She wants something from me. I can't—" He whirled on her. "Am I supposed to feel this sudden attachment to her? Because I don't!"

Her expression flickered with something that looked almost like pain, and it took her a long time to answer.

"I doubt she expects that right away. Maybe you could start just by getting to know her. She makes quilts, and she's an amazing artist. But she doesn't know that about herself."

"I guess." He jerked his hands from his pockets and did exactly what he'd been trying to avoid since last Friday. "I'm going stir-crazy. There's this place about twenty miles away. Let's get out of here."

He saw right away that she was going to refuse, and he didn't blame her. At the same time he couldn't be alone now, so he whipped the notebook off her lap and pulled her to her feet. "You'll like it."

An hour later the two of them were soaring over the Au Sable River in a sleek little German-built glider.

Chapter 18

Sexual daydreams and fantasies are normal.
They're even a healthy way to pass time while
you're waiting for the right person to come along.

"My Secret Sex Life"
for Chik

"IT'S NICE THAT KEVIN FINALLY DECIDED TO SPEND SOME TIME WITH
you. Maybe he'll agree to marriage counseling." Amy finished putting the strawberry jam cake on a Wedgwood plate
and regarded Molly with her familiar pitying expression.

"We don't need marriage counseling," Kevin snapped as
he came through the door with Marmie padding at his feet.
They'd just gotten back from their gliding adventure, and his
hair was windblown. "What we need is that cake. It's five
o'clock, and the guests are waiting for tea."

Amy moved reluctantly toward the door. "Maybe if you'd
both pray . . . "

"The cake!" Kevin growled.

Amy gave Molly a look that indicated she'd done her best
but that Molly was hopelessly doomed to life without sex.
Then she disappeared.

"You're right," he said. "That kid *is* irritating. I *should* have
given you a hickey."

This was a topic Molly definitely didn't want to discuss,
and she focused all her attention on arranging the tea tray.
She hadn't had time to change out of her rumpled clothes or

straighten her own windblown hair, but she forced herself not to fidget as Kevin took a few steps closer.

"In case you were worried, Daph . . . My ears have just about recovered from that scream."

"You were heading right for the trees. And I didn't scream." She picked up the tray and shoved it at him. "I squeaked."

"One hell of a squeak. And we weren't anyplace near the trees."

"I believe that our female guests are anxiously awaiting you."

He grimaced and disappeared with Marmie.

She smiled. She shouldn't have been surprised that Kevin was an experienced glider pilot, although she wished he'd mentioned it *before* they'd taken off. Despite their afternoon together, things weren't much better between them. He hadn't said a word about his interviews that morning, and she couldn't bring herself to ask. He'd also been strangely jumpy. Once she'd accidentally bumped into him, and he'd sprung away as if she'd burned him. If he hadn't wanted her with him, why had he invited her?

She knew the answer. After his confrontation with Lilly, he hadn't wanted to be alone.

The woman who was causing his turmoil slipped into the kitchen through the back door. Uncertainty was written all over her face, and Molly's heart went out to her. During the drive back to the campground, she'd brought up Lilly's name, but Kevin had changed the subject.

She remembered what he'd said earlier at the cottage. *Am I supposed to feel this sudden attachment to her? Because I don't!* It had been a pointed reminder that Kevin didn't like close attachments. She'd begun to realize how skillful he was at keeping people away. Oddly enough, Liam Jenner, for all his obsession with privacy, was less an emotional recluse than Kevin.

"I'm sorry about your cat," Molly said. "It was an impulse. Kevin needs lots of excitement." She traced the edge of the cut glass serving plate. "I want him to enjoy the campground so he won't sell it."

Lilly nodded slowly. Her hands slipped in and out of her pockets. She cleared her throat. "Did Kevin tell you about our conversation?"

"Yes."

"It wasn't exactly a rousing success."

"But not quite a failure either."

A heartbreaking flicker of hope appeared on her face. "I hope not."

"Football is a lot simpler than personal relationships."

Lilly nodded, then toyed with her rings. "I owe you an apology, don't I?"

"Yep, you do."

This time Lilly's smile had something more to it. "I was unfair. I know it."

"Darn right you were."

"I worry about him."

"And the damage a man-eating heiress might do to his fragile emotions, right?"

Lilly looked down at Roo, who'd come out from under the table. "Help me, Roo. I'm scared of her."

Molly laughed.

Lilly smiled then sobered. "I'm sorry I misjudged you, Molly. I know you care about him, and I can't believe you'd deliberately hurt him."

Molly suspected Lilly's opinion would change if she knew the circumstances behind their marriage. Only her promise to Kevin kept her from telling her the truth. "In case you haven't figured it out yet, I'm on your side. I think Kevin needs you in his life."

"You'll never know how much that means to me." She gazed toward the door. "I'm going in for tea."

"Are you sure? The guests will be all over you."

"I'll manage." She straightened her posture. "I've had enough of hiding out. Your husband is going to have to deal with me one way or the other."

"Good for you."

By the time Molly reached the sitting room with a plate of cookies and another teapot, Lilly was chatting graciously with the guests who'd surrounded her. She had her heart in her eyes whenever she looked at Kevin, but he avoided looking back. It was almost as if he believed that any sign of affection toward her would somehow trap him.

Molly's childhood had taught her to beware of people who weren't emotionally open, and his guardedness depressed her. If she were smart, she'd rent a car and drive back to Chicago this very night.

An elderly woman from Ann Arbor who'd checked in earlier that day appeared at her elbow. "I've heard you write children's books."

"Not so much anymore," she replied glumly, thinking about the revisions she still hadn't done and the August mortgage check she wouldn't be able to write.

"My sister and I have always wanted to write a children's book, but we've been so busy traveling that we never can seem to find the time."

"There's more to writing a children's book than just finding the time," Kevin said from behind her. "It's not as easy as people seem to think."

Molly was so startled she nearly dropped the cookie plate.

"Kids want a good story," he said. "They want to laugh or get scared or learn something without having it shoved down their throats. That's what Molly does in her books. For example, in *Daphne Gets Lost . . .* " Off he went, describing with uncanny accuracy the techniques Molly used to reach her readers.

Later, when he appeared in the kitchen, she smiled at him.

"Thanks for defending my profession. I appreciate it."

"People are idiots." He nodded toward the baking supplies she was setting out for breakfast the next morning. "You don't need to cook so much. I keep telling you I can order from the bakery in town."

"I know. I enjoy it."

His gaze drifted over her bare shoulders and lacy camisole top. He lingered there for so long she felt as if he were running his fingers over her skin. A silly fantasy, she realized, as he made a grab for the biscuit tin where she'd just deposited the leftover cookies. "You seem to enjoy everything about this place. What happened to all those bad memories of summer camp?"

"This is how I always wanted a summer camp to be."

"Boring and lots of old people?" He bit into a cookie. "You've got strange taste."

She wasn't going to argue with him about this. Instead, she asked the question she'd been postponing all afternoon. "You haven't said anything about your interviews this morning."

He scowled. "They didn't go as well as I wanted. The first guy might have been a great chef once, but now he shows up drunk for interviews. And the woman I interviewed put so many restrictions on when she could work that she'd have been useless."

Molly's spirits soared, only to sink as he went on.

"I've got one more candidate coming in tomorrow afternoon, though, and she was great on the phone. She didn't even mind a Sunday interview. I figure we can train her on Monday and leave here by Wednesday afternoon at the latest."

"Hooray," she said glumly.

"Don't tell me you're going to miss falling out of bed at five-thirty in the morning?"

Amy giggled in the hallway. "Troy, don't!"

The newlyweds were getting ready to check in before they left. Every afternoon right after tea they raced back to their apartment, where Molly was fairly certain they jumped into bed and made very noisy love before they had to return to the B&B for the night.

"Lucky us," Molly muttered. "Now we can get lectured on our sexual inadequacies by both of them."

"Like hell." With no warning Kevin grabbed her, pushed her against the refrigerator, and crushed his mouth to hers.

She knew exactly what he was doing. And while this might be better than her hickey idea, it was a lot more dangerous.

His free hand caught her leg beneath the knee and raised it. She snaked it over his hip and curled her arms around him. His other hand dipped under her top and covered her breast. Just as if he had the right.

It was all for show. She told herself that as she parted her lips and let his tongue slip into her mouth. He felt as if he somehow belonged here, inside this one small part of her, and she wanted to kiss him forever.

The kitchen door thumped, reminding her they had witnesses. Which, of course, was the whole point. Kevin drew back a few inches, not even far enough for her lips to cool. His eyes never left her mouth, and he kept his hand on her breast.

"Go away."

A gasp from Amy. The thud of the door. The sound of quickly retreating footsteps.

"I—I guess we showed them," Molly breathed against his mouth.

"I guess," he replied. And then he started kissing her all over again.

"Molly, I— Oh! Excuse me . . . "

Another quick thud of the door. More retreating footsteps, this time Lilly's.

Kevin muttered a dark curse. "We're getting out of here."

His voice held the same note of determination she'd heard in television interviews when he promised to dominate Green Bay. He released Molly's leg. His hand slipped more reluctantly from her breast.

She'd gotten herself right back where she wasn't supposed to be. "I really don't think—"

"No more thinking, Molly. I'm your husband, damn it, and it's time you start acting like a wife."

"Like a— What do you—"

But Kevin was fundamentally a man of action, and he'd done enough talking. Shackling her wrist, he hauled her to the back door.

She couldn't believe it. He was abducting her to have . . . *Forced Sex!*

Oh, jeez . . . Fight back! Tell him no!

She knew from watching Oprah exactly what a woman was supposed to do in this situation. Scream at the top of her lungs, drop to the ground, and start kicking her assailant as hard as she could. Oprah's authority had explained that not only did this strategy have the advantage of surprise, but it used a woman's lower-body strength.

Scream. Drop. Kick.

"No," she whispered.

Kevin wasn't listening. He was dragging her across the garden and along the path that ran between the cottages and the lake. His long legs ate up the ground just as they did when he was trying to beat the final whistle. She would have stumbled if he didn't have such a tight grip on her.

Scream. Drop. Kick. And keep screaming. She remembered that part. You were supposed to keep screaming the whole time you were kicking.

The idea of dropping to the ground was interesting. Counterintuitive, but it did make sense. Women couldn't compete with men when it came to upper-body strength, but if the male assailant was standing and the woman dropped . . . A shower of hard, fast kicks to the soft parts . . . It definitely made sense.

"Uhm, Kevin . . . "

"Be quiet, or I swear to God I'll take you right here."

Yes, this was definitely Forced Sex.

Thank goodness.

Molly was so tired of thinking, so tired of fighting what she wanted so much. She knew it was a lousy reflection on her personal maturity that she needed to believe that the decision had been taken out of her hands. Even crummier to regard Kevin as a sexual predator. But at twenty-seven she wasn't yet the woman she wanted to be. The woman she intended to be. By the time she was thirty, she was absolutely certain she would have taken charge of her own sexuality. But for right now let him do it.

They were bump, bump, bumping down the path, passing Fairest Lord Jesus, passing Noah's Ark. Lilies of the Field lay right ahead.

She reminded herself of Kevin's shortcomings as a lover and vowed she wouldn't say a word to him about them either during or afterward. He wasn't a naturally selfish person. How was he supposed to know about foreplay when he'd had all those women servicing him? And a little slam, bam, thank you, ma'am would be a good thing. Those feverish nighttime images that had been robbing her of sleep would finally fade in the harsh glare of reality.

"Inside." He jerked open the cottage door and gave her a push.

She had no choice in the matter. No choice at all. He was bigger, stronger, apt to turn violent at any moment.

Even for an imaginative person that was a stretch.

She wished he hadn't let her go, but she liked the way he'd braced his hands on his hips. And his glare definitely looked threatening.

"You're not going to start giving me crap about this, are you?"

This posed a dilemma. If she said yes, he'd back off. If she said no, she'd be giving him permission to do something she knew she should resist.

Luckily, he wasn't done being angry. "Because I'm sick of it! We're not kids. We're two healthy adults, and we want each other."

Why didn't he stop talking and just drag her to the bedroom? If not by the hair, then at least by the arm.

"I'm packing all the birth control we're going to need . . . "

If only he'd said he was packing a gun and he'd turn it on her if she didn't lie there and let him do what he wanted. Except she wanted to do a lot more than just lie there.

"Now, I suggest you march your little butt right to the bedroom!"

The words were perfect, and she loved the way he jabbed his finger toward the door, but the expression in his eyes was beginning to look less like anger and more like caution. He was getting ready to back off.

She hurried to the bedroom. She couldn't make too much of this, couldn't let it be too important. She was a beautiful slave girl forced to give herself to the ruthless (but gorgeous) man who owned her. A slave girl who needed to get her clothes off before he beat her!

She pulled off her top so that she was standing before him in her bra and shorts, which weren't really shorts but gauzy harem pants. Harem pants he was going to rip from her body if she didn't take them off first.

She bent her head and kicked away her sandals. Then she pulled her shorts—harem pants—over her legs and cast them aside. When she looked up, she saw her owner standing in the bedroom door, a slightly befuddled expression on his face, as if he couldn't believe it was going to be this easy. *Ha!* Easy for *him*! He wasn't staring death in the face!

She was wearing only her bra and panties. Lifting her chin, she gazed at him defiantly. He might possess her body, but she'd never let him have her soul!

He moved toward her, his confidence restored. Of course he was confident. She'd be confident, too, if she had an army of guards stationed right outside the door, ready to drag a disobedient slave girl to her death if she didn't submit.

He stopped in front of her and gazed down, his green eyes raking her body. If she'd left her top on, he would have torn it off with his dagger . . . no, his *teeth*!

He burned up her skin with those imperious eyes. What if she didn't please him? Such a merciless master demanded more from her than simple submission. He demanded cooperation! And (she'd just remembered) he'd vowed to have her dearest friend, the gentle slave girl Melissa, tortured to death if he was displeased. No matter how it destroyed her pride, she must satisfy him!

To save Melissa.

She lifted her arms and cradled his magnificent jaw between her hands, desperately trying to gentle this barbarian. She leaned forward and pressed her innocent lips to his cruel ones—cruelly, cruelly . . . sweet.

She sighed and teased him with the tip of her tongue. When he opened his mouth, she invaded. How could she do anything else when she had poor, gentle Melissa's life to protect?

His hands splayed over her bare back, moved up to the clasp of her bra. Her skin quivered. The clasp fell open.

He gripped her shoulders and took over the kiss. Then he tugged off her bra and cast it aside.

His mouth left hers. His jaw scraped her cheek. "Molly . . . "

She didn't want to be Molly. If she were Molly, she'd have

to grab her clothes and put them right back on, because Molly wasn't self-destructive.

She was only a slave girl, and she bowed her head submissively as he drew back and gazed down at her naked breasts, now exposed to his predatory emerald eyes. She shivered and waited. Cotton rustled as he drew his T-shirt—his silken robe—over his head and tossed it aside. She squeezed her eyes shut when he pulled her against him, his conqueror's chest pressed to her naked, defenseless breasts.

Tremors swept over the sensitive skin as he began to nibble kisses, like a golden slave's collar, around her throat, then down to the breasts that no longer belonged to her. They were his. Every part of her body belonged to him! Her knees grew weak and sagged. She wanted this so much, but she needed desperately to hold on to her fantasy.

Master . . . Slave girl . . . His to do with as he wished. Mustn't anger him . . . Let him—oh, yes—extend the trail of kisses over her ribs to her navel, her stomach, gliding over her hipbones as his thumbs caught the elastic on her panties.

Concentrate! Envision those cruel lips! Those cutting eyes! The dreadful penalty the slave girl would pay if she didn't ease her legs open so he could slip his hand between them. Her merciless master . . . Her savage owner . . . Her—

"There's a bunny on your panties."

Even the most creative mind couldn't have held a fantasy together against that dark, husky chuckle. She glared at him, then grew uncomfortably conscious that one of them still wore a pair of khaki slacks while the other wore only a sky blue pair of bunny panties.

"What if there is?"

He straightened and rubbed his fingers over the front of the panties, making her shiver as he gave the little bunny a pat. "Just wondering."

"They were a present from Phoebe. A surprise."

"They sure surprised me." He nuzzled her neck while he

continued patting her bunny. "Are these the only ones?"

She sucked in her breath. "There . . . might be a few more."

He splayed his other hand across her bottom and massaged. "You got the badger dude on any of them?"

She did. Benny, with his cute little badger mask. "Could you stop . . . talking . . . and get back to . . . ahh . . . conquering."

"Conquering?" He slipped one long finger beneath the elastic leg band.

"Never mind." She sighed as he rubbed. Oh, that was wicked. She eased her legs open and let him go where he wanted.

And he wanted to go everywhere.

Before she knew it, her panties were gone, along with his clothes, and they were naked on her bed, too impatient to pull down the quilt.

Their play turned serious much too soon. He gripped her shoulders and pulled her on top of him—the servicing position. She wiggled up his body, caught his head in her hands, and kissed him again, hoping to slow him down.

"You're so sweet . . . " he murmured in her mouth.

But he was impossible to distract. He caught the back of her knees and spread them over his hips. Here it came. She braced herself for his thrust and bit her lip to keep from yelling at him to *take his time, for Pete's sake, and stop acting as if the ref just blew the two-minute warning!*

She'd promised herself she wouldn't criticize, so she sank her teeth into the hard muscle of his shoulder instead.

He made a low, hoarse sound that might have been pain or pleasure, and the next thing she knew she was on her back and he was hovering over her, those green eyes wicked.

"So the bunny lady wants to play rough?"

With two hundred pounds of muscle? Oh, I don't think so.

She started to tell him she'd only been trying to distract

him so he wouldn't be so quick on the trigger, but he shack-led her wrists and made a dive for her breast.

Ahhhhh . . . It was torture. Agony. Worse than agony. How could one mouth cause so much havoc? And she didn't ever want it to stop.

He brushed his lips over the slope of her breast. He grazed the nipple, moved to the other breast, where he did the same. Then, without warning, he began to suckle . . .

She writhed against him, but he didn't release the wrists he'd imprisoned in one hand. Leaving the other free to roam.

It meandered from breast to belly, then lower, brushing through the curls. But that proved to be a tease because he quickly moved on to her inner thighs.

They fell open.

He stayed where he was.

She twisted, trying to force those tantalizing fingers away from her thighs to the part of her that throbbed so much she thought she would die.

He didn't take the hint. He was too busy tormenting her, too busy playing at her breasts. She'd heard that women could have orgasms just from this, but she hadn't believed it.

She'd been wrong.

The shock wave caught her by surprise, thundered through her, and pitched her into the sky. She didn't remem-ber crying out, but she heard the echo and knew she had.

He slowed. She shuddered against his chest, breathed him in, tried to understand what had happened to her.

He stroked her shoulder. He kissed her earlobe. His whis-pered breath tickled her hair. "A little quick on the trigger, aren't you?"

She was mortified. Sort of. Except it had felt so good. And been so unexpected. "An accident," she managed. "And it's your turn."

"Oh, I'm not in any hurry . . . " He picked up a lock of her hair, drew it to his nose. "Unlike some people."

The sheen of perspiration on his skin, the way he pressed against her thigh, told her he was in more of a hurry than he wanted to admit. A very *big* hurry. Funny . . . she hadn't remembered that about him. Not exactly. She remembered that it had hurt. And now that she thought about it, there'd been a moment when she'd thought she might be too small.

No time like the present to find out if that was true.

She scooted on top of him.

He scooted her back off. Dawdled at the corner of her mouth. When was he going to get to the slam, bam part?

"Why don't you just lie back and rest for a while?" he whispered.

Rest? "Oh, I definitely don't—"

He caught her shoulders, nestled his thumbs in her armpits, started that trail of kisses again. Only this time he kept going.

Before long his hands were at her knees, pushing them far apart. His hair brushed her inner thighs, so sensitive now that she quivered. And then he claimed her with his mouth.

The gentle suction . . . the sweet thrusts . . . She couldn't breathe. She caught his head, pleading. Her hips buckled as the waves seized her once again.

This time when she'd calmed, he didn't tease her. Instead, he grabbed the condom she'd forgotten about, eased his body over hers, and gazed down with those green eyes. His skin was hot beneath her hands, and the blaze of late-afternoon sun streaming through the window burnished him with molten gold. She felt his muscles quivering beneath her palms as the effort to hold back became too much for him. Still, he gave her all the time in the world.

She opened . . . stretched to accept him.

He filled her slowly, kissing her, soothing her. She loved him for the careful care he was taking, and slowly, her body accepted his.

But even when he'd buried himself, he didn't ram at her. Instead, he began a slow, silken thrusting.

It was delicious, but it wasn't enough, and she realized she no longer wanted his restraint. She wanted him free and wild. She wanted him to luxuriate in her body, to use it for his pleasure. Wrapping her legs around him, she grasped his hips and urged him on.

The leash he'd held on his self-control snapped. He plunged. She moaned and met his thrust. It was like being burned in a fire of the senses.

He was too big for her, too strong, too fierce . . . Absolutely perfect.

The sun burned hotter until it exploded. They flew together into a brilliant crystalline void.

He'd never made love to a woman with a bunny on her panties. But then, there was a lot about making love with Molly that was different from anything he'd experienced. Her enthusiasm, her generosity . . . Why should he be surprised?

Kevin slid his hand over her hip and thought about how good it had been, even though she'd acted strange at first, almost as if she were trying to convince herself to be afraid of him. He remembered the way she'd stood before him in her bra and bunny panties, with her head high and shoulders back. If an American flag had been waving behind her, she'd have looked like a very sexy Marine Corps recruiting poster. The few, the proud, the cottontailed.

She stirred in his arms and snuffled her nose against his chest, burrowing like one of her storybook pals. But despite the snuffling, the burrowing, and the bunny panties, Molly had been every inch a woman.

And he was in big trouble. In one afternoon, he'd undone everything he'd been trying to accomplish by ignoring her.

She slid her hand from his chest to his belly. Here and

there the last shafts of sunlight glazed her hair with little reddish sprinkles like the ones she'd used on yesterday's sugar cookies. He forced himself to remember all the reasons he'd tried so hard to keep her at a distance, starting with the fact that she wasn't going to be part of his life much longer, which could very well piss off her sister, who happened to be the owner of the team he intended to take to the Super Bowl this year.

He couldn't think about all the ways a team owner had of making it tough, even for her star player, not right now. Instead, he thought about how much passion had been locked up inside the small, quirky body of this woman who was and wasn't his wife.

She snuffled again. "You're not a bust-out. As a lover, I mean."

He was glad she couldn't see his smile, because giving her even the smallest advantage generally meant he ended up swimming in the lake with his clothes on. He settled for sarcasm. "I sense a tender moment coming on. Should I get a handkerchief?"

"I just mean that— Well, after last time . . . "

"Don't tell me."

"It was all I had for comparison."

"For the love of—"

"I know it's not fair. You were asleep. And unwilling. I haven't forgotten that."

He tucked her closer and heard himself say, "Maybe it's time you did."

Her head shot up, and she looked at him with a million emotions on her face, the main one being hope. "What do you mean?"

He rubbed the back of her neck. "I mean, it's over. It's forgotten. And you're forgiven."

Her eyes filled with tears. "You mean it, don't you?"

"I mean it."

"Oh, Kevin . . . I—"

He sensed a speech coming on, and he wasn't in the mood for any more talk, so he started making love to her all over again.

Chapter 19

Yes!

*Notes for Chik article,
"Do Jocks Only Want One Thing?"*

MOLLY SAT IN THE GAZEBO STARING OUT AT THE COTTAGES AND daydreaming about last night instead of getting ready for the community tea she'd invited everyone to attend on the Common that afternoon. She'd driven into town after breakfast to buy an extra cake along with some soft drinks, but refreshments were the last thing on her mind. She was thinking about Kevin and all the delicious things they'd done.

A car door slammed, distracting her. She looked up to see the paragon he'd been interviewing settle behind the wheel of an aging Crown Victoria. Molly had caught a glimpse of her as she'd arrived for her interview and hated her on sight. Just one look at the no-nonsense reading glasses dangling from a chain around her neck told Molly this woman's cookies would never burn on the bottom.

Kevin appeared on the front porch. Molly automatically waved to him, then wished she hadn't because it made her seem too eager. If only she were one of those sublimely mysterious women who could control a man with the flicker of an eyelash or a single smoldering glance. But neither flickering nor smoldering was her strong point, and Kevin wasn't a man to be controlled anyway.

Roo saw him coming across the Common and scampered to meet him, hoping for a game of catch. Molly's skin grew hot just watching him. Now she knew exactly what every part of the body underneath his black polo shirt and khaki slacks looked like.

She shivered. She didn't doubt he'd enjoyed making love with her last night—she'd been pretty darned good, if she did say so herself—but she knew it hadn't meant the same thing to him that it did to her. He'd been so . . . everything— tender, rough, thrilling, and more passionate than even her imagination could have invented. This was the most danger- ous, the most impossible, the most hopeless crush she'd ever experienced, and last night had made it worse.

Suddenly Kevin stopped walking in midstride. She saw right away what had caught his attention. A nine-year-old boy stood on the edge of the Common holding a football. His name was Cody. His parents had introduced him yester- day when they'd checked in to Green Pastures.

Kevin might not know they finally had younger guests. Between going up in the glider in the afternoon, then locking themselves in the bedroom at the cottage, he wouldn't have seen the children, and she hadn't thought to mention it.

He began walking toward the boy, Roo following along. His stride picked up as he got nearer, until he stopped in front of the child. Molly was too far away to make out what he was saying, but he must have introduced himself because the boy froze up a little, the way kids did when they found themselves in the presence of a well-known athlete.

Kevin rubbed the boy's head to settle him down, then slowly took the football from him. He tossed it back and forth in his hands a few times, spoke to the boy again, then gestured toward the center of the Common. For a moment the boy simply stared at him, as if he couldn't believe what he was hearing. Then his feet flew, and he raced out to catch his first pass from the great Kevin Tucker.

She smiled. It had taken a few decades, but Kevin finally had a kid to play with at the Wind Lake Campgrounds.

Roo joined in the game of catch, yipping at their ankles and generally getting in the way, but neither of them seemed to mind. Cody was a little slow and endearingly awkward, but Kevin kept encouraging him.

"You've got a good arm for a twelve-year-old."

"I'm only nine."

"You're doing great for nine!"

Cody beamed and tried harder. His legs pumped as he ran after the ball, then tried unsuccessfully to duplicate Kevin's form when he tossed it back.

After nearly half an hour of this he finally began to tire, but Kevin was too caught up rewriting history to notice. "You're doing great, Cody. Just relax your arm and put your body into it."

Cody did his best to comply, but he began to dart yearning glances toward his cottage. Kevin, however, focused only on making sure this boy wouldn't suffer the same kind of loneliness he had.

"Hey, Molly!" he called out. "You see what a good arm my friend has here?"

"Yes, I see."

Cody's sneakers were starting to drag, and even Roo was looking tired. But Kevin remained oblivious.

Molly was just getting ready to intervene when the three O'Brian brothers—ages six, nine, and eleven, as she recalled—came running out from the woods behind Jacob's Ladder.

"Hey, Cody! Get your suit on. Our moms said we could go to the beach!"

Cody's face lit up.

Kevin looked thunderstruck. She really should have remembered to tell him that several of the families checking in yesterday had kids. She experienced a sudden, irrational hope that this somehow would make him change his mind about selling the place.

Cody hugged the football to his chest and looked uneasy. "It's been nice playing with you, Mr. Tucker, but . . . uh . . . I have to go play with my friends now. If it's okay?" He edged away backward. "If you . . . can't find anybody else to play with, I guess—I guess I can come back later."

Kevin cleared his throat. "That's okay. You go on with your friends."

Cody was off like a shot with the three O'Brian boys following.

Kevin approached her slowly. He looked so disconcerted that Molly bit her lip to keep her smile within reasonable boundaries. "Roo'll play with you."

Roo whimpered and crawled under the gazebo.

She rose and walked to the bottom of the steps. "Okay, I'll play with you. But don't throw hard."

He shook his head in bewilderment. "Where did all these kids come from?"

"School's finally out. I told you they'd show up."

"But . . . how many are here?"

"The three O'Brian boys, and Cody has a baby sister. Two families have one teenage girl each."

He sank down on the step.

She held her amusement in check as she sat next to him. "You'll probably meet them all this afternoon. Tea in the gazebo will be a nice way to kick off a new week."

He didn't say anything, just gazed out at the Common.

She considered it a tribute to her maturity that only a small bubble of laughter escaped. "Sorry your playmate ran away."

He stubbed the heel of his sneaker in the grass. "I made a fool out of myself, didn't I?"

Her heart melted, and she rested her cheek against his

shoulder. "Yes, but the world could use more fools like you. You're a very nice man."

He smiled down at her. She smiled back. And that's when it hit her.

This wasn't a crush at all. She'd fallen in love with him.

She was so horrified, she jerked away.

"What's wrong?"

"Nothing!" She started to chatter to cover up her dismay. "There's another family. More children. Checking in today with . . . some kids. The Smiths. They didn't say how many—how many kids. Amy talked to them."

In love with Kevin Tucker! Please, not that! Hadn't she learned anything? She knew from her childhood how impossible it was to make someone love her, yet she'd once again fallen into that old, destructive pattern. What about all her dreams and hopes? What about her Great Love Story?

She felt like burying her head in her hands and crying. She wanted love, but he only wanted sex. He stirred beside her. She was glad of the distraction, and she followed the direction of his gaze across the Common. The O'Brian boys were chasing each other while they waited for Cody to change into his swim trunks. Two girls who looked as though they were about fourteen came walking up from the beach carrying a boom box. Kevin took in the kids, the boom box, the old trees, the sherbet-colored cottages.

"I can't believe this is the same place."

"It's not," she managed. "Things change." She cleared her throat and tried to block out her turmoil. "The woman you hired. Is she starting tomorrow?"

"She told me I had to fire Amy first."

"What? You can't! She's finishing all her work and doing everything you ask! Besides, that patronizing little twit's terrific with the guests." She shot up from the step. "I mean it, Kevin. You should make her cover up her hickeys, but you can't fire her."

He didn't respond.

Molly grew alarmed. "Kevin . . . "

"Relax, will you? Of course I'm not going to fire her. That's why that old biddy drove off in a huff."

"Thank God. What was her problem with Amy?"

"Apparently Amy and her daughter went to high school together and never got along. If her daughter's like her mother, I'm on Amy's side."

"You did the right thing."

"I guess. But this is a small town, and I've reached the end of a very short list. The college kids have all gone to work on Mackinac Island for the summer, and the kind of person I need to hire isn't interested in taking a job that's only going to last through September."

"That's your answer, then. Keep this place and make the job permanent."

"That's not going to happen, but I do have another idea." He stood and looked down at her, his eyes doing a sexy dance and his mouth curling in a smile. "Did I mention that you look real good naked?"

She shivered. "What idea?"

He spoke lower. "Do you have any animals on your panties today?"

"I forget."

"Then I guess I'll have to look."

"You will not!"

"Yeah? Who's gonna stop me?"

"You're lookin' at her, jock boy." She jumped from the top step and raced across the Common, glad for the excuse to run off her turmoil. But instead of heading toward the B&B, where the presence of the guests would keep her safe, she darted between the cottages and toward the woods where she'd be . . . unsafe.

Roo loved this new game and scampered after her, yipping with excitement. It occurred to her that Kevin might not be following, but she needn't have worried. He caught her at the edge of the path and pulled her into the woods.

"Stop it! Go away!" She slapped at his arm. "You promised you'd carry those card tables out to the gazebo."

"I'm not carrying anything until I see what's on your panties."

"It's Daphne, okay?"

"I'm supposed to believe you're wearing the same underpants you had on yesterday?"

"I have more than one pair."

"I think you're lying. I want to see for myself." He dragged her deeper into the pines. While Roo circled them barking, he reached for the snap on her shorts. "Quiet, Godzilla! There's some serious business going on here."

Roo obediently quieted.

She grabbed his wrists and pushed. "Get away."

"That's not what you were saying last night."

"Somebody'll see."

"I'll tell them a bee got you, and I'm taking out the stinger."

"Don't touch my stinger!" She grabbed for her shorts, but they were already heading for her knees. "Stop that!"

He peered down at her panties. "It's the badger. You lied to me."

"I wasn't paying attention when I got dressed."

"Hold still. I've just about found that stinger."

She heard herself sigh.

"Oh, yeah . . . " His body moved against hers. "There it is."

Half an hour later, just as they were emerging from the woods, a very familiar-looking Suburban came barreling around the Common. Kevin told himself it was just a coincidence as he watched it screech to a stop in front of the B&B, but then Roo barked and raced toward it.

Molly let out a squeal and began to run. The car doors opened, and a poodle that looked like Roo jumped out. Then came the kids. It seemed like a dozen, but it was only four, all of them Calebows who were rushing his not-so-estranged wife.

Dread pooled in the pit of his stomach. One thing he knew: Where there were Calebow kids, there were bound to be Calebow parents.

His steps slowed as the luscious blond owner of the Chicago Stars slithered from the driver's side of the car and her legendary husband emerged from the passenger side. The fact that Phoebe had been driving didn't surprise him. In this family, leadership seemed to shift back and forth according to circumstances. As he approached the car, he had an uneasy premonition neither of them would like the circumstances at Wind Lake.

What were those circumstances? For almost two weeks now he'd been acting crazed. Training camp was a little over a month away, but he was either laughing with Molly, getting mad at her, freezing her out, or seducing her. He hadn't watched any game film in days, and he wasn't working out enough. All he could think about was how much he loved being with her—this sassy, aggravating kid-woman who wasn't beautiful, silent, or undemanding, but a pain in the ass. And so much fun.

Why did she have to be Phoebe's sister? Why couldn't he have met her in a bar? He tried to imagine her in glitter eye shadow and a cellophane dress, but all he could see was the way she'd looked that morning in her underpants and his T-shirt. Her bare feet had been hooked over the rung of a chair, her pretty hair tousled around her face, and those wicked blue-gray eyes had shot trouble at him over the rim of a Peter Rabbit cup.

Now Molly hugged her nieces and nephew, apparently forgetting that her clothes were rumpled and she had pine needles in her hair. He didn't look much better, and any astute pair of eyes could see what they'd been up to.

There were no eyes more astute than the ones belonging to Phoebe and Dan Calebow. All four of them rotated toward him.

He slipped his hands into his pockets and played it cool. "Hey, there. Nice surprise."

"We thought so." Phoebe's polite response stood in marked contrast to the warm way she used to greet him, while Dan's expression was assessing. Kevin beat back his uneasiness by reminding himself that he was untouchable, the best quarterback in the AFC.

But the Chicago Stars had no untouchables as long as the Calebows were at the helm, and right then it flashed through his mind exactly how this could play out if he wasn't careful. If they decided they wanted to keep him away from Molly, he'd be called into the front office one day soon and hear that he was part of a big-ticket trade. A lot of struggling teams would be more than happy to give up some top draft choices for an All-Pro quarterback, and before he knew what had happened, he'd find himself playing for one of the league's bottom-dwellers.

As he watched Dan taking in the pine needles stuck to Molly's hair, a mental picture flashed through his head of himself barking out signals for the Lions in the Silverdome.

Molly hugged the kids who were chirping around her. "Are you surprised to see us, Aunt Molly? Are you surprised?"

"Roo! Kanga's here to play with you!"

" . . . and Mom says we can go swimming in . . . "

" . . . fell off the monkey bars and got a black eye!"

" . . . this boy calls her every day, even though . . . "

" . . . then he threw up all over the . . . "

" . . . Dad says I'm too young, but . . . "

Molly's attention shifted from one child to the next, her

expression flickering from sympathy to interest to amusement without missing a beat. This was her real family.

The sharp ache took him by surprise. He and Molly sure weren't a family, so it wasn't as if he'd been cut out of anything. He was just having a leftover reflex from his childhood, when he'd dreamed about being part of a big, messy crowd like this one.

"Omigosh!" Molly squealed. "*You're* the Smiths!"

The kids squealed back and pointed their fingers at her. *Gotcha, Aunt M!*

Kevin remembered Molly's earlier comment that a family named Smith was checking in today. Meet the Smiths. His sense of dread grew.

Molly gazed at her sister, who was holding Roo the Fierce. "Did Amy know who you really were when she took the reservation?"

Tess giggled. At least he figured it was Tess, because she wore a soccer jersey while her look-alike scampered around in a sundress. "Mom didn't tell her. We wanted to surprise you!"

"We get to stay all week!" Andrew exclaimed. "And I want to sleep with you!"

Way to go, Andy boy. You just tossed good ol' Uncle Kevin right out on his ass.

Molly rumpled his hair and didn't reply. At the same time she reached for the quietest Calebow.

Hannah had been standing a little off to the side, as she usually did, but her eyes sparkled with excitement. "I thought up a whole new Daphne adventure," she whispered, barely loud enough for him to hear. "I wrote it down in my spiral notebook."

"I can't wait to read it."

"Can we see the beach, Aunt Molly?"

As Dan took the keys from Phoebe, he turned toward Kevin. "Maybe you could show me the cottage so I can start unloading."

"Sure." Just what he didn't want to do. Dan was on a mission to assess how much damage Kevin had done to his precious Molly. But when it came to damage, Kevin felt as if he were the one who'd suffered a head wound.

Molly pointed toward the cottage on the other side of the Common. "You're staying in Gabriel's Trumpet. The door's unlocked."

Kevin walked across the grass while Dan drove around. They did a catch-up on the team as they unloaded, but he knew Dan fairly well, and it didn't take the Stars' president long to say what was on his mind.

"So what's going on here?" Dan slammed the tailgate on the Suburban harder than he needed to.

Kevin could be as in-your-face as Dan, but he decided it was smarter using Molly's "dumb" ploy. "The truth is, I've been having a bitch of a time." He picked up a laundry basket filled with beach toys. "I didn't think it was going to be so hard to get someone to run this place."

"Dad!" Julie and Tess came running up, followed by Andrew. "We need our suits so we can go swimming before the tea party this afternoon."

"Except Aunt Molly says I get to drink lemonade," Andrew declared, " 'cause I don't like tea!"

"Look at our cottage! It's so cute!" Julie raced to the door as Molly and Phoebe approached with Hannah.

Molly looked tense, and Phoebe regarded Kevin with eyes as chilly as a Lions uniform in the middle of a losing Detroit November.

"The lake's freezing, girls," Molly called out to the twins on the porch, trying to act as though everything were normal. "It's not like the pool at home."

"Are there water snakes?"

The question had come from Hannah, who looked worried. Something about her had always gotten to Kevin. "No snakes, kiddo. Do you want me to go in with you?"

Her smile flashed a thousand watts of gratitude. "Would you?"

"Sure. Get your suit on, and I'll meet you there." He didn't want to leave Molly alone with the enemy, so he said, "Your aunt'll come along. She loves swimming in that old lake, don't you, Molly?"

Molly looked relieved. "Sure. We can all go swimming together."

And wasn't this going to be a whole new way to have fun?

He and Molly waved cheery see-you-laters to the Calebows. As they walked away, he thought he heard Dan muttering to Phoebe, but he caught only one word.

"Slytherin."

Molly waited until they were far enough away before she let her agitation show. "You have to get your things out of the cottage! I don't want them to know we've been sleeping together."

After the way they'd looked coming out of the woods, he figured it was already too late, but he nodded.

"And don't let Dan get you alone again. He'll just give you the third degree. I'll make sure one of the kids is always around when I'm with Phoebe."

Before he could reply, she took off toward the cottage. He kicked at a clump of gravel and headed for the B&B. Why did she need to be secretive? Not that he wanted her to say anything—things were rocky enough as it was. But Molly didn't have to worry about being traded to Detroit like he did, so why didn't she tell them to go to hell?

The more he thought about it, the more her attitude bothered him. It was okay for him to want to keep this private, but somehow it wasn't okay for her.

Chapter 20

In olden days a girl who liked a boy always made sure he won when they played cards and board games.

"Playing Rough"
article for Chik

THEY CHANGED OUT OF THEIR SUITS IN TIME FOR MOLLY'S TEA IN the gazebo, which she'd decided to hold at three o'clock instead of five because it would be better for the kids. She complained to Phoebe that the paper plates and store-bought cake disqualified her from a photo spread in *Victoria* magazine, but Kevin knew she cared more about having a good time than bringing out the good china.

He nodded at Lilly, who'd walked over with Charlotte Long and Charlotte's friend Vi. He'd already noticed the cottage residents shielding her from the curiosity of the more transient guests at the B&B. He thought about going over to talk to her, but he couldn't think of what to say.

Molly kept herself surrounded with scampering poodles and noisy kids. She had a red heart barrette in her hair, pink jeans, a purple top, and bright blue laces in her sneakers. She was a walking rainbow, and just looking at her made him smile.

"George!" Molly bounced up and down waving at Liam Jenner as he got out of his pickup around four o'clock and walked toward them. "George Smith! Thanks for coming."

Jenner laughed and walked over to give her a hug. He might be old, but he was a good-looking son of a bitch, and Kevin wasn't crazy about the way he and the bunny lady were hanging on to each other.

"You've got to meet my sister. She used to run a gallery in New York, but I won't tell her who you are."

Yeah, right. Molly's eyes flashed the mischief jitterbug, but Jenner was oblivious. *Sucka.*

As the artist headed toward Phoebe, he walked right past Lilly. Maybe Liam had gotten fed up with all her early-morning rejections at the kitchen table. Kevin couldn't figure it out. If Lilly didn't like being around him, why did she keep showing up for breakfast?

He glanced from Lilly to Molly and tried to pick the exact moment when his long practice of surrounding himself with low-maintenance women had exploded in his face. He slammed his ball cap down on his head and promised himself he'd watch game film tonight.

The men wanted to talk football, and Kevin and Dan complied. Around five some of the adults began to drift away, but the kids were still enjoying themselves, and Kevin decided he'd put up a basketball hoop tomorrow. Maybe he'd buy some rubber rafts for the beach. And bikes. The kids should have bikes while they were here.

Cody and the O'Brian boys came running up, their faces sweaty and clothes grimy. Exactly the way a kid should look in the summer.

"Hey, Kevin! Can we play softball?"

He could feel the smile spreading all over his face. A soft-ball game on the Common, right where the Tabernacle had once stood ... "Sure we can. Listen up! Everybody who wants to play softball, raise your hand."

Hands went up all over the place. Tess and Julie raced forward, and Andrew started to yell and hop. Even the adults were interested.

"A softball game is a wonderful idea," Charlotte Long chirped from her lawn chair. "Get everything organized, Kevin."

He smiled at her poking. "You want to be a captain, Cody?"

"Sure."

He looked around for another captain and started to pick Tess, but something about the way Hannah was sitting at her father's feet cuddling the poodles got to him. He'd seen her hand inch up, only to settle back into her lap. "Hannah, how about you? Do you want to be the other captain?"

Kevin was startled to see Dan drop his head and groan.

"No, Kevin!" Tess and Julie cried together. "Not Hannah!"

Molly surprised him most of all—the bunny lady, who was supposed to be so damn sensitive around kids. "Uh . . . maybe it would be better if you picked somebody else."

What was wrong with these people?

Luckily their callousness didn't faze Hannah, who jumped up, smoothed down her shorts, and gave him a smile that looked exactly like her aunt's. "Thank you, Kevin. They hardly ever let me be captain."

"That's because you—"

Phoebe laid her hand over Tess's mouth, but even she looked pained.

Kevin was disgusted with all of them. Nobody was more competitive than he was, but he'd never stooped low enough to make a little kid feel bad just because she wasn't athletic. He gave her a reassuring smile. "Don't pay any attention to them, sweetheart. You'll be a great captain. You can even choose first."

"Thank you." She stepped forward and surveyed the crowd. He waited for her to choose either him or her father. She surprised him by pointing toward her mother, a woman who played so badly that the veterans on the Stars' team had gotten in the habit of scheduling dental appointments just so they'd have an excuse to leave the team picnic before the annual softball game.

"I choose Mom."

Kevin bent closer and lowered his voice. "In case you weren't sure, Hannah, you can choose anybody you want, including guys. That means your dad. Me. Are you sure you want to choose your mom first?"

"She's sure." Dan sighed from behind him. "Here we go again."

Hannah gazed up at Kevin and whispered, "Mom gets her feelings hurt because nobody ever wants her on their team."

Tess cut right to the bone as only an eleven-year-old could. "That's because she sucks."

Phoebe sniffed and patted her team captain's shoulder, conveniently forgetting her earlier lack of support. "Pay no attention, Hannah. A winning attitude is far more important than natural ability."

Unlike Hannah, Cody was no fool, and he chose natural ability over that winning attitude. "I pick Kevin."

Dan rose from his lawn chair and moved closer to his daughter. "Hannah, honey, I'm over here. Don't forget about me. I'll get my feelings hurt if you don't choose me."

"No you won't." Hannah gave him a blazing smile, turned away, and fastened her eyes on Lilly, who'd been talking about gardening with some of the older women, and as far as Kevin could remember, hadn't raised her hand. "I pick you."

"Me?" Lilly looked pleased and stood. "Lord, I haven't played softball since I was a teenager."

Hannah smiled up at her mother. "This is going to be an exc'llent team. Lots of winning attitude."

Cody, not one to let any grass grow under his feet, chose Dan.

Once again Kevin stepped in, trying to help Hannah out by pointing toward the oldest of the O'Brian boys. "I was watching Scott toss the football around earlier. He's a pretty good athlete."

"Save your breath," Dan muttered, and sure enough, Kevin saw Hannah's third choice coming the minute he noticed Andrew's lower lip sticking out.

"I choose Andrew. See, Andrew, just because you're only five doesn't mean nobody wants you on their team."

"I'll take Tess," Cody countered, right on the mark.

"And I'll take Aunt Molly!" Hannah beamed.

Kevin sighed. So far Cody had one current NFL quarterback on his team, one former NFL quarterback, and one of the most athletic little girls in northern Illinois. Hannah, on the other hand, had her mother, the worst softball player in history; her little brother, who had a lot of heart but, at five, not much skill; and Molly, who was . . . well, Molly—the lady who tipped canoes, tried to drown herself, and in general hated sports.

Cody's next choices included the teenage girls who'd been kicking a soccer ball earlier with Tess, the middle O'Brian—who was built like a tank—and both his physically fit parents.

Hannah chose the six-year-old O'Brian, a kid Kevin was fairly certain he'd seen hiding his security blanket in the shrubs. She redeemed herself by picking her sister Julie, who at least was a dancer and coordinated, and then Liam Jenner, although her reasoning wasn't too sound. "Because he drew a beautiful picture of Kanga and Roo for me." While Cody filled in the rest of his team with the younger adults, Hannah chose every oldster who wanted to play.

It was going to be a bloodbath.

The boys ran to their cottages to get the equipment, Mr. Canfield—whose arthritis had been acting up—volunteered to umpire, and everybody soon settled into place.

Hannah's team was up at bat first, and Kevin found himself on the pitcher's mound facing the six-year-old who'd tucked his security blanket in the forsythia. Kevin made the mistake of glancing over at Molly and wasn't surprised to see her give him a look that clearly said, *If you're the kind of man who can strike out Linus, then you're not the man I thought you were, and you can forget all about getting me naked anytime in the foreseeable future,* comprenez-vous?

He walked the kid.

Hannah sent up Andrew next, and Kevin put a soft one over the plate. Andrew missed, but he had a great swing for a little kid, and as Kevin watched an expression of mulish determination settle over his face, he knew he'd just caught a glimpse of what Dan Calebow had looked like at the age of five. Because of that, his next pitch was harder than he intended, but Andrew was game, and he gave it his best.

Molly, on the other hand, shot him a look that had "dickhead" written all over it. *He's five, you idiot! Just a little boy! Is winning so important that you're going to strike out a five-year-old? You're definitely not ever, ever going to see another pair of bunny panties for the rest of your life! No way, no how. Adiós, muchacho!*

Kevin gave him another soft one, and Andrew banged it into short right. The oldest O'Brian kid didn't know how dangerous even a kindergarten Calebow could be, and he was caught napping. As a result, Linus made it to third, and Andrew settled in with his dad on second.

Dan ruffled his hair.

"Kevin?" Hannah called out politely. "Mr. McMullen's up next. He wants to know if it's okay if he uses his walker?"

And didn't that just say it all.

Finally it was Cody's team's turn to bat, and Kevin was up. Near the pitcher's mound he saw Little Hannah Goodheart huddled with the Four Horsewomen of the Apocalypse: Molly, Phoebe, Lilly, and Julie. Finally the females dispersed, leaving their pitcher on the mound.

Molly, the bunny lady.

Kevin couldn't contain his grin. Now, this was more like it. And guess what, boys and girls? Benny the Badger was showing little Daphne no mercy.

Molly tried to stare him down, but he could tell she was nervous. Damn right. All-American. MVP. Heisman candidate. All-Pro. Good reason to be nervous.

He stepped up to the plate and smiled at her. "Just try to keep the ball away from my head, sweetheart. I like my good-looking nose right where it is."

"That," Dan said from behind him, "was a mistake."

Yeah, right . . .

Molly went through a few gyrations that were supposed to pass for a warm-up. Kevin tapped his bat to the ground and waited for the pitch, thinking how cute she looked. Better than cute. Her lips were all rosy where she'd bitten them, and her breasts pressed against her purple top the same way they'd pressed against his chest the night before. As she released the ball, her sweet little rear end wiggled inside those tight pink jeans the same way it had wiggled against—

The ball sailed past him while he was distracted. *Whoa . . . what was that about?*

"Strike one!" Mr. Canfield called out.

A fluke, that's all. A lapse in concentration brought on by too little eye on the ball and too much eye on the doll. He stepped away from the plate.

She knew it was a fluke, too, because she started gnawing at that bottom lip again and looking even more nervous than before. That made this a good time to start playing a few mind games. "Nice pitch, Daphne. Think you can do it again?"

"I doubt it."

She was definitely nervous. Definitely sexy. He loved the way that lady made love, with her whole heart and every part of her body.

Her butt wiggled. Oh, he remembered what that wiggle felt like.

The ball came fast, but this time he was ready for it—except it dropped unexpectedly at the last instant, and his bat met nothing but air.

"Exc'llent, Aunt Molly."

"Thank you, Hannah."

Kevin couldn't believe it.

"Nice going," Dan grumbled from behind him.

Molly stroked the inner slope of her breast with her index finger. The tip of her tongue flicked over that puffy bottom lip. God, she was making him hot! As soon as this game was over, he was dragging her back into the woods, family or not, and then he'd show her a real game.

She wound up, and just as she released the ball, looked right at his crotch. He instinctively stepped away to protect himself. As a result he missed most of it and tapped a feeble roller back to the mound. He started to run. She threw to Julie on first base, who caught it with something that looked like a pirouette from *Swan Lake*.

He was out. *Out!* He looked from the ballerina to the bunny lady and tried to take it in. Molly's eyes flicked from his face to his crotch. And then she grinned. "Did I ever tell you I went to summer camp for nine years?"

"I believe you mentioned it." He couldn't imagine any summer camp teaching that particular trick. The queen of the mischief-makers had thought it up all by herself.

By the end of the first inning Molly had given Cody an easy pitch, walked Dan, and struck out the oldest O'Brian kid, along with his father.

Jocks 0, Last Kids to Be Chosen in Gym Class 2.

She sauntered past him as her team came in from the field. "Nice day."

"I thought you said you weren't any good at sports."

"I said I didn't *like* sports, jock boy." She flicked his chest. "There's a difference."

He couldn't let her get away with that one, so he gave her

some prime NFL sneer. "Next time you stare at my zipper, jock girl, you'd better be on your back."

She laughed and ran off to join her team.

Lilly was first up. She was all Guccied in coordinating colors with diamonds flashing from her rings and bracelets. She kicked away a pair of leopard-print sandals, slipped off sunglasses with interlocking C's at the hinges, and grabbed the bat. She took a couple of practice swings, then stood up to the plate as if she owned it. Right then he knew that he hadn't gotten all his athletic ability from the rodeo rider.

She arched an eyebrow at him, and her eyes caught the light. Green like his.

I know you're my real mom and I love you very much . . .

He didn't try to burn her. Instead, he sent it nice and easy over the plate. She took a great swing, but she was rusty and didn't catch it all.

"Foul ball!"

He gave her the same pitch again, and this time she caught it clean. The bat cracked against the ball, and as her team whooped, she made it to second. He was startled by the burst of pride he felt.

"Nice going," he muttered.

"Past my prime," she said.

Captain Goodheart was up next, all solemn and serious, with the same worried look on her face he sometimes saw her aunt wearing. Hannah's straight brown hair was a little lighter than Molly's, but they had the same stubborn chin, the same slight tilt at the eyes. She was a serious kid, as well as being neat. Her American Girl T-shirt didn't show any sign that she'd been playing with a couple of poodles and eating chocolate cake. He spotted a tiny notebook sticking out of the back pocket of her shorts, and something inside him melted. She seemed more like Molly's daughter than Dan and Phoebe's. Was this the way his little girl would have looked?

Out of nowhere his throat tightened.

"I'm not very good," Hannah whispered from the plate.

Oh, man, not that . . . He was dead meat. He threw wide.

"Ball one."

She looked even more worried. "I'm better at drawing. And writing things. I'm pretty good at writing things."

"Cut it out, Hannah," her insensitive jerk of a father called from second base.

Kevin had always considered Dan Calebow one of the best parents he'd ever known, which just proved how wrong he could be. He shot him a quelling look and threw a lob so soft, so gentle, that it didn't make it to the plate.

"Ball two."

Hannah bit her bottom lip and spoke in a helpless whisper. "I'll be so glad when this is over."

Kevin melted, and so did his next pitch, just as it passed over the plate.

Hannah bunted it with a choppy little swing.

Kevin went after the ball, but he didn't hurry so he could give her enough time to make it to first base. Unfortunately, Cody missed the catch, and she made it to second.

He heard a chorus of cheers go up and saw Lilly slide home, Gucci pants forgotten.

Last Kids to Be Chosen in Gym Class 3, Jocks 0.

He cocked his head at Hannah.

"I'm not a very good batter," she said in her lost-little-girl voice, "but I can run really fast."

"Brother," Dan said in disgust.

Kevin was about to say something comforting when the little girl exchanged a look with her aunt that just about knocked him off his feet. It was only a smile. But it wasn't an ordinary smile. Oh, no. It was a sly little hustler's smile!

An expression of such perfect understanding passed between niece and aunt that he nearly choked. He'd been conned! Hannah was a world-class mischief-maker, just like Molly!

He turned on Dan, who looked faintly apologetic. "Phoebe and I still aren't sure if she plans it ahead of time or if it just happens."

"You should have told me!"

Dan gazed at his youngest daughter with a combination of irritation and fatherly pride. "You had to see this for yourself."

Sports sometimes had a way of making everything clear, and right then it all fell into place—from Molly's almost drowning and the incident with the canoe to Marmie's uncharacteristic trip up into that tree. Molly had been stringing him along from the very beginning. Cody came forward, clearly unhappy with his pitcher's lackluster performance, and the next thing Kevin knew, he was standing on second base while Dan took over at the mound.

Hannah the Con Artist exchanged a sly glance with Molly, and Kevin saw why. It was Phoebe's turn at bat.

Oh, and didn't the good times just start to roll then? There was more butt wiggling, lip licking, and breast thrusting than anybody under the age of consent should be allowed to witness. Dan started to sweat, Phoebe cooed, and the next thing he knew, the Stars' owner was perched on first while Miss Hannah claimed third.

It had turned into a bloodbath.

The Jocks finally managed to beat the Last Kids to Be Chosen in Gym Class, but only because Captain Cody was smart enough to replace Dan with Tess, who was immune to butt wiggling, plus being nobody's fool. Tess made short work of the nursery set and politely but firmly put the oldsters out to pasture. Even she, however, couldn't stop Aunt Molly from hitting a homer in the last inning.

For someone who hated sports, Molly sure did know how to handle a bat, and the way she ran the bases left Kevin so aroused he had to bend over and pretend he was rubbing away a leg cramp to keep from embarrassing himself. As he rubbed, he remembered how crowded Molly's bed would be this week with all the kids snuggling up against her. The way he understood it, this was Julie's night, tomorrow it would be Andrew's, then Hannah's, then Tess's. Maybe he could sneak into the cottage after bedtime and kidnap Auntie M. But then he remembered her telling him Julie was a light sleeper.

He sighed and resettled his ball cap on his head. Face it. There wasn't going to be any joy in Mudville tonight. Mighty Kevin had struck out.

Chapter 21

The woods were spooky, and Daphne's teeth chattered. What if no one ever found her? Thank goodness she'd brought along her favorite lettuce and marmalade sandwich.

Daphne Gets Lost

LILLY LEANED BACK INTO THE CHAISE AND LISTENED TO THE TINkling of the wind chimes hanging from the redbud tree that grew next to the patio. She loved wind chimes, but Craig had hated them and wouldn't let her hang them in her garden. She closed her eyes, glad the guests at the B&B seldom visited this quiet spot just behind the house.

She'd finally stopped asking herself how long she was staying here. When it was time to leave, she'd know. And today had been such fun. When she'd slid into home plate, Kevin had almost seemed proud of her, and at the picnic he hadn't deliberately avoided her the way Liam had.

"Hiding out from your adoring public?"

Her eyes snapped open, and her heart skipped a beat as the man she thought about far too much came out the back door of the B&B. His hair was shaggy, his clothes the same rumpled khaki shorts and navy pocket T-shirt he'd worn earlier at the picnic. Like her, he hadn't yet cleaned up from the softball game.

She gazed into those dark eyes that saw too much. "I'm recuperating from this afternoon."

He sank into the cushions on the redwood chair next to her. "You're a pretty good softball player for a girl."

"And you're a pretty good softball player for a sissy artist."

He yawned. "Who are you calling a sissy?"

She stopped herself from smiling. She did too much of that when they were together, and it encouraged him. Every morning she told herself she'd stay in her room until he left, but she'd go downstairs anyway. She still couldn't believe what she'd done with him. It was as if she'd been under a spell, as if that glass-enclosed studio had been part of another world. But she was back in Kansas now.

She was also mildly irritated by how much he'd enjoyed himself without her. If he hadn't been laughing with Molly, he'd been flirting with Phoebe Calebow or teasing one of the children. He was a gruff, intimidating man, and the fact that they hadn't been frightened of him somehow annoyed her.

"Go get cleaned up," he said. "I'll do the same, then take you out to dinner."

"Thanks, but I'm not hungry."

He gave a weary sigh and rested his head against the back of the chair. "You're hell-bent on throwing this away, aren't you? You're not going to give us a fighting chance."

She eased her legs over the side of the chaise and sat straighter. "Liam, what happened between us was an aberration. I've been alone too much lately, and I gave in to a foolish impulse."

"Just time and circumstances, is that it?"

"Yes."

"It could have happened with anyone?"

She wanted to agree, but she couldn't. "No, not with anyone. You can be attractive when you put your mind to it."

"So can a lot of men. You know there's something between us, but you don't have the guts to see what it is."

"I don't need to. I know exactly why I'm attracted to you. It's an old habit."

"What do you mean by that?"

She twisted her rings. "I mean that I've been there and done that. The alpha male. The stallion who rules the herd. The take-charge prince who makes all Cinderella's troubles go away. Men like you are my fatal weakness. But I'm not a penniless teenager anymore who needs someone to take care of her."

"Thank God. I don't like teenagers. And I'm too self-centered to take care of anyone."

"You're deliberately minimizing what I'm trying to tell you."

"That's because you're boring me."

She wouldn't let his rudeness distract her, especially since she knew it was calculated to do just that. "Liam, I'm too old and too smart to make the same mistake again. Yes, I'm attracted to you. I'm instinctively drawn to aggressive men, even though it's their nature to run roughshod over the women who care about them."

"And here I thought this conversation couldn't become any more infantile."

"You're doing it right now. You don't want to talk about this, so you're belittling me to try to get me to shut up."

"Too bad it's not working."

"I thought I'd finally gotten smart, but obviously I haven't, or I wouldn't be letting you do this." She rose from the chaise. "Listen to me, Liam. I made the mistake of falling in love with a controlling man once in my life, and I'll never do it again. I loved my husband. But, God—sometimes I hated him more."

She hugged herself, astonished that she'd revealed something to him she could barely admit to herself.

"He probably deserved it. He sounds like a son of a bitch."

"He was just like you!"

"I seriously doubt that."

"You don't think so?" She jabbed her hand toward the

redbud tree. "He wouldn't let me have wind chimes! I love wind chimes, but he hated them, so I wasn't permitted to hang them in my own garden."

"Good judgment on his part. The things are a nuisance."

Her stomach clenched. "Letting myself fall in love with you would be like falling in love with Craig all over again."

"I really resent that."

"A month after he died, I hung a set of wind chimes outside my bedroom window."

"Well, you're not going to hang them outside our bedroom window!"

"We don't have a bedroom window! And if we did, I'd hang as many sets there as I wanted!"

"Even though I've expressly asked you not to?"

She threw up her hands in frustration. "This isn't about wind chimes! I was just giving you an example!"

"You're not getting off that easily. You're the one who brought the subject up." Now he was on his feet. "I've told you I don't like the damn things, but you've said you're going to hang them up anyway, is that right?"

"You've lost your mind."

"Is that right or not?"

"Yes!"

"Fine." He gave a martyr's sigh. "If it's that important to you, go ahead and hang the damn things. But don't expect me not to complain. Bloody noise pollution. And I'll expect you to give in on something that's important to me."

She clutched her head. "Is driving me crazy your idea of seduction?"

"I'm trying to make a point. One you seem unable to understand."

"Enlighten me."

"You're not going to let any man run roughshod over you, not anymore. I just tried, but you wouldn't let me, and if I can't do it, no one can. You see? We don't have a problem."

"It's not that simple!"

"What about me?" He touched his chest, and for the first time he looked vulnerable. "What about my fatal weakness?"

"I don't know what you mean."

"Maybe if you'd think about someone other than yourself, you would!"

His words didn't sting as Craig's would have. Liam's were intended to goad her, not to wound. "You're impossible!"

"What is a man like me supposed to do, tell me that. I don't know how to pull my punches, and I'm too old to learn, so where docs that leave me?"

"I don't know."

"Strong women are my weakness. Tough women who don't fall apart just because a man doesn't always say what they want to hear. Except the strong woman I'm falling in love with doesn't want to put up with me. So where does that leave me, Lilly?"

"Oh, Liam . . . You're not falling in love with me. You're—"

"Have a little faith in yourself," he said gruffly. "In the woman you've become."

She felt trapped by his brutal honesty. He didn't know what he was saying. The person he saw when he looked at her wasn't the person she felt like inside.

He moved to the edge of the patio, his hands in his pockets. "You've been slamming doors in my face for long enough, I think. I love you, but I have my pride, too."

"I know that."

"The painting's almost done, and I'd like you to see it. Come to my house on Thursday evening."

"Liam, I—"

"If you don't show up, I won't come looking for you. You're going to have to make a decision, Lilly."

"I hate ultimatums."

"I'm not surprised. Strong women usually do." He walked away.

* * *

Kevin spent most of the next two days trying to catch Molly alone, but what with his trips into town for bikes, attending to the guests, and the kids who kept popping up every time he stuck his head out the door, he didn't have the opportunity. Twice Dan tried to talk to him, but the phone interrupted once and a guest's dead car battery the other time. By Tuesday evening he was so grouchy and out of sorts that he couldn't concentrate on the game film he'd stuck in the office VCR. Five weeks to training camp . . . He nudged Roo off his lap and got up to go to the window. It wasn't even seven o'clock, but a few rain clouds had rolled in and it was getting dark. *Where the hell was she?*

Just then his cell phone rang. He snatched it from the desk. "Hello."

"Kevin, it's Molly."

"Where have you been?" he snarled. "I told you I wanted to talk to you after tea today."

"I spotted Phoebe coming up the front walk, so I dodged out the back door. She's getting more persistent. Then I ran into Tess, and she started talking to me about a boy who likes her."

Yeah? Well, what about the boy who likes you?

"The thing is . . . after Tess left, I decided to take a walk in the woods by myself, and I started thinking about this idea I have for Daphne. One thing led to another, and the next thing I knew, I was lost."

For the first time all day he relaxed. "You don't say." As he loosened his grip on the phone, his stomach rumbled. He realized he hadn't eaten anything since breakfast, and he headed into the kitchen to fix himself a sandwich. Roo trotted along.

"Lost in the woods," she said with emphasis.

"Wow." He tried to keep the smile from his voice.

"And now it's getting dark."

"It sure is."

"It also looks like rain."

He glanced out the window. "I was just noticing that myself."

"And I'm scared."

"I'll bet." He tucked the cell phone under his chin and pulled some lunch meat from the refrigerator, along with a jar of mustard. "So you found a nearby convenience store and called me?"

"I happened to bring Phoebe's cell phone along."

He grinned and grabbed a loaf of bread from the pantry. "Smart of you."

"At camp we were taught to wear a whistle around our neck if we went walking alone. Since I didn't have a whistle . . . "

"You took a cell phone."

"Safety first."

"God bless the power of telecommunications." He went back to the refrigerator for some cheese. "And now you're lost. Have you looked for moss on the tree trunks?"

"I didn't think of that."

"It grows on the north side." He began to assemble his sandwich, enjoying himself for the first time all evening.

"Yes, I believe I remember hearing that. But it's a little dark to see."

"I don't suppose you tucked a compass in your pocket, or a flashlight?"

"That didn't occur to me."

"Too bad." He slapped on some extra mustard. "You want me to come look for you?"

"I'd really appreciate it. If you bring your phone along, I might be able to direct you. I started out on the path behind Jacob's Ladder."

"That'd be a good place for me to start then. Tell you what—I'll call you from there."

"It's getting dark fast. Would you mind hurrying?"

"Oh, sure, I'll be there before you know it." He discon-nected, chuckled, and settled down to enjoy his sandwich, but he'd barely managed three bites before she called back. "Yeah?"

"Did I tell you I might have sprained my ankle?"

"Oh, no. How'd you do that?"

"Some kind of animal hole."

"Hope it's not from a snake. There are some rattlers around here."

"Rattlers?"

He reached for a napkin. "I'm walking by Jacob's Ladder right now, but somebody must be running a microwave, be-cause I'm getting interference. I'll call you back."

"Wait, you don't have my num—"

He disconnected, gave a whoop of laughter, and headed for the refrigerator. A sandwich always tasted better with beer. He whistled to himself as he popped the cap and settled back to enjoy.

Then it struck him. What the hell was he doing?

He snatched up his cell phone and punched in Phoebe's number from memory. There'd be plenty of time later to teach her a lesson. This was the first chance he'd had in two days to get her alone. "Hey, Molly?"

"Yes."

"I'm having a little trouble finding you." He tucked the phone under his chin, grabbed the beer, along with what was left of his sandwich, and headed out the back door. "Do you think you could scream?"

"You want me to scream?"

"It'd be helpful." He took another bite of sandwich and hurried toward Jacob's Ladder.

"I'm not really much of a screamer."

"You are in bed," he pointed out.

"Are you eating?"

"I need to keep my strength up for the search." He waved at Charlotte Long with his beer bottle.

"I'm fairly sure I'm near the creek. At the end of the path that starts right behind Jacob's Ladder."

"Creek?"

"The creek, Kevin! The one that runs from the woods across the meadow. The only creek there is!"

She was beginning to sound snappish. He took a sip of beer. "I don't remember a creek. Are you sure?"

"Yes, I'm sure!"

"I suppose I'll recognize it when I see it." Kids were running around on the Common. He stopped for a moment to enjoy the sight, then returned to his mission. "The wind's really started to kick up. I can hardly see the path."

"It's not that bad here."

"Then maybe I'm going the wrong way."

"You took the path behind Jacob's Ladder, right?"

He tossed the rest of his sandwich into a trash container and stepped onto that exact path. "I think so."

"You think so? Aren't you paying attention?"

Definitely snappish.

"Just keep talking. Maybe I'll be able to tell how close I'm getting by the reception."

"Can you hear the creek?"

"Which creek is that again?"

"There's only one!"

"I hope I can find it. I don't even want to imagine how terrible it'd be if you had to spend the night in the woods by yourself."

"I'm sure that won't happen."

"I hope not. Whatever you do, don't start thinking about the Blair Witch."

"The Blair Witch?"

He managed a choking noise, then a monster moan, and disconnected.

It didn't take long for his phone to ring again.

"My ribs are aching from laughter," she said dryly.

"Sorry. It was just a squirrel. But it was huge."

"If you don't play right, I'm going home."

"Okay, but you'd better not be wearing anything more than shoes and a hair ribbon when I find you."

"I don't own a hair ribbon."

"That'll be one less thing for you to take off, then, won't it?"

As it turned out, she was still dressed when he spotted her, but that didn't last for long. They tumbled naked into the soft meadow grass, and as the rain began to fall, their laughter faded.

He drugged himself on her kisses, and as he entered her soft, welcoming body, he glimpsed something that felt almost . . . holy. But the illusion was too fragile to survive the primitive demand of his body.

The rain drummed on his back. Her strong fingers dug into his shoulders—demanding. The rain . . . this woman . . . Her pleasure spiraled beneath him, and he lost himself.

As one day slipped into the next, Molly behaved like a woman possessed. On Wednesday she lifted her skirt for Kevin in the office while the guests gathered for tea. That same night she escaped another of Phoebe's arrangements for a private chat and met him in the woods behind the cottage. The following morning he dragged her into the pantry just as Troy was coming through the kitchen door, then had to cover her mouth because she started making too much noise. Later she hauled him into a deserted cottage, but as he lifted her onto the kitchen table, her muscles finally rebelled from the strain of so many awkward positions, and she winced.

He pressed his forehead to hers and took a shaky breath,

struggling for control. "This is nuts. You've had enough."

"Are you kidding? I'm just getting started, but if you can't keep up with me, I understand."

He smiled and kissed her. Oh, she loved those slow kisses. He caressed her breasts and her thighs, trying to take more care, but they were dancing with danger, and she wouldn't let him. Before long she forgot all about her aching muscles.

That evening they sidestepped the Calebows' dinner invitation by announcing that they had to drive into town for supplies, but when they returned to the campground, they discovered their luck had run out. Phoebe and Dan were waiting for them on the steps of the B&B.

Chapter 22

One day this bad guy came to Nightingale Woods. He was realy bad and mean, but he pretended to be Benny's friend. But only Daphne knew he was realy bad. So she told Benny, "Hes not your friend!!!!!"

Daphne Meets a Bad Guy
by Hannah Marie Calebow

MOLLY HEARD KEVIN'S QUIET CURSE AND FIXED A SMILE ON HER face. "Hey, you guys. Escape the kiddies for a while?"

"They're playing flashlight tag on the Common." As Phoebe came down the steps, she took in Molly's rumpled dress.

Molly needed her wits about her, but the fact that she was still missing her underwear put her at a disadvantage. "I hope Andrew's going to be all right. You know how fast he disappears."

"Andrew's just fine," Dan said. "There's not much trouble he can get into around here."

"You have no idea," Kevin muttered.

Phoebe tilted her head toward the lane that led past the beach. Her oversize Stars sweatshirt and jeans didn't quite hide the power player beneath. "Mrs. Long volunteered to keep an eye on all of them. Let's take a walk."

Molly flexed her shoulders. "I think I'll pass. I've been up since five-thirty, so I'm a little tired." From making love three times today. "Maybe tomorrow."

Dan's voice rang with Southern steel. "It won't take long. And there are a couple of things we want to discuss."

"Your vacation is almost over. Why can't you just relax and enjoy the rest of it?"

"It's a little hard to relax when we're so worried about you," Phoebe replied.

"Well, stop worrying!"

"Calm down, Molly," Kevin said. "If they want to talk, I'm sure we can spare a few minutes."

What a suck-up. Or maybe he'd decided it was time to play a risky new game. She'd known from the beginning that he wasn't sneaking around because he was afraid of Dan and Phoebe. He was doing it because he loved taking chances. "You might have the time, but I don't."

Dan reached out for her arm just as he'd done since she was fifteen, but Kevin shot forward and blocked his way. She didn't know who was the more astonished, herself or Dan. Had Kevin interpreted the gesture as a threat?

Phoebe recognized the signs of antlers clashing, and she moved to her husband's side. The two of them exchanged one of their glances, and then Dan set off toward the lane. "Right now. Let's go."

The moment of reckoning was finally here, and there was no escaping it. Molly could imagine the questions they were going to ask. If only she could figure out how to answer them.

They headed silently past the beach and the last of the cottages, then along the edge of the woods. When they reached the split-rail fence that marked the end of the campground, Dan stopped. Kevin stepped slightly away from Molly and rested his hips against a post.

"You've been here for two weeks," Phoebe said as she let go of Dan's hand.

"Two weeks ago Wednesday," Kevin replied.

"The campground is beautiful. Our kids are having a wonderful time."

"It's nice having them here."

"They still can't believe you bought all those bikes."

"I enjoyed doing it."

Dan lost patience. "Phoebe and I want to know what your intentions are toward Molly."

"Dan!" Molly cried.

"It's all right," Kevin said.

"No it's not!" She glared at her brother-in-law. "And what kind of sexist Southern crap is that anyway? What about *my* intentions toward *him*?" She didn't exactly know what those intentions were beyond keeping the real world at bay by staying in Nightingale Woods for as long as she could, but she had to face Dan down.

"You were supposed to be getting an annulment," Phoebe said. "Instead you ran off together."

"We didn't run off," Molly replied.

"What else would you call it? And every time I try to talk to you about it, you dash away." She jammed her hands into the pockets of her jeans. "This is the fire alarm all over again, isn't it, Molly?"

"No!"

"What fire alarm?" Kevin asked.

"Never mind," Molly said hastily.

"No, I want to hear this."

Phoebe betrayed her. "When Molly was sixteen, she pulled the fire alarm at her high school. Unfortunately, she hadn't seen any sign of a fire."

Kevin regarded her curiously. "Did you have a good reason?"

She shook her head, feeling sixteen all over again.

"So why did you do it?"

"I'd rather not go into this now."

He tilted his head toward Dan. "You always talk as if she's perfect."

"She is!" Dan barked.

Molly smiled despite herself, then bit her lip. "It was an

aberration. I was an insecure teenager testing Phoebe and Dan to make sure they'd stick by me no matter what I did."

Kevin's eyes took on a speculative gleam. "So did they evacuate the school?"

Molly nodded.

"How many fire trucks?"

"My God . . . " Phoebe muttered. "It was a serious offense."

"It's a Class Two felony," Molly said glumly, "so it got fairly nasty."

"I'll bet." Kevin turned back to the Calebows. "Fascinating as this is—and I'll admit it's pretty fascinating—I don't think that's what you want to talk about."

"This isn't a big deal!" Molly exclaimed. "Two weeks ago Kevin showed up at my place because I'd missed an appointment with the attorney. I hadn't been feeling well, and he decided some fresh air would do me good, so he brought me up here."

When Phoebe wanted to, she did sarcasm better than anyone. "You couldn't just take her for a walk?"

"Didn't think of it." Unlike Phoebe, Kevin wasn't going to tell Molly's secrets.

But Molly had to be truthful about this part. "I've been seriously depressed, but I didn't want you to know how bad it was. Kevin's a fairly dedicated do-gooder, even though he tries to fight it, and he told me if I didn't go with him, he'd drive me out to your place and dump me on the two of you. I didn't want you to see me like that."

Phoebe looked crestfallen. "We're your family! You shouldn't have felt that way."

"I'd already upset you enough. I'd been trying to pretend I was all right, but I just couldn't do it any longer."

"She wasn't all right," Kevin said. "But she's gotten better since she's been here."

"How long are you planning to stay?" Dan's expression was still suspicious.

"Not much longer," Kevin replied. "Another couple of days."

His words made Molly's chest hurt.

"Do you remember Eddie Dillard?" Kevin went on. "He used to play for the Bears."

"I remember him."

"He wants to buy the place, and he's driving up tomorrow to check it out."

Molly's stomach turned over. "You didn't tell me that!"

"Didn't I? I guess I was preoccupied."

Preoccupied having sex with her. But there'd been plenty of time between their erotic workouts for him to have mentioned this.

"We can leave right after that," he said. "I just talked to my business manager this afternoon, and he finally found someone in Chicago to take over for the rest of the summer, a married couple who've done this before."

He might as well have slapped her. He hadn't even told her he'd asked his business manager to look in Chicago. She felt more betrayed than when Phoebe had mentioned the fire alarm. He knew she'd hate this, so he'd neglected to mention it. There was no real communication between them, no common goal. Everything she didn't want to accept about their relationship was right there in front of her. They might share sex, but that was all.

Phoebe nudged a clump of chicory with her toe. "And then what happens?"

She couldn't stand hearing Kevin say it, so she said it for him. "Nothing happens. We file for a divorce and go our separate ways."

"A divorce?" Dan asked. "Not an annulment?"

"Grounds for an annulment are limited." Molly tried to sound impersonal, as if this had nothing to do with her. "You need to prove misrepresentation or duress. We can't, so we'll have to get a divorce."

Phoebe looked up from the chicory clump. "I have to ask . . . "

Molly knew right away what was coming and tried to think of a way to stop it.

"The two of you seem to get along . . . "

No, Phoebe. Please don't.

"Have you considered staying married?"

"No!" Molly jumped in before Kevin could respond. "Do you think I'm crazy? He's not my type."

Phoebe's eyebrows shot up, and Kevin looked annoyed. She didn't care. She was filled with an awful desire to hurt him. Except she couldn't do it. Phoebe was Kevin's boss, and his career meant everything to him.

"Kevin didn't have to bring me up here, but he did it anyway because he knew I needed help." She took a deep breath and reminded herself he'd forgiven her and that she owed him this. "He's been wonderful, extremely kind and sensitive, and I'd appreciate it if the two of you stopped being so suspicious of him."

"We aren't—"

"Yes you are. It's put him in a difficult position."

"Maybe he should have thought about that when he was dragging you into the woods on Sunday," Dan drawled. "Or was he too busy being kind and sensitive?"

Kevin got that tight look around his jaw again. "Exactly what are you trying to say, Dan?"

"I'm saying that if helping Molly was just a humanitarian gesture on your part, you shouldn't be sleeping with her."

"That's it!" Molly exclaimed. "You just crossed the line."

"It's not the first time, and I'm sure it won't be the last. Phoebe and I watch out for our family."

"Maybe you should watch out for somebody else in your family," Kevin said quietly. "Molly's asking you to respect her privacy."

"Is it her privacy you're worried about or your own?"

Antlers were clashing again, but Molly didn't care. "You keep forgetting that I'm not accountable to you any longer. As for my relationship with Kevin . . . In case you haven't noticed, we're not even sleeping under the same roof."

"And I wasn't born yesterday," Dan said stubbornly.

Molly could no longer hold back. "How about some simple courtesy, then? I've spent the past twelve years pretending I don't see the two of you grope each other, pretending I don't hear the two of you at night when you make—believe me—*way* too much noise. The fact is, Kevin and I are married at the moment. We'll be getting a divorce soon, but we don't have one yet, so whatever is or isn't going on between us isn't a topic for discussion. Do you understand me?"

Phoebe was looking increasingly upset. "Molly, you're not the kind of person who can take sex lightly. It needs to mean something."

"You're damn right it does!" Dan whirled on Kevin. "Did you forget that she just had a miscarriage?"

"Back off." Kevin's lips barely moved.

Dan saw he wasn't getting anywhere there and zeroed in on Molly. "He's a football player, and it's part of the mentality. He may not intend to, but he's using you."

Dan's words stung. He understood what it was to love a woman, so he recognized how shallow Kevin's feelings for her were.

Kevin shot forward. "I told you to back off."

Molly couldn't let this go on any longer, so instead of crying as she wanted to, she went on the attack herself. "Wrong. I'm using *him*. I lost a baby, my career's in the toilet, and I'm broke. Kevin's my distraction. He's my reward for twenty-seven years of being a good girl. Now, do you have any more questions?"

"Oh, Molly . . . " Phoebe chewed her bottom lip, and Dan looked even more upset.

Molly lifted her chin and glared at both of them. "I'll give him back when I'm done with him. Until then leave me alone."

She'd almost reached Lilies of the Field before Kevin caught up with her. "Molly!"

"Go away," she snapped.

"I'm your *reward*?"

"Only when you're naked. When you have your clothes on, you're a cross to bear."

"Stop being a wise-ass."

Everything was falling apart. Eddie Dillard was showing up tomorrow, and Kevin had found someone else to run the campground. Even worse, there was nothing that could make him care about her in the same way she cared about him.

He touched her arm. "You know they mean well. Don't let them get to you."

He didn't understand that they weren't the ones who were tearing her apart.

Lilly refused to look at the clock as she moved away from the window. The Calebows had finally managed to corner Kevin and Molly, but she couldn't imagine that the confrontation had been productive. Her son and his wife didn't seem to know what they wanted from their relationship, so she doubted they could explain it to her family.

Lilly had liked the Calebows immediately, and their presence these last five days had helped lift her heavy heart. They obviously loved Molly and, just as obviously, saw Kevin as a threat, but Lilly was beginning to suspect that Kevin was as big a danger to himself as he was to Molly.

Nine-thirty . . . She headed for the armchair in the corner where she'd left her quilting but picked up a magazine instead. She hadn't been able to work on her quilt since Sunday, when Liam had issued his ultimatum. And now it was Thursday.

Come to my house on Thursday evening. . . . If you don't show up, I won't come looking for you.

She tried to build up some resentment against him, but it didn't work. She understood exactly why he'd done it, and she couldn't blame him. They were both too old to play games.

9:34 . . . She thought about Kevin taking over the bedroom downstairs. She liked falling asleep knowing they were under the same roof. When they passed each other in the hallways, they smiled and made small talk. At one time that would have been more than she could have hoped for. Now, it wasn't enough.

9:35 . . . She concentrated on flipping through her magazine, then gave up and paced the floor. What good were life lessons if you didn't pay attention to them?

At ten-thirty, she forced herself to get undressed and put on her nightgown. She got into bed and stared at the pages of a book she'd been enjoying only a week earlier. Now she couldn't remember anything about it. *Liam, I miss you so . . .* He was the most remarkable man she'd ever met, but Craig had been remarkable, too, and he'd made her miserable.

As she reached across the bed and turned off the light, her world had never seemed smaller or her bed lonelier.

Eddie Dillard was big, genial, and coarse, the kind of man who wore a gold chain, burped, scratched his crotch, carried a wad of bills held together with a big money clip, and said . . .

"You duh man, Kev. Isn't he, Larry? Isn't Kev here the man?"

Oh, yes, Larry agreed, Kev was definitely the man.

Dillard and his brother had shown up late that morning in a black SUV. Now they were sitting around the kitchen table eating salami sandwiches and belching beer while Eddie gloated over the prospect of owning his own fishing camp and Larry gloated over the prospect of running it for him. To Molly's dismay, they all seemed to regard it as a done deal.

This would be a place, Eddie said, where a man could put up his feet, relax, and get away from being "pussy-whipped by his wife." This last was uttered with a wink, clearly signaling (one man to the other) that no woman pussy-whipped Eddie Dillard.

Molly wanted to throw up. Instead, she jammed a tiny bar of French-milled soap into one of the bird's-nest baskets they used in the bathrooms to hold toiletries. She didn't know whom she disliked more, Eddie or his revolting brother Larry, who planned to live upstairs in the house while he ran the fishing camp.

She glanced over at Kevin, who was leaning against the wall sipping from a longneck. He didn't burp. When Eddie had arrived, Kevin had tried to get rid of her, but she wasn't going anyplace.

"So, Larry," Eddie said to his brother, "how much you figure it'll cost to paint these frou-frou cottages?"

Molly dropped one of the tiny, frosted-glass shampoo bottles. "The cottages were just painted. And they're beautiful."

Eddie seemed to have forgotten she was there. Larry laughed and shook his head. "No offense, Maggie, but it's gonna be a fishing camp, and guys don't like fruit colors. We'll just paint everything brown."

Eddie pointed at Larry with his longneck. "We're only painting the cottages in the middle, the ones around that whadyacallit?—that Common. I'm gonna tear down the rest of them. Too much upkeep."

Molly's heart stopped. Lilies of the Field wasn't on the Common. Her pink, blue, and yellow nursery cottage would be torn down. She abandoned the toiletry baskets. "You can't tear those cottages down! They're historic! They're—"

"The fishing's real good around here," Kevin cut in, shooting her a frown. "Large- and smallmouth bass, perch, bluegill. I heard a guy in town talk about a seven-pound pike he pulled out of the lake last week."

Eddie patted his stomach and belched. "I can't wait to get out on that boat."

"This lake is too small for what you want," Molly said desperately. "There's a strict limit to how big an outboard motor you can use. You can't even water-ski."

Kevin shot her a pointed look. "I don't think Eddie plans to cater to the water-skiing crowd."

"Nah. Just fishermen. Roll out of bed in the morning, give everybody a coffee thermos, a bag of doughnuts, and some beer, then send 'em out on the lake while the mist is still on the water. Come back after a coupla hours for brats and beer, take a nap, play some pool . . . "

"I think we should put the pool table out there." Larry pointed toward the front of the house. "Along with a big-screen TV. Once we tear down all the walls between the rooms, everything will be together—the pool table, TV, the bar, and the bait shop."

"*Bait shop!* You're putting a bait shop in this house!"

"Molly." Kevin's voice sounded a warning note, and Eddie tossed him a pitying look. Kevin narrowed his eyes at her. "Maybe you'd better go check on Amy."

Ignoring him, she zeroed in on Eddie. "People have been coming here for years. The campground needs to stay the way it is, and the bed-and-breakfast, too. The house is filled with antiques, and it's in wonderful condition. It even runs at a profit." Not much of one, but at least it paid for itself.

Eddie gave an open-mouthed laugh that revealed too

much of his salami sandwich. He jabbed his brother. "Hey, Larry, you want to run a bread-and-breakfast?"

"Yeah, sure." Larry snorted and reached for his beer. "As long as I can have a pool table, satellite TV, and no women."

"Molly . . . out. Right now." Kevin jerked his head toward the door.

Eddie chuckled as the little woman was finally put in her place.

Molly clenched her teeth, then drew her lips into a stiff smile. "I'm leaving, darling. Just make sure you clean up after your friends. And last time you washed dishes, you splashed—so don't forget to wear your apron."

Now *that* was pussy-whipping!

After dinner Molly pleaded an upset stomach to the munchkins and told them they'd have to sleep in their own cottage. Since it was their last night here, she felt guilty, but she didn't have any choice. She changed into jeans, turned out the lights, and curled up in the chair by the open window. Then she waited.

She didn't worry about Kevin dropping in. He'd gone to town with the Dillards, where, if there was any justice, he'd get drunk and end up with a world-class hangover. Also they hadn't spoken all afternoon.

During tea she could see right away that he was angry with her, but she didn't care because she was angry right back. *You duh man . . . You duh big dumb jerk!* Selling the campground was bad enough, but selling it to somebody who intended to destroy it was unconscionable, and she'd never forgive herself if she didn't at least try to put a stop to it.

Lilies of the Field was too isolated for her to be able to see the men when they returned from town, but the campground was quiet enough that she knew she'd hear them. Sure enough, a little after one in the morning the sound of a car engine drifted through the window. As she straightened in the chair, she wished there weren't so many loopholes in her plan, but it was the best she had.

She pulled on her sneakers, grabbed the flashlight she'd swiped from the house, and left Roo behind so she could set to work. Forty-five minutes later she let herself inside Lamb of God, where Eddie and Larry were spending the night. She'd checked it out earlier, right after the men had left for town, to see which bedroom was Eddie's. Now it smelled like stale liquor.

Moving closer, she gazed down at the big, dumb, drunken lump under the covers. "Eddie?"

The lump didn't move.

"Eddie," she whispered again, hoping she didn't wake up Larry, too, since it would be easier dealing with only one of them. "Eddie, wake up."

Fumes came off him as he stirred. Someone this gross shouldn't be allowed in Nightingale Woods. "Yeah . . . yeah?" He wedged open his eyes. "Whatzu . . . "

"It's Molly," she whispered. "Kevin's estranged wife. I need to talk to you."

"Whadya . . . whatzabout?"

"About the fishing camp. It's very important."

He started to lever himself up, then fell back into the pillow.

"I wouldn't bother you if it weren't important. I'll just step outside while you put some clothes on. Oh, and you don't need to wake Larry."

"Do we hafta talk now?"

"I'm afraid so. Unless you want to make a terrible mistake." She hurried from the room, hoping he'd get up.

A few minutes later he stumbled out the front door. She put her fingers to her lips and gestured for him to follow. Sweeping her flashlight across the ground, she cut across the edge of the Common, then headed back toward Lilies of the Field. Before she got there, however, she turned into the woods and headed toward the lake.

The wind had picked up. She felt a storm brewing and hoped it didn't hit until she was done with this. He loomed next to her, a big, hulking shape.

"What's going on?"

"There's something you need to see."

"Couldn't I see it in the morning?"

"That'll be too late."

He swiped at a branch. "Shit. Does Kev know about this?"

"Kev doesn't want to know."

He stopped walking. "What do you mean by that?"

She kept her flashlight pointed at the ground. "I mean that he's not deliberately deceiving you. He's just ignored some things."

"Deceiving me? What the hell're you talking about?"

"I know you thought I was being silly today at lunch, but I was hoping you'd listen to me. Then we could have avoided this." She started walking again.

"Avoided what? You'd better tell me what's going on here, lady."

"I'll show you instead."

Eddie stumbled a few more times before they finally reached the water. The trees whipped in the wind, and she braced herself. "I hate being the one who has to show you this, but there's a . . . problem with the lake."

"What kind of problem?"

She slowly swept the flashlight beam along the edge of the water, just where it lapped the shore, until she found what she was looking for.

Dead fish floating in the water.

"What the hell . . . ?"

She played the light over the silver bellies of the fish before turning the beam back onto the bank. "Eddie, I'm so sorry. I know you have your heart set on a fishing camp, but the fish in this lake are dying."

"Dying?"

"We have an environmental disaster going on. Toxins are leaking into the water from a secret underground chemical dump. It'll cost millions to fix the problem, and the town doesn't have the money. Since the local economy depends on tourists, there's a big cover-up going on, and no one will publicly admit there's a problem."

"Fuck." He grabbed the flashlight and shone it back on the floating fish. Then he snapped it off. "I can't believe Kev would do this to me!"

This was the most glaring loophole in her plan, and she tried to overcome it with dramatic presentation. "He's in denial, Eddie. Terrible, terrible denial. This was his childhood home, his last link with his parents, and he simply can't face the fact that the lake is dying, so he's convinced himself it isn't happening."

"How does he explain the damn dead fish!"

A very good question, and she gave it her best shot. "He stays away from the water. It's so sad. His denial is so deep that—" She gripped his arm and went into full Susan Lucci. "Oh, Eddie, I know it's not fair to ask you to do this, but do you think . . . ? Could you just tell him you've changed your mind and not confront him about this? I swear he wasn't deliberately trying to deceive you, and it'll tear him apart if he thinks he's destroyed your friendship."

"Yeah, well, I'd say he has."

"He's not well, Eddie. It's a mental problem. As soon as we get back to Chicago, I'll make sure he gets psychotherapy."

"Shit." He sucked in his breath. "This is gonna blow the hell out of his passing game."

"I'll find a sports psychotherapist."

Eddie wasn't a complete fool, and he asked her about the

underground dump. She expanded her story to include as many buzz words from *Erin Brockovich* as she could still remember and made up the rest. When she was done, she dug her fingernails into her palms and waited.

"You sure about all this?" he finally said.

"I wish I weren't."

He shuffled his feet and sighed. "Thanks, Maggie. I 'preciate it. You're all right."

She slowly released the breath she'd been holding. "You, too, Eddie. You, too."

The storm hit just after Molly collapsed in bed, but she was so tired she barely heard it. It wasn't until the next morning when a series of thuds on the front steps awakened her that she forced open her eyes. She blinked and looked at her clock. It was after nine! She'd forgotten to set her alarm, and no one had awakened her. Who'd fixed breakfast?

"Molly!"

Uh-oh . . .

Roo scampered into the room, and then Kevin appeared looking like a gorgeous storm cloud. So much for hoping the loopholes in her plan wouldn't come back to haunt her. Eddie must have confronted Kevin after all, and now there was going to be hell to pay.

She sat up in bed. Maybe she could distract him. "Just let me brush my teeth, soldier boy, and then I'll take you to paradise."

"Molly . . . " His voice sounded a low warning note, the same note she'd heard on Nick at Nite when Desi confronted Lucy. Molly had some 'splainin' to do.

"I have to pee!" She jumped up, flew past him to the bathroom, and shut the door.

The flat of his hand smacked the panel. "Come out here!"

"In a minute. Did you want something?"

"Yeah, I want something, all right. I want an explanation!"

"Oh?" She squeezed her eyes shut and waited for the worst.

"I want you to explain why there's a frickin' *tuna* in my lake!"

Chapter 23

It's true. Guys don't think the same way girls do,
and this can lead to trouble.

"When Guys Won't Listen"
for Chik

OH, BOY . . . MOLLY STALLED AS LONG AS SHE COULD—BRUSHING
her teeth, splashing water on her face, straightening her tank
top, and retying the drawstring on her pajama bottoms. She
half expected him to charge in after her, but apparently he
didn't see the need, since the window had been painted shut
and the only other way out was through him.

A bath was too much to hope for. Besides, it was way past
time to face the music. She'd edged open the door and saw
him leaning against the opposite wall ready to pounce.
"Uh . . . what were you saying?"

He carved out the words with his teeth. "Would you care to
explain why, when I walked down to the beach after breakfast this morning, I found a *dead tuna* floating in the lake?"

"A change in fish migration patterns?"

He grabbed her arm and pulled her toward the front
room. Another bad sign. At least in the bedroom she'd have
had a fighting chance.

"I seriously doubt that migration patterns are going to
change enough for a saltwater fish to end up in a freshwater
lake!" He pushed her down onto the couch.

She should have gone back to the lake last night and fished out the fish, but she'd assumed they'd stay where they were until they sank. They probably would have if it hadn't been for the storm.

Okay, enough messing around. Time for some righteous indignation. "Really, Kevin, just because I happen to be brighter than you doesn't mean I know everything about fish."

Probably not her best strategy, because his words bristled with splinters. "Are you going to look me in the eye and tell me you don't know anything about how a tuna got in that lake?"

"Well . . . "

"Or that you don't know why Eddie Dillard came up to me this morning and told me he wasn't going to buy the campground after all?"

"He did?"

"And what do you think he said to me before he drove away?"

"Just a guess: 'You duh man'?"

His eyebrows shot up and his voice grew as soft as an assassin's footsteps. "No, Molly, he didn't say that. What he said was 'Get some help, man!' "

She winced.

"Now what do you suppose he meant?"

"What was it he said again?" she croaked.

"Exactly what did you tell him?"

She fell back on the Calebow kids' technique. "Why do you think *I* told him something? There are lots of people here who could have said something to him—Troy, Amy, Charlotte Long. It's not fair, Kevin. Every time something happens around here, you blame me."

"And why do you think that might be?"

"I have no idea."

He leaned down, braced both his hands on her knees, and

brought his face inches from hers. "Because I've got your number. And I've got all day."

"Yes, well, I don't." She licked her lips and studied his earlobe, perfect just like the rest of him, except for a small red tooth mark she was fairly sure she'd put there. "Who fixed breakfast this morning?"

"I did." He spoke softly, but the pressure on her knees didn't ease. He definitely wasn't letting her up. "Then Amy came in and helped me. Are you done stalling?"

"No . . . yes— I don't know!" She tried to move her legs, but they weren't going anywhere. "I didn't want you to sell the campground, that's all."

"Tell me something I don't know."

"Eddie Dillard is a fool."

"I know that, too." He stood up, but he didn't back away. "What else have you got?"

She tried to stand herself so she could let him have it, but she was pinned in by his body. It made her so agitated she wanted to scream. "If you know that, how could you have done this in the first place? How could you have stood there and let him talk about painting the cottages brown? About tearing down *this* cottage—the cottage you're standing in right now!—and then turning the B&B into a bait shop?"

"He could only do those things if I sold the campground to him."

"If you—" She whipped her legs around him and jumped up. "What are you saying? Omigod, Kevin, what do you mean?"

"First I want to hear about the tuna."

She gulped. The moment she'd conceived her plan, she'd known she'd have to tell him the truth. She'd just hoped it wouldn't be quite so soon. "All right." She backed away a few steps. "Yesterday I bought some fish at the market, and last night I put them in the lake, and then I woke up Eddie and took him to see them."

A pause. "And you told him *what* exactly?"

She made eye contact with his elbow and talked as fast as she could. "That an underground chemical dump was leaking into the lake and killing all the fish."

"An underground chemical dump?"

"Uh-huh."

"An underground chemical dump!"

She took another quick step backward. "Could we talk about something else?"

Oh, jeez, that made his eyes flash fourteen different shades of mad. "Eddie didn't happen to notice that some of those fish shouldn't have been in a freshwater lake?"

"It was dark, and I didn't let him have a really good look." Another quick step backward.

Countered by a quick step forward from him. "And how did you explain away my trying to sell him a fishing camp on a *contaminated lake*?"

Her nerves snapped. "Stop looking at me like that!"

"Like I might wrap my hands around your neck and squeeze?"

"Except you can't, because I'm your boss's sister."

"Which only means I need to come up with something that doesn't leave marks."

"Sex! There are couples who think that having sex when they get really angry with each other is a turn-on."

"And you know this how? Never mind, I'm going to take your word for it." He reached out and snared the front of her top.

"Uh . . . Kev . . . " She licked her lips and gazed up into those glittering green eyes.

He splayed his hand across her bottom. "I seriously suggest you don't call me that. And I seriously suggest you don't try to stop this either, because I really, *really* need to do something physical to you." He shoved himself against her. "And everything else I'm thinking about will put me in jail."

"O-okay. That's fair." As soon as she was naked, she'd let him know what else she'd said to Eddie.

But then his mouth crushed hers, and she stopped thinking altogether.

He didn't have the patience to take off his own clothes, but he stripped her, then slammed and locked the bedroom door in case any little Calebows decided to come visit their Auntie M.

"On that bed. Right now."

Oh, yes. As fast as she could get there.

"Open your legs."

Yes, sir.

"Wider."

She gave him a couple of inches.

"Don't make me have to ask you again."

She slid up her knees. It would never be like this for her again. Never again would she feel so absolutely safe with a dangerous man.

She heard the sound of his zipper. A rough growl. "How do you want it?"

"Oh, shut up." She reached out and opened her arms. "Shut up and come here."

Seconds later she felt his weight settling over her. He was still angry, she knew that, but it didn't stop him from touching her in all the places she loved to be touched.

His voice was low and husky, and his breath stirred a lock of hair near her ear. "You're making me crazy, you know that, don't you?"

She pressed her cheek to his hard jaw. "I know. I'm sorry."

His voice grew softer and tighter. "It can't—we can't keep . . . "

She bit her lip and held him tight. "I know that, too."

He might not understand that this was going to be the last time, but she did. He drove deep and high inside her, just the way he knew she liked. Her body arched. She found her rhythm and gave him everything. Just once more. Just this one last time.

Usually, when it was over, he drew her onto his chest, and they cuddled and talked. Who'd been more magnificent, her or him? Who'd made the most noise? Why *Glamour* was superior to *Sports Illustrated*. But this morning they didn't play. Instead, Kevin turned away, and Molly slipped into the bathroom to clean up and dress.

The air was still damp from the storm, so she pulled a sweatshirt over her shorts and top. He was waiting on the screen porch, Roo at his feet. Steam curled from his coffee mug as he gazed out into the woods. She huddled deeper into the warmth of the sweatshirt. "Are you ready to hear the rest of it?"

"I guess I'd better be."

She made herself look at him. "I told Eddie that even though you were selling this place, you were still emotionally attached to it, and you couldn't stand the thought of something happening to the lake. Because of that, you were in denial about it being contaminated. I said you weren't deliberately deceiving him; you couldn't help it."

"And he believed this?"

"He's stupider than dirt, and I was pretty convincing." She trudged through the rest of it. "Then I said you had a mental problem—I'm really sorry about that—and I promised I'd make sure you got psychiatric help."

"A mental problem?"

"It was all I could come up with."

"Other than butting out of my business?" He slammed down his mug, sending coffee sloshing over the table.

"I couldn't do that."

"Why not? Who gave you permission to run my life?"

"No one. But . . ."

His temper had a long fuse, but now it fired. "What's *with* you and this place?"

"It's not me, Kevin, it's you! You've lost both your parents, and you're determined to keep Lilly at arm's length. You don't have any brothers and sisters—any extended family at all. Staying connected with your heritage is important, and this campground is all you have!"

"I don't care about my heritage! And, believe me, I have a lot more than this campground!"

"What I'm trying to say is—"

"I have millions of dollars I haven't been stupid enough to give away—let's start with that! I have cars, a luxury house, a stock portfolio that'll keep me smiling for a long time. And guess what else I have? I have a career that I wouldn't let an army of self-serving do-gooders steal from me."

She clenched her hands together. "What do you mean by that?"

"Explain something to me. Explain how you justify spending so much time minding my business instead of taking care of your own?"

"I do take care of it."

"When? For two weeks you've been plotting and scheming over this campground instead of putting your energy where it belongs. You have a career that's going down the toilet. When are you going to start fighting the good fight for your rabbit instead of lying down and playing dead?"

"I haven't done that! You don't know what you're talking about."

"You know what I think? I think your obsession with my life and this campground is just a way of distracting yourself from what you need to be doing with your own life."

How had he managed to turn the conversation? "You don't understand anything. *Daphne Takes a Tumble* is the first book on a new contract. They won't accept anything else from me until I revise it."

"You don't have any guts."

"That's not true! I did all I could to convince my editor she'd made a mistake, but Birdcage won't budge."

"Hannah told me about *Daphne Takes a Tumble*. She said it's your best book. Too bad she'll be the only kid who gets to read it." He gestured toward the notepad she'd left on the couch. "Then there's the new one you're working on. *Daphne Goes to Summer Camp*."

"How do you know about—"

"You're not the only sneak. I've read your draft. Other than some blatant unfairness to the badger, it looks like you've got another winner. But nobody can publish it unless you follow orders. And are you doing that? No. Are you even forcing the issue? No. Instead, you're letting yourself drift along in some never-never land where none of *your* troubles are real, only mine."

"You don't understand!"

"You're right about that. I never did understand quitters."

"That's not fair! I can't win. If I make the revisions, I've sold out and I'll hate myself. If I don't make them, the Daphne books are going to disappear. The publisher will never reprint the old ones, and they sure won't publish any new ones. No matter what I do, I'll lose, and losing's not an option."

"Losing isn't as bad as not fighting at all."

"Yes it is. The women in my family don't lose."

He gazed at her for a long time. "Unless I'm missing something, there's only one other woman in your family."

"And look what she did!" Agitation forced her to move. "Phoebe held on to the Stars when everybody in the world had written her off. She faced down all of her enemies—"

"Married one of them."

"—and beat them at their own game. Those men thought she was a bimbo and wrote her off. She was never supposed to have ended up with the Stars, but she did."

"Everybody in the football world admires her for it. So what does this have to do with you?"

She turned away. He already knew, and he wasn't going to make her say it.

"Come on, Molly! I want to hear those whiny words come out of your mouth so I can have a big cry."

"Go to hell!"

"Okay, I'll say it for you. You won't fight for your books because you might fail, and you're so competitive with your sister that you can't risk that."

"I'm not competitive with Phoebe. I love her!"

"I don't doubt that. But your sister is one of the most powerful women in professional sports, and you're a screwup."

"I am not!"

"Then stop acting like one."

"You don't understand."

"I'm starting to understand a lot." He circled his hand over the back of one of the farmhouse chairs. "As a matter of fact, I think I've finally got it."

"Got what? Never mind, I don't want to know." She headed for the kitchen, but he moved in front of her before she could get there.

"That thing with the fire alarm. Dan talks about what a quiet, serious kid you were. The good grades you got, all the awards you earned. You've spent your whole life trying to be perfect, haven't you? Getting to the top of the honor roll, collecting good-conduct medals like other kids collect baseball cards. But then something happens. Out of nowhere the pressure gets to you, and you flip out. You pull a fire alarm, you give away your money, you jump in bed with a total stranger!" He shook his head. "I can't believe I didn't see it right away. I can't believe nobody else sees it."

"Sees what?"

"Who you really are."

"Like you'd know."

"All that perfection. It's not in your nature."

"What are you talking about?"

"I'm talking about the person you'd have been if you'd grown up in a normal family."

She didn't know what he was going to say, but she knew he believed it, and she suddenly wanted to run away.

He loomed in the door between her and escape. "Don't you see? Your nature was to be the class clown, the girl who ditched school so she could smoke pot with her boyfriend and make out in the backseat of his car."

"What?"

"The girl most likely to skip college and—and run off to Vegas to parade around in a G-string."

"A G-string! That's the most—"

"You're not Bert Somerville's daughter." He let out a bark of rueful laughter. "Damn! You're your mother's daughter. And everybody's been too blind to see it."

She sagged down on the glider. This was silly. The mental meanderings of someone who'd spent too much time inside an MRI machine. He was trying to take everything she understood about who she was and turn it topsy-turvy. "You have no idea what you're—"

Just like that, she ran out of air.

"What you're—" She tried to say the rest, but she couldn't because deep inside her something finally clicked into place.

The class clown . . . The girl most likely to ditch school . . .

"It's not only that you're afraid to take a risk because you're competing with Phoebe. You're afraid to take a risk because you're still living with the illusion that you have to be perfect. And, Molly, trust me on this, being perfect isn't in your nature."

She needed to think, but she couldn't do it under those watchful green eyes. "I'm not— I don't even recognize this person you're talking about."

"Give it a few seconds, and I bet you will."

It was too much. *He* was the bonehead, not her. "You're just trying to distract me from pointing out everything that's screwed up about you."

"There's nothing screwed up about me. Or at least there wasn't until I met you."

"Is that right?" She told herself to shut up, this wasn't the time, but everything she'd been thinking and trying not to say spilled out. "What about the fact that you're afraid to make any kind of emotional connection?"

"If this is about Lilly . . . "

"Oh, no. That's way too easy. Even someone as obtuse as you should be able to figure that out. Why don't we look at something more complicated?"

"Why don't we not?"

"Isn't it a little weird that you're thirty-three years old, you're rich, moderately intelligent, you look like a Greek god, and you're definitely heterosexual. But what's wrong with this picture? Oh, yeah, I remember . . . You've never had a single long-term relationship with a woman."

"Aw, for the . . . " He sprawled down at the table.

"What's with that anyway?"

"How do you even know it's true?"

"Team gossip, the newspapers, that article about us in *People*. If you ever did have a long-term relationship, it must have been in junior high. Lots of women move through your life, but none of them gets to stay around for long."

"There's one of them who's been around way too long!"

"And look at what kind of women you choose." She splayed her hands on the table. "Do you choose smart women who might have a chance of holding your interest? Or respectable women who share at least a few of your—and don't even *think* about arguing with me about this—a few of your rock-bottom-conservative values? Well, surprise, surprise. None of the above."

"Here we go with the foreign women again. I swear, you're obsessed."

"Okay, let's leave them out of it and look at the American women the PK dates. Party girls who wear too much makeup and not enough clothes. Girls who leave drool marks on your shirts and haven't seen the inside of a classroom since they flunked dummy math!"

"You're exaggerating."

"Don't you see, Kevin? You deliberately choose women you're predestined not to be able to have a real relationship with."

"So what? I want to focus on my career, not jump through hoops trying to make some woman happy. Besides, I'm only thirty-three. I'm not ready to settle down."

"What you're not ready to do is grow up."

"Me?"

"And then there's Lilly."

"Here we go . . . "

"She's terrific. Even though you've done everything you can to keep her at arm's length, she's sticking around, waiting for you to come to your senses. You've got everything to gain and nothing to lose with her, but you won't give her even a little corner of your life. Instead, you act like a petulant teenager. Don't you see? In your own way you're as freaked by your upbringing as I am about mine."

"No I'm not."

"My scars are easier to understand. I had no mother and an abusive father, while you had two loving parents. But they were so different from you that you never felt connected to them, and you still feel guilty about it. Most people could push it aside and move on, but most people aren't as sensitive as you."

He sprang from the chair. "That's bullshit! I'm as tough as they come, lady, and don't you forget it."

"Yeah, you're tough on the outside, but on the inside

you're so soft you squish, and you're every bit as scared of screwing up your life as I am."

"You don't know anything!"

"I know that there's not another man in a thousand who would have felt honor-bound to marry the crazy woman who attacked him in his sleep, even if she was related to the boss. Dan and Phoebe might have held a shotgun to your head, but all you had to do was place the blame where it belonged. Not only wouldn't you do that, but you made me swear not to either." She pulled her cold hands into the cuffs of the sweatshirt. "Then there's the way you behaved when I was miscarrying."

"Anybody would have—"

"No, anybody wouldn't have, but you want to believe that because you're afraid of any kind of emotion that doesn't fit between a pair of goalposts."

"That's so stupid!"

"Off the field you know something's missing, but you're afraid to go looking for it because, in your typically neurotic and immature fashion, you believe something's wrong inside you that'll keep you from finding it. You couldn't connect with your own parents, so how can you ever make a lasting connection with anyone else? It's easier to focus on winning football games."

"Lasting connection? Wait a minute! What are we really talking about here?"

"We're talking about the fact that it's time for you to grow up and take some real risks."

"I don't think so. I think there's a hidden agenda behind all this mumbo jumbo."

Until that moment she hadn't thought so, but he sometimes saw things before she did. Now she realized he was right, but it was too late. She felt sick.

"I think you're talking about a lasting connection between us," he said.

"Ha!"

"Is that what you want, Molly? Are you angling to make this a real marriage?"

"With an emotional twelve-year-old? A man who can barely be civil to his only blood relative? I'm not that self-destructive."

"Aren't you?"

"What do you want me to say? That I've fallen in love with you?" She'd meant to be scathing, but she saw by his thunderstruck expression that he'd recognized the truth.

Her legs felt rubbery. She sat on the edge of the glider and tried to think of a way out, but she was too emotionally battered. And what was the point when he'd see through it anyway? She lifted her head. "So what? I know a one-way street when I run into it, and I'm not stupid enough to drive down it in the wrong direction."

She hated his shock.

"You are in love with me."

Her mouth was dry. Roo rubbed against her ankles and whimpered. She wanted to say this was just another variation on her crush, but she couldn't. "Big deal," she managed. "If you think I'm going to cry all over your chest because you don't feel the same way, you're wrong. I don't beg for anybody's love."

"Molly . . ."

She hated the pity she heard in his voice. Once again, she hadn't measured up. She hadn't been smart enough or pretty enough or special enough for a man to love.

Stop!

A terrible anger filled her, and this time it wasn't directed at him. She was sick of her own insecurities. She'd accused him of needing to grow up, but he wasn't the only one. There wasn't anything wrong with her, and she couldn't keep living her life as if there were. If he didn't love her in return, that was his loss.

She shot up from the glider. "I'm leaving today with Phoebe and Dan. Me and my broken heart are skulking back to Chicago, and you know what? We'll both survive just fine."

"Molly, you can't—"

"Stop right now, before your conscience gets cranked up. You're not responsible for my feelings, okay? This isn't your fault, and you don't have to fix it. It's just one of those things that happened."

"But . . . I'm sorry. I—"

"Shut up." She said it quietly because she didn't want to leave in anger. She found herself moving toward him, watched her hand go to his cheek. She loved the feel of his skin, loved who he was despite his all-too-human frailties. "You're a good man, Charlie Brown, and I wish you all the best."

"Molly, I don't—"

"Hey, no begging me to stay, okay?" She managed a smile and stepped away. "All good things come to an end, and that's where we are." She made her way to the door. "Come on, Roo. Let's find Phoebe."

Chapter 24

It's a bunny-eat-bunny world.

Anonymous children's book editor

ONLY THE PRESENCE OF THE KIDS MADE THE TRIP BACK TO CHICAGO bearable. It had always been difficult for Molly to hide her feelings from her sister, but this time she had to. She couldn't taint Phoebe and Dan's relationship with Kevin any further.

Her condo was musty from having been closed up for nearly three weeks and even dustier than when she'd left. Her hands itched to start scrubbing and polishing, but cleaning chores would have to wait until tomorrow. With Roo scampering ahead, she carried her suitcases to the sleeping loft, then forced herself back down the steps to her desk and the black plastic crate that held her files.

Sitting cross-legged on the floor, she pulled out her last contract with Birdcage and flipped through the pages.

Just as she'd thought.

She gazed up at the windows that stretched all the way to the ceiling, studied the mellowed brick walls and cozy kitchen, watched the play of light on the hardwood floors. *Home.*

* * *

Two miserable weeks later Molly stepped from the elevator onto the ninth floor of the Michigan Avenue office building that held the offices of Birdcage Press. She retied the cardigan around the waist of her red-and-white checked gingham sheath and made her way down the corridor to Helen Kennedy Schott's office. Molly had long ago passed the point where she could turn back, and she only hoped the concealer she'd dabbed under her eyes hid the shadows.

Helen rose to greet her from behind a desk cluttered with manuscripts, galleys, and book covers. Even though the weather was muggy, she was dressed in her customary editorial black. Her short gray hair lay neatly against her head, and although she wore no makeup, her nails shone with slick crimson polish. "Molly, it's wonderful to see you again. I'm so glad you finally called. I'd nearly given up trying to get hold of you."

"It's good to see you," Molly replied politely, because no matter what Kevin said about her, she was, *by nature*, a polite person.

A strip of the Chicago River was visible through the office window, but the colorful display of children's books on the shelves drew Molly's attention. As Helen chatted about the new marketing manager, Molly spotted the bright slender spines of the first five Daphne books. Knowing that *Daphne Takes a Tumble* would never join them should have felt like a stab in the heart, but that part of her was too numb right now to feel anything more.

"I'm so glad we're finally having this meeting," Helen said. "We have lots to talk about."

"Not so much." Molly couldn't prolong this. She opened her purse, drew out a white business envelope, and set it on the desk. "This is a check reimbursing Birdcage for the first half of the advance you paid for *Daphne Takes a Tumble*."

Helen looked stunned. "We don't want the advance back. We want to publish the book."

"I'm afraid you won't be able to. I'm not making the revisions."

"Molly, I know you haven't been happy with us, and it's time to sort this out. From the beginning we've only wanted what was best for your career."

"I only want what's best for my readers."

"We do, too. Please try to understand. Authors tend to look at a project only from their perspective, but a publisher has to look at the larger picture, including our relationship with the press and the community. We felt we had no choice."

"Everybody has a choice, and an hour ago I exercised mine."

"What do you mean?"

"I published *Daphne Takes a Tumble* myself. The original version."

"You published it?" Helen's eyebrows shot up. "What are you talking about?"

"I published it on the Internet."

Helen erupted from her chair. "You can't do that! We have a contract!"

"If you check the fine print, you'll see that I retain the electronic rights to all my books."

Helen looked stunned. The larger publishing houses had plugged this hole in their contracts, but some of the smaller presses like Birdcage hadn't gotten around to it. "I can't believe you did this."

"Now any child who wants to read *Daphne Takes a Tumble* and see the original illustrations will be able to do it." Molly had planned a big speech, complete with references to book burning and the First Amendment, but she no longer had the energy. Pushing the check forward, she rose from her chair and walked out.

"Molly, wait!"

She'd done what she needed to, and she didn't stop. As she headed for her car, she tried to feel triumphant, but she mainly felt drained. A college friend had helped her set up the Web site. In addition to the text and drawings for *Daphne Takes a Tumble,* Molly had included a page that listed some of the books various organizations had tried to keep out of children's hands over the years because of their content or illustrations. The list included *Little Red Riding Hood,* all the Harry Potter books, Madeleine L'Engle's *A Wrinkle in Time, Harriet the Spy, Tom Sawyer, Huckleberry Finn,* as well as the books of Judy Blume, Maurice Sendak, the Brothers Grimm, and Anne Frank's *Diary of a Young Girl.* At the end of the list, Molly had added *Daphne Takes a Tumble.* She wasn't Anne Frank, but she felt better being in such wonderful company. She only wished she could call Kevin and tell him that she'd finally fought for her bunny.

She made a few stops to pick up supplies, then swung onto Lake Shore Drive and headed north to Evanston. The traffic was light, and it didn't take her nearly long enough to get to the moldy old brownstone where she now lived. She hated her second-floor apartment with its view of the Dumpster behind a Thai restaurant, but it was the only place she could afford that would take a dog.

She tried not to think about her little condo, where strangers had already moved in. Evanston didn't have many loft conversions available, and the building had a waiting list of people anxious to buy, so she'd known it would sell quickly. Even so, she hadn't been prepared for it to go in less than twenty-four hours. The new owners had paid her a premium to sublease while they waited for the final paperwork, so she'd had to scramble to find a rental, and here she was in this dismal building. But she had the money to repay her advance and settle her bills.

She parked on the street two blocks away because her Slytherin landlord charged seventy dollars a month for a parking spot in the lot attached to the building. As she climbed the worn steps to her apartment, the El tracks shrieked just outside the windows. Roo greeted her at the door, then scampered across the worn linoleum and began to bark at the sink.

"Not again."

The apartment was so small that she had no place for her books, and she crawled over the packing boxes on her way to the kitchen sink. She gingerly opened the door, peered inside, and shuddered. Another mouse quivered in her Hav-A-Heart trap. The third one she'd caught, and she'd lived here for only a few days.

Maybe she could get another *Chik* article out of this— "Why Guys Who Hate Small Animals Aren't Always Bad News." Her cooking piece had just gone into the mail. At first she'd called it "Breakfasts That Won't Make Him Puke: Scramble His Brains with Your Eggs." Just before she'd slipped it into the envelope, she'd come to her senses and substituted "Early-Morning Turn-ons."

She was writing every day. As devastated as she was about everything, she hadn't given up and gone to bed the way she'd done after her miscarriage. Instead, she was facing her pain and doing her best to live through it. But her heart had never felt emptier.

She missed Kevin so much. Each night she lay in bed staring at the ceiling and remembering how his arms had felt around her. But it had been so much more than sex. He'd understood her better than she'd understood herself, and he'd been her soul mate in every way but the one that counted. He didn't love her.

With a sigh that came from the bottom of her being, she set aside her purse, slipped on the gardening gloves she'd bought along with the trap, and warily reached under the sink for the handle on the small cage. At least her bunny was hopping free and happy in cyberspace. Which was more than she could say about the rodent.

She let out a squeak as the frightened mouse started

scampering around the cage. "Please don't do that. Just be quiet, and I promise I'll have you in the park before you know it." Where was a man when you needed one?

Her heart contracted in another achy spasm. The couple Kevin had hired to take over at the campground would be in place by now, so he was probably back in town partying with the international set. *Please, God, don't let him be sleeping with any of them. Not yet.*

Lilly had left several messages on her answering machine wanting to know if Molly was all right, but she still hadn't returned them. What could she say? That she'd had to sell her condo? That she'd lost her publisher? That her heart had suffered a permanent break? At least she could afford an attorney now, so she had a shot at being able to get out of her contract and sell her next Daphne book to another publisher.

She held the cage as far away as she could and retrieved her keys. She was on her way to the door when the buzzer sounded. The mouse had given her the heebie-jeebies, and she nearly jumped out of her skin.

"Just a minute."

Still holding the cage at arm's length, she stepped around another book box and opened the door.

Helen charged inside. "Molly, you ran out before we could talk. Oh, God!"

"Helen, meet Mickey."

Helen pressed her hand to her heart, the color bleaching from her face. "A pet?"

"Not exactly." Molly set the cage on a packing box, but Roo didn't like that. "Quiet, pest! I'm afraid this isn't the best time for a visit, Helen. I have to go to the park."

"You're taking it on an outing?"

"Releasing it."

"I'll—I'll come with you."

Molly should have enjoyed seeing her sophisticated former editor so discomposed, but the mouse had discomposed her, too. With the cage held far from her body, she led the way outside and began winding through the back alleys of downtown Evanston toward the park by the lake. Helen, in her black suit and heels, wasn't dressed for either the heat or stumbling around potholes, but Molly hadn't invited her to come along, so she refused to take pity.

"I didn't know you'd moved," Helen called from behind. "Luckily, I ran into one of your neighbors, and he gave me your new address. C-couldn't you release it somewhere closer?"

"I don't want him to find his way back."

"Or use a more permanent trap?"

"Absolutely not."

Although it was a weekday, the park was filled with bicyclists, college students on Rollerblades, and children. Molly found a grassy area and set the cage down, then hesitantly reached for the latch. As soon as she sprang it, Mickey made his leap for freedom.

Straight toward Helen.

Her editor gave a strangled cry and leaped up on a picnic bench. Mickey disappeared into the shrubbery.

"Beastly things." Helen sagged down on the tabletop.

Molly was feeling a little wobbly-kneed, too, so she sat on the bench. Beyond the edge of the park, Lake Michigan stretched to the horizon. She gazed out and thought of a smaller lake with a cliff for diving.

Helen pulled a tissue from her purse and dabbed at her forehead. "There's just something about a mouse."

There were no mice in Nightingale Woods. Molly'd have to add one if she ever found a new publisher.

She gazed at her old editor. "If you've come here to threaten me with a lawsuit, you're not going to get much."

"Why would we want to sue our favorite author?" Helen pulled out the envelope that held Molly's check and set it on the bench. "I'm giving this back. And when you look inside, you'll see a second check for the remainder of your advance. Really, Molly, you should have told me how strongly you felt about the revisions. I'd never have asked you to make them."

Molly didn't even try to respond to that piece of Slytherin crapola. Nor did she pick up the envelope.

Helen's tone grew more effusive. "We're going to publish *Daphne Takes a Tumble* in its original version. I'm putting it on the winter schedule so we have time to line up promotion. We're planning an extensive marketing campaign, with full-page ads in all the big parenting magazines, and we're sending you on a book tour."

Molly wondered if the sun had gotten to her. "*Daphne Takes a Tumble* is already available on the Internet."

"We'd like you to remove it, but we'll leave the final decision up to you. Even if you decide to keep the Web site, we believe most parents will still want to buy the actual book to add to their children's collections."

Molly couldn't imagine how she'd been so magically transformed from a minor author to a major one. "I'm afraid you'll need to do better than this, Helen."

"We're prepared to renegotiate your contract. I'm sure you'll be pleased with the terms."

Molly had been asking for an explanation, not for more money, but she somehow got in touch with her inner tycoon. "You'll have to deal with my new agent about that."

"Of course."

Molly had no agent, new or old. Her career had been so small that she hadn't needed one, but something had definitely changed. "Tell me what's happened, Helen."

"It was the publicity. The new sales figures just came out two days ago. Between the press coverage of your marriage and the SKIFSA stories, your sales have soared."

"But I was married in February, and SKIFSA went after me in April. You're just noticing?"

"We spotted the first rise in March and another in April.

But the numbers weren't all that significant until we got our end-of-the-month report for May. And the preliminary June figures are even better."

Molly decided it was a good thing she was sitting down, because her legs would never have held her. "But the publicity had died down. Why are the numbers shooting up now?"

"That's what we wanted to find out, so we've spent some time on the phones taking with booksellers. They're telling us that adults originally bought a Daphne book out of curiosity—either they'd heard about your marriage or they wanted to see what SKIFSA was so upset about. But once they took the book home, their kids fell in love with the characters, and now they're coming back to the stores and buying the whole series."

Molly was stunned. "I can't believe this."

"The kids are showing the books to their friends. We're hearing that even parents who've supported SKIFSA's other boycotts are buying the Daphne books."

"I'm having a hard time taking this in."

"I understand." Helen crossed her legs and smiled. "After all these years you're finally an overnight success. Congratulations, Molly."

Janice and Paul Hubert were the perfect couple to run a bed-and-breakfast. Mrs. Hubert's eggs were never cold, and none of her cookies burned on the bottom. Mr. Hubert actually enjoyed unstopping toilets and could talk to the guests for hours without getting bored. Kevin fired them after a week and a half.

"Need some help?"

He pulled his head out of the refrigerator and saw Lilly standing just inside the kitchen door. It was eleven at night, two weeks and one day since Molly had left. It was also four days since he'd fired the Huberts, and everything had turned to crap.

Training camp started in a couple of weeks, and he wasn't ready. He knew he should tell Lilly that he was glad she'd stayed to help out, but he hadn't gotten around to it, and it made him feel guilty. There'd been something sad about her ever since Liam Jenner had stopped showing up for breakfast. Once he'd even tried to mention it, but he'd been clumsy, and she'd pretended not to understand.

"I'm looking for rapid-rise yeast. Amy left a note that she might need some. What the hell is rapid-rise yeast?"

"I have no idea," she replied. "My baking is pretty much limited to box mixes."

"Yeah. Screw it." He shut the door.

"Missing the Huberts?"

"No. Only the way she cooked and the way he took care of everything."

"Ah." She gazed at him, amusement temporarily overriding her unhappiness.

"I didn't like how she treated the kids," he muttered. "And he was making Troy nuts. Who cares if the grass gets mowed clockwise or counterclockwise?"

"She didn't exactly ignore the kids. She just didn't pass out cookies to every scamp who showed up at the kitchen door like Molly did."

"That old witch shooed them off like they were cockroaches. And forget about taking a few minutes to tell the kids a story. Is that too much to ask? If a kid wants to hear a story, don't you think she could put down her damn Lysol bottle long enough to tell 'em a story?"

"I never heard any of the kids actually ask Mrs. Hubert to tell them a story."

"They sure as hell asked Molly!"

"True."

"What's that supposed to mean?"

"Nothing."

Kevin opened the lid on the cookie jar, but closed it again when he remembered the ones inside were store bought. He reached into the refrigerator for a beer instead. "Her husband was even worse."

"When I heard him tell the kids not to play soccer on the Common because they were ruining the grass, I figured he might be doomed."

"Slytherin."

"The B&B guests did love the Huberts, though," she pointed out.

"That's because they don't have kids here like the cottage people do."

He offered her a beer, but she shook her head and got a water tumbler from the cupboard instead. "I'm glad the O'Brians are staying for another week," she said, "but I miss Cody and the Kramer girls. Still, the new kids are cute. I saw you bought more bikes."

"I forgot about the rug rats. We needed some Big Wheels."

"The older kids all seem to be enjoying the basketball hoop, and you did the right thing hiring a lifeguard."

"Some of the parents are a little too casual." He carried his beer over to the kitchen table, took a seat, then hesitated. But he'd already put this off long enough. "I really appreciate the way you've been helping out."

"I don't mind, but I do miss Molly. Everything's more fun when she's around."

He felt himself growing defensive. "I don't think so. We've had lots of fun without her."

"No, we haven't. The O'Brian boys keep complaining, the old folks miss her, and you've been grouchy and unreasonable." She leaned against the sink. "Kevin, it's been two weeks. Don't you think it's time to go after her? Amy and Troy and I can take care of the place for a few days."

Didn't she realize he'd already thought about this from a hundred different angles? There was nothing he wanted more, but he couldn't go after her, not unless he wanted to settle down forever as a married man, and that was something he couldn't do. "It wouldn't be fair."

"Fair to whom?"

He poked at the label on the bottle with his thumbnail. "She told me . . . She has feelings."

"I see. And you don't?"

He had more feelings than he knew what to do with, but none of them were going to make him lose sight of what was most important. "Maybe in five or six years things will be different, but I don't have time right now for anything but my career. And let's be realistic—can you see Molly and me together long-term?"

"Without any trouble."

"Come on!" He shot up from his chair. "I'm a jock! I love being active, and she hates sports."

"For someone who hates sports, she's an excellent athlete."

"She's okay, I guess."

"She swims beautifully and dives like a champ."

"That's just from summer camp."

"She plays an excellent game of softball."

"Summer camp."

"She knows everything about football."

"That's only because—"

"She plays soccer."

"Just with Tess."

"She's studied martial arts."

He'd forgotten about that kung fu move she'd put on him last winter.

"And she told me she'd played on her high school tennis team."

"There you go. I hate tennis."

"Probably because you're no good at it."

How did Lilly know that?

Lilly's smile looked dangerously sympathetic. "I'd say you're going to have a hard time finding a woman who's as athletic and adventurous as Molly Somerville."

"I'll bet she wouldn't go skydiving."

"I'll bet she would."

Even to his own ears he sounded sulky. And Lilly was right about the skydiving. He could almost hear the sound of Molly's screams when he pushed her out of the plane. But he knew she'd love it as soon as her chute popped.

He still felt queasy about her falling in love with him. And angry, too. This had been temporary right from the beginning, so it wasn't as if he'd led her on. And he sure hadn't made any promises. Hell, half the time he'd barely been civil.

It was the sex. Everything had been fine up until then. If he'd kept his pants zipped and his hands to himself, she'd have been fine, but he hadn't been able to do that, not when they were together day after day. And who could blame him?

He thought of the way she laughed. What man wouldn't want to feel that laughter under his lips? And those blue-gray eyes with their wicked tilt were a deliberate sexual challenge. How could he have thought about anything except making love when they were turned his way?

But Molly knew the rules, and great sex wasn't a promise, not in this day and age. All that crap she'd handed out about his not making emotional connections couldn't have been more wrong. He had connections, all right. Important ones. He had Cal and Jane Bonner.

Whom he hadn't talked to in weeks.

He gazed at Lilly. Maybe because it was late and his defenses were down, he found himself telling her more than he intended. "Molly has some opinions about me I don't share."

"What kinds of opinions?"

"She thinks . . . " He set down his beer bottle. "She says I'm emotionally shallow."

"You are not!" Lilly's eyes flashed. "What a terrible thing to say!"

"Yeah, but the thing is—"

"You're a very complicated man. My God, if you were shallow, you'd have gotten rid of me right away."

"I tried—"

"You'd have given me a few pats on the shoulder and promised to send me a Christmas card. I'd have been satisfied and driven off into the sunset. But you're too emotionally honest to do that, which is why my being here has been so painful for you."

"That's nice of you to say, but—"

"Oh, Kevin . . . you mustn't ever think of yourself as shallow. I love Molly, but if I ever hear her say anything like that about you, she and I are going to have words."

Kevin wanted to laugh, but his eyes were starting to sting, and his feet were moving, and the next thing he knew, his arms just opened up. Leave it to a man's mother to come to his defense when the chips were down, even if he didn't deserve it.

He gave her a fierce, possessive hug. She made a sound that reminded him of the mew of a newborn kitten.

He hugged her closer. "There are some things I've been wanting to ask you."

A shaky sob against his chest.

He cleared his throat. "Did you ever have to take music lessons and stink at the piano?"

"Oh, Kevin . . . I still don't know one note from another."

"And do you ever get a rash around your mouth when you eat tomatoes?"

Her grip on him tightened. "If I have too many."

"And what about sweet potatoes?" He heard a hiccuped sob. "Everybody likes them but me, so I wondered . . . " He stopped because it was getting hard for him to speak. At the same time, pieces inside him that had never quite fit began to come together.

For a while they simply held each other. Finally they began to talk, trying to catch up on three decades in one night, stumbling over their words as they filled in the blanks. By unspoken consent they avoided only two topics: Molly and Liam Jenner.

At three in the morning, when they finally parted at the top of the steps, Lilly stroked his cheek. "Good night, sweetheart."

"Good night—" *Good night, Mother.* That's what he wanted to say, but it felt like a betrayal of Maida Tucker, and he couldn't do that. Maida might not have been the mother of his dreams, but she'd loved him with all her heart, and he'd loved her right back. He smiled. "Good night, Lilly Mom."

The waterworks really opened up then. "Oh, Kevin . . . Kevin, my sweet little boy."

He drifted off to sleep with a smile on his lips.

When the alarm forced him out of bed a few hours later to start breakfast, he thought about the night before and the fact that Lilly would be a permanent part of his life now. It felt good. Exactly right.

But nothing else did.

As he made his way down to the gray, empty kitchen, he told himself there was no reason to feel guilty about Molly, but that didn't seem to matter to his conscience. Until he figured out some way to make amends, he'd never be able to stop thinking about her.

Then it came to him. The perfect solution.

Molly stared at Kevin's attorney. "He's giving me the campground?"

The attorney shifted his weight closer to the center of the packing box that held Molly's computer. "He called me first thing yesterday morning. I'm finalizing the paperwork now."

"I don't want it! I'm not taking anything from him."

"He must have known you'd react that way, because he said to tell you if you refused, he'd let Eddie Dillard bulldoze the place. I don't think he was kidding."

She wanted to scream, but it wasn't the attorney's fault that Kevin was high-handed and manipulative, so she controlled her temper. "Is there anything to prevent me from giving the campground away?"

"No."

"All right, I'll accept. And then I'm giving it away."

"I don't think he'll be too happy about that."

"Hand him a box of tissues."

The attorney was young, and he gave her a halfway-flirtatious smile, then gathered up his briefcase and made his way through the furniture to the door. In deference to the July heat, he wasn't wearing a suit coat, but her apartment didn't have air-conditioning, and there was a damp spot on his back. "You might want to get up there fairly soon. Kevin's left, and there's no one in charge."

"I'm sure there is. He hired someone to take over."

"They didn't seem to work out."

Molly wasn't a swearing person, but she could barely hold back a big one. She'd had only forty-eight hours to get used to being a successful children's book author, and now this.

As soon as the attorney left, she crawled over the couch to retrieve her phone and call her new agent, the best contract negotiator in town. "Phoeb, it's me."

"Hey, big-time author! Talks are going well, but I'm still not satisfied with the up-front money they're offering."

She heard the relish in her sister's voice. "Just don't bankrupt them."

"It's so tempting."

They chatted about the negotiations for a few minutes before Molly got to the point, doing her best to say it without choking. "Kevin's just done the sweetest thing."

"Walked blindfolded in front of speeding traffic?"

"Don't be like that, Phoebe." She was definitely going to strangle on this. "He's a great guy. As a matter of fact, he's given me the campground as a surprise."

"You're kidding."

Molly gripped the receiver tighter. "He knows how much I love it there."

"I understand that, but . . . "

"I'm going to drive up tomorrow. I'm not sure how long I'll stay."

"At least this will get you out of that fleabag apartment until we finish negotiating your contract. I suppose I should be grateful."

It had been humiliating telling Phoebe that she'd been forced to sell her condo. To her sister's credit, she hadn't offered to bail Molly out, but that didn't mean she'd kept quiet.

Molly got off the phone as soon as she could and glanced over at Roo, who was trying to keep cool under the kitchen table. "Go ahead and say it. My timing sucks. If I'd waited two weeks, we'd still be in our old place basking in air-conditioning."

It might have been her imagination but Roo looked censorious. The traitor missed Kevin.

"Let's get our chores done, pal. First thing tomorrow we're taking off for the North Woods."

Roo perked up.

"Don't get too excited, because we're not staying. I meant it, Roo, I'm giving the place away!"

Except she wouldn't. She kicked a dish box aside, wishing it were Kevin's head. He'd done this out of guilt. This was his way of trying to make it up to her because she'd fallen in love with him and he didn't love her back.

A great big pity present.

Chapter 25

Daphne wasn't speaking to Benny, and Benny didn't care, and Melissa couldn't find her movie-star sunglasses, and it had started to rain. Everything was a big mess!

Daphne Goes to Summer Camp

LILLY STOPPED JUST INSIDE THE B&B'S KITCHEN DOOR. MOLLY HAD fallen asleep at the table. Her head rested on her arm, her hand lay by her sketch pad, and her hair spilled across the old oak tabletop like overturned syrup. How could Lilly ever have believed she was a dilettante?

Since Molly had returned to the campground ten days ago, she'd finished the illustrations for *Daphne Goes to Summer Camp*, started a new book, and written an article for *Chik*, all that in addition to cooking and tending to guests. She couldn't relax, even though she'd told Lilly her new contract had finally given her financial stability. Lilly knew she was trying not to dwell on Kevin and understood her quiet suffering. She could have strangled her son.

Molly stirred and blinked, then looked up and smiled. There were shadows under her eyes. They probably matched the shadows under Lilly's own. "Have a nice walk?"

"I did."

She sat up and tucked her hair behind her ears. "Liam was here."

Lilly's heart skipped a beat. Other than catching a glimpse

of him in town a few days after he'd issued his ultimatum, she hadn't seen him in weeks. Instead of growing easier, their separation had become more painful.

"He brought something for you," Molly said. "I had him put it in your room."

"What is it?"

"You probably should see for yourself." She picked up a pen that had fallen to the floor, then began to fiddle with it. "He asked me to tell you good-bye."

Lilly felt chilled, even though the kitchen was warm. "He's leaving?"

"Today. He's going to live in Mexico for a while. He wants to experiment with the light."

She shouldn't be shocked. Had she expected him to sit around waiting for her to change her mind? Anyone who understood Liam Jenner's art knew he was fundamentally a man of action. "I see."

Molly rose and gave her a sympathetic look. "You've screwed up so bad."

"So badly," she retorted, in one of those leftover reflexes from life with Craig.

"Not that I could survive without you, but, with Kevin gone, why are you still here?"

Lilly had made plans to meet Kevin in Chicago soon. Neither of them wanted to keep their relationship a secret, and Kevin had already flown to North Carolina to share the news with his friends, the Bonners. He'd also told Cal's brothers, their wives, and the guy sitting next to him on the plane, according to their last phone call.

Lilly yearned to see him again, but she couldn't bring herself to leave the campground yet. She told herself she was staying because of Molly. "I'm hanging around to help you out, you ungrateful little twit."

Molly carried her water glass to the sink. "Other than that."

"Because it's peaceful here, and I hate L.A."

"Or maybe because you can't make yourself walk away from Liam, even though you've treated him like crap and you don't deserve him."

"If you think he's so wonderful, take him yourself. You have no idea what it's like being married to a controlling man."

"Like you couldn't have him eating out of your hand if you wanted."

"Don't you take that tone of voice with me, young lady."

"You're such a dork." Molly smiled. "Go upstairs and see what he left you."

Lilly tried to sweep from the kitchen in a diva's huff, but she knew that Molly wasn't buying it. Her son's wife had the same kind of open, honest charm as Mallory. Why couldn't Kevin see what he'd turned his back on?

And what about the man she'd turned her back on? She still couldn't work on her quilt. All she could see now when she looked at it were scraps of fabric. There were no more surges of creative energy, no more glimpses of the answers to life's mysteries.

She made her way past the second-floor landing to the narrower flight of stairs that led to the attic. Kevin had tried to get her to move into one of the larger rooms, but Lilly liked it up here.

As she slipped inside, she saw a large canvas, taller than it was wide, leaning against the end of her bed. Even though it was wrapped in brown paper, she knew exactly what it was. The Madonna she'd admired so much that afternoon in his studio. She fell to her knees on the braided rug and, holding her breath, pulled away the paper.

But it wasn't the Madonna at all. It was the painting Liam had done of her.

A sob rose in her chest. She pressed her fingers to her mouth and scrambled back. He'd been brutal in his depiction of her body. He'd shown every sag, every wrinkle, every bulge that should have been flat. The flesh of one thigh lapped the edge of the chair where she was seated; her breasts hung heavy.

And yet she was glorious. Her skin was luminous with a glow that seemed to come from deep inside, her curves strong and fluid, her face majestically beautiful. She was both herself and Everywoman, wise in her age.

This was Liam Jenner's final love letter to her. An uncompromising statement of feelings that were clear-sighted and fearless. This was her soul exposed by the brilliant man she hadn't been courageous enough to claim as her own. And now it might be too late.

She grabbed her keys, flew down the stairs, and ran outside to her car. One of the children had drawn an elaborate rabbit in the dust on the trunk. Then she realized that the drawing was too sophisticated. More of Molly and her mischief.

Too late, too late, too late . . . The tires hissed as she sped from the campground toward his glass house. While she'd been putting up barriers against a dead husband she hadn't loved in years, he'd gone after what he wanted.

Too late, too late, too late . . . The car jolted over the ruts at the top of the lane, then steadied as the house came into view. It looked empty and deserted.

She jumped out, rushed to the door, and leaned on the bell. There was no answer. She banged it with her fists, then raced to the back. *He's going to Mexico . . .*

The glass-enclosed studio rose above her, a tree house for a genius. She could see no signs of life inside, none in the rest of the house either.

Behind her the lake sparkled in the sunlight, and the sky floated blue and cloudless above, the perfect day mocking her. She spotted a door off to the side and rushed toward it, not expecting it to be open, but the heavy knob turned in her hand.

Everything was quiet inside. She moved through the back of the house into the kitchen, then made her way to the living room. From there she mounted the catwalk.

The arch at the end beckoned her toward his sacred space. She had no right to enter, but she did.

He was standing with his back to the door packing tubes of acrylics into a carrying case. Like the other time she'd been here, he was dressed in black—tailored slacks and a long-sleeved shirt. Dressed for traveling.

"Do you want something?" he growled without looking up.

"Oh, yes," she said breathlessly.

He finally turned, but she saw by the stubborn set of his jaw that he wouldn't make it easy.

"I want you," she said.

If anything, his expression grew more arrogant. She'd badly dented his pride, and he needed much more.

She reached for the hem of her linen sundress, pulled it over her head, and tossed it aside. She unsnapped her bra and discarded it, slipped her thumbs beneath the waistband of her panties, pushed them down, and stepped out of them.

He watched her silently, his face revealing nothing.

She raised her arms and slid her hands into her hair, lifting it from the nape of her neck. She crooked one knee, turned slightly from the waist, and eased into the pose that had sold a million posters.

With her age and her weight, standing before him like this should have been a travesty. Instead, she felt powerful and fiercely sexual, just as he'd painted her.

"You think that's all you have to do to get me back?" he scoffed.

"Yes. I do."

He jerked his head toward an old velvet couch that hadn't been here last time. "Lie down."

She wondered if he'd posed another model on it, but instead of feeling jealous, she felt a stir of pity. Whoever the woman might have been, she hadn't possessed Lilly's powers.

With a slow, certain smile, she made her way to the couch. It sat beneath one of the studio's skylights, and light showered her skin as she lay upon it.

She wasn't surprised to see him grab a palette and tubes from the case. How could he resist painting her? Resting her head against one of the rolled arms, she settled with perfect contentment into the soft velvet while he worked, squeezing out the paint. Finally he gathered brushes and came toward her.

She'd already noted his quickened breath. Now she saw the fire of desire burning behind the genius in his eyes. He knelt before her. She waited. Content.

He began to paint her. Not an image on canvas. He painted her flesh.

He drew a soft brush fat with cadmium red across her ribs, then added Mars violet and Prussian blue at her hip. He dappled her shoulder and belly with orange, cobalt, and emerald, clamped a discarded brush between his teeth like a pirate's dagger and stippled her breast in ultramarine and lime. Her nipple beaded as he swirled it with turquoise and magenta. He pushed open her thighs and adorned them with aggressive patterns of viridian and blue-violet.

She felt his frustration growing along with his desire and wasn't surprised when he tossed the brushes aside and began to use his hands on her, whorling the colors, claiming her flesh until she could no longer bear it.

She sprang to her feet and pulled at the buttons on his shirt, smearing it with the stigmata of Renaissance gold he'd dabbed in her palms. No longer content to be his creation, she needed to re-create him in her image, and when he was naked, she pressed against his flesh.

The hot pigments blended and fused as she imprinted herself upon him. Once again there was no bed, so she pulled the cushions from the couch and kissed him until they were both breathless. Finally he drew back far enough so she could open herself to him. "Lilly, my love . . ." He entered her as fiercely as he created.

The paint made her inner thighs slip against his hips, so she gripped tighter. He plunged harder and faster. Their mouths melded with their bodies until they stopped being two people. Together they tumbled off the edge of the world.

Afterward they played with the paint and exchanged deep kisses along with all the love words they needed to say. Only when they were in the shower did Lilly tell him she wouldn't marry him.

"Who asked you?"

"Not right away," she added, ignoring his bluster. "I want to live together for a while first. In perfect bohemian sin."

"Just tell me I don't have to rent a cold-water flat somewhere in lower Manhattan."

"No. And not Mexico either. In Paris. Wouldn't that be lovely? I could be your muse."

"My darling Lilly, don't you know you already are?"

"Oh, Liam, I love you so. The two of us . . . an atelier in the Sixth Arrondissement owned by an old lady in ancient Chanel suits. You and your genius and your wonderful, wonderful body. And me and my quilts. And wine and paint and Paris."

"They're yours." He laughed his great lusty laugh and soaped her breasts. "Did I remember to say that I love you?"

"You did." She smiled the depth of her feelings into those dark, intense eyes. "I'll hang a set of wind chimes under the eaves."

"Which will keep me awake, so I'll have to make love to you all night."

"I do love wind chimes."

"And I do love you."

*   *   *

With a sense of detachment Kevin watched the indicator on the Ferrari's speedometer climb. *Eighty-seven . . . eighty-eight.* He shot west on the tollway past the last of Chicago's suburbs. He'd drive all the way to Iowa if he had to, anything to make this restlessness go away so he could concentrate on what was important.

Training camp started tomorrow morning. He'd drive until then.

He needed to feel the speed. The sizzle of danger. *Ninety . . . ninety-one.*

Next to him the divorce papers that had arrived that morning from Molly's lawyer slid off the seat. Why hadn't she talked to him before she'd done this? He tried to steady himself by remembering what was important.

He had only five or six good years left . . .

Playing for the Stars was all that counted . . .

He couldn't afford the distraction of a high-maintenance woman . . .

On and on he went, until he was so tired of listening to himself that he pressed the accelerator harder.

It had been one month and four days since he'd seen Molly, so he couldn't blame her for the fact that he hadn't stepped up his workouts as he'd planned or watched all the game film he'd intended to. Instead, he'd gone rock climbing, run some white water, done a little paragliding. But none of it satisfied him.

The only time he'd felt remotely content was when he'd talked to Lilly and Liam a few days ago. They'd both sounded so happy.

The wheel vibrated beneath his hand, but he'd felt a bigger rush going cliff diving with Molly.

Ninety-five. Or what about the day she'd flipped the canoe? *Ninety-six.* Or when he'd climbed the tree after Marmie? *Ninety-seven.* Or just watching the mischief flash in her eyes.

And when they'd made love. That had been the rush of a lifetime.

Now all the fun was gone. He'd gotten more thrills riding a bike at the campground with Molly at his side than he was getting going ninety-eight in a Ferrari Spider.

Sweat trickled under his arms. If he blew a tire right now, he'd never see her again, never have a chance to tell her she'd been right about him all along. He was exactly as afraid as she'd said.

He'd fallen in love with her.

Just like that the empty spaces inside him filled up, and he took his foot off the accelerator. As he sagged back in the seat, he felt as if his chest had caved in. Lilly had tried to tell him and so had Jane Bonner, but he hadn't let himself listen. Molly was right. He'd secretly believed he couldn't measure up as a person in the same way he measured up as a player, so he hadn't tried. But he was way too old to keep living his life underneath leftover shadows.

He slipped into the right lane. For the first time in months he felt calm. She'd told him she loved him, and now he knew exactly what that meant. He also understood what he had to do. And this time he intended to do it right.

Half an hour later he rang the Calebows' doorbell. Andrew answered wearing jeans and an orange inner tube. "Kevin! Do you want to go swimming with me?"

"Sorry, buddy, can't do it today." Kevin slipped past him. "I need to see your mom and dad."

"I don't know where Dad is, but Mom's in her office."

"Thanks." He ruffled Andrew's hair and made his way through the house to the office in the back. The door was open, but he knocked just the same. "Phoebe?"

She turned and stared at him.

"Sorry for barging in like this, but I need to talk to you."

"Oh?" She kicked back in her chair and extended her chorus-girl legs—longer than Molly's but not nearly as enticing. She wore white shorts and pink plastic sandals printed with purple dinosaurs. Despite that, she looked more formidable than God, and when it came to the world of the Stars, she was just as powerful.

"It's about Molly."

For a moment, he thought he saw speculation in her expression. "What about her?"

He stepped into the room and waited for an invitation to sit down. It didn't come.

There was no way to ease into this, and no reason he should. "I want to marry her. For real. And I want your blessing."

He didn't get the smile he expected. "Why the change of heart?"

"Because I love her, and I want to be part of her life forever."

"I see."

She had a perfect poker face. Maybe she didn't know the way Molly felt about him. It would have been just like Molly to try to protect him by hiding her feelings from her sister. "She loves me."

Phoebe didn't look impressed.

He tried again. "I'm fairly sure she's going to be happy about this."

"Oh, I'm sure she will be. At first anyway."

The temperature in the room dropped ten degrees. "What do you mean by that?"

She rose from the desk, looking much tougher than someone wearing plastic dinosaur sandals should. "You know we want a real marriage for Molly."

"So do I. That's why I'm here."

"A husband who'll put her first."

"That's what she's going to get."

"The tiger's changing his stripes awfully quickly."

He didn't pretend not to know what she meant. "I'll admit it's taken me a while to figure out that my life needs to be about more than playing football, but falling in love with Molly has readjusted my viewpoint."

Her expression of cool skepticism as she came around the side of the desk wasn't encouraging. "What about the future? Everyone knows how you feel about the team. You once told Dan that you'd like to coach after you retire as a player, and he got the idea you eventually want to move into the front office. Do you still feel that way?"

He wasn't going to lie. "Putting the game into perspective doesn't mean I want to throw it away."

"No, I don't imagine it does." She crossed her arms. "Let's be honest—is it Molly you want or is it the Stars?"

Everything inside him went still. "I hope you don't mean what I think you do."

"Marrying into the family on a permanent basis seems like an efficient way to make sure you eventually get to the front office."

The chill that crept through him went all the way to his bones. "I said I wanted your blessing. I didn't say I needed it." He began to walk away, only to have Phoebe's next words slap him from behind.

"If you go near her again, you can kiss the Stars good-bye."

He turned, not believing what he heard.

Her eyes were cold and determined. "I mean it, Kevin. My sister's been hurt enough, and I won't let you use her to fulfill your long-term plans. Stay away from her. You can have the team or you can have Molly, but you can't have both."

Chapter 26

Daphne was in a very bad mood. It followed her around while she baked her favorite oatmeal-strawberry cookies, and it stuck to her side when she talked to Murphy Mouse, who'd moved into the woods a few weeks before. Even the big pile of shiny new coins jingling in her pink backpack didn't make her feel better. She wanted to run to Melissa's house for cheering up, but Melissa was planning a trip to Paris with her new friend, Leo the Bullfrog.

Most of all Daphne was in a very bad mood because she missed Benny. He made her angry sometimes, but he was still her best friend. Except she wasn't his best friend anymore. Daphne loved Benny, but Benny didn't love her.

She sniffed and wiped her eyes with the strap from her electric guitar. His new school started today, and he'd be having so much fun that he wouldn't even think about her. He'd be thinking about touchdowns instead, and all the girl rabbits who'd be hanging out by the fence wearing tube tops and trying to entice him with foreign phrases and puffy lips and bouncy breasts. Girls who didn't understand him like she did, who were impressed with his fame and money and green eyes, and didn't know that he loved cats and needed entertaining sometimes and didn't hate poodles nearly as much as he thought, and that he liked to sleep cuddled around her with his hand—

Molly ripped the paper from her yellow pad. This was supposed to be *Daphne's Bad Mood*, not *Daphne Does Dallas*. She gazed out across Bobolink Meadow and wondered how some parts of her life could be so happy and some parts so sad.

The sweatshirt she'd spread in the grass had bunched under her bare legs. It was Kevin's. As she straightened it, she tried to concentrate on the happy parts of her life.

Thanks to her new contract, she was financially secure for the first time since she'd given away her money, and she was bursting with ideas for new books. The campground and B&B were filled to capacity, and the more responsibility she gave Amy and Troy, the more they were able to handle.

Their feelings toward the place had become as proprietary as her own, and they'd asked her to consider converting the attic into an apartment where they could live year-round. They wanted to keep the B&B open all winter for cross-country skiing and snowmobile enthusiasts, as well as city people who simply felt like enjoying winter in the country. Molly had decided to let them do it. When Kevin had been searching for someone to run the campground full-time, he'd overlooked the obvious.

She hated how much she missed him. He probably didn't even think about her. She knew now that was his loss. She'd offered him her most precious possession, and instead of holding on tight, he'd thrown it away.

She snatched up her writing pad. If she couldn't work on *Daphne's Bad Mood*, she could at least make a list of groceries for Troy to pick up in town. Amy was baking her new specialty for tea—dirt cupcakes, which were chocolate cupcakes topped with green coconut frosting and Gummi Worms. Molly was going to miss Lilly's help with the guests, although not nearly as much as she'd miss her companionship. Her mood lifted a little as she thought about how happy Lilly and Leo the Bullfrog were.

She heard a movement behind her and set aside the notepad. One of the guests had found her hiding place. So far that morning she'd made restaurant reservations, drawn maps to antique stores and golf courses, unstopped a toilet, taped up a broken window, and helped the older kids organize a scavenger hunt.

Giving in to the inevitable, she turned—and saw Kevin coming around the fence at the bottom of the meadow.

She forgot to breathe. The frames of his silver Rēvos glinted, and the breeze tousled his hair. He wore a pair of khaki slacks with a light blue T-shirt. Only as he came closer did she see a picture of Daphne printed on the front.

Kevin stopped where he was and stood there simply gazing at her. Molly sat crossed-legged in the meadow with the sun shining on her bare shoulders and a pair of yellow butterflies fluttering like hair bows around her head. She was all the dreams he'd lost at dawn—dreams of everything he hadn't understood he needed until now. She was his playmate, his confidante, the lover who made his blood rush. She was the mother of his children and the companion of his old age. She was the joy of his heart.

And she was gazing at him as if a skunk had just wandered out of the woods.

"What do you want?"

What had happened to *Kiss me, you fool?* Riiiight . . . He pulled off his sunglasses and tried a little of the old playboy smile. "So how's it going?"

Had he really said that? Had he really said "how's it going?" He deserved everything she was going to throw at him.

"Couldn't be better. Nice T-shirt. Now get off my property."

So much for the woman who'd wished him all the best the last time they'd been together. "I, uh . . . heard you might be selling the place."

"When I get around to it."

"Maybe I'll buy it back."

"Maybe you won't." She stood up, and a few blades of grass stuck to the side of one of those legs he loved to touch. "Why aren't you at training camp?"

"Training camp?" He slipped his sunglasses into his shirt pocket.

"Veterans are supposed to report this morning."

"Damn. I guess I'm in trouble then."

"Did Phoebe send you here?"

"Not exactly."

"Then what's going on?"

"I wanted to talk to you, that's all. Tell you some things."

"You're supposed to be at training camp."

"I think you already mentioned that."

"One phone call and I can find out why you're not there."

He hadn't wanted to do this yet, and his hands found their way into his pockets. "First, maybe you'd better hear what I have to say."

"Give me your cell phone."

"It's in the car."

She grabbed a sweatshirt he seemed to remember belonged to him and marched toward the fence at the bottom of the meadow. "I'll call from the house."

"I'm AWOL, okay? I'm being traded!"

She spun around. "Traded? They can't do that."

"They're crazy, and they can do just about anything they want."

"Not without throwing away the season." She twisted the

arms of his sweatshirt into a knot at her waist and charged toward him. "Tell me exactly what happened. Every word."

"I don't want to." His throat felt tight and his tongue clumsy. "I want to tell you how pretty you are."

She regarded him suspiciously. "I look just like I did the last time you saw me, except my nose is sunburned."

"You're beautiful." He moved closer. "And I want to marry you. For real. Forever."

She blinked. "Why?"

This wasn't going the way he'd planned it. He wanted to touch her, but the frown marks between her eyebrows made him think twice. "Because I love you. I really do. More than I ever could have imagined."

Perfect silence.

"Molly, listen to me. I'm sorry about what happened, sorry it's taken me so long to figure out what I want, but when I was with you, I was having too good a time to think. After you left, though, things weren't so good, and I realized that everything you said about me is right. I was afraid. I let football become my whole life. It was the only thing I was sure of, and that's why I got so reckless this year. There was something missing inside me I was trying to fill up, but I went about doing it the wrong way. But there sure isn't anything missing inside me now, because you're there."

Molly's heart was pounding so loudly she was afraid he could hear. Did he mean it? He looked as if he meant it—worried, upset, more serious than she'd ever seen him. What if he really meant it?

As a child who'd been emotionally abused, she had a strong survivor's instinct, and it kicked in. "Tell me about the trade."

"Let's not talk about that now. Let's talk about us. About our future."

"I can't talk about the future until I understand the here and now."

He must have known she wasn't going to let it go, but he

still tried to sidestep. "I've missed you so much. Without you, I stopped being happy."

It was everything she'd wanted to hear. And yet . . . "All I have to do is call her."

He wandered toward the fence. "All right, we'll do it your way." He braced a hand on the top rail. "I wanted to try to set things right with them once and for all, so I went out to the house. Dan wasn't around, but I saw Phoebe. I told her I loved you and that I was going to ask you to marry me for real. I said I wanted her blessing."

Molly needed something to hold on to, but there wasn't anything around, so she sank down in the weeds, drew her knees to her chest, and concentrated on sucking in air.

He gazed down at her. "You could look a little happier."

"Tell me the rest."

"Phoebe didn't like it." He pushed himself away from the fence, the lines around his mouth deepening. "As a matter of fact, she hated it. She accused me of using you as an insurance policy toward my retirement."

"I don't understand."

"Everybody knows I want to coach eventually, and I've talked to Dan about his front-office work."

Molly finally got it. "She said you were using me to guarantee your future with the Stars. Is that it?"

He erupted. "I don't need a guarantee! I proved myself a long time ago! There's not a player in the league who knows more about the game than I do, but she looked at me like I was a no-name parasite. Molly, I understand that you love your sister, but football's a game about winning, and I have to tell you right now that I've lost all respect for her."

Her legs had regained enough strength for her to stand. "There's more, isn't there?"

His expression was a mixture of anger and confusion, as if he couldn't comprehend how a life made of gold could have developed any tarnish. "She said I could have you or the

Stars, but not both. She said if I saw you again, my career with the team was over. If I stayed away, I still had my job."

Something warm opened up in Molly's heart. "And you believed her?"

"You're damn right I believed her! And it's her loss! I don't need the Stars. I don't even want to play for them anymore."

Her loving, interfering sister . . . "She was scamming you, Kevin. This whole thing's a scam."

"What are you talking about?"

"She wants me to have a Great Love Story like she had with Dan."

"I saw her face. This wasn't any scam."

"She's very good."

"You're not making sense. What do you mean that she wants you to have a love story? I'd already told her I loved you."

"She's a romantic. Almost as much as me. An ordinary love story isn't good enough. She wants me to have something I'll remember my whole life, something to pull out and examine if you forget to send flowers on our anniversary or get mad because I put a dent in the car."

"I'm sure you understand what you're talking about, but I don't have a clue."

"If you were a woman you would."

"Well, excuse me for having a—"

"Words are wonderful, but every once in a while a few women are lucky enough to have something extra, something unforgettable." This was so basic to her that she had to make him understand. "Don't you see? Dan saved her life! He was willing to give up everything for her. Because of that, Phoebe always knows she comes first with him—ahead of football, ahead of his ambition, ahead of everything. She wanted me to have the same thing with you, so she convinced you that you had to choose."

"I'm supposed to believe that she jeopardized the entire

team just to force me into making some kind of grand romantic *gesture*?" He was starting to shout. "I'm supposed to *believe this*?"

Kevin loved her! She could see it in his eyes, hear it in his frustration. He'd been willing to give up the team for her, and her heart sang. But the sound was almost drowned out by another noise—one as unexpected as it was inevitable.

The clang of a fire alarm.

She tried to ignore it. Even though she knew Kevin's career with the Stars was as secure as ever, he hadn't known it, and the fact was, he'd been willing to make the sacrifice.

Yes, her heart was definitely singing. Yes, this was a moment she could spend her entire life reliving. A moment that was perfect.

Except for the fire alarm.

She refused to listen to it. "You seem a little angry."

"Angry? Now, why would I be angry?"

"Because you thought Phoebe kicked you off the Stars."

"You forget that I don't *care* about the Stars anymore. You forget that I want to play for a team with an owner who understands that the point of the game is *winning*, not jeopardizing millions of dollars in revenue so her star quarterback can play Sir Galahad!"

The fire alarm clanged louder. "Then you didn't make much of a sacrifice."

He was a champion, so he could spot the blitz coming from a mile away, and his expression grew wary. "This is important to you? This whole romantic-gesture thing?"

Clang . . . Clang . . . Clang . . . "I have to get ready for tea."

"I haven't done enough? You want something more?"

"Not at all."

A muffled curse, and then he swept her into his arms and began carrying her toward the woods. "How's this for a romantic gesture?"

She crossed her arms over her chest, crossed her ankles, a

perfect portrait of petulance, but she felt sick. "If this involves naked bodies, it's sex, not romance."

Unfortunately, he set her down instead of kissing her until he'd drowned out the sound of a thousand fire alarms. "You think I don't know the difference between sex and romance? You think because I'm male, I'm obtuse."

Her Great Love Story was on a downhill spiral because of a fire alarm that had grown so loud she wanted to cover her ears. "I guess only you can answer that question."

"All right, here's what I'm going to do." He took a deep breath and met her gaze straight on. "I'll win the Super Bowl for you."

She realized he meant it, and little starbursts of happiness exploded inside her—each one punctuated by the noise of the alarm. Right then she understood that she was facing the fundamental question of her life, a question that had its roots in the heart of a little girl who'd been emotionally abandoned when she was much too young. Kevin Tucker was strong enough to slay dragons for her and strong enough to win the Super Bowl for her, but was he strong enough to love her even when she wasn't lovable? She needed an answer that would quiet the fire alarm forever.

"It's only July, loser," she sneered. "By Super Bowl Sunday I'll have forgotten your name."

"I seriously doubt that."

"Whatever." She scratched a mosquito bite, looked bored, and spoke the ugliest words she'd ever said. "My mistake. I really don't think I love you after all."

Horrified, she began to snatch it back, then stopped because he didn't look upset, only calculating.

"Liar. Have you ever heard of the Saxeten River Gorge?"

"Can't say as I have." Had the fire alarm lost a few decibels? "It sounds boring. Did you hear me say I didn't love you?"

"Yeah. Anyway, it's in Switzerland, and it's as treacherous as they come. But I'm prepared to rappel to the bottom, and once I get there, I'll carve your initials in the rock."

Yes, definitely not as loud. She tapped her foot in the grass. "Touching, but Switzerland's almost as far away as the Super Bowl. Besides, when it comes right down to it, all you're talking about is a little graffiti, right?"

"There's a sport called parapenting. You parachute off a mountain peak—"

"Unless you're going to write my name in the sky on your way down, don't bother."

His eyes lit up.

"On second thought," she said hastily, "you'd probably misspell it. And the closest mountains are on the other side of the state, so what about the here and now? Okay, maybe I do love you, but truth is, champ, all this Iron Man stuff might impress the guys in the locker room, but it won't get you babies and home-cooked meals."

Babies and home-cooked meals! A family that was all hers. And a man who satisfied her to the very depths of her soul.

Just like that, the fire alarm went still forever.

"So we're going to play hardball," he said.

Kevin understood her better than anyone on earth. He understood her so well that he still hadn't thrown up his hands and stomped away. She listened to the glorious silence inside her and wanted to weep with the joy of knowing that this man's love didn't have to be earned with perpetual good behavior.

"I was willing to give up the Stars for you," he reminded her, his expression shrewd. "But I guess that's not good enough . . . "

"Oh, yes . . . " Kevin without the Stars was unthinkable.

He didn't take his eyes off her. "So I'll have to give you something more."

"Not necessary." She smiled her love at him. "You passed the test."

"Too late." He grabbed her hand and began pulling her back toward the campground. "Come on, sweetheart."

"No, really, Kevin. It's all right. I was just— It's the fire-alarm thing. I know it's neurotic, but I wanted to be sure you really loved me. I—"

"Could you walk a little faster? I'd like to get this over with so we could start working on one of those babies you mentioned."

A baby . . . And this time it would be all right. She realized he was pulling her toward the beach. "You don't have to—"

"We'd better take one of the rowboats. Not that I don't trust you in a canoe, but let's face it, you've got a spotty record."

"You want to go out on the lake? Now?"

"We have unfinished business." He led her onto the dock. "You're still looking for that great romantic gesture."

"No I'm not. Really! I've already had the most romantic gesture you could possibly make. You were willing to give up the Stars for me."

"Which didn't impress you."

"More than you can imagine. I've never been so impressed."

"Could have fooled me." He stepped down into the row-boat tied to the end of the dock, then pulled her in with him. "Apparently I still haven't met the Dan Calebow Standard."

"Oh, but you have." She sat on the seat. "I was just be-ing . . . careful."

"You were being neurotic." He untied the line and picked up the oars.

"That, too. So do we really need to take to the high seas?"

"Oh, yeah." He began to row.

"I didn't mean it. When I said I didn't love you."

"You think I don't know that? And you can tell me how romantic I am when we get to the middle of the lake."

"I'm not being critical, but I don't imagine you'll be able to do anything too romantic out there."

"That's what you think."

She loved him so much that it wasn't hard to humor him. "You're right. Rowing us to the middle of the lake is a very romantic gesture."

"I do know my romance."

He didn't have a clue about romance, but this sweet-talking son of a preacher man knew everything there was about love. Daphne rippled on his chest with the movement of his muscles as he rowed. "I like your T-shirt."

"If you're right about your sister—which I hope you are, even though I swear I'm going to report her to the commissioner—I'll have them made up for all the guys on the team."

"Maybe not your best idea."

"They'll wear 'em." He smiled. "I'll make a concession to the defense, though, and put Benny on theirs. And congratulations on saving your books. Lilly told me all about it over the phone. I'm sorry you had to sell your place, but it would have been too small for both of us anyway."

Molly thought of the big old Victorian farmhouse on the outskirts of Du Page County she'd heard Phoebe mention was up for sale. It would be plenty big enough.

"I think we're about in the middle," she said.

He looked behind him. "Just a little farther. Did I tell you how deep it was out here?"

"I don't think so."

"Really deep."

She could feel her smile spreading all over her face. "I'm hopelessly in love with you."

"I know that. It's my own hopelessly-in-love feelings that are in question."

"I promise I won't ever question them again."

"Let's make sure of that." He shipped the oars, and they drifted for a while. He looked at her and smiled. She smiled back.

Her heart felt as if it had somehow gotten lodged in her

throat. "You're the most steadfast man I've ever known, Kevin Tucker. I can't imagine why I thought, even for a moment, that I needed to test you."

"Every once in a while you go crazy."

"Phoebe calls them 'incidents.' And today was the last one. I risked throwing away the most important thing in my life, but I won't make that mistake again." Her eyes filled with tears. "You gave up the Stars for me."

"I'd do it again. Although I sincerely hope I don't have to."

She laughed. He smiled, then looked serious. "I know you don't love football the same way I do, but, driving up here, I kept thinking about coming out of the huddle and looking over toward the fifty-yard line." He touched her cheek. "I saw you sitting there just for me."

Molly could see it, too.

"The wind's picked up," he said. "It's getting colder."

The sun shone in the sky as well as in her heart, and she knew she'd never be cold for the rest of her life. "I'm fine. Perfect."

He nodded toward the sweatshirt that was still wrapped around her waist. "You'd better put that on."

"I don't need it."

"You're shivering."

"That's from excitement."

"Can't be too careful." The rowboat wobbled a bit as he stood and drew her up in front of him, where he unfastened the sweatshirt and pulled it over her body. It was so large it came to her knees. He pushed a lock of hair behind her ear. "Do you have any idea how precious you are to me?"

"Yes, I really do."

"Good." Quick as a flash he crossed the empty sleeves in front of her like a straitjacket and tied the cuffs in the back.

"What are you—?"

"I love you." He brushed a kiss across her lips, picked her up, and dropped her over the side.

She was so astonished that she took a mouthful, then had to kick furiously to get to the surface. With her arms imprisoned, it wasn't easy.

"There you are," he said when she bobbed up. "I was getting worried."

"*What are you doing?*"

"Waiting till you're ready to drown." He smiled and eased back down on the seat. "And then I'm going to save your life. Dan did it for Phoebe, and I'm going to do it for you."

"Dan didn't try to *murder her first!*" she screamed.

"I go the extra mile."

"Of all the stupid—" She caught another mouthful, coughed, and tried to say more. Unfortunately, she was sinking back under.

He was in the water waiting for her when she came up— hair dripping in his eyes, Daphne plastered to his chest, his green eyes dancing with the sheer pleasure of being alive, in love, and having such a good time. There was no woman on earth who could entertain him the way she could. And no woman who would ever love him more.

Which didn't mean she was giving in without a fight. "By the time you save me," she pointed out, "I'll be too tired to do anything but sleep."

Seconds later she watched the sweatshirt sink to the bottom of the lake without her.

"That was fun." Kevin's smile was a mile wide, and his eyes were misty with something other than lake water.

"Not in front of the children." Her eyes were misty, too, as she tugged off his Daphne T-shirt.

They made love in the shadow of the rowboat, holding on to the gunwale and each other, choking and gasping, first one of them underwater and then the other, two daredevils who'd found their perfect mate. Afterward they gazed into each other's eyes, not saying anything, just feeling peaceful and absolutely perfect.

Epilogue

Found in a notebook tucked under the gazebo at the Wind Lake Campground. Author unknown— although there are suspicions.

ALL THE ANIMALS IN NIGHTINGALE WOODS GATHERED FOR THE christening. Daphne wore her second-best rhinestone tiara (she'd misplaced her best at a road rally). Benny polished his mountain bike until it shone. Melissa dazzled with a swirly scarf from the rue Faubourg Saint-Honoré, and her new husband Leo the Bullfrog created a beautiful painting in honor of the occasion.

The ceremony took place under a shady tree. The animals waited until it was over to scurry out from the shadows of the gingerbread cottages and move among the guests, invisible to all but the very smallest of humans.

Victoria Phoebe Tucker blinked down at Benny from her perch on her father's shoulder, her green eyes alive with curiosity. *What's up, dude?*

"What's up yourself?"

Hey, you look familiar.

"I know your dad pretty well."

Daphne hopped forward. "*Bonjour*, Victoria Phoebe, and welcome to Nightingale Woods." She cast an admiring glance at the frothy confection of white lace and pink ribbons that enveloped the baby and draped her father's large, tan arm. Victoria Phoebe already had an eye for fashion. "I'm Daphne, and this is Benny. We stopped by to introduce ourselves."

"And see if you wanted to play some football," Benny added.

Victoria Phoebe stuffed a pink ribbon from her christening cap into her mouth. *You might have noticed I'm sort of tied up right now.*

"Sarcastic like her mother," Murphy Mouse noted.

Victoria Phoebe's father reached up to retrieve the ribbon. She went after his hand and took a few chomps on her favorite teether, his brand-new Super Bowl ring. He kissed her forehead and exchanged a special smile with her mother, who stood at his side. Nearby her Aunt Phoebe gazed happily at the new family that her special talent for deception had helped create.

"I don't recognize all of the big people," Leo the Bullfrog said, "but I sure know the little ones—the Calebows and Bonners, the Denton children from Telarosa, Texas, and isn't that a Traveler over there?"

Victoria Phoebe liked being in the know, and she abandoned the Super Bowl ring to point out some of the adult guests. *All those giant men are Daddy's playmates. And over there are Uncle Cal's brothers with the mommies and kids. Aunt Jane is talking to Uncle Dan right now. She's pretty nice, but she tried to write something on my leg last night when she was holding me, and Daddy had to take her pen away.*

"We've had complaints before," Daphne said. "Your mother looks particularly fetching."

And she smells totally awesome—like flowers and cookies. I love my mom. She tells the best stories.

"Like, duh," Benny said.

Daphne poked him, but Victoria Phoebe was snuggling into her father's neck and didn't notice. She peeked back up. *This is my daddy dear. He says I'm his very special girl, but not* to tell Mommy, except he always says it in front of her, and then they laugh.

"You have very nice parents," Melissa observed politely.

I know, but they kiss my cheeks too much. I'm getting chapped.

"I remember Rosie Bonner used to complain about the same thing."

Rosie Bonner! Victoria Phoebe grew indignant. *Last night she tried to hide me in the litter box because I was getting too much attention, but Hannah distracted her with a cookie. I loooove Hannah.*

"She's always been our special friend," Daphne said. "We played with her a lot when she was your age."

Don't you play with her now?

The animals exchanged glances. "Not in the same way," Benny said. "Things change. Stuff happens."

Victoria Phoebe was a future summa cum laude, so not much got past her. *What kind of stuff?*

"Children can only see us when they're very young," Melissa explained kindly. "As they get older, they lose the power."

That bites.

"But they can read about us in books," Murphy Mouse added, "which is nearly as good."

"Books that are making your mother a ton of money," Leo pointed out. "Although not as much as my paintings."

Victoria Phoebe grew huffy. *Forgive me very much, but reading doesn't hold a lot of appeal at the moment. I'm still trying to cope with diaper rash.*

"Definitely sarcastic," Celia the Hen clucked.

Daphne, who appreciated sarcasm, decided it was time for more explanation. "Even though you won't be able to see us as you get older, Victoria Phoebe, we'll be around watching out for you and all your brothers."

Brothers?!

"We're sort of like guardian angels," Melissa interjected hastily.

"Furry ones," Benny added.

"The point is," Daphne said patiently. "You'll never be alone."

Exactly how many brothers? Victoria Phoebe asked. And then, *Oops! Gotta go!* as her father passed her over to her mother.

The creatures watched Kevin pick up a glass of lemonade from the table under the trees. "I'd like to propose a toast," he said. "To all our friends and the family that means so much to me. Especially to my mother, Lilly, who came into my life at just the right time. And my sister-in-law, Phoebe, who is almost as good at matchmaking as she is at running a football team." He turned, cleared his throat, and sounded sniffy. "And to my wife . . . the love of my life."

Victoria Phoebe peered around her mother's arm. *Here they go with the kissing again. Right now it's just each other, but they'll get to me and my cheeks next.*

Sure enough, they did.

Daphne gave a blissful sigh. "Now we're at the very best part of being in the book business."

"The happy ending," Melissa said, nodding in agreement.

"Way too much kissing," Benny grumbled. And then he brightened. "I got an idea. Let's go play some football!"

Which they did. Right before happily ever after.

Dear Readers,

If you haven't had enough of the Chicago Stars and the Bonner family, I'm delighted to tell you a trip to your local bookstore will fix that. You can read Phoebe and Dan's story in *It Had to Be You*, where Molly also makes her first appearance. That book will lead you to Bobby Tom Denton's story in *Heaven, Texas*. And what about Gabe, the mysterious Bonner brother on the run from himself in Mexico? His story, along with sexy Pastor Ethan's, is in *Dream a Little Dream*. Finally, if you'd like to catch up with Molly, Kevin, and little Victoria Phoebe, find a copy of *Match Me If You Can*.

I love hearing from my readers, and it's not hard to find me. Simply visit *www.susanelizabethphillips.com* to learn more about the Chicago Stars, the Bonner family, and all the rest of my books.

Happy reading,